CONTEN

PART ONE   1

CHAPTER I: A New Alliance   3

CHAPTER II: A Foreshadowing Of Things To Come   13

CHAPTER III: At The Court Of Fools   22

CHAPTER IV: The Burned Witch's Lair   31

CHAPTER V: Of Troubled Souls   41

CHAPTER VI: A Chase Renewed   49

CHAPTER VII: Into the Forest   56

CHAPTER VIII: Under Eaves Again   65

CHAPTER IX: After The Slaughter   92

CHAPTER X: Devils With White Faces   104

CHAPTER XI: An Awkward Homecoming   121

CHAPTER XII: A Renewed Pursuit   130

CHAPTER XIII: Ichor And Blood   140

CHAPTER XIV: The Witch Queen's Bower   158

CHAPTER XV: A Soul Sold   188

CHAPTER XVI: Of Beasts and Men   200

CHAPTER XVII: Of Love and Hate   231

CHAPTER XVIII: The Witch Hunter's Quarry   240

PART TWO 269

CHAPTER I: An Audience With Royalty 271

CHAPTER II: The Shield Queen's Hall 289

CHAPTER III: Spared and Ensnared 310

CHAPTER IV: A Dream Shattered 320

CHAPTER V: Of Sour Times 324

CHAPTER VI: A Tryst For New Lovers 335

CHAPTER VII: The Warband Musters 344

CHAPTER VIII: A Palace Coup 348

CHAPTER IX: The Trail Grows Cold 354

CHAPTER X: In Search of Prey 359

CHAPTER XI: Throwing Down the Gauntlet 369

CHAPTER XII: When Brave Knights Tilt 378

CHAPTER XIII: Blood on the Horizon 398

CHAPTER XIV: Of Duelling Hearts 402

CHAPTER XV: A State Funeral 422

CHAPTER XVI: When Houses Clash 431

In loving memory of my father, who sought the Judgment of Azrael ten years ago

WARLOCK'S SUN RISING

Book Two of the Broken Stone Chronicle

DAMIEN BLACK

PART THREE 451

CHAPTER I: The Warrior-King's Passing   453

CHAPTER II: An Invasion Stalled   463

CHAPTER III: Of Birds and Men   468

CHAPTER IV: A Road Rejoined   476

CHAPTER V: A Brawl Beneath The Rafters   487

CHAPTER VI: A City Under Siege   509

CHAPTER VII: Where Dead Kings Walk   515

CHAPTER VIII: A Spell Broken   541

CHAPTER IX: Unwelcome Tidings   559

CHAPTER X: A Regency Disputed   564

CHAPTER XI: In Search Of Succour   572

CHAPTER XII: Another Close Shave   581

CHAPTER XIII: A Wedding Of Reavers   593

CHAPTER XIV: A Hard Road For Sick Wayfarers   600

CHAPTER XV: A Throne Secured   608

CHAPTER XVI: The Final Stretch   617

GLOSSARY OF NAMES 623

Acknowledgements 641

Farov Islands

Sea of Valhalla

ers

Cravern

Cravern Estuary

Realms of Northalde, Thraxia and Vorstlund

(being part of the northerly Free Kingdoms)

Wyvern Sea

The Empire →

Urring

Free City of Meerborg

Lothan Monastery

Groukalos Castle

Loanfluss R.

Glimmerholt

Merkstaed

Dulsinor

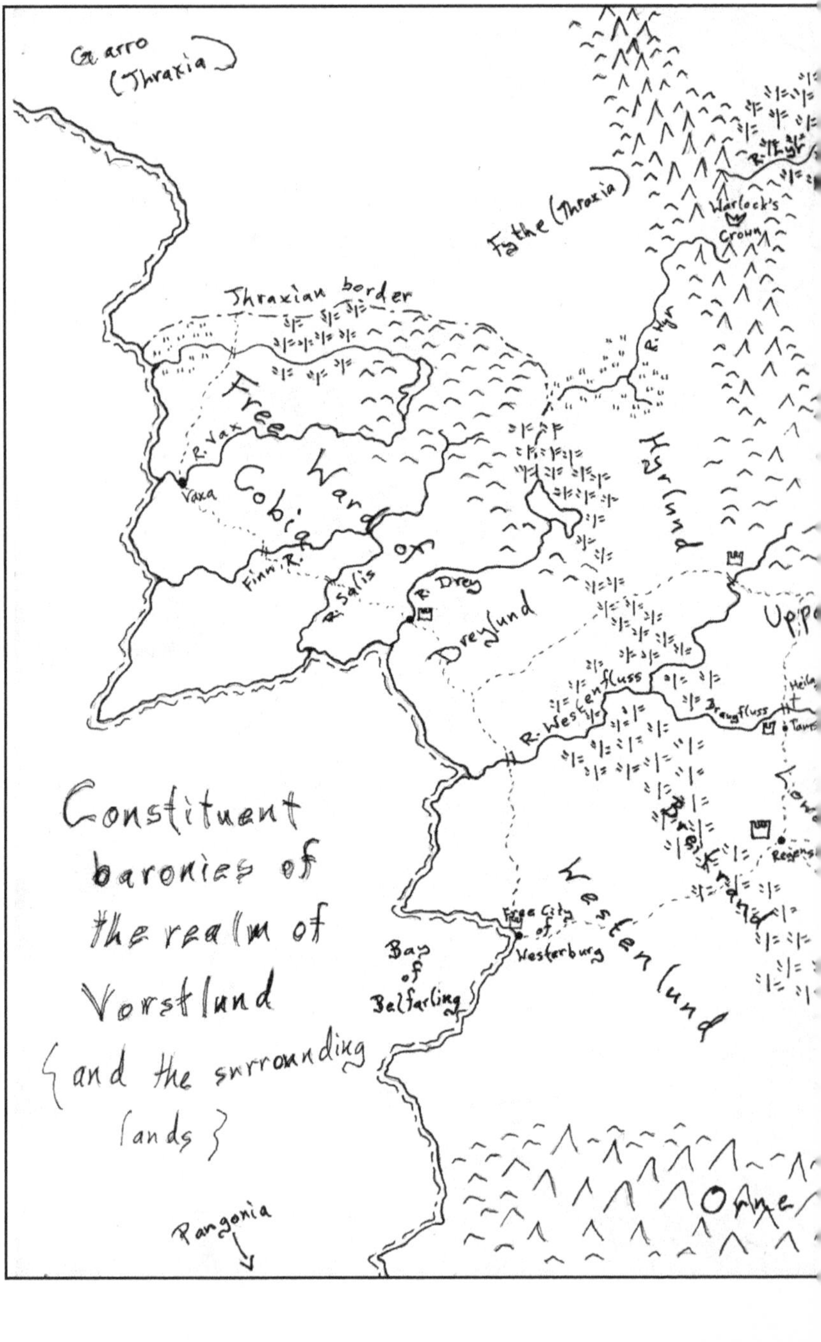

Garro (Thraxia)
Fythe (Thraxia)
Warlock's Crown
R. Hyr
Thraxian border
Free Ward of Cobia
R. Vax
Vaxa
Finn R.
R. Salis
R. Drey
Dreylund
Hyrlund
R. Westenfluss
Braugfluss
Free City of Westerburg
Bay of Belfarling
Westenlund
Constituent baronies of the realm of Vorstlund
{and the surrounding lands}
Rangonia

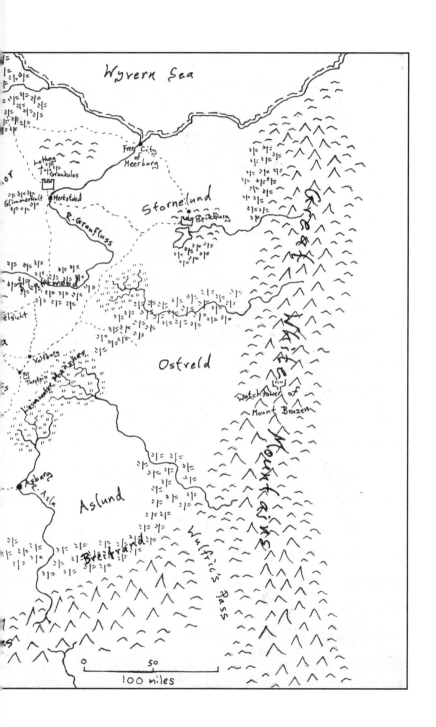

Wyvern Sea

Free City of Heerborg

Lothan
Grankolos

Glimmerholt Merkstadt

R. Graufluss

Storneland

Beckburg

or

elsickt

a

Wermod

Valfborg

Tarstein

Ostreld

s

Watchtower of
Mount Brazen

Asborg
R. Asla

Aslund

Breikrand

Wulfric's
Pass

Mountains

0   50
100 miles

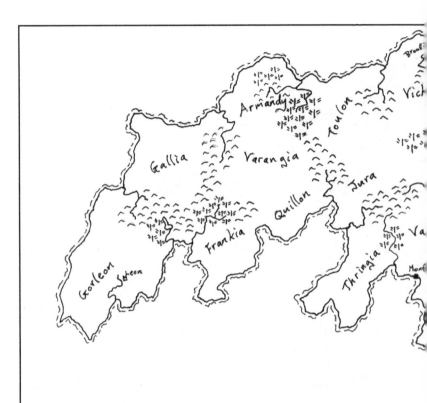

Kingdom

of

Pangonia

50

100 miles

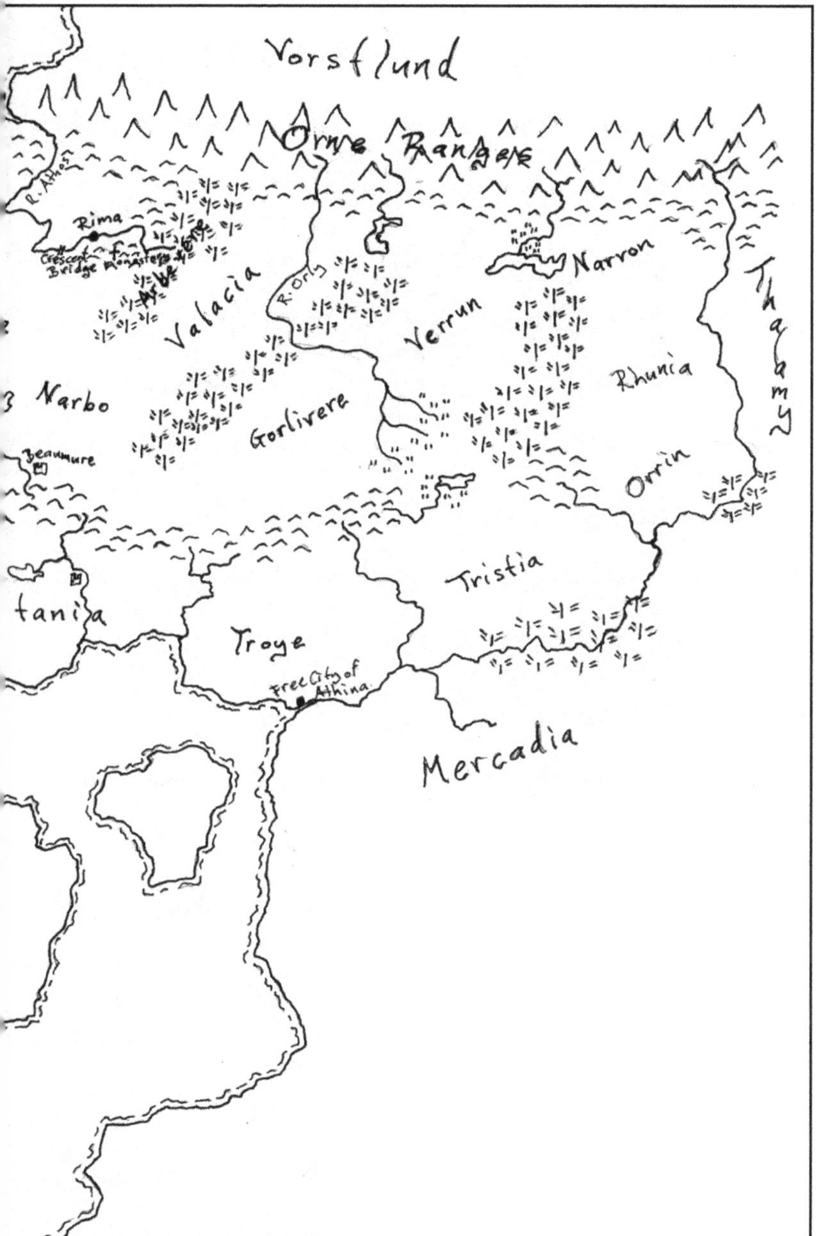

Vorsflund
Orme Ranges
R. Athos
Rima
Crescent Bridge
Monastery
Valacia
R. Orly
Verrun
Narron
Thamy
Rhunia
Narbo
Gorlivere
Beaumure
Orrin
Tristia
Troye
Free City of Athina
Mercadia

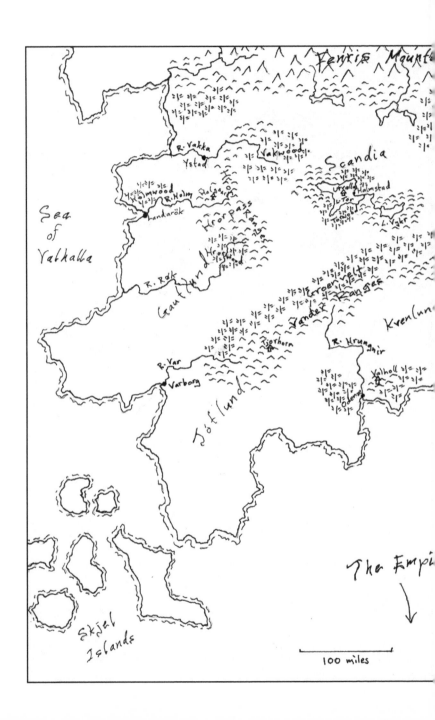

Fenris Mountains

R. Vakka
Ystad
Vakwood

Scandia

Holmwood
R. Holm
Holdgard
Urzolla Halmstad
L. Tor
Tor
L. Vakr

Handarök

Hror Pass
Gautland

Sea
of
Valhalla

Hroor
gard

Groen velt
Zander Ranges

Kren lund

R. Rök

Sjorhorn

R. Hrungnir

R. Var
Varborg

Jötlund

Valholl
Odense

Skjel
Islands

The Empi

100 miles

Randeor
Hjaldring

Utpass Utgard

Sea

The Frozen

Principalities

{being the domain

of the

Ice Thegns }

PART ONE

⤛ CHAPTER I ⤜

A New Alliance

The grizzled thegn approached the tree stump and stared at its shorn bloody top. With the resignation of a warrior about to meet the gods, he knelt in the coarse sedge and bowed his head. The youth next to him raised his axe and placed its dripping blade across the back of his neck. The fighters around them clashed weapons against shields one last time, their bloodthirsty yells mingling with the crackling of fires as the palisade burned.

Gripping the axe more tightly, the lordling shouted above the din, his voice cutting through the roaring of throats and the sound of steel hitting oak.

'Thegn Hardrada, you are found wanting in the eyes of Tyrnor,' he cried. 'Your warriors we have gifted with the sleep of the sword – now it is your turn to taste the blood ember! Have you anything to say?'

Hardrada did not reply. With a curt nod, his executioner raised the axe and brought it down. He felt a thrill shoot through his wiry frame as the thegn's head shot free of its body, borne on a tide of gore. As the headless corpse slumped to the ground besides the others, he turned to bellow at his cheering seacarls: 'All hail Guldebrand, new Ice Thegn of the lands of Jótlund, crowned in blood before the Great Reaver!'

'All hail!' thundered the five-hundred strong host clustered on the hill. Most of the warriors who had followed Guldebrand across the Hrungnir River into his rival's lands were more seasoned than him. But today he had shown his leidang that he was no spoilt princeling. He had done his share of killing in battle, and meted out a warrior's death to the surviving losers.

'Now Middangeard stands empty of Hardrada and his last loyal seacarls,' he said, addressing Walmond, his under-thegn. 'What of his family?'

Walmond pointed with his axe towards the burning outhouses lying on the rugged plains around the hillock. 'We found them in yonder granary stores,' he said. 'Being hidden by slaves amidst the provender. We brought them up to the hall while you were finishing the executions.'

Walmond, his right-hand man: twice his age and size, but loyal to a fault. He would reap the reward of that loyalty, now he served an ambitious ruler.

Guldebrand nodded, then raised his voice again so his bloodied seacarls could hear him. 'We shall not be unmerciful towards Hardrada's kith and kin – Gunnehilda and her bairns shall sup with us this night! As for the slaves, they shall meet the fate of all bondsmen who dare oppose made fighters. Crucify them.'

Many of the seacarls grunted in approval. It was well. Guldebrand had been thegn for just half a dozen seasons, but he knew when to be ruthless. A true thegn carved out his reputation on the flesh of corpses made by his own hand. A true thegn must always be feared first – and then respected. He had respected Hardrada, but that hadn't stopped him taking advantage of his weakened position to raid his lands. Fear kept one's rivals away: fear and only fear. Respect was for the priests and farseers.

Guldebrand raised his eyes to the darkening firmament. For one last time he let his sweeping gaze take in the butchered bodies of Hardrada's leidang scattered about the hill. Beyond them pillars of smoke rose from the burning palisade and town, carving ugly rents against the sky.

Inhaling deeply, he felt his heart soar as the sound of slave women crying and screaming met his ears. Not all his warriors had stayed to watch the executions. The ravishings had begun.

Turning to look at the high hall crowning the adjacent hill he gestured towards it. 'Let us repair inside, and feast and drink! Tjórhorn shall ring with music and laughter one last time before we burn it to the ground!'

Another cheer. Guldebrand felt his father's blood coursing through his veins. In a lightning stroke he had doubled his lands, achieving what the old man never had in thirty years. A good effort for someone of sixteen summers.

✛ ✛ ✛

A few hours later and Guldebrand was presiding over a debauch. The hall was filled with smoke from the firepits and warriors carousing to the sound of pipe and horn and drum as frightened slaves played for the victors. Tjórhorn was two storeys high, the uppermost housing Hardrada and his family's private quarters. Shrieks and grunts could be heard from above the crooked rafters of the low ceiling. Hardrada's rooms were being used for the ravishings, a normal part of any conquest; victorious seacarls were entitled to use a beaten lord's slave women for their pleasure. He would have his turn shortly – there were plenty of terrified wenches refilling horns of wine and mead from leather gourds who hadn't been taken yet.

But first as ruler of a newly extended principality he had to observe due ceremony, feasting his seacarls while he divided new lands among them.

Raising a horn to his beardless lips he quaffed another draft. It was fine wine, from Pangonia – Hardrada's tastes had been good, say what you like about his recklessness in war. Perhaps it was the strong ruby vintage, brought across the Sea of Valhalla, that had impaired the old man's judgement.

'Those of you who have elected to stay on Hardrada's lands shall be given a plot equal to twice your former share in Kvenlund,' he declared after banging down his horn for silence. 'Your former plots shall be given to those who have chosen to return home. The year-tithe I shall extract from all new domains, in accordance with custom.'

Another drunken cheer resounded across the reeking hall, briefly drowning out the music and screams from upstairs. Every fighting man present had doubled the extent of his lands. Guldebrand had just done likewise with his income. There was good strong wine from the civilised mainland and meat aplenty. There were comely wenches there for the ravishing.

What was not to like?

'A toast to our leader, young in years but old of mind and stout of heart like his father,' bellowed Holgaar Breakshield, getting unsteadily to his feet. 'A worthy successor to Gunnar Longspear!' Though shorter than average, Holgaar's broad shoulders and knotted muscles gave him a fearsome aspect.

Another cheer; more wine and mead flowed. Guldebrand relaxed back into the high chair as a slave refilled his horn. She wasn't the best-looking wench, but that didn't bother him over much. Sometimes it was fun to ravish the ugly ones too, just for the sake of it. He felt a thrill course through his loins as he glanced sidelong at her lumpy curves. The wine was going to his head. Yes, it would be time for a good ravishing right soon. But first he had one more piece of business to attend to...

Turning to look at the pale-faced noblewoman sat next to him he cracked a smirk. 'Why Gunnehilda, you've barely touched your meat,' he said affably. 'And yonder wine-cup looks over full methinks. Has something spoiled your appetite?'

The seacarls within earshot laughed at the jibe. Without raising her head, the ash blonde widow murmured: 'I never saw much value in the death-feasting. I would fain rather you left me to tend my grieving children and mourn my husband's passing in private.'

'Ah, but that is where you and I differ, you see,' replied Guldebrand, leaning forwards and grinning more broadly. 'You have no respect for tradition. The customs of the Northlands demand that the vanquished's kin are feasted by his conquerors, as a sign of magnanimity in victory.'

Getting to his feet he raised his horn and cried: 'And I am not magnanimous in victory?'

'JA!!!' came the chorus of answers. You could count on your seacarls for the desired response when you'd just enriched them.

From one of the rafters a raven suddenly dislodged itself, flying through the smoke towards the entrance-way. Guldebrand glared blearily after it. Weren't ravens in victory-time supposed to forebode ill? He pushed the thought from his fevered mind as he turned to address Hardrada's widow again.

'Your husband, for all his merits, had grown... weak about the head,' slurred the young thegn. 'For what kind of idiot would stake two thousand fighting men on a mad adventure, leaving his lands barely defended and ripe for conquest?'

'Perhaps Hardrada was spending too much time betwixt the sheets!' yelled a seacarl. 'A man who spends over much seed abed loseth his reason!'

More laughter. That was an old joke but an enduring one.

'Perhaps,' laughed Guldebrand. 'Yet who could blame the old man if so? For is his widow not passing fair?'

More hoots and jeers cut through the reeking air, made pungent by the crammed bodies of sweating men.

'Have you brought me here to honour me, or humiliate me?' asked Gunnehilda coldly, still not looking up from her platter. Next to her cowered her two young sons, aged four and six summers apiece. Hardrada had taken wife late.

The young thegn put a hand to his mouth in mock disbelief. 'Humiliate you?' he gasped. 'Why no, sweet lady, I've brought you here to *congratulate* you – for your newfound freedom from that doting greybeard you called husband. We shall find you a more suitable bedfellow – one who doesn't throw away his lands to back the losing side in a Northlending civil war!'

'Perhaps Hardrada was not as foolish as you think, Thegn of Kvenlund-Jótlund.'

The cold voice cut across the din. It was not loud, yet something in its icy timbre was enough to silence the assembled warriors and still the music. Only the crepitant fires and shrieking women upstairs could be heard now.

'Who speaks?' said Guldebrand, suddenly feeling nervous. Instinctively he raised his hand to the neckline of his byrnie, his fingers groping towards the pomander he wore beneath.

'One who would counsel you, if you have ears to listen.'

A tall figure made its way between the rudely arrayed tables, the uneven light of the braziers showing naught but cloak and kirtle and walking staff.

'And who might you be?' queried Guldebrand sharply, a hand straying to the haft of his axe, as he inwardly berated himself for his nervousness. What was there to be nervous about? He was sitting in a hall of victory surrounded by made men at his beck and call. Yet still he felt a slight tenseness; something was pressing at the edge of his psyche. His hand moved from the axe back to the sour-smelling pomander of herbs.

The stranger had drawn level with his table. All eyes were on him now. Even the sound of rutting upstairs seemed to have abated.

'I was an adviser to the late lord of this hall,' replied the shadowy figure, drawing a sharp look from Gunnehilda. 'In fact it was I who counselled Hardrada to throw his lot in with the Northlending rebels on the mainland.'

'You!' Gunnehilda had risen to her feet, and now stared at the stranger with accusing eyes. 'You it was who fostered this misfortune, with your silver-tongued guile! You are scarcely more welcome than my husband's killers, Ragnar of the White Eye.'

The stranger muttered a word in a foreign tongue. Harsh-sounding and wicked it was; Guldebrand felt a shiver run through him, as though a Gygant had caught him in its frosty glare. The smoke suddenly seemed to congeal and grow thicker; the flames guttered, throwing the hall momentarily into blackness. When the lights flared up again a tall figure in shimmering sea-green robes stood before them. Where a

second ago he had clutched an ordinary walking staff, he now held
a three-pronged trident fashioned from metal of an alien hue. He
stared at Guldebrand with his one good eye.

'Tamer of oceans,' said Guldebrand cautiously, slowly drawing
out the pomander and pressing it to his nostrils. 'Perhaps I should
thank you for leading Hardrada astray. It would have been a hard-
fought victory without your help.'

'Or no victory at all come to that,' replied Ragnar impatiently.
'I did not come here to bandy words, Guldebrand the Beardless.
Expanding your domains was never my original intention.'

Guldebrand felt his young face flush. He didn't like hearing his
epithet. Was it his fault Longspear had died before he'd been old
enough to grow a beard? He had killed made men and ravished their
women – surely that made him man enough.

'But expanded them I have,' he sneered back. 'In fact I'd say I've
been rather more successful in battle than you have, ocean-tamer. Radko
the Farseer reports many dead berserkers on a foreign field, while
the Northlending rebels you supported share the grave with them.'

'Ah, so you still use the services of that hedge wizard?' Ragnar
shot back, his sightless eye catching the light with an eerie sheen.
'How else has my erstwhile apprentice served you?'

'With a charm to ward off your witcheries, my silver-tongued
friend,' smirked Guldebrand. 'So don't be thinking to subdue me to
your will with the sorcerer's speech, as you did Hardrada.'

'Ah, a pomander of abjuration,' hissed Ragnar. 'So my old
understudy did learn a few things after all. But you should have no fear
– I shall not need the power of Enchantment to convince you to enlist my
services. You will quickly see the benefit in allying yourself with me.'

'And why should the Thegn of Kvenlund-Jótlund do that?'
barked Walmond. 'Given what happened to his predecessor.'

Holgaar lurched to his feet angrily, pulling his axe free. 'By your
leave, Guldebrand, let me show this apostate priest a steel welcome.
He is banished from the Principalities for following the Left-Hand
path! I say we send him on his way!'

A few dozen throats voiced what the men thought of that.
Northlanders were more tolerant of sorcerers than the mainlanders
with their strange sacrificial peace-god, but practising black magic
spelled trouble in most places.

An impulse seized Guldebrand. 'You stand accused of
demonolatry on my lands, Ragnar of the White Eye,' he said. 'How
plead you to these charges?'

Ragnar stared at him inscrutably. Guldebrand couldn't tell if he was surprised or not. 'I plead neither guilty nor innocent,' replied the mage curtly. 'I have not come here to waste time with legal – '

'Nonetheless, you *do* stand on my land,' persisted Guldebrand. 'Accused of a capital offence. If you will not plead one way or the other it makes no difference – you still must fight before the gods. In sight of Tyrnor shall your guilt or innocence be determined! Holgaar, as you have levelled the accusation, you shall fight for the prosecution. Clear a space!'

The hall became a flurry of activity. Seacarls loved watching a fight as much as they relished being in one. Within a few short minutes Guldebrand was presiding over a makeshift circular space between the tables. Holgaar had taken down his broad target shield from the wall to complement his axe. Ragnar had not moved. He stood stock still, facing Guldebrand with the same inscrutable expression on his disfigured face.

Holgaar loped into the middle of the circle, coming between his liege and the unwelcome sorcerer. He still looked somewhat unsteady on his feet, but even on the wrong side of a few horns Breakshield was a formidable opponent.

Guldebrand banged his horn on the table again for silence. Getting to his feet he said: 'At my command, begin. The gods shall determine who has the right of this.'

Slowly and deliberately, Ragnar stalked into the middle and squared off against Holgaar, who had already dropped into a battle stance. Turning his peculiar trident to point at his enemy's chest, he said in a low deep voice: 'Thegn Guldebrand, is this what you want? I have no wish to cause quarrel with you.'

Guldebrand took another whiff of the pungent herbs about his neck. He could sense a subtle power pushing behind the words. He guessed from what Radko had told him about magic that the mage would be visualising the abstract symbols of the sorcerer's script, trying to placate him using the power of Enchantment, one of the Seven Schools of Magick.

'Think not to charm your way out of this, White Eye,' he said evenly. 'And don't waste your time trying to pacify Holgaar – I'll just send another warrior against you, and not even you could hope to enthral all my men.'

Ragnar scowled, his cool demeanour broken for the first time. 'So be it,' he snarled, dropping into a fighting stance of his own.

'Fight!'

Holgaar lunged at the priest with a roar. Sidestepping the attack Ragnar called out more of the strange words of magic, the air suddenly cooling as he pronounced the unnatural syllables. A subtle change came over him: he moved more quickly, while his robes seemed to undulate about his spidery form with an elemental life of their own.

Time and again Holgaar rushed him, but each time the priest dodged aside with a nimbleness that defied his age. The assembled warriors called out encouragement to Holgaar, cursing each time the warlock averted another attack. Gradually Holgaar began to tire. Lashing out with another fierce swipe, he cried out in frustration as yet again the axe blade bit naught but shimmering robes.

That was the moment Ragnar chose to counter-attack.

With astonishing speed he darted forwards, bringing his trident up over his shoulder and down towards Holgaar's sweat-streaked face. Instinct borne of years of hard combat saved his life, and he brought his shield up to protect his head. The three prongs buried themselves in the shield and Ragnar pronounced another syllable. Holgaar and several of the nearest watching warriors gasped as a blue light coruscated the length of the trident, suffusing the shield and turning it into a slab of ice. Pulling the weapon free Ragnar twisted agilely on his heel, bringing its weighted butt round in a dazzling arc and shattering the shield into tiny fragments.

Lurching backwards Holgaar brought his axe around in a defensive swipe, but drink and fatigue had the best of him, and Ragnar parried the blow easily before attacking again. Holgaar managed to counter the first three strikes with parries of his own, but the fourth found a way past his guard and pierced his mail shirt, goring his chest and finding his heart. With a gasp of agony Holgaar sank to his knees. Ragnar pronounced another few syllables and the hall erupted with gasps of dismay as blue light suffused Holgaar.

When the warlock wrenched his trident free, it was from an ice statue that kneeled on the floor, its face frozen in a grimace of death.

Ragnar turned to face Guldebrand. His robes returned to normal, if clothing that constantly changed hues could be called normal.

'I stand cleared of all charges of demonolatry,' he said. 'By the customs of our people you must now show me due hospitality.'

'Don't listen to him!' cried Walmond, reaching for his own axe. 'Yon mage would have your soul in his icy grip with his honeyed words and magick-making! He may have the Lord of Oceans at his back, but he speaks with the tongue of Logi the Trickster God!'

'Stay your hand, Walmond,' replied Guldebrand. 'I've just lost one good seacarl, I'll not lose another. Let's hear what the White Eye has to say.'

'I thank you for your courtesy, Thegn Guldebrand,' said Ragnar. 'What I have to say is this: how many strong men have you left behind in Kvenlund?'

Guldebrand sneered again. 'Think you that I would make the same mistake as Hardrada? I left one good fighting man for every one I took with me. Asmund Steady-hand won't find my lands undefended!'

'Asmund's hands are steady about the plough not the axe,' retorted Ragnar, getting a grudging laugh from some of the warriors. Guldebrand's other neighbour was hardly the most formidable of the Ice Thegns, and had averted conquest only through clever diplomacy and timely tribute-paying.

'He is ageing and heirless, and commands but seven hundred warriors – even less than your tally,' Ragnar went on. 'Hardrada was the greatest of the southern thegns, until our... venture went awry. I shall not lie to you, Thegn Guldebrand – I serve a darker master than you could hope to fathom, and he is displeased with me. The King of the Northlendings proved far more resilient after years of peace than any would have thought. My loss has proved to be your gain... and the initiative you have shown is promising.'

'Promising of what, White Eye?' laughed Guldebrand. 'Do you really expect me to follow you on a madcap adventure as Hardrada did? A man with twice as many swords met with slaughter at the hands of our mainland cousins. I now sit upon half the southern Principalities, and no man shall take it from me.'

'That is where you are mistaken,' replied Ragnar. 'Oldrik Stormrider was the most powerful of the Ice Thegns along with Hardrada. Now you sit upon his erstwhile rival's lands. Think you that he will let you enjoy such good fortune uncontested? The Stormrider consolidated his Principality before you were born, Guldebrand the Beardless – he is no stranger to battle and has tasted the fruits of victory many times ere now. When word reaches him he will come marching south and sailing down the coast to relieve you of your new possessions – and your head.'

That last remark provoked uproar amongst Guldebrand's drunken seacarls. The wily mage had got his attention though. Banging down his horn, the thegn said: 'Get to your point, Ragnar, for doubtless you have one.'

Ragnar stroked his iron-grey beard and smiled a frosty smile. Was it the wine or were there hints of blue and green in the priest's hair too? The warlock continued: 'Until today, five Thegns ruled the Frozen

Principalities. Now, thanks to your efforts and those of the Northlending King, but four remain. These lands have not been shared between so few leaders since the Treaty of Ryøskil. The time is ripe, Thegn Guldebrand.'

'Ripe for what?'

'Are you so easily sated by a quick victory? Or perhaps strong drink has addled your youthful mind, cunning as it is. I see potential in you, Guldebrand, more than that ageing fool Hardrada.'

'I told you not to bother with flattery, Ragnar,' said Guldebrand. 'Potential for what, I wonder? To be another of your pawns?'

'I would not presume to insult your intelligence,' replied Ragnar. 'I propose an alliance of equals. Hardrada is not the only Ice Thegn to have broken with the Treaty of Ryøskil. The Stormrider's seacarls prey on ships from the mainland now, and rumour has it Magnhilda is planning something similar.'

'What of it?' barked Guldebrand. 'Let Magnhilda and Oldrik take to the seas if they wish. I have more than enough lands now – and I will defend what I have rightfully taken!'

'You disappoint me, Guldebrand. I had not realised your ambitions were so small.'

'Small!? I've just doubled my lands!'

'Aye, and what if I told you there was a way to double them again, and again after that?'

'With more raids against the mainlanders I suppose? Forgive me, White Eye, but the last time you persuaded an Ice Thegn to attack the Northlendings it didn't work out too well.'

'Which is why I won't counsel the same thing again,' said Ragnar, ignoring the laughter from Walmond and the other seacarls. 'No, let the mainlanders be for now. I had something closer to home in mind.'

'Oh yes of course,' smirked Guldebrand, 'defending myself against the Stormrider as you said – but what do I need your help for?'

'Still you think too small,' replied Ragnar with an impatient shake of the head. 'I wouldn't have you sit here and wait to defend. I would have you take the initiative again and attack.'

'You'd have me do battle with the Stormrider? A man who commands close on five thousand warriors? To what purpose?'

'To accomplish what has not been achieved in the Principalities for hundreds of years and unite the Northlanders under one Magnate.' The warlock's sightless eye seemed to glow with a light of its own as he pointed at the thegn with his trident. 'The gods have spoken, and they mouth your name from the stormy halls of Gods-home. Guldebrand the Beardless, I would make you King of the Frozen Wastes.'

⊷ CHAPTER II ⊷

A Foreshadowing Of Things To Come

From the parapet of the inner sanctum both monks watched the novices spar in the dusty courtyard below.

'His quarterstaff technique is barely passable,' observed the older monk.

'He has other talents,' replied Horskram. He watched keenly as Adelko backed away from his older opponent, parrying his deft strokes with increasing difficulty. The adept's mind flashed back to the clearing by Lake Sördegil, when Adelko had nearly lost his life to a Northland brigand. Only the intervention of the squire Vaskrian followed by his own had saved his life on that occasion. Horskram supposed he had that much to thank the foolish hotblood for.

'So you say…' the Abbot's words sounded weighty with scepticism. Horskram felt his impatience rise but checked himself. After all he was on Prior Aedric's holding: Ørthang Monastery, the Argolian Order's southern outpost in Northalde. Built on the edge of a sweeping plateau, it overlooked the plains of Saltcaste as they stretched languidly towards the Wyvern Sea.

It was all conquered land, its dead lord's heirs disinherited. Even now the Knights of the White Valravyn would be harrying outlaws, the remnants of Thule's disbanded levy, from its fields and meadows.

'What more assurances can I give you?' asked the adept, turning to look at the Abbot in the fading sunlight. 'On numerous occasions he has showed unusual proficiency in the Scriptures – when we exorcised Belaach from the girl Gizel at Rykken, against the horror sent to pursue us at Landebert's homestead, during its attack on the Valravyn's headquarters at Staerkvit. And then at Thule Castle he saw through the Sea Wizard's deceptions. He has barely seen fifteen summers, yet already he shows psychic prowess that a journeyman would envy.'

He was repeating himself now, and he hated repeating himself. Was this his fate, to constantly strive against timid sceptics within his own Order? He suppressed the thought: it was prideful and unbefitting an Argolian. And yet his temper was scarcely improving with old age...

'Yes, I do not doubt your testimony,' said Aedric, tugging at his long white beard. At four score winters, he was one of the Order's oldest members. 'And the youth's powers are indeed prodigious for his age, all the more so given that he joined the Order later than many. However, I do not think that constitutes enough evidence to name him a hierophant – many novices show early promise and become skilled adepts and journeymen without earning such high praise.'

'Yes, I seem to recall you saying much the same about me, when my powers were growing. But nowadays no one doubts my status, not even Hannequin himself.'

Aedric scrutinised him in the greying light. 'Be careful of pride and vanity, Horskram – for such are the workings of Azathol.'

Horskram sighed wearily. Even as he had spoken, he'd known the older monk would invoke the Second Prince of Perfidy to admonish him.

'I am but an instrument of Reus' will, and hold no hubris in my heart for the part He has allotted me,' he replied firmly. 'I am merely pointing to the fact that you are a sceptic – and sceptics are rarely convinced in the first instance.'

'With good reason! Jonus of Sceptus was a sceptic... why his teachings gave rise to the very word. And he was accounted among the wisest of his days.'

Horskram resisted the urge to roll his eyes. Aedric was fond of quoting the Thalamian philosophers, and enjoyed showing off his loremastery of the Golden Age. His sixth sense told him there was more than a hint of pride about the older monk himself. But then it was all too easy to cast stones at others, as the Prophet said.

'Yes well, I shall leave quoting the great philosophers of the Era of City States to you, Prior Aedric – I am far more interested in what the Farseers of Norn had to say.'

'Prophecy? You would have me put aside the philosophers of the Golden Age for false prophets who lived in Second Age of Darkness?'

'They called themselves farseers and not prophets for a reason – they never claimed heritage from the Unseen.'

'They lived in pagan times, and worshipped the archangels as gods,' Aedric reminded him.

'As did the folk of Sceptus' time,' countered Horskram. 'And the Farseers of Norn predicted the coming of the Creed to these shores.'

'Depending on how one reads their sayings,' said Aedric, showing no signs of giving up his scepticism.

'Prophecies are always open to interpretation,' replied Horskram. 'But their last farsight sounds familiar enough, don't you think? "A youth shall come from the cold mountains of the land of the Reaver Kings, middling of stature and timid of manner, the son of smiths, but touched by the Unseen. He shall be led by one wiser in years and bearing similar gifts, yet the novice shall surpass the master."'

As if on cue a shout went up from the courtyard. Adelko lay sprawled in the dust, his opponent pressing his iron-shod quarterstaff to his throat.

'All right, that's enough combat practice for today!' cried Brother Cedric, ceasing the four dozen novices in his class with a wave of the hand. 'Return your staves to the barracks and prepare for the evening meal! Adelko – tarry a while, I need to talk to you about your footwork!'

'I notice the Farseers say nothing about his skills as a warrior,' commented Aedric dryly.

'He has other far more important gifts,' replied Horskram stubbornly.

'Time will tell how many,' the Abbot contented himself with saying.

Horskram suppressed another sigh. His lore of the philosophers of Ancient Thalamy fell short of Aedric's, but he remembered the words of Tachymus well enough: *when two scholars disagree, no amount of arguing shall bring one over to the other, for 'tis faith not reason that separates them.* And perhaps the Abbot had a point – if he was right about the youth, time would indeed bear out his theory.

'There are other matters I would seek your counsel on,' said Horskram, changing the subject.

'Oh really?' queried the Abbot, raising a bushy white eyebrow. 'You seem fairly resistant to all my counsels today – my views on the jumbled words of false prophets who may or may not have lived eight hundred years ago aside, you don't seem set on following even my most practical advice. I've already told you that this plan to seek a witch in the Argael so you can forge an alliance with her against Andragorix is folly beyond – '

'Yes, yes,' interjected Horskram, his impatience rising again. 'I have half a dozen good swordsmen with me, one of them accounted

the best in the realm. Together Adelko and I have proved our
spiritual fortitude. After all we've survived, I think you can safely
say our security has not gone unthought upon.'

'Your preoccupation with security does not escape me, Brother
Horskram – it was so acute I practically had to divine your mission
for myself. You might have trusted me with your story from the
outset – given I'm sheltering you and your hungry swordsmen.'

'Forgive me, Prior Aedric, but hard events taught me what
happens when the Order does not guard its reputation. I still hold
that the fewer who know of what transpired at Ulfang the better
for all of us.'

He felt a spasm of phantom pain as events of twenty years ago
came surging back. His old scars throbbed, as they always did at
such moments. He felt all of his sixty winters and more – though the
years had been kind to his body, they had been less so to his spirit.
He could only hope and pray his years of devotion would grant him
eternal rest in the Heavenly Halls.

'The Purge was a black time for all who love the Order,' Aedric
was saying. 'Even one such as I who escaped the worst of its excesses.
Yet you are wrong to fear for the Argolians' standing in the eyes of
others – why, was it not established that the very Temple itself was
guilty of the demonolatry it so wrongly accused you of?'

'And so you think that if anything, it should be the perfects who
fear what others believe about them,' replied Horskram. 'And yet
bitter experience tells me it is not so – the True Temple stands absolved,
its mortal sins cleansed on Regus Square in Rima a generation ago.
Not so the Argolian Order! There are still many who believe 'twas
naught but deviltry that allowed us to "turn the tables" on our
accusers, as the Arch Perfect of Strongholm put it so eloquently.'

'And so you would have us keep the fragment theft a secret... that
and the fact that we guarded such a dread heirloom in the first place.'

'Aye, that I would, Brother Aedric – even if it means practising
secrecy within our own ranks. Our enemies are not limited to the
clerics of the Temple. The King of Pangonia might be wily enough
not to repeat the mistakes of his father and call for another Purge,
but he is not exactly friendly to us either.'

'That does not make him an enemy.'

'No, not in itself,' Horskram allowed. 'But I've heard it said he
desires a new crusade, and that means he must ally himself with the
Supreme Perfect. Who knows what His Supreme Holiness might ask
in return? And while we're on the subject of so-called holy wars,

don't forget about the Bethlers – they have ever been displeased with our Order for refusing to endorse the Pilgrim Wars.'

Aedric snorted derisively. 'What that bunch of sword-wielding fanatics thinks is of no concern to me, Brother Horskram – the Bethlers are a perversion of all monastic orders and an insult to the Creed.'

'And they are the most powerful religious organisation in the southerly Free Kingdoms,' Horskram reminded him. 'Ah Aedric, you focus too much on what is right and think not enough of what is *real*. The Temple commands lands and fighting men, as do the Bethlers and the King of the Pangonians – that is what counts in this godless world, not whose hearts are closest to Reus.'

Aedric frowned. 'So cynical...! You have wandered the realms of mortalkind over long – it has hardened your heart.'

'It has done nothing of the kind – it has rather opened my eyes.'

Both monks fell silent. The sun began to slip behind the Hyrkrainian ranges to the west. The brooding peaks had been an almost constant companion on the adept's journey from the Highlands. They had provided little in the way of cheer, he noted ruefully.

The circular courtyard stood empty, Adelko and the other novices having shuffled off to the refectory. This was located to the north side of the monastic compound with the storehouses and chapel, opposite the barracks and living quarters of the journeymen and novices. The monastery was similar to Ulfang, though somewhat smaller. The cloisters surrounding the inner sanctum were adjoined by buildings housing the monastery's two dozen adepts. The sanctum's walls were a little higher than Ulfang's and commanded a spectacular view over the plains. On a clear day it was even possible to make out the roiling blue dunes of the distant sea.

Presently the Abbot turned to look at Horskram. 'We must go to eat now – what else did you want to ask me about?'

'It can wait until after supper – the Farseers of Norn aren't the only ones whose prophecies we must consider.'

Aedric raised an eyebrow again. 'Oh no?'

Horskram did not turn to look at him as he replied. 'The demon Belaach and the Fays of Tintagael both gifted us with prophecy... meaning we must also weigh the words of immortalkind.'

The Abbot sucked in a sharp breath. 'Horskram, this is a serious matter – why did you not tell me of this along with the rest of your story this morning?'

'I thought you might have already divined it,' replied Horskram wryly, though he scarcely felt mirthful.

'This is no occasion for levity,' said the Abbot. 'Bad enough you let yesterday elapse before giving me details of your mission, but you keep this from me until now? And what else do you guard I wonder?'

Not half so much as I would like, reflected Horskram sourly. But there had been little keeping the Abbot at bay – as one of the eldest and wisest Argolians, Aedric had a keener sixth sense than most. Not even a hierophant could keep him off the scent for long.

'I am giving you the sum of all I have to tell,' replied Horskram cautiously. 'I needed to measure your reaction to the rest first.'

'To divine if I am friend or foe, I suppose!' exclaimed Aedric. 'Well I trust you are finally satisfied as to my trustworthiness. Now hear this,' – he raised a gnarled finger and wagged it at Horskram – 'I may not be possessed of your gifts, but while you shelter behind my walls I outrank you, hierophant or not! So give me the rest of your story – or you and your knightly bodyguards can go and beg their bed and board elsewhere.'

Horskram stared at him, mastering his anger with some difficulty. Aedric had never been easily cowed, unlike Sacristen who always deferred to him. But his sixth sense told him the octogenarian could be trusted.

Closing his eyes he cast his mind back to the last day of the exorcism in Rykken, sifting through strands of memory until the demon's prophecy bubbled to the surface:

Hell's Prophet shall reawaken/the Five and Seven and One shall lead the hosts of Gehenna to victory

Silver shall be tarnished black as night/the fires will rise and consume all in their path/the righteous shall moan beneath the scourge

Those who oppose us shall scream for eternity/the flesh shall be broiled from their bones/their souls shall be bound in burning brass

For the war of worlds is coming...

The adept opened his eyes. He felt sick, but then recalling the words of demonkind was a sickening experience. The horizon seemed to have darkened behind the Abbot, throwing the mountains into stygian gloom. The banner bearing the lectern motif of the Order flapped noisily in a rising wind.

'A demon's word is never to be trusted,' said the Abbot after another silent pause. 'Not even in defeat. It will twist the truth always.'

Horskram nodded. 'And yet once uttered its words should never be ignored – for there is always useful advice contained therein. If one can decipher one's way past the innate lies and trickery.'

Aedric frowned, tugging thoughtfully at his beard. 'On the surface, Belaach's words appear straightforward in their prediction – Hell's prophet is the Priest-King of Varya, Ma'amun; the Five and Seven and One respectively correspond to the Five Tiers of the Kingdom of Burning Brass, the Seven Princes of Perfidy, and Abaddon himself.'

The Abbot made the sign of the wheel. Horskram followed absently, his mind now thoroughly engaged with the puzzle that had troubled him since Rykken.

'… the rest of it is a simple assertion of future victory, in this war betwixt the mortal world and the Other Side that the fiend predicts,' continued Aedric. 'Where is the trickery?'

'Where indeed?' asked Horskram.

'There is nothing there suggesting a course of action,' rejoined the Abbot after another pause. 'The words aren't intended to mislead in that way. Belaach was compelled in defeat to give up a glimpse of the future, as he sees it… to share with mortals an insight a demon possesses into what will be.'

'… but he is concealing it deliberately. That's the deception,' said Horskram, catching on.

'I think so,' said the Abbot. 'He isn't trying to lead you down a blind alley. After grappling with you for five days he knew you were too wise for that. So he's settled for hiding the truth in his own words. He's given you a prophecy you can't use.'

'Unless we can decipher it.'

'Indeed. I will meditate upon this matter after supper. What of the Fays?'

Again Horskram cast his mind back. The eerie words of the Faerie Kindred caused him less discomfort than those of Belaach, though tapping into their otherworldly essence scarcely felt pleasant. Their lambent forms flitted through his mind's eye as he recounted their words.

'Twelve verses!' breathed Aedric. 'Never before have the Faerie Kindred shared so much with mortalkind.'

'The Farseers of Norn predicted as much,' Horskram pointed out. '"The two hierophants shall come unto the realm of sylvan kings / Half a hundred lines of prophecy shall be bequeathed them by the Fay Folk."'

'And it is the last verse that proved so instrumental in young Adelko's undoing of the Sea Wizard's deception at Thule,' said Aedric, pointedly ignoring Horskram's reference to the Farseers.

'I said his powers were remarkable.'

'His insight certainly,' mused the Abbot. 'The Fays have advised you well, for to seek Strongholm surely saved your skins and kept your mission alive. And their dire predictions dovetail with Belaach's own... The Faerie Kindred fear the return of Ma'amun, or another incarnation. And rightly so, if the Headstone is reunited and all the hosts of Gehenna return to the mortal vale led by the Fallen One.'

The old monk shuddered and made the sign again. This time Horskram was too preoccupied to follow suit.

'The verses trouble me in other ways,' said the adept, before repeating the third and fourth stanzas:

Oh mortal wise beyond your time,
Gifted with reckoning sublime!
The Vylivigs salute your mind,
So far above your meagre kind!

Your Order has ne'er seen your like,
Brave monk your time shall come to strike,
Forces of darkness are abroad,
Not all shall take an open road!

'Why surely Brother Horskram, you would welcome acknowledgement of your cherished status?' asked the Abbot sarcastically.

Horskram shook his head. 'You do me a disservice, Brother Aedric – for I do not believe the Fays were addressing me.'

'So you believe this is yet another endorsement of your young disciple?'

'Aye. I am considered blessed among our Order, but there are others whose powers overmatch mine – Grand Master Hannequin and Malthus of Montrevellyn. No, the Fays' words suggest the advent of one among us who surpasses all that have come before. Adelko could be such a one – his powers are yet untested and far from full fruition.'

'Far indeed,' replied the Abbot, resuming his scepticism. 'Too far to make any such pronouncements. The youth is not the only promising novice in the Order.'

'Granted,' Horskram had to allow. 'And yet I think it is another indicator – the Fays have not led us astray thus far. They have as much to lose from the coming holocaust as ordinary mortalkind.'

The Abbot looked sharply at Horskram. The adept sensed a meeting of their six senses: both monks had been talking for a while and were by now attuned to one another.

'What else about the stanzas concerns you?' asked the elder monk.

Horskram turned to look across the darkening plains. Hardy though he was, up at the sanctum's summit the dusk air carried a chill he felt all too keenly.

'The last couplet... the part about dark forces not taking an open road,' he said presently. 'Something in it unsettles me... there is still far too much we don't know about our enemies.'

'Indeed – all you have fathomed thus far is that this Sea Wizard was in the employ of Andragorix, and that another witch in Thraxia may or may not be allied to him. You still have not divined his whereabouts. The couplet states the obvious – your enemies come at you unawares, this has been the case since the outset of your mission.'

Horskram shook his head. 'That is all true enough, but I believe there's something more to it than that... the Fays are trying to tell us something else, in their roundabout way.'

The Abbot sighed. 'Well, both conundrums will have to wait until after evening prayers,' he said. 'Now 'tis time we supped. You are due to leave at daybreak tomorrow and should eat – it's another four days' ride to the Argael.'

The Abbot turned to leave, gingerly taking the stairs that led back down to his private chambers. Horskram lingered a few moments longer, staring at the diminishing horizon, but the blackened landscape told him nothing. Heaving a tired sigh he followed Aedric down the stairs, feeling the weight of his mortal sins and unsolved problems with every step.

⊷ CHAPTER III ⊷

At The Court Of Fools

From the Seat of High Kings, Abrexta the Prescient gazed coolly at the court she had subjugated. Beside her the mortal king she had bewitched slouched, one bejewelled hand clasped loosely about a goblet of wine, the other holding her supple waist tightly. The rich ruby liquid dripped from the goblet's golden lip and splashed across the flagstoned floor of the hall, drowned out by the clashing of arms. Both knights wielded their greatswords clumsily. But then that was hardly surprising given that each had a hand tied behind his back. The pots and pans lashed to their hauberks were also bound to make elegant movement difficult, or any movement come to that.

Abrexta smiled thinly, sipping from her own goblet as she reflected on the subtle joys of Enchantment. By far her favoured of the Seven Schools, it had given her the power to control a kingdom, or the city that hosted its ruling house at least; even now, as King Cadwy stirred beside her, she kept the stylised images of a caged bird and hooked fish clear in her mindset, while wordlessly intoning the Sorcerer's Speech.

Her elan had grown apace in recent years. Dozens of others, all lords or men of high office, now danced to her tune. Those she had not been able to enthral had been despatched by those she had.

One by one she named her high-born thralls in the language of magic, the age-old speech taught to the Varyans by the Unseen in days far gone, when gods had walked the earth and the very Gygants trembled at their passing. As she did, she visualised the syllables dancing to and fro amidst the symbols occupying her central mindset.

So accomplished had she grown at her art that Abrexta could keep her perverted litany going whilst gazing on the mortal fight of flesh before her, and register excitement as Sir Mordàen struck Sir Aédan across the head. It was an ill-timed blow from a weapon designed for two-handed use, but enough to draw a torrent of blood from the older knight's forehead and send the cooking pot lashed to it skittering across the flagstones. Sir Aédan gasped and crumpled to his knees, his own sword slipping from his hand as his grey beard turned dark red.

The throng of courtiers tittered and clapped sycophantically. Abrexta marvelled at the capricious ways of men, that so few needed ensorcelling to do one's bidding. Enthral the men at the top, and the rest fell into line of their own free will.

The knights had both professed loyalty to the Seat of High Kings, each accusing the other of fomenting treason. Some men were more resistant to Enchantment than others, and she had to be careful not to over-stretch her powers, so she had resorted to more conventional methods to learn the truth. With access to the palace spies that had been easy enough – both men were plotting rebellion but had been rivals for years. That rivalry had spurred them to try and do away with each other.

Such foolishness. Had they reconciled their grievances the two bannermen might have caused her some trouble, for each commanded twenty lances. As it was, they had delivered themselves straight into her hands. The death duel to decide the truth of the matter had been her idea, conveyed silently to the King who had pronounced judgment after hearing them. The details – that they should fight one-handed, with half the royal kitchens strapped to them, and a skinful of Pangonian red forced down their throats for good measure – had been Cadwy's own notion. A man ensorcelled could still come up with ideas of his own: it pleasured her daily to see what whim would take the King next, just as it pleasured her nightly to see what deviant new practice he would suggest abed.

Perhaps she had done the King a favour by enthralling him – all those freakish fancies he had never dared indulge before she entered his life, why the poor fool had never had so much fun.

All the same, as Aédan gasped and bled and Mordàen loomed above him, Abrexta felt the need to return her focus to bending Cadwy's will. Even now she could feel the vestiges of honour fighting her urge to give the command. Shutting her eyes she silently gave the order in the Sorcerer's Tongue...

'Kill him,' said the King.

Mordàen brought the blade down again, missing by inches and jarring the weapon from his hand as it glanced off a pan strapped to Aédan's shoulder. The younger knight fell on the older, drawing a dirk from his belt. Aédan had no time to draw his own but instead grabbed his assailant's wrist, both knights making an awful clattering sound as they grappled on the floor like lamed beggars fighting over a coin.

More sniggers from the courtiers. The King relaxed back into his throne, pulling her closer as he drained his cup. Like the palace it rested in, the Seat of High Kings was constructed of interlocking branches, their natural forms bent by faerie magick into shapes that mortals could use. The Palace of Bending Branches and the ancient sorcery that still held it fast in place was testimony to a near-forgotten time, long before the coming of the Creed, when descendants of the druid clans of Skulla and Kaluryn had practised the Right Hand Path in leafy glades and worshipped the Moon Goddess openly on starlit nights. Some loremasters claimed that in those days mortalkind had wedded the Fays, whose lucent hands had helped build the preternatural edifice that overlooked the mundane wooden houses of Ongist.

How fitting then that this city should fall under her sway, for was she not the descendant of faerie union with mortalkind? Had not Yathaga the Three-Eyed prophesied the return of the Kindred to the Seat of High Kings more than a hundred years ago? The great witch had been burned at the stake in Market Circle for her troubles, before the stern-eyed Argolians who had brought her to so-called justice.

Abrexta felt her heart harden at the memory. She turned to kiss the King full on the lips and, resting his shaggy-maned head on her shoulder, gazed across the smoky hall and out of a broad palace window. The palace was built on giant stilts that allowed it to straddle the River Rundle and gave it a commanding view of the city around. Ongist fell in a disarrayed jumble down the hills on either side of the river towards the thriving port and harbour at its edge. It was home to some forty thousand souls, most of whom eked out a miserable existence that would have been unknown in the times when mortals mingled with faerie-kind. She could see Market Circle about halfway down, crammed with unwashed hawkers trading rotting meats, threadbare textiles and other soiled goods.

Such is the bounty of the Palomedian calling, she reflected bitterly. How different to the days of Bendigedfryn and his ilk! Back then, lesser god-things had taught men and women to coax the treasures of the soil from the earth's rich bosom. Starvation and disease had been virtually unknown.

A yowling brought her attention back to the fight. Mordàen had managed to overpower his wounded opponent, driving his dagger past his mailed shirt and deep into his breast. As the older knight expired in a twitching heap, his killer hauled himself unsteadily to his feet and stared as keenly at the King as his drunken eyes would allow.

'I hath vanquithed my thoe,' the younger knight slurred. 'My innothence ith provthed in the eyeth of the Almighthy.'

But the Almighty had no place in a court ruled by a pagan witch.

Even now Abrexta could feel her royal lover fighting her, an old sense of justice struggling to shrug her off. Intensifying her mindset she visualised a hand clutching a heart, another of the hieratic symbols of the Sorcerer's Script she had memorised to perfection. As she did, she spoke her next command in the Language of Magick.

'The King deems the fight unjustly won, and the King's word is law,' said Cadwy obediently. 'Sir Mordàen, you are guilty of murdering a loyal subject, and the sentence is death. Throw him in the river.'

Mordàen's cries of protest were drowned out by a ripple of applause as knights, ladies and other favourites dutifully showed their appreciation. Four heavy-set men-at-arms stepped forwards to carry out the sentence, disarming the drunken exhausted knight before dragging him over to a window overlooking the Rundle. Sir Mordàen gave a truncated scream as the serjeants cast him into the river, sinking without trace beneath the uncaring waters as pots and pans and armour dragged him down to a wet grave.

With a flourish Cadwy called for more wine and music. The sound of fiddle and drum and bagpipes filled the hall as minstrels struck up a lively tune. Abrexta felt a flush of pleasure – at least that was one thing the Palomedians with their One-God-In-Two hadn't diminished: the musical tradition of her foremothers remained as strong as ever.

The witch felt a tugging at the fringes of her consciousness. The others were trying to break free, encouraged by her distraction with the King. That was always the danger with Enchantment – though her powers were second to none in Thraxia, even she had her limits. Focus too much attention on one thrall, and the others might strive to resist her will. Intensifying her mindset she pictured a wide net cast across many fish... and the minds under her spell returned to quiescence.

The King was drinking more wine at her unspoken suggestion, which would make him more easy to control: she would need him in pliant mood for the next phase of her plan. Abrexta was about to broach the subject when a commotion at the entrance caught her attention.

She recognised the man: Sir Jalis of Brychon, a senior bannerman from
Gaellentir. The knight was exchanging hot words with the serjeant-at-
arms, who would not let him pass beneath the antlered lintel.

Lord Braun of Gaellen... the three lords of Dréuth could be counted
on to make trouble, but Slànga Mac Bryon and Tíerchán Mac Thoth
would take care of that problem in due course. Her apprentices served
her interests there, hedge witches who had ingratiated themselves
with both clan leaders. She had planned on using her Scrying to
communicate with them later today – but now it looked as though one
of Braun's men was bringing her fresh news himself.

'Let him pass,' cried Cadwy across the revelry, following her
suggestion. 'I would have news of the north.'

Scrying was a drain on her elan – if she could avoid using any,
all to the better. The day would come of course when her energies
would be limitless. When Morwena's Doom and the power to
harness its forces was recovered, an army and more would march
to her lightest whim.

Sir Jalis came huffing and puffing up the hall's slanted approach
– the Fays had spurned mortal symmetry in their designs – rudely
elbowing aside the King's toadies. Too stubborn by far to enthral
and too old to seduce, the stocky knight was a problem she would
fain be rid of. All in good time.

'My greetings to the First Man of Clan Cierny,' hollered Jalis, his
protocol sounding at odds with the debauch unfolding around him.
Serving wenches moved among the courtiers with trays of wine and
sweetmeats, the more comely ones being groped by drunken knights.
Others were cavorting manically to the insistent strains of music as
retainers lit hanging fire baskets to ward against the coming chill of
dusk. Though it was early summer, nights were still cold this far north.

That said, the Palace of Bending Branches afforded more warmth
than any stone keep. Some put it down partly to the same magic
that had warped living bough and bole into the hybrid like of
rafter, gable and pillar; others put it down to the patchwork quilt of
overlapping hangings that festooned the hall.

Her fay ancestors could claim no credit for that: the montage of
dyed deerskins had been commissioned by King Bann, the first of his
name, who had brought the ways of chivalry to Thraxia three centuries
ago. A flaring brazier glanced across a nearby clutch of skins portraying
the heroic Sir Tantris riding through the Bruinwood in pursuit of
Antalix, the two-headed golden stag who had belonged to the Cloven-
Hoofed God. Sir Tantris, as renowned for his singing and hunting as

he had been for his skill with sword and spear, had ended his days begging the streets after King Bann had his eyes put out and banished him for seducing his wife Ylayne. The King hadn't thought fit to put that ignoble deed on the deerskins lining his hall, Abrexta noted wryly.

Her attention was drawn sharply back to Jalis as he began to say something of interest.

'Lord Tarneogh's forces have been overrun,' the knight was saying. 'Last we heard the highlanders burned Daxor Keep to the ground and razed the town. The only survivors will be those taken as slaves. Our scouts report Tíerchán and the Death's Head are already striking south-west – they mean to pin down Lord Cael at Varrogh while Slangà marches round the tip of Lake Halfrein and hits us from the south. They're too many in numbers – for the umpteenth time, Your Majesty, send knights to help us! Dréuth is all but lost!'

If the courtiers nearby were alarmed by that, they gave no indication of it. But then that was exactly what Abrexta wanted – surround the King with the useless and incompetent, to make sure nothing deviated from her plan.

And according to her plan, Dréuth must fall.

'I am sorry Sir Jalis,' said Cadwy, echoing her suggestion. 'I can give no thought to it – my bachelors have already been despatched down south. The lords of Tul Aeren are giving me trouble about the latest taxes.' The King sounded as though he had conceded a trifling loss at dice.

'Tul Aeren?!' Jalis' eyes bulged with disbelief. He was still kneeling. Cadwy had not bade him rise. 'We've a highland uprising in the north – a few truculent barons can't be a priority, you're about to lose the northern reaches of the realm to pagan savages!'

A dancing courtier, the worse for drink, caught his foot on the forgotten corpse of Sir Aedàn. Arms flailing, he sent a tray of sweetmeats crashing to the floor as he fell. Laughter erupted from the nearby courtiers.

'Nonsense,' replied the King, laughing with the others. 'The southerly reaches of the realm are richer and must be pacified first. Then I'll see to it that reinforcements are sent north – *if* I deem Dréuth worth saving.'

That raised a few more sniggers. Abrexta had made sure whoever the King picked as favourites, northerners were not among them.

'Worthy...!' Sir Jalis rose, forgetting himself. 'Do you think they'll stop with Dréuth? Our lands sit directly north of yours – once Slangà and Tíerchán reunite over our corpses you'll have an army of highland screamers banging down the walls of Ongist!'

'Let them come,' answered the King, his voice hardening. 'They'll find the knights of the First Clan more than a match for them, even if the so-called Lords of Dréuth aren't man enough to beat them on their own. Now begone from my hall, before I have you horsewhipped for your impudence!'

Sir Jalis stared at the ensorcelled King, then shot Abrexta a venomous glance.

If looks could kill, she thought coolly.

She had half a mind to have Cadwy clap him in irons, but thought better of it – there was little to gain in sending the old knight to languish in the dungeons with others who had dared oppose her. She'd see to it that her highland allies disposed of him.

'The King is tired, and grows weary of your heckling presence,' she said imperiously, meeting Jalis' eye. 'You would do best to return to your homeland, and defend yourselves as best you can. We have more pressing matters at hand, as you can see.' She indicated the debauch with an extravagant sweep of her arm.

Sir Jalis' eyes bulged so much she thought they might pop out of his fat head. He seemed about to say something but checked himself, instead managing a half bow before turning and stalking out of the hall.

'Deftly handled my loving liege,' she purred in his ear, allowing a white hand to drop to Cadwy's thigh. 'More a buffoon than a knight, that one – and you mustn't trouble yourself with the north. You are right to focus on the south, and here – your personal demesnes that are the heart of the kingdom.'

She felt the King flush and stiffen with pleasure as she pressed herself closer to him, her raven tresses mingling with his own. She felt his crown of gold and emeralds, fashioned to resemble mythical beasts of the faerie time she so yearned to bring back; its cool surface felt good against her cheek. Though a woman she was as tall as Cadwy, a man of middling stature at best.

'Yes,' he mumbled, staring distractedly at his empty wine cup. 'I have all I need here. We shall have a tourney to celebrate summer's awakening in a fortnight, and I shall preside over much pageantry and merry-making.'

His voice was beginning to slur and he sounded like the knight he had just executed. The light from the baskets was offset by the thick smoke emitting from them. They were curious contraptions wrought of a metal that was strangely light, said to be a vestige of the forgotten artisanry the island folk had brought with them over the Tyrnian Straits, after the Wars of Kith and Kin an age of men ago.

The Island Realms... the next part of her plan hinged on the ancient land of her ancestors. All of her unnaturally long life she had yearned to see those shores, since Yathaga had told her of the druid clans and their primeval powers. She had learned those same powers at the feet of the old witch.

'Your judicious taxes shall bring in much revenue,' she said. 'More than a tourney warrants. I had more ambitious plans in mind.'

Cadwy blinked, staring ahead blankly at the dancing courtiers. Several knights had already made their way to the side of the hall with serving wenches, and now clasped them in lusty embraces. The music set her heart racing – that, and the thought of her next venture.

'Yes...' murmured the King. 'I had wondered what we were going to use the money for.'

Abrexta felt a slight resistance behind the words. She'd had little difficulty enchanting Cadwy when he had taken her to the Royal Cot; he had been a lonely and melancholy man, still mourning the loss of his wife three summers ago. But she had many more men enthralled now.

She mouthed more words in his ear, nibbling it as she pictured a hand clutching a heart. 'Wonder no more, my loving liege – for I shall tell you! For too long now our harbours have but welcomed the cogs of other lands, contributing few of their own to the great seas that lash this blessed realm. Our ancestors were once great mariners, in days long gone when the Moon Goddess smiled on Curufin and Orbegon.'

Cadwy stirred. She could feel pride kindle in his breast. 'You speak of the Exiled Clans, who founded this realm,' he said, turning to look at her. His grey eyes had recovered a hint of their old keenness. She intensified the hieratic symbol in her mindset as she continued: 'Aye, my loving liege, of that age I speak – and its like has never come since! Would you fain not look upon the return of such an epoch, under your reign?'

Cadwy nodded slowly, the keenness fading from his eyes as a misty look came over them. 'Aye, my love, that I would... but how?'

He looked pathetic, so weak-minded and confused. She pressed: 'Think not of these petty land wars – what is there in the rough hinterlands worth fighting for? I would have you reign over lands more fruitful – aye a very empire, one taken by sea!'

Cadwy looked at the floor. 'By sea? Thraxia has not dared build a fleet since the War of the Cobian Succession.'

'Yet our shipwrights have not forsaken their age-old craft.'

Cadwy shook his head. 'Our craft falls far short of our ancestors' – my uncle's failure to defeat the Cobians bears testament to that.'

'The ships were well constructed enough, 'twas the admirals who were to blame! With the right leadership, a new Thraxian fleet would be a force to be reckoned with.'

'And where would we find such men? My uncle banished his admiralty for their abject failure five years ago – we've had precious little new talent coming through the ranks since.'

'Look south to your former foes, my loving liege. Cobia has a great maritime tradition, yet it is a small country with few opportunities – its mariners often seek service in the Mercadian navy. Give them a reason to look north.'

The King stared at her. 'You'd have me commission a fleet, and crew it with Cobian sea captains? How much gold shall I need to persuade them to betray their own country?'

She felt like laughing in his face. Had this fool really reigned for more than two years before she enthralled him? Suppressing her mirth she met his eye. 'I am not suggesting you commission a new fleet to attack Cobia,' she said patiently. 'I mean for you to send it *west*, across the Tyrnian Straits... the time has come to take back the lands our ancestors were so unjustly banished from two millennia ago. Conquer the Island Realms – and reunite the Westerling race!'

The King gawped. Not even Enchantment could hold back his initial misgivings. 'Art thou mad? The Straits are haunted, the Islands themselves protected by ancient magicks! Some even say the Archangel Kaia still visits their shores to speak by moonlight with the druid caste!'

She could feel his fear, but underneath that she sensed another powerful emotion: the innate lust for power that all kings felt. Channelling her mindset she pictured a roaring lion rearing over a huddled figure, superimposed above the fish and hook symbol.

Even as Abrexta spoke she knew she had him.

'Let me worry about the ghosts and the druids, my loving liege. Raise the taxes. Commission the fleet. Solicit the Cobians. For too long have we lived in the shadow of our neighbours – Thraxia's time has come.'

Favouring the King with a last lingering kiss, she pulled away and drained her goblet. She felt the blood of her fay ancestors pounding in her temples as the wild music strained against the gnarled ceiling. All about them the courtiers swirled, dancing to the tune she had set.

⊷ CHAPTER IV ⊷

The Burned Witch's Lair

For the third night running Adhelina awoke in a cold sweat, breathing heavily as she calmed herself and struggled to remember her dreams.

The pale-faced figures had returned to haunt her sleep again, their lipless mouths cracked open in silent yowls as they reached for her with two-fingered hands. That part was always the same, lumpen forms hunched over them in the moonlight as they cowered together. This time it was Anupe who was first to fall, swallowed up by the ogrish fiends as they devoured her silently... There was never any sound.

Feeling the sweat trickle down her back the heiress of Dulsinor pressed both hands tightly to her temples. She closed her eyes and remembered.

She had seen other things too – this time it had been a party of knights being swallowed up by a surging forest whose branches and roots moved... then a great castle, a white flag hanging limply from its battlements... The scene had shifted again, and she had been as a bird, flying high above the lands of the earth, a range of mountain peaks to the west... another forest... to its north another party of knights carrying a chequered banner, then directly below her to the south three slightly smaller figures riding. Behind them another group of mounted warriors rode in hot pursuit, a bright banner streaming in the wind like hot tongues of flame... The scene had shifted again and she and Hettie had been back in the clearing, watching Anupe get torn apart by the horrible white monsters...

The sound of coughing drew her attention back to the waking world. Hettie lay curled up on her makeshift cot next to her, shivering beneath the fur skin that served as a rude blanket. She was moaning softly in her sleep. Was she having strange dreams too, Adhelina wondered?

She pressed a white hand gently to her oldest friend's forehead. It felt damp and clammy. The simple she had placed in a pomander around her neck was a day old; she would need to make a new one. She was nearly out of St Clepticus' Weed; she had some Tincture of Launacum she could use instead, but it wasn't as effective against the Sweating Sickness...

Hettie stirred. Her fever had not yet broken, but it wasn't as bad as it had been the previous week. That was something to be grateful for. She was eighteen summers but the Sweating Sickness had been known to kill others as young and strong as her. Reaching into her medicine pouch Adhelina began to prepare the last of the weed, silently praying it would be enough to break her fever.

She shivered in the damp. Their resting place was hardly the best for a sick patient, but what choice had they had? Two days after the fight with the brigands Hettie had taken poorly, and out in the wilderness of Dulsinor they had been lucky to find the hollow where the burned crone lived. A series of low caves set deep into a hillside covered with tumbleweed and briars, at least it was well concealed. They were just half a day's ride from the main road connecting Meerborg to the Argael and could have made it to the nearest inn, but it seemed like too much of a risk to take. Two damsels, one of them sickly, and a foreign freesword would attract too much attention; by now Balthor and his men would be in the Free City, putting the word around. They could not take the risk that someone might see them and realise who they were...

Adhelina bit her lip fretfully as she doused the Clepticus' Weed in a little water from her gourd and refilled the pomander. The pungent smell of the herb rose gently as she wrapped it anew and tied it gently around her lady-in-waiting's neck. They had been here a tenday now, and she had not felt much safer than she would have done at a roadside inn.

True, the burned crone seemed to want little to do with the wider world, and had taken them in without much fuss. Perhaps she was lonely and grateful for the company. But there was something unnatural about her; the glint in her eyes as she looked at them beneath disfigured eyelids made Adhelina feel uneasy.

The crone's dwelling wasn't much better. It was dead of night, yet Adhelina had lit no taper before preparing her friend's simple: the grotto was illuminated by an orb of glass hanging from the middle cave containing a swirling liquid that emitted a blue-green light. This dimmed and grew stronger seemingly of its own will but never went out. The damsel had read enough accounts of Argolian witch hunters to suspect Alchemy, the Seventh School of Magick.

Hettie's breathing eased as the fresh simple took effect, her coughing subsiding. Touching her friend's forehead again Adhelina felt the heat ease slightly. Rummaging around in her medicine pouch she produced a dried bunch of Lonefrick's Cap. She'd boil another dose in hot water this afternoon; that should help some more with the fever. It was a strong plant and she couldn't risk using it more than once a week, because the side effects could be severe: rashes and sores in minor cases, bleeding and death in extreme ones.

A low mumbling drew her attention away from her herbs. It was coming from beyond the entrance to the cave she shared with Hettie, past the middle one where Anupe slept, her calloused hand still resting on her drawn falchion. Pulling her cloak around her Adhelina stepped gingerly towards the entrance, crouching low to avoid banging her head against the rough ceiling. The smell of dank earth was all about her.

Stopping at the entrance-way joining her cave to Anupe's, she looked past the Harijan's sleeping form. There were two more exits: one led back towards another cave that served as an antechamber and looked onto the overgrown hollow where their horses were tethered; the other led to the burned crone's part of the grotto.

That was where the mumbling was coming from.

Adhelina closed her eyes and tried to focus her hearing. Was the crone talking in her sleep? The words weren't distinct enough to make out, but even so the heiress of Dulsinor felt sure they were not in any tongue she knew. A shiver caressed her spine; her clothes stuck to her flesh clammily.

Adhelina gave a start as she felt a hand grip her wrist. Looking down she saw Anupe had rolled over and was brandishing her blade.

'What are you doing?' the outlander asked in a hoarse whisper.

'Just listening...' replied Adhelina, regaining her composure.

'To what?'

'Our host... just listen.'

Both women waited in silence for a few seconds. The words stopped then came again, low and sibilant and strange. Adhelina did not like them, whatever they meant.

'I do not care for this place,' said Anupe, reading her thoughts. 'The sooner Lady Freihertz is well enough for moving the more I shall like it.'

'At least we should be safe from Sir Balthor and his men,' said Adhelina. 'While we've been stuck here he's probably given up the search and gone back to Graukolos.'

'Explaining your strange vanishing to his lord,' said the mercenary, sitting up and stretching. The pungent smell of steel and leather on a woman was still hard for Adhelina to get used to, but she felt grateful for the freesword's protection.

'My father won't stop at that,' said Adhelina. 'Even now he will be mustering a wider search – he commands a hundred bachelors and twice that number of serjeants, plus landed vassals. Our plan was a good one when we had time on our side. Now...'

'You are right,' said the Harijan. 'This delay is not in our interest. So why do you not follow my counsel – '

'I'm not leaving her here,' snapped Adhelina. 'As I told you more than a week ago, I will not abandon Hettie to face my father's justice alone.'

Anupe shook her head exasperatedly. 'Very well, then you will leave us in a difficult position instead.'

Their argument was interrupted by a sound. A winged shape suddenly flew from the crone's cave. It crossed the middle cave in the blinking of an eye, before disappearing out of the far exit to be swallowed up by the night sky.

'What was that?' breathed Adhelina.

'I am not sure,' replied Anupe. 'A bird... or something else. Perhaps it is time I spoke to our host.' The Harijan got up agilely, and began stalking towards the crone's cave.

Hettie called out behind them.

Adhelina turned back to see to her friend. Hettie sat up, coughed and shook her head. The heiress of Dulsinor reached out and touched her forehead. It was cool.

'Why Hettie, your fever's broken!' she said. 'Thank Reus, you're on the mend!'

Hettie managed a small smile in the eerie light. 'Thanks to your efforts, milady. I recognise a pomander of herbs when I smell one.'

'And sharp as ever!' said Adhelina delightedly, a warm wave of relief washing over her. Hettie would need another day or two of rest, but she was out of danger.

'But where on earth are we?' asked Hettie, looking around the grotto. 'I don't remember much... how long have I been sick?'

'Your fever was at its worst ten nights ago,' explained Adhelina. 'We had to tie you to the saddle and brought you here, to this place. We're still in the wilderness, about a half a day's ride from the road to Meerborg. You've been in and out of consciousness for a good tenday.'

'A tenday?' replied Hettie, startled. 'But that will mean... Won't Balthor have realised we aren't in Meerborg?'

'Oh Hettie, rather too sharp for your own good!' said Adhelina fondly. 'Don't worry yourself about such things for now, just concentrate on getting well. We're quite safe, we're in this place...' She trailed off, wondering how safe they really were.

They were distracted by a sharp yell. Loping back to the centre Adhelina saw Anupe emerge from the crone's cave, dragging their host by a tuft of grey hair.

The Harijan flung her roughly to the ground.

'Speak!' she commanded. 'I like not your witch ways. What creature flew from your cave just now?'

'There wasss no creature,' hissed the crone, her deformed mouth cracking an ugly grimace. 'You sssaw a ssshadow, nothing more.'

She would have been tall for her sex and large of body, but decades of living in the grotto had hunched her back. Besides that the crone's scarred skin gave her a shrivelled aspect that belied her true size. Her deerskin robes were soiled with earth, her burned face topped by sparse tufts of hair.

Anupe menaced the crone with her falchion.

'Do not insult me – I know my own eyes and ears,' she said, yanking her into an upright position. The middle cave was the largest but both women still had to stoop.

The burned crone spat at Anupe's feet and said nothing. The Harijan flung her back to the ground and pressed the tip of her blade against her throat.

'You are a witch,' said Anupe, gesturing at the cave's jumbled contents. It was crammed with assorted odds and ends, rubbish the crone had collected over the years – broken stools, worn crates, a splintered barrel, lengths of twine, a pair of cracked lanterns, threadbare cloth, soiled bearskins, mildewed sacks, an assortment of shattered ceramic bowls and gourds... their strange host did not lack for company, if inanimate objects could be said to be company.

'How many have you tricked with your sorcery over the years?' she demanded. 'No ordinary hermit would keep such things.'

The burned crone narrowed her eyes, looking all the more hideous in the pulsing light of the orb. 'Then why do you ssstay?' she hissed. 'Leave me be if you don't like what you sssee.'

'That we shall, now that my friend is better,' interjected Adhelina. 'But first you must tell us what you are up to. I heard you mumbling to yourself before yon winged apparition flew from your cave – explain yourself, or my bodyguard shall not be merciful.' As if to emphasise her employer's words, Anupe stepped forward and placed a booted foot on the crone's broad flat chest.

'I have not troubled you,' said the crone. 'Shelter and ressst for your friend you begged. Thisss I gave you. I even offered you tea but you refusssed. I did not even asssk for a share of your meat. Thisss isss how you repay me?'

'As to your blandishments, I am glad we tried them not,' said Adhelina. 'For Reus knows what your potions contained and I see no herbs here that I recognise. You haven't troubled us 'tis true, but night and day you've watched us keenly. What have you learned?'

Adhelina caught Anupe flashing her a look. She knew she was taking a risk, but instinct told her the crone already knew more than she should.

The crone remained tight-lipped. The sight of Anupe's razor-sharp blade seemed not to frighten her. Perhaps she did not think a woman capable of killing, though Adhelina knew better. Or perhaps she had already suffered so much that death held few terrors for her.

The Harijan must have been thinking along the same lines, for she said: 'Milady, please fetch me a taper from my things over yonder, I would have a more natural light.'

Glancing at the bundle next to her Adhelina nodded. 'Hettie, be so kind as to give our freesword what she requests.' These were emergency circumstances, but the heiress of Dulsinor still ought not to fetch and carry.

Hettie did as she was asked and produced a taper and tinderbox. Following the Harijan's instructions she clumsily struck up a fire. All the while the crone struggled to be free but Anupe dropped her falchion and wrestled her to the ground, pinning her arms behind her before lashing them together with some of the twine.

As Hettie approached with the flaring taper she gave vent to a hideous shriek. Adhelina was scarcely surprised; she had shrunk back into the furthest corner of the cave every night when Anupe had cooked them meat after hunting. Their peculiar host seemed to survive on a diet of nuts, roots and berries.

'Now I think you will tell us what we want to know,' said Anupe, dragging her upright and forcing her to face the flames. 'Or do you want to feel the fire again?'

'Noo, noo, NOOOOO!' shrieked the crone hysterically. 'Not the FIRE, pleassse! They burned me sssso badly, they would have killed me!! The monksss rescued me from the fire only to burn me again! Not the fire, *not the fire*, NOT THE FIRE!!!'

The significance of her words was not lost on Adhelina. Peering at the crone in the firelight she could see it – virtually invisible against the rumpled flesh of her forehead, but still just about discernible if you really looked for it.

'Why she's been branded,' she said. 'One can barely notice it against her scars. She's been tried by Argolians and found guilty. She is a witch!'

'Now tell me something I do not know,' said Anupe.

'We will not hurt you,' said Adhelina. 'But you must tell us what you know and what you have done. Otherwise you really will burn to death this time.'

She felt a pang of guilt. She didn't like any kind of cruelty, but what choice did they have? She would be free of her bondage to the loathsome Herzog her father wanted her to marry – even if that meant doing unpleasant things.

'I heard you and the freessssword talking last night,' spat the crone. 'Sssomething about getting out of Dulsssinor, and your father being a powerful man, and ssstoping at nothing to find you... and then I realisssed who you were. It had been many yearsss since I sssaw you, and you were but a girl-child back then.'

Adhelina's eyes narrowed further. 'Who are you?' she barked.

'One who would fain ssserve your father again,' replied the witch. 'I wasss a chambermaid at Graukolosss, and I lived in the village of Lanfrig nearby. My mother'sss sssister lived in the Glimmerholt, and practisssed sssorcery. 'Twas from her feet I learned...'

A sly self-satisfied smile crossed the witch's face. At a nod from Anupe, Hettie brought the taper closer so she could feel the flames. Anupe had to hold her even more tightly to stop her frantic squirming.

'What did you learn?' pressed Adhelina.

'I tried to transsssform my wages – copper into sssilver, but I could not. The disssscipline of merging Transsssformation with Alchemy isss a difficult one to massster alasss... My neighboursss found me out, and took hold of me. Sssome were for burning me on the ssspot, othersss wanted to call the Argolians. Both sssides had their way... Only the arrival of two friarsss sssaved me, but I wasss half burned ere they intervened. Then they tried me, and I wasss found guilty of practisssing Right Hand sssorcery. They branded me a witch and the Eorl banished me from Graukolosss and all the landsss for ten leaguesss about, on pain of death.'

'Your punishment was justly deserved,' replied Adhelina firmly. 'But why were you not bound in links of cold iron, as the penalty for witchcraft stipulates?'

The burned witch looked at her with admiration. 'Very clever, the heiresss of Dulsssinor isss well read indeed.'

'Save your flattery and answer my question.'

'My posssessions were impounded by the Argolians, but I had another cache of paraphernalia buried in the woodsss near where my aunt usssed to live. I went there and recovered it – among other thingsss was a concoction I had made that would render itsss drinker sssubject to itsss maker's wishes. After that it wasss just a matter of finding a vagabond, sssomeone who would trick a sssmith into drinking it. My ally knocked the sssmith out and robbed him after he freed me from the iron. I found thisss place and have lived here ever sssince, but I have grown lonely in the wildernesss. I would fain return home.'

'And you think my father will lift your banishment if you turn me in?'

The witch favoured her with an ugly smile. 'It can't hurt to try now can it, sssweetie?'

'And so what was the spell you were using just now? What creature did you conjure up to tell my father of our whereabouts?'

'Ah, sssso clever! What a shame the Argolians don't accept women, you would have made a fine witch hunter...!'

'Enough of your cheek – answer my question or by Reus I really will have you burned!'

'It wasss no creature, jussst an ordinary bird of flight. It's carrying a little messsage to your father.'

'What did the message say?' The witch squealed as Hettie waved the brand at her, doing her best to look menacing. Her drawn sick face looked ghastly enough in the flickering light.

'I sssaid the heiresss of Dulsssinor isss here, with a freessssword and high-born companion. I sssaid I would wait by the broken well ssseven leaguesss from the eassst road to Meerborg every day at noon for one hour. I sssaid gold would loosssen my tongue easssily enough.'

Adhelina's lip curled in disgust. 'I can't expect a commoner to have honour, but your avarice is sickening.'

'This broken well, where is it?' asked Anupe.

'Not far,' replied the witch. 'Half a league eassst of here, towardsss the main road.'

'And this message of yours, it said nothing else?'

'Nothing – I would not wish to reveal everything before I wasss sssure of my reward.'

'No indeed, you have proved most clever in this regard,' replied Anupe, pulling her dirk from her boot and plunging it into the crone's back.

The witch's dying scream drowned out the damsels' own cries before she expired in a twitching heap, the dagger buried in her heart.

'We could not leave her alive to tell them more when they arrive,' said the Harijan, ignoring their horrified expressions as she pulled her blade free of the spurting wound. 'At least she did not die by the fire.'

'That was an ugly deed and an unjust one!' protested Adhelina. 'I said she would come to no harm if she helped us!'

'She helped us by dying,' replied the Harijan, before cleaning her bade coolly and returning it to its scabbard. 'Now, let us get our things together and get gone from this strange place. Lady Freihertz will have to ride, and finish her recovery in the saddle. My guess is a bird can fly to Graukolos in a few days. That means most likely we will have this Balthor on our backs again within a week – there was enough information in that note for him to guess as to our whereabouts. We must get to the Argael with all haste.'

Stepping lightly over the corpse the outlander began packing up her things.

Adhelina and Hettie exchanged shocked looks. But what was there to say? The Harijan had the right of it, and no amount of talking would bring the dead back. Adhelina felt her heart sink. How many more lives would her bid for freedom cost?

Her oldest friend clearly sensed her misgivings. 'Try not to think too much, milady,' she said, drawing closer. 'She's right – we need to get out of here right away. There'll be time aplenty for reflecting when we're on a ship to Meerborg.'

Adhelina smiled weakly, then frowned. 'Will you be all right? Your fever's only just broken – ideally you should have had another day or two of rest.'

Hettie smiled back, trying to look hardy. 'I'll just have to do my recovering in the saddle, as Anupe said. At least the worst is over – and besides, some fresh air and exercise will do me some good I trow.'

'Thank Reus you're well again Hettie,' said Adhelina. 'I don't know what I'd do without you.'

'You'd probably be on a dromon bound for the Empire by now,' answered Hettie ruefully.

'We'll get there yet, Hettie, you'll see.'

Her friend smiled again but could not hide the sadness in her eyes. Their old life already seemed a thousand miles away.

They packed their things in silence. In less than an hour they were following a trail out of the hollow where the burned witch had lived and died. It was a clear summer's night and the stars were a welcome relief after the eerie light of the grotto. Anupe rode ahead, holding the taper aloft to light their way.

Adhelina's mind flashed back to the nightmares that had awoken her, and she suppressed a shiver. She suddenly had a sense of the three of them caught up in a tiny halo of light, surrounded on all sides by a darkness that had no earthly compass.

Perhaps that's all there is to a life, she thought dolefully.

⚔ CHAPTER V ⚔

Of Troubled Souls

A delko picked at his food. He was normally always hungry, and the monks of Ørthang ate just as well as those of Ulfang, but he had no appetite. The refectory was somewhat smaller than Ulfang's, and bereft of the statues he had found so appealing. Thinking on the one of St Ionus that had been his favourite, he thought it strange the patron saint of travellers should be absent now – he had become quite the voyager since leaving his monastic home in the Highlands.

Ørthang was altogether less impressive, and housed half the number of Argolians, but it was alike enough to bring on another bout of homesickness. He missed his brother Arik, so briefly rediscovered.

But more than that, he missed the feeling of innocence.

Since leaving Ulfang he had encountered spirits, devils, freeswords and faeries; he had seen war in all its horrors and even had a hand in its outcome. He was leading the life of adventure he had always dreamed of... and while he couldn't deny it thrilled as much as it horrified him, he also felt a lingering sadness that hadn't been there three months ago. He was sharing his mentor's fate, becoming bound up in events greater than himself – and getting blood on his hands. Not literally perhaps, but Horskram's hard words at Salmor had struck home.

He'd had a say in whether men lived or died, and that changed you.

The other novices treated him with a mixture of curiosity and awe: even leaving most of it out, his story had been enough to leave half of them dumbstruck. And yet he'd just got a pasting from a novice of seventeen summers who reminded him of Yalba, his loudmouth friend from Ulfang.

A life of adventuring only changed you so much, he reflected wryly – for all the trials he'd survived, he was still a near hopeless fighter.

He thought back to the exorcism that had started it all. He still recalled the demon Belaach's power, how it had tried to torment him, opening up dark pockets in his mind in an effort to quash his soul and break his will. The Psalms had kept him going on that occasion, and many others.

But now he began to feel gnawing doubts that were very much his own: had he done the right thing, choosing to be an Argolian?

The sound of a bell brought Adelko from his uncomfortable reverie. The evening meal was over, and it was time for prayers. Getting up with the rest of the novices, he glanced over at the corner table where his companions sat. Seeing Vaskrian, Sir Braxus and the four raven knights put him in mind of the refectory at Ulfang again, when he had looked over furtively at the freeswords guarding the merchants who had stopped to visit.

Back then he had looked upon fighting men with fear and unease: now they were his friends, bosom companions who would die protecting him if need be. And yet Horskram had told him on the eve of the march to war that a true Argolian could never be friends with such men, no matter the cause... Never mind that his mentor had once been a crusader and done his fair share of killing.

Adelko felt a tightness in his chest that he hoped prayer would diminish. His mind, restless at the best of times, was riven with conflicting thoughts. The aches and pains from his quarterstaff bout seemed trifling in comparison. He'd had worse. The cut to his forehead had healed, as had the gash in his side: though he couldn't look at that scar without a chill of horror as he remembered the Hag in Tintagael.

As the two hundred monks of Ørthang filed outside and made their way across the twilit courtyard towards the chapel, Adelko wondered grimly what his fifteenth summer held in store. Somewhat more than his fourteenth, he suspected.

✣ ✣ ✣

Vaskrian watched the monks file out of the refectory. He felt satisfied. He'd had his fill of good food and watered wine, but that wasn't the real reason why.

His war wounds still ached – his *war* wounds. The pain brought him an intense pleasure. He'd fought in battles and survived, killing his share of fighters. He thought back to the clearing on the way to Harrang, when Sir Branas had forced him to put Derrick out of his misery. He still felt bad about that, truth be told. Not a good kill. It hadn't felt... knightly.

But this time around was different. He'd slaughtered rebels, men fighting against their King. He'd fought on the *right* side, and the

Almighty had witnessed that and brought the Loyalists a resounding victory. He'd played his part, a small one maybe, but enough to raise a humble squire in estimation.

He glanced sidelong at his new master. Sir Braxus of Gaellen – a Thraxian and a foreigner, there was no denying it. But a foreigner who'd promised him great rewards, if he served well. That was a damn sight more than his last two guvnors had offered. He felt a surge of excitement and reached for the hilt of his sword... before remembering he'd left it in his lodgings, along with the rest of his weapons and armour. He'd wanted to wear his mail shirt to supper, it was made by Strongholm smiths and of the finest quality. But Braxus was having none of it: warriors or no, they would abide by the rules of the Argolian Order.

That annoyed him. Monks! All good and well for healing the sick or fighting evil spirits, but what gave them the right to tell fighters to abandon the tools of their trade?

Still, he had befriended one of them... Adelko, funny sort of chap with his round face and goggle eyes. Always talking about things Vaskrian didn't understand, like history and languages and doing the right thing. And yet he liked the lad. He didn't talk down to him like so many others; he never criticised him for his ambitions to become a knight, even though he obviously disapproved of violence. And the night before the battle at Linden, when he'd thanked him for saving his life... it would have been much better coming from a fine-looking damsel, but it had been right nice all the same. That was what knights were supposed to do: crush rebels and robbers and protect the weak and defenceless.

In fact it was just about the best reason for killing someone he could think of.

Vaskrian looked past his master at Sir Torgun. His hero. The knight's rugged face looked serious and troubled. The squire couldn't think why, he had everything going for him: the best knight in the land, serving in its most prestigious order (an order he longed to join someday).

And now he was sharing the road with him, on a madcap quest that belonged in bard's song.

The thought of it sent another thrill through his wiry frame as the six of them rose to leave the refectory. Strictly speaking Sir Braxus was in charge of his combat training, but he hoped to sneak a few tips from Sir Torgun here and there. After all he was the best swordsman in their company, and it paid to learn from the best.

Following his master out into the courtyard Vaskrian felt a twinge of unease. Yes, it was a madcap quest... he still struggled to

remember what had happened to him in Tintagael. Bard's song –
hadn't he met someone in that cursed forest, a knight who'd served
in the time of Thorsvald the Hero King, celebrated himself in verse?
He shook his head. No, that was impossible – Thorsvald had lived
and ruled more than a hundred years ago, the Thirteen Knights who
had met their end in Tintagael were long gone...

Or were they? The forest was haunted, after all. Oh why couldn't
he remember?

'What ails thee?'

His guvnor was looking at him keenly in the gloaming.

'Nothing, Sir Braxus, just... I was thinking about Tintagael.' He
found it hard to lie to his new master, the foreigner was far too
perceptive for that.

'Well don't,' replied the Thraxian. 'From what I know of the
Faerie Kindred, the less you dwell on their ways the better. Just be
thankful you survived your journey through that accursed place
– few do from what I've heard. Now let's away to bed – we've a
long day ahead of us on the road tomorrow, you'll need to check
everything so we can set off at first light.'

Vaskrian nodded and did as he was told. For once the mundane
duties of squirehood didn't bother him over much – he didn't like
thinking about the forest, and any distraction was welcome.

✠ ✠ ✠

Braxus sighed as he lay down on his pallet while his squire busied
himself checking their equipment. A disused storage room in one
of the monastery's outhouses, hardly lodgings fit for men of noble
birth. But that was the Argolians for you. They had long followed
nobody's rules but their own – small wonder so many powerful
people despised them.

And here he was, taking orders from one. A merry band of
adventurers they were, and there was no doubt who was in charge.
Horskram of Vilno.

Braxus had no reason to like the man. He was arrogant and
conceited; always so sure of himself, bereft of any manners. The
Thraxian hadn't forgotten the way the old monk had spoken to him
on the morning of the march to war. Just who did he think he was?
His father Lord Braun had always respected the secretive order of
monks – that in itself was enough reason to dislike them.

But what choice had he had? The Northlending King had played
him skilfully; he dared not return to Thraxia empty-handed, and

if this fool's errand was the only chance of getting Freidheim to consider giving military aid to his countrymen, so be it.

Braxus shifted uncomfortably on his pallet in the flaring light of the taper Vaskrian had lit. All the same, there *was* something afoot… Abrexta's witcheries were the cause of his homeland's woes, of that he was certain. Without her sorcerous meddling King Cadwy would have despatched reinforcements to aid the northern lords against Slangà and his highlanders long ago. The Sea Wizard was gone who knew where, but he'd clearly had a hand in the civil war of the Northlendings… And Horskram's tale of horror from the Highlands to Strongholm bore all the hallmarks of a Left-Hand warlock hell-bent on destroying anyone in his or her path. Wherever he was, this Andragorix certainly seemed to fit the description.

His knowledge of the Headstone of Mammon was hazy, and he liked it that way. Tales of that legendary age of sorcerer-kings had never made him feel anything but uneasy. But piecing together everything Horskram and King Freidheim had told him, it looked for all the world as if he was caught up in events that went beyond the borders of a single country.

Reus damn it, by the looks of it someone was trying to bring the whole of the Free Kingdoms under their control.

At any rate, that was the message he'd given to Vertrix for his father. He doubted the old man would give it much credence, he reflected bitterly: just another excuse for his wayward son to remain wayward.

Thinking on his compatriots brought a pang of homesickness over Braxus. Even now the seven of them would be taking ship back to Thraxia, and Reus knew what state the kingdom would be in by the time they returned. Would there even be a home to come back to? Between them Slánga and Tíerchán had fielded a formidable force of hate-filled highlanders; and thanks to that sorcerous bitch Abrexta the northern lords wouldn't hold out for much longer.

Vaskrian returned from the stables having fed the horses, and gestured at the taper. Braxus nodded curtly. His squire extinguished the light, and the heir of Gaellentir turned over and closed his eyes, silently praying for Morphonus to grant him the sweet release of sleep.

✠ ✠ ✠

Torgun sat on an uneven stone that jutted out from the perimeter wall of the monastery, sharpening his sword. He knew he should get some rest, but there was no sleep in him tonight. Glancing up at the dark skies, he wondered if the stars would look any different in the lands they were journeying to. A loremaster had once told him they did if you went far enough south, but Torgun had paid him little heed. What concern had he for foreign climes, when lifelong duty would keep him at home in Northalde where he belonged? Even his errant days venturing beyond the King's Dominions had seemed like a great journey.

Now his King had told him his duty lay elsewhere, beyond the borders of the very realm he had sworn to serve. His heart yearned for high adventure and Freidheim's word was law, but he felt sad all the same. He didn't like the thought of leaving Northalde, especially not in the aftermath of a war. The southern provinces would be crawling with remnants of Thule's levy, causing trouble for ordinary commoners.

You were made for greater things than harrying outlaws... the King's words came back to him. Perhaps he was, but that wasn't for him to say. And surely protecting His Majesty's subjects was more important than winning glory?

Freidheim had spoken to him of a plot to rule realms that lay behind the war they had just won. Torgun had seen enough at Staerkvit to be convinced that some awful devilry was in the air – for only a black magician could conjure up such foul fiends. The thought of it sent a rare shiver down his spine.

He didn't like that feeling, not one little bit.

No mortal man would ever instil fear in his heart, of that he was certain. He had slain dozens of brave fighters in his young life; injured and ransomed and unhorsed hundreds more.

But warlocks and demons and wadwos – they were a different story. He'd faced all three, and had hated fighting them. Mortal men could be killed or vanquished, you could beat them in a fair fight. But the powers of the Other Side... that was a different matter. He'd seen the demon at Staerkvit slay dozens of his comrades effortlessly – without the prayers of Horskram and his understudy, who knows how many more would have died?

Running his whetstone up and down his broad blade, he glanced across at the monks leaving the chapel and heading back to their quarters. This was *their* kind of fight – knights weren't supposed to engage the supernatural.

Putting the whetstone down he hefted his sword. It was larger than the usual size: even a strong knight would struggle to wield it one-handed, yet he used it with ease. And he'd had to hack with all his might just to inflict a slight wound on the horror at Staerkvit.

His mind went back to when he'd travelled the kingdom as an errant, before joining the White Valravyn. In his nineteenth summer, he had fought a duel with a sorceress in the Laegawood. Halga Bloodmouth, the local woodfolk called her. She had preyed on them for weeks, stealing their children to use in her awful sacrificial rites. An Argolian had been sent to apprehend her, but died trying: his mangled corpse had been found hanging from a tree. Torgun had been staying with the woodfolk when they heard that news: he had jumped at another chance to win more renown and set off in search of her.

He had found her living in a disused fort on the western edges of the woods. He soon learned the reason for her name. Looking at his sword glinting in the starlight he remembered how he had drawn it and approached the witch, offering her one chance to surrender and come quietly. She had laughed in his face, an awful scratching sound. Clearly the woman was out of her wits, driven mad by the unclean powers she had channelled.

As he had advanced on her she had spat on the ground between them. Her saliva was red and there was far too much of it... he could see it now, dropping in thick gobbets on the long grass between them, burning and cracking the bright green blades. The gobbets had bubbled up and expanded as the witch spoke words in an unnatural tongue, clumping together in a red miasma before turning into a host of blood-coloured scorpions.

He had barely survived, being stung several times as he crushed them one by one in his huge mailed fists. Only his iron constitution had saved him, and as Halga had approached him to cut his throat with a silver knife, he had grabbed up his sword and plunged it into her belly. Even then it hadn't been over. Mouthing a spell through dying lips, the witch had transformed her spilled entrails into a swarm of serpents. It had taken all of his last strength to cut them to ribbons before he passed out.

He'd been found by the woodfolk, who tended him. It had taken him a couple of tendays to recover physically, and even now he sometimes had nightmares.

Apart from anything else, killing a woman did not sit easily on his conscience – even an evil one like that who had given up her soul to the Fallen Angel. He hadn't earned his spurs to kill women. And now he was off to find another witch in another forest, this time to seek an alliance – against yet another sorcerer. Torgun felt his temples throbbing. Thoughts of warlocks and witchery made his head spin.

He missed Hjala too – he'd known it was a mistake rekindling their romance. Now he had that to deal with too, but then chivalrous knights were supposed to yearn after a true love, he supposed. Reaching into his tunic he pulled out the token she had given him on their last night together – a platinum amulet fashioned to resemble one of the rearing unicorns of the Ingwin coat of arms. A precious gift from a peerless lady. Holding it gave him renewed peace of mind, and he began to be ashamed of his fearful thoughts of the Other Side.

Standing up, the young knight sheathed his sword. Yes, he ought to be grateful – war and quest were the stuff of knighthood after all. His King had been right, he was certainly made for this sort of thing. But walking back towards his lodgings, Sir Torgun could not shake the feeling that he had left a simple life of service behind forever.

⤙ CHAPTER VI ⤚

A Chase Renewed

'I think we've found it.' Sir Redrich's face looked flustered as he pushed back through the undergrowth. Sir Balthor was hardly surprised – riding cross country through the wilderness was bad enough at the best of times, never mind on a hot day like this. Dismounting from his courser, he felt the sweat trickling beneath his armour. It was just a light byrnie but all the same it itched in the heat.

'Step aside, let me see,' he ordered curtly, nudging past the other knight into the clearing. There it was, just as the mysterious hermit's message had said it would be – an old well, broken and disused.

'Well I don't see any sign of a hermit,' he growled.

Sir Redrich squinted up at the sun, trying to fathom its position behind the thick clouds. 'She said noon – by my reckoning we're about an hour early.'

Early. Balthor hated that word even more than he hated riding cross country. A nobleman was never early, nor should he rush, unless it was an emergency. Well technically speaking this *was* an emergency, but all the same it galled him – to rush to get somewhere only to wait... on a commoner, of all things!

He would never live it down – he was the greatest knight in Dulsinor, he deserved better than this.

All told, it had been a horrendous few weeks. First of all failing to find any clues as to the theft from the Werecrypt, then letting the runaway heiress elude him. He had visited every merchant house in Meerborg, describing the Stonefist's daughter and her lady-in-waiting over and over till the words became tedious to utter. Stuck in the bustling stink of the Free City, having to ask – *ask* – the merchant class for help. Insupportable! Didn't they know who he was? Not even its brothels and taverns had been enough to relieve his pains.

Worse still, after all that he'd returned empty handed. The Eorl had lost his temper and rebuked him in front of everyone who mattered, calling him a blockhead and a damned incompetent.

The look on Sir Urist's face had made it twice as bad – the Marshal had loved every minute of it.

And then the strange message had arrived: *Two runaway damsels I am keeping at my homestead in the wilderness, one is sick and cannot move. A foreign freesword protects them. If this interests you, meet me by the broken well seven leagues south of the Meerborg road to the Argael. I shall wait there for one hour from noon every day.*

The castle perfect Tobias had said the handwriting was ungainly, not in a fine hand. The odd commoner did learn how to write, but they were usually city-dwellers. That had prompted much speculation, but Balthor had heard all he needed to hear on the matter. *Commoner.* To go through all that wasted effort only to be trumped by some peasant living in the middle of nowhere – insufferable!

When the Eorl had despatched him a second time, warning him not to return empty handed again, Sir Urist had actually dared to smile. Balthor couldn't wait for this summer's tournament – he'd see to it that he unhorsed the Marshal a second time, maybe break a few more bones. That would wipe the smile off his face! But the Graufluss Bridge Tourney felt a long way away – if indeed it would go ahead at all now. No, he corrected himself quickly, it would – because this time Sir Balthor Lautstimme would not fail. He would bring back the Eorl's headstrong daughter, if he had to tie her to his blasted saddle.

Just what on earth was Her Ladyship playing at anyway? Overindulged by the Stonefist, that was the problem. His Lordship had never got over his wife's death, everyone about the castle knew that. Spoiled – read far too much, who knew what black arts she had learned in those books of hers? Must have used some kind of magic to escape in the dead of night like that. And what business did one of noble birth have reading anyway? Leave that to the perfects and the loremasters. Balthor couldn't read a word, and he was fiercely proud of that.

Sir Wilhelm and Sir Rufus pushed their way through the undergrowth to join them in the clearing. The three knights were the same ones assigned to him on his first pursuit of Lady Markward. They were all young, inexperienced, beneath his dignity: he deserved better company. Had the Eorl done it deliberately, he wondered, just to irk him? He was sick of the sight of their faces. They had better show some respect.

'Where are the horses?' he barked. For the sake of speed they weren't travelling with squires, so they had no one to see to things like tethering their steeds. He hated travelling without a squire – that was beneath his dignity too. The greatest knight in Dulsinor, bereft of a squire? He would never live it down!

'I've tethered them, they aren't going anywhere,' said Sir Wilhelm. He was the oldest of the three but still Balthor's junior by some ten winters. Balthor didn't care for his tone. It had been Wilhelm's suggestion to travel cross country, rather than take the long route by road through Meerborg. As if he hadn't known to do that himself, unpleasant as it was.

'See to it that they don't,' replied Balthor sternly. 'Bad enough we've had to dismount for half the journey since we left the road, I'll be right wroth if we have to walk back all the way!'

The young knight nodded wordlessly, but Balthor could tell by the look in his eyes that he was thinking something all right. Shared the same name as the Eorl, that was the trouble with Sir Wilhelm – gave him ideas above his station. But he knew the man's family, oh yes: as the younger son of a minor vassal he would never be more than an ordinary bachelor.

Needed bringing in line, this one.

'Well, I'm hungry,' he said. 'This ride has left me famished. Go and fetch us some victuals, we'll not meet this peasant on empty stomachs.'

Wilhelm's gaze hardened and he seemed about to say something when Sir Rufus spoke up.

'I'm only knighted recently,' he said. 'I don't mind seeing to our victuals. Not so long since I was doing it anyway.'

That kind of remark made Balthor sick. At twenty summers Rufus was the youngest, but that gave him no excuse to act like a squire. What had possessed the Eorl to give this weakling spurs?

'Yes well, why don't you get to it then,' he sneered. 'You obviously miss your squirehood.'

Rufus gawped at that but turned to comply. Wilhelm's face did not lighten though Redrich laughed at the jibe. Yes, right attitude that one. Perhaps he'd make something of himself, if he deferred to his betters. As for Rufus, he had no sympathy. Since when were knights supposed to conduct themselves like meek maids? He blamed that Code of Chivalry that had come out of Pangonia, during the time of King Vasir-whatever-his-name-was. A knight should stand proud and boast of his deeds – what was the point in doing them otherwise?

Presently Rufus returned and the four of them sat down to eat. Cured meats and hard cheeses washed down with weak wine – hardly the groaning boards of Graukolos, but it would have to do. The sun climbed steadily to its zenith and Balthor began to feel drowsy. Abruptly he stood up. Couldn't be seen nodding on the job. Had a reputation to maintain, dammit. Where was that wretched peasant?

✠ ✠ ✠

An hour passed. Balthor felt the tension growing in him like the Wasting Sickness. Another wild goose chase – he could not return to the keep like this, he was finished if he did.

'Perhaps we should check the lands that lie about here,' suggested Wilhelm, as if reading his thoughts. 'Surely this commoner would not have picked a meeting place too far from home?'

'Yes, yes, I was just going to say that,' snapped Balthor. 'Let's start by checking the edges of the clearing, perhaps there's another trail.'

There was. It was hidden behind more undergrowth, heading roughly in a south-westerly direction. It was too narrow for their horses, so they left Sir Rufus tending them and made their way in single file.

Balthor felt his confidence rise as they pushed their way into an overgrown dell another hour later. A cave mouth gaped from a rock face opposite, above which a thicket of trees grew raggedly, their branches blocking out the sunlight. That made it all the easier to see the faint blue-green light spilling from the entrance.

'Better draw swords,' muttered Balthor. 'I like not the look of yon cave.'

The whisper of steel reassured him instantly; he always felt better with a sword or spear in his hand. With that and iron links about his body, he would gladly take on the Known World.

The mouth was low and they had to crouch to enter. The cave they were in led straight into another one, piled with an assortment of rubbish. The strange light was coming from a glass globe hanging from the ceiling of the second cave. Balthor felt sure he didn't like it. A glance at the others' faces told him they were thinking much the same.

Lying beneath the globe was something he could understand – a dead body.

'She's been burned badly,' said Redrich after they had inspected the corpse. 'But she was stabbed – in the back by the looks of things.'

'Do you think I'm blind?' said Balthor. 'There are two more caves, we had better search them and now!'

They soon had enough to piece things together. In the rear cave they found a filthy cot and a rude wooden desk with scraps of parchment and a quill and ink on it. Strange-looking paraphernalia too – flasks and phials, with curious instruments fashioned from silver. And finally, in a worn old chest beneath the desk, two tomes covered in strange symbols that made Balthor queasy when he tried to look at them.

The side cave had proved just as illuminating: what looked like used poultices of some sort and traces of dried herbs. Signs of a healer. And a shawl, finely embroidered, though stained by the road. Not something most commoners could afford.

They hauled their findings out into the dell and gathered about them.

'Signs of our runaway damsels, the work of a freesword, and a dead witch, by the looks of things,' said Sir Wilhelm.

'Yes, I was going to say that,' said Balthor. 'Well it looks as though the witch was our informant – that's how she was able to command a crow to send message to the castle. And the freesword has killed her in retaliation, by the looks of things.'

The expression on the other knights' faces suggested they already knew that. Best to take the lead, show his authority.

'Search the dell. Let's see if there are any clues as to which direction they took.'

Another trail besides the one they had entered by struck out east, back towards the main road. The dell itself was clustered with horse dung – the damsels and their bodyguard had stayed here a while.

They followed the trail for half an hour before finding more evidence.

'More horse dung,' muttered Balthor. 'They're headed for the main road – let's get back to Rufus and our horses, quick sharp!'

He felt a sense of relief as he gave the order. He hated travelling on foot like a common serjeant – that was beneath his dignity too.

In fact, what didn't he hate about this wretched detail? He was supposed to be hunting and feasting and tourneying – not running around the wilderness searching for damned horse dung! Was this his reward for proving himself Dulsinor's greatest knight? Perhaps he should seek service elsewhere.

✢ ✢ ✢

The sun was low in the sky by the time the four of them reached the main road. Sir Balthor was wheeling his horse around towards Meerborg when Sir Wilhelm grasped his reins. Balthor shot him a fierce look and he quickly let go.

'What is it now?' he roared. He had a mind to knock the young knight from the saddle. He knew who he'd be challenging to a duel of honour come the Graufluss Bridge Tourney.

'I don't think she's going to Meerborg,' said Wilhelm, meeting Balthor's furious stare with difficulty.

'Whatever do you mean? Isn't it obvious what the Lady Markward intends – she wants to take ship from the port! She means to get out of Vorstlund altogether, though Reus knows why!'

'With all due respect,' replied Wilhelm, licking his lips. 'I think the Lady Markward is too shrewd for such an obvious move.'

'Obvious! Are you calling me – '

'She must realise His Lordship will have sent men to warn the merchant houses of the Free City by now,' pressed the knight.

Balthor was reaching for the hilt of his sword when Sir Redrich spoke up.

'Sir Balthor, I believe there is sense in what Sir Wilhelm says – the Lady Markward has ever been known for her wits and learning. Given her delay, it is far more likely that she plans to escape the country by fleeing through the Argael, to Northalde.'

'To Northalde! Have you lost *your* wits?!' There's a bloody civil war going on in Northalde!'

'Aye, and last time I checked, Vorstlendings weren't on either side,' put in Wilhelm, his courage returning.

'If her plan be to escape the realm, she has a much better chance of doing it by fleeing north – even if that means entering a country at war,' said Redrich.

'I think Redrich and Wilhelm have the right of it, sire,' stammered Rufus. The weakling even talked like a squire.

Balthor bit his lip and stared up the highway towards the north. The Argael lay a day's hard ride away from them. Like any forest, it was said to be peopled by strange things – Woses and witches and Reus knew what else. Going in that direction meant leaving Vorstlund behind and heading into foreign territory. The comforts of the keep suddenly seemed very far away.

But what choice did he have? Much as he hated to admit it, the other three were probably right – Adhelina of Dulsinor was far too clever and headstrong to head tamely back into the simple trap he'd baited for her in Meerborg. Damn the cunning of women, if only the Eorl had been blessed with a living son!

Twice he had returned to Graukolos a beaten man, outfoxed. There wouldn't be a third time. He was the greatest knight in Dulsinor, and he had a reputation to live up to.

Wheeling his courser around again he barked another order. 'We ride northwards – should be able to reach the town of Bergen by nightfall, we'll requisition fresh steeds there.'

The four knights set off up the road at a gallop. As they left a spray of dust in their wake, Sir Balthor resigned himself to the hand the Unseen had dealt him: now he was Dulsinor's greatest knight *errant*.

He'd better have something good to boast about when this miserable business was done.

⊷ CHAPTER VII ⊶

Into the Forest

Hettie tried to pay attention as they rode along the highway. She felt sick and tired, but all the same she wanted to remember the land she was leaving forever. They had left the wilderness behind some two leagues before reaching the main road; on either side of it stretched well-tended fields, ears of corn and wheat waving gently in the late afternoon breeze. Homesteads dotted about the countryside sent willowing spires of smoke into the summer skies, as peasant wives began cooking the evening meal for their husbands working the fields. Sheep and cows were being herded back to their pens; off in the distance she could make out a party of riders returning to a high-beamed hall, a manor belonging to a vassal of the Eorl.

Dulsinor in bloom. The thought of it made her feel sicker still. Why oh why had her dearest friend driven her to this? Hettie felt sure she was not made for a life of wandering; hearth and home and loyal service were the things that moved her. And yet it was precisely the last of these that had set her on this sorrowful path.

Adhelina was riding next to her, the road being broad enough for two. She glanced at Hettie and pursed her lips.

'Anupe,' she called to the freesword riding a few paces ahead of them. 'We must seek a proper bed for the night, at Bergen. Hettie needs rest if she is to complete her recovery.'

The Harijan did not slow as she replied. 'As I have already said, we do not know how far this Balthor has spread news of your escape. If we stay the night at the town, there is no telling who we may find there.'

'And as I said before, I sincerely doubt Balthor will have ventured so far. He would have headed straight to Meerborg, it's the obvious choice. Bergen lies on the borders of the realm.'

'Yes, he may not have been there himself, but perhaps he sent word… These fields are well-tended, the ground soft. The weather is warm, and you have enough clothing – less the shawl you foolishly left behind.'

Hettie felt a twinge. 'I'm sorry... we were in a rush, and it's hard to think straight when you're not well.' She didn't know what else to say.

'Don't apologise Hettie,' said Adhelina firmly, before addressing the Harijan again. 'This is exactly why we need to get her a bed for the night. Her fever may have broken but she's still fragile and needs proper rest!'

'She will get all the rest she needs,' replied Anupe. 'I will find us some trees to camp under – I have seen plenty of... what was the word you taught me?'

'Copses,' supplied Adhelina, looking impatient.

'Yes, copses,' rejoined the outlander. 'You should be happy – this is the last you will see of your homeland, you should enjoy it while you can.'

'She is impossible,' hissed Adhelina, seething. 'I've a good mind to release her from service.'

'Don't do anything on my account,' croaked Hettie. Her throat felt as though it had been scoured by a whetstone. 'I'll be all right. And Anupe has a point – we've come this far and we don't want to risk being caught now.'

They rode on in silence, passing only a couple of mendicant perfects and a few itinerant labourers. The sun lowered in the sky and with the onset of dusk a chill returned to the air. Hettie began coughing and spluttering. Her limbs felt as though they were made of lead. She clutched the reins tightly, hoping she wouldn't slide off her horse.

'That's enough!' cried Adhelina after half an hour. 'We're stopping at Bergen, that's a *command*, Anupe. While you are in my service you will do as I say.'

The Harijan wheeled her courser around to face them. Her eyes glinted dangerously beneath her hood. 'Very well, but in the event of your capture I want something now, for my pains. If you will not listen to me – '

'Yes, here...' Adhelina reached into the folds of her cloak and tossed over a jingling purse. 'It's not much – as I told you my treasures are in a strongbox at Meerborg. But if it will allay your fears of not getting paid, so be it.'

The freesword hefted the purse thoughtfully. 'Very well,' she replied. 'If you will not be moved on this, we will do as you say. But do not say – '

' – you didn't warn us,' Adhelina finished for her wearily. 'Yes, I understand. In any case, I've thought of a way to do this and minimise our risk.'

'Oh yes? I am all ears, as you say...'

'If Balthor sent word as far as Bergen he would have done it from Meerborg – that was before the witch sent her message to Graukolos, so he would only have included Hettie and me in his description. A foreign freesword stopping at an inn for the night won't attract any suspicion – so you scout the place first. If there are no knights or other people in service to my father staying there, we'll know it's safe. In that case you secure us a room for the night and come and fetch us – you'll have to do that now anyway, seeing as you have all my money.'

The outlander gave one of her short barks that Hettie supposed was laughter. 'So the heiress of Dulsinor has thought of everything, as usual! Yes then, it shall be as you say. But if I think it is unsafe – '

' – then we make do with a copse for the night.'

With a curt nod the mercenary pocketed the purse.

✣ ✣ ✣

The twinkling lights of Bergen greeted them about an hour after sunset. Hettie knew a little of the town. It had some five hundred souls, mostly traders who thrived on commerce with travelling merchants from Northalde and the woodfolk of the Argael; furs, ale, timber and iron tools mostly changed hands for meat, cheese and woollen garments. The town wasn't protected by a wall or stockade: one of Wilhelm's bannerets had his holding nearby, and commanded a dozen knights and a like number of men-at-arms.

Hettie bit her lip. That was good for the town's security, less good for theirs. She supposed Sir Bertram's knights and serjeants were likely to stop and enjoy a stoop or seven when not patrolling their liege's demesnes... She felt bad, it was as if she were the cause of their taking yet another risk.

The road continued straight through Bergen, its wooden houses clustered on either side in hotchpotch fashion. One or two were painted bright colours, but most were a simple dun-brown; Vorstlendings tended not to be showy in prosperity.

'Both of you wait over there, by yonder trees,' said Anupe, pulling her hood down tightly. 'I will return shortly.'

Hettie shivered in the gathering breeze, wrapping her cloak about her. A flock of birds could be heard squawking in the distance. She hoped they weren't ravens – her mistress said the Northlendings believed them to be an omen of doom. She felt as though they were already half in Northalde: this was the closest she'd ever come to leaving Vorstlund.

Presently Anupe returned.

'We have a room for the night – lodgings have a separate entrance, which means you can avoid passing through the taproom.'

'Who did you see there?' asked Adhelina. 'Anyone we should know about?'

'Just a couple of serjeants, but they were so drunk they didn't even notice me.'

Hettie felt relief wash over her. Adhelina smiled: 'Reus bless the intemperance of the Vorstlendings! Probably Bertram's soldiers, drinking themselves into a stupor. Well at least that's something we don't have to worry about!'

The inn was halfway up the road. It was divided into two buildings, the taproom and lodging house. A rickety flight of wooden stairs attached to the outside of the latter took them up to their chamber on the top floor. Anupe had chosen well, though it was small and cramped, with just enough room for a bed and a space on the floor for the Harijan. They ordered supper to be brought up but Hettie was too tired to eat. Curling herself up on her half of the bed, she felt a delicious release flood her aching limbs. In a few moments she was fast asleep.

✣ ✣ ✣

She woke to feel Adhelina prodding her gently. Sunlight was peering through cracks in the crude shutters.

'Breakfast is here,' said her mistress. 'I've ordered extra for you – you didn't eat last night.'

Hettie fell ravenously on the food. It was good Vorstlending fare: boiled eggs and cheese and bacon, with a hunk of crusty bread and a mug of weak ale to wash it down. After that she felt much better.

'How long was I asleep for?' she asked.

'Too long,' put in the Harijan, picking at her food. 'It is well past sunrise and we need to be going if we want to reach the forest before sunset.'

'Here, drink this,' said Adhelina, proffering a phial with green liquid in it. Hettie could see herbs swirling around inside it.

'It's a tincture I prepared while you were sleeping, it'll help with your symptoms.'

Hettie grimaced as she swallowed the liquid. Her mistress' concoctions were rarely tasty.

'Best to leave some ale for after,' quipped the Harijan, seeing the look on her face.

Gathering up their things they made their way down to the stables, which were an annex of the lodging house. They hadn't been able to avoid being seen by the ostler, but Hettie could only hope they wouldn't be unlucky enough to have problems with a stablehand twice. The lad seemed flushed and preoccupied; perhaps he was new to the job.

All to the better, thought Hettie.

They rode out of the yard and back onto the main road. As they left the inn Hettie saw a man relieving himself outside the taproom. He glanced up at her and leered. Judging by his rough green breeches and jerkin he looked to be a woodsman, probably come from the Argael to trade.

She turned her head away quickly and focused on the road leading out of town, but it felt as though his eyes were still staring at her back. Despite feeling much better, she shivered again.

✤ ✤ ✤

It was late afternoon when the Argael began to impose itself on the horizon. Just a dark smudge of green at first, it soon loomed large, stretching across their line of sight. Gazing at the oaks Adhelina felt a sense of triumph, mingled with trepidation. They were nearly out of Vorstlund, but she knew that Hettie's misgivings about the ancient forest were not entirely misplaced.

It had once been much larger, before the rise of the Free Kingdoms brought on the Great Clearing, as mortalkind emerged from the Second Age of Darkness and strived once more to carve a civilisation from the wildernesses of Urovia. Disparate communities of charcoal burners and huntsmen – known as the woodfolk – had settled beneath its eaves during that time.

But they shared the Argael with far older things.

The Wadwos – or Woses as they were sometimes called – had lived there for millennia, long before the Reaver Kings had settled the mainland. Mostly solitary creatures, they preyed on woodfolk and travellers alike, but could be overcome by weight of numbers. For that reason few merchants dared take the road between Northalde and Vorstlund without a strong party of freeswords. Outlaws too had been known to take refuge in the forest, and *elementi* were said to dwell in its innermost reaches, where not even the woodfolk dared venture.

That part of the forest had been taken over by a mighty woods witch, so it was told, decades ago – perhaps even a hundred years past, according to some legends. Argolian testimonies she had read named her a Right Hand practitioner – not entirely evil, but one who commanded the spirits of nature and expected to be left alone. According to these reports the Earth Witch had put a glamour on the stretch of forest she ruled, suffering none to enter freely: the Girdle of the Earth Witch, they called it. Maps Adhelina had looked at indicated the road they took passed east of the Girdle, joining up with that from Graukolos before striking roughly north-west towards Northalde.

That suits, she thought. *I've no wish to beard a witch in her lair.*

A glance at Hettie told her that she was thinking much the same and none too pleased about their chosen direction. But there was nothing else for it – as long as they stuck to the main road and didn't detour too far from it, they had a good chance of getting through unharmed.

Or that was what she told herself anyway.

✢ ✢ ✢

At sunset they stopped to take their last meal of the day at the forest's edge. Anupe had insisted, saying they would need their strength in case the worst should happen, but Adhelina could scarcely eat she was so nervous. Gazing back down the highway she kept expecting to see Balthor and a company of knights thunder into view.

No, she kept reminding herself, *we must have at least two days on him.*

They finished supper and remounted. Anupe had lit a taper to light their way as they penetrated into the gloom of the forest. The road remained broad, but the trees blocked out much of the sky. It felt cool beneath the densely packed leaves; the fragrance of forest smells was delicious in her nostrils. Adhelina felt glad, thinking of the abundance of herbs and good growing things that the Argael must be home to... never mind all the Wadwos and witches and nature spirits.

That reminded her of something. Nudging her courser into line with Anupe's, she reached into her saddlebag and produced a small jar of ointment.

'Here, take this,' she said, proffering the jar. The mercenary raised an eyebrow.

'It's a tincture I prepared from Wose's Bane, when we were staying at the burned witch's grotto – I'd been meaning to give it to you sooner, but we've been quite distracted.'

'Thank you,' said the freesword, taking the jar. 'What is it?'

'It's poison to any Wadwo,' explained Adhelina. 'Rub a small amount on your blades – a slight gash should be enough to pass it into a Wose's bloodstream. They won't last long after that, if the tome I read tells true.'

The mercenary cracked a grin. 'Well, the runaway lady is certainly full of surprises! I thank you for your gift – let us hope I do not find a use for it.'

'No indeed,' said Adhelina. The dark forest suddenly seemed less welcoming.

✛ ✛ ✛

Stars were peeping through silhouetted branches when they came to a trail leading off to the left.

'We should stop here for the night,' said Adhelina. 'There are blockaded clearings off the road, built years ago to protect travellers against Woses and roving outlaws.'

Anupe nodded and they struck off the road. Adhelina felt her nerves jangling – *don't stray too far* – but a minute later she felt relieved to see the stockade.

Her relief was quickly dispelled. It was constructed of barked logs running the perimeter of the clearing – but half of what used to be the gate was hanging off its hinges, with the rest scattered across the clearing. Anupe's taper told a similar tale as they inspected further – a great breach had been gouged at the far end, two logs smashed to splinters.

'Those were logs of oak,' said the Harijan. 'These Wadwos must have the strength of giants.'

'Bloodstains...' said Adhelina, staring at the dark smears lashed across the beams.

'They are old at least,' said Anupe, holding up the torch and looking closer.

'Let's be gone from this place,' wailed Hettie. 'I told you we shouldn't have come he-'

'Na mun is gawn nawhere,' a strangely accented voice rang out through the night. 'Nee na *wummun* neither.'

The three of them wheeled their horses around. Standing in the entrance was a stocky man, dressed in green garb and carrying a longbow. Two other men in similar attire, likewise armed, stepped into the clearing just behind him.

Anupe drew her blade. 'Impressive,' she breathed. 'I didn't hear a thing. Not easily do men fool the ears of a Harijan.'

The lead figure frowned. 'What's she seyin'?' he asked, addressing the damsels. 'Funny accent, canna ken a word she sez.'

'You're woodfolk,' said Adhelina slowly. 'Our bodyguard is an outlander, her accent will be strange to you.'

'*My* accent?' put in the Harijan, but Adhelina ignored her.

'We seek passage through the forest, nothing more. We want shelter for the night, in the morning we will be on our way.'

'Aye, that mebbe,' replied the lead woodsman. 'But things 'ave chenged roon' these parts, 'n' we canna be trustin' anybody nowadays.'

'We are peaceful travellers, our bodyguard is just doing her – *his* – job protecting us. Anupe, lower your blade!'

'That I will do when they lower their bows,' replied the Harijan, nudging her horse forwards.

It was an unusually rash move for the swordswoman.

'*Draw*,' said the lead woodsman. In a heartbeat three shafts were pointing at the outlander's heart. Anupe pulled her horse up. It whickered skittishly, steam escaping its nostrils into the night.

Adhelina felt her pulse racing. Woodsmen seldom interfered like this with travellers. What was going on? She began to wonder if the apparent Wadwo attack had been so long ago after all.

'Milady, there's more of them!' exclaimed Hettie. Adhelina turned to see another three woodfolk push their way in through the rent behind them. Fanning out, the newcomers nocked and drew.

Anupe glanced backwards and forwards.

'Perhaps you will miss and kill each other,' she offered dryly, enunciating her words so they could understand.

The leader gave a brown-toothed grin and said: 'Nah, think not sirrah. Woodfowk dunna miss, not at this range.'

'What do you want with us?' barked Adhelina. It was clear that they were outnumbered and outmanoeuvred: she couldn't see even the skilful Harijan winning now. Besides, she did not want to hurt the woodfolk – despite their behaviour, everything she had heard about them suggested they were mostly honest people.

'Ah canna sey that until we've tekken ye back t'oors fer questionin',' replied the leader. 'The headman'll be wantin' a word wit' youse – not often ye see two rich ladies 'n' a lone freesword travellin' through oor woods. But strenge fowk fer strenge times, as they say.'

He made a clucking sound. The two men next to him sheathed their bows and slowly approached Anupe.

'Four arrows still trenned on ye, try anythin' 'n' yer all dead,' he said. 'So I'll thank ye te come quietly down offa them 'orses. Dunna worry – they'll be tekkin' good care o'. Woodsman's promise.'

'I think we'd better do as he says,' said Adhelina, quickly translating for Anupe's benefit. 'If they just want to question us, I don't see any need for bloodshed.'

'For once I agree,' sighed Anupe. 'A Harijan hates surrender, but I like not these odds.'

Once they were down the leader nodded at them and made another clucking sound.

'Now we need t' search ye fer yer weapons,' he said. Four woodsmen still had their arrows trained on them.

Anupe glanced at Adhelina, her eyes glinting beneath her hood. 'It'll be all right,' she said, trying to sound reassuring.

They searched them all closely, but seemed interested only in Anupe's weapons, leaving everything else in their possession.

Definitely not outlaws then – something to be grateful for, thought Adhelina.

She was just thinking this when the woodsman searching Anupe suddenly pulled back her hood. Their captors' eyes widened when they saw her face.

'Well, well,' breathed the leader. 'A wummun wha kens how t'use a blade... strenge times, strenge fowk *indeed*.'

He gave a nod to the other woodfolk, who had shouldered their bows and drawn long hunting knives. Now they surrounded the three women in a loose circle.

'C'mon lads,' said the leader. 'Let's be 'avin ya. There's Woses aroond as like as not, an' ah dunna fancy bein' caught oot in the open wi' these numbers.'

The woodfolk steered them back out of the stockade, before striking west into the forest away from the main highway. It was not long before the Argael had taken them into its hoary bosom, and all sight of it had vanished.

Why do we always have such trouble sticking to the road? Adhelina wondered disconsolately.

⊷ CHAPTER VIII ⊷

Under Eaves Again

'And that,' said Braxus, brushing his fingers lightly over the strings of his lyre, 'is how Bendigedfryn tricked the sorceress Myrca into parting with the golden apple.'

Everyone applauded, save for Horskram, who was sat on a tree stump at the other end of the stockaded clearing, deep in thought as usual. Vaskrian clapped loudest of all. There was no denying his guvnor's skill behind the strings, and he sang like an angel. It cast his mind back to the day they'd met, atop the King's palace at Strongholm.

But Torgun frowned. He looked confused. 'Your skill at music is unsurpassed, Sir Braxus,' he said courteously. 'But I'm not sure I can applaud the song's sentiments.'

Braxus raised an eyebrow. 'Oh, and why is that?' he inquired.

'This trickster hero you describe... why he uses nothing but base methods to steal the apple from the witch! Surely you must know some nobler songs?'

Braxus rolled his eyes. 'That isn't the point, Sir Torgun – Bendigedfryn needs the apple to cure the Princess Olwen of her sickness. Myrca is a selfish woman who only wants to keep it so she can treasure it. Bendigedfryn is using trickery, aye, that I'll grant you. But he's doing so for the greater good.'

'I still don't see why good song should be spent celebrating the deeds of a trickster,' said Torgun, still frowning. 'Though as I said, your skill at harp is unsurpassed.'

'It's a lyre, not a harp,' said Braxus, laughing.

Adelko quickly hid a smile, though none of the raven knights laughed back. Aronn stared stonily at the Thraxian. Torgun looked away, losing interest in the conversation. The Chequered Twins exchanged bemused glances.

Vaskrian felt the food he'd just eaten sitting heavily in his gut. They had been on the road for nearly a week now, and tensions between his master and his countrymen seemed to be running as high as ever. But then how could knights sworn to defend the realm be expected to take a liking to a foreigner whose people had made war on theirs for generations?

And that foreigner just happened to be his new guvnor.

Getting to his feet he set about clearing up Braxus's trencher and knife. It was a clear summer's night and the stars and moon were shining brightly overhead.

They had reached the Argael without much incident – that had been a disappointment of course, he'd been hoping they would bump into some of Thule's former levymen. The battle for Salmor already seemed a long way away, and he was itching for a good scrap.

The only thing of note had been the awful ruin they had passed on the northern skirts of the forest. Who knew how long it had been there – Adelko said it was thousands of years old. Vaskrian hadn't liked the look of it one bit. It had reminded him of the broken tower they'd seen after leaving Tintagael: the stones hadn't looked right, all funny angles and bizarre shapes that hurt his eyes to look at. It hadn't been a tower this time: the novice had whispered it was possibly a fragment of an ancient city that had survived the Breaking. Whatever that was.

At any rate, it all had something to do with this mad quest they were on. If they didn't find this evil sorcerer and stop him, maybe the people who had built that ruin would come back. Whatever: it all sounded like mumbo-jumbo to him. All Vaskrian needed to know was where the next fight was.

As he cleaned his master's utensils, he wryly reflected that maybe the next fight would take place here, between knights who were supposed to be allies. He didn't like that thought at all: which side would he be on if that happened?

Horskram stirred from his reverie, getting up and approaching the fire to warm his hands.

'Now you are done entertaining yourselves, I would suggest an early night,' he said, without looking at any of them. 'We'll need to detour from the main road tomorrow, and that will mean leading our horses and travelling on foot.'

'And you're sure this woodland commune you mentioned will help us?' asked Aronn. 'Last I heard the forest dwellers aren't too welcoming of strangers.'

'They should be minded to help me at least,' replied the adept. 'I know their headman well. I once saved his nephew from possession, not to mention banishing several Terri that were terrorising them a few winters ago.'

'Terri?' Aronn's ruddy face looked perplexed. No wonder, Vaskrian thought – the old monk was even harder to understand than Adelko.

'Earth spirits,' clarified Horskram. 'There's a good deal more to be found in this part of the world than many others – my services have often been sought here.'

'So in other words,' put in Braxus, packing away his lyre, 'they owe you one.'

Horskram favoured him with a flat stare. 'If by that, sir knight, you mean they are indebted to me, then yes. We'll leave our horses with them for safekeeping and collect them when our business here is done. The Earth Witch's Girdle is at the heart of the forest – we'll need a local guide to find it.'

'And what do you plan on saying to this Earth Witch once we do find her?' asked Braxus. 'From what I know of magi, they don't take kindly to strangers wandering in and asking them for help. Especially not if those strangers happen to include an Argolian friar.'

'If the rumours we have heard be true, the Earth Witch is fighting for her territory against another wizard – only one versed in the black arts could hope to control and unite the Wadwos. Our interests therefore should dovetail – we both want Andragorix apprehended or dead. She'll help us.'

Braxus frowned. 'Assuming the warlock behind the Wadwos *is* this Andragorix. We don't know for certain he is – you said yourself the demonologist likes to play with words.'

Horskram's eyes were bright pinpoints in the firelight, his face set grim as he answered: 'Aye, that he does, Sir Braxus. But unless I've misjudged him, he is longing for this confrontation. He wants me to find him – so he can be revenged for the injuries he suffered last time we met.'

'Injuries inflicted on him by a Thraxian knight who died fighting him, if my memory serves,' said Braxus. 'I hope I don't make it two!'

Horskram said nothing to that, but returned to gazing at the fire. Vaskrian hoped the Thraxian didn't die too – that would make it three dead guvnors in a row for him. He didn't fancy garnering a reputation as the Cursed Squire of Hroghar.

They all turned in shortly after that. Vaskrian didn't fall asleep immediately, but stayed awake staring up at the stars thinking about what had been said.

Wadwos – they hadn't met any yet, but it seemed likely they would. Sir Torgun had killed one in single combat, before he joined the White Valravyn. He said it had been hugely strong and hardy as an ox, though clumsy and ill disciplined. It had taken him several sword strokes to kill it – and Torgun was the strongest knight in the realm. The thought of that made Vaskrian feel unusually nervous. What kind of fight would that make for? Reckless though he was, he wasn't sure he wanted to find out.

Where were those outlaws, Reus damn it?

⁜ ⁜ ⁜

Adelko woke to the sound of birdsong and the feel of sunshine on his face. Yawning, he sat up on his pallet and stretched.

The Argael certainly wasn't as creepy as Tintagael – he was thankful for that much at least. He had been secretly dreading another haunted forest; nightmarish memories of the realm of the Faerie Kings still clustered at the back of his mind.

Seek sanctuary beneath the trees...

The words of the sylvan lords, spoken in rhyme and riddle in the heart of their spectral kingdom. He shivered despite the clement morning, lurching to his feet to banish the recollection.

They weren't seeking sanctuary this time in any case, he reflected grimly as he went over to join the others for breakfast – if Horskram's guess proved right they were seeking the endgame. If Andragorix was here somewhere, lurking beneath the eaves of the Argael, this was their chance to apprehend the mad mage and put everything right.

He felt more uneasy at that thought than anything else. His sixth sense told him that the outcome of the next few weeks would be anything but straightforward. It also told him his mentor was thinking much the same.

He glanced over at Horskram, who was busy checking their horses. Ever since Salmor, he had felt increasingly attuned to the old monk. And he sensed that the adept was anything but sure of himself. He hid it well – portraying an aura of steely confidence that had all the others convinced. Except perhaps Sir Braxus. Adelko's sixth sense also told him there was more to the foreign knight than met the eye – he had a keen intelligence that none of the other fighters in their group possessed. Perhaps that was why Horskram had decided to enlist him. Not that he showed much sign of respecting the Thraxian on that account. But then Horskram rarely showed signs of respecting anyone – he had even seemed pushy with his king at times.

Horskram, always so difficult to get along with.

Still, that didn't change matters – they were headed into grave danger together again, and that meant he had to try and clear up the bad blood between them. Before any of it got spilled.

Packing up camp they left the clearing, following the trail back to the main path and retaking it southwards. Adelko nudged his steed into line with Horskram's. The adept said nothing, staring fixedly ahead.

They continued like that for a while before Adelko screwed up his courage and spoke.

'When will we reach the woodfolk settlement you mentioned, Master Horskram?' he asked.

'Before sunset, assuming the road remains good all the way to the turning we need.'

Silence followed.

'My quarterstaff technique still needs a lot of improvement,' Adelko tried, hoping for a better response. 'Funny, given everything we've been through.'

'You have plenty of warrior friends now – I am sure they can help you with your footwork.'

'I'm sorry Master Horskram, I understand why you don't want me to befriend these people...' He lowered his voice, glancing back timidly at the six armed men that rode behind them. 'But they've pledged their *lives* to protect us. I can't just ignore them.'

'I am not asking you to ignore them. I am asking you to remember your vows, and keep them at a distance. You're an Argolian – we do not take men of the sword as our bosom companions. Even if they are sworn to protect us.'

'But they're on our side – they're fighting the good fight, aren't they?'

Horskram sighed, that same weary sigh. 'There is no such thing as a good fight. If you still do not understand that, there is little point in our having this conversation.'

His mentor lapsed back into silence. Adelko could sense the pain in him, the anguish and conflicted feelings. He felt a sudden pity for the old monk.

And yet the novice's next words sounded pitiless enough.

'Then... how do you live with what you've done? When you were a crusader?'

Horskram seemed ready for that question though. 'By striving not to be the man I once was, every day. As I told you outside Strongholm, I have repented my sins.' He paused, then added: 'And that means realising what you have done, and accepting the pain that comes with it. Only by going through that pain can you emerge from it.'

'Then... why do you seem so troubled still? I can feel it... you're, well, conflicted.'

'Did I not make myself clear at Salmor? One does not have to wield a sword to cause the deaths of men. One can take decisions, or influence those of other people, that will result in just the same... As you have already begun to do.'

Adelko felt a stab of guilt. How foolish to hope his mentor would not bring that up.

'But if the alternative would have been worse...'

His mentor's face remained unsmiling beneath his cowl. 'And can you say for sure it would have been? Right and wrong, good and evil, loyalist and rebel – these are terms that mortal men have conceived. Only the Almighty knows all, and sees the true face of things as they are. The rest of us but see through a glass darkly, as the Prophet sayeth.'

'But the Prophet himself took sides, and spilled blood, before he saw the error of *his* ways,' said Adelko.

'Aye, true enough,' allowed Horskram. 'But in the end he achieved his goals through peaceful resistance – and self-sacrifice.'

That got Adelko thinking. Palom's campaign of boycott had flummoxed the Thalamian Empire, damaging its already fragile revenues. It was a less emphasised part of the Scriptures, but true enough: the Redeemer had stood up to the Emperor by ordering his followers to stop attacking legions, down their tools, and refrain from engaging in commerce. It had worked – until the Empire had caught Palomedes, dragged him back to Tyrannos in chains, and executed him publicly. Deprived of its leader, the movement he started had crumbled. But the seed of his message survived, thanks to the Seven Acolytes, and slowly spread its way across Urovia. Thus had the Creed been born.

'Palom's message is clear enough to those that have eyes to see,' continued Horskram. 'If you forsake violence and greed, and are prepared to forgo the comforts of civilisation for a time, you can bring a tyrant to his knees – without using bloodshed.'

'... and yet here we are, answering violence with violence, supporting one ruler over another just because they seem less bad than the alternative,' said Adelko, finally catching on. 'We might stop the worst from happening, but we're not really improving things either.'

'Just so,' said Horskram, perhaps a hint of respect returning to his voice. 'We may defeat Andragorix or we may not, but either way we still fall far short of the example Palom set us, and the world he envisaged.'

Another thought occurred to Adelko. 'And yet as one of the avatars, surely Palom should have known better than to begin his campaign with violence?

'Palom was indeed an avatar – one of the Unseen descended to earth in mortal form,' Horskram agreed. 'The same Unseen who taught magic to mortals in the first place. They are far from perfect themselves – they have made many errors in their time.'

'And yet we revere many of them as archangels,' put in Adelko.

'Angel and demon – another construct of the mortal mind,' replied Horskram. 'The peoples of the Golden Age saw them as gods and goddesses, the pagan Northlanders still do. The *Unseen*... the clue is in the name, Adelko. The pagans "saw" the Unseen as they *wanted* to see them. Perhaps we still do the same.'

'But... that's blasphemy,' gawped Adelko.

'The perfects of the so-called True Temple would have you believe that,' said Horskram. 'But in truth, these terms are all relative. Yes, Virtus, the angelic avatar of courage, is certainly more wholesome than demonic Zolthoth, who represents wrath. Yet many a warrior has called upon the one only to be poisoned by the other.'

'But... that isn't the fault of Virtus,' argued Adelko. 'That's Zolthoth undermining him.'

'And the Scriptures teach that Zolthoth is a dark emanation of Virtus – he was *born* of him, Adelko. Even if you discount that, how many warriors in history have showed courage on the battlefield, only to shed blood? One does not have to be in the grip of rage to kill – in fact, the less enraged a fighter is, the better he kills.' Horskram nodded back towards the others. 'Ask any of them, except perhaps Vaskrian, and they will tell you as much.'

Adelko frowned. Horskram was making sense, but the novice didn't like what he was hearing. It made him feel troubled and confused.

'So... you don't think we should revere the Seven Seraphim then? Or the rest of the archangels? Is that no better than calling them gods?'

'I did not say that,' replied Horskram firmly. 'No – the reason we call the Unseen angels or demons and not gods is precisely because they are not flawless, nor do they operate autonomously. All of them come from Reus – but at least the angels still follow His command, or try to as best they can, unlike Abaddon and his followers.'

'And yet if the Unseen are manifestations of Reus, who is all-knowing, how can they have made such flawed decisions?'

'Perhaps now you understand why your sixth sense is telling you I am conflicted,' said the adept, more sadly than anything else.

Adelko was about to ask another question but Horskram quickly added: 'That is enough theology for today. Think on what you have learned from this discussion – and think twice before you befriend yon swordsmen.' Flicking the reins, he nudged his horse ahead of Adelko's to forestall any more questions.

He needn't have feared on that account. The novice felt more relieved than anything else: his urge to question things was usually compulsive, but this time it was making his head hurt.

Steering his thoughts elsewhere, he reflected that at least he appeared to have mended fences with his mentor somewhat; some of the tension between them had ebbed away. Focusing on the feel of his horse ambling beneath him, and the sound of birdsong in the trees, Adelko fell into a meditative state. As his painful thoughts dropped away from him, he felt a welcome calmness wash over him like warm water.

✣ ✣ ✣

The afternoon was growing old when the first signs of trouble made themselves known. Corpses of freeswords littered the road, their light armour no protection against the myriad strokes that had cut them down. There were five in total. Besides them were the hewn bodies of two other men, their fine robes spattered with blood.

But it was the last corpse that brought a stab of pity to Torgun's heart: a girl of no more than ten summers, her terrified eyes frozen and sightless.

He made the sign before dismounting with the other knights to investigate. Merchants sometimes travelled with their families, if they felt well protected enough to take the risk.

Poor souls – they must have had no inkling of the dangers they were heading into. He didn't think much of the merchant class, but they hadn't deserved to die like that. Especially not a blameless girl.

Swallowing his rage at the unchivalrous deed, Sir Torgun bent to examine the corpses and swore silently he would bring justice to her killers if he could.

'They're dressed well, but not as richly as a Northlending merchant,' said Sir Aronn. 'That probably means they were Vorstlendings, travelling from the south.'

Torgun nodded. That made sense – the Vorstlendings were known for their dislike of excessive finery.

'That explains why they were travelling with a child and not more strongly protected,' he said. 'News of our war and the outlaws probably hadn't reached them.'

It had to be Thule's former levies: the merchants' purses had been slashed open, there were no signs of any horses or other treasures. Unless Wadwos had taken to thieving as well as slaying.

'Over here! There's a blood trail leading off the road – one of them must have survived.'

Braxus was standing by the side of the highway, pointing at a dark smear that led off into the woods.

Torgun went over to look, pushing his conflicted thoughts about Braxus away. He was grateful for the Thraxian's help and did not doubt his strength or courage... but all the same there was something of the rogue about the foreigner's manner, and that didn't befit a true knight. He didn't trust him.

'He or she must have crawled into the forest after they left,' said Torgun. 'Judging by their wounds they were greatly outnumbered... no one could have escaped while the brigands were still here.'

Sir Braxus nodded. 'Perhaps best if we leave it – no sense in jeopardising our mission for someone who probably didn't survive long in any case.'

Sir Torgun stared at him disapprovingly. 'I'll not abandon a man until I know for sure he is dead. If the outlaws did this, they are my responsibility – two thousand of Thule's levies escaped, and I will bring them to justice wherever I can.'

Horskram leaned over his saddle to address Torgun. 'I agree with Sir Braxus – we already knew there was a risk of outlaws, and gain nothing by detouring here. The turning we need is but an hour's ride away. We must press on.'

Sir Torgun frowned. He did not like to take issue with an Argolian, and Horskram was well respected. But he liked shirking his duties less. 'Master monk, our responsibility as knights of the White Valravyn – '

' – expired the minute you left the kingdom,' Horskram finished for him. 'You're sworn to protect me, on an oath to the King himself need I remind you? We leave the bodies where they lie and carry on – when we get to the woodlanders I'll have them bring the bodies back so we can give them the Last Rites.'

Sir Torgun looked from Braxus to Horskram, suppressing feelings of resentment. He hated to admit it, but the old monk was right. He had sworn an oath, and his king's word was law.

Sir Aronn wasn't done yet though. 'I say no man's vow should keep him from following his knightly duties,' he protested. 'And this man could help us if he still lives!'

'How?' sneered Horskram. 'By telling us he and his godless friends were set upon by outlaws? I think we have gathered as much.'

'What if they were Wadwos?' persisted Aronn. 'A survivor could tell us.'

'It makes no difference,' said Horskram. 'We know the dangers we face. And Wadwos fight better at night, their pale skins like not the sunlight. So the longer we delay the more chance we have of meeting them before we reach the settlement.'

Sitting up, the adept flicked his reins and began steering his mount past the bodies. 'This isn't a discussion,' he said. 'So get back on your horses. We leave the bodies where they lie.'

Heaving a frustrated sigh, Sir Torgun retook the saddle. Sir Aronn exchanged a look with him as he did likewise, his eyes blazing.

As they picked their way around the fly-encrusted corpses, Sir Torgun caught the dead girl's eyes again.

Was this really better than harrying outlaws?

✣ ✣ ✣

Horskram brooded in the saddle as they made their way through darkening eaves. They had reached the turning in good time. The trail they now followed was narrow and they had to ride single file, but at least the oaks were tall enough that they could remain mounted.

It had pained him to leave the bodies behind, their dead souls unavenged. But it was more important to get to the settlement, so their remains could be brought back for the Last Rites and those dead souls could seek the Judgment of Azrael.

This was no time for chivalrous heroics in any case – their mission was far more important than bringing outlaws to justice.

Always a choice betwixt bad and worse... he reflected gloomily on his discussion with the novice. He had to hope it had instilled some sense in the youth – if he was right about him, he had to ensure Adelko did not fall into iniquity. Too often those chosen by Reus to do His work had slipped into darkness themselves, seduced by the trickery of Abaddon as they tried to walk the path of the righteous...

A flurry of movement caught his eye, breaking his thoughts. A spiral of condensed air, shaped like a flying tornado, whipped through the branches, causing them to wave manically. Ahead of him

Sir Aronn yelled as one of them slapped him in the chest, causing him to lurch backwards. His panicked horse reared and whinnied.

'Do not be alarmed,' he said, as the knight steadied his mount and instinctively reached for his sword. ''Tis but an Aethus – a spirit of the air. Let it pass and it shall do you no harm.'

Sure enough the air spirit skittered off through the woods, leaves shuddering in its wake.

'I like not this cursed wood,' snarled Aronn, clutching the reins. 'I would fain be in open country again.'

'If you think this is bad, you should try Tintagael,' replied the adept with a wry smile. 'At least here the Elementi do not serve a malign and controlling power – not until we reach the Earth Witch's Girdle at least.'

'Your words give me little comfort, master monk,' replied Aronn, nudging his horse into a canter again.

Horskram glanced over his shoulder to make sure the others had not lost their composure. Adelko rode directly behind him; the novice seemed unruffled, though he muttered a prayer. Given all he had seen, that was unsurprising: the lad's spiritual fortitude had grown and the lesser forces of the Other Side held few terrors for him nowadays. Behind Adelko rode Braxus and Vaskrian, the Chequered Twins bringing up the rear. They hadn't seen enough to cause them any alarm.

'There's smoke burning up ahead!' called Sir Torgun from the front of their column.

'Cooking fires, or sign of war?' Horskram called back.

'Looks like cooking fires – charcoal burners, most like.'

Horskram felt relieved. Glancing up through the trees he saw patches of fading blue that told him sunset was approaching. They had reached the settlement not before time.

A stout party of armed woodfolk was waiting for them as they made their way into the clearing surrounding it. Columns of smoke from the charcoal fires Torgun had reported could be seen drifting above its stockaded walls. A dozen bowmen stood on its ramparts, arrows trained on the newcomers.

The party below, about another dozen strong, was armed with rude clubs and hunting knives. Their leader raised a hand as he recognised Horskram.

'Stan' down lads,' he called to the others, who lowered their bows. 'It's Brother 'orskram, in company o' armed men, 'n ravens at that. There ent no King's law this far south, as well ye know.'

'Have no fear, Alfrech, they come not in service of the King's law, but in service to me,' Horskram reassured him. 'We seek shelter for the night and a word with Olfach.'

Alfrech scratched his straggly brown beard. 'Olfach passed last winter – 's Hala who's in charge now,' he said. 'She'll be wantin' a word wi' you now yer 'ere, ye better come in.'

Turning, the woodsman placed two fingers in his mouth and whistled. The single gate creaked open. Dismounting, Horskram motioned for the others to do likewise and passed in. They tethered their horses and made their way to the meeting place.

At first glance the village was much the same as he remembered it: a few dozen low wattle huts crammed together, with no thought for order. A camp of tents might have been better organised. But his sixth sense told him more. There was a palpable aura of unease about the place – its ten score inhabitants were clearly frightened, more than he had ever seen them.

Passing further in, he noticed fresh wood on the west side of the stockade. That part of the wall had been newly rebuilt. Beside it were a handful of huts under construction.

A recent attack, he thought. *No wonder they're scared.*

A space in the midst of jumbled huts constituted the meeting place. Here a ring of tree stumps surrounded a large fire. Hala was sat on one of them next to the other village elders. She was a spidery woman of about fifty-five winters. She had ever been a fierce old harridan; he was far from surprised to see her as headwoman.

Horskram knew that wouldn't make his next job any the easier.

Alfrech and his men sat down around the fire, gazing intently at the strangers who now joined them. Other woodfolk gathered around the fringes of the circle, men and women and children staring curiously. Dusk was creeping in. The adept felt his tenseness increase a notch as he took a seat with the rest of the company.

'So what brings you 'ere this time, brother?' Hala asked pointedly. 'We could use yer 'elp right enough – one o' yer brothers was 'ere last month. Had another attack o' Terri.'

Horskram nodded. He wasn't surprised – if all they had heard was true, the Rent Between Worlds would be wider than usual thanks to the proximity of two powerful sorcerers clashing. That meant more spirits could pass through from the Other Side.

'How many this time?' he asked.

'Some 'alf a dozen,' the headwoman answered. The expression on her sharp face did not change but Horskram could sense the fear, though she hid it well enough from her people. 'They tore down 'alf the west side o' the stockade, swallowed up a dwelling each. Lost several good folk wi' them.' She shook her head sadly. Several elders exchanged grim glances.

'Who was the Argolian?'

'Sed 'is name was Tomas o' Einbeck, 'ad a novice wi' him too.'

Horskram nodded again. 'Aye, I know him – from our chapter in Dulsinor, a few leagues south of the forest. Good man, highly experienced. You were in safe hands.'

'Aye, master monk, tho' it took 'em near a week to get the job done. Had a couple o' fire spirits too, din't mek matters any the easier – nearly burnt down the granary. Thank Reus for the Argolians – they put a stop to 'em before they could do some real damage.'

Hala made the sign.

'Saraphi?' queried Horskram. 'That's unusual – fire spirits usually prefer to manifest in hotter climes.'

'It ent just us 'ave 'ad problems wi' such,' put in Alfrech. 'At night we see lights blazing, from deeper in the forest. Those of us who've had a mind to go south've heard strenge screaming... chantin' and such like. We dunna think to go there na more.'

The grizzled old hunter made the sign himself.

'So, everything we have heard is true then?' pressed Horskram. 'The Earth Witch stirs from her lair beyond the Girdle, fights another warlock?'

'Aye, as much as we kin gather oorselves,' said Alfrech. 'Wadwos on the warpath, like never before. Somethin' behind that, never seen 'em this organised before. Brother Tomas said it 'ad to be some sort o' black magic, tamin' beastfowk like that. We canna fight 'em like this.' Worry was now written across his weathered features. 'Before, when it were just one or two, solitary like, strength in numbers always kept us safe. But now... some o' my men 'ave spotted 'em lately. They're *armed*, Brother 'orskram. Marchin' in time t' sound o' drums – we 'ear them sometimes, mostly at night.'

'At least we've not got the worst o' it,' rejoined Hala. 'The further into the forest ye go, the closer ye get to the Girdle... not 'ad contact wit' a fair few settlements for some months now.'

'And on top o' all that, we've 'ad run-ins wi' outlaws, robber fowk from up your way,' cut in one of the elders. Horskram recognised him: a scrawny hunched old fellow, about seventy winters. What was the man's name? Old age was catching up with Horskram too.

He suddenly realised there was silence. All were waiting for him to speak.

He felt the same old weariness. Always others looking to him for advice, the way forward. Wise Master Horskram, vanquisher of spirits and sorcerers, counsellor to kings and saviour of the common folk. He sometimes wished he wasn't a hierophant, though he knew it was blasphemous to spurn the gifts of the Almighty.

'Let us consider our problems one at a time,' he said slowly. 'First, have you had any further encounters with elementi or other supernaturals since Brother Tomas left?'

Hala shook her head. 'No 'orskram, praise be to the Prophet, that we 'aven't. Not so far anyway.'

'That is good,' replied the adept. 'And what of the Wadwos? Have any of them launched an attack?'

'No, we've just 'ad sightings, on huntin' and foragin' parties south o' 'ere,' said Alfrech.

'And the outlaws?'

'That's a different story,' he replied. 'We fought a band o' them six nights ago – killed two of oor lads but we managed to get the better o' them, killed three before the rest fled. There were only seven o' them to oor twelve, we dunna go out in smaller groups nowadays.'

'How far out were your huntsmen?' asked Horskram.

'About half a day from 'ere,' replied Alfrech. 'Why d'ye ask?' he added, catching the look in Horskram's eye.

He told them of the slain party of freeswords and merchants.

'That's not so far from 'ere,' muttered Alfrech. 'Not a million miles from where our boys fought neither.'

'Do you know anything more?' asked the adept. 'We can fathom that the Wadwos have a leader, but what about the outlaws?'

'We were 'opin' you could tell us more about that,' said Hala, fixing him with another stare.

There was no keeping the truth from her, Horskram decided reluctantly. He told them of the war against Thule and his disbanded levies.

The elder whose name he had forgotten let a whistle escape his haggard lips. 'Two thousand levymen – armed n' trained,' he said. 'We'll not be thankin' you Northlendings for that in a hurry.'

Discontented muttering filled the clearing as the villagers registered the unwelcome news. Horskram felt his tension rise with their anger.

'Not all of them will have made it as far as here,' he said, doing his best to mollify the woodlanders. 'Many will have been taken down by King Freidheim's men as they fled through the southern provinces.'

'Not so many as we would like,' interjected Sir Torgun. 'They had a head start on us while we were finishing off Thule's last forces at Salmor, and few would have been foolhardy enough to linger long in the realm once they knew he was defeated.'

Horskram glowered at the young knight. Did he always have to be so damned honest?

The muttering had grown to a steady chatter as the village erupted into fearful speculation. Hala called for silence.

'Let Brother 'orskram speak,' she said. 'He's 'elped us in the past, and not let us down yet.'

Horskram took a deep breath as the chattering died down and all eyes returned to him. He would have to manage this next part delicately.

'The outlaws we can only give you so much help with,' he said, choosing his words carefully. 'Any we encounter we will certainly bring to justice – you have the word of Sir Torgun here, Commander in the Order of the White Valravyn, who considers it his personal responsibility.'

Torgun stood and nodded curtly at the elders. He was seemingly oblivious to the fact that his sentiments were being manipulated, but out of the corner of his eye the adept caught Sir Braxus giving him a wry smile.

'However, I believe that the more pressing problem is this clash of warlocks and all the dangers it is bringing to your door,' the adept continued. 'In fact what brings me here is a black magician I am hunting. I believe he is responsible both for provoking the Earth Witch and uniting the Wadwos. My intention is to seek him out and...'

His mind suddenly flashed back to Roarkil.

Sir Belinos of Runcymede cooked beside him... Andragorix lay on his back, blood spurting from the bloody stump where his hand had been... Horskram raised his quarterstaff, poised to strike at the mad mage's throat... But on the point of dealing the death blow he was swept back to another place, far from where he stood, a windswept desert where men clashed and bled in the sand...

Flashbacks within flashbacks...

Horskram tore his mind back to the present.

'... stop him,' he finished. His words sounded flat and lame in his own ears, but Hala seemed not to have noticed.

'Well, your fellow brother hinted that it might be black magic, but if so where is this other warlock?' she inquired, making the sign again with the rest of the elders. Talking openly about Left-Hand sorcerers was enough to spook even the woodfolk, who had spent their lives living next to a witch.

'I have yet to divine his exact location,' replied Horskram, recovering his composure. 'But was hoping you might be able to help me in this matter.'

Hala was looking at him suspiciously now. 'Well, we're all ears, master monk,' she said thinly.

Horskram met her dark eyes as he said: 'Clearly the Earth Witch is no friend to this other warlock. I intend to seek her help to find him. Once he is dealt with, there will be an end to this sorcerous war and things should hopefully return to normal.'

'You mean to travel beyond the Girdle?' asked Hala, incredulous. 'An Argolian friar, sworn to oppose sorcerers?'

'Strange as it seems, my enemy's enemy is my friend,' replied Horskram wryly. 'But you are right. It is not a move I would ever have considered until now, and as such I do not know that part of the Argael well.'

He paused a moment, then added: 'And that is why I have come here – to ask you to provide guides to take us there.'

The villagers resumed their muttering. The elders just looked at one another, more surprised than anything else. But Hala kept looking at him with hard eyes.

'You think to ask if we can send some more o' oor men into danger, just when we need every strong 'and about us?' she scoffed. 'I'm sorry, brother 'orskram, but we'll be doin' no such thing.'

'A couple of good men is all I need,' the adept persisted. 'Think what you stand to gain – if I can persuade this Earth Witch to help us defeat the other warlock, not just your village but all the woodfolk will stand to benefit!'

'Aye, and if ye don't, I've lost another couple o' good men,' replied Hala. 'And ye've just brought me news o' more outlaw killin's not far from 'ere.' She shook her head. 'I'm sorry, I canna do it. We've lost enough people as is.'

Damn her fierce old hide! He had known this would be difficult the minute he'd learned Hala was in charge. If only Olfach was still –

'Master Horskram, is the gate closed?'

Adelko had sprung suddenly to his feet and was looking anxiously back towards the clearing entrance.

Horskram glanced at Alfrech, who nodded. Getting up the adept walked over to stand next to the novice. His own sixth sense was buzzing, but he had put that down to the villagers' unease.

'What is it, lad?' he said softly. 'What do you sense?'

'... danger,' said Adelko, still looking back towards the gate, which was obscured by the huts. 'Something or someone coming, from the direction we took I think. Whatever it is, it knows where we are and it means us harm.'

The adept had seen enough of his understudy's progress not to ignore him on these occasions.

'We are about to be attacked,' he declared, unsheathing his quarterstaff. 'Hala, get any woodfolk too young or old to fight safely indoors! Alfrech, double your archers on the walls – facing the way we came from – and gather the rest of your able-bodied men and women about you. Sir Torgun – lead the rest of our group with me! We'll be the vanguard.'

The young knight nodded and gave a curt command. As one, the four ravens stood and drew swords. Braxus and Vaskrian did likewise, a keen light burning in the squire's eyes. Adelko fumbled at his quarterstaff, unslinging it awkwardly.

'Come on,' Horskram said. 'Let's get up on yon wall, see what our eyes can tell us.'

The two monks dashed up the wooden stairs to the crest of the stockade. It was barely the height of two men, but that would have to do. Nudging for space on a walkway now thronged with huntsmen bending their bows, Horskram peered out into the gloaming.

The trees were densely packed about the settlement, with only a short stretch of cleared land between their fringes and the stockade. From their vantage point the trail was barely visible, covered by a shroud of green darkened by deepening night.

'Looks like our eyes will tell us nothing,' muttered Horskram.

They waited. Glancing down behind him the adept saw Torgun and Braxus and the rest of their company standing at the head of some fifty woodfolk before the gate. A few archers had taken up positions on the other three sides of the stockade, just in case. The rest of the villagers were scrambling fearfully back into their huts.

They waited.

Then he saw them, faint pinpricks of light at first, gradually thickening and growing stronger. Torches.

'Extinguish our lights!' Horskram cried. 'Don't give them a target!'

'He's right,' said the archer next to him, a woman of about thirty summers. There were a few tapers burning, stuck into makeshift sconces along the top of the stockade. The cry went up and one by one the torches on the wall winked out, plunging them into deeper gloom. Only the fire burning in the meeting place and the stars and moon remained to keep stygian dark at bay.

The lights grew steadily stronger, then winked out all at once.

'They've had the same idea,' growled Horskram. 'They're being led by someone who knows what they're doing.'

'I think I see some of them, they must be at the clearing's edge,' said a woodsman with keener night-sight than most.

'How many do you see?' called out Sir Torgun.

Horskram shushed him. 'Too many to tell.'

'Wait,' said Adelko. 'I'm getting something else... more of them, coming from the north. I don't think they're close yet.'

Horskram had to marvel at the novice's growing powers. Reus Almighty, but the lad's sixth sense was *specific.*

'They mean to outflank us,' said Horskram. 'You,' – he gestured at the woodsman next to him – 'take half the archers here and move them around to face north. Keep bowmen on the other sides as well, they may be coming at us from different directions.'

The woodsman complied and the walkway was a flurry of activity, men and women stepping surefootedly despite the darkness. The two monks remained with the main party facing the trail.

They had no sooner changed their position than their attackers emerged from the trees – dark forms loping through the night like hungry wolves. The archers on the wall brought several down screaming, but targeting moving men at night was hard work even for woodfolk, and most reached the stockade.

Horskram realised their next move as the stockade resounded with dull thunks.

'Grappling hooks!' he cried. 'They're trying to scale the walls!'

Hurriedly some of the woodfolk dropped their bows and pulled out hunting knives, trying to cut the ropes in time. The first wave fell, grunting and cursing as they hit the ground, but quick as a flash another wave of men were at the walls. Horskram peered out at the dimming line of trees. He could make out more shapes flitting from them.

'There's too many of them!' he yelled. 'They'll overrun us – Torgun, open the gate and engage them before it's too late!'

'Master Horskram, they're coming from the north side too now!' Adelko cried. Flashing a sideways glance, Horskram saw more outlaws dashing from the trees towards the stockade. The ground in that direction stretched a bit longer from the woods; the archers managed to cut down several before the others made the walls. But there were many more behind.

'There must be a hundred of them at least!' he cried. 'Somebody's got this lot organised.'

That hardly surprised him. Thule had spent years training his levies – for pressed commoners they had fought well, almost on a par with the regular soldiers who served the barons. At least they weren't heavily armed: the glint of moonlight caught the odd stud on a leather jerkin, but that aside they carried the same light axes and short swords as they had to war.

Still, that was more than the woodfolk could claim – deprived of the chance to use their bows, with their hunting knives and clubs they would be little match for their assailants.

The gate creaked open below. Looking down he saw Sir Torgun and the others lined up in a defensive semi-circle, ready to receive attack. Behind and around them the rest of the woodfolk clustered. Horskram could almost feel their fear as a solid thing; he wished for once he didn't have his sixth sense.

The outlaws poured in. Stealth gave way to battle now, and angry war cries rang through the night air.

'Adelko, stay here!' the adept barked. 'I don't want a repeat of the Laegawood – no heroics, do you understand me?'

Adelko nodded. He was learning to recognise his limitations. The adept turned to the archers. 'The rest of you, pick off as many as you can from up here and don't engage unless you have to – they may be holding others in reserve under the trees.'

The man and woman he had spoken to nodded dumbly, probably wondering how a monk knew so much of war. That knowledge had cost his soul many a pain, but Horskram scarcely reflected on that as he bounded back down the stairs.

The ground before the gate was already littered with corpses. Sir Torgun alone appeared to have cut down three outlaws, his powerful sword strokes looking effortless in the half-light; next to him Sir Aronn struck down another robber, a trail of blood and brains following him as he fell to the ground shrieking. Sir Braxus disabled one attacker with a shield barge, sending the man tottering back spitting teeth before the Thraxian's sword found his gut. The Chequered Twins and Vaskrian looked scarcely less impressive, and their blades had made three more spurting corpses when Horskram reached them.

Despite their best efforts, sheer weight of numbers had been enough for the attackers to push past their ring of steel: woodfolk screamed as the outlaws hacked and gouged at them with the fury of desperate men.

Horskram caught one as he lunged towards a woodlander, causing him to double up with a blow to the midriff. Reversing his quarterstaff, he knocked him senseless with a blow to the head. He felt his gut tighten as it always did in those situations: one more life taken and he would most likely be beyond Purgatory. Stepping over the outlaw he engaged another head-on, pushing him back with a series of rapid strikes.

The fight surged on. The tide of outlaws gradually abated as the villagers and their protectors held firm. A second wave clustered beyond the gate, some trying to scale the stockade.

Horskram felt his tension ease slightly as he sent another outlaw spinning away from him in a spray of blood, his nosebone shattered. They were turning the tide, his plan of engagement had worked! If the archers on the walls could hold off the others...

A great crashing sound put paid to that hope. With horror he saw the wall by the side of the gate collapse, men toppling to the ground amidst the frayed timbers. In their wake a great furrow suddenly appeared in the earth, heading towards him with an alarming speed.

Stepping back the old monk felt his sinews strain as he narrowly avoided tumbling into the chasm that suddenly appeared next to him.

Reus' teeth – a Terrus, now of all times!

There was a flash of light behind him. Turning he saw an explosion of fire from the meeting place. Great tongues of flame reached high up into the air, descending with a rush on the nearest hut. The sound of screams erupted as the hut was consumed by the conflagration.

A Saraphus as well – it couldn't be...

And then he knew.

I can still send other agents to trouble you... Words spoken in a chamber at Salmor castle two weeks ago.

'Andragorix,' snarled Horskram through gritted teeth.

All hell was breaking loose. Another wave of outlaws was pouring through the breach made by the Terrus, outflanking the knights and descending on the terrified woodfolk in a rain of steel and blood. A voice crying out caught his ears – he looked up to see Adelko hanging onto the stockade walkway for dear life, right next to where the section had fallen in. More screams erupted behind him as the fire spirit attacked another hut, its occupants burning alive as it went up like a barrel of pitch. Torgun and the others were hard pressed now, each of them taking on two or three foes. More screams, muffled ones, came from the great rift ploughed by the Terrus as outlaw and woodsman alike fell into its depths.

The chasm closed on the hapless victims, crushing them pitilessly as it shifted towards the monk. Lurching backwards, Horskram felt his back collide with a hut as he intoned the words of the Psalm of Earth's Calming:

Spirit of the Other Side
Thou hast crossed the great divide
Set by He who made the earth
And brought it to its ancient birth!

Spirit from beyond the rent
'Tis He commands thee to relent
These rocks and stones are not thine own
Return now to immortal bourne!

The chasm stopped short of the monk's trembling feet, like an invisible dog being pulled on a leash. Horskram let it have another couple of verses:

Spirit of the Other Side
Thou hast broken rules decreed
By Him who made the forests wide
And all the lands that sprouted seed!

Spirit from beyond the rent
Your trespass 'gainst Him now repent
These rocks and stones are not thine own
Relinquish now usurpéd throne!

Shutting out the din of conflict, Horskram closed his eyes and focused on the words. He spoke them in Decorlangue, the ancient tongue of the Redeemer, but the true power of such things lay in the conviction *behind* them: he was calling on Reus Almighty, invoking His power through the same words spoken by Palom a thousand years ago.

Even so, he knew he could not hope to banish a Terrus right away – the most he could do was drive it off, beyond range of the words that called it back to its preternatural realm.

A rumbling at his feet told him it was working as the elemental raged, sending stones and sods of earth skittering up in all directions. Reaching inside his habit Horskram closed his hand about the phial at his neck, trusting to the Redeemer's blood to lend him power as he chanted the final verses:

Spirit of the Other Side
Return across the great divide
Seek the forests and the dales
Of thine own immortal vale!

Spirit from beyond the rent
By unclean powers thou wert sent
Pay no heed to mortal call
Obey the laws of the Lord of All!

A great howl went up from the broken ground. Full of sadness it was, like a ravenous beast denied its prey. Horskram opened his eyes and the Terrus was gone, the chasm closing up as suddenly as it had opened. Only a scar across the land showed it had ever been.

Horskram's eyes widened. He had just *banished* an earth spirit – at the first attempt! He muttered a brief prayer, clutching the phial more tightly. The Redeemer's blood didn't abjure an elemental the way it would a demon, yet still the relic's power could not be doubted.

And he would need it again, right soon.

Many more of the huts towards the other side of the settlement were now burning. Dashing towards the meeting place, he saw several screaming figures running pell-mell, burning alive under the Saraphus' pitiless touch. The spirit itself could be seen now, flittering from one fire to another, a vaguely humanoid form with tongues of flame shaped like talons.

He sucked in a deep breath as he prepared to utter the Psalm of Flame's Quenching. Saraphi were the most malevolent of elementi, their wild and reckless psyches the hardest to banish.

He was about to intone the words when things went from bad to worse. From out of the fires dotted about the settlement another three spirits leaped, launching themselves towards villagers who had broken off from the battle to try and douse the flames killing their women and elders and children.

As fresh screams erupted about him Horskram clutched the phial again and summoned his resolve. His task now seemed impossible, but perhaps the Redeemer's blood would save them.

✢ ✢ ✢

The female woodlander grasped Adelko by the arm and yanked him back onto the shorn end of the walkway. Just then an outlaw hauled himself over the stockade, clutching a knife between grinning teeth.

His thanks turned to a yell of warning. The huntress turned rapidly and stabbed down hard with her own knife. The outlaw screamed as its point found his eye, sinking in up to the hilt. He toppled backwards taking her blade with him, but she quickly caught his as it slipped from his mouth.

Adelko looked feverishly about him. Outside the stockade the outlaws were abandoning the dangerous climb, pouring instead through the gap. On the other side his companions fought bravely, though for every brigand they cut down another appeared in his place.

His sixth sense told him the presence of magic had increased sharply and his eyes told him as much: he could see Horskram backing away towards a hut, a Terrus boring its way through the ground after him as it crushed men to death in its wake. Towards the centre of the village a Saraphus was wreaking havoc, burning huts and villagers as it leapt to and fro in a fiery dance of death.

Suppressing his nausea, he forced himself to concentrate. Who needed his help most?

The woodlanders on the walkway next to him were making light work of the last climbers on the walls. Their fellows down on the ground were faring worse, being no match for Thule's hardened levies at close range.

To make matters worse, some woodfolk had broken off from the melee to try and save their families burning in the huts.

I can't help much in a fight, but I can help there, he decided.

'I need to get down!' he yelled at the woman who had saved him. The stairs he had come up by had been smashed by the Terrus.

'There's another set, on the opposite side!' the woodlander yelled back, turning her aim on the outlaws fighting inside the compound. At least with the fires she should have a chance of distinguishing friend from foe.

Adelko ignored the curses of the other bowmen as he clumsily barged past them. Reaching the other stairway he took it two steps at a time, tripping and tumbling down the last few to land in a sprawling heap at the bottom. Grabbing his quarterstaff he hauled himself up and approached the burning huts.

As he neared them bright flares suddenly hurt his eyes. He gasped as another three Saraphi burst into life, descending mercilessly on the woodfolk. Dropping his quarterstaff he pulled out his copy of the *Holy Book of Psalms and Scriptures* and fumbled for the correct page. He'd never banished an elemental, and weeks of adventure had left little time for study.

Praying the fire spirits wouldn't target him, he found the page and prepared to read. At that moment a sonorous voice cried out. His mentor, reciting the same psalm. Hurriedly he joined his voice to Horskram's:

Spirits of the Other Side
Thou hast crossed the great divide
Set by He who gave men means
To warm their halls and cook their meat!

Spirits from beyond the rent
'Tis He commands thee to relent
Desist from speaking fiery tongues
In bourne where thou hast ne'er belonged!

Strong and clear their voices rang together. The dancing figures shimmered and flickered, pausing in their awful depredations and swarming overhead like angry fireflies. He felt the heat from the burning huts, felt the sweat pour from his body, soaking his habit. The stench of charring flesh clogged his nostrils.

Gagging, he struggled his way into the next verses:

Spirits of the Other Side
Thou hast broken rules decreed
By Him who made the fires high
That shine on earth and plain and tree!

Spirits from beyond the rent
Your trespass 'gainst Him now repent
Quench these ravaging tongues of flame
Return to spirit world in shame!

The spirits burned indignantly as they streaked to and fro across the dark firmament, their zigzagging forms cutting trails of blazing light across Adelko's vision. Wiping his sopping brow he prepared to read the last verses, trying to synchronise his words with Horskram's:

Spirits of the Other Side
Return across the great divide

Seek the sun that never sets
No more thy master's patience test!

Spirits from beyond the rent
By unclean powers thou wert sent
Pay no heed to mortal call
Obey the laws of the Lord of All!

The four spirits stopped moving, coalescing into a single sheet of roaring flame. It undulated above them, growing weak and diaphanous: Adelko fancied he could now see past it to the stars and sky. He felt an arcane power fighting them both, a malign will beyond the summoned elementals struggling to reconstitute their elan.

Feverishly they repeated the verses, their voices growing more synchronised as they attuned to one another. The elementi roared wrathfully, sounding like the burning huts only ten times stronger. Even the fighters paused a few seconds to look up: mortal men awed enough by supernatural conflict to momentarily stop killing each other. The conjoined fire spirit stretched across the skies, growing fainter still, its flames turning red, then blue. As one Horskram and Adelko called out the final line of the psalm, repeating it over and over.

And then the elementi heaved a great sigh, and were snuffed out like a candle.

Adelko felt his sixth sense stab his mindset violently. He turned to see an outlaw leering over him, his axe poised to strike. The axe came whistling down and Adelko hurled himself out of the way, slipping and falling over.

His limbs suddenly felt heavy. He had used so much energy, channelling the power of the Redeemer, and the heat had taken its toll: his movements felt lethally slow as he tried to roll out of the way of the next strike. He was dimly aware of Horskram shouting, running towards him, but he was too far away. Another shape flickered against the crackling huts...

With an ugly belching sound the outlaw fell next to him. A long knife was buried in his back. Looking up he saw the female woodlander from the wall gazing down at him, a wry smile on her lips.

'That's twice I've saved yer skin, Northlending,' she said, reaching down to pull the blade free.

He made to sit up and reply, but suddenly felt himself falling backwards into a soft, dark pit. Blackness closed around the edges of his vision, and he knew no more.

✠ ✠ ✠

Vaskrian's arms ached. He was more than a match for any single outlaw, but there were a lot of the curs and trying to kill people who outnumbered you was tiring work. Especially the last one – he'd virtually had to hack the wretch to pieces to get him to give up the ghost.

Another brigand fell with a cry as Braxus struck him down with a clever riposte, circling his blade away from his opponent's and piercing his chest with a lightning thrust.

Good move. He'd have to get his guvnor to teach him that one. It looked like less work than cutting a man to red ribbons.

The two of them leaned against each other, recovering their breath. The woodfolk had rallied somewhat since their huts had stopped exploding: that and the slaughter they'd made had evened up the odds somewhat, giving them a brief respite.

It was all too brief. A pair of outlaws cut down another couple of woodfolk and turned to seek new foes, a murderous glint in their feral eyes.

Vaskrian and Braxus exchanged a brief look, nodded, and charged as one.

Blood was running down the fuller of Vaskrian's blade, making the squire's hand slick, and his grip was unsteady as he crossed swords with the outlaw, an ugly man with a bald head and scar running across his upper lip. He nearly let go of the hilt – the outlaw pressed forwards on the counter but Vaskrian moved agilely back, remembering the footwork Braxus had taught him.

He waited for the brigand to press him, then stepped nimbly to the left and in. Regaining his grip he aimed a downwards thrust at the brigand, who only had time to gape as the blade punctured his thigh and severed an artery. Vaskrian wrenched the weapon free and watched with satisfaction as his foe fell screaming, a fountain of blood pouring from his leg.

Was that four or five he'd killed? He hated losing count.

Braxus was still engaged. Vaskrian was about to help him but his guvnor had things under control. Blocking an axe swipe with his shield he pushed quickly back: the outlaw, a burly man, was clearly surprised by the slim knight's strength. He took a couple of steps back, allowing the Thraxian to come at him, sword raised high. The brigand steadied himself, anticipating an overhead strike... but at the last moment Braxus switched directions, bringing his sword round and down in a powerful cut. The brigand staggered back on one leg, the other one staying where Braxus had severed it just below the knee. The outlaw crashed to the ground, his eyes rolling up into his head.

Vaskrian scanned the skirmish, hungrily seeking another foe as his second wind blew fast upon him.

Sir Torgun's blade was a blur as he clashed with three brigands; the squire gawped as he stabbed one in the mouth, transfixing the back of his skull, while knocking another senseless with his heavy kite. The third outlaw scarcely had time to press his own attack before the blond knight whirled to face him, using the momentum of movement to slice him across the top of the face. The man fell in a wash of blood that spurted from a wide slit where his eyes had been.

Torgun's footwork was rock solid, his face a mask of concentration. In fact he hardly seemed bothered at all, as if the fight bored him. Vaskrian had never seen a man his size move with such speed. His hero was truly astonishing to watch.

Not that he'd be watching him much more tonight. There was always a turning point in any battle, large or small; that one last casualty that broke a side... and this was it.

Thule's deserters had come expecting easy plunder, to butcher a bunch of frightened woodfolk: they hadn't expected six of the best swords the Free Kingdoms had to offer. Even the timorous woodfolk had found their courage, fighting ferociously to save their homes and kin, clearly inspired by having great warriors in their midst. And the archers remaining on the walls picking them off had helped the cause too. Vaskrian supposed the strange fires had been useful like that – but what in the Known World had caused them?

The squire didn't bother to cut down any more as the remaining outlaws turned tail and fled. The memory of Derrick's death still haunted him, truth to tell: he wanted to avoid dishonourable killings wherever possible.

Besides that, he was exhausted.

Sitting down amidst the corpses he let out a satisfied sigh. All in all, a good day for him. More valour to his credit.

The wailing of women drifted through the smoke. Maybe not so good for these poor woodland folk, but still you had to look on the bright side – at least they hadn't shared the fate of their dead family and friends.

His rest was rudely interrupted by his guvnor, telling him to come and help douse the fires. With a sigh Vaskrian heaved himself back on to his feet.

It really was hard work, being a hero.

⇥ CHAPTER IX ⇤

After The Slaughter

A delko awoke to darkness. Where was he? He had dreamed strange dreams. He had walked through blood-soaked fields, beneath a foreign sun. Armed men rode at him on all sides. Some cast spears at him; others levelled crossbows and fired. But none of the missiles hit him, glancing harmlessly away as he calmly deflected them one by one...

That was all he could remember.

He sat up. His body ached and his soul felt weary. As his eyes grew accustomed to the light he realised he was in a hut; a sliver of sunshine peered beneath a flap of hide covering the window overlooking the rickety cot he had slept in.

A hut... of course. As memory flooded back to him he stumbled to his feet and pushed his way through a deerskin hanging across the low doorway. Bright sunlight stabbed his eyes. He blinked, a familiar stench filling his nostrils. As his vision cleared he realised what the smell was.

Death. He had seen enough of it during the war, and now Azrael's bounty lay sprawled across his line of sight again.

The hut was on the edge of the meeting place. The fire had been cleared away to make space for corpses. At least fifty were there, most of them covered in fly-encrusted gashes and other horrible wounds, some no more than charred husks. Reaching inside his habit for a rag, he pressed it to his mouth and nose.

Looking closer he saw that the bodies were piled on a huge pyre. Sat on the tree stumps ringing it were his companions. They were alive at least – though all of them except Torgun bore light wounds and every one of them was heavily bloodstained.

Wailing and sobbing met his ears, coming from the other huts. The surviving woodfolk, mourning their dead. His eyes returned to the funeral pyre. One of the charred corpses looked to have been a small child, of no more than five summers.

Letting go of the rag he leaned against the hut and was sick.

'You'll need to pull yourself together, lad – we must give these unfortunates their Last Rites.'

He looked up to see his mentor standing over him. A rare but wan smile crossed his face. 'Be of some cheer, Adelko – but for your help last night, it might have been us seeking the Heavenly Halls too.'

The novice pulled himself upright, his stomach churning. He tried to take some comfort from Horskram's kindly words.

'So many of them... It's not as bad as the war, but still...'

'There's a bigger mound outside the walls – we gave as good as we got, Adelko!' Vaskrian had come over. His left arm was swathed in a bandage, but he could still move it and didn't seem overly bothered.

'I don't think I need to see it,' replied Adelko, surprised at his curtness. He was beginning to see Horskram's point of view. A hundred people slaughtered, what was there to be so damned cheerful about?

The squire must have sensed his mood. 'Well, I'm off to see about breakfast, for me an' the guvnor – fighting's hungry work. Glad to see you're on the mend anyway, Horskram says you did really well against those spirit things.'

Adelko shook his head as he watched his controversial friend stroll off. He half expected Horskram to say something, but he held his peace. The novice's sixth sense told him he was pleased, in his own way.

'Here is your scripture book,' he said, handing it to Adelko. 'You know the passage we need. We'll proceed as soon as the woodlanders bring the others back.'

'The others?'

'The murdered freeswords and merchant family we found on the road,' Horskram reminded him. 'I did promise them a decent funeral too, godless though they were in life.'

Adelko nodded numbly. More corpses were the last thing he wanted to see.

Gradually the meeting place filled up with woodfolk, many of their ashen faces streaked with tears. Hala had survived – though she looked as though she had aged twenty winters – but of Alfrech there was no sign. He was not with the party that returned with the bodies of the freeswords and merchants either. Adelko supposed glumly he was somewhere on the pyre.

One face among the sortie did catch his eye though. It was the female woodlander who had saved his life. He was about to step

forward and thank her when Sir Torgun sprang to his feet with a cry
of dismay. The sortie had brought back the bodies from the road in
two litters, one for the mercenaries and another for the merchants.
Striding over to the latter, he pointed at one of the bodies.

'Where did you find this one?' he asked the nearest woodsman.

'Not far off the trail, jus' like ye sed, sir knight,' he replied
grimly, shaking his head. 'Sad business, that an' the girl. Boy
couldna been older n' eight summers.'

Torgun rounded on Horskram, rare fury crossing his rugged features.

'A boy of eight summers,' he said accusingly. 'A lad we could
have saved from bleeding to death alone in the woods.'

His words hung heavy in the air.

'For all we know he might have bled to death long before we reached
them,' replied Horskram stoutly, though Adelko's sixth sense told him
his mentor was pained. 'In any case what's done is done. We've just
saved a settlement from being slaughtered – why don't you think on
that instead, sir knight? Now if you'll excuse me, I have souls to shrive.'

Horskram beckoned Adelko over, ignoring Torgun's burning
stare. Sir Aronn glared at the old monk as he adjusted a bandage about
his thigh, while the Chequered Twins muttered darkly to one another.

Adelko tried to focus on preparing as they stripped the corpses and
added them to the pile. His voice sounded thin and reedy in his ears as
they gave them the Last Rites, Hala weeping silently as she lit the pyre.

'What about the outlaws?' Adelko asked his mentor once the
ceremony was over. 'Don't we need to dispose of their bodies too?'
Thick black smoke from the pyre smeared the blue summer skies.

'Such men deserve no help on their journey to Azrael's shores,'
replied his mentor sternly. 'The Angel of Death shall give them just
retribution when he despatches them to Gehenna.'

Adelko could sense his mentor was still upset about the dead boy.

'I meant getting rid of the bodies is all,' he added tentatively.

But Horskram shook his head. 'Nay, we leave them there –
as discouragement to other outlaw bands. These poor folk have
suffered enough.'

Adelko pictured the pile of corpses rotting in the sun, and was
thankful he did not live in the settlement.

✠ ✠ ✠

'So you see the value in what I was trying to tell you,' said Horskram.
'I am convinced the *elementi* who brought so much harm to your
village were sent by the very warlock I am hunting. You must send

a guide with us to seek the Earth Witch – this blasphemous duel of sorcerers must be stopped!'

Hala nodded. She appeared to have recovered her composure, though the sadness had not left her face – she had lost two nephews and a brother.

'Aye, I ken that right enough... just thinkin' who to send is all.'

A silence fell about the meeting place. The pyre had burned down, leaving naught but ashes and charred remains. These had been covered with a tarpaulin. On the morrow the woodfolk would scatter them across the forest, as was their custom.

'I'll show yon adventurers t' Girdle.'

All turned to look at the speaker. Adelko recognised her instantly.

'Ah, young Adelko's saviour,' said Horskram. 'Events prevented our being properly introduced. And you would be?'

'Me name's Kyra,' replied the huntress, leaning on her stout bow of yew. 'At yer service.'

Horskram frowned. 'Though I am grateful for what you did, I would fain not take a woman into danger,' he said.

'Beggin' yer pardon, master monk, but ye've brought me enough danger as 'tis, what wi' this wizard ye're on about sendin' spirits to trouble us on your account.'

The other woodlanders exchanged amused glances and comments at that. Clearly this Kyra had a reputation for speaking her mind.

'Tek no offence,' she continued. 'It was only a matter o' time 'fore we ran int' trouble anyway. Yer right – this mad war needs stoppin'. If I can 'elp ye do that, I will. Don't be worryin' 'bout bringin' me no trouble, Brother 'orskram – I ken the risks right well.'

The adept nodded. 'Very well, you've proved your usefulness already – so be it. I have not seen you before though... how long have you lived here?'

'Long enough,' replied the huntress. 'But I'm not 'ere often. I travel the forest more n' most. A better tracker an' marksman ye'll not find for leagues around.'

Dusk was gathering in. The woodfolk got up and made their way back to their huts to mourn the dead. Soon only Kyra remained, staring impassively at the adventurers she had now joined.

'I haven't had the chance to thank you for saving me,' said Adelko, rising and approaching her shyly.

Kyra nodded curtly. 'Think nowt on it, young sirrah – an Argolian friar should always be spared, where possible. An' we 'aven't even met any Woses yet – we'll need your holy prayers all the more.'

The novice cringed inwardly. So far as he knew, Wadwos – though the results of the Elder Wizards' frightful experiments – felt no terror at the Redeemer's words. Cold steel was what was needed against them – that and a lot of courage. He wasn't sure he possessed either.

'What made you decide to follow me?' he asked the huntress. 'Down into the village I mean.'

Kyra shrugged. 'Ye looked like ye needed some 'elp is all. Ye're over young to be in the thick of things, Adelko.'

She looked at him, not unkindly. She was tall for a woman, and slender, though her plain hard-set features told of a rough life. She was in early middle age and her dark hair was already streaked with grey.

'Maybe I am at that,' the novice sighed. 'I always longed for adventure... Then Horskram took me on as his second and I got what I wanted.'

He stopped speaking, the sound of crickets suddenly loud in his ears.

The woodlander cracked a humourless grin.

'Not always s'good is it? Gettin' what ye want.'

Adelko shook his head. 'No, not always.'

Thanking her again, he went to help Horskram ready their things. His stomach growled as he realised he had not eaten all day. He was usually always hungry, but the stench of death had not left his nostrils.

✦ ✦ ✦

They left the settlement at first light. Their horses remained behind; the woodland paths Kyra now took them on meant journeying on foot. As much as he wasn't looking forward to getting footsore again, Adelko was glad to leave the village. It was another clear summer's day, and he gratefully buried himself in the verdant richness of the Argael, a welcome antidote to the horror and slaughter he had just witnessed. He wondered grimly if he would ever get used to seeing such things: he hoped he never had to.

They marched in loose formation, following the huntress as she took them through the densely clustered oaks. The ground dipped after a while, falling in irregular shelves. That made for harder going of course: the novice glanced over more than once at the knights in their heavy mail, marvelling at their hardiness. They were carrying injuries too, albeit light ones, but not a word of complaint escaped their lips.

Not a word – though his sixth sense told him Sir Torgun and the other ravens were far from happy. It wasn't the rigours of the journey that bothered them either. He wondered how they were going to overthrow a warlock with a supernatural army at his beck and call when they could not even agree with each other.

Around midday they stopped at a stream to take food and rest. The mood was still sour, and no one spoke.

He found himself sitting next to the Chequered Twins. Doric and Cirod were a curious sight, exactly the same in every way but for their hair. Doric's was jet black, whilst Cirod's was a shock of white.

His mentor had warned him not to befriend these men, but something had to be done to lighten the mood. It was more than his sixth sense could bear.

'Your hair, sir knights... how did it come to be different colours?'

He was half expecting them to ignore him, but both twins exchanged smiles.

'Well,' started Doric, 'we used to be exactly the same.'

'Our hair was brown,' added Cirod.

'But our mother could never tell us apart.'

'We were so alike, you see.'

'So one day she prayed to Reus...'

'... asking Him for help.'

'She went to the High Temple at Strongholm...'

'... especially so she could do it.'

'The next morning when she awoke...'

'... my hair was lighter than Torgun's...

'And mine as dark as yon woodland wench.'

Adelko blinked. 'You're joking... a miracle made you the way you are?'

The two young knights exchanged smiles again.

'Well yes, I suppose...

'... you could call it that.'

Aronn strode over from behind them, grasping both twins by the shoulder. The three of them were all tall after the manner of pure-blooded Northlendings, though Aronn was a shade bigger.

'Their hair may be different, master monk,' he said, his ruddy face creasing as he grinned. 'But when I knock their heads together, they both bleed red right enough!'

The twins shrugged him off, the three of them laughing.

'He might try that,' said Doric.

'But he'd have to fight us both,' added Cirod.

'Perhaps I should put it to song,' said Braxus, joining the conversation. *'The Tale of the Chequered Twins*, it has a certain ring to it...'

'Aye, but you won't get past the first verse, with these two,' quipped Aronn. 'Try me instead, Thraxian, I'm a finer sword than this pair of amateurs put together!'

'Yes, you're good at carving up outlaws, that much I've seen,' deadpanned Braxus with a wry smile. 'How about *The Red Faced Butcher of Brigands?*'

Aronn scowled at that. For a second Adelko thought things were going to turn ugly, but the Chequered Twins started laughing, and Aronn couldn't help but join in.

He felt his spirits rise. Surely this was the way it was meant to be – adventurers were supposed to share a joke or two when they weren't trying to avoid being killed. Or that's how it had always seemed in the lays anyway. He glanced around, hoping to get the others involved, but Horskram was consulting Kyra about the way ahead, while Vaskrian was busy cleaning utensils in the stream. Torgun sat apart, leaning against a tree and staring moodily at the flowing water as he sharpened his sword.

Well, at least he'd got some of the company talking. It was a start.

✠ ✠ ✠

They pressed on deeper into the forest, their footfalls monotonously crunching through moss and sedge as they meandered steadily towards its heart. The air grew stiflingly hot and oppressive; Adelko continually shifted his habit, his pudgy frame sticky beneath the coarse brown wool.

The ground levelled out gradually; they must be in a deep wide basin of land, covered in a thick blanket of trees. Large black spiders scuttled away as they pushed through webs that crisscrossed the oaken boles, their gossamer forms catching stray shafts of sunlight that dappled the humid earth beneath his feet. Occasionally a flash of scarlet greeted his eyes as frightened squirrels fled their coming; red robins and bluetits joined their flapping forms to the riot of colour. The Argael was intoxicating, an assault on his young senses, but at least it felt natural unlike the horrible presence of haunted Tintagael.

As the sun set and darkness began once more to steal through the branches, Kyra and Horskram called a halt for the day.

With a groan of gratitude Adelko sank down against the nearest tree-trunk, delicious rest seeping through his limbs.

'How much farther until we reach the Girdle?' Horskram asked Kyra as they began unpacking their things for the night.

'Another day an' we should reach it,' she replied, pulling two strips of dried meat from her pack. 'But ye'll 'ave to find another way in, unless yer prayers can turn rivers an' tame earth.'

Horskram eyed her sharply. 'What do you mean?'

'I dunna roam idly, master monk,' said the huntress, taking a swig of water from her skin as she chewed greedily on the meat. 'I've been t'Girdle, seen it wi' me own eyes. Woses bin tryin' to get past it fer weeks now.'

Horskram's eyes narrowed. The others were all looking at her too, save for Vaskrian who was making a small fire.

'Explain,' said the adept.

'Didna want to talk 'bowt such in front o' the others,' began Kyra. 'They're scared enough as 'tis. But there's those of us woodfowk say we should unite 'gainst the Woses – we've got a band o' us together, try an' pick 'em off as best we can. Problem is they dunna seem to tek much notice o' our arrows, 'less ye get 'em right int' eye. So we've also been keepin' a watch on t'Girdle, tryin' to find some way o' gettin' in to talk to the Earth Witch. We've a mind to form an alliance wi' her, same as you. We need her 'elp as bad as you do.'

The huntress paused. Vaskrian's fire cracked and spluttered into life. Grateful as he was for added warmth and light, Adelko wondered if fires were such a good idea. Braxus had clearly thought along similar lines, ordering his squire to make it a small one.

'The Woses 'ave the Girdle surrounded,' the woodlander went on. 'It's protected by a magic river, runs in a perfect circle around 'er realm. Anyone tries to cross wi'out her say-so, river rises up an' drags 'em down. Some've said they can see figures made o' water inside it.'

Horskram nodded. 'Lymphi – water spirits that she commands. Go on.'

'Then there's a ford, seems like it's made o' natural earth. But it's a trap – some o' us saw a group o' Woses try an' use it to cross – the ford just opened up beneath 'em and dumped 'em in the river.'

'More Terri,' Horskram frowned. 'The Earth Witch is using elemental magic to protect herself from Andragorix's servants.'

'Wait a minute,' put in Braxus. 'Weren't we attacked by an earth spirit the other night? Who's to say the Earth Witch wasn't behind that one too?'

Horskram shook his head. 'Unlikely. She has no interest in attacking the woodlanders – '

' – unless they come prying into her realm,' pressed Braxus. 'Which by the sounds of it, some of them have been.' The Thraxian shot Kyra an accusing glance.

'We've not 'ad the chance to pry, not yet,' said Kyra. 'We searched the whole Girdle for another way in. Gettin' past the Wadwos is difficult but not impossible – they're camped at regular intervals and we've 'ad to sneak between 'em. But there's no other way in, none that we've found anyway.'

'So we're looking at a stand-off,' mused Horskram as the flames from the fire thickened, sending shadows skittering across the trees. 'She can't get out, and they can't get in.'

'There's more, master monk,' Kyra went on. 'As I said, we managed to get close enough to observe, an' the Woses 'ave built these catapults, see. They're not so big, but they fill 'em up with bales o' burning pitch – then they throw 'em into the Girdle. We saw 'em do it one night, an' fire spirits jumped out, like fires o' Gehenna – started burning trees on t'other side o' river...'

'What about the water spirits in the river?' asked Braxus, his green eyes keen in the firelight. The other knights and Vaskrian were just staring, looking utterly bewildered. Adelko began to perceive Horskram's wisdom in bringing the Thraxian along – he certainly seemed more at ease dealing with supernatural foes than the Northlending knights.

'Aye, I were comin' to that,' rejoined Kyra. 'They rises up out o' the river right enough, an' soaks the catapults, then they flows back across it to fight the fire spirits int' Girdle. That's when the Woses try an' cross the river – they've not succeeded yet but we've watched 'em do it a few times. Every time, they get a bit closer t'other side.'

'Andragorix is clever – and powerful,' said Horskram, frowning. 'He is slowly wearing her down, counting on his elan being stronger than hers. He knows it is only a matter of time before he breaks past her defences.'

Adelko felt it was his turn to speak up. 'Why does he need the Wadwos and their catapults?' he asked. 'He sent Saraphi to attack us directly, why not do the same with the Earth Witch?'

'Her defences are long established, and probably powerful enough to stop Andragorix manifesting Saraphi directly on her territory,' explained Horskram. 'Either that or she is counter-scrying – using her arts to block his efforts to detect her exact location.'

Adelko nodded, recalling the fiend sent by Andragorix to pursue them across the wildernesses of Northalde and how uncertain a discipline demonology had been. That lack of perfect control had probably saved their lives – but only just. The thought of what the warlock could do with the Headstone of Ma'amun reunited sent a shiver down his spine.

'So how are we going to get to her?' asked Braxus. 'Even if she does need our help, she won't let us in without knowing who we are.'

'We must hope her Scrying tells her enough to work out that we are here to help.' Horskram's face looked grim in the firelight. Adelko didn't need his sixth sense to tell him his mentor was far from happy with that plan.

'Kyra, are there Wadwos camped near the bridge?' asked Braxus.

The huntress nodded. 'Aye, out o' renge o' the water spirits, but not far off.'

'Well you say arrows don't bother them over much – I suggest we find out how they take to swords of cold steel,' said the Thraxian. 'We ambush a Wadwo camp, kill them all and take a bag of beastmen heads as a peace offering to the ford. She should let us in then.'

Sir Torgun and the other ravens nodded their approval. Here at last was something they could understand.

'They're abowt twenty strong,' warned Kyra. 'Ye'll 'ave yer work cut owt for ye.'

'What about this woodlander rebellion you're part of?' asked Braxus. 'Can we get them to help?'

Kyra bit her lip. 'Difficult to say... Madogan, he's our leader, says he dunna want t'engage hand to hand 'till there's more o' us. He's no coward, but he's a cautious man... says we can't risk losing all on a straight fight. Reckon he's right too, beggin' yer pardons – us woodfolk aren't used to fightin' like that. To be o' any use we'd need to outnumber 'em at least three to one.'

Sir Torgun slammed a huge fist into his palm. 'I'll not wait on common folk, however hardy and brave!' he cried. Adelko started. The tall knight was rarely this animated, even in battle. 'This is a job for true knights, and our duty is clear,' he declaimed, standing and gazing around him. 'We must engage these creatures, even if the odds be against us! I have slain one before, they are not invincible.'

'One aye, but twenty...' mused Aronn. 'I quail before no man, but those are long odds.'

'Then we shall have to shorten them with our strong right arms,' replied Torgun stubbornly. Adelko exchanged glances with Horskram. Clearly Northalde's greatest knight was feeling the pressures of adventuring – the novice could feel the yearning for action pouring from him.

'For once I agree with Sir Torgun,' said Braxus. 'What choice do we really have? We knew this quest wouldn't be easy.'

'Quest?' snorted Aronn. 'Sounds more like a suicide mission to me – but I'm with you. If there's fighting to be done I'll not shy away from it!'

The Chequered Twins merely nodded in agreement.

'There's one thing I've left to tell ye,' said Kyra, her voice dropping slightly. 'One other trick the Earth Witch has up 'er sleeve, it may 'elp us or it may not.'

All eyes turned to the huntress again.

'Some o' our lot 'ave reported sightings... o' somethin' else.' Her dark eyes looked fearful in the uneven light cast by the crepitant flames. 'Group o' the lads were trackin' a small band o' Woses, abowt a tenday ago. They were planning on ambushing 'em towards break o' day, Wadwos preferrin' to fight at night. Anyway, they followed 'em to a clearin'. Beastmen were settin' up camp when something came at 'em from the darkness. Lads said it were huge, twice the size o' a Wadwo, an' they're big enough! Smashed three o' 'em to pieces before a Wose gets out a drum, starts bangin' it...'

She paused again, reflecting. 'It were right strenge, cos we've been 'earin' that a lot recently,' she went on. 'Woses dunna normally go in fer marchin' but then they've never been organised before, so we'd just assumed it were part o' that. Anyway, lads said the thing 'eard the sound and gave an 'orrible scream, started runnin' – came straight towards them, an' they panicked an' fled.'

'What happened to the rest of the Woses?' asked Horskram.

'They must've pressed on instead o' campin' int' clearing. By the time the lads regrouped they were long gone. Tracked 'em till early morning, but by the time they caught up wi' 'em they'd rejoined one o' the camps abowt the Girdle. That made too many o' 'em fer a small band o' woodfowk to take. Still at least this thing, whatever it was, did some damage for us.'

Horskram rubbed his beard. He looked genuinely puzzled. 'How did the woodfolk describe this apparition?'

'It were dark, an' everythin' 'appened so quickly,' answered Kyra. 'Said it were almost part o' th'earth, shaped like a man, but definitely no mortal.'

'Another Terrus?' suggested Braxus. 'She is called the Earth Witch after all...'

Horskram shook his head. 'Nay, a Terrus possesses the earth and manipulates it, a blasphemous entity that spurns the natural laws set down by the Almighty. But I've never heard of elementi using the earth to take humanoid form. By Reus, what deviltry is this?'

'Well, whatever it is, seems it might be on our side,' suggested Kyra, though she plainly looked unsettled.

'Or it might be on nobody's side but the Earth Witch's,' said Horskram, giving voice to Adelko's thoughts.

Silence followed. An owl hooted, giving them all a start. The faces of the company looked tired and fretful, shadows streaking lines across their faces as flames danced across firewood.

'Everyone eat and get some sleep,' said Horskram. 'Sir Torgun, I'll leave you to organise the night's watch. And put that blasted fire out!'

Shrugging, Vaskrian rose to obey after getting a nod of assent from Braxus. Adelko rolled out his pallet before fishing around in his pack for food and water.

Lying down after a snatched supper he was soon asleep. But as was so often the case, it didn't last. More strange dreams came to trouble him, of white-faced ogres wreathed in hot fires devouring men and women clad in green. Above them loomed a vast shadowy figure, its tenebrous form quenching the fires one by one. Its shadow grew as it did, devouring all in its path. The last fire winked out...

Adelko woke with a start. He strained his ears above the snoring of his comrades, fancying he could hear the distant beating of a great drum. But there was nothing, save for the occasional hooting of the lone owl.

Turning over on his pallet, he prayed to Morphonus for dreamless sleep, and drifted off again.

⊷ CHAPTER X ⊷

Devils With White Faces

'Beggin' your pardon, sir knight, but I've not had anyone of that description stayin' here in the past few days. We've had the odd freesword passing through, but no high-born women.'

The innkeeper looked apologetic enough, and didn't seem to be holding anything back.

Balthor frowned. He might have known. The heiress was far too sly to leave such an obvious trail. Reus damn the cunning of women! Heaving an impatient sigh, he ordered food and rooms for the night. They had ridden hard to reach Bergen before the Wytching Hour; it was late, and he was tired.

'We'll be needing fresh horses too,' he declared. 'I claim them as the Eorl's agent, according to the laws of the land. Their owners shall be duly compensated.'

The innkeeper nodded, his floppy hat bobbing ridiculously. At least the man was obedient; he would brook no more arguments today, especially not from a commoner.

The four knights sat down at a table in a corner to eat. The taproom was virtually empty. Far fewer folk were travelling than was normal at this time of the year: rumours had been filtering out of the Argael in the past few weeks, of woods witches and Woses and frightened woodfolk.

Well the rumours didn't scare him, Balthor thought defiantly as he took a spoonful of gristly stew. No, it was the absence of good food and the other comforts of Graukolos that troubled him. Perhaps he was getting too old for errantry. He'd have to see about things when he got back, try to dislodge that cur Urist from his job as marshal perhaps. Just as he'd dislodged him from the saddle.

He was busy enjoying that thought when a shadow fell on him. Gazing up coldly he saw a woodland trader standing before him, dressed in the green apparel of the forest folk.

'Can I help you?' he asked curtly, taking a swig of ale.

'Reckon I can at that, sir knight,' said the blond-haired man, an ugly grin creasing his leathery skin.

'Well then, state your business and be quick about it,' said Balthor, wondering what the churl could possibly say that might interest him.

'I saw two wummen an' a freesword leavin' 'ere two nights ago,' said the woodsman.

Balthor put his mug down and exchanged glances with Sir Wilhelm next to him.

'You're quite sure?' asked Balthor. 'Describe them to me.'

The woodsman did so. It sounded like the Eorl's daughter and her lady-in-waiting, though of course he had no idea what their mysterious new bodyguard looked like.

'Well that settles it,' said Balthor, pushing away his wooden bowl and starting to rise. 'We'll take the new horses now and ride through the night.'

He reached into his money pouch for a coin. 'Here, for your trouble, churl,' he said, proffering the silver mark.

The woodsman took it but did not leave.

'Beggin' yer pardon, sir knight, but I reckon I can be o' more 'elp than that.' The grin had not left his face.

Another opportunist. Balthor was about to push him aside to go and talk to the innkeeper when Sir Wilhelm said: 'Explain yourself.'

Balthor rolled his eyes, seething inwardly, but listened as the woodsman spoke. 'The Argael's not what it used to be – ye may've 'eard o' the Woses and the Earth Witch – '

'We have, villein, and such things hold no terrors for true knights of Dulsinor,' snapped Balthor. 'Now, if you'll – '

'Beggin' yer pardon, sir knight,' the woodlander held up greasy hands apologetically, 'but whoever them wummen are, they're not likely t'get far along the road – these are bad times fer the woodfolk, an' we've grown right wary o' foreigners. Soon as they stop for food an' rest, they'll be apprehended most like. Merchants and such we let pass, once we're sure o' their business. But anyone lookin' suspicious gets taken in fer questioning.'

The woodsman paused, looking from Balthor to Wilhelm, then added: 'And, beggin' yer pardon, but two high-born ladies an' a foreign freesword travellin' together sounds pretty suspicious t'me.'

The woodsman paused again. 'Go on,' said Balthor. 'Get to your point, churl.'

'Well, sirrah, me point is, if they gets taken in they wulna be easily tracked by them as dunna ken the forest – an' I ken it right well, ye take my meanin'... I can track anyone, an' I ken all the settlements in the south side o' the Argael. An' I can speak the language.'

Balthor frowned, scratching at his beard. Perhaps the churl had a point there. He could barely understand him – and this was a woodsman used to dealing with civilised folk.

'You are offering your services as a tracker and guide then,' said Sir Wilhelm. 'How much?'

'Five silver marks a day is all I ask,' said the woodsman, grinning again.

Balthor spluttered indignantly. The cheek of the man! 'Three silver marks, and not a penny more,' he said sternly, leaning in to emphasise his point. He was a head taller than the woodsman, and got the desired effect.

'Aye, aye,' said the churl, holding up his hands again. 'Three silvers a day it is then. I'll take the word o' true knights as bond on that.'

'You shall indeed,' said Balthor, pushing past him. 'We'll get going right away. You'd best saddle up your horse then – what is your name?'

'Ratko, sirrah,' replied the woodsman, giving a half bow that seemed too insincere for Balthor's liking. 'At yer service.'

'You'd bloody well better be,' Balthor shot back, striding over to the innkeeper.

Not even time to finish a miserable meal – knight errantry clearly wasn't all it was cracked up to be. That settled it: when he got back to Graukolos he'd make it his next mission to oust Sir Urist. He could still see the Marshal smirking at him.

✣ ✣ ✣

The five of them tore up the highway, pausing at brief intervals so Ratko could double check it for hoof marks. So far things had gone according to plan. They had been in the forest for a day now. Her Ladyship and her companions had entered the forest and not deviated. Or so the churl said – there were other hoof marks too, though Ratko said those belonged to larger groups, and only one set indicated a party of three.

This Ratko had better know what he was about – Balthor would have his head otherwise.

It was late in the evening when they reached the first of the stockaded clearings the tracker had mentioned. Part of it was smashed in.

'Woses,' breathed Ratko, a look of fear entering his face. 'They've been doin' that more n' more, teamin' up and breaking down our barricades. Never seen 'em so organised, so *crafty*.'

'Yes, well never mind the Wadwos,' said Balthor, taking a pull from his skin. The watered wine tasted good after another long hard ride. 'Do your job.'

Ratko dismounted and began to study the clearing and the trail leading to it.

'They stopped 'ere, alright,' he said, his face buckling up as he scrutinised the ground carefully in the torchlight. 'An' there were others too... woodfolk, judgin' by the footprints. We tread a lot more lightly than outsiders.'

The woodlander continued to check around the gap and the entrance. He seemed to make up his mind about something, nodding to himself.

'Well?' Balthor asked impatiently.

'Nearly done 'ere,' said Ratko. 'Just need to go back and check the main road again.'

He returned shortly. 'Aye, they was taken from 'ere, jus' as I said they would be,' he announced. 'Their 'oof marks dunna continue past this clearin', an' over 'ere...' he gestured beyond the breach, 'they continue, but they're lighter. That means they dismounted an' led their 'orses into the wood.'

'So where will they have been taken?'

'The nearest settlement's abowt a league from 'ere. That's where they'll be, most like.'

'Assuming the woodlanders are still keeping them,' put in Sir Wilhelm. 'We've made up some of the time they had on us, though not all.'

'Well then what are we waiting for?' barked Sir Balthor. 'Let's get a move on!'

Following Ratko, they led their horses out of the clearing and into the forest. As they did Balthor caught a sound. Not a forest sound, but something... rhythmical. He paused momentarily, training his ears on it. Were those *drums* he could hear? Strange...

Shaking his head he pressed on, following Ratko deeper into the gloom-shrouded trees.

✢ ✢ ✢

'This is impossible!' cried Adhelina, pacing up and down inside the cramped hut. 'We've been here two days now – when are they going to see sense and let us go?'

'These wood people are a suspicious bunch,' said Anupe, sitting back against the wattled wall. She looked maddeningly relaxed, resting her hands on her knees. 'I think meeting a female freesword has made them even more nervous, though I am impressed to see they teach their women to hunt. That is something at least.'

Adhelina shot the Harijan a fierce glare. 'Well, I'm not interested in how they treat their womenfolk just now, Anupe – I'm far more concerned with how they're treating us!'

'We have been well fed and they have not harmed us,' replied Anupe, unruffled. 'I am sure they will soon realise we are not a threat and let us go. They must all agree on something before they decide what to do. In the Empire they have a word for it, though I do not know it in your tongue.'

'Democracy,' sighed Adhelina. She had read about it. They had experimented with it in some parts of the Thalamian Empire, later in its history, before the Emperor had abolished it. It was still practised to some extent in the Urovian New Empire, where Anupe had served before coming to Vorstlund.

Quite frankly, she wasn't at all sure it was a good idea. If you let everyone have a say, how on earth did you get things done?

'We could be waiting here forever until they reach a decision,' she said, echoing her own thoughts. 'What in the Known World has them so skittish?'

'Wadwos and witches, that's what,' put in Hettie. At least the two days' forced rest had done her good, the old healthy colour was back in her cheeks. Some of it drained out of her as she spoke now though. 'I said it wasn't a good idea, coming to the forest. If folk who've lived here all their lives are this scared, it can't be without good reason.'

'Yes well, we're here now, Hettie, so there's not much point in talking about what we should have done.'

She was snapping now, and she hated snapping, especially at her dearest friend. But she had to admit, perhaps Hettie was right.

'At least Balthor isn't likely to find us now,' said the heiress, trying to lighten things.

'Unless he bumps into the same people as we did,' said Anupe. 'No – there is no point in worrying about what might happen. Best just to sit and wait.'

The Harijan closed her eyes, relaxing more fully. Adhelina eyed her bodyguard with a mixture of envy and resentment. Hettie said nothing more and returned to peering out of a gap between the single window's edge and the flap of deerskin covering it, trying to fathom some clue as to what their captors were up to.

Adhelina resumed her pacing. They had not touched her things and she still had her herbs... she wished she had some Silverweed to make a tincture with, just like she used to in the old days for fun. Getting royally intoxicated on the gifts of Kaia seemed like a very good idea right now.

Several more hours slipped by. Woodfolk acting as their gaolers brought them the evening meal, refusing to answer any questions. Adhelina was just beginning to think about sleep when the fur skin blocking the door was thrown aside. One of the village elders, Harns, stepped in. He was joint headman along with his wife, Hilda. They had both led the questioning on the first night of their stay. Adhelina had remained tight-lipped, refusing to divulge their true identities or the nature of their business. She supposed that hadn't helped allay their suspicions, but if she told the truth there was every chance they would be escorted straight back to Dulsinor.

She hadn't come this far only to be thwarted by a bunch of charcoal burners and hunters.

'We've been talkin' 'bout what to do wi' you,' began Harns. He was a shy, timorous man, clearly unused to dealing with prosperous foreigners.

'I know that full well,' replied Adhelina sternly, trying to use her status to her advantage. 'You spent all of last night discussing us, it would have been nice to have been invited. Now a third night is on us – I hope you have agreed to see sense and let us be on our way.'

Harns looked at the earthen floor as he replied: 'The elders 'ave agreed to 'ear your story again. They're waitin' for ye in the meeting place now.'

Adhelina rolled her eyes. 'Another interrogation? We have *told* you our story – we belong to a rich merchant family in Meerborg, and are travelling to Northalde to do trade. Yon freesword is our bodyguard, an unconventional one I'll grant but still... You are delaying us, please let us go!'

'Well, we'll be seein' about that,' replied Harns, turning to leave the hut. 'If ye'll just follow me, beggin' yer pardons.'

Four armed woodfolk fell in around them as they exited. A gaggle of villagers clustered about them on the short walk to the meeting place.

Wonderful, thought Adhelina. *Another audience.*

Making their way to the meeting place they sat down on tree stumps by the fire. Hilda, Harns and the other elders joined them, along with the leader woodsman who had apprehended them. She had learned his name was Ludo.

Impatiently she repeated her story, taking care not to deviate from the original. Harns and Hilda exchanged glances, before the headwoman spoke.

'We've checked yer things,' she said. 'Lot o' jewellery an' fine things. Seems more like somethin' a *noblewoman* would carry.'

Adhelina felt her heart rise to her mouth as she felt Anupe's dark eyes turn upon her. So that little deception was at an end: no more pretending her wealth was secreted away in a strongbox in Meerborg.

'And not many a merchant we know would trust 'is daughter to carry 'is wares, even if jewellers ye be,' put in Ludo, forestalling her next deception. 'We dunna ken rightly what business brings ye into the forest, but clearly it ent *trade*.'

Adhelina licked her lips. She was at a loss for what to say next, and the Harijan's burning stare wasn't helping her to concentrate.

'Who goes there?'

The call came from a sentry on the gate. All turned in its direction.

Hilda held up her hand for silence. 'Visitors,' she said grimly, before lapsing into dialect and addressing the rest of the village. She spoke too quickly for Adhelina to follow, but her meaning was clear enough. The young and old began hurrying back towards their homes, while the rest of the woodfolk strung their bows and drew hunting knives.

Their four guards closed around them. 'Yer t'go back to yer quarters,' said Hilda. 'This meet's postponed.'

They were halfway back when a loud voice called out from the other side of the stockade.

'We travel on the business of the Eorl of Dulsinor! One of your people has brought me here to make inquiries. Let us in!'

Adhelina's pulse quickened. Only one man in all the Eorldom had a voice that loud. Balthor Lautstimme.

The sound of another dialect speaker came from beyond the wall. The guard nodded and motioned for the gate to open. In they strode, Sir Balthor and three other knights, one of whom looked familiar. Before them came another woodsman, a trader most likely.

'Wait, bring 'em back,' said Hilda. 'Looks like yon visitors might 'ave the answer to oor riddle.'

A minute later they were all standing in the clearing. Sir Balthor stared at her, his flame-coloured hair catching the firelight. 'Lady Markward, I am charged by the Eorl of Dulsinor, your father, with bringing you back to your rightful home,' he declaimed. 'You have unlawfully fled Graukolos without his consent. This ends now.'

'This man is lying,' she tried desperately. 'I have never seen him before in my life! Clearly he is an opportunist, seeking to spirit us away and rob us in the night. You will not release us into his charge.'

Silence greeted her words, which hung hollow in the night air. The fire popped and crackled, wordlessly mocking her efforts.

'Well,' deadpanned Ludo. 'I ken who *I* believe.'

All eyes were on her. She felt her anxiety slip away to be replaced by despondency. Balthor was right: her escape attempt was over.

And then they heard it, drifting through the shadowed trees. *Boom-boom, boom-boom-BOOM...* A simple but solid rhythm, growing stronger with every beat.

The woodfolk flew into a flurry of panicked motion.

'Woses!' cried Ludo. 'They're comin' fer us – everyone at their posts!'

Adhelina and Balthor stood and stared in bemusement as the woodlanders left them, some dashing to take up positions on the stockade while others stood guard by the huts. The settlement was suddenly alive with wailing and shouting.

Sir Balthor drew his sword and strode across the clearing towards Adhelina.

'It seems fate puts one more obstacle in my way,' he said pompously. 'You're to stay here until this business is done – you are under my protection now, and I will not let you out of my sight. Is that understood?'

Adhelina nodded dumbly. She was normally quick-minded and resourceful, but events had happened so rapidly.

Balthor turned to address Anupe, registering some surprise at her appearance. 'And who might you be?' he asked curtly.

'I was guarding your mistress – until recently,' she said, letting the last word drop venomously. Adhelina squirmed inside.

'A woman bodyguard?' scoffed Balthor. 'That'll be the day. Well, whoever you are, your services are no longer required.'

'That may be the case, but I am still owed monies, which I intend to claim,' replied the Harijan, a dangerous tone entering her voice. 'But first things first...'

Suddenly dashing over to where Hilda was yelling orders at the woodsfolk, Anupe grabbed her and hissed something in her ear. Hilda took a step back, blinked, and pointed at a nearby hut. Anupe nodded and loped off towards it.

'Men, with me,' cried Balthor. The other knights gathered about her and Hettie, drawing their swords and unslinging their shields.

'No one moves from this spot – we protect the heiress of Dulsinor, or die trying.'

You could say one thing for Balthor – he was brave and loyal. Arrogant and stupid, but brave and loyal nonetheless.

Boom-boom, boom-boom-BOOM... The drums were sounding loudly now. Archers on the walls bent their bows. Was it a trick of the light or were some of them trembling? Adhelina made the sign and silently prayed they would survive the night.

'They have a battering ram!' screamed one man on the walls. 'Shoot them down – ' He broke off screaming as something hit him in the chest, sending him crashing into the nearest hut. He rebounded and fell to the ground in a twisted heap. The stone that had hit him thunked to the ground next to him.

Adhelina gawped. It was the size of a large chest.

Boom-boom, boom-boom-BOOM...

Another volley of great stones came flying over the top, some finding targets and others crashing through thatched roofs, crushing screaming villagers inside.

There came a great thunk – the gate shuddered backwards, spitting splinters. A few seconds passed and the same again, the stout bar holding it in place cracking. Desperate woodfolk on the walls nocked and drew... the head of one exploded as a huge log smashed into his face, sending him careening off the walkway in a shower of blood made black by night.

Adhelina and Hettie joined hands instinctively as the gate smashed in two at the third sally, the battering ram's iron tip puncturing through it and splitting it from head to toe. It had to be the size of a fully grown oak tree.

Even Balthor and his knights looked scared now. One of them, the youngest, began shaking. A pungent smell pierced the air. With shock and disgust Adhelina realised he had soiled himself.

And then they were through.

Adhelina's eyes widened as her dreams came flooding back to her. They were even more terrifying in the flesh: great lumpen forms standing a man and a half tall, clad in greasy black leather and clutching awful-looking weapons in two-fingered hands – giant mattocks, pick-axes, war hammers... tools to kill made with no thought for the skill or grace of fighting.

Their faces were barely humanoid, devoid of all expression. Soulless black eyes peeped out from under pronounced square brows, two slits for a nose and lipless mouths that opened now, and only now, to give vent to a primal, animal scream that Adhelina hoped she would never hear again. Long thick blood-red tongues waved between broken teeth as the Wadwos caught their scent.

She felt Hettie's hand slip from hers as her friend fainted. Tearing her eyes away from the loathsome creatures, Adhelina knelt beside her. Pulling her head into her lap, she fumbled around in her travelling pouch, searching for some tincture of St Darrin's Cap to revive her friend. She had a feeling they might be doing some running before too long.

✤ ✤ ✤

'Hold!' cried Balthor as the Wadwos began laying about them, cutting an ugly red swathe through the hapless woodfolk. 'We stay where we are until they attack us – protecting Her Ladyship is our priority.'

He could sense his men's fear. That was little surprise – he could sense his own too. But behind that, there was also excitement. If he survived this and lived to tell the tale, his reputation would surely be restored.

Sir Balthor the Wadwo-Slayer. That would wipe the smile off Urist's face for good.

'Remember your bard song,' he said to the others, trying to keep his voice even. 'They're hugely strong but clumsy. If we stick together in formation we can beat them.'

'What about our horses?' said Sir Wilhelm. 'We stand a better chance if we're mounted.'

They had left those tethered to the wall by the gate. They were rearing and whinnying frantically now, straining at the leash and desperate to be gone.

'They're too panicked,' Balthor barked back. 'Nobody moves, we stand our ground I say!'

They watched grimly as the desperate battle unfolded. There were ten beastmen, some sprouting arrows where the archers had shot them. There were about forty or fifty armed woodfolk in all, though their numbers were being whittled down fast. Of their guide there was no sign.

The woodlanders surrounded the Wadwos in groups of four and five. A couple of groups had thought to use ropes to bring their huge opponents down: two or three sturdy men pulled on a lasso about a Wose's neck while the others took advantage of the distraction to hack and stab furiously at its legs. One fell to its knees, letting go of its mattock… only to smash the men holding the lasso with a great sweep of its arms, scattering them like rushes. The others cutting at it panicked and ran as it picked up its weapon and got to its feet. It loomed over the men it had knocked down, pulverising the head of one as he struggled to get up, squashing it into his body like a concertina and sending bloody shards of skull spattering across the nearest hut wall.

The second Wadwo didn't fare so well. As it struggled with its lasso another woodlander on the wall jumped onto its back, stabbing deep into the monster's neck. Pale ichor burst from the deadly wound, and the Wadwo fell to its knees expiring. The man paid bravely for his courage: reaching back the dying Wose grasped him by the arms, pulling him over its head and smashing him to the ground with a sickening thud. He cried out and lay still.

The rest of it was carnage. Blood and brains spattered the Wadwos as they felled one woodsman after another with crushing blows. Balthor normally enjoyed watching a good fight, but this was a sickening spectacle.

Two beastmen broke off from the melee and stalked towards them, leaving a dozen dead and dying men in their wake.

Now it begins, he thought, clutching his sword and shield more tightly. 'Four on two, not bad odds for true knights of Dulsinor,' he said, doing his best to rally the men. 'One distracts and defends, the other attacks – go for the back of the knees if you can! Bring 'em down, then go straight for the head or throat! Don't waste any time with body blows.'

The Woses screamed again as they loped into a lumbering charge. Sir Redrich next to him prepared to receive attack, Balthor moving agilely to the side and behind him. The monster brought its mighty pick-axe down in a vicious arc towards the knight – at the last moment he dodged aside and the weapon sprayed turf as it buried itself in the ground.

Stepping in around him, Sir Balthor hacked at the monster's knee. The stroke was slightly off and it hit just below, biting through leather and deep into its calf. It screamed and wrenched the pick-axe out of the ground, sweeping it around with staggering strength. Balthor stumbled back, the lethal blow narrowly missing his chest. Redrich stepped in with a downwards thrust, piercing the creature's foot. It cried out and tottered as he pulled the blade free, pus-coloured ichor spurting from the wound.

Like lightning Balthor was on it again. The tension of the road and all the miseries it had brought suddenly burst from him in a wrathful tide, and roaring a war-cry he hacked and stabbed at it in quick succession, slicing its kneecap in two before piercing its groin. The Wadwo tumbled to the ground, grabbing him and yanking him down with it.

This close he could smell its body, like stale horse urine it was. He gagged and thrashed desperately as it tried to pull him into a crushing embrace. Balthor was stronger than most men, but now he felt like a frantic child.

Its arms closed around him like a vice and all his deeds flashed before his eyes...

With a yowl the creature flung its arms up to its face, arching its back as Redrich's sword found its eye. The knight's two-handed thrust pinned its head to the dark earth; the thing convulsed once, twice, then lay still.

Balthor rolled away from the gargantuan corpse and pulled himself up again, scrabbling for his sword. A glance told him all he needed to know. Sir Rufus lay unmoving on the ground, a red ruin where his face had been. Sir Wilhelm was hard pressed, his shield arm hanging limply at an awkward angle, grimacing as he struggled to dodge furious swipes of his Wadwo's war hammer. Sir Redrich ran at it from the rear, thrusting at its leg behind the knee. It yowled as his sword point found its mark. Lifting up its leg and hopping backwards, it collided with Redrich and barged him to the ground. With a ferocious snarl Balthor stepped in and hacked viciously at the Wose's ankle on its good leg. It yowled again more loudly and toppled over. The three knights circled it and rained blows on it, ichor spraying up and spattering their surcoats and faces. Balthor felt like vomiting by the time the thing was finally slain.

Gathering his composure he looked around for the damsels, the tumult of the wider battle momentarily forgotten. Adhelina was dragging Hettie to her feet; she appeared to have regained consciousness, though she wore a stunned expression on her face.

'There are more coming!' shouted Wilhelm, yanking Balthor's attention back to the battle.

Turning he saw the ground before the smashed gate carpeted with mangled flesh and crushed bones. The woodlanders had managed to bring another beastman down, but the six others were making light work of the remainder. He spared a moment of admiration for common men who had chosen to lay down their lives in defence of their families, and steeled himself. The Woses seemed barely to notice their injuries, though they all bled from numerous gashes and punctures.

He knew this was the end. Not even three brave knights could hope to best twice their number of such strong creatures, and Wilhelm was hurt badly.

'Stand your ground,' he muttered, feeling the fire at his back. 'We protect Her Ladyship or die trying.'

The beastmen lumbered towards them, their dead black eyes and white faces devoid of emotion. The three knights prepared to make a heroic end of things.

At least he'd go down in troubadour's song for this, Balthor reflected grimly as the fiends closed on them.

A spinning silver flash caught his eye. One of the Wadwos stopped short, a dirk suddenly sprouting from its arm. Balthor thought little of it – a last futile effort by a woodsman – but the creature suddenly keeled over, thrashing around fitfully and making a sickening gurgling sound.

'Anupe!' he heard Adhelina exclaim behind him, but he had little time to reflect on what that meant as the five remaining beastmen engaged them.

Wilhelm was the first to fall, a scream dying as quickly as it had exited his lips as a mattock caught him in the chest, crumpling his ribcage. He kneeled in the dirt, a tide of blood erupting from his mouth and washing over his surcoat. A second backwards sweep nearly took his head off, twisting it around on its neck with a horrible tearing sound.

Two of the creatures loomed above him, one wielding a hammer, the other clutching what looked like an anvil welded to an iron rod.

At least they have a sense of humour, he thought wryly as they tried to crush him like a fly. Ducking with a speed born of desperation, he felt a stinging in his ears as the crude weapons struck each other with a deafening clang. Gripping his sword in both hands he drove it up through the groin of one, the point exiting from its lower back. The creature gave vent to a great ululating cry, lurching back and wrenching the blade from his hand.

Spinning around Balthor tried to duck the next swing he knew was coming... but saw instead his second assailant had fallen to the ground and was thrashing around in agony just as the other had done. Standing behind it was the female mercenary, her falchion blade slick with grey gore.

Another scream reached his ears as he snatched up Rufus' sword. Whirling around he saw Sir Redrich go flying through the air, smashing against a hut and collapsing in a broken heap. Three Woses left. Two of them closed on him and the foreign freesword.

His swung at him with a great scythe. Without thinking he brought his shield up, yelling in pain as the blade smashed through the oak, slicing open his forearm.

Dodge don't parry you fool, he berated himself as the thing yanked the scythe free and prepared for another swing. Spurring himself on he stepped inside its guard, aiming a lethal thrust at its midriff just below its boiled leather jerkin.

But this one was smarter and quicker than the others, and took two great strides backwards out of range; Balthor's sword point scraped harmlessly against tough hide. The Wadwo brought the scythe up and around, slicing downwards. That caught him off-guard – he had been expecting another methodical sidewise swipe. He threw himself to one side and tried to counter attack, but the thing anticipated and changed its position, circling around to follow his own movement and keeping him at bay with another swipe.

Behind it he could see the freesword dancing and whirling with breath-taking speed, but two of the fiends were on her now and she could do nothing but stay on the defensive.

He locked eyes with his adversary. He had half expected to see some look of recognition, of respect for a worthy foe, but its dead pinpricks showed nothing. The Wose's mouth hung open, its unnaturally long tongue lolling sideways in a silent leer as it came at him again.

Again and again it pressed him, driving him back, pursuing him remorselessly around the fire. He tried to counter attack but he was growing tired; the days of hard riding had taken their toll.

Out of the corner of his eye he glimpsed the two damsels, slowly edging their way towards their horses by the exit.

Of course, their *horses*...

He wouldn't recapture the Lady Markward, and he wouldn't survive the night, but maybe he could buy the Eorl's daughter some time, give her a chance to flee. He owed his liege that much at least.

Gripping his sword and shield with renewed vigour, he snarled a curse at the loping Wadwo.

'Come then, you bestial cur,' he said with all the venom he could muster, 'let's see what you're really made of.'

His sudden attack caught the monster off-guard. It stepped back, parrying his frenzied strokes with its scythe, the blade scouring chips from the treated hardwood. He didn't care where he hit it now, any bit of damage before it finished him off would do.

His last blow sliced a finger, half severing it. The Wose gave an angry hissing sound and let one hand go of the scythe.

Now was his chance. Stepping in close again he tried the same trick as before, crouching low and aiming a thrust up at its vitals. His opponent seemed to be expecting the move however; the Wadwo abandoned the scythe and brought its huge fist down towards his head, not bothering to defend itself.

Too late he realised he had overstretched himself, been too quick to press his advantage. Everything seemed to slow down suddenly: he could see his sword speeding towards the creature's gut, firelight glinting on Rufus' unsoiled blade as the Wadwo's fist came down towards his unarmoured head...

There was an explosion of light. A thousand tiny needles suddenly buried their hot points in his skull. He felt his grip on the sword relax just before it reached the Wadwo, the hilt slipping from his fingers and vanishing into nothingness as his senses left him.

✢ ✢ ✢

Adhelina struggled to get Hettie to stay with her. All about them was pandemonium, as terrified villagers too young or old to fight poured from their huts and sought refuge in the forest. Glancing behind her she saw there were just three Wadwos left, one menacing Balthor on the other side of the fire, the other two swatting at Anupe as men might try to crush an irritating wasp.

'Come on Hettie, for Reus' sake!' Adhelina yelled in her friend's ear. Her lady-in-waiting stumbled on beside her. The simple had been enough to revive her but not fully to recover her wits – Adhelina cursed the fireside tales that had planted such seeds of fear in Hettie's mind, although she was terrified too.

With some difficulty they reached their horses. Adhelina struggled to calm them, but it was hard work doing that alone.

Glancing over her shoulder she could see the village was nearly empty. Of Balthor there was no sign. She felt her heart in her mouth as the third Wadwo stalked back around the fire, clutching a scythe in one hand.

Anupe must have seen it too, for without a second thought the Harijan darted nimbly between the two Woses attacking her, before breaking into a mad dash for the stockade and vanishing between the huts. Her attackers seemed about to pursue her when the beastman with the scythe addressed them in a guttural tongue. With horror Adhelina realised it was pointing at her.

The two Woses turned and lumbered towards them, mercilessly clubbing down a pair of elderly woodfolk as they did. She recognised one of them: Harns, his scrawny limbs twitching as he expired in a heap.

'Hettie, for Reus' sake, MOVE!' screamed Adhelina, grabbing her friend and yanking her towards a horse.

Something in her voice must have stirred her. Hettie blinked, looked back once, and scrambled for the horse's reins. Silently mouthing a prayer, Adhelina did the same. The beasts were still terrified and extremely skittish. She struggled to take the saddle, falling twice before finally managing to hoist herself onto the mare's back.

A huge shadow fell across her. A horrid stench filled her nostrils as a clammy two-fingered hand grasped her by the neck and lifted her off the horse. She kicked and punched frenziedly, finding a strength and fury she never knew she had, but she might as well have been rain lashing the stormy seas. The other beastman had Hettie in its grasp too; her oldest friend had fallen into a paroxysm of fear, trembling uncontrollably.

The creatures bound them fast together with thick ropes they carried on their backs, tying their hands and feet as well. As Adhelina registered that they were being spared, she found pity in her heart for the less fortunate village elders: the third Wadwo stalked about the compound, hewing down stragglers with its scythe, a monstrous reaper bringing in a harvest of blood.

When it was done it barked another command at the two guarding them. Adhelina could only watch as they ransacked the village, despatching a handful of old folk and infants they found cowering in huts. She could not look as they dashed the heads of babes against wall and tree trunk. A few of the younger womenfolk had stayed, unable to leave their children behind; the Wadwo gathered these up in its huge arms like bundles of wheat and brought them over to where the damsels were. They trussed them up as well.

They found little enough of value that belonged to the woodfolk, but Adhelina's saddlebags laden with her valuables were added to the pile.

Not that I'll be needing them any more, she thought, more sadly than anything else. Lying on the ground next to Hettie, she felt the terror ebb out of her to be replaced by a great weariness. Her bid for freedom from the world of men had led her – and her best friend – into a world of monsters. She wanted it to be over.

The three surviving Wadwos returned to them. One lifted up the damsels and the wailing woodswomen, slinging them effortlessly over its huge shoulders. The second picked up a sack they had put their spoils in. The third, the one with the scythe, now carried a large hide drum, which hung from its shoulders by a leather strap.

As their inhuman captors shambled from the settlement they had raped, the one with the drum started up a rhythm in time to their loping gait.

Boom-boom, boom-boom-BOOM...

As the noise filled her ears, Adhelina shut her eyes and wondered why they were still alive. Then the answer came to her, as her copious reading bore fruit once more. A stab of renewed fear, far worse than terror of death, lanced through her body.

The heiress of Dulsinor stifled a scream, and prayed feverishly for deliverance.

⊷ CHAPTER XI ⊷

An Awkward Homecoming

Sir Vertrix watched from the deck as the crooked rooftops of Ongist slid into view. To either side of the River Rundle the wooden houses tumbled down the hillsides, levelling out as they reached the city centre. Crowning the grander stone buildings of that district he could see the Palace of Bending Branches, perched on its curiously fashioned stilts straddling the river and swaddled in banners sporting a green stag and bear rearing at one another on a sky blue background. The coat of arms of the Ruling Clan Cierny inspired him with little reassurance under the circumstances.

He could hear the sounds of bustling clamour cutting across the lapping waters with increasing intensity as the market squares and trading streets opened for business. Not long after that he caught the reek of it, borne on the brisk wind: fish, offal, dung, burning charcoal, the sweat of many men and animals.

The old knight hated cities, but then any respectable knight did in his opinion. Men of arms were men of the country; cities a necessary evil. At least Strongholm had benefited from its position by the sea, a fortuitous location that cleansed it of its urban stench. Ongist boasted forty thousand souls' worth of that stench – a loremaster had once told him that was its population. Twice that of the Northlending capital, but all superiority over its age-old rival ended there. Ongist made for a poor enough sight after the proud buttressed city of the Northlendings: its dilapidated walls, their dark stones unevenly crammed one atop the other, said as much; likewise the crooked streets it dubiously protected, left half in gloom thanks to the lurching storeys of the buildings unsteadily lining them like woozy drunkards.

We couldn't organise an orgy in a brothel, he thought disparagingly, *no wonder they always beat us at war*.

He turned to look at his squire. Gormly looked much the same as he always did, hard as a stone and little more expressive. He could sense a gladness to be home in him though; Gormly hadn't been any happier to find himself on foreign soil than his master.

'Well, we're not in the part of it we want to be, Gormly,' the old knight sighed. 'But at least we're back in Thraxia.'

Gormly nodded deferentially. 'We'll take to the saddle as soon as we've docked, just like you said sire – should be no more than a week's hard ride. We'll be home soon enough.'

'If there's a home to return to!' said Vertrix with a humourless laugh.

And by the sounds of the news they had received in Port Grendel, there might well not be.

Bad enough that they'd had to return home without Sir Braxus, who'd got it into his head that going on some madcap adventure with that Argolian friar was the only way to get the Northlending King to send military aid to Thraxia; bad enough that it had fallen to him, Sir Vertrix, to deliver this unwelcome news to the young knight's father, Lord Braun. Then they'd docked at Grendel, intending to retrace their outbound journey up the river, only to be told the lands to the southeast had been overrun by Slangá Mac Bryon. If the highland rebels from the Brekken Hills had overrun the surrounding countryside, Reus knew what his ally Tíerchán had done from the Whaelen Hills that neighboured Gaellentir – they had barely been able to hold them off when they'd left on their mission to Strongholm. And that had been well over two months ago.

Vertrix felt anxiety gnaw at his innards as he thought on that. It was an all-too familiar feeling by now; they had been forced to spend nearly an extra week at sea, trading in their carrack for a cog leaving Grendel for Ongist. A week to churn over the news, wondering what had befallen kith and kin at home.

On top of all that now they had to return to whatever was left of that home via the troubled capital. It was the last thing he wanted, but they hadn't been left with much choice: to have any chance of making it to Gaellentir they would have to approach from the south and hope the lands held by Lord Cael hadn't been overrun yet.

Of course, in happier times reporting to the King would have made perfect sense under the circumstances. But given everything that had happened, who knew what kind of reception their news would get. Since Abrexta had entered his life, Cadwy had seemed completely indifferent to the plight of the northern wards.

'Go and fetch Bryant and Regan,' he muttered, trying to take his mind off possible future events. 'And make sure everything is prepared –

the sooner we're off this wretched ship and out of Ongist the better
I shall like it!'

Gormly nodded curtly and dashed off to see it done. Vertrix
returned to staring at the walls of Ongist, growing across his vision
and clouding his mood further.

The harbour was a riot of activity. Yard-arms and great wheeled
cranes were loading and unloading goods from the cogs, carracks,
sloops and barges that vied for a space at Ongist's crowded wharf.
Shipcraft was one thing Thraxians did do well, Vertrix reflected – but
that hadn't stopped them losing the War of the Cobian Succession
nearly a decade ago. Despite its being fought primarily at sea.

He sighed heavily, weighed down by his gloomy thoughts. It
was a miracle the realm was still together – come to think of it,
it barely was thanks to Abrexta and her sorcerous meddling. Sir
Braxus had also hinted at a darker conspiracy when he had pressed
the parchment scroll upon him, with strict instructions that it be
delivered straight to Lord Braun's hand: wizards had been behind
the civil war in Northalde, wizards were behind the strange mission
the young knight had chosen to accept, and those same wizards
might well have something to do with Abrexta.

'Wizards here, wizards there,' muttered Vertrix as the ship
slowly creaked in to dock at one of the many jetties jutting out from
the wharf. 'Wizards every blasted where.'

Sir Regan, who had just joined him with the others, glanced at
him quizzically. 'What was that?' the raven-haired knight asked.
There was a sharpness in his voice that wasn't often found in
the easy-going youngster; the thigh injury he'd picked up in the
Northlending civil war still hadn't healed and he was reduced
to limping. But then the last few weeks had been trying for all
of them.

'Ah, 'tis naught,' said Vertrix, hastily dissembling. 'Just
wondering what state the realm's in, what with the highlanders up
north and things as they are down here.'

'It's in a state of change is what it is,' said Bryant, striding over
from the starboard side. 'Why don't you both come and look at this?'

The urgency in his voice brooked no delay. Ongist did most
of its maritime trade on the north side of the Rundle; the south
was typically reserved for the warehousing of goods owned by the
wealthy merchants.

Until recently that was. Vertrix took a sharp breath as he registered the sight: a hundred skeletal ship frames lined the waterfront. They were in the early stages of construction, but their purpose was unmistakable.

'War galleys,' he breathed. 'More than I've seen since our last military disaster. Seven Princes, what in the Known World is Cadwy playing at now?'

'Cadwy, or Abrexta?' asked Regan pointedly. 'Building warships when what we need is a land army to face off the highlanders! This has her mark all over it, the conniving bitch.'

Vertrix favoured the young knight with a sour glance. He despised Abrexta as a witch and a danger to the realm, but he still didn't hold with disrespectful talk of women. Regan and Braxus were notorious – or rather celebrated – for their conquests, but the old knight didn't approve. In his day chivalrous knights hadn't done that sort of thing. Or he hadn't anyway. Longing for his wife Rihanna surged up in him. He'd missed her so. That feeling quickly turned to sickness at the thought of what might have happened to her while he was away.

Banishing the thought he said: 'Sharp words will avail us nothing – this isn't our concern anyway. We've to get back up north as quickly as we can.'

'Shouldn't we try to find out more first?' put in Bryant. 'Folk here are likely to have heard more since we left Grendel.'

Vertrix nodded reluctantly. 'Aye, start asking questions as soon as we're off the ship – but don't take too long about it, Bryant! I don't want to stay here any longer than we have to. Something tells me it won't go well for us if the King's men learn we are here.'

Bryant frowned at that but said nothing more. Vertrix fidgeted with his sword belt fretfully. Here they were, dodging their King to get back to a homeland that had probably been pillaged thanks in part to that same monarch. The world had turned upside down.

Longshoremen released the poles holding their cog clear of the jetty, permitting it enter a space opened up by a sloop embarking on its latest voyage. The ship docked and sailors lowered the gangplank at the captain's call. Their squires led their horses down onto the jetty – all except poor Paidlin, who limped along glumly behind them. His leg was healing well and he had escaped the horrors of gangrene, but he was a wretched sight stumbling down the gangplank, nearly letting go of his crutch as he slipped.

Vertrix caught him and helped him down. 'Easy now, lad,' he said. 'Takes a while to get used to an injury like that. Don't rush.'

'Aye sir,' replied the former squire, looking even more downcast.

The old knight had no more words of comfort. But how did you comfort a promising young noble who'd been crippled for life at fifteen summers?

The harbour was a swarming throng of merchants and sailors, with a smattering of harlots for good measure. Ignoring them all with a distasteful grimace, Vertrix scanned the crowded market stalls and taverns, trying to tell if anything had changed.

Ongist felt chaotic – but then it had always seemed that way, even before Abrexta. There were no port officials to register their arrival, but that was all too typical of the disorganised Thraxians. Now he was immersed in its noise, he could hear the strains of fiddle and lyre more clearly. The sound raised his spirits somewhat. Music, that was another thing Thraxians actually did well. He'd heard enough of the Northlending bards at Stronholm to last a lifetime – half of them played renditions of Thraxian songs anyway, badly.

He was just thinking that perhaps it wasn't so bad to be home after all, when Bryant came bustling over. He had just been talking to a group of rugged-looking men.

'Well, what news?' asked Vertrix, the others gathering round.

'Not good,' replied Bryant, as stoical as ever. 'Yon men are fur traders, from the north. Say they escaped with their lives by a cat's whisker, highlanders came at them on the western fringes of Liathduil. Only their horses saved them.'

'Liathduil?' exclaimed Regan. 'Redeemer's wounds, that means they've crossed the Burryn!'

'We fathomed as much at Grendel,' said Vertrix, impatiently waving him to silence. 'That's why we didn't retrace our steps and sail back down the river, remember? Go on, Bryant, what else?'

Bryant's face was set grim as he answered. 'Lord Tarneogh is dead, and so are most of his retainers. Tíerchán's lot overran Daxtir more than two weeks ago. They razed the place to the ground and killed every soul for leagues about. Clan Joyce has been wiped out.'

'Pagan savages!' snarled Vertrix. 'What about Gaellentir?'

It was the question he feared to ask most, but they had to know if they were about to ride into a death trap.

A flicker of hope crossed Bryant's face. 'The traders haven't heard anything fresh for a week, but last they heard it still stands, though Slangá has it surrounded and many of the lands about have been scoured. The highlanders have Lord Cael penned in as well.'

Vertrix shut his eyes tightly, trying to think above the noise of the city. One of the northern wards conquered and the other two hanging on for dear life under siege. It wouldn't be long now.

Opening his eyes he let out a deep breath. 'Let's saddle up – we've no time to lose.'

The other knights just stared at him. 'Well, what are you waiting for?' he barked.

Regan made an awkward face. 'I'm not one for sounding disloyal, Sir Vertrix, but... they're surrounded. How in Gehenna are we going to get into Gaellen?'

'And even if we could,' added Bryant, 'what good would it do? Risk our lives just to tell Lord Braun that our mission has failed, no knights from Northalde, his son isn't coming back...'

'He is coming back!' snapped Vertrix. He took another breath and ran his hands through thinning grey strands of hair. He was usually unflappable: Sir Vertrix of Cornach, a safe pair of gauntlets in any situation. But he was at a loss as to how to deal with this one. It just kept going from bad to worse. He had to admit, the other two were probably right. Even if by some miracle they did get past the highlanders, what good would it do?

'We're still Lord Braun's vassals,' he persisted stubbornly. 'And if that means dying with him, so be it.'

'Unless we try to change things here,' said Bryant, speaking slowly as if giving voice to an incipient idea. 'We demand an audience with the King, try to convince him – '

'And he'll just ignore us, like all the other ambassadors we've sent!' barked Vertrix. 'And don't you think he might want to know how we came to be down here?' He lowered his voice so their squires and any passers-by wouldn't hear him. 'What do we tell him? That we've just returned from a secret voyage to try and have him overthrown, for his own good?' He shook his head. 'Nay, we're as likely to find ourselves dangling on the end of a rope as anything else if we go anywhere near Cadwy while he's in this state.'

Bryant was about to reply when a hue and cry went up the length of the harbour.

'HANGINGS! MORE HANGINGS! Market Circle, there's more hangings!'

Drunken sailors and curious shoppers started moving up towards the circle, which lay just off the waterfront. An ugly swarm of commoners was soon pushing its way into it. How city folk loved a good hanging.

'I think we need to see this,' said Sir Bryant. 'Might give us an idea of how badly the resistance movement is doing.' At least the knight had rediscovered his deadpan humour.

'Market Circle lies on our quickest route out of this rathole in any case,' said Vertrix. 'But I'll be damned if I'm going there on foot with the rest of this rabble! Gormly, help Paidlin mount, the rest of you saddle up now!'

A few minutes later and they were jostling their way none too gently through the throng into the circle. It felt good to sit a horse again after so long at sea, but even that pleasure was quickly soured by the spectacle that greeted them.

'Redeemer's wounds, that's Lord Math's son!' exclaimed Sir Regan, recognising one of the bloodied men on the scaffolding. Squinting at the young man's face Vertrix saw he was right. Sir Gwydion of Cerdigion, a future lord of Low Umbria, was about to meet a traitor's death.

At least there was one small crumb of comfort – that meant the rest of the realm was starting to wake up, realise that something had to be done. Perhaps news of the situation in the northern wards had finally reached them, spurring them into action. And the lands of Low Umbria lay directly south of the King's Fold: this uprising had been close to home.

Vertrix scanned the other faces as the hooded executioner put ropes around their necks. There were seven in all, but he only recognised two others – Father Nynniaw, the Senior Perfect of Low Umbria, and Prior Máel, head of the Argolian chapter there. The Order had been suppressed in lands directly ruled by the King, though clearly Máel had refused to heed to the royal decree.

These were illustrious men – something of note had happened.

'The Low Umbrians revolted again,' said a nearby merchant in response to his question. 'Only this time it was more serious, the whole province rose up in arms against the King. They marched on Ongist – His Majesty's forces met them in an open field south of the Rundle and won. Took these seven prisoner, killed many more. The rest they put to flight.'

'What's happened since?' pressed Vertrix.

'He's got knights occupying the lowlands of Umbria now, last I heard anyway,' replied the merchant, twisting a mustachio.

'And the north, what of the north?' pressed Vertrix. 'We just heard they're close to being overrun.'

'Aye, that's right,' replied the merchant. 'The word is King Cadwy's parlaying for peace with the highlanders.'

'Peace? Since when did lowland Thraxians make peace with pagan rebels?'

The merchant lowered his voice, leaning in across the saddle of his piebald pony so Vertrix could hear. 'Rumour has it His Majesty's consort has... contacts among the highlanders. Some are even saying the King plans to make a gift of the northern wards to the pagans, allow them to settle there permanently if they don't encroach any farther south.'

The merchant appeared unruffled. But then such wretches didn't care who owned the land or ran the country, so long as they could sell to them. Suppressing the urge to yank the preening trader from his pony, Vertrix thanked him curtly and turned to whisper the news to Bryant and Regan.

'This isn't right,' said Regan. 'If these are traitors, the King should be here to preside over the execution!'

'What's been right with the realm of late?' said Sir Vertrix. A herald was proclaiming their wrongdoings, detailing the sentence of death by hanging, drawing and quartering. 'Reus knows how many so-called traitors Cadwy's executing nowadays – he's probably too busy disporting himself upriver on his damned pleasure barge to bother doing it in person!'

'Keep your voice down!' hissed Bryant. 'Half the circle will hear you!'

'Think so?' cried Vertrix bitterly above the crowd, now baying for blood. 'Listen to them – blasted churls, they'll cheer anything that gives them respite from their sorry lives! Never mind that these poor devils are dying for their country!'

With a sneer of disgust the old knight wheeled his horse around, barging a couple of sailors out of the way. One of them glared up at him fiercely, but Vertrix matched his stare, putting a hand to his sword hilt for good measure. The salty cur soon remembered his place.

'Come along!' he barked at the others. 'I'll not tarry here and watch good men die as sport for whores and drunks – let's away, we've seen enough!'

By the time they had pushed their way through to the other side of the circle, the hangings had begun. It wouldn't end for the poor devils there – that was only the beginning of their torment. Out of the corner of his eye Vertrix caught the executioner preparing long knives for the drawing as the condemned men danced the gallows dance; at least he'd not have to see their entrails get spilt.

The winding street led away from the heart of the city, slowly ascending towards the perimeter walls. More folk were coming to watch the executions; he drove his steed through them, cursing all the way, looking back once to check everyone was still following him.

The sickening spectacle at Market Circle had settled it for him. Even if there was little hope left up north, he'd be damned if he would die here like those men. Put a sword in his hand and a field beneath his feet, give him a chance to see Rihanna one last time at least. He'd married late in life and his two sons were barely of squiring age; they lived in a manor just a few leagues from Gaellen. He could only pray they had made it to the safety of the castle.

Yes, he'd die fighting to be with them, the Fallen Angel take this cursed city and its stench –

That thought died as he rounded a corner and saw a dozen mounted serjeants led by a haughty-looking knight. All had their swords drawn and bore the King's coat of arms. The winding street was wide enough for three abreast at most, but even so the odds weren't in their favour. Besides that, fighting the King's soldiers was likely to get you killed even if you won.

Vertrix had the uncanniest feeling that they had been waiting for them. The others pulled up short behind him, and his worst fears were realised when the knight spoke. 'Sir Vertrix of Cornach,' he declaimed, 'I arrest you and your retinue in the name of the King.'

'Who says I am such?' replied the old knight coolly.

'The coat of arms on your tabard,' replied the haughty knight smugly. 'An old knight with a running grey deer on a green background was the description I was given. You seem to fit it remarkably well.'

Vertrix cursed inwardly. It hadn't even occurred to him not to wear his surcoat. He prided himself on keeping a cool head under fire, but subterfuge wasn't his style.

'I see,' he replied, doing his best to sound unperturbed. 'And may I know on what charges my men and I are being arrested?'

The knight's smile was icy as the royal guards nudged their steeds towards them, mail armour jingling and hooves clattering on the rude cobblestones.

'Treason.'

⊷ CHAPTER XII ⊶

A Renewed Pursuit

Balthor gasped as a torrent of cold water slapped him from unconsciousness. Sitting up with a start he blinked and looked around. Corpses of men and monsters littered the ground about him. Standing over him was the foreign mercenary, clutching an empty bucket she had just emptied over his head.

His head... a low throbbing reminded him of his fight with the chief Wadwo. Shaking it free of water and feeling waves of pain shoot through his skull, he wiped his face and stared up at her.

'Now is not a time to be resting,' said the freesword dryly.

A sudden panic rose in him. 'The ladies you were guarding...'

'Are not here,' the outlander finished for him. 'They have been taken, I think, though the gods only know why.'

With some effort Balthor hauled himself up. His whole body ached, but that hardly bothered him. He was still alive – though Her Ladyship remained unaccounted for.

The dead bodies of his comrades caught his eye. He felt suddenly ashamed that he had thought so ill of them – they had fought valiantly, as befitted true knights. Well, perhaps Rufus had been found wanting – but how many young fighters had been unlucky enough to face such fiends?

Gazing at the loathsome corpses of the Wadwos, their pale ichor looking even more sickly in the morning light, he shuddered and made the sign.

'Tell me what happened,' he said.

'After you fell I realised I could not win against three of yon beasts,' answered the freesword. 'So I escaped.'

Balthor fixed her with a quizzical stare. 'Why did you come back?'

The strange woman shrugged her shoulders. 'To see what I could find.'

Such lack of valour and loyalty was all that could be expected from a pagan foreigner, and a woman at that, so Balthor let it go and pressed her for more information.

'Her Ladyship... yon damsel you were protecting – did you see what happened to her?'

'I think she tried to flee with the rest of the villagers,' replied the mercenary. 'Though clearly she did not get far – her horses are still here.'

Balthor cursed loudly. 'Then they are lost to us!' he cried. 'With the woodfolk gone we cannot hope to track them through this wretched forest.'

The freesword stared at him inscrutably. Damned foreigners, impossible to know what they were thinking.

'I have something to show you,' she said. 'Come with me.'

✢ ✢ ✢

Flinging aside the hide entrance to the hut, the freesword revealed her treasure with a triumphant flourish. He was bound and gagged and looked even more unkempt than usual, but it was unmistakably Ratko, their erstwhile guide.

'I found him hiding under a pile of firewood,' explained the mercenary. 'He must have avoided the beast creatures, but a Harijan's senses are not so easily fooled!'

Balthor turned to look at her, momentarily forgetting Ratko, who had started yelling into his gag.

'A what? Just who are you anyway?'

'My name is Anupe, at your service. I come from a land where women learn to fight as men do, only better. My story is too complicated to explain here.'

Balthor had no wish to hear it. 'And why are you "at my service"?' he barked. 'What's your interest in all of this?'

'I have still not been paid,' replied Anupe. 'The lady you seek owes me money – and if I am not mistaken those Wo-Wos or whatever you call them took her riches with her.'

The knight glared at her. 'And what makes you think I will help you get your money?'

She shrugged again. 'You are a man of honour are you not? I have helped you so far, and will help you more – in this country I understand a man of honour pays what he owes.'

Sir Balthor frowned. He had to admit she had a point, although doing business with a woman was extremely distasteful, especially this kind of business.

'Very well,' he frowned. 'Let's get this churl untied and get us gone – they have a half day on us already.'

✠ ✠ ✠

The Wadwo tracks were easy enough to follow. They took them in a south-westerly direction, further off the main road and deeper into the heart of the forest. That had meant leaving their horses behind. It pained the proud knight to leave the fine courser he'd requisitioned from one of Bergen's richer merchants, but they didn't have much choice: the woods were far too dense.

Following closely behind Ratko he kept a close eye on him, his sword drawn and pointed at the small of his back. He had balked when they told him his next task, and tried to run off. But Anupe was swift as a deer, and she had brought him to the ground before he managed twenty paces. After that Balthor had loomed over him and put the fear of Reus into the churl. His head was still pounding and he was furious and upset – he'd had a good mind to carve the tracker up there and then, but of course they needed him.

Ratko pulled up short as they reached an overgrown dell. The trees parted a little here. Balthor was grateful for the flash of azure skies. It was stiflingly hot; the sun had risen to its zenith above the treetops and they were all drenched in sweat after their forced march.

'What is it?' snarled the knight, with more viciousness than was necessary.

'It looks like they were joined by others here,' breathed the tracker.

The knight exchanged glances with Anupe and cursed. 'Well, how many?' he asked.

'Looks like another three or four,' replied the woodlander after studying the tracks a little longer.

Balthor felt his heart sink. The odds had turned against them yet again.

'Well, we'd best press on then,' he sighed. 'We need to catch up with them before any more of the fiends join them!'

'Wait,' said Anupe suddenly. 'I have something here that might help put things in our favour again.'

Reaching into the folds of her cloak she produced a jar of green ointment.

'Dammit woman, we've no time for your pagan ways now,' spluttered Balthor.

'This is no work of mine,' replied the freesword coolly, 'but made by the very lady we seek. It is a treatment made from a plant you call Wose's Bane... it helped me kill several of the beast people.'

Of course... Her Ladyship and her blasted obsession with herbalism. Well, he'd seen her cure and treat enough knights at Graukolos, she could be trusted on that score at least.

'All right,' he said, somewhat bashfully. 'How does it work?'

'You apply it to your blades, it should last for at least one battle,' explained the freesword.

Balthor grudgingly snatched the pot and sat down to daub his sword and dagger.

Redeemer's wounds – now he was going into battle with poisoned weapons! Errantry *definitely* wasn't all it was cracked up to be.

✢ ✢ ✢

They spent the rest of that day and the next travelling hard, barely stopping to eat and sleep. Balthor should have been exhausted by now, but a fire burned in him that stubbornly refused to go out – he was damned if he'd be outdone by a woman and a churl in matters of endurance. He had a reputation to maintain: he was still the greatest knight in Dulsinor, and if he had to die to keep that epithet alive so they could put it on his tombstone, then so be it.

He was thinking that for the umpteenth time towards evening when they began to hear a sound, dull and rhythmic and repetitive.

Boom-boom, boom-boom-BOOM…

'That'll be the Woses,' said Ratko, his voice shaking. 'They play 'em drums at night.'

'Redeemer be praised, we've caught up with them!' said Balthor. 'They won't be expecting us – if we strike fast enough and this blasted herb poison works, the day may well be ours!'

'We should get closer to them first, unawares,' said Anupe. 'See for sure how many they are.'

'All right,' said Balthor. 'You, churl – is there another dell up here? If they've taken to low ground for the night we can get the advantage of height against them.'

Ratko shook his head. 'Aye, there's a dell a'right, but they wilna be stoppin' now, sirrah – Woses prefers to travel at night. Most like, they'll be eatin' now.'

'What do they eat?' asked Anupe curiously. Balthor repressed a shudder – he was half expecting to hear that they feasted on mortal flesh, but the answer surprised him.

'Far as we ken, naught but trees an' roots an' such,' said the woodlander. 'Right strange fowk, yon beastmen.'

'They are *not* folk,' said Sir Balthor severely. 'They are ogrish fiends, and we'll soon send them to Gehenna where they belong!' He gripped his sword feverishly. 'Lay on, dammit!'

✢ ✢ ✢

Flattening themselves against the sedge they peered down into the dell. It was wider than the previous one; stars peeped from the clear night skies in the aftermath of dusk, a sickle moon slowly waxing towards gibbousness.

We'll reap a fine harvest underneath that sickle, thought Balthor, though in truth he knew he was just trying to console himself. For a glance told him his fears had been justified. About the clearing lurched half a dozen beastmen, tearing branches off trees and crunching them between broken teeth. They had kindled a small fire in the middle of the dell. Next to it lay a large hide drum.

He had to pray the Wose's Bane and element of surprise would be enough to turn the tide; the tracker was clearly petrified out of his wits and would be of little use in a fight.

At least the damsels were still alive: they were slumped in the centre of the clearing, lashed together back to back beside a small group of terrified woodswomen who were also bound. One of the beastmen lumbered over to them, pulling a gourd from its belt. Grasping Hettie it unstopped the gourd and poured a white liquid down her throat, spilling half of it on her bosom.

'Milk!' he hissed as the Wadwo served Adhelina with the same. 'So they're feeding them at least – keeping them alive, but for what?'

'If all goes well, we will not need to find out,' said Anupe, slowly reaching for her dirk and preparing to throw it. 'I can take down one of the creatures now – then we rush them. Hopefully we can kill two more before they react, then it is just three against two.'

Balthor bit his lip. They couldn't be sure of that – the dell was wide, its ground uneven. The leader with the scythe was there: it had already proven to be a shrewder opponent than its cumbersome form implied.

Then he noticed something. The leader was clutching its scythe in both hands, with no sign of the injury he had inflicted on it.

'They heals very quick if ye dunna kill 'em outright,' said the tracker, when Balthor asked him. His sweaty face was pale and gaunt.

'Reus' teeth, why didn't you tell us that in the first place?' hissed Balthor. 'I've a good mind to – '

'Wait!' whispered Anupe. 'Listen…'

The Woses had heard it too; they were now looking up from their strange meal. Their ears looked like cauliflowers but their hearing was evidently quick enough.

Then he heard it too.

Boom-boom, boom-boom-BOOM…

More drums. A Wadwo seized the drum and started beating the same rhythm, timing its responses to the growing sound.

Boom-boom, boom-BOOM...

Boom-boom, boom-boom-BOOM...

'More of them!' said Anupe. 'Coming from the other side of the dell I think!'

'Then now is the time!' said Balthor, starting to rise.

Anupe grabbed him and yanked him back down. She was surprisingly strong for such a slight woman.

'No!' she hissed. 'They are too close – we'll be overrun before we can kill these ones and rescue the ladies.'

She was right. A minute later another four beastmen burst into the dell, loping down from the forest fringe to join their comrades. They were dressed in the same greasy boiled leather, and carried the hotchpotch weapons typical of their kind: one of them had fashioned a giant club from a sapling, bound with iron loops sprouting long crude nails.

This one appeared to be the leader of its band. It approached the Wadwo with the scythe, and the two giant creatures cracked their heads against one another.

'A painful way of saying hello,' quipped the Harijan.

'Is this a time for joking?' Balthor rounded on her. 'There's ten of them now – this is a fight we can't win!'

'It would appear not,' she replied, looking as serene as ever. He hated that – women were supposed to swoon at first sign of danger, not react calmly to it all the time. He felt like strangling the outlander.

'So what do you suggest?' he demanded, struggling to keep his voice down so they wouldn't be heard above the Wadwos' guttural grunts as they greeted one another.

'That we wait,' said Anupe, pushing her dirk back into its scabbard. 'We cannot kill them now so let's keep following them until we get a better chance... If what yon woodsman says is true they will soon leave after eating, if you can call that eating.'

The knight glanced at the tracker. The dirty woodlander clearly looked relieved that the fighting had been postponed.

Presently the Wadwos took up their spoils and the women and set off again, one of them putting out the fire with a stomp before leaving. They moved in single file beneath the trees now, the one holding the damsels and woodfolk in the middle while the two drummers kept up their monotonous twinned rhythms, one at either end of the misshapen column.

Stepping lightly down into the dell after them, the three of them followed the beastmen at a distance. Balthor mouthed a silent prayer as they did, wondering why the Wadwos were keeping the women alive.

✢ ✢ ✢

They pushed on hard through the night. At least it was cooler now; the drop in temperature brought renewed vigour to Balthor's limbs. He hadn't pushed himself this much since the last war; much as he hated to admit it, years of carousing had softened him up. Perhaps the archangel Stygnos had set him on this path to teach him a lesson, he reflected grimly: being the greatest knight in Dulsinor should be no easy life. Dawn was starting to gift the trees with shape and colour when he noticed them beginning to thin. The twin drums could still be heard, relentlessly beating a path ahead of them.

'Where are we?' he asked the tracker. 'It feels like we're leaving the Argael.'

'We are,' replied Ratko. 'If they carry on this way, they'll lead us t'mountains.'

The Hyrkrainians. Balthor wondered wryly how the beastmen would manage, deprived of their precious tree-food. It struck him as strange – the Wadwos were native to the Argael, and there were few sightings of them beyond its confines. Just where was this mad chase leading them?

He didn't like to dwell on that. The creatures had shown no signs of splitting up. That still meant ten armed beastmen to fight at the end of an exhausting journey. He thought of the castle troubadour back at Graukolos. Whatever lay Baalfric Swiftfingers composed to mark his heroic death, it had better be good.

The ground started to rise steadily as the trees thinned out some more. Ignoring his aching limbs Balthor pressed on, trying to use the beastmen's rhythm as a marching tune. It gradually got lighter, then the drumming stopped abruptly.

'Can you still follow them?' Anupe asked the tracker.

'Aye,' replied Ratko. 'Light's good enough to follow their tracks now.'

The sun was rising on the rugged green foothills of the mountains when they broke cover of the Argael an hour later. Picking their way through rock-strewn slopes they stopped as they saw it: further up the hills, set against the backdrop of the dizzying slopes was a crude fort fashioned from logs. The warband of beastmen they had been following could now be seen, loping up towards it.

'Well I'll be buggered,' breathed Ratko as they ducked behind a large boulder out of sight. 'Yon beastfowk've built themselves a bloody castle.'

'I take it this is not normal for such creatures?' asked Anupe.

The woodlander shook his head emphatically. 'Ye can say that again – normally they live in caves, jus' two or three o' 'em. Why, now they're almost behavin' like *men*.'

'I am glad you do not think they are behaving like women,' replied the Harijan dryly.

'And I'm glad you still find time for jokes,' snarled Balthor. 'We should have attacked them in the dell – now what in Seven Princes do you suggest we do?'

The question was rhetorical – he had no interest in a woman's opinion on warfare. Although he had to admit the foreigner's stamina was impressive. He felt as though his whole body was on fire. At least he was only wearing a light mail shirt: a full-sized hauberk would have made the ordeal even harder to bear.

The freesword appeared to be taking his question literally though. 'We need to try to get around, to yon hills higher up,' she said, pointing. 'That way we can spy on them.'

Sir Balthor followed her finger. She was right: beyond the fort the hills continued to rise steadily upwards to meet the mountains proper. There was a ridge overlooking it that snaked a crescent from its far side towards where they crouched.

'Yes, we can reach the end closest to us if we strike out due west from here,' he said. 'We can probably get up there by noon, if we push ourselves. Though Reus knows what we'll do once we're up there!'

He turned to look at the fort again. The warband had reached its gate; a single beat of a drum sounded, reverberating off the peaks and slopes. The gate slowly creaked open, and the Wadwo raiding party disappeared inside, taking the damsels and woodswomen with them.

And then suddenly he knew. His gut lurched as fireside tales from his childhood came back to him.

'Redeemer's mercy, they're going to dishonour them!' he exclaimed.

The other two looked at him quizzically.

'I remember my governess used to tell of Wadwos preying on wayfarers in the Argael,' he said. 'The men they would butcher, but sometimes they would take the women alive... so they could beget more of their monstrous kind on them!'

Suppressing his revulsion he made the sign.

'This makes sense,' said Anupe, nodding slowly. 'In my land we do the same, with men, so that our people can survive.'

Balthor shot her a disgusted look.

'Aye, we know them tales,' said Ratko. 'They've done it t'our wummenfowk long enough. Were only the odd vanishin' until recently – but lately there's been more an' more gone missin'.'

'Why didn't you say so in the first place?' Balthor demanded.

The tracker quailed before his wrath. 'I didna want t'say till we could be sure,' he stammered. 'An' truth to tell, I dunna like to dwell on such things.'

Balthor shook his head, his disgust complete. The tracker's cowardice was despicable, even for a commoner.

'We can't abandon them to that fate – we must storm the gate,' the knight said. 'I'd sooner die than have that on my conscience!'

'Wait, sir knight, I weren't finished yet,' said Ratko. 'We kens the 'abits o' Woses right well, after all these years. They dunna breed until the moon's full, so they say. We've time on our 'ands.'

Balthor reflected on that. The churl's counsel was better late than never. And he was right – his governess had always said something about a full moon. He'd always thought her a frightful old woman, telling tales like that to young nobles, but now he thanked her from the bottom of his heart. Full moon was about a week away. It didn't leave much time, but maybe just enough...

'All right,' he said. 'I can get back to Graukolos, raise the Eorl's forces...' His voice trailed off as he realised he didn't have his horse. There was just wilderness dotted with farmsteads between where they were and the castle, with precious little opportunity to requisition a swift courser. It would take him at least a week just to reach Graukolos on foot, and by then it would be too late.

'Dammit!' he swore, cursing hard truth. 'I don't have enough time to get there and back with enough men to storm this blasted fortress.'

'There might be another way,' said Ratko, a keen light entering his beady eyes. 'Some o' the woodfowk are puttin' together a resistance movement, I ken the fellow Madogan who's leadin' it an' where 'is base is. If I kin get word to 'im, he'd come 'elp us.'

Sir Balthor glared at him suspiciously. He still did not trust the shifty tracker.

'And why should we trust you?' he asked, giving voice to his thoughts. 'Who's to say you won't disappear as soon as we let you out of our sight?'

For the first time since he had met him, Ratko looked indignant. 'I may not be the bravest or noblest like you, sir knight,' he said, 'but these're oor wummenfowk they're dishonourin' too.

Besides that, I'd sooner be a messenger than gettin' int' thick o' it wi' you two.'

Sir Balthor paused to consider that. The tracker was a coward and a base rogue – but only the most depraved of men would stand by and let their women be ruined by such monsters. Flawed as he was, the commoner probably wasn't that bad he decided.

'All right,' he said, 'how soon can you get them back here?'

'Their camp's abowt a day from 'ere, might tek 'em another day or two to muster enough men, but as soon as they know what's goin' on they'll be keen enough to get 'ere. Last I 'eard, Madogan 'ad no idea abowt this fort.'

'Good,' said Balthor, clapping him on the shoulder with enough force to make him stumble. 'We'll wait for you on yonder ridge – it's wide and long enough to hold a host of men, a perfect spot for your woodland archers. Now get you gone – and Reus speed you on your way!'

The woodlander nodded and bounded off back down the slopes towards the forest.

'You really think he can be trusted?' asked Anupe. 'He could have told a story to save his skin.'

'Maybe, but what choice do we have? Without ready aid of men Her Ladyship and her companion are doomed anyway.'

'You are probably right,' said Anupe. 'Well we have at least three days until he returns, I suggest we use them to find out as much as we can about our enemies.'

As they scrabbled up towards the ridge, Sir Balthor felt delicious hope returning to him. It was a desperate plan, leading a ragtag band of forest churls against a host of monsters – but it might just work. And if it did, his reputation would soar. The Eorl would reward him with a banneret's seal and double his lands for this. The greatest knight in Dulsinor? Nay, he might well be considered the greatest knight in Vorstlund if he pulled this off.

Sir Balthor allowed a wolfish grin to cross his features as he loped up the rocky hills.

⊷ CHAPTER XIII ⊷

Ichor And Blood

'They've picked their spot well,' muttered Sir Aronn. 'A hundred yards of open ground and a river at their backs – no chance of surprising them by day.'

Sir Torgun frowned. His friend was right: from where they were crouching the land broke abruptly, tumbling towards the River Lyr at a steep incline with naught but rocks and the odd tree for cover. Beyond its grey waters the forest resumed, a great blanket of oak obscuring the horizon even from their high vantage point. The Woses had pitched camp on the open scree by the river's edge, right next to a ford that crossed it. Two of the creatures on sentry duty, sat on boulders while their comrades slept the day away in log huts. He wondered at the strength that had driven the boles of wood through the hard shingle into the unyielding earth below.

But this was no time for admiring a loathsome enemy.

'We'll have to wait for dusk,' he said. 'That way we've a chance of closing with them as they're waking up. Perhaps we can slay a few before they realise what's happening.'

'I thought you said Wadwos are weaker by day?' asked Aronn. 'Wouldn't it make sense to attack them now, while the sun's still up?'

Sir Torgun shook his head. 'Much as I value your opinion, Sir Aronn, I must disagree. The one I fought came at me by day – it was no weakling I can tell you! If we attack them now it's at least three to one against us – yon woman and the monks will be of no use in this fight.'

'I will be,' disagreed Kyra, 'but only if we kin get closer – it'll need to be close range for me to start puttin' arrows through their thick skulls.' She seemed equally comfortable with the Vorstlending and Northlending tongues, but then the woodland dialect was a mishmash of the two and other influences.

'And how will you do that with no light?' asked Sir Braxus pointedly. 'If we're to catch them while they're waking we can't wait for them to start a blasted fire!'

The huntress made a face at that, but said nothing.

Sir Torgun frowned, turning back to scan the camp again. The catapult Kyra had mentioned was there: fashioned from logs and sitting on wheels, waiting to be hauled over the ford. Besides it were what looked like a couple of barrels, covered with a heavy wet tarpaulin. Most likely for the pitch: the tarpaulin was there to stop anyone setting it on fire with a couple of well-placed fire arrows.

The beastmen had thought of everything. Someone was definitely controlling them – it was uncanny how much like regular soldiers the once-mindless monsters had become. Horskram said they had been bred for that purpose long ago, by a race of mighty warlocks who had something to do with the quest they were on. Few sorcerers since, if any, had relearned how to master the creatures. Until now.

'Well, we'd better get back to Horskram,' said Torgun, 'give him his report.'

The four of them slunk back behind the cover of the trees and went to rejoin the others.

✣ ✣ ✣

A couple of hours later the six of them were loping down towards the camp, doing their best to move quietly in their armour.

Sir Torgun caught a glimpse of the Hyrkrainians to the west, bathed in the orange glow of sunset; the river parted the forest to allow a knuckled sliver of the ranges to peep through. As they moved from tree to tree and drew nearer the camp, he could make out hulking figures emerging from the huts in the fading light. His boots occasionally dislodged small stones as he picked his way downwards, but the sound of the fast-flowing river should hopefully obscure that.

A quick glance told him the others had taken up their positions. In accordance with their plan, they were behind half a dozen of the nearest trees, swords drawn and shields ready.

They waited. Then the sound came, a whistling that imitated a lark. Responding to the signal, Vaskrian tossed a leather bag towards the camp. It landed some ten paces away from it. The sentries looked up sharply, peering out towards the sound. Still behind the tree, the squire lit a taper and threw it towards the bag. It wasn't a perfect throw, but it didn't need to be: it landed several paces away from the bag, enough to shed light on it.

As one they broke cover and dashed towards the camp, some fifty paces separating them and their targets. There came a searing noise as a flaming arrow arced across the twilit skies, striking the bag dead centre. It erupted in a ball of fire.

They roared battle cries as they closed on the Wadwos. Torgun felt his heart soar – their plan had worked! They'd managed to get a light for Kyra to see by, and hadn't lost the element of surprise.

Closing on a sentry he cleaved off both its legs with two mighty strokes before it could even take a swing at him. The joy of battle was on him now: he moved like lightning and struck like a tempest. Sir Aronn was getting stuck into the other, his sword ringing off its crude spiked mace before he found its guts with a sidewise stab.

There were twenty at least, but most of these had just got up and didn't have their weapons on them. Ululating cries cut across the gurgling river as the other four hacked and gouged at the beastmen, cutting down several before they could arm. Another arrow struck a Wose in the neck; with a roar it turned to face the attack, before a second shaft buried itself in its eye.

By the time the Wadwos started fighting back there were around fifteen left.

Three of these circled Sir Torgun, already spattered with their ichor, which clogged his nostrils with its stink. He lunged at one, a great brute wielding a makeshift morning star fashioned from a chain and anvil with knife blades welded to it. It curled the thing around, trying to sweep him aside like chaff, but Torgun anticipated the move with a sideways duck, his torso tracing an invisible horseshoe as he came back up several paces to the left of where he'd been. The creature barely had time to register that it had been flanked before he cut its arm off at the elbow.

The next one lunged at him with a pike but Torgun had spotted it from the corner of his eye as he'd come up from his duck; twisting on his heel he turned away and let the polearm bite thin air, throwing up his shield to parry a hammer blow from the third Wose as he stepped in and stabbed the second in the midriff, punching through its armour and finding its entrails. The hammer blow splintered his kite in two, but Strongholm mail and his hugely strong arm were enough to withstand the partly turned blow, though it shook him from head to toe. He wrenched his blade free from the second Wose, a mess of grey guts following in its wake.

The last Wadwo raised its warhammer in both hands, but Torgun hurled himself at it before it could strike, shoulder barging it in the chest.

The move would have been sheer folly from a lesser knight, but Torgun wasn't much smaller than a Wadwo. The beastman staggered back and Torgun brought his sword around in a whirling arc, driving its point through the beastman's heart and burying the blade up to the hilt in its chest. He pushed down on its corpse with his foot as it fell to the ground, pulling his blade free and tossing aside his cloven shield in one easy movement.

In an instant he took in the scene. Aronn had felled another but was hard pressed by two more; blood ran from a gash in his head. The Chequered Twins had one left each, having made corpses of two more, but the Thraxian and his squire were struggling, being pushed back by five of the monsters. Several of these sprouted arrows, but none of Kyra's shafts had found another eye.

He was about to dash over and help them when he heard a great cracking sound. Turning to look across the river, he saw a huge manlike figure come crashing out of the woods. As it stepped into the water, sending up a huge cascade, Sir Torgun mouthed a silent prayer.

✛ ✛ ✛

From their vantage point overlooking the Wadwo camp, Adelko watched the battle unfold. Next to him Kyra nocked and drew, while Horskram muttered prayers.

He felt completely powerless. It reminded him of the battle at Linden Castle, when he'd been unable to do anything to help his friends. In a way this was worse: here he could actually see the people he cared about, albeit as shadows against the burning bag of pitch. Every time a Wadwo swiped at one of them his heart lurched into his mouth.

Their plan had been a good one, but perhaps not good enough. He could make out Braxus and Vaskrian, backing away beyond the fringes of the light, a pack of bloodthirsty beastmen baying after them. The raven knights seemed to be faring better, but even with Sir Torgun on their side victory was beginning to look doubtful.

Kyra swore as another arrow missed its target. They had picked a spot that allowed her to shoot at close range, but trying to hit a moving target in the eye with only a small fire to see by was nigh impossible. Frankly he was amazed she had managed to fell one of the creatures.

The huntress was nocking another arrow to her bowstring when they heard a loud crashing sound from the woods. Adelko followed it and gawped as a giant humanoid figure stalked out of the trees and began crossing the river. It moved with unnatural jerky movements that were eerily fast for a thing of its size; as it stepped across the Lyr into the light he could see it more clearly. It appeared to be fashioned of dark wood, roughly humanoid but angular in form; some strange matter covered its barky hide, though he could not tell what it was at such a distance.

'Ye Almighty!' breathed Horskram, abandoning his prayers. 'That is no Terrus!'

The wooden giant moved to attack the party of Wadwos menacing Vaskrian and Braxus. A few gargantuan steps and a swipe of its huge arm sent the nearest one flying into a hut, collapsing a wall. Another Wose broke off its attack, lurching towards a drum that rested against the side of the hut, while another two hacked at it ferociously. The thing scarcely noticed their assault, knocking one off its feet with a glancing blow.

'It's the wood demon I told ye of!' exclaimed Kyra, who had stopped shooting. 'It's on our side!'

'Demons are never on anyone's side but their own,' said Horskram. 'Adelko, come with me – do you remember the Psalms of Banishing and Abjuration?'

Adelko blinked quizzically. He was fairly confident he did – he had used them at Rykken to save Gizel, and again at Landebert's hut on the Brenning Wold to save their own skins. But something didn't add up – in all his studies at Ulfang, he'd never heard of demons taking such a peculiar form.

'What kind of demon possesses a wooden statue?' he asked as they began to scramble down the slopes towards the river.

'A very rare kind,' said the adept over his shoulder. 'Yon horror is a Golem – an evil spirit bound to a statue fashioned by a warlock to do its bidding. Once bound they are nigh impossible to banish, but we must try!'

The Wadwo reached the drum. Slinging it over its head the beastman began beating on it. The Golem paused. It was crushing the first Wose into the hard ground with its amorphous broad foot while holding the second above its head, ready to smash it into the ground as it hacked desperately at it with a crude axe.

The drum beats resonated across the dusky skies. The Golem tottered backwards and wavered, making more curious jerky movements... Then with a horrible high-pitched scream it hurled the Wadwo at its companion beating the drum. The Wose crashed into its fellow, the two of them falling in a sprawling heap. In an instant the thing was on them. It brought its foot down on the drum, smashing it and crushing the chest of the Wadwo beneath it. Hauling itself to its feet the other Wose turned to run, but the Golem caught it by a leg, swinging it round into another hut and breaking its back.

The knights and Vaskrian launched themselves at the remaining beastmen with renewed vigour. Thanks to the Golem the odds were evening up fast, but Horskram was even more frantic in his efforts to reach the skirmish, shouting down to the others: 'RETREAT! In Reus' name, GET OUT OF THERE!'

But his words were lost in the din of combat. Adelko caught his foot on a rock and stumbled, swearing impiously as he tripped and fell to the rough ground.

Horskram rounded on him. 'Get up!' he shouted. 'This is no time for blaspheming, Adelko! I need you in the purest of spirits if we have a chance of besting this thing!'

'But you said yourself the Psalms probably won't work,' Adelko spluttered, picking himself up. 'There must be some other way of beating it! What about that drum?'

'Yon drum lies in broken splinters, boy, this is no time for contemplation!'

'But it must not like it for a *reason...*'

'Tis probably some magic of Andragorix's,' snarled Horskram. 'We've no time for this – unless you really do have one of your bright ideas!'

His mentor was staring at him. It was too dark up on the slopes to see his face, but Adelko's sixth sense told him Horskram was actually waiting for him to suggest something.

His mind flashed back to his childhood. He was at the celebration feast in Narvik. Balor the headman had been saved by Horskram and he had just met the adept for the first time. He could picture it clearly, his kith and kin sat around the clearing drinking and eating, some of the younger lads and lasses getting up to dance as Ludo Sharpears and his brothers took the music up a notch...

Down by the river the fighting raged on as Horskram continued to stare at him.

✣ ✣ ✣

Vaskrian darted to one side as a Wose swiped at him with a woodcutter's axe. The blow would have taken his arm off at the shoulder, but he was beginning to find his courage again. Whatever that demon-thing was, it had probably just saved his life: he and Braxus were left with just one beastman each, a fight they could actually win.

He circled around it, changing directions to try and confuse his opponent and employing everything the Thraxian knight had taught him about footwork. His initial tactic had been to try and wear the thing out and then step in to attack, but the loathsome creature wasn't tiring.

With a guttural cry it launched itself at him again. Vaskrian dodged another swipe and circled around again. He was much faster than it, but he couldn't get close enough to counter, and if the Wadwo wasn't tiring he certainly was. He stopped moving and crouched down to receive its attack, sweat dripping off his face. The wood demon was cutting a swathe through the remaining Wadwos; it wouldn't be long before the others could come and help.

That was the last thing he wanted – a Wadwo scalp would be a nice addition to his growing kill-list.

Glad of a still target, the Wose launched itself at him. Vaskrian clutched his sword in both hands, holding his nerve. He'd wait till the last moment, then dodge aside and get it on the counter – he'd seen Braxus and Torgun use the same manoeuvre, surely it would work for him...

There was a flash of movement behind the Wose. It suddenly arched its back, dropping its weapon and roaring in agony as a blade appeared from the top of its groin just below the waistline. It took two steps forward and fell to its knees. A second later its head shot off its huge shoulders, borne on a tide of pus-coloured gore.

Sir Braxus stood behind it, a rakish grin on his face. Behind him lay the twitching carcass of another Wadwo.

'Can't win 'em all, squire of mine,' he said. 'Glory takes time to earn.'

✠ ✠ ✠

Sir Braxus turned to see how the others were faring. The last two Wadwos were being brought down. The Northlendings were butchering one like a slab of meat, its body quivering into lifelessness at their feet. Their strange saviour had just dispensed of the other, bringing its huge fists together and crushing its ribcage like a wicker doll before kicking its corpse dismissively into the nearest hut.

'In the name of Palom, GET OUT OF THERE!'

Horskram's voice tore through the darkness. By the sounds of it he was somewhere up on the slope, though Braxus couldn't see him beyond the fading circle of light; the flames from the burning pitch were starting to fade.

The wooden apparition turned to look at the four knights it had just saved. Its face was carved in an ugly totem. Braxus was reminded of the carvings of Tarnelion, a haunted island off the coast of Thraxia once home to a cult of devil-worshippers who practised human sacrifice. He had never visited it and didn't want to, but he'd read about it in his father's library. He had an unpleasant feeling this was something similar. Its eyes were two stones that seemed to glow with a green light of their own; its entire body was carved with strange symbols that hurt his eyes to look at.

Crouching suddenly it swept an arm at Sir Doric, catching him square in the chest and sending him flying. With a cry of rage Sir Cirod launched himself at the wooden giant, his blade carving uselessly at its gigantic legs. Only then did Braxus realise that the attacks of the Wadwos had not left a scratch on it.

With astonishing speed and strength the apparition brought its fist down on Cirod's collarbone, shattering it. He barely had time to cry out before it caught him with its second fist, his head erupting in a shower of blood and bone and brains.

Torgun and Aronn backed off aghast as the thing came after them, Cirod's brains spattered across its unyielding form.

'This is a fight we can't win,' said Braxus, turning to his squire. 'Let's...'

His voice trailed off as he saw Vaskrian staring at his sword. The blade was shimmering with a keen green light. It matched the colour of the wood demon's eyes.

'Where in Reus' name did you get that blade?' he gawped.

'It was my father's,' replied the squire. 'The Fay Folk of Tintagael took it from me and did something to it...'

'A magic blade, now I've seen it all!' cried Braxus. He glanced over to where the Northlending knights were desperately trying to hold the thing off. They moved a lot faster than the Wadwos, but it only seemed a matter of time before the Golem pulverised them.

'All right, dammit!' cursed Braxus. 'I'll join the others – try to distract it while you get behind it, see what that faerie blade can do!'

Dashing towards the fray he yelled a war cry. Vaskrian began circling around, trying to get in position to attack it from the rear.

'Keep distracting it!' cried Braxus to the others, hoping the demon couldn't understand him. 'Get it facing this way and make sure it doesn't turn around, we're going to try something!'

✠ ✠ ✠

Adelko scrabbled frantically up over the lip of the incline to rejoin Kyra. The huntress nocked and drew, sending another flaming arrow into the Golem's chest.

'Damn thing wilna burn!' she cried. 'Seven Princes, yon knights've 'ad it!'

'Not if we can help it!' breathed Adelko. 'Where are our things?'

The huntress looked at him blankly.

'Our travelling gear!' he yelled. 'I need to get to Braxus's things, where are they?'

'Their over t'other side, where we left 'em,' she replied, looking baffled. 'Why...?'

'There's no time to explain – you move a lot faster than me. Do you know the wooden case, the one the Thraxian carries around with him?'

She paused, then nodded. 'Aye, I think so... the one wi' them funny clasps – '

'That's the one,' the novice cut her off. 'You need to go and fetch it, then get it down to Sir Braxus.'

She glanced back down to where the Thraxian was rolling on the ground, having just dodged another bone-crushing swipe.

'He seems a bit distracted right now...'

'Master Horskram will take care of that,' replied Adelko breathlessly. 'Just get the case and bring it down there!'

The huntress nodded, put down her bow, and bounded off towards the ridge of trees.

Adelko turned back to watch the desperate fight, hoping it wouldn't be too late.

✠ ✠ ✠

Braxus lurched up from his roll, dropping into another crouch as the thing swung at him again. Sir Torgun took advantage to dive in and strike at it. He'd never seen a mightier sword arm than the Northlending's, but the blow glanced off its thigh harmlessly.

We're dead, he thought. Then he saw a flickering shape, moving out of the darkness and into the shrinking circle of light.

Maybe not yet...

With a bellow Sir Aronn ran at it, suddenly pulling up short and moving backwards quickly, trying to goad it. The Golem took the bait: he narrowly avoided being clubbed by a fist slick with blood and ichor, but stumbled and fell backwards to the ground. The thing loomed above him, its giant angular frame cutting pitilessly across the darkening skies. It raised a huge foot and stamped down hard. Aronn rolled aside at the last minute but yowled as he collided with a rock.

Braxus and Torgun drove in together, both slashing frantically at the Golem's legs. It swung at the Northlending, catching him a glancing blow on the shoulder. It was enough to send the huge knight careening sideways like a spinning top. Braxus stepped backwards, inviting it to follow him. Vaskrian inched closer in behind it, the sword shimmering in his hand...

'Braxus, stay out of this fight!'

The Thraxian knight jumped, nearly losing his concentration as Horskram moved in behind him.

'Reus teeth, you'll get us both killed!' Braxus snarled, without taking his eyes off the wooden fiend. It stepped forwards with a horrible speed, bringing its fists in towards both men and trying to squash them like flies. Braxus threw himself at the old monk, bringing the pair of them down. Two giant fists smashed together above them with a resounding crack.

Vaskrian chose that moment to attack. Dashing nimbly towards it he hacked furiously at the thing's ankle. It let out another horrible scream as the blade bit deep, tottering sideways and crashing into a hut, crushing its beams like twigs. Jerking itself into a sitting position it lashed out at the squire with its uninjured foot, keeping him at bay long enough to get to its feet again.

It limped now as it stalked towards them, moving gingerly on its wounded ankle. The strange blade had bit deep, and a viscous sap-like substance oozed from the wound.

'That cursed blade won't be enough to kill it,' said Horskram as they picked themselves up. 'You're to fall back and meet Kyra.'

Braxus spared him a glance as the Golem limped towards them. 'In Reus' name, why?'

'She has your lyre,' replied the monk, moving back as it closed on them. 'When she gives it to you, play for your life!'

'What?!' cried Braxus, ducking another swing. His auburn locks waved as though in a gust of keen wind; the thing had missed him by a hand's breadth.

Torgun and Aronn had regained their feet and now rejoined the fray.

'Just do it!' snarled Horskram. 'We'll keep it distracted for now!'

Utterly bemused, the Thraxian fell back beyond the light, which had nearly guttered out. Another flame caught his eye: Kyra, bounding down the slope towards him, a taper clutched in one hand and a case in the other. His lyre.

'Here,' she gasped when she reached him. 'Yer lyre, Horskram says ye're to play it now!'

'I know,' muttered the Thraxian, hurriedly unfastening the clasps. This was without a doubt the strangest day of his life.

✛ ✛ ✛

Vaskrian trembled as the thing towered over him. His blow had cut deep and it had lost a lot of its speed, but now it was focusing all its attacks on him, ignoring the others as they tried to distract it.

It struck at him with both fists in quick succession, dislodging hard earth and pebbles as he weaved desperately from side to side. Dashing between its legs he struck it a passing blow, but he was in motion and couldn't get full force behind it without the right footwork. He felt a sickening feeling knife through him as it screeched again, a horrid inhuman sound that put him in mind of the demon they'd fought in Northalde. More sap oozed from the wound, this one to its inner thigh, but it was no more than a scratch. It tried to catch him a backwards blow as he ran out from under its legs, but the swipe was ill timed and just missed him.

They both turned to face each other. The knights had given up trying to distract it with their own useless blades – the demon clearly had eyes only for him.

'Vaskrian, toss me your blade!' cried Sir Torgun. 'This is a knight's job!'

The words stung him. But if his hero was saying them, they were probably true. Besides, not even he was reckless enough to believe he could take on a demon of folklore in single combat.

He threw the blade at Torgun's feet. The knight snatched it up just as the demon changed tack, lurching towards him with its carved fists. Sir Torgun stepped aside and sliced its forearm. Another horrid screech told them they had drawn blood. Or sap, perhaps.

The fire guttered and went out. Vaskrian caught another at the edge of his vision. Glancing over he saw Kyra holding a taper while Braxus clutched…

… his *lyre?*

His eyes returned quickly to the Golem. Plunged into gloom it looked like a giant shadow etched against the evening skies, with two points of light for eyes. Was it his imagination or were the strange symbols on its body also traced with a faint illumination?

Torgun prepared to take another run at it as it loomed over him.

The notes drifted plangently through the dark, the lyre's soft cadence eerily at odds with the ghastly scene around them. Braxus began to sing:

My name is Sir Magwich, I cannot be slain
Though true knights have tried and giants would fain
I bear the girdle of Olwen, the witch of Gwenhyfyr
'Tis her magic protects me, from bow, blade and spear!

The notes resonated loud and clear, though Vaskrian fancied his master's voice quavered a little. The Golem gave vent to another shriek, this one long and lingering, as though it were trying to drown out the music. Stepping back it began moving around jerkily, as it had done before. It looked almost frantic.

Torgun wasn't a man to waste an opportunity. Launching himself at the Golem with a war-cry he hacked furiously at it, sending splinters flying as he cut at its knees. The thing's legs were the size of tree trunks, but the knight's strength was kindled by a mighty rage. The demon tried to run but fell with a crash, its head landing in the river with a splash as its bleeding legs gave way beneath it.

'This is for Doric and this is for Cirod!' Sir Torgun roared, clambering onto its back as it thrashed around desperately.

Braxus kept playing and singing:

Ye can meet me on horseback, ye can fight me afoot
Ye can cut me to ribbons, from branches to roots
But while I wear the girdle of crimson brocade
I'll ne'er meet Azrael, nor fall to his blade!

Torgun hacked at the Golem furiously with Vaskrian's enchanted blade, carving rents across its back and head and shoulders. The faint light from the marks on its body began to grow fainter, its struggles weaker.

Her grammarie it binds me, my flesh is encased
In words of a litany no mortal can trace
I'll fight in the wars and seek danger in quest
But ne'er shall I bleed from the swords of the best!

Torgun raised the blade high above his head in both hands. He drove it down into the Golem's back, piercing it where its heart should have been. Its thrashing subsided into quivering, its screech dying off and becoming a strange high-pitched whining sound.

'Step back from it Torgun!' cried Horskram. 'The animating spirit is leaving the body!'

His fury spent, the Northlending knight slumped backwards. The Golem had stopped moving altogether, the sigils covering its body had lost their light and its eyes had gone dark. A hissing sound could be heard now; in the gloom Vaskrian thought he could make out some kind of vapour exiting the wound caused by Torgun's death blow. A horrendous stench filled the air, making him gag.

✤ ✤ ✤

Braxus stopped playing as he saw the thing expiring. 'Worst audience I've ever had,' he muttered, as he went to pack up his lyre.

✤ ✤ ✤

Torgun knelt beside Sir Doric as he struggled to breathe his last. The Golem's blow had crushed his chest; blood poured from his mouth as he tried to speak.

'Peace, Sir Doric,' said Torgun, taking a gauntleted hand in his own. He was trying to be stoical as all noble Northlendings should, but watching an old comrade die was never easy.

Doric tried to stare at him, his glazed eyes weak and distant in the light of Kyra's taper.

'My brother... is he...?'

'He speeds towards the Heavenly Halls,' said Sir Torgun, an unwanted tear forcing itself down his cheek. 'You'll be with him shortly.'

Doric stared up at the darkened heavens. He looked confused.

'Aye...' was all he said.

Torgun was about to tell him they would honour both their memories in troubadour's song... then he realised the knight was dead. He closed Doric's eyes and rose, wiping his tears away.

Horskram and Adelko began intoning a prayer. The sound of music drifted across the wrecked camp once more; Braxus had taken out his lyre again and begun to play a dirge.

Sir Torgun listened in silence for a while, then walked over to the Thraxian. Braxus looked up at him and stopped playing.

'Your music saved us tonight, strange as that seems,' said the Northlending. 'My thanks are due – and the thanks of the Order too.'

The Thraxian shrugged. 'Think nothing of it, sir knight. I am sorry for your loss.'

Torgun remained staring at him, trying to decide if he could ever like the foreign knight. Then he said: 'Yon tune you were playing just now, a right fine sound it has. Do you think you could put words to it... for the Chequered Twins, I mean?'

Braxus shrugged again. 'It is an old score in my land,' he replied. 'A traditional piece we play at funerals... but I don't see why not. When I find the time I'll do so. It's a while since I composed anything new anyway.'

Sir Torgun didn't see why any of that was relevant, but nodded curtly and put a broad hand on Braxus' shoulder. Perhaps he had been wrong to misjudge him; the foreigner was brave, even if he was a Thraxian.

'Thank you,' he said softly, before walking away.

Vaskrian had started building a fire. Sir Aronn was binding up his head wound, his face even sourer than usual. Horskram approached him and started talking about giving the Chequered Twins their Last Rites. Torgun wasn't sure why brave men needed extra prayers to earn their rightful place in the Heavenly Halls, but he respected the Argolians enough to trust their judgement in the matter.

Evening deepened into night as they chopped wood for a funeral pyre, using the smashed logs of the huts and the Wadwos' axes. When it was ready they doused it in pitch from the barrels underneath the tarpaulin, before placing the mangled bodies on it next to each other. The monks intoned the Last Rites, bidding the fallen fighters swift passage to the Judgment of Azrael.

When it was done, Torgun approached the pyre with a flaming brand. He tried not to look at Cirod, a shattered skull slick with pulped brains where his head had been. He hated burning high-born men, but the ground was too hard for a proper burial.

'Does anyone have anything to say?' he asked. Nobody did. Torgun lit the pyre and stepped back. Overhead the waxing moon seemed to mock them with its sickle mouth. He tossed the brand onto the pyre and made the sign, holding his splayed hand across his breast and bowing his head as orange tongues consumed his friends.

Thoughts of battles and tourneys, carousing and feasting, and jokes shared on the training ground at Staerkvit ghosted across his memory. He felt a deep sadness tinged with bitterness. Dying in the field fighting mortal men was one thing; being broken like a doll for sport by an inhuman monster was another. What would he say to their poor mother when he returned to Northalde? Not all her prayers would bring them back now.

Unbidden, another tear slid down his rugged cheek.

✠ ✠ ✠

Vaskrian sat on a rock by the fire staring at his sword. Torgun had returned it to him, though he wasn't sure it was much use now except as an heirloom. Whatever faerie magic it possessed had been used up against the Golem; he now clutched the same tatty old blade his father had given him, covered with dints and notches.

Perhaps it was for the best. You didn't want to get a reputation for using magic after all. Still, he wasn't looking forward to fixing it and now it was back to normal it felt clumsy in his hand.

They were all sat around the fire. Braxus was next to him, drinking from a wineskin. They had left the bulk of their supplies back at the settlement with their horses, but the Thraxian had thought to bring some cheer.

'You did well against yon apparition,' he said, passing the skin to his squire. 'And the Wadwos. A fine reputation you're garnering yourself.'

Vaskrian nodded. His mentor was trying to cheer him up with kind words – and he had earned the praise – but he didn't feel much joy of it. The funeral had put him in melancholy spirits and he was tired.

'Think I need a new sword,' was all he said.

'No need to worry about that,' said Aronn, overhearing and getting up. He disappeared into the darkness before returning with a scabbarded blade.

'Knights of the Order don't take their swords to the grave with them,' explained Aronn. 'Strictly speaking they're property of the Order – but seeing as you've no fit weapon...'

He proffered the sword.

Vaskrian hesitated. Taking a dead man's sword, it didn't feel quite right.

'Take it, lad,' said Aronn gruffly. 'You've more than earned it.'

The scabbard was plainly decorated but made of sturdy, dark leather bound in iron. Taking the sword he unsheathed the blade. It was of the finest quality – forged by the bladesmiths of Staerkvit, who rivalled those of Strongholm. Its balance was perfect, the edge razor sharp. The hilt was just long enough to facilitate two-handed use if needed. At the centre of the crosspiece was a motif bearing the emblem of the Order. Most knights would have been proud to call it their own.

Magic or no magic, it wasn't a poor successor to his last sword.

'I... thank you,' breathed the squire.

Aronn clapped him on the shoulder. 'Don't thank me – just give me a swig of that wine!'

Vaskrian handed him the skin and resheathed the sword. He'd try it out tomorrow, when the time was right.

'So whose bright idea was it to play the thing music?' asked Aronn, resuming his seat and taking a swig.

'Adelko had one of his... revelations,' said Horskram. 'I must confess I had thought yon drums imbued with some spell to drive off the Golem.'

Aronn raised an eyebrow. Horskram motioned for Adelko to speak up.

'I just remembered the night Master Horskram and I met,' said the novice, looking bashful, 'back in my home in the Highlands. Horskram had cast out an evil spirit for us, and we were celebrating, the whole village. Ludo was playing – he was our local troubadour if you like, him and his two brothers. I could hear them playing as if it were yesterday, on the fiddle, pipe and... drum.'

Horskram picked up the thread, shaking his head as Aronn proffered the wineskin: 'When he told me that, I realised the Unseen had sent him a revelation, to aid us in our time of need! The Golem is a rare demon indeed, and few have heard of it – many years have passed since I read of it at the Grand High Monastery in Rima. I had quite forgotten its weakness.'

'Music?' queried Aronn, still looking disbelieving.

'Just so,' said Horskram, nodding. 'For some reason the evil spirit that animates the Golem's body cannot abide the sound of music – strains that are so pleasing to mortal ears cause it unendurable torments. I recalled yon Thraxian and his lyre, and knew then we could defeat it.'

'So the Woses were usin' drums as protection from that thing?' asked Kyra as Aronn tossed her the wineskin.

'Aye,' confirmed Horskram, 'otherwise the Earth Witch's servant would doubtless have caused them a lot more trouble.'

'Is that who summoned it then?' asked the huntress.

'I can't see who else it would be,' replied the adept. 'Only a warlock of some craft could fashion a Golem and conjure up its animating spirit. And it's unlikely to be Andragorix if he's armed his Wadwos with drums to defend them against its attacks.'

Sir Torgun looked up at that, anger suddenly streaking his face. He had been staring despondently at the ground, but he was paying attention now.

Vaskrian tensed as his hero slowly stood up.

'You mean to say that *thing* that just killed two of ours was controlled by the sorceress we seek?'

The tall knight was staring at Horskram, his eyes frosted over with icy rage. Vaskrian exchanged glances with his guvnor, who was frowning now. Nobody else spoke.

'Aye, it seems that way, Sir Torgun,' replied the adept. 'Seeking an alliance with a witch sickens me as much as – '

'We will *not* seek an alliance with her!' exclaimed the knight, his hand moving to the hilt of his sword. 'We will seek her *death* instead, and be revenged on her!'

Horskram also rose, his eyes hardening. 'We will do no such thing,' he said. 'Our mission is to find and eliminate Andragorix, by any means necessary.'

'Then I say a pox on our mission!' snarled Aronn, also rising. 'Knights of the White Valravyn do not let their brothers go unavenged!'

'Need I remind you that you are under orders from your King, whose command your Order serves?' the adept shot back.

That was enough to give Sir Torgun pause, but Sir Aronn's blood was up. 'And who set him up to give that command, eh, Brother Horskram?' he snarled. 'You and your secretive missions – you've done nothing but bring ruin on us with your mad quest to kill this warlock!'

'This warlock will kill us all if we don't stop him!' yelled Horskram. 'Do you think I like doing this? Trying to get past some blasted magic girdle to cosy up to a witch whose kind I've spent half my life fighting?'

Horskram held the burly knight's gaze. Adelko could sense a battle of wills between them, while Sir Torgun seemed to be fighting one all of his own.

'If we don't find this woods witch and make peace with her, then their deaths will have been for nothing!' cried the adept. 'Like it or not we need her help, so there'll be no bloodfeud with her while our mission stands, do you hear me? Now sit down and drink your wine, I've finished arguing.'

Sir Aronn's eyes blazed. He bunched a fist and stepped towards Horskram, but Sir Torgun laid a restraining hand on his shoulder. Sir Braxus got up, his face set grim, hand on his own sword hilt as he eyed the Northlending darkly.

'Peace, Sir Aronn,' said Torgun, his voice softening. 'Much as it pains me to admit it, the Argolian is right. We'll seek an alliance with her – *for now*.' The broad-shouldered knight shot Horskram a meaningful look. 'But know this, Brother Horskram – when that alliance is done, we will seek her out again and have her answer for her crimes.'

'That we shall,' replied Horskram. 'Rest assured, she will answer for her crimes: conjuring a Golem is Left-Handed magic and her truce with our Order is forfeit on that account. You want revenge? You'll get it, and I'll help you to get it – *after* we've dealt with Andragorix.'

'Ye shouldna say that,' warned Kyra, her face growing anxious. 'They say the Earth Witch can see an' hear everythin' that 'appens in these woods.'

'Have no fear on that count,' said Horskram, sitting down again. 'Scrying allows a sorcerer to see across space and time, but you can only hear someone if they are also using a tool to talk to you.'

He returned the huntress's blank look with a sombre stare. 'Never mind,' he said irritably. 'On second thoughts, pass me that wineskin – a man needs a blasted drink once in a while.'

Vaskrian felt tension melt into relief as the knights sat down. In fact he almost smirked as the adept snatched the skin off the woodlander and took a swig. It was nice to know the crusty old monk was human after all.

It was nicer still to know they weren't about to start carving each other up, or not tonight anyway. He glanced at his new sword, dearly bought with a brave man's life. It deserved a better first fight than that.

⊷ CHAPTER XIV ⊷

The Witch Queen's Bower

Adelko woke to find Horskram shaking him. Blinking away sleep he sat up. It was still dark: the sun had not yet risen.

'We need to get moving,' said the adept. 'The Wadwos have been attacking the Girdle, they might send a scout to reconnoitre with the company we slew.'

The novice stretched and got up. They had moved back to their original spot on the fringe of the trees overlooking the river. Next to him Kyra and Vaskrian were preparing a hasty breakfast. Ignoring the rumbling in his stomach he wandered over to the edge of the trees. Columns of smoke rose above the forest canopy across the river, dark smears against the deep grey skies; he could make out flickers of orange here and there, presumably fires caused by Andragorix's Saraphi.

His gaze shifted to the camp. The ruined log huts and Wadwo corpses were sprawled across the pebbly ground; the Golem lay face down in the river unmoving. Another demon vanquished, sent back to Gehenna and the city of burning brass. Adelko wondered what chance mortalkind ever had against a foe that could not be killed, only banished.

Horskram called him over to eat, and he gratefully abandoned the thought. He was starving – they had not eaten since yesterday afternoon.

✛ ✛ ✛

The skies were lightening when they crossed the ford and re-entered the forest. The catapult they left burning, having covered it with pitch and set it alight. As they pressed on through the trees Adelko felt his sixth sense jangling painfully; the strong presence of powerful sorceries, growing ever closer.

After an hour they broke cover of the trees and reached the Girdle. The ground dropped away vertically, a deep smooth-sided chasm cut by a wide fast-flowing river that curved away to either side. He could well believe it was not natural: the feel of it was all wrong, the flow too steady, the curvature too perfect. Glancing down into the waters he tried to see if could spot the humanoid shapes that Lymphi sometimes took, recalling the water spirit he'd glimpsed in the Brekawood. That had been three months ago, though it felt like a lifetime now.

But he saw no such thing. The waters just continued to flow, mechanically and methodically. They had a lucent silvery tinge to them, as if they were made of light not liquid; it reminded him of the strange colours of Tintagael, and that made him shiver. Next to him Vaskrian clutched the hilt of his new sword, his face suddenly pale and taut.

Before them a ford stretched across the river. It looked every bit as unnatural as the Girdle itself: it was far too high, a sliver of earth and rock that stood in defiance of the natural law of things. Only sorcery could have kept it from tumbling in upon itself.

'How did the Wadwos get down to cross?' he asked Kyra.

'They use ropes and grapples for the most part – then they tries to swim across.'

'Swim?' asked Braxus, incredulous. 'Since when do beastmen know how to swim?'

'Thus were they designed, in ages long ago,' supplied Horskram. 'A race of super-soldiers should be able to meet everything nature throws in one's path.'

Adelko gulped, remembering how he had almost drowned in the Warryn. Tearing his eyes from the eerie river he looked across the chasm.

On the other side the forest continued, but not as they had known it. Where before had been only oaks now there was a riot of different species: yews, birches, ashes, beeches, elms and many others he had never seen before clustered riotously at its lip, some of them threatening to tumble over into the river below. They were all suffused in a silken web of gossamer, its silvery colour matching the waters of the Girdle.

Pagan sorcery though it was, he had to admit it was beautiful. Nothing like Tintagael, it smacked of a paradise on earth... though of course that was a blasphemous concept.

Something had marred that beauty though: dotted about the canopy he saw charred husks, some of them still smouldering. Above the trees tendrils of smoke continued to mar the blue skies.

'All right, Sir Braxus,' said Horskram. 'It was your idea, so you may as well do the honours.'

The Thraxian nodded and motioned to Vaskrian for a sack he had taken from the Wadwos. The squire handed it to him and the knight emptied its contents before the edge of the river. Some twenty lumpen heads caked with crusted ichor tumbled onto the ground.

'Earth Witch!' cried Horskram in his sonorous voice. 'We come with an offer of alliance – look upon these heads as proof of where our loyalties lie. Grant us an audience!'

'I thowt ye said she canna hear us?' said Kyra.

'She probably can't,' admitted Horskram. 'But this close to her borders she may have spies that can. The Earth Witch is said to have command over creatures of the animal kingdom.'

Adelko peered across the Girdle again. He could see the odd bird flitting to and fro, but the magic river was wide and it was hard to tell even what species they were.

They waited. Nothing happened.

'This witch is no friend to anyone but herself,' growled Aronn. 'We've come on a fool's errand, Horskram.'

'It's too far across to throw a rope,' said Braxus. 'We'll not get any further unless this Earth Witch is prepared to trust us.'

'Small wonder she dunna, seein' as 'alf of you wants to kill 'er now,' muttered Kyra.

They soon fell to arguing after that. Eventually Horskram shouted them all down.

'Peace!' he cried. 'Let me think.'

The adept sat down and began muttering, stroking his circifix. He was speaking in Decorlangue, but Adelko couldn't make out what he was saying.

Abruptly the old monk stood up. Placing his quarterstaff and pack on the ground he said: 'Everybody stay put. No one follow me.'

Horskram stretched out his arms to either side of him and stepped forward onto the rocky bridge.

'No, Master Horskram!' gasped Adelko. 'The Terri, you'll fall in!'

But the adept ignored him, and continued to walk slowly across the bridge. It was wide enough for two to pass, so he wasn't in danger of losing his footing, but Kyra's stories had Adelko expecting the bridge to slough apart beneath his mentor at any second.

As he walked across Horskram began reciting scripture, though Adelko was unfamiliar with the passages: 'Reus Almighty, thy humble servant bends to thy will; thy immutable laws he embraces.

Though the servants of Abaddon assail me I shall not be frighted; the bright wings of the archangels shall be my shield; they shall carry me across fields of fire, through winds of want, above waters of despair. The moaning earth shall not consume me, though Ma'alfecnu'ur send a thousand pestilences to torment it!'

'Now he sounds like my father on Rest-day,' quipped Braxus. Torgun nudged him sharply. 'Peace!' he whispered. 'I like this quest no more than you, but an Argolian's prayers should not be mocked!'

The Thraxian shook his head and shot a wry glance at Vaskrian.

The adept continued to step forwards, raising his voice: 'Let Ta'assaswazelim visit us in his wrath! Let Zolthoth afflict us with cruel torments! Let Nurë's reckless fire be unbridled! Let Aqualcus and Celestian conspire to bring gust and wave tearing across the fair face of Kaia's green earth! I shall not yield nor quail, for thou art with me!'

The adept continued to tread slowly forwards. Adelko fancied he could see the slender knife of rock begin to shudder. He didn't like to mingle his poor prayers with Horskram's, so he clutched his own circifix tightly. The others exchanged worried glances; the smile had vanished from Braxus's lips, and Torgun and Aronn made the sign.

Oblivious, Horskram continued to advance, thundering the sacred words: 'Reus Almighty, I beseech thee in the Redeemer's name, send the Seven Seraphim to guard thy humble servant from the meddling iniquities of the Unseen! Let their foul sorceries die on their lips, let them choke on their blasphemous words and see their dark arts unframed! Though all the hosts of Gehenna stretch shadows across the mortal vale, thy light SHALL DISPELL THEM ALL!'

No sooner had he said the final words than the bridge began to fall away. A hundred rumbling voices were suddenly heard, their chthonian mutterings like an incipient avalanche as the narrow sliver began to shatter and crumble.

'He's done for now,' breathed Kyra. 'Got the Earth Witch right angry with 'is prayers he 'as!'

'No, look!' shouted Adelko. 'He isn't falling!'

The bridge continued to cascade in great fragments, tumbling into the waters of the Girdle. But Horskram remained exactly where he was, seemingly suspended in mid-air. He had stopped walking and stood stock still, his arms still spread out. Adelko noticed he was clutching an item in each hand: his silver circifix in one, and the phial containing the Redeemer's blood in the other.

'Ye Almighty!' breathed Sir Torgun, kneeling and making the sign again. 'It's a miracle!'

They all followed suit except Sir Braxus who remained standing, glaring suspiciously at the adept who was now apparently standing on thin air.

Horskram turned and looked at them. A merry twinkle was in his eyes, a broad grin on his face. He suddenly looked younger than Adelko had ever remembered seeing him.

'Oh come, come,' he said lightly. 'No need for all that. Just a devoted follower of the Almighty being rewarded for his faith!' He stamped his foot on where the bridge had been but a moment ago. It sounded as though he was stamping on the ground. 'There's nothing to fear,' he said, still smiling. 'Naught but good green earth here – just as the Almighty intended it to be! You're all quite safe.'

The others exchanged fearful glances. Adelko was the first to step up to the lip. He squinted down at the river. Was that *grass* he could see at his feet? It appeared ever so faintly, a shimmering vision as if glimpsed in a dream. His head spun. Horskram was still standing there, beckoning to him and smiling.

'Wait,' said Braxus. 'What if it's another trap? An illusion to convince us all to cross and share his fate?'

Adelko paused at that. Then he shut his eyes, focusing on his sixth sense. He could still detect the pervasive presence of powerful magic, but it seemed to have receded slightly. He imagined himself looking towards where Horskram was standing. All he saw were grass and sedge and weeds, and beneath those, cool damp earth...

Keeping his eyes shut, he took a step forwards.

He felt something solid beneath his foot. He took another step forwards, then another. By the time he opened his eyes he was standing next to Horskram, who was still smiling. Looking down he could see the waters of the Girdle, swallowing up the last fragments of the ford in its silvery gullet. He was suspended directly above it, with nothing to support him: the ghostly ground had vanished.

'It's safe!' he called, still feeling very strange.

They crossed in single file, Horskram leading the way. At the other side was a semi-circular clearing that abutted on the Girdle's edge; some of its trees had been reduced to piles of cinder, breaking up what would have been a pleasing sense of symmetry. From the opposite side of the clearing a path led, picked out in small green gravel and lined with moonstones on either side.

From up this path a squirrel appeared, its red furry form looking oddly normal as it scurried in their direction.

Normality wasn't likely to last long in a place like this. Sir Aronn gawped as it ran up to him and shimmied up his hauberk before perching on his shoulder.

'Yon creature seems to have taken a liking to you,' chuckled Braxus. 'Probably thinks you're another squirrel, what with your ruddy complexion.'

'Mebbe ye shouldna have given him yer wine last night,' said Kyra, her eyes meeting the Thraxian's. The knight's eyes lingered on her rather longer than Adelko thought necessary.

Cursing, Aronn reached up to grab it, but the squirrel darted out of reach, scurrying up onto his head and nestling in his curly hair. The knight growled and was about to make another grab at it when Horskram stopped him.

'Wait, it's probably a messenger sent by the Earth Witch,' said the adept. 'Let's watch what it does.'

Sure enough, the squirrel hopped lightly off of Aronn's head, scurrying back down his hauberk and then up the path. It stopped at ten paces and turned back to look at them, cocking its head.

'It wants us to follow it,' said Horskram.

'Led by a knight-loving squirrel into the heart of a witch's lair,' said Braxus. 'I'm not sure even I have the craft to put that into song.'

They followed the squirrel, their boots crunching on the gravel as it led them deeper into the Girdle. They were certainly in need of a guide. The path led into a veritable maze of zigzagging routes, all picked out in the same green gravel and moonstones; without the peculiar squirrel's help they would almost certainly have been lost. The trees were as varied as ever, though many had been badly burnt. They passed through open courtyards, decorated with rock pools and fountains; these teemed with animals that seemed possessed of the same queer intelligence as their guide, foxes and birds and wolves that appeared to whisper to each other as they passed. The whole place was suffused with silvery light that mingled pleasingly with the natural green and brown of the forest. Not all of it was so pleasant to look upon though: many times they entered scorched clearings that had fallen victim to Saraphi.

The noon sun was putting the odd wreath of cloud to flight by the time they reached their destination. Adelko's sixth sense told him they had reach the heart of the Girdle. He had half expected to see a glorious palace constructed of vines and boughs, but there was just a wide cave mouth from a shelf of rock that lined the opposite side of the clearing they were in. The path they had followed was the only entrance.

The squirrel ran up to the cave and was swallowed up by its dark mouth. They waited, sweltering in the midday heat.

Minutes slid by, and then a figure appeared from the cave. She was unnaturally tall for a woman, of a height with Aronn, and her body was thin and bony. A long cascade of white hair tumbled down her back, held in place by a circlet made of intertwining twigs punctuated with small white flowers. Her skin was the colour of the earth, though her features were Urovian, hard and angular like her body. It was hard to tell her true age, though she did not seem young. Her eyes were a russet red colour and conveyed an old sadness and world-weariness.

She wore a green robe that at first he assumed to be decorated with embroidered leaves; as she stepped towards them Adelko realised they *were* leaves, bound together by some invisible force. They rustled softly as she drew level with them. Silver bracelets clinked on her wrists, and on her long slender fingers were rings carved of different types of wood.

'Who disturbs my realm?' The words were spoken absently, as if her attention were elsewhere. Her eyes roved over them, fixing on nothing and no one in particular.

'People who would help you,' answered Horskram.

'Really?' She turned her strange eyes on the adept as if noticing him for the first time. 'Freebooters I see, all but one an outsider. Freebooters who destroyed my Golem I might add, weakening my defences in time of war.'

Sir Aronn stepped forward angrily. 'That thing you call a defence slew of two our brothers! We were busy ridding this forest of the beastmen who plague it when yon demon attacked us!'

The Earth Witch gazed at him vacantly. Her face betrayed no emotion as she spoke: 'A Golem is not easily controlled, sometimes it runs amok. My apologies for your loss.'

'Apologies!' exclaimed Sir Torgun. 'Those men now seek the Heavenly Halls thanks to your demon and you offer us... apologies!'

The Earth Witch favoured him with a crooked smile. 'The Heavenly Halls are the paradise of your faith are they not?' she asked. 'Then mourn them not – for they are in a better place than this if your beliefs be true.'

With a metallic whisper Aronn's sword left its scabbard. 'You kill our comrades and now you dare to mock us?' he snarled. 'By my troth, there'll be a reckoning for this, *now*.'

A harsh syllable dropped from the witch's mouth. Adelko's sixth sense flared, and he immediately thought of the forbidden books in the Abbot's sanctum back at Ulfang. The grass around Aronn's feet suddenly grew large and long, snaking up around his legs. He gasped as it closed on him at the waist, holding him fast. Sir Torgun whipped out his own blade and was on her like lightning, but before he could strike the Earth Witch uttered another word and evaporated into a wreath of pale mist. The knight's sword sliced uselessly through it.

'Put up your sword!' Horskram commanded. Aronn began to cry out as the blades of grass, horribly enlarged, started to constrict him. Braxus drew his dirk and began hacking at them, but they were tough as old roots and he could not work at them fast enough. Aronn writhed, dropping his sword and trying to tear them apart with his bare hands.

Sir Torgun did as he was told. The mist coalesced on the other side of the clearing next to the cave, resuming the Earth Witch's natural form. If that was her natural form.

'You are unwise to trouble me in my realm,' she said calmly, as though nothing much had happened. 'Sheathe your blades and I'll spare yon knight.'

The giant grass relaxed its grip on Aronn as blades were returned to scabbards. It wasn't crushing him any more, though it still held him tightly.

'We mean you no harm,' said Horskram, holding up his hands. 'My bodyguards are understandably distraught over their loss – it would help if you did not provoke them on the matter.'

The Earth Witch rustled back towards them, the leaves she wore catching the sunlight and shimmering like emeralds.

'Their loss?' she asked distantly. 'And what about my loss? Yon Golem took me many months to fashion – do you know how many hours I spent carving the magic words into its body? All that time... lost.' She came to a halt, gazing off into the distance.

'I understand the Sorcerer's Script is not easy to master,' replied Horskram carefully. Adelko could sense his mentor struggling to hide his revulsion. 'And that you have lost a vital protector. But we are here to seek an alliance – we share a common enemy, one we would both see destroyed. If we unite and succeed, you will have no further need of... such protectors.'

Adelko could almost hear the adept gritting his teeth as he spoke.

'Aye?' she replied. 'And who would this *common enemy* be, pray tell?'

'I think you know the answer to that question full well – Andragorix Silfrmund, the most notorious Left-Hand warlock these lands have seen in generations. I have been hunting him for many years now.'

'That doesn't surprise me,' she answered, sounding cold now. 'Your kind are always hunting witches... such as I am.' She held his gaze.

'The Argolian Order has never tried to meddle in your affairs,' said Horskram diplomatically. 'We have left the Earth Witch at peace within her Girdle.'

She laughed at that, though there was no humour in the sound. 'At peace? Aye, only because my Girdle protects me.'

'It did not do so just now,' countered the adept, dropping the pretence of cordiality.

'You are unusually gifted, that I'll allow,' she said. 'You and your apprentice.' Adelko started as she turned cold eyes on him. 'Prophecies have foretold of both your coming.'

The novice didn't have time to reflect on that, for Horskram cried: 'Then in Reus' name, why are we standing here parlaying if you knew of our coming?'

She returned her gaze to the adept. 'The prophecies didn't necessarily say your coming would be a good thing. And even if it is, I had to be sure – the Farseers of Norn were somewhat vague, like most of their ilk.'

'Well, here we are,' said Horskram, raising his arms with mock levity. 'The ones the pagan prophets predicted, in all our shabby glory! Now will you accept our offer of help and tell us what you know about Andragorix or not?'

'That depends,' she replied coolly, glancing again at Adelko. 'What kind of help are you offering?'

Horskram sighed impatiently. 'We need your Scrying if we are to find Andragorix. Tell us where he is, and we will seek him out and kill him for you.'

Hearing his mentor talk about killing people always unsettled the novice; he also sensed a rising tension in Horskram at the mention of the word.

The Earth Witch stood silently for a few moments, then nodded. 'All right, I accept your offer.' She nodded towards Aronn. 'Can young hotspur there be trusted to keep his sword sheathed?'

Horskram turned and looked pointedly at Aronn. His eyes were like burning coals, his face flushed blood-red, but he nodded.

'Good.' The Earth Witch turned towards the cave, muttering another word. The grass retreated, sinking back into the ground and resuming its normal size. Sir Aronn picked up his sword and sheathed it with an exaggerated gesture.

'Follow me,' she said, disappearing into the cave.

✣ ✣ ✣

Inside it was dark and dank. The air had a musty smell and it was cold; Adelko felt his sweat freeze unpleasantly. A faint light could be seen at the back of the cave, which sloped downwards at a gentle incline. It was coming from a peculiar moss that glowed with a dull green light. It reminded him of the Golem's eyes and he made the sign.

The back of the cave was a rock wall, but another word from the Earth Witch and it suddenly parted like liquid, revealing a rough passageway that continued downwards before bending to the right. He had never heard the language of magick used out loud before; the sound was hateful to the ear. He wondered how wizards ever got used to hearing it, let alone speaking it. Perhaps his mentor was right and there was no such thing as a good witch.

The rock wall slicked back into place behind them. Everyone was on edge, but Kyra looked petrified. Adelko guessed she had grown up hearing tales of the Earth Witch and her forbidden realm within the Girdle.

The passage twisted and wound back on itself like a rough spiral staircase. The temperature gradually rose again as they went deeper into the bowels of the earth.

Eventually the tunnel levelled out and stopped turning. They followed it for several hundred paces before it opened out into a large cavern. They were standing on a shelf of rock, overlooking a rippling pool that spanned the entire length and breadth of it. In the middle was a small island on which sat a chair carved of stone that appeared to be set into it. Before the chair a slim rocky finger jutted upwards, in what Adelko supposed was a makeshift lectern.

But it was the ceiling that caught his eye. Hanging from it were dozens of upside-down trees; strange glowing fruit hung from their boughs, casting a multi-coloured radiance across the pool, which shimmered and sparkled as it caught the myriad hues. Adelko thought of the folk tales his mother used to tell him, of how the North Wind would carry impious wanderers off to a fabled kingdom at the end of the rainbow. The more learned called it Celestian's Seat, after the archangel who controlled the winds and weather. He felt he must surely be there now, so vivid and varied were the colours that stabbed his eyes.

'Quite the spectacle is it not?' asked the Earth Witch, a hint of pride entering her voice. 'You'll get used to it, your eyes just need time to adjust.'

She murmured a few more words in the language of magick. The water bubbled at her feet, sending motes of coloured light skittering in all directions. A narrow ford arose from the pool, fastening seamlessly onto the island and lip of rock they stood on.

'Follow me,' she said again, walking across the ford.

The island was about the length of two men in diameter. They clustered around the seat as the Earth Witch sat down before the finger of rock. Atop it was a small white orb of crystal, perfectly smooth. The chair and lectern were carved with scenes of sybaritic abandon, fauns and satyrs and nymphs cavorting amongst trees. Such faerie races had seldom been seen in the mortal vale since the waning of the Golden Age. Adelko wondered how old the chair was. Or the woman who sat on it for that matter, if woman she really was.

Another word and the ford slowly disappeared again. The Earth Witch turned to look at Sir Aronn, as if to say *don't even think about killing me if you want to get off this rock.* The burly knight just stared at her hatefully.

'Now,' she said, turning back to face the pool. 'I'll tell you what I know – and show you too.'

The Earth Witch laid her fingers gently on the orb as she muttered another incantation. This time it was longer: Adelko fancied she was almost singing the words, though not to any earthly cadence. The lights above them suddenly changed colour to a silvery white, while the pool ceased to move and became a shimmering mist.

The mists swirled and eddied for a minute while the Earth Witch continued to chant. Then they parted. Before him clear as day Adelko could see the lands of the earth spread out, as if from a bird's eye view. He sucked in his breath as he realised they were looking at the Hyrkrainian Mountains, where they sloped down to meet the borders of the Argael. He mumbled a prayer.

The Earth Witch muttered another word or two and moved her hand over the orb. She appeared to be using it to move the conjured image around: the vista grew suddenly larger, homing in on a stretch of foothills at the southwest corner of the forest. Next to him Vaskrian leaned over and retched into the pool. Kyra stumbled against the back of the chair, clutching at it with white hands.

'That is a common reaction to a first experience of Scrying,' said the witch without looking up. 'Try not to be sick into the pool, it interferes with the vision.'

His stomach churning, Adelko could see what looked like a wooden settlement on the foothills. Beside it a path snaked up into the mountains.

'Wadwo fortress,' explained the Earth Witch. 'That's his first line of defence. They built it six months ago, must be about two hundred of them garrisoned there. It looks like they've been taking prisoners too – women only as far as I can tell, that means Andragorix probably has them breeding.'

'Breeding?' asked Sir Torgun.

'Aye, Wadwos live hundreds of years, but they have no womenfolk of their own. And they can only breed with mortal women when the moon is full.'

'Ye Almighty!' breathed the knight, making the sign.

'The trail it guards takes you up into the ranges proper,' she continued, ignoring him. 'As far as I've been able to tell, this is where he's got himself holed up.'

The scene switched in a blur as she shifted it up past the trail to the upper ranges. 'The peaks aren't so high in this stretch of the mountains, you can probably get there in a couple of days on foot.'

Muttering a few more words she touched the crystal and changed the angle so that they were looking at the mountains from the side. The scene blurred some more as she brought it into sharper focus, and then they were looking at where the trail emerged onto a broad rocky plateau. The shelf was crowned by five huge shards that stabbed the azure skies. They were fashioned from strange looking stones of alien hues, in bizarre interlocking patterns that made no sense to look at.

'Those are just like the stones of the Watchtower we saw at Tintagael,' breathed Adelko, 'and the ruins we passed just before we entered the Argael!'

'The Warlock's Crown they call it,' said Horskram. 'Another relic of the blasphemous civilisation built by the Varyans.' He made the sign.

'Was it another one of their watchtowers?' asked the novice, his curiosity returning to him.

'No one knows for sure,' answered the Earth Witch. 'Could be, or it might even be a former palace or some other building. It's been millennia since the Varyans walked the Known World, too long for us ever to know the truth.'

In the centre of the plateau between the gigantic shards was a vast crater. The vision was flickering now; it was hard to see, but it looked as though there were several layers of floor below ground level.

'My guess is he's taken up residence in what used to be the basement or dungeon. The ground beneath the rock will be honeycombed with chambers, although as you can see much of it is ruined. He'll be in there somewhere, most likely towards the bottom depending on how many levels have fallen in.'

'You can't get us in further for a better look?' asked Horskram.

The Earth Witch shook her head. 'No. He's counter-scrying, I can't get past the shards.'

'How did the two of you come into contact?' asked the adept.

'He approached me about a year ago,' replied the witch. 'Said he had something big in play. I've endeavoured to have as few dealings with the man as I can - his soul is depraved beyond all reckoning and he gives sorcerers a bad name - but he was just as arrogant as I remember him.'

'You don't need to remind me of his character,' said Horskram. 'What big something did he mention?'

Adelko's sixth sense was quickening by the second. His mentor was hungry now, yearning for further evidence of the warlock's crimes.

'He wouldn't divulge details unless I agreed to join him - said something about a great power returning, and a new age of sorcerer-kings. He wanted me to work for him, subdue the woodlanders and help him unite the Wadwos into an army.'

'What was this army purposed for? Did he say?'

'He didn't go into specifics, but he suggested that in the next couple of years he would have the northerly Free Kingdoms under his control. Said I could have the run of Vorstlund, he would control Northalde, and someone else would have Thraxia.'

'Reus' teeth, he's talking about Abrexta!' snarled Sir Braxus.

'So what did you tell him?' asked Horskram, ignoring the knight.

'I told him I wanted no part of his grand schemes,' replied the witch. 'I've more than enough with my own realm here in the Girdle. The beasts and birds of the forest are all I seek to govern, Friar Horskram, though you might find it hard to believe that. I want no part in the doings of mortal men.'

'I imagine your response pleased him,' said the adept, steering the subject back to Andragorix.

'Oh yes, he showed his true colours then - started screaming at me, saying he'd tear down the Argael one tree at a time if I didn't change my mind. I told him if he wanted a war he could come and get me. I didn't reckon on his being able to enthral the Wadwos on his own.'

'His powers have grown since I last fought him,' said Horskram. 'What else did he say?' Both Adelko and his mentor could sense there was more.

'I was coming to that,' replied the Earth Witch. 'Before things turned ugly and he was still trying to convince me to join him, he mentioned that he had an apprentice who would help him win over the Ice Thegns. He also said he had a special task in mind for me.'

Horskram raised an eyebrow. 'A special task?'

'Aye, said he needed someone to help him get at the druids and marcher lords, in the Westerling Isles.'

She paused, still staring at the pool.

'Go on,' the adept pressed.

'Again, he wouldn't go into specifics, but I had an inkling of what he was talking about... I studied at Kell, you see, a long time ago.'

Adelko's sixth sense was at breaking point. He felt he had to speak.

'You're not telling us everything you know,' he said softly.

'No I'm not,' she replied, unfazed. 'Because you're not either.' She turned to look at Horskram. 'You say you've been hunting this Andragorix for years, and only now you seek my help? There's more to this than a personal vendetta between you and one warlock. I know full well what the druids guard on Kaluryn – and if a madman like that is trying to get his hands on it, then these are dangerous times for all of us.'

She closed her eyes, suddenly looking very tired. The image in the pool flickered and went out. The light in the cavern slowly recovered its previous fluorescence.

'I don't just use this thing to see across space, but then you probably know that,' she continued. 'The opaque curtain of time can be parted too, on occasion, and I've had glimpses of things to come.' A sadness entered her voice. 'This is the future I've feared most of all. So why don't you tell me your story, and I'll tell you as much as I can that will help you.'

Horskram paused, glanced at Adelko, and nodded. 'Not here,' said the adept.

The novice understood right away – Horskram didn't want everyone to know, especially not newcomers to the mission like Kyra.

'Very well, let's go to my quarters.' The Earth Witch stood and spoke another word. Another ford rose, this one connecting to a second lip of rock in a different part of the cavern. A tunnel led off from it.

'Do you have to pass through here every time you want to go out?' asked Braxus as they crossed the bridge and stepped onto the shelf. 'Must be very inconvenient.'

The sorceress favoured him with a dusky smile as she led them up the corridor. It was lit with the same pale green moss as the entrance.

'There's more to my little grotto than meets the eye, sir knight,' she said. 'I'm only showing you what I want you to see.'

She said no more on the subject and the Thraxian shared a puzzled look with Adelko as they followed her.

The tunnel zigzagged its way upwards before emerging into a chamber lit by more glowing fruit, this time hanging from vines that lined the walls and appeared to grow directly out of the rock. The floor was decorated with rugs that detailed more sylvan forest scenes, and chairs and tables carved from wood were dotted about. On the tables were silver trays bearing fruits and sweetmeats and ceramic amphoras. On the chairs were delicately embroidered silk cushions. Those caught Adelko's eye: they were quite rare in the northerly Free Kingdoms.

'At least those blasted Pilgrim Wars of yours were good for something,' said the sorceress as she caught him eyeing them. 'Contact with the Sassanians has given you Urovians some of the finer things in life, even if you had to butcher thousands to get at them.'

'You're not an Urovian then?' asked Adelko.

The sorceress stared darkly at him, indicating the subject wasn't up for discussion. Adelko dropped it.

She ushered them into seats. 'Refresh yourselves with food and wine,' she said. 'Don't worry, I haven't magicked it. Most of it comes from my vinyards and gardens, the meat is provided by animals who have agreed to sacrifice themselves for the good of my realm.'

The adventurers exchanged wary glances, then sat down to eat and drink. Adelko fell on it hungrily enough – right now he didn't care if it was magicked, truth to tell. It tasted good. The wine was a rich tawny colour and delicious.

When they were done the sorceress rose. 'Now I think it is time you and I spoke together, Friar Horskram.' Adelko noticed she didn't refer to him by his usual honorific – but then he supposed the Earth Witch acknowledged no masters.

The adept got to his feet. 'Sir Torgun and Sir Braxus, you should accompany Adelko and me, the others can stay here.'

Adelko felt his heart surge. *Adelko and me...* It was good to know his mentor had no doubts about bringing him along to secret councils any more.

The sorceress led them out through another tunnel. This one ended in stairs that climbed straight upwards before exiting into a chamber fashioned from hanging gardens. Sunlight was streaming through oval windows, their shapes formed by vines overlaid with thatch-eaves.

Adelko blinked – he was sure they hadn't come up far enough to be above ground again. There was more to her grotto than met the eye all right.

The rocky ground beneath their feet was perfectly smooth. Bumblebees and hornets buzzed to and fro, and bluetits and red robins fluttered amongst the leaves and branches. The verdant walls of the strange chamber were suffused with the same silvery gossamer substance that permeated the entire Girdle.

In the middle of the chamber was a round wooden table, bearing an embossed carving of Kaia in her mortal form of a curvaceous woman at its centre. Around it were half a dozen wicker chairs. Another amphora was perched on a smaller table with earthenware cups next to it.

'You are right to be cautious,' said the Earth Witch when her four guests had sat down. 'This sort of thing shouldn't be so openly discussed.'

'You'll get no disagreement from me there,' said Horskram.

She poured them each a cup of wine before taking one for herself and sitting down.

'Well, you have your privacy – and a stoop of my finest wine. Now is the time, I think.'

The adept nodded and took a sip before telling her their story. By now it was a long one, and Adelko was pleasantly buzzing his way into his third cup when his mentor was done.

'Those are fearful tidings,' sighed the Earth Witch. 'My foreboding was not misplaced.' Through his tipsy fugue Adelko sensed considerable anxiety in the sorceress. 'So Andragorix did want help getting the third fragment – in fact that was probably his real reason for soliciting my aid, he's doing a fine job of controlling the Wadwos and subduing the woodlanders by himself.'

'You mentioned you studied in the Island Realms?' pressed Horskram.

'Yes, I know all about their magic defences. I would have been a valuable tool,' she said, anger entering her voice for the first time.

'Well at least he won't be getting your help,' said Horskram.

Braxus leaned forwards. 'What about Abrexta? She's closest to the Islands – could she be his next attempt to get at the druid clans and the fragment they're keeping?'

The Earth Witch nodded. 'It's quite possible. I wasn't aware of her before – I'll try and scry on her, see what I can find out.'

Braxus sat back, nodding and taking a sip of wine. He looked somewhat relieved. Adelko sensed he was deeply troubled about his homeland, and desperate for something he could bring back to his father.

'What about the Vorstlendings?' put in Sir Torgun. 'If Andragorix is planning to send a Wadwo army to attack them, shouldn't we warn them?'

'If we succeed in our mission we won't have to,' said Horskram. 'His hold on the beastmen will be released and they'll revert to type.'

'It explains the abducted women though,' added the Earth Witch. 'He's obviously trying to breed a Wadwo army – the things develop very quickly, growing to maturity within a year or two. Normally they rarely breed, but with someone controlling them...' She made a disgusted noise. 'It doesn't even bear thinking about. Those poor women – most of them won't survive childbirth, if you can call such abominations children.'

'All the more reason to stop him, and right soon,' said Horskram. 'Yon fortress lies on our path. We'll raze it to the ground – Kyra knows the leader of the resistance movement, we'll reconnoitre with them on our way there.'

'Aye, I've kept an eye on Madogan,' said the Earth Witch. 'Brave man. I tried to help him where I could with my Golem until...' She let her words trail off as a hint of ice entered her tone. Sir Torgun's face hardened.

'Never mind,' interjected Horskram quickly. 'What else can you tell us about Andragorix's defences?'

'They are hard to assess,' she replied. 'It depends on how much elan he has left over from controlling the Wadwos and summoning Saraphi to attack me. I would have thought that would be enough to keep him occupied – exhausted for that matter – but given what you've just told me...' She shook her head. 'He conjures up two demons – one to steal the fragment at Ulfang, another to try and kill the pair of you – then conjures yet another to make off with the fragment at Graukolos... and all this while he was contending with me too? You say you fought him several years ago – I'm amazed you survived, if he's grown this powerful!'

'I barely did,' conceded Horskram. 'But no... you're right. He's much more powerful now than he was back then. What I don't understand is *how*... the Headstone is useless until it's reunited. Where has he got this extra power from, to get at it in the first place and threaten you?'

The Earth Witch tapped her fingers thoughtfully against her cup. 'That riddle might be answered by another,' she said.

Horskram looked at her quizzically. 'What do you mean?'

'This bid to reunite the Headstone, after hundreds of years... No one has attempted it until now.'

Horskram shrugged. 'What of it?'

The sorceress pursed her lips. 'Seven hundred years, and not one single attempt,' she said. 'Ask yourself why – there's been plenty of accomplished warlocks in that time, and no few who would have been mad enough to try it.'

Horskram shrugged again. 'Morwena thought she could do it – why she even went to the trouble of enthralling Søren so he could recover it for her in the first place!'

'Aye, Morwena was always ambitious, and vain, and power-hungry,' said the sorceress, her eyes hardening. 'But she knew what she was doing. She had to have been confident of being able to use the thing before going to all that trouble to get it. She lived in the Watchtower of the Valley of the Barrow Kings, who were there before the Islanders... That would have given her access to all the ancient learning of the Elder Wizards. So she must have believed she could actually learn to wield the power of the Headstone.'

Horskram looked surprised. 'I was always under the impression that the Headstone was its own guide, so to speak – the words set down on it – '

'... are the most potent ever written in the Sorcerer's Script,' the sorceress finished for him. Aye, that much is common knowledge among us sorcerers. But to learn to use them you need to have knowledge from another source...'

Adelko thought back to the day long ago in Narvik when Horskram had placed his first book in front of him. A book to tell you how to read other books...

'Like a manual you mean,' said the novice. 'For learning how to read?'

'Exactly,' said the Earth Witch, catching his eyes with her own. He felt as though she were probing him, appraising him in some way...

She looked back at Horskram as he exclaimed: 'Reus' teeth, how could I have been so blind! You're right!'

'Loremasters tell that Ashokainan also coveted the Headstone,' continued the sorceress. 'He too lived in a former Watchtower, in the Great White Mountains that guard the lands you call the Empire. He tried to ensorcell Antaeus on one of his voyages, to get him to recover it for him.'

'I've never heard of such an account,' argued Horskram. 'According to the loremasters I've studied, Antaeus lived more than two millennia ago. Ashokainan is said to have been hundreds of years old, but that would still place him centuries after Antaeus.'

The Earth Witch shook her head. 'He lived for well over a thousand years until Søren slew him,' she said.

'So you say...' Horskram still looked dubious. He didn't like being shown up on his lore, especially not by a pagan sorceress. 'In any case, what relevance does he have to Morwena?'

'Don't forget Morwena sent Søren to kill Ashokainan, as one of his Seven Deeds – he was an unwanted rival you see, she wanted him out of the way. How convenient that the Watchtower was destroyed along with him – according to some accounts, by Søren's own hand at Morwena's behest.'

'... so no one else could get their hands on the texts needed to use the Headstone.'

'Exactly. Of course the same thing happened to the Watchtower of the Valley of the Barrow Kings when Søren killed Morwena.'

'Which leaves only one Watchtower intact and inhabited,' finished Horskram.

'Where is that?' asked Adelko.

'Somewhere in the Hot South,' said the sorceress. 'In the Sultanates of Sassania.'

'I know of it,' said Horskram. 'But the warlock who dwells there is by all accounts a recluse, much like yourself. He meddles not in the affairs of mortalkind, and suffers none to approach him.'

'Just so,' said the Earth Witch. 'But by the looks of it, Andragorix has somehow got his hands on this ancient knowledge. If he's spent the past three years poring over grimoires written by the Elder Wizards themselves, and not just diluted copies...'

'... that explains his increased powers,' said Horskram.

'Well,' put in Sir Braxus, 'you'd better tell us about the last time you fought him, Horskram. Give us some idea of what to expect at least.'

'That I'll do when the time is right,' said the adept, though he looked severely troubled.

'Be of some cheer,' said the Earth Witch. 'Your powers must be considerable to get past my defences, and that talisman you carry should give you some protection from his sorceries.'

Horskram's eyes narrowed. 'The blood of the Redeemer is no talisman, but a relic of our faith,' he said darkly.

'The two are no different to me,' replied the Earth Witch, unruffled. 'People see things in whatever form suits them...'

Adelko had to smile at that. His mentor had hinted at this much, during their talk of theology in the Argael. Horskram glanced at him disparagingly; perhaps he sensed what his novice was thinking. But he said nothing more on the matter.

'I think we have spoken enough,' said the sorceress. 'I'll need to rest before I try to learn more about this Abrexta – Scrying is draining work, especially when you've a wizards' war to fight on top of it. You should all do the same - you'll need your strength for the trials to come. I noticed many of you are carrying injuries too, I'll see to those as well before you leave.'

Sir Torgun glared at her, distrust and hatred scored across his face.

'Oh for Kaia's sake, what are you expecting, sir knight?' she demanded. 'Healing potions that turn you into zombies? I'm a skilled herbalist as well - I was thinking more along the lines of King's Wort and Marius' Weed, nothing your lily-white Marionite monks would be ashamed of using.'

Torgun said nothing, but turned away with a disgusted expression. The sorceress ignored him pointedly. 'Oh and that reminds me,' she added as they all rose to leave. 'I'll give you some Wose's Bane to take with you - should give you an edge against the Wadwos. I'll make sure you've enough to give to Madogan as well.'

Adelko glanced out of a window just before he took the stairs back underground. He could see the riotous canopies of the Girdle, pocked with black craters that still smoked. Beyond that he caught a glimpse of the mountains. He searched briefly for the tell-tale shards of the Warlock's Crown, but they were out of sight. For now.

✣ ✣ ✣

Adelko lay on his back, staring up at the stars with sleepless eyes. Dark dreams had chased him from his sleep; he could not remember their form, only flickering shapes now pressed at the penumbra of his consciousness, shapes that made him think of shadow and steel and blood.

Next to him his companions snored with an abandon he could only envy. The Earth Witch had shown them to a glade after tending their wounds and feeding them again. The lush grass was of such texture as he had never seen before; his feathered bed in the King's palace at Strongholm could not have been more comfortable.

Not that it had availed him much in the way of rest. He was sitting up and thinking about exploring the Girdle when he caught a movement from the corner of his eye. Turning he nearly jumped out of his skin as he saw the Earth Witch standing over him, seemingly appeared out of nowhere.

She raised a bony hand to her brown lips. 'Don't wake the others. I need to speak with you, and that squireling friend of yours, alone. Go and wake him.'

The novice got to his feet and went over to do her bidding, his curiosity instantly getting the better of him. Truth to tell, he wasn't entirely surprised she wanted a private audience with him – she obviously thought he was significant in some way – but he had not expected her to take an interest in Vaskrian. What on earth could she want with the rakehell squire?

He shook Vaskrian awake. The squire turned over, his eyes flicking open as he grabbed Adelko by the habit.

'Calm down!' hissed Adelko. 'It's just me... The Earth Witch wants a word with us.'

Vaskrian blinked and sat up, struggling to bring his sleepy eyes into focus. 'Do you think it's a trap?' he asked nervously, glancing over at her and back at Adelko. His hand strayed to the dirk he kept in his boot, something he'd picked up from Braxus.

The novice shook his head. 'I don't think so,' he whispered. 'My sixth sense says we're probably safe with her.'

The squire stared at him. 'Your what?'

'Never mind, let's go with her, find out what she wants!'

The Earth Witch was standing at the edge of the glade, her tall dark form almost blending in with the trees. She motioned for the youths to follow her up a gravelled path.

It took several twists and turns, passing through several courtyards. The woods were eerily quiet; no owls hooted, no foxes scurried from the bushes. Even the leaves were silent.

Eventually she stopped at a hexagonal clearing bordered with moonstones. At its centre was a dais fashioned from what looked like the shorn trunk of an old oak tree, its sides carved with the fauns and other forest spirits Adelko had become used to seeing.

She led them over to it. The top of it had been hollowed out into a low basin. The Earth Witch held her hands over it and murmured softly. The basin slowly filled up with water.

'Long ages have passed since the Moon Goddess sailed to the Island Realms,' she said softly, as if speaking to the woods themselves. 'Before that the lives of the Islanders were harsh and bleak, as they scratched a living from the unyielding rock and hard soil. The First Age of Darkness was upon us then, and all mortalkind had to pay the price of the Elder Wizards' folly.'

The water stopped just a finger's breadth from the lip of the basin. Touching its surface the sorceress muttered an incantation. The waters began to shimmer and glow as the pool had done in her subterranean lair.

'Kaia re-gifted mortalkind with the language of magick, teaching her priest-folk the Sorcerer's Script,' she went on, still as if speaking to no one in particular. 'They became the druids, and under her tutelage they ushered in an age of plenty – fruit was coaxed from the trees, the earth became rich and fertile, and all on the Islands shared in the cornucopia. For my people it was a golden age, enough to rival that of the City States of Thalamy or the Hierocracy of Sendhé far to the south.'

Adelko plucked up the courage to speak. 'But we're taught that's blasphemy,' he said. 'Using magic to alter the laws of the natural world. Only Reus has the right to do that.'

'Aye, so I have heard it said by the learned of your faith,' answered the witch. 'A divine intervention by the Lord Almighty Himself, what you would call a miracle.'

'That's right,' said Adelko, though for some reason he felt unsure of himself.

Perhaps sensing that, she turned her red eyes on him and said: 'But for us there is no such distinction – even the Creed acknowledges that the Unseen, all the angels and archangels and spirits of the Other Side, are but emanations of your One God's essence. They are of Him, and therefore calling on their power is no different to calling on the deity you call Reus.'

'I see...' Adelko had never heard it put like that before. It seemed to make sense, and yet it went against everything he had been taught. He wondered what Horskram would say if he were here now.

'I have watched you from afar for some time now, both of you in fact,' she continued, staring pointedly at Vaskrian. The squire was looking fit to drop back off to sleep again. 'As I said earlier, Scrying gives me the power to see across space and time, though often I am granted just a fleeting glimpse, and see through a glass but darkly.'

'The Redeemer said that,' said Adelko. 'Horskram quoted that part of the Scriptures a few days ago.'

'Your mentor is far wiser than most of his kind,' said the sorceress. 'His inner struggles as he searches for the truth are doubtless painful to him. If only he could fully accept that truth has more than one facet.'

'What do you mean?' asked Adelko.

'For you there is but one god, and what we pagans call gods are in fact no more than his servants and enemies, demons and angels and so forth. But what if both were true? What if the One God could be the Many as well? All existing at the same time, separate as your individual limbs are, and yet part of an integrated whole.'

She continued as Adelko reflected on her words: 'A mortal man has many moods: he can be kind, or wroth, or sad, or joyful. He can seem like a different man when a different mood is on him, yet ultimately he is the same man is he not?'

'I suppose so...' said Adelko. Vaskrian was staring at the trees, clearly bored. The novice wondered why she had brought him along.

Seemingly oblivious, the Earth Witch went on: 'Think on the many moods of your One God, Adelko. If Reus sees all, then He must have known what strife He would bring forth when he gave birth to Abaddon and his future followers aeons ago... If Reus created all, then perhaps He must answer for everything in the Universe: good, bad and indifferent.'

'But that's blasphemy!' cried Adelko.

'You are still unable to let go of your beliefs,' she replied. 'The things you learned in the monastery have shaped your mindset. But you were born for far more than merely learning at the feet of others, Adelko of Narvik – in time, if you survive, you will learn far more. You will learn how to judge for yourself the nature of things, and if my Scrying be true, it is your destiny to impart that knowledge to others.'

'What about this quest,' he asked. 'Andragorix, the Headstone fragments, all of that? Am I... *was* I, destined to be part of all that?'

'That I cannot say for sure,' answered the sorceress. 'All I can say is that this quest, as you call it, will be the making or breaking of you – it will be the crucible that forges you into the person I think you really are... Or it will be the conflagration that destroys you.'

'The demon Belaach said something about conflagration in his prophecy,' said Adelko, shivering suddenly in the night air.

'Do not mention that name here!' said the Earth Witch sharply. 'Bad enough I had to bind a demon to that wooden manikin to try and save my realm.'

'They're very angry with you for doing that,' said Adelko. 'Horskram says it's Left-Hand Magic, that – ' He stopped in mid-sentence. He didn't want to betray his mentor, but he felt something odd happening. He was becoming attuned to the Earth Witch, not as hunter and criminal, but as an understanding of... equals?

'Ah yes, another cardinal error of your faith,' said the Earth Witch. 'Left hand and right, black and white, good and evil – always so simple. Life is never that simple.'

She turned to Vaskrian. 'You have also been marked out,' she said. 'The Farseers of Norn spoke of another youth that would play a part in the struggles to come. In fact you already have – twice now you've saved your friend's life. Though I'm not sure why you were chosen – you seem like a passing reckless young man to me.'

The squire stared back at her defiantly. 'If I'm reckless it's because I'm brave,' he said. 'I fear no man – I even dealt your precious Golem a tidy blow.'

'Ah yes, using faerie magic by the looks of things,' she mused. 'For all your appearances to the contrary, you are clearly no ordinary squire. The Farseers had it thus: "At his right hand shall come another young in years, sullen eyed and resentful, strong but reckless. He shall be low born but rise high, yet no man shall honour him with title for his deeds. The seas shall rise in arms at his call, the earth shall be stained with the blood of his enemies. He will deal death to the foes of the chosen one, a raven shall fly at his back, the sweet taste of victory shall sour in his mouth."'

'That doesn't sound so good,' said Vaskrian gloomily.

'Remember what I said – truth has more than one facet,' replied the sorceress cryptically.

'But all I want is to be a knight!' Vaskrian spluttered. 'It's all I've ever wanted!'

'And why do you wish to be a knight?' retorted the Earth Witch. 'So you can kill with "honour", as your master does?'

'That's exactly what I want,' persisted Vaskrian, growing red-faced and angry. 'I can fight as well as any high-born man my age, why should I miss out just because I wasn't born some blueblood's son?' His eyes were filled with rage and resentment now. Adelko sensed a deep pain and longing in his friend. He wished he could help him somehow.

'You want overly well methinks,' said the sorceress. 'Do you think having "sir" attached to your name will make you a better fighter, or a better person? Will it bring back that poor squire you so shamefully murdered?'

Vaskrian gawped. 'How did you know...?'

'As I said, I have been watching you both for a long time,' replied the Earth Witch. 'I fear you're going to get a lot more blood on your hands before you grow up.'

'Derrick was a cur!' snarled Vaskrian. 'A stuck-up knight's son who couldn't fight half as well as he talked – he deserved to die!'

The Earth Witch looked at him sadly. 'I don't share the traditions of the Northlanders, but you really do have a raven at your back, Vaskrian of Gaellen. Strange that the gods should have chosen someone like you to guard Adelko on his journeys.'

She reached into the pool and pulled something from its shimmering depths. It was a small hollowed out crystal pendant; a mist writhed within it, changing colour from grey to blue and back again.

'I think you should wear this,' she said. 'I've seen some of what lies ahead and it's for me to play a small part in the Farseers' prophecy. Here, take it.'

'I'll have no truck with your pagan ways, witch!' cried the squire. 'I've already heard enough from – '

The sorceress stared at him. Her concentration seemed to be elsewhere. 'I... said... *take it.*'

Vaskrian reached out dumbly and took the pendant, putting it around his neck and tucking it into his jerkin.

'Now go back to the glade,' she said. 'I'll have Burrow guide you.'

She murmured something and the red squirrel appeared from the trees. Bidding Adelko a confused good night, the squire turned and followed it back up the trail.

'You used magic to make him take the pendant,' he said accusingly. 'I could sense you doing it!'

'I don't like using Enchantment unless I really have to,' said the Earth Witch. 'It isn't my favourite of the Seven Schools. But yon youth is clearly impossible. Why he's been chosen I've no idea – the ways of the gods are strange.'

The Earth Witch turned and touched the pool again, conjuring up a vision from its shimmering surface.

'I want to show you something,' she said. 'One last thing before you go back to bed.'

'A glimpse of my future?' asked Adelko uncertainly. At the monastery he had learned that using Scrying for such purposes was very dangerous – men could drive themselves mad trying to avert their possible futures, sometimes even bringing their doom about through doing so. But right now he wasn't sure if anything he had learned was actually true or not. He wished his mentor were here to guide him.

'Not exactly,' replied the witch. 'Yours is a rare spirit, Adelko of Narvik. I want to help you understand your gifts better.'

Placing both hands in the pool she cupped them and raised some water, offering it to him.

'Drink,' she said.

'I... no, I won't! That's Alchemy you're practising, I'm an Argolian and it's forbidden – '

'*Drink.*'

He could feel her pressing at his will now, visualising the abstract symbols of the Sorcerer's Script as she tried to get him to do her bidding. He began mouthing the Psalm of Abjuration to counter the effect. Slowly he felt the force subside, though the sorceress did not move.

'Drink, Adelko of Narvik – if I can't compel you, perhaps I can persuade you. Remember what I said about there being more than one truth. I am only trying to help you.'

He felt an anguish come over him. He knew it was wrong, but his curiosity burned in him. Something in him longed to know, as it had always done... He felt an unseen truth beckoning him with an invisible hand.

'Would you be standing here now if you hadn't stepped across your Abbot's threshold three moons ago?' she pressed relentlessly. 'Your hunger after forbidden things is what set you on this path in the first place – drink, Adelko of Narvik, it is your destiny to seek truth in all its forms!'

No power of enchantment compelled him now, only his unquenchable thirst for knowledge, the same thirst that had seen him burrowing through dark corners of the world for the past year. Bending forwards he took a sip of water from the sorceress's earthy hands. It tasted oddly sweet, not like fruit or any other kind of sweetness he had ever experienced. The liquid was ice cool as it slipped down his throat...

✥ ✥ ✥

Everything dropped away from him with a sharp *crack*. As he had done outside Tintagael, he suddenly saw himself from afar, standing in the clearing with the Earth Witch near the middle of the Girdle; around it the clustered eaves of the Argael stretched in all directions. The vision receded further, and he could see the slopes of the Hyrkrainians as he had done in the pool, the Wadwo fortress studded against a hillside. There were two tiny figures on a ridge overlooking the fort, on the other side from the trail it guarded...

The vision rushed away from him, and the Free Kingdoms were spread out like a vast map, the seas looking strangely still. He continued to hurtle backwards, the lands and seas condensing into a blue-green orb surrounded by endless stars in an ocean of night... Back he went, soaring with a speed that confounded comprehension, the stars fading and blackness closing around him...

He opened his mouth to scream but no sound came. He sensed rather than saw the next series of visions: hosts of berserker

armies clashed swords and shields against an icy tundra painted
in a wash of crimson, a blond youth standing before them roaring
triumphantly; in a baking desert under a hot sun, exotic-looking
soldiers rode in thick columns, their multi-coloured turbans blazing
in the light; at their head rode a dark-skinned warrior, short in
stature but proud and confident; a host of knights dressed in white
stood ready to meet them, and above both armies in the orange skies
a great serpent coiled around a giant wheel, crushing its spokes...
Far to the west a fleet of high-prowed ships put out to sea, sporting
a banner emblazoned with a green stag and a bear, pulling steadily
towards a horizon where ghosts moaned and tumbled beneath the
foamy waves and strange black stones loomed at the fringes of a
mist-shrouded island... Countless leagues away lay another island,
atop it a blasted city, vaster than any he could have imagined, its
broken edifices mocking the natural composition of the stormy skies;
in their midst a tower soared... a lone figure swathed in dark robes
stood atop it next to another stone, carved with hieratic symbols
that burned his psyche...

He felt a thousand ideas conflicting, grating and jarring at one
another as ambition ran wild, hunger for power marrying thirst for
blood in a tidal wave of suffering. A multitude of voices cried out
'I have the right of it!' and many more screamed, tortured souls
begging for mercy as they exited their broken bodies; beyond them
loomed another city, even vaster, its towers of burning brass casting
long shadows across a fiery host whose forms were made of naught
but fire and cinder...

He soared past the brass city and his anguish dropped away
as he found himself on a bright unending plain, surrounded by
beautiful forms of white and pink who whispered softly to him:
'The choice is yours.' He opened his mouth to answer and a colossal
black angel appeared before him, blindfolded. Countless eyes both
open and shut nestled in the fearful plumage of its great wings.

'YOU HAVE CHOSEN,' it thundered. 'THE UNALTERABLE
LAW HAS BEEN ALTERED/NOW EVERYTHING MUST CHANGE.'

The visions of heaven and hell dropped away in a heartbeat. He
was floating in a void... Then stars and suns started to take form
about him, giant vapours condensing into gigantic belts made of light
and dust. He saw another orb of blue and green, shaped much like the
first, and as he hurtled towards it he saw continents shaped like those
of the first, yet different somehow... Iron dragons coursed across
alien skies at terrifying speed, spitting fire on all below; ordinary

folk ran terrified from their dwellings as they were consumed in the conflagration about them. Above the skies, in two vast semicircles of thrones set into the firmament, sat a host of angels and demons.

'Help these people!' he cried at the angels. But the angels were silent and unmoving. He turned to the demons and saw they were the same, staring impassively at the spectacle below. Turning back to follow their gaze he saw more iron monsters crawling over the face of the earth, crushing all in their path... great towers belched up plumes of smoke, clogging the darkening skies with their poisonous fumes... in the cities people dressed in strange clothing gathered at vast marketplaces, jostling with each other for goods that had no shape or form beneath looming towers of glass that were impossibly straight and smooth.

'Help these people!' he cried at the city folk, but no one listened.

Beyond the lands, strangely bare and bereft of forests, the seas roiled and churned, their waves heavy and thick with tar; dead fish floated across their slick surfaces... back on the bare plains he saw vast herds of animals brought to the slaughter; a charnel stench clogged his nostrils as they were given up to vast metal giants for sacrifice... across the land millions of mouths were opened... many fed greedily at a giant trough covered in numbers that constantly changed; many more moaned and wept... some were faced to the heavens and prayed.

But no one listened, and no one answered.

The black angel appeared before him again. 'YOU HAVE CHOSEN, NOW EVERYTHING MUST CHANGE/THE CRAFT OF MORTAL MEN SHALL OUTSTRIP THE WIZARDRY OF OLD/YET ALL SHALL MEET ME IN THE END.'

The angel grew larger, filling up his sight. He felt himself falling into an endless darkness, one that stretched far beyond the glinting stars into an abyss of nothingness...

✤ ✤ ✤

His eyes flicked open. He was lying on the floor of the clearing. The Earth Witch was cradling his head in her lap. She smelled of damp earth and roots. Overhead the skies were lightening, mellowing at the rose-fingered touch of dawn.

'It is over,' she said softly. 'Now you have seen what lies ahead.'

'But... it's hideous!' said Adelko. 'Even if we stop Andragorix... everything will change, and not for the better.'

'Aye,' she said sadly. 'Everything will change. But remember what I have told you – truth has more than one facet. You have seen a vision of many possible futures. Not all may come to pass.'

'But I saw such horrid things,' he said. 'And it was my fault! Because of choices I made... I can't be responsible for that!'

'We are not privileged to choose our destiny,' replied the Earth Witch. 'In other times and places it will be called pre-determinism, the simple law of cause and effect.'

Adelko got up. He felt uncomfortable lying in a woman's lap, even such a strange woman as the Earth Witch. It stoked up desires he wasn't supposed to entertain.

'Cause and effect?'

'One action precedes another, therefore everything is predestined to happen. Another way of looking at fate. Many truths, Adelko: if you take nothing else away from tonight, remember that.'

'But why try to stop Andragorix?' he persisted. 'If we're all doomed anyway to live in a world without faith or magic... We'll be abandoned.'

The Earth Witch sighed. She suddenly looked very old. 'Or free, depending on how you look at it. No miracles, no magic, no divine interference of any kind. Just us, left to our own devices.' She paused, sitting silently, lost in thought.

'But no,' she said after a while. 'Ours is not the luxury to choose between good and evil either. All we have before us are choices, decisions we'll make influenced by probability. If we stop Andragorix, whatever hellish vision of the world you've seen may come to pass, or it may not. It may not even have been our world you saw.'

That would have stunned Adelko yesterday but now he nodded. 'Yes, that's true... I had the idea of there being, well, many worlds in our Universe, not just the one.'

'Or even many Universes,' replied the Earth Witch. Then she sighed again, shaking her head slowly as if to clear it. 'No, if we don't stop Andragorix, the probability is that he really will visit hell on earth. So that's why we have to try. But even if we succeed, there's no guarantee of any kind of paradise on earth either. Just less chance of it becoming hell – as far as we know.'

She shut her eyes tightly. Adelko could see and sense her struggling with powerful emotions.

A sudden thought struck him. 'How old are you? When you spoke of Morwena, it sounded almost as if you knew her.'

The witch opened her eyes and looked at him keenly. 'I did,' she said softly. 'I studied with her at Kell, hundreds of years ago.'

Adelko lurched upwards, making the sign.

'Calm down, for Kaia's sake,' she said, suddenly irritable. 'I'm not one of the undead! I'll go to the grave, and sooner than you think. But it's true I've had a longer life than most mortals.'

'Then the rumours are true!' exclaimed the novice. 'About your father being a Terrus.'

'According to other tales, it's my Alchemy that keeps me alive – strange potions I've learned to concoct here in my mysterious realm,' she laughed. 'Or perhaps I made a pact with a demon, so the other tale goes – some even say I'm a demon myself!'

She rose, tall and majestic in the growing light. 'Many truths, Adelko, many truths – and often we see only what we want to see. Your job from now on is to try and get past that, if you can.'

Adelko nodded, mulling over her words. Another question occurred to him as he got up to leave with her.

'What will happen to you and your Girdle? If the visions I've seen and the prophecies you believe in come to pass? If there's no more magic, I mean.'

'I'll fade, and so will my realm. But at least it will be a gentle death, not like the one Andragorix has planned.'

'I'm sorry,' said Adelko. 'I'm not supposed to say it, but your realm is beautiful.'

'I notice you don't say the same about me!' she mocked. 'In any case, don't be sorry: I've had a good long run here in the mortal vale. Godshome calls to me more loudly each day – my time will come soon, and I'm ready for it. As for my realm... well, the birds and beasts got on tolerably well before I came to watch over them. Perhaps they'll remember a few of the things I taught them after I'm gone.'

She beckoned for him to follow her from the clearing. Following her Adelko wondered if he would be among the last mortals ever to see the Earth Witch's Girdle. Perhaps there existed another one like it, in another world somewhere; the thought of that lightened his heart a little as he trudged back to rejoin his sleeping companions.

⊱ CHAPTER XV ⊰

A Soul Sold

The boy whimpered, struggling feebly at the manacles that bound him to the strangely sculpted wall. Andragorix ignored him as he stirred the viscous liquid he had just collected in a jar, mixing it with tincture of Tyrnor's Foil. On its own the tincture was a powerful stimulant; mixed with the boy's blood and his own seed it would give him the strength he needed to continue his work.

'Please...' the boy managed to whisper, the manacles clinking as he writhed in agony. 'I want to go home! Let me go home...'

Andragorix put the jar down on a raised stone slab. Angels and demons had been carved around its borders with a craft lost to mortalkind millennia ago. Walking over to the boy, he stroked his hair and bent to whisper in his ear.

'I'm sorry,' he said. 'Did I go overly hard on thee just now? Be thankful I didn't have to open another vein.'

He stroked the bleeding boy with his one living hand; the other shone brightly in the light from orbs of crystal set into the sculpted mouths of demons and angels lining the undulating walls. It was hard to believe the Varyans had worshipped both side by side: though the demons were a later addition, their beautiful forms gradually crowding out their horrid angelic opposites. A perfect metaphor for the progression of the Elder Wizards' mighty civilisation.

The boy flinched, whimpering more loudly as he tried to move away. The manacles bound him to a round alcove that looked like a gigantic sucker. Andragorix felt his lust return as he gazed on the boy's naked form. Dozens of cuts crisscrossed the lad's body. He would endure many more before Andragorix was done with him.

He kissed the boy's filthy matted hair. He began wailing, a desperate sound full of pain and bereft of hope. Andragorix shut his eyes, pleasure coursing through him as he drank it in. The sins of the Seven Princes were his chief delight; body and soul he had lived them for many years now.

'On second thoughts,' he said. 'Your frail body might not survive another turn so soon. I wouldn't want to curtail your suffering.'

Look at you, so sick and depraved – why don't you just kill yourself and go straight to Gehenna if you're so keen to serve its King?

He looked at the ring on his flesh hand, the bulbous red gem swirling with pale mist as his mother's shade berated him.

'Still doubt your son, eh mother?' he said, smiling a sickly smile.

You're no son of mine! the disembodied voice spat. His binding spell allowed his mother to convey her thoughts and emotions empathically. *You should have burned years ago – what a pity that friar didn't succeed in bringing you to justice. May he do so this time!*

'I'll rip him apart before he does!' screamed Andragorix. He tended to speak out loud to her, even though all he needed was to think the words. 'I'll drink his blood and chew on his marrow! I'll tear out his eyes and cook them after I've strangled him with his own entrails!'

You are mad, replied his mother coldly. *To think I taught you the clean ways of the Right-Hand Path for you to come to this – drinking your own seed and buggering small boys! You are an ABOMINATION!*

Something snapped in him then and he suddenly started crying. 'Oh mother, I'm sorry!' he sobbed. 'I didn't mean to kill thee, you just make me so *angry!* Why must you anger me so?'

Anger you? Why you've been angry all your life, she sneered. *Couldn't stand up for yourself against the village boys who tormented you, and now you despise the world. You say you'll rule it one day, but you can't even rule yourself! Given up body and soul to gross passions! You are WEAK!*

His sorrow hardened into anger that quickly condensed into a ball of white-hot rage. The wrath of the archdemon Ta'ussuswazelim coursed through him. 'I'LL SHOW YOU!' he screamed. 'I'll show you how weak I am when I'm sitting at Abaddon's right hand and ruling his Kingdom on Earth!'

His mother's ghost sneered again. *You'll never rule anything while you serve another – by all the gods, why don't you unbind me and let me seek my rest?*

'No,' said the warlock, his voice dropping to a sibilant hiss. 'I'll not, mother! I'll keep you here by my side so you can watch my triumph! Now be silent, you wretched whore.'

Picking up the jar he strode over to another counter. It was like the first, only much larger. His alchemical apparatus lay sprawled across it; a convoluted web of glass and wood, silver instruments dotted about it. Pouring the mixture into a shallow dish, he touched the wick with his silver hand and muttered a word in the language of magick, visualising the abstract symbol of flame from the Sorcerer's Script. An orange tongue leapt from his metal fingers and lit the wick beneath the dish.

He felt a wave of weakness washing over him. He probably shouldn't waste his elan using Thaumaturgy to light a burner, but he'd soon have more than enough to keep him going. And he would need it too – there was much to be done.

As the mixture sizzled in the pan, he began to chant the incantation: his weakness increased as he channelled the powers of Alchemy, but he knew well enough to ride it out. When it was near boiling he lifted the pan off with his silver hand and poured the hot mixture back into the jar. Muttering a final few words, he swallowed the contents in one thick glob.

He felt renewed power course through him as the concoction took immediate effect. His limbs almost rippled with vigour and he felt his elan return to him. He moved towards the sucker-shaped exit with a poise and grace that a skilled dancer would have envied.

The lights went out as he left his laboratory, leaving the boy moaning in darkness.

The corridor turned like a snake; it had taken him a while to get used to the Varyans' lack of concern for mortal symmetry, but then the Varyans had been more than mortal. What unearthly beauty they had wrought! Even the benighted latter-day sages had the gumption to call it the Platinum Age – there had been nothing like it since.

But there would be again, and right soon. When he took full control and put his plans into operation, a new era would dawn – an era of hell on earth. A hell he would rule.

The thought of that, and the potion coursing through his veins, brought up a welter of intense emotions. He felt the archdemon Invidia taking him in her cloying embrace, filling him with fierce ambition that would never be quelled until every soul moved according to his will.

The corridor emerged into another chamber. Its ceiling had partly fallen in, providing natural light from the stars above. He only used the chamber at night; he increasingly disliked the sun.

Like his laboratory the chamber followed no geometric shape, the sculpted angels and demons chasing its walls as they intertwined with one another in a stone dance of madness. There were other friezes here too: of strange cityscapes that spurned the architecture of those masons who had come after, buildings that somehow managed to stay upright despite their bizarre forms. Some of them were doubtless scenes from Varya itself, the age-old citadel of the Elder Wizards. He would take up his rightful place there, at the Hour of All's Ending.

For now he had to make do with this lowly ruin: but at least he was getting closer to his birthright.

'One step at a time,' he muttered to himself as he approached the dais at the centre of the chamber and mounted the staircase that coiled around it. The steps were wide and deep and seemed to twist back on themselves... yet somehow conveyed the climber unerringly to the summit. More evidence of the mind-bending sorceries of the Elder Wizards.

Andragorix was well accustomed to the dizzying effect and he hopped up the giant steps two at a time, his limbs galvanised by Alchemy. The Varyans had been tall of stature, taller even than the Northlending nobles he was descended from. Thought of the father who had disowned his illegitimate son caused hatred to burn inside him. It was a hatred he had happily carried over towards all Northlendings. He would be revenged on the whole bloody pack of them! That idiot Ragnar had let him down badly: now was his next chance to deliver up the Kingdom of Northalde. He wouldn't get a third.

In the middle of the dais crouched a statue of a demon, its amorphous body carved to resemble decaying rolls of putrid flesh resting on four thick legs that ended in molluscan feet. Stone eyes set at odd angles peered from all sides of its bloated form. Where its head should have been there sprouted a tentacular maw. The statue was shockingly detailed – a manifestation of Ma'alfecnu'ur, the avatar of corruption and disease. The tentacles were supposed to represent his insidious essence, but Andragorix had found another use for them.

The maw was tilted and clutched a polished silver mirror of unremarkable design. Leaning in, Andragorix breathed on it and muttered the incantation for Scrying, visualising a hawk, an ear and an eye in quick succession. The vapour from his breath swirled on the mirror, becoming a vortex of shimmering quicksilver. From its centre a vision slowly began to take shape, gradually spreading outwards in increasing concentric circles until it covered the surface.

The frosty features of Ragnar appeared before him.

'Well, ocean-tamer, you'd better have good news for me this time,' said Andragorix, staring at him with unmasked contempt.

'I do, my liege,' replied Ragnar, nodding courteously. 'I have found a champion among the Northlanders – Guldebrand Gunnarson is both ruthless and cunning. He already has Jótlund in his grasp and now seeks an alliance with the thegns of Scandia and Utgard against Oldrik Stormrider.'

'Well see he doesn't spend too much time parlaying! I want the Frozen Principalities united under one Magnate – under *our* control – and ready to attack the mainlanders by next spring.'

Again Ragnar nodded. 'The Thegn of Utgard will be readily cowed. The Shield Queen of Scandia will need more persuading, but I am confident she will agree to throw her lot in with us once we make our proposal. With three thegns against him and my sorcery to contend with, not even the Stormrider will be able to resist us.'

'Promises of that nature I've heard before!' snarled Andragorix, feeding on his anger like a draft of coarse wine. 'You had better hold to this one, or there'll be one less warlock to trouble the realms of men!'

'It shall be as you say, my liege,' replied the White Eye. His tone was subdued, his expression deferential, but Andragorix knew better. Half a chance and his understudy would seek to use Enchantment to ensorcell him. But that could never happen, for Andragorix was already bound to a far darker master.

'The King of Gehenna sees all,' Andragorix reminded him. 'You would do well to abide by your own words. Serve me better than you did last time, and you shall have rule over the Frozen Wastes. Fail, and I shall find other uses for you, perhaps as one of my undead.'

'And how go Your Worship's experiments?' asked Ragnar, stilling the flash of anger that crossed his face.

'Well enough,' lied Andragorix. 'Concern yourself with the subjugation of the Ice Thegns – and let me worry about mobilising the dead.'

'It will be as you say, my liege,' replied Ragnar.

'Excellent. Now get thee gone – report back to me at the next quarter of the waxing moon.'

Without waiting for a reply he mouthed another incantation, visualising a closing gate. The mirror shimmered and returned to quicksilver and the mage's face disappeared.

Andragorix repeated the first spell, tapping his silver fingers against the statue's maw. He shouldn't disrespect such a sacred object, but he wasn't in the most patient of moods. As before the mirror shimmered, another face growing from its centre.

'Abrexta, how speed we in Thraxia?' he asked. He felt his loins harden as he looked on the witch's fair features. He would have her – in every way possible – when the time was right.

'My liege,' replied the sorceress in silky tones. 'We are speeding well, though my elan is sorely stretched – I cannot ensorcell many more.'

'Have I not taught you the art to bolster your powers?' snapped Andragorix. 'I give you the tools to get the job done, and all you have for me are complaints!'

The enchantress scowled. 'I like not your tone, Andragorix, and have no wish to bleed small children and mingle their vital juices with mine own.'

Andragorix didn't care for her sarcastic tone. One to watch, this Abrexta – perhaps offering her Thraxia wasn't such a good idea. He could always have her despatched to the Island Realms to rule there instead once the war was over, where she would be well out of the way.

'The Master's teachings are not for the faint-hearted,' he leered. 'Perhaps I have misplaced my faith in you... We shall see! In the meantime, give me your report.'

'King Cadwy has commissioned a fleet to attack the Island Realms,' she said. 'The northern wards are hard pressed – Daxtir is defeated and Gaellen has nigh fallen. After that only Varrogh remains. I'm already suing with the Highlanders for peace in return for the lands they have conquered. But news of the uprising we put down in Umbria has reached the southern wards... we've heard rumours they plan to unite and wage a war of resistance against the King's Fold. I need your help – is it ready yet?'

'Patience, my sweet sorceress,' crowed Andragorix. 'This is no mere mortal I am trying to enthral – such powers have not been harnessed since the Elder Wizards! Rest assured I shall be sending you the help you need soon. The southern Thraxians won't cause you much trouble once they find themselves harried from the rear. That should leave you free to consolidate your grip on power in the King's Fold and focus on the war with the Islanders. When will the fleet be ready?'

'If all things go according to plan, the new fleet should be ready to sail on the autumn tides.'

'That's cutting it a bit fine,' said Andragorix. 'You know well enough how soon the ice comes that far north.'

'Have you an incantation that allows for the swifter crewing and building of ships?' she asked pointedly.

'Very well, but no later!' he spat, wishing he could violate her then and there. He caught the expression on her face.

'What is it now?'

'We've had a complication,' said Abrexta. 'A group of knights was arrested in Ongist, several days ago. They are part of the original party sent out with Lord Braun's son.'

'The one who went to Strongholm and ended up getting involved in the Northlending war?'

Abrexta nodded. Her Scrying had allowed her to spot the knights and track their movements, but without being able to hear them, their purpose had remained uncertain. An audience with the Northlending King probably meant they were seeking military aid against the Highlanders though. What a pity the hedge witch was unversed in Demonology. Andragorix's elan had been too stretched to take care of it himself.

'Yes, what of it?' he asked.

'We've charged him with treason, but he's denied all charges.'

'So have him tried and executed and be done with it. I hardly care if he was guilty or not.'

Abrexta licked her lips. 'We can't actually prove the charges against him, and if I have him executed...'

Her voice trailed off.

'Well?' barked Andragorix.

'The knight who leads the party is one Sir Vertrix, a distinguished veteran and highly thought of at court. If I have him killed out of hand, it could provoke an uprising in Ongist and the rest of the King's Fold. I've already told you I'm stretched to breaking point, and politically we're on a knife-edge up here. Making a truce with the Highlanders is going to be very unpopular, especially after we've let them run amok up north.'

'I thought we'd arranged the antidote to that – a campaign to take back the Thraxians' ancestral homeland on the Islands, to set to rights the banishment of their ancestors?'

'It will be a popular move if we proclaim it in the right way,' Abrexta allowed, 'but you don't appreciate the situation here. I've had all the King's most trusted advisers killed, enthralled, banished or imprisoned. I've made sure he sits by idly while the north falls to the Highlanders. I've had to quash several rebellions already, executing more respected lords and knights along with senior members of the Temple and the Argolian Order. Even if that's all technically happening on the King's orders, there's only so much the people can take. If I send Vertrix and his men to the block without just cause, it could be the final straw... I need more time, to build the fleet and distract the populace with promises of a fresh war. I can't kill him now.'

Andragorix stifled his rage and frustration, forcing himself to think. He felt his temples pounding as the potion's effects reached their peak.

'Very well,' he said after a few moments. 'Keep him and his men under arrest for now. Try to enthral at least one of them if you can – locked up in Ongist and far away from their doomed liege, they shouldn't be able to cause much trouble if you keep a close eye on them.'

'It will be as you say, my liege.'

The witch looked relieved. It galled him to have use such weaklings as thralls, lesser mages who scarcely deserved to be part of his glorious new world order. But he needed them – for now.

'Good, get thee gone. Report back to me at the next quarter.'

He mouthed the closing spell and Abrexta disappeared.

Descending from the dais he was about to head over to his study but changed his mind. Looking at the sorceress had inflamed his loins again: he would fain have something more fleshy than a half-starved boy to sate his appetites. The archdemon Satyrus possessed him, filling him with dark desires.

Making his way through meandering corridors he entered his bedchamber. It was sparsely decorated, save for the intricate Varyan friezes. Those were glorious enough to look at, but Andragorix hankered after more traditional finery – silks and gold and jewels as befitted the future prince of the world. But his master had compelled him to secrecy, until the time was right. It pained him to think that his Wadwos were being wasted butchering woodlanders and hillfolk – he longed to see his army bring back real spoils from burning keeps and smashed castles. Then he would live like the king he was.

Thoughts of wealth faded as he looked upon the chamber's sole occupant, lust for earthly riches giving way to lust for unearthly flesh.

Reclining on a rude bed was a naked woman, her translucent skin glowing over slender curves in the still light of the glowing orbs. She was impossibly beautiful, in a way that no mortal woman ever could be.

'What is your pleasure today, my lord?' asked the Succubus, gazing at him with hooded, exotic-looking eyes. She addressed him directly in the language of magic, using its darker modes that were favoured by demonkind.

'Darker skin,' said Andragorix, walking over to the bed. 'Larger breasts, fuller figure.'

The demon complied, her slim body filling out to accommodate his wishes, the skin deepening until she had the tawny complexion of a Sassanian beauty.

'Very good,' hissed the mage, pulling up his black mantle and mounting the bed. He felt his loins stiffen as she opened her legs and he descended on her. '*Very good…*'

✣ ✣ ✣

When it was over he rolled off the Succubus and walked over to a rough table. It had been pillaged from a mountain village by his Wadwos and was more a block of wood. He tried to ignore it as he helped himself from a jug of wine, throwing in a few pinches of ground Silverweed for good measure. He knocked the drink back, gasping as lights danced at the corners of his eyes and a pleasant buzzing filled his head. He shouldn't mix ordinary intoxicants with magic potions, but it gave him pleasure to do so.

'Chreosoaneuryon, my favourite of the Seven Princes,' he laughed, invoking the archdemon of intemperance. 'I'll see those loyal to me disport themselves unto their very deaths when thy kingdom cometh. At least they'll die with smiles on their faces!'

'My lord was lusty today,' said the Succubus. 'A fine performance, I look forward to your next visit.'

'I'm not interested in your pleasure,' snarled Andragorix. 'Be silent and trouble me no more – I didn't summon and bind you for your conversation.'

Slamming the cup down he stalked from the chamber.

✣ ✣ ✣

Several hours later Andragorix stretched and rose from the pile of scrolls before him. He had copied them diligently from the original, taking pains to make sure the hieratic symbols of the Sorcerer's Script were perfectly represented. Comparatively speaking, that had been the easy part: were it not for the potion he would have passed out as he strived to master the complex symbols, perfecting their pronunciation and visualisation.

Exiting his study he made his way over to the part of the ruin he was using for his latest experiment. Two Wadwos guarded the entrance. Like the rest of the place it didn't follow any particular shape. Whatever door had stood there was long destroyed, but that didn't concern him: the Wadwos were enthralled to him thanks to the powerful gramarye he had copied down and learned.

And to think Abrexta complained of enthralling mortal men. He had never had much use for Enchantment, thinking it more for women, though his mother had taught him the basics. But learning to ensorcell the Wadwos had taxed him, taking long months of diligent study. And now he was trying to enthral something far older and more powerful.

But that was a task for another day. Striding into the chamber he motioned for the Wadwos to enter another next to it.

The chamber was empty save for a rack along the far wall, which contained vials of liquid, a pot of brushes and stirrers and several mixing bowls. The stench of decay permeated the chamber, coming from next door. It had made him gag at first, but as his studies of Necromancy progressed he had become used to it, and then grown to love it.

'Bring me a dozen,' he said, addressing the Woses in their guttural tongue. Learning it had been part of his studies, but fortunately the language was simple and easily mastered.

Andragorix prepared another concoction as the beastmen complied with his command, dragging corpses of hillfolk in differing stages of decomposition from the next chamber and arranging them around the mage in a circular pattern.

When it was done he bent to each one, pouring a drop of black liquid into their mouths as he muttered the necessary incantation. Finally, taking up another mixture he had prepared and a small brush, he painted a hieroglyph on each one's head in blood red. Necromancy was one of the hardest Schools to master, and if one wished to bind the spirits of the dead to their bodies a considerable knowledge of Alchemy was also required, to prepare the constituent body.

Taking up his position in the middle of the corpses he began to recite the incantation he had been studying. He visualised the symbols as he spoke them: a tomb opening; a humanoid figure trapped within a ribcage; Azrael, the Angel of Death, his wings clipped. Raising his hands he began turning slowly, anticlockwise, stopping briefly each time he faced a corpse. It was the Wytching Hour, the best time to cast the spell: powered flowed into him, siphoned from the Other Side. From deep in his psyche, Andragorix felt rather than heard tormented souls shrieking as he tried to drag them back into their rotting bodies.

Over and over he repeated the ritual, turning and reciting the words as he visualised the symbols again and again, trying to picture them perfectly in his mind as the scrolls had instructed. He felt Azrael fighting him from Azhoanarn, the Place of the Dead, where the souls of the unshriven were doomed to roam until the Hour of All's Ending. Shutting his eyes tightly and ignoring the sweat pouring down his slender frame, he pushed harder...

Something gave. Opening his eyes the warlock saw the corpses around him twitching. Repeating the incantation he pushed harder, trying not to get distracted, to keep focused on the visualisations...

One of the corpses slowly sat up. Then another. Andragorix felt himself strained to breaking point. His nose began to bleed and his head started to tremble, feeling as though it might explode at any second.

Harder and harder he pushed...

More corpses sat up. One or two were trying to drag themselves to their feet. His whole body trembled. The pain was unbearable.

With a gasp he collapsed, his mind letting go of the symbols. His link with the Other Side was severed. The corpses slumped back to the ground, lifeless.

From where he lay Andragorix tried to give vent to a scream of frustration, but all that came out was a gasp. Motioning to the Wadwos he ordered one to help him up while the other dragged the bodies back into the other room.

'Too... many,' he stuttered, speaking to himself more than the Wose that pulled him up like a rag doll. 'Can't manage more than six. What a fell army.'

The Wadwo took him back to his room. Ignoring the Succubus, he collapsed on the bed and fell into a coma-like sleep.

✢ ✢ ✢

Hours later Andragorix left his chambers and made his way over to the main exit. Passing through the asymmetrical doorway he ignored the Wadwos guarding it as he emerged into a vast crater. It was open to the skies; overhead the stars were beginning to fade, sucked up by the encroaching dawn. The floor was strewn with huge fragments from the original building whose fractured basement he now occupied; he paid little heed to the broken chunks of alien architecture as he made his way over to a vast grate on the other side of the crater.

The grate was the size of a great hall of men. Two more Wadwos guarded it, though they would be able to do little if the magic binds that held the thing below should fail.

'How is our guest – sleeping?'

The Wadwo grunted in the affirmative.

Squatting down beside the grill the warlock gazed between the gigantic bars at the juddering form beneath, its snores sending a great rumbling up through the thick stone floor. Satisfying himself that all was well, he nodded and returned to his chambers, anxious to avoid the first touch of dawn.

Enough of Necromancy for a while: tomorrow he would turn his energies to Enchantment, much as he despised it. He could not yet raise the dead in numbers, but if he could master the necessary incantation he would send one foe with the power of an army to trouble the realms of men.

⊷ CHAPTER XVI ⊷

Of Beasts and Men

The morning clouds rubbed their giant backs together, deepening to dark grey as they threatened a summer squall. Sir Braxus shifted uncomfortably in the humidity, readjusting his hauberk and tabard. He'd taken advantage of their brief pause the previous day to take them off, for the first time since leaving Salmor. The thought of bathing his face and hands in one of the Girdle's many fountains seemed already a distant one as its mistress bade the seven of them farewell.

'Goodbye and good luck,' she said, staring at them impassively with her strange red eyes as she stood before the cave where they had first met her. 'You're going to need it, but if the prophecies prove true then the gods should favour you.' She looked at Adelko and Vaskrian as she said this, though Braxus couldn't fathom what she meant by that.

Witches. They were all alike, when it came down to it. He didn't think this one was altogether much different from Abrexta, judging by everything he'd heard about her.

'Thank you for your help,' replied Horskram, keeping things diplomatic. 'We'll do everything in our power to use it to destroy our mutual foe – and may the Prophet be with us!'

Was it his imagination or had the old monk emphasised the word 'prophet' in response to her invocation of the pagan gods? This was a strange alliance and no mistake – the sooner it was done, the better.

Sir Torgun stepped forward. Braxus had a sinking feeling the diplomacy was about to come to an abrupt end.

'I shall not deny that you have helped us, and given us food and shelter and tended our wounds,' said the towering knight. 'But know this – the White Valrayvn still holds you responsible for the deaths of two of its knights. We shall not let that deed go unaccounted for.'

The Earth Witch's lip curled in a half-sneer. 'Return if you can and seek justice as you see fit, by all means,' she said. 'But something tells me you shall not tread a path of vengeance back here, though both your roads shall be dark and bloody.'

Sir Aronn glowered and moved a gauntleted hand to his sword hilt.

'What mean you by that?' he snarled, but Torgun put a restraining hand on his arm.

'Only time will tell,' she contented herself with saying, before looking away. 'You must leave now. Burrow will show you out.'

The squirrel appeared from beneath the skirts of her leafy robe and scurried past them, turning and cocking its head. The creature was looking at them expectantly.

'Let us be gone,' muttered Horskram, turning to go.

Braxus was last to leave. He was just following the others out of the clearing when the Earth Witch called him back.

'A quick word, sir knight, before you leave.'

He turned and approached her, rather more quickly than he felt was right.

She stared at him inscrutably, a smile playing on her lips. 'There is much of my kin in you, Braxus of Gaellen,' she said. 'Your blood traces back to the Exiled Clans... true island folk.'

'Tell me something I don't know,' he replied affably. Was she *flirting* with him? She looked old, yet young at the same time. He felt his loins stir in spite of himself. He hadn't been with a woman since leaving Salmor – a long time for someone like him. Why, he had even been staring at Kyra yesterday, and she was no beauty.

The Earth Witch reached into the folds of her bizarre robes. 'Perhaps in happier times we might have known each other better,' she said in a voice that was strangely neutral. 'I want you to take this. Call it a token of... a partnership that never was.'

'I could always come back after we're done,' he said, smiling broadly and feeling suddenly giddy. A desire to have the sorceress right then and there shot him with a jolt.

'Maybe you will,' she said, still smiling as she handed him her gift. He stared at it. A bronze brooch, shaped like a round shield, with an embossed silver hawk on it. 'I think you should wear this on your cloak, sir knight. It matches the colours of your tabard.'

'I... yes, certainly,' he replied, snatching the proffered brooch as though it were a king's ransom. 'I'll wear it at all times!'

Her smile crooked a little. 'Good, see that you do.' She suddenly looked past him up the trail. 'I think your companions are leaving you behind,' she said. 'You'd better go and catch up with them.'

'Yes, I better had!' he exclaimed, turning without another word and striding up the path. He was still clutching the brooch tightly when he drew level with Vaskrian.

'Everything all right?' his squire asked him.

'Aye...' replied the knight, feeling confused, though he didn't know exactly why. 'Of course. Now let's get out of this place, while we still can!'

Even as he was saying that, his hands were reaching up to fasten the brooch to his cloak. He had the strangest feeling that they weren't his hands at all.

✢ ✢ ✢

Burrow led them back to the clearing that overlooked the waters of the Girdle. It was the same as they had left it. No new craters marred its edge, and everything appeared much as it had when they first entered. Adelko had been half expecting to come under attack by night, to wake to the sound of trees erupting into balls of fire as Andragorix sent Saraphi to torment his foe, but the night had been strangely still and calm – though certainly not uneventful for him.

He had barely had time to take stock of his strange vision. Already it was fading in clarity, though he knew it would linger in his psyche, a perpetual source of food for thought. His strange conversation with the Earth Witch crowded at the forefront of his mind instead, particularly her parting words.

Many truths, Adelko, many truths – and often we see only what we want to see. Your job from now on is to try and get past that, if you can.

The bridge was still there. Burrow stopped before them and cocked his head towards it, before scurrying off into the undergrowth. Gazing at it and mulling over the Earth Witch's counsel put the novice in mind of a question he had been meaning to ask his mentor.

'So when you crossed this bridge the first time, after you said those Psalms, was it a miracle?' he asked Horskram as they crossed back over.

'No, though for now it will be in our interests to let yon knights believe it was,' said Horskram in a low voice. 'Technically a miracle would be petitioning the Almighty to revoke the laws of nature on one's behalf.'

'Like what sorcerers do when they tap the powers of the Unseen using Thaumaturgy?' queried Adelko. 'When Andragorix conjures up his fire spirits for instance?'

'Just so. I didn't do that – in fact my prayers did just the opposite. They channelled the Almighty's powers to reverse the unnatural alterations the Earth Witch made to this forest with her witcheries.'

Horskram's voice hardened at the last word. He clearly had not relished the alliance or any of the past day's events. All save one that was.

'You seemed so happy when you did it,' said Adelko.

'Aye, I was!' replied his mentor with rare levity. 'The Psalm of Gramarye's Quenching is a joyous passage, a celebration of the Redeemer's might over all the misguided teachings of the Unseen. To master it and feel its sacred power coursing through your soul is a rare privilege.'

'The Unseen – by that you mean the Archangels as well as the Archdemons,' said Adelko, remembering the Earth Witch's words.

His mentor's face darkened. 'Not even the Archangels are all-wise or all-knowing, Adelko, as we have discussed on previous occasions.'

And perhaps neither is the Almighty Himself, Adelko longed to reply. But he kept that thought private – he didn't think it wise that his mentor should learn of his conversation with the Earth Witch.

'I'd never heard it before you spoke it,' he contented himself with saying.

'That is because few know it,' said Horskram. 'Even most adepts seldom master it.'

'So... I imagine you'll be using it, against Andragorix?'

Horskram nodded as they reached the other side and waited for the others to join them. Kyra took the lead now, taking them back into the forest and steering a course south-west. Their next destination was the resistance camp she'd spoken of – without the help of Madogan any attack on the Wadwo fort guarding the path to the Warlock's Crown would be futile.

'I'll use it as well as I can,' replied his mentor when they were on their way again. 'Though it was not enough to defeat him utterly the last time we met.'

Adelko sensed a sadness in the old monk. He guessed the death of Sir Belinos of Runcymede, the pious knight who had helped him against Andragorix last time, still weighed heavily on his conscience.

'Be of good cheer, Master Horskram,' he ventured. 'At least this time we have the blood of the Redeemer to aid us.'

Horskram's face darkened again as he replied: 'And even that may be cancelled out by his increase in power, though we should be safe enough from his demonic servitors thanks to the succour it gives us.'

Another question occurred to Adelko.

'I thought the Golem was a demon,' he said. 'Why didn't the Redeemer's blood help us then?'

'Perhaps it would have – we didn't have to find out, Reus be praised,' replied Horskram. 'But the Redeemer's blood is at its most powerful against demons in bare form. A demon bound to an earthly substance is harder to turn – the ways of magic and the means to fight them are not always easily grasped. That is why we cannot rely solely on its power alone – we will have to work hard at our recitals too!'

'... we? But I don't know the Psalm of Gramarye's Quenching... and you said most adepts never master it. I'm just a novice.'

Horskram turned to look at him, his blue eyes twinkling in a stray ray of sunlight as they pushed through a thicket behind Kyra.

'Correct on all three counts,' he said. 'But I will not expect you to master it, or even to learn it. When we confront Andragorix, I will lead the recital. You must join your voice to it as best you can – I shall need your elan! Every bit counts.'

'So why didn't you bring more friars with you? When we stopped at Ørthang you could have enlisted more support.'

'You are forgetting the need for secrecy. I can't have everyone in the Order knowing of our mission.'

'Why not?' Adelko called after him, stopping short as his habit got caught in the thicket. 'Why always this need for secrecy?'

'The Fallen One's servants are everywhere,' said Horskram, without slowing. 'The fewer who know of what we're up to, the better!'

Disentangling himself, Adelko stumbled after his mentor. He considered pressing him for more answers, but his sixth sense told him a familiar story. The adept was done talking for the nonce, and that meant no more questions.

✠ ✠ ✠

'Who goes there?'

Sir Torgun brandished his sword, angling his body to present a more difficult target. He missed his kite shield, left in splinters by the fight with beastmen.

Disappointment fell on him like a wet shroud as five woodlanders entered the clearing in response to his challenge, clutching their long yew bows. Dawn wasn't far off and he had taken a double turn on watch; he rarely needed more than four hours' sleep a night and wasn't tired.

On the contrary, he burned with energy.

Fury at the unavenged deaths of his brethren still consumed him. He didn't like getting angry: it led to conduct unbefitting a chivalrous knight, so he needed something to channel it. Another fight would do handsomely – preferably with a mortal foe.

But there was no sense in fighting these honest folk, especially not if they were natural allies against the unnatural foe they marched to face.

'Well met, sirrah,' said one of them, eyeing his surcoat warily. 'What brings raven knights t'Argael?'

'We seek your leader, one Madogan,' replied the knight, nudging Aronn awake with his boot. 'One of your folk guides us to him.'

'Oh aye?' asked the woodsman as the five of them edged forwards, fanning out to surround him. They still had not let go of their bows, and arrows remained nocked to strings. A cowardly way to approach combat, but you could only expect so much from commoners and Torgun knew better than to judge such men harshly.

'We mean you no harm,' the knight said, sheathing his sword and relaxing his stance.

Sir Aronn had pulled himself to his feet and was blinking sleep away. 'Go and wake the huntress,' said Torgun softly. 'Probably best if she talks to them.'

Favouring the woodfolk with a surly glance, Aronn did so.

'Kyra,' said the leader when she had been fetched. 'Sorry fer sneakin' up on ye like that, canna be too careful nowadays.'

'Think nowt on it, Rafe,' replied the huntress. 'Ye did the right thing. Where's Madogan? Is he near? We've a tale fer 'im an no mistake.'

'He's got us camped towards the outskirts of the forest,' answered Rafe. 'We've a tale fer you an' all. We'll take ye to him.'

✤ ✤ ✤

Shadows were lengthening through the forest by the time they reached another stockaded clearing. It was larger than any Sir Torgun had seen yet; an outer perimeter had been hastily constructed around the original set of walls. The young knight cast a keen eye over the defences. It was no castle, but the woodfolk had done what they could with the resources at their disposal. The inhabitants of the Argael had long enjoyed independence from either realm at its borders, and they guarded it fiercely.

Rafe whistled at the guards on the outer wall, who let the drawbridge down. It opened inwards, straddling a ditch lined with stakes surrounding the inner wall. The gate was hauled open for them as they marched into the compound.

There were no dwellings, only four long low buildings that Torgun guessed doubled up as storehouses and barracks. Standing in the middle of these was a group of woodlanders, holding close conversation. They parted as the newcomers approached.

Sir Torgun spotted the leader straight away. Something in his bearing marked him out. He was taller than the others, with blond hair and a close-cropped beard and moustache, handsome enough after his own fashion. The woodlanders were a mix of Vorstlending, Northlending and the ancient tribes who had been there before the First Reavers. It looked as though Madogan had a fair streak of Northlending in him. Sir Torgun hoped that would make him easier to deal with.

Madogan nodded at the new arrivals. A scouting party had encountered them during the afternoon, so their arrival wasn't a surprise.

'Welcome back, Kyra,' he said, ignoring his guests. 'aven't seen you in a month o' Restdays.'

'I've brought us some 'elp,' replied the huntress. 'And I've some news fer you.'

'I've some news fer *you*,' said Madogan. 'We've found the Woses, where they're based. They're not even in the woods.'

Kyra looked surprised. 'How did ye ken?'

'Dunna ken if ye've met Ratko,' he said, introducing a shifty-looking woodlander standing next to him. 'Sez he found their fortress, on the outskirts o' the forest, a day away from 'ere.'

Horskram cleared his throat loudly. 'Perhaps some introductions might be appropriate?' he said pointedly.

Madogan turned as if noticing him for the first time. 'Madogan Steadyhands, at yer service,' he said brusquely. 'An' you?'

Horskram introduced them.

'That's a motley band an' no mistake,' said Madogan. 'So what brings such men to our troubled lands?' He had returned his grey eyes to Kyra.

'Probably best if we talk to you in private,' she said.

One of the woodlanders spoke up at that. He was an ill-favoured looking fellow, with a face like an anvil and eyes that squinted meanly.

'Why should we trust this wanderin' slattern?' he spat. 'Always got to do it yer way, 'aven't ye Kyra?'

'Aye, I have,' she replied. 'Got a problem wi' that, Baldo?'

'Aye, I do,' said Baldo. 'Had a problem wi' you ever since ye killed yer 'usband, my cousin. Ye should've hanged long time ago.'

There were some mutterings at that. Torgun could tell some were on Kyra's side, but most seemed to sympathise with Baldo. His instincts already told him whose side he was on. His hand moved deftly to the hilt of his sword as Kyra rounded on her cousin.

'There's good reason why I didna hang, as well ye ken!' she yelled. 'Ereth Hunter was a womanising drunk who beat me black an' blue, till I put a stop to it. The reeve found me not guilty o' murder ten summers ago, and that should be an end to it!'

Baldo's eyes narrowed even further, if that was possible. 'Found ye not guilty, yet banished ye from yer community,' he growled. 'I'll not be a party to any ploy o' yours, Woses or no Woses.'

He spat on the ground and turned to leave.

'I suggest you apologise to yon woman before you leave.'

Sir Torgun's words were quiet and calm, and all the more dangerous for that. Dozens of pairs of eyes turned to look at him uncertainly. Horskram's rolled as he resigned himself to another conflict. But Sir Torgun was damned if he would let a woman, even a common one, stand abused.

'Begging yer pardon, sir knight, I meant no offence,' said Baldo, taking in the knight's huge frame.

'Really?' said Sir Torgun mildly. 'It seems to me you did. Chastising a woman who has been exonerated by court of law is not acceptable. Though the King's law doesn't apply here, I am still sworn to oppose injustice in all its forms. Your behaviour just now was as uncouth as it is unfair. Therefore I think it behoves you to apologise.'

Baldo blinked. Kyra was staring at the knight incredulously. Torgun guessed she wasn't used to having members of the nobility speak up for her. Or speak to her at all, come to that. But as far as he was concerned justice was for everyone, not just the high-born.

'It be... what?' replied Baldo, looking perplexed now. The word 'behoved' obviously wasn't in his vocabulary. Communicating with common folk could be tricky.

Madogan, who had said nothing but watched the proceedings with an amused smile, chose that moment to intervene.

'I think, Baldo, what the knight is sayin' is ye should say sorry, afore he cracks yer thick skull apart.' Laughter erupted around the compound. This Madogan was clearly well liked by his men. That boded well: it was important to know one had charismatic leaders on one's side going into battle.

'The Code of Chivalry forbids me to duel with a commoner in any case,' Sir Torgun reassured him. 'Therefore, if you really will not apologise, I suggest a bout of fisticuffs. I'll tie one hand behind my back to make it a fairer fight.'

Sir Aronn and Madogan were both grinning broadly. Horskram exchanged glances with Braxus and shook his head. Baldo turned pale and took a step back. 'No... no, that wilna be necessary, sir knight...' he stuttered. 'Kyra, I'm sorry fer what I said. It wilna happen again.' He stumbled against a tree stump and nearly fell over. More laughter filled the clearing.

'That's alright,' said Kyra, laughing with the rest. 'It's not yer fault ye're a born fool with a walnut fer a brain. Now be off wi' ya, we need to speak wi' Madogan.'

Baldo turned and practically ran for the nearest building.

'Now I ken I can trust ye,' said Madogan, smiling at the knight. 'The ravens 'ave a reputation fer justice, and we'll be needin' all the good fighters we can get. Follow me if ye will, sir knight, an' tell us what ye know.'

✛ ✛ ✛

'We've about an' 'undred and forty men an' women ready to fight,' said Madogan, leaning on his bow.

His face was set grim in the light of the charcoal braziers. Vaskrian couldn't blame him – they were doing their best to hammer out a good battle plan, but it looked for all the world as though this wasn't going to be a fair fight. But then what was fair about the world? He pushed away his gloomy thoughts and forced himself to concentrate as Madogan went on.

'Better marksmen ye'll not find in the Free Kingdoms, but at close range it'll be a slaughterhouse an' no mistake.'

'We'll take care of the fighting at close quarters,' said Sir Torgun. 'Just place as many archers as you can on the ridge overlooking the fort. We'll goad the beastmen out to fight us, then you pick them off with poisoned arrows. Because of their size they should present easy targets even when we're in a melee with them.'

Kyra had already broken out the Wose's Bane that the Earth Witch had given them. There was enough for two or three arrows per archer, plus their own blades.

'Aye, but we've no idea 'ow many o' them are in there,' said Madogan, still looking deadly serious. 'An' yer only six – countin' the Vorstlendin' knight an' this foreign freesword – plus some forty o' the stronger lads I'll send wi' ye, the ones that 'ave a chance o' fightin' hand t'hand. Woses 'ave the strength o' two men at least, chances are the odds won't favour ye.'

'Then you'd better shoot straight, and you'd better shoot fast!' said Sir Aronn. 'If what yon woodland trader says is true, they'll have to cover several hundred paces of broken ground to reach us, with little in the way of cover. That should give you time to even up those odds before they close on us.'

Vaskrian fingered the hilt of his fine new sword. He'd need its workmanship right soon by the looks of things. The Earth Witch's words returned to him. *You too have a part to play...* He should be overjoyed. He'd always thirsted for glory, now it looked as though the Almighty Himself had marked him out for something big.

Yet no man shall give you a title for your deeds...

That thought filled him with despondency. Was that his fate, to take part in a great quest and never get credit for it? Typical, just typical. Life wasn't fair. The rest of the war counsel faded into the background as he sank into a melancholy mood. He was bored of listening to talk in any case. He just wanted to get the next battle over with: another thankless task set before him.

Perhaps he'd quit service after the battle was done, take a job as a freesword. Maybe he wasn't destined for title and glory, but at least he could earn a decent living selling his blade to the highest bidder. He sighed at the thought. Frustrated ambition was a bitter draught to swallow and no mistake.

Reus damn the Earth Witch and her unearthly ways! What man in his right mind would ask to know his future?

✢ ✢ ✢

'Look!' Anupe caught Balthor's sleeve, gesturing towards the lip of the Argael. Peering in that direction he could see groups of lithe-looking bowmen dressed in green emerging from the trees.

'They've come!' she said excitedly. 'Three days as he said – perhaps I was wrong to suspect our friend.'

'How many?' asked Sir Balthor. It was getting dark, but there was still just enough light to see by. They had spent a frustrating two days camped out on the ridge, struggling to assess the foe as best they could. Judging by its comings and goings, and movements within the compound, there had to be at least two hundred beastmen garrisoned there.

Of their captives he'd only seen one sign, and that had been enough: what looked like the corpses of two women, their blood-spattered bodies dragged from a low building at the far end of the compound and burned on a pyre. He'd guessed they had just given birth to Wadwos, an experience few if any could survive.

The thought of the same thing being done to Her Ladyship and her friend made him sick. He yearned for combat, the chance to rescue them from such a horrid fate.

Now that chance had come.

'Well over a hundred I think,' said the Harijan, her quick eyes providing the answer to his question. Balthor felt cold fear clutch his innards with icy hands, his hot excitement receding at its touch. He knew from hard experience that wouldn't be nearly enough.

Then he caught a glint of dying sunlight on armour.

'Looks like they have some knights with them,' he mused, some hope returning to him.

'Some of yours?' asked Anupe.

'No,' he replied. 'I can't see their coats of arms at this range, but the colours aren't familiar. Let's get down there and find out who they are.'

It took them several hours to scrabble back down from the ridge, clambering over the hard knuckled terrain by light of stars and moon. Balthor glanced upwards several times at the latter, but of course it was nowhere near full yet.

A guard posted on the woodlanders' camp challenged them as they arrived. They had set up on a stretch of broken slopes just where the forest's edge petered out into rocks and shrubs. Glancing up at the fortress he could see torchlight flaring on its ramparts, but if the waking Wadwos had seen their attackers, they gave no indication of it.

'I am Sir Balthor Lautstimme, Dulsinor's foremost knight, sworn sword to the Eorl of Graukolos,' he declaimed. 'I sent my employee, one Ratko of the Argael, to fetch you.'

He heard muttering. There were hardly any lights across the camp; an amorphous mass of silhouetted forms were all that told of the woodland force.

'A'right,' came the response. 'Come through. We've a dozen arrows trained on ye, so dunna think o' tryin' nowt.'

A sentry escorted them to the middle of the camp. A steady night breeze was blowing, billowing up Balthor's surcoat. He hoped there would be none of that tomorrow, it would be bad for the archers.

As his eyes adjusted to the lack of light he could see more than half the company were making ready to march, bows and quivers slung across backs and cloaks wrapped tightly around them. Someone struck tinder to taper and his eyes blinked as the sudden light blinded him momentarily.

When his vision cleared he found himself surrounded by a motley band of adventurers. Two Argolian friars, a richly-dressed knight accompanied by a lean squire, Ratko and another pair of woodlanders, two more knights wearing chequered cloaks, Northlending by the looks of them... He recognised the older monk.

Horskram of Vilno had stayed at Graukolos on several occasions. Balthor felt sure he didn't like the haughty secretive monk, who had rarely deigned to speak to him. He also recognised the emblem on the Northlending knights' surcoats. What in Reus' name was the Order of the White Valravyn doing this far south? King Freidheim's sworn knights seldom left his Dominions, never mind Northalde.

He introduced himself formally and the men staring at him did likewise. They spoke in Decorlangue now, the common tongue used between high-born peoples throughout the Free Kingdoms. He translated into Vorstlending for the benefit of Anupe, inwardly cursing. He hated foreign languages, why couldn't everybody just speak bloody Vorstlending?

'My thanks for coming,' he said, addressing Madogan in his own tongue when the introductions were done. The high speech of Old Thalamy would be quite beyond a commoner.

'My thanks fer spyin' on 'em fer us,' replied the woodland chieftain affably. Balthor didn't care for the commoner's tone. 'How many d'ye reckon are up there?'

'Hard to say for sure,' ventured Balthor. 'At least two hundred.'

The woodlander whistled. Horskram translated for his foreign companions, who exchanged grim looks.

'Look, what are you doing here?' Balthor asked Horskram, who spoke his own language fluently. 'What concern is it to a bunch of Northlendings and a Thraxian what happens in the Argael on the Vorstlending side of the border?'

'That tale would be over long in the telling,' replied the monk. 'Suffice to say for now we are very much on your side.'

Madogan gave a low whistle and the woodlanders began marching off, their inky forms moving against the craggy slopes as they began the ascent towards the ridge.

'We attack at dawn, so best to get some rest now,' said Sir Torgun. Stepping forwards he clasped hands with Sir Balthor. 'It will be an honour to fight alongside Dulsinor's greatest knight.'

Balthor returned the grip, suddenly feeling a little unsure of himself. So far as he could tell the Northlending wasn't being sarcastic. He could barely admit it even to himself, but next to Sir Torgun he felt like a child.

'Aye,' he said, recovering his composure. 'There'll be a bloody morning and no mistake.'

The woodlander holding the taper extinguished it, and Balthor went by starlight to find a space to rest as best he could.

✤ ✤ ✤

A cowl of brooding clouds covered the rising sun as the archers took up their positions. Sir Balthor hastily ran a whetstone across his blade before joining the foreign knights who would be his allies in the coming conflict.

Sir Torgun had briefed him of the battle plan over a snatched breakfast in the pre-dawn light. It sounded simple enough, but then oftentimes simple strategies were all it took to win the day. Sir Balthor fervently hoped this would be one of those days. He glanced at his blade, but it showed no signs of the Wose's Bane. He supposed that was a good thing: hopefully it should make the Wadwos even more likely to take the bait.

Madogan gave the order and his men dipped their arrows in the makeshift braziers before them, then drew the flaming shafts to their lips. Did some of those burning arrow points tremble slightly as they pointed accusingly at the leaden skies? He could hardly blame the commoners if so: even noblemen of courage would quail before such a foe. The thought of poor Sir Rufus flashed through his mind, his sightless eyes fixed in terror as they peered from his mangled corpse.

'Fire!' The command was appropriately worded. Balthor prayed no such thing would be caused by the volley. He wasn't here to rescued the charred corpses of high-born maidens.

The flaming arrows curled a graceful arc, their trails blazing across the grey firmament before dipping down into the compound like a vicious claw. Many shafts lodged in the walls, but some made it over the ramparts, which appeared to be unmanned. It was too far to hear if the Wadwos were discomfited; perched on its rock-strewn slope, the fortress stared impassively down at its attackers.

Madogan repeated the command and another fiery wave crested the hills. Sir Balthor glanced nervously up at the ridge overlooking the fortress. The bulk of the woodlanders lined it, crouched down to conceal themselves as best they could.

A third volley fell on the fortress. A few tendrils of smoke could be seen, wafting up above the wooden walls. Sir Balthor prayed for the damsels' safety. No winds disturbed the smoky wreathes as they ascended to the stony heavens: at least his prayers on that count had been answered.

A flash of movement came from the fortress. Its gate creaked slowly open.

'They've taken the bait!' cried Sir Torgun, who appeared to have assumed command. 'Switch arrows now!'

Madogan repeated the command and the woodlanders knocked arrows dipped in Wose's Bane to their bows. On the ridge the others could be seen doing likewise. The ridge wasn't deep but it was long enough to fit the hundred men and women who lined its rocky lip. Balthor held his breath and returned his gaze to the fortress.

They began to emerge, in an orderly column two abreast.

'They're in contempt of us,' remarked Sir Braxus. 'They think we can't harm them from such a distance.'

'It's only their lust for blood that draws them out,' said Madogan. 'That'll be their downfall.'

Or you hope as much, thought Sir Balthor, minding the commoner's shaking voice. He raised the shield he'd taken from Sir Rufus and brandished his sword. Let the woodfolk have their turn with their bows; good strong knights would finish the work with cold steel. Well, cold steel and poison for monsters.

The Wadwos had chosen their spot for a fort well. Perched atop a flat shelf of land, it overlooked the only pass up into the mountains for leagues. The rocky hills that stretched up to meet it flattened out, giving it the perfect vantage spot.

As the Wadwos drew towards its edge and he saw how they planned to make use of that advantage, his heart quickened.

'Hold steady!' cried Sir Torgun, also spotting it. 'Madogan, give the order now!'

'Release!'

Another rain of shafts arced up and down towards the beastmen. They did not even try to avoid them as they hurtled down towards them, but stepped over to the lip of rock and let go of their burden.

There were some forty in the sally. Each one clutched a round rock the size of a man's chest. Letting these go the white-faced creatures gave a unified yell as they watched them tumble down towards their attackers.

The arrows found their mark just then. Half the beastmen dropped, convulsing as the poison took effect. The other half began moving back towards the gate but were struck down by another volley from the archers on the ridge. Not all the bowmen up there were aiming outside the fortress. He guessed more of the beastmen were assembled in the compound.

The first sally was wiped out, but that was small consolation to their killers as dozens of boulders crashed down the slopes towards them.

'Down!' yelled Madogan. 'Flatten yourselves to the ground!'

Not all the woodlanders had the presence of mind to obey his order. Several screamed as they suddenly shot backwards, their bodies transformed into bloody masses of bone and flesh wrapped around great balls of rock. Not all those who obeyed in time were lucky either: a few unfortunates were crushed into the hard rock as they lay. When the surviving company rose there were scarcely more than thirty left.

Another sally of Woses came pouring out of the gate, moving swiftly now. Pausing to hurl more rocks down the slopes, they drew weapons and came loping down in the wake of their tumbling phalanx of stone. This second attack was too swift to give them time to fire another volley.

Pressing himself behind a narrow dip in the rock, Balthor tensed as another boulder crashed off it just inches above his head, careening upwards on the rebound before landing a few feet downwards from him and continuing its descent towards the line of trees below him.

Looking up he saw at least fifty Wadwos pouring down towards them, their horrible ululating cries filling the air between them.

Reus dammit, why weren't the others on the ridge giving them another volley? Then he had his answer. The winds had started blowing. Hard. Glancing at the ridge he saw several archers plummeting off it as they were swept to their deaths by what looked like flying tornadoes. Those that weren't being menaced directly had no hope of a clear shot in the suddenly fierce winds.

'Battle formation!' cried Sir Torgun. 'They're nearly on us!'

The beleaguered woodlanders got to their feet. Many were trembling visibly.

'You heard the man!' shouted Madogan. 'Do as he says!'

A thin line of some twenty five woodsmen prepared to receive attack. Sir Balthor stood at the forefront with the other knights and the sinewy looking squire, who was obviously hell-bent on making some kind of a name for himself.

A horde of beastmen twice their number and nearly twice their size hurtled down the hills towards them...

'Now!' cried Sir Torgun. Madogan echoed his command in his own tongue, and all of them flattened themselves to the ground again. The beastmen tried to check themselves and pick off the prone targets, but the laws of nature were against them. Their heavy forms crashed onwards, staggering as they struggled to right themselves and turn to face the enemy that was now behind them.

As one they rose and tore down towards the beastmen, striking and gouging at their legs and torsos, taking full advantage of the sudden height and initiative their unorthodox tactic had gifted them. Some two dozen beastmen went down, convulsing horribly. The others regrouped and began lashing about them, spattering blood far and wide as their giant weapons found flesh and bone.

Screaming his family war-cry, Sir Balthor lost himself in the fury of battle. An anarchic tapestry of white and red seemed to envelop him like the work of some mad artist as he plunged himself into the fray. All thought of tactics was gone. He laid about him like a madman himself, leaving it to the archangel Ezekiel to decide whether he should live or die. The winds whipped furiously around him, the unnatural weather seeming to echo his unbridled battle rage.

✠ ✠ ✠

Adelko squatted on the large flat-topped boulder they had picked for a vantage spot, silently mouthing words from the *Holy Book of Psalms and Scripture*. The first volleys had been fired, though from where they were he could not tell if the fortress had been affected. He and Horskram were positioned to the southwest of their comrades; from there they had a clearer view of the ridge, but between them and the fortress the rocky land surged upwards and inwards from the path it guarded before cutting back on itself sharply. They were positioned just at the tip of that point, guaranteeing them some security from the Wadwos. It wouldn't have been a good spot for archers or fighting, but it was perfect for keeping an eye on one's allies and intervening with sacred words of prayer if needed.

And needed they were, before long.

'Just as I expected, a timely intervention from our sorcerous quarry,' said Horskram, indulging a ribald turn of phrase. 'Get up, Adelko, and summon your fortitude. It's time for us to get involved.'

It was true enough. The Aethi had coalesced out of nowhere, just above the ridge. He could discern the faintest of humanoid forms within the tornadoes that suddenly assailed the archers, sending some to screaming deaths and scattering the shafts of the rest like twigs caught up in a gale.

Taking a deep breath, he joined his voice to Horskram's as he began reciting, focusing on the words on the page and his master's psyche simultaneously:

Spirits of the Other Side
Thou hast crossed the great divide

Set by Him who made the gales
That sweep across the glades and dales!

Spirits from beyond the rent
'Tis He commands thee to relent
Still your stormy voices keen
Share silence with thy lords Unseen!

He could feel the spirits fighting him, struggling to ignore the divine ordinance he and his mentor now invoked. The Aethi continued to envelop the woodlanders in swirling clusters, sweeping several more off the ridge. Pushing the spectacle from his mind, he pressed on with the Psalm:

Spirits of the Other Side
By He who sends the winds from high
To bring the rains that nourish seed
I command thee cease thy screed!

Spirits from beyond the rent
Thy trespass 'gainst Him now repent
End this stormy ruinous lust
Or see thy breath choke in the dust!

His soul and Horskram's intertwined, becoming one and not one, separate and consubstantial; acting together in concert as one entity, yet not the same. It was one of the great contradictory mysteries of their Order, but Adelko had little time to ponder it as they pushed, their words bolstered by a growing spiritual fortitude. The air spirits receded, giving the woodlanders a breathing space as they bent their essences to combating the words sent to banish them:

Spirits of the Other Side
Return across the great divide
Despoil no more the fair wide lands
That Reus gave to mortal man!

Spirits from beyond the rent
By unclean powers thou wert sent
Pay no heed to warlock's call
Obey the laws of the Lord of All!

Now the Aethi were weaving frantically amongst one another, conjoining and separating in the blinking of an eye as they struggled to abjure the sacred recital. The winds they commanded began to disperse, losing their cogency as they dispersed and flurried in all directions.

Adelko felt beads of sweat collect on his forehead as he and his mentor repeated the litany...

✣ ✣ ✣

Sir Balthor stepped back from his freshest corpse, sucking in lungfuls of air as he thanked Ezekiel for the briefest of respites. All around him was mayhem. Corpses of beastmen and woodlanders quilted the uneven ground, though it was obvious that the latter outnumbered the former. All the woodfolk were dead save for Madogan and a couple of the strongest of them. The Wadwos crowded around them, gore-drenched weapons raised high. The foreign fighters were still alive, though probably not for much longer. Sir Balthor had just enough time to shed the shattered remnants of his shield and grip his sword in both hands as two beastmen lunged at him...

The foremost arched its back, crying out as it fell to the ground convulsing. An arrow sprouted from its back. The second glanced towards the ridge as another shaft buried itself in its shoulder.

More arrows fell around them, coming like a long-wished for deluge in time of drought. Beastmen fell to the ground as the poisoned tips worked their natural magic. It was only then that Balthor realised the wind had dropped. Just above the ridge the tornadoes had coagulated into a whorling miasma of silvery air, the once-humanoid shapes within them congealing into one another and losing all semblance of form.

'Ezekiel be praised!' he muttered, though he wasn't sure the avatar of just war was an appropriate archangel to invoke.

The others were exchanging glances, leaning exhaustedly against each other as they paused to catch their breath back. The Woses were breaking ranks, some of them lumbering back towards the fort while others crashed down towards the cover of the trees. Anything to escape the deadly shafts that now assailed them.

The archers on the ridge had rallied quickly and were grouping themselves into three lines of fire. The group on the far side fired into the fortress itself while the middle swathe cut down another sally of Woses descending towards them. The third focused its fire on the ones that had been on the point of slaughtering them.

'They've only enough for three shots each!' yelled Madogan, a bloodied arm hanging limply from his side. 'We'd best be abowt it if we want to rescue our wummenfowk!'

That was enough for a second wind (one they'd hopefully be masters of, Reus willing). Balthor joined his war-cry to the others as they surged up towards the fortress.

✠ ✠ ✠

Kyra pushed the stinking Wadwo corpse off her and peered after the band of warriors as they pushed up towards the fort. She half expected to be shot by a stray arrow but the Woses were fleeing towards the forest and her kinsmen and women were focusing their precious poisoned arrows on targets further up the slopes and inside the fortress.

The time for playing dead was over, and she had no wish to share the Argael with the fleeing brutes. Hauling herself up, she began scrabbling after the knights.

She stopped short and fell as someone grabbed her heel. She rolled over, expecting a dying Wadwo to come at her. She barely had time to register surprise as Baldo launched himself on top of her. In his hand was a sharp knife, stained with ichor.

'Had the same idea as me, hey?' he snarled, leaning down heavily on her and driving the knife-point towards her. She grabbed his wrist, squirming frantically and trying to get him off her.

'Thowt ye'd play dead, well now ye'll be dead fer real,' he said, grinning as spittle dropped from crooked yellow teeth into her face. 'It's time fer real justice too!'

She struggled some more, crying out, but no help came. In a straight fight she would have been confident of beating Baldo, but he was stronger than her and it was only a matter of time before his blade found her throat.

'Quit yer crowing,' she managed to gasp. 'I'll not beg fer mercy from the likes o' you.'

'And ye'll be gettin' none neither,' he grinned, pushing the knife closer to her throat. She felt its soiled blade touch her skin, a drab of ichor from it running down her neck. It felt strangely cold. With her last strength she let out another scream for help. No archers came to her aid. They were concentrating on the Wadwos and probably too far away to discern what was going on in any case. She closed her eyes and tried to be brave...

Suddenly the pressure lifted off her. She opened her eyes and saw Baldo's head and the upper half of his torso jerk upwards. A flash of silver, and a red smile opened across his distended throat. He fell to one side, gurgling horribly as a torrent of blood poured down his chest.

Standing over her was the strange warrior woman who had joined their party with the knight from Vorstlund. In one hand was a dirk stained tip to hilt with red. The other was extended towards her.

'Get up,' she said in her accented Vorstlending. 'Let's join the others before your folk shoot us too.'

Taking her hand she let the mercenary pull her up. It felt tough and warm in hers. Kyra flushed with pleasure at its touch, though she didn't have time to entertain that notion.

'I thought you were with the others?' she said as they began ascending the slope together.

'I was,' said the freesword over her shoulder. 'But I heard you screaming so I came back to help you. I've been keeping an eye on you.'

Kyra barely had time to register the twinkle in that eye before the outlander turned back to face the burning fortress.

✣ ✣ ✣

Adhelina shut her eyes tightly, wishing she could do the same with her ears. The wailing of the women had reached a crescendo, a hideous cacophony that sounded like a chorus of banshees. Some part of the fort was on fire: she could smell the smoke permeating through the logs of the long low room they were chained up in, hear the crackling of flames outside. Mingled with that she could make out the beastmen shouting at each other in their guttural tongue. Next to her Hettie slumped against the wall, too terrified to do more than shiver and cry. Further up the room a girl of fourteen summers smashed her head rhythmically against the hard oak, moaning incoherently. Her filthy matted hair was red and hid the blood well.

She heard prayers among the wailing. Not prayers for deliverance, but prayers for deliverance from life itself. And who could blame them? About half the hundred women crammed together like carcasses of rotting meat were with child.

With child. The heiress of Dulsinor felt like cursing language itself for its sheer inadequacy at evoking such an awful state. For the umpteenth time she tried not to look at their horribly distended bellies, their limbs painfully emaciated as the unclean lives they incubated sapped the strength from their bodies. Worst of all were their dead eyes. She had seen that look before, having treated women dishonoured during her father's last war.

Was it worse, she wondered, to be ravished by actual monsters than men made monstrous by war?

The end result certainly appeared to be. She had seen two of the victims give birth in the past couple of days; the bloodstains were still on the space of floor where they had been. Seeing that had left a chill of horror on her heart that Adhelina knew she would carry forever; likewise she would never forget the demented screams as the doomed mothers had thrashed around, dying as they brought abominations into the world.

The women had been taken from the Argael and nearby mountain villages, or that was as much as she had been able to glean from Gerta, one of the few captives besides herself to have retained her sanity.

'Something's definitely happening,' she called over to Gerta, trying desperately to kindle some hope. 'It sounds like they're under attack.'

'Aye, but it'll tek a small army to get us out o' here,' replied Gerta. She was about five and twenty summers and had been taken with Adhelina and Hettie. She had not yet been ravished. 'Best pray it's fightin' men sent by yer father.' Adhelina had dropped all pretence of secrecy: it hardly seemed to matter any more.

She mouthed a prayer, imploring Stygnos to gift her with fortitude. She bore herself with all the pride and courage of a high-born Vorstlending, yet the heiress of Dulsinor had felt herself stretched almost to breaking point since their capture.

Feverishly she clutched at straws. The moon would not be full for another week or so. That gave them time... Judging by the sounds of it, a rescue attempt was indeed under way.

But would it be enough?

'Hettie, try to be strong,' she whispered, leaning in as close to her friend as her chains would permit. 'Someone's coming – we're going to be rescued!'

Rescued. The absurdity of it crushed her. All her life she had read of romantic escapades, knights in gleaming armour saving damsels in distress, and now she was living the dream. What a dream to live out! Somehow it had never occurred to her, in the fancies of her callow youth, that this would be her part in any such tale – to wait passively while strong men came to pluck her from a hideous fate.

But in the past few weeks she had tasted something far more precious. *Freedom.* The freedom of an open road, the chance to choose her own fate. That had been torn from her as abruptly as she had found it.

'And so the dreams of old become reality, and put the new ones to flight,' she murmured to herself, perversely savouring the bitterness.

No, it wasn't the bitterness she savoured: it was the fact that she still had the presence of mind to *be* bitter, and not simply terrified.

The cries outside were increasing. The smoke was thickening. Perhaps it would be better if they burned: even that seemed preferable to the fate that awaited them if the gallant rescue attempt should fail.

Pulling at her manacles with all her waning strength, Adhelina added her voice to the terrible chorus, giving vent to a long, agonised scream of frustration.

✣ ✣ ✣

Sir Balthor pounded up towards the gate. Blood was streaming from a cut in his forearm where a beastman had cloven his shield, but he did not care. The archers on the ridge had managed to pick off most of the Wadwos charging down towards them, and the rest were falling back towards the fort.

Darting past a writhing beastman he closed the distance, his legs burning as they drove him up the last few yards. A Wadwo was dragging the gate to, trying to shut them out. He spared a glance for the others, who had stopped to cut down the last of the sally.

Diving through the narrowing gap he stopped and spun on his heel, slicing at the back of the Wose's knee. It fell with a cry and the gate stopped moving.

Gazing around the compound he took it in. To his left, the wall overlooking the pass was ablaze; an attempt by the Woses to extinguish the flames had been abandoned as the archers peppered them. Over to his right an enclosure piled high with vegetation was also on fire, presumably their food supply. The corpses of dead and dying beastmen littered the floor. There were two long low buildings flush to either wall, both of them burning. Another located against the far wall caught his eye: the surviving beastmen, about a dozen strong, were retreating inside it.

He prayed the captives were in that one. Turning to the gate he heaved it open to let the others through. The archers had ceased firing, whether to avoid shooting them or simply because their poisoned arrows were spent he could not say.

Dashing over towards the first roaring building he checked it, then the other. No screams of women burning alive came from either, thank Reus.

Sir Torgun and the rest burst into the compound and drew level with him. Balthor pointed at the last building with his sword.

'The last of them are taking refuge in there,' he said. 'We must rescue the women before this place burns to the ground!'

Sir Torgun nodded. Blood was pouring from a wound in his shoulder, but he had about as much mind for injuries as Balthor did. The battle joy was on them: that special feeling where a man could revel in his anger like an intoxicant.

As one they dashed towards the building. Their enemies stood waiting for them, clutching their cruel weapons as they prepared to make a last stand. You could say one thing for the beastmen, they were brave after their own fashion.

Torgun and Balthor took the wide doorway together, tearing through it swords awhirl. He saw only a flurry of black and white as a beastman launched itself at him. The others pushed in behind them and soon the building was flooded with cries and screams that mingled horribly with the desperate wailing of the women chained against the walls.

✢ ✢ ✢

Andragorix watched as his first line of defence crumbled. The burning fort flickered across the silver mirror as the fires spread across the walls, its doomed precinct a pyre for its garrison. Ignoring the disappointing spectacle he pushed further, keeping the symbol of a stylised ogre with an iron collar about its neck firmly in mind as he struggled to order the Wadwo serjeant to do his bidding.

Break cover/fight now.

He could feel its natural stubbornness resisting him, the atavistic urge to protect its young stirring it up to mutiny.

Leave the young/attack the invaders.

The warlock bent his will, focusing his elan on taming the rebellious creature. He could feel its resistance as a point of tension in the middle of his head.

Leave the young/fight now.

Keeping the symbol firmly in mind, he simplified the command. *Fight now/fight.*

The point in his head intensified, then suddenly gave way as the creature succumbed to his will. Andragorix smiled evilly as a trapdoor concealed by earth slid open in the middle of the compound.

✢ ✢ ✢

Kyra moved to a corner of the room, trying to find a mark. She was useless in a straight fight against such fiends, but she had enough Wose's Bane left for one arrow. They were evenly matched in numbers, but the poison they had applied to their blades had mostly worn off; the surviving beastmen would need to be hacked to death. One of the devils lunged at Anupe, its hammer raised high.

Time to repay a favour, thought Kyra coolly as she drew the arrow to her lips. The shaft went through the beastman's mouth and into the back of its throat. It lurched backwards and fell to the floor thrashing. The outlander spared her a fleeting nod of thanks before turning to help Madogan, who was on the verge of being sliced in two by a huge meat cleaver. Her falchion found the back of its leg; Madogan stepped in and buried his hatchet in its kneecap. The thing slumped to its knees and the two of them closed on it, cutting it to grey-white ribbons.

A glance about the room told her a similar story. All the other woodfolk lay dead, but the knights had triumphed. Sir Aronn buried his blade in the last one's chest as it struggled to stand up on its one good leg. Vaskrian and Braxus had just brought down another, their bodies drenched in sweat and ichor. Sir Torgun stood over the corpses of two he had made, breathing heavily.

A flurry of movement caught her eye. Turning she saw another six of the creatures, loping towards them from a dark pit previously hidden by a concealed trapdoor.

'There's more o' them!' she yelled, ducking back behind the doorway. She'd put the last of her Wose's Bane on her hunting knife; she slashed the first one's calf as it tore into the room. It fell convulsing and the others poured in after it. It seemed a strange rage was on these ones, something she hadn't seen in the others. Backing off into the corner again she scrabbled for her bow and hoped she'd find an eye.

✤ ✤ ✤

Sir Balthor turned as Kyra yelled a warning. He had been about to look for the heiress of Dulsinor but the fighting wasn't over yet. His arms throbbed. He'd just hacked his beastman to pieces, a frenzy coming over him that he'd never known was in him. He prayed he'd find that frenzy again as he closed with yet another.

It took a swipe at him with a hammer. He was well accustomed to fighting Wadwos by now, and ducked it smartly, stepping in for a lunge. It took the blade straight in its gut. He was about to pull it free when the creature did something unexpected. Abandoning its weapon it reached down and caught his arm. A cruel twist sent an explosion of pain through Balthor as he heard his elbow snap.

This one was larger than most. Without letting go of his arm it reached down and put a clammy two-fingered paw on top of his head. His temples exploded as it tightened its vice-like grip on him, stark bright lights bursting across his vision. From somewhere very far away he heard a female voice scream his name. He struggled with his one good arm to find his dagger, but it was on the other side of his belt and his fingers felt distant and clumsy. He felt the sinews in his neck tear as his head turned impossibly. His eyes went black as they swivelled around forcibly to face the other wall. A bolt of lightning tore up from his spine and through his skull, a searing pain that abruptly terminated in nothingness.

✤ ✤ ✤

Adhelina screamed as she watched the Wadwo tear Balthor's head off his shoulders. It barely seemed to notice his sword stuck hilt-deep in its stomach. Flinging body and head aside, it lurched towards a ruddy-faced knight who had just brought down one of its comrades. A bandage on his head had come apart, and fresh blood stained his curly blond hair. The Wadwo launched itself at him with bare fists. Another blond knight, dressed in the same surcoat and even taller than his comrade, attacked it from the side. She watched with her heart in her mouth as the two knights hacked and gouged the beastman into dying submission. Just behind them an auburn-haired knight and a chestnut-haired youth were doing much the same. Anupe and a woodlander with a broken arm were faring less well, until their beastman fell back, an arrow buried in its eye up to the feathers. It fell with a crash and suddenly it was over. No more beastmen remained.

The woodlander with the broken arm slumped to the ground with a groan and passed out. Six exhausted men and women stood panting in the middle of the hut. The fires crackled and smoke wafted in. The women around them screamed with panic.

If she was doomed to play the part of a rescued damsel, she would play it her way.

'Well don't just stand there!' she yelled. 'Get us out of here, before this place burns down!'

✤ ✤ ✤

Adelko stared at the smoky ruins of the fortress. A pile of cinders was all that remained of it, that and a hecatomb of monstrous corpses. The woodlanders from the ridge had arrived and begun to take care of the bodies of the slain. Others had joined them on the shelf of rock that the battle had won them.

The women who had fallen victims to the Wadwos were an awful sight. They had been freed, but looking on their sooty faces, streaked with tears and blood, he knew they would never be truly free again.

And that was just the ones who had not been violated. Those had more pressing problems than their future wellbeing.

'I will not preside over the slaughter of innocent women,' said Sir Torgun hotly. 'No matter how foully they have been used.' A dangerous light was in the young knight's eyes as he faced the others. Adelko didn't need his sixth sense to tell him more violence could be pending if matters did not go well.

'There's no choice, sir knight,' said Madogan, his arm in a sling. His face looked pale and drawn and sorrow clouded his eyes. 'They wilna survive childbirth if we leave 'em as is. Least we can do now is give 'em a clean death.'

A chorus of throats echoed that sentiment, the woodfolk who weren't busy seeing to the dead.

'We cannot and will not put blameless women to the sword!' cried Torgun. 'It would be an act of gross dishonour!'

'Aye, and an act o' mercy too,' put in Madogan. 'We care not fer knightly honour – we'll do it, save ye gettin' yer lily white noble hands dirty.' He fixed the knight with a pointed stare.

'Show respect to a nobleman!' snarled Sir Aronn. 'Especially one who's just saved your lives.'

Madogan met the angry knight's stare, but said nothing.

'There is another way.'

All eyes turned to the noblewoman they had just rescued. She was sat apart from the others, her lady-in-waiting's head cradled in her lap.

'We're all ears, Lady Dulsinor,' said Horskram courteously. Brief introductions had been made.

'My things were rescued by Anupe,' she said. 'Among my valuables is a pouch of medicine.'

'Beggin' yer lordly pardon,' said Madogan. 'But what medicines can help these poor wenches?'

'I have Abaddon's Root,' replied the noblewoman. 'When distilled, it can be used to make a concoction that induces abortion.'

Now it was Horskram's turn to get angry. 'Use of such herbs spurns the Almighty's gift of life,' he said sternly.

'Then why did He create them in the first place?' replied Adhelina, meeting his gaze with her cool green eyes. Though her travelling clothes were torn and her face was scratched, she still looked every inch the noblewoman. Adelko could see she was very beautiful, but truth to tell after all these years he still didn't see what all the fuss was about where women were concerned.

Others in his party felt very differently. He could sense a surge of passion course through Sir Torgun as he stared at her. Likewise Sir Braxus was gazing at her with no uncommon interest.

'I don't think Reus would mind if we... put such abominations out of their misery,' Adelko found himself saying. 'After all, He didn't create the Wadwos did he?'

Or did He, indirectly? he wondered just then. His conversation with the Earth Witch still lingered in his mind. But he gave no voice to that thought as Horskram rounded on him.

'I'll thank you to keep your peace, Adelko of Narvik,' he snapped. 'Just because you've proved yourself once again against yon air spirits doesn't give you the right to twist the words of Scripture! Our Prophet himself said to kill life in the womb is an act of murder. Do you dare deny this?'

'No,' replied the novice, surprised at his firmness of tone. 'I deny that the Prophet had inhuman monsters in mind when he said those words.'

Horskram held his gaze, then turned away with a disgusted gesture. He could feel their souls conflicting. It was just the opposite of the feeling he'd had on the rock when they had banished the Aethi together.

'I'm no perfect,' said Kyra, 'but I say yon monk is right. We should give Her Ladyship the chance to save our wummen.'

'Aye,' said Madogan, hope returning to him. 'If she can save their lives, who cares what happens to Wadwos in the womb?'

The woodfolk nodded their assent. No one in their group barring Horskram seemed to disagree.

'Very well,' said the adept darkly. 'But let it be noted that I did not condone the use of such a baleful herb. It was one of Abaddon's creations when he had a hand in making the world.'

'That was before he fell into darkness,' pointed out Adhelina. 'And the Author of All Evil created many things that live upon the face of the earth – even goats! Do we spurn their milk for the same reason?'

Horskram shook his head and stalked off. Adelko stared after him, nonplussed. He had just watched as they threw burning pitch into the secret cellar, burning the infant Woses before they could grow to full size. What was so different about killing them in the womb? If anything Adhelina's way seemed more humane – and it might save dozens of mortal lives too.

'Your teacher seems not to like difficult students who have ideas of their own,' said Anupe, tightening the straps on her pack next to him. The Harijan was in cheerful spirits. He had watched as Adhelina handed over several fistfuls of gold and silver jewellery, much of it studded with gems.

'I see you got your pay then,' said Adelko sullenly. He didn't care for levity right now.

'Yes, finally,' replied the mercenary, ignoring his tone. 'Anupe the Harijan gets her reward for all her hard work.'

'I'd like to talk to you, about where you come from,' said the novice, keen to change the subject. 'I've read about the Harijans, but the books I looked at date from Ancient Thalamy and didn't say much.'

'That is because we keep ourselves as secret as we can,' replied the warrior woman. 'But I like a man who speaks up for women, as you did just now. So perhaps before I go, I will tell you some things about our people.'

'Go?'

The Harijan shrugged. 'My services are at an end. What the Lady Dulsinor does from now on is her business. Tomorrow I will journey east, to take ship for the Empire.' She patted her money pouch, now stuffed with precious rings and other valuable trinkets. 'I should be able to fetch enough coin for a horse and other things.'

Adelko sensed relations between employer and hireling had been a tad strained of late.

'Are you sure you won't stay?' he asked. 'I think we're going to need fighting men... and women of course.'

Anupe chuckled. 'Oh ho! I think I have had enough adventures in the Free Kingdoms for a lifetime! I thank you for your offer, Adelko of Narvik, but I want to get back to a country that is less strange than this one!'

Adelko was about to ask her what she meant by that when Kyra approached them. 'We'll set up camp here and make some food, will ya help me gather some firewood?' she asked the Harijan. Adelko was shocked when his sixth sense registered the same kind of feelings he had detected in Torgun and Braxus whenever they looked at Adhelina.

Anupe favoured Kyra with a vulpine grin. 'For you, anything!' she beamed. Kyra smiled back shyly and the two of them strode off together. Adelko suddenly realised he was blushing. If his sixth sense was right, he knew what his mentor would have to say about that blossoming friendship.

✤ ✤ ✤

The sun had long set behind the looming mountains when they sat down to supper. Another funeral pyre had been built and more Last Rites had been said. The Woses had been burned too, if only to get rid of the stink of them. Despite their losses the woodfolk were in high spirits – a great victory had been won and Madogan was confident of using it to increase recruits and flush the remaining Woses out of the Argael for good.

Of all this Sir Torgun was but peripherally aware. As he sat by the cooking fire watching the meat roast and running his whetstone up and down his blade – badly blunted after striking through the chains that had bound the women captives – he found his eyes flicking towards Lady Adhelina of Dulsinor time and again. She looked a little less sad and drawn now that her lady-in-waiting had recovered, though that poor damsel could barely utter a word and was obviously still overcome by all the horrors she had lived through.

Sir Torgun felt sure that he had never seen anyone so ravishingly beautiful in all his life. And the way she had spoken to Horskram, so proud and defiant and caring... Beautiful on the outside and inside, she could have walked straight out of a Pangonian romance: surely not even the age of King Vasirius had produced such a perfect maiden!

He longed to speak with her, but knew that now probably wasn't the right time – she was busy tending her friend, and had just finished administering to the poor women whose lives she had saved. Best to leave her to recuperate and make an introduction later, she'd earned some rest.

As he gazed upon her strawberry blonde tresses that seemed to mirror the firelight, Sir Torgun realised that Princess Hjala no longer mattered to him as she once had. That revelation shocked him. Almost.

✤ ✤ ✤

Sir Braxus idly plucked his lyre and stole glances at the Vorstlending stunner that the archangel Ushira had happily put in his way. The woodlanders had broken out some ale, and spirits were rising. It wasn't nearly as tasty as Thraxian mead, but it warmed his belly just the same. Passing the skin to Vaskrian he glanced over at the Lady Markward and wondered how he could woo her. Now obviously wasn't the time to strike: she'd been through too much and his suit would quickly turn cold if ill-timed.

But woo her he would, as soon as the opportunity presented itself. For here was a damsel to drive out thought of all others. Taking in her supple curves, which even her baggy riding clothes barely hid, Sir Braxus inhaled sharply. Every wench he'd ever bedded, high-born and low, receded into the back of his mind; once-treasured memories now assuming the run of ordinary recollections.

It would be a wooing of wooings, one he'd write a song about: a song that would be sung in halls long after they were both gone. It wasn't only her looks that had him hooked, it was her spiritedness too... how he'd loved it when she'd spoken up against the pompous monk, beating him at his own games of logic and scholastics. Why she'd even had his timorous novice rebelling against the crusty old adept! Here at last, he was sure, was something he'd never yet found: a match of equals, someone worth keeping in his bed for longer than a few weeks.

Brushing his fingers across the lyre strings, he acquiesced gladly as one of the woodlanders asked him to play. He hoped she was paying attention as he struck up his best tune.

✣ ✣ ✣

Andragorix watched the mortal chaff celebrating around the fire with hatred in his heart. That did not bother him: hatred was always in his heart and he enjoyed the feeling. But now it was mixed with the feeling of having been beaten. And that he did not relish at all.

At the edge of the silver mirror he caught his dearest foe staring glumly into the fire. He had expected the wily Argolian to get past his fortress of course, but not by razing it to the ground. But then that was Horskram of Vilno: a constant thorn in his side, hell-sent by the King of Gehenna to test him.

'Oh Horskram, why so glum?' he asked the mirror. 'I'll give thee plenty to be sad about once I'm done!'

He murmured the words of the closing spell and the mirror went dark. There was no starlight: he had not thought to order the Wadwos to pull aside the great sheet of stone he used to block out the sun when he needed to scry by day.

And a long day it had been. He felt exhausted. Marshalling the Wadwos and summoning the Aethi had drained his elan, not to mention the constant Scrying. He was for bed, another dose of Morphonus' Root, and dreamless sleep. Pulling back his cloak he touched the pommel of the sword at his belt and murmured a word. A grey light sprung from it, enough to guide him back to his chambers.

His duel with Horskram had forced him to put aside his sorcerous studies: tomorrow would be spent preparing for their final encounter. But anything that concerned Horskram was a worthy reason to pause in his plans for world domination. He almost felt his silver hand tingle as he walked through dark corridors that twisted with a madness even he envied.

Yes, killing the Argolian and all his companions would be almost as good as bringing the Known World to its knees.

⊷ CHAPTER XVII ⊷

Of Love and Hate

Kyra buried herself deeper in the cloak, pushing her body up against Anupe's. The Harijan's body felt hard and warm against hers. Basking in its glow she kissed her new lover full on the lips. Somewhere beyond the thicket they had chosen for their tryst a couple of birds took flight, their wings flapping as they screeched into the close night air.

'Are ye always this forward?' she asked, pulling her mouth from Anupe's.

The Harijan frowned, her nut-brown skin creasing above her dark eyes. It was a quizzical gesture that she was learning to love fast. 'Sorry,' she asked. 'What do you mean "forward"?'

'What I mean,' said Kyra, rolling her eyes, 'is d'ye always just grab a wummun ye like?'

'Usually,' smirked the freesword. 'Especially the ones that I know are willing.'

Kyra opened her mouth in shock, not sure if her foreign lover was joking. 'Ye're terrible,' she grinned, kissing the Harijan again.

'So terrible,' agreed Anupe, stroking her breast and moving her calloused hand down towards her thighs. Kyra felt a thrill of pleasure. Living amongst the tight-knit and deeply conservative woodfolk, she so rarely got the chance to indulge her true desires.

The sound of a twig snapping brought their amorous reprisal to an abrupt end. Anupe stiffened beside her, and not with arousal. The Harijan's hand emerged from beneath the cloak and snaked deftly towards her unsheathed falchion.

'Sure I saw 'em sneakin' off in this direction together.'

'Pair o' slatterns, we'll be doin' the Almighty a favour. We'll see 'em hang fer this, *and* Baldo.'

'Mebbe 'ave some fun wi' em first?'

The men laughed. It sounded like there were three of them at least. Silent as a fox, Anupe stood and wrapped the cloak around her, motioning for Kyra to lie still. Kyra did no such thing. Wrapping herself in her own cloak, she grabbed her bow and pulled an arrow from its quiver.

'Think I see it, over there.'

Torchlight permeated the folds of the thicket.

'Are you looking for someone, gentlemen?'

Three men stopped short as Anupe stepped out to face them, Kyra following close behind.

'If I were you I would look away,' said Anupe coolly. 'Any man who sees my natural form must pay with his life. Old Harijan custom.'

'Get 'em!' yelled the first woodlander. That was his death sentence. Without waiting for them to come the Harijan darted forwards, her blade flashing. By the time Kyra had nocked and drawn two of them lay dying while the third was crouched over, covering his eyes.

'Dunna kill me, please!' he wailed. 'I didna look, I swear I didna!'

Anupe's lip curled in disgust as she raised her bloody falchion. Kyra stepped in front of her.

'Dunna do it, there's been enough bloodshed as 'tis,' she breathed.

That was all the wretch needed. Springing to his feet he bounded back towards the camp, screaming blue murder. Silhouetted figures on night watch could be seen against the camp fire.

'Now see what he will do!' snarled the Harijan. 'Your pity has got us in real trouble!'

'We're in trouble already – they must 'ave seen ye do fer Baldo,' replied Kyra, not best pleased with her lover's quick temper. 'C'mon, let's get dressed an' go face the music. Madogan'll put this right, I ken 'im right well.'

She bit her lip as Anupe stomped off to put her clothes on. She and Madogan had been friends for years, but this might overreach the boundaries of that friendship.

✠ ✠ ✠

Adhelina had been busy since before dawn, giving the fifty or so women in her care another dose of Abaddon's Root. It would take two or three administrations each morning before it took effect – assuming Wadwos responded the same way as mortal children in the womb. There wasn't much in the way of comfort for the poor blasted creatures, though Madogan had sent men off to fetch wood and tarpaulin to construct a makeshift hospice.

She spared a glance across the panorama gifted her by the rising sun. The Argael was spread out like a green velvet blanket, a perfect match to the blue skies that enfolded it. To her left and right the grey-white peaks of the Hyrkrainians stretched, their rocky buttressing a pleasing contrast to the soft lushness of the trees that stretched up to greet it.

Adhelina sighed. The world was a beautiful place. And yet she had seen so little of it. And what she had seen of late had by turns horrified, appalled and terrified her. *A rich table set with poisoned dishes* – that was how the Thalamian poet Thracian had described the mortal vale, upon his return from the Wars of Unity that had seen the ancient city-states consolidated under the warrior king Thalamus.

'It is a fair view is it not?'

She turned, startled at having her reverie broken. The Thraxian knight was standing next to her, a pleasant smile on his lips. She had been introduced to him, but so much had happened she'd barely registered his name.

'Sir Braxus of Gaellen, at your service,' he said with a courteous bow, as if reading her thoughts.

'Lady Adhelina of Dulsinor, at yours,' she replied formally in Decorlangue. She cursed inwardly. The knight seemed charming enough, but right now the last thing she wanted to do was converse with a stranger.

'How go things with your patients?' he asked. 'I trust they will fare well in your able hands.'

'The *women*,' she replied pointedly, 'fare gravely, as befits the hideous ordeal they have been subjected to.'

'Please forgive me, I had not intended any offence,' said the knight, the smile not leaving his lips. 'You are right of course, my question was clumsy and foolish. Truth to tell, though I've seen the horrors of war many times, I've never seen such as this. I know not quite what to say.'

Adhelina sized him up, trying to work out if he was being sincere or not. She found herself thinking of Sir Agravine, the bachelor at her father's keep who used to flirt with her. The Thraxian was certainly handsome, after the fashion of his people, and obviously had a flair for dress: even his travelling clothes were richly seamed, the green woollen breeches and tunic matching the colour of the canopy she had just been admiring. Both were embroidered delicately with silver thread depicting vines and leaves.

'In truth I know not what to say either,' she confessed in a low voice. 'Half these poor souls are probably too far along to survive in any case, and as for the others, I doubt if they'll ever be whole in mind or body again.'

'You're doing the right thing,' said Braxus, turning to gaze at the landscape. 'If half of them survive to enjoy but half the fruits of life, that will be better than the alternative.'

Adhelina glanced at him sidelong. He *did* sound sincere, and he was saying all the right things. Even his body language, turning away from her so as not to pressure her with his gaze, seemed well mannered. Perhaps too well mannered. Knights did not just stroll up to noblewomen they barely knew to make idle conversation, she knew that much.

'Where will you go next?' she asked, trying to get him on the back foot. 'You're on some kind of mission with the Northlendings connected to those beastly creatures, I've gathered that much.'

'I'd expect a woman of your perspicacity to gather that much and more,' he said, turning to look at her again. His eyes were the colour of his clothes and sparkled. Adhelina had mixed feelings. On the one hand his persistent compliments were starting to feel a little contrived, annoying even. On the other it was nice to be complimented on her intellect rather than just her looks, as was usually the case with knights who approached her.

She met his gaze, pointedly waiting for an answer to her question.

'I'll be pressing on with the Northlendings,' he said. 'I'm bound to them by oath until we root out the warlock responsible for the beastmen.'

She looked at him quizzically. Her thoughts returned instantly to the theft at her ancestral home weeks ago. 'A warlock you say? Tell me more, I want to know.'

'I can't,' he sighed. 'You're clearly a well-educated woman, Adhelina of Dulsinor, so you know how these quests tend to go – sworn to secrecy until done. Especially when there's an Argolian leading it!' He suddenly became agitated. 'I like not these mountains – the sooner we're done with this business the better I shall like it.'

Adhelina was about to say something when she heard a cry. It was Hettie. Dashing over she saw her friend had awoken from a nightmare, he face drenched with sweat.

'There Hettie, nothing to be afraid of!' she said. 'You're here, safe with me.'

'Their white faces...' was all Hettie managed to say. She was staring ahead, looking for all the world as though a Wadwo were standing right in front of her.

'... are gone for good,' supplied Adhelina, hoping that wasn't a lie. 'Men from the woods led by knights fought them and won. We're safe Hettie! Here, lie back and I'll fix you something.'

She was already reaching for her medicine bag. She had given her tincture of St Elenya's Node; it was good for treating those suffering from shock and deep trauma, but it hadn't seemed to do much so far. She resolved to double the dose.

'May I be of any assistance, my lady?' inquired Sir Braxus. She had almost forgotten he was there.

'Yes, as a matter of fact, you can,' she said. 'I need to boil a preparation for my lady-in-waiting. Can you get that fire over there lit please?'

'Certainly,' replied Braxus, before putting his fingers in his mouth and whistling. 'Vaskrian! Over here!' he cried, switching to Northlending. 'Stop showing off with your new sword, there's a fire that needs lighting.'

The Thraxian's wiry squire came over to see to it. Strange that a Thraxian should take a foreigner into service, but Adhelina had little time or inclination to pry into the matter.

Braxus was staring across the plateau at the woodlanders' camp now. Glancing up from her preparations she saw that they were gathered in a circle, debating something furiously. The Northlendings were involved too, and the argument appeared to be getting quite heated.

'What's that all about?' Sir Braxus asked his squire. Her Northlending was good enough to follow their conversation; they didn't write much that was worth reading, but in her youth she had insisted on learning the tongue spoken by their closest neighbours.

'Search me,' replied Vaskrian, not looking up from the fire. 'Something to do with that outlander who joined us for the fighting. Apparently she killed two woodlanders last night.'

Adhelina turned to look at him. 'Anupe, you mean? What on earth happened?'

'Don't know, my lady,' said the squire, acknowledging her with a courteous nod as befitted her station. 'They're accusing her of killing another fellow, during the battle yesterday. One of the other woodlanders is involved too – Kyra her name is, she guided us here. Not really my business to interfere.'

She didn't care for the squire's sullen tone. Nor did his master by the looks of things, for just then Sir Braxus said something angrily in Northlending. It was too quick for her to follow, but she gathered his meaning when Vaskrian favoured her with a half bow and said: 'My apologies for any insolence offered, I meant no offence.'

'None taken,' replied Adhelina tersely.

'Your fire is ready,' he added, before stalking off.

'Please forgive my squire,' said Sir Braxus. 'He's an angry young man, unused to being around his betters. I'm doing my best to gentle him, but such things take time.'

She nodded absently. She didn't really care about his squire. Right now she was fixated on getting Hettie's medicine down her, and heading straight over to see what kind of trouble her erstwhile bodyguard had got herself into.

✢ ✢ ✢

'I say they should hang!' cried one woodlander, to a chorus of angry approval.

'There'll be no hanging without a trial,' said Madogan firmly, raising his good arm for silence. He barely got it. The blood of the woodfolk was up.

'Never mind a hanging, we should burn 'em!' cried one woman. 'They were ruttin' on each other, it's a sin! I say they're witches!'

'Witches?' cried Madogan, rounding on her fiercely. 'An' who are you te sey that, Ulla?' He gestured towards where Horskram stood frowning, rubbing his beard and deep in thought. 'Perhaps the Argolian would like to give 'is professional opinion on the matter?'

Horskram cleared his throat. 'They are certainly not witches,' he said. 'And the venal sins of mortal men – and women – are of no concern to my Order. Likewise, I have no judicial authority in murder trials. This is your business, I'm afraid.'

Sir Torgun had held his peace for long enough. The two women were doubtless strange, and he didn't approve of their behaviour in the slightest, but they had fought alongside him nonetheless.

'I say these women deserve a fair trial,' he ventured. 'They may have broken your laws, but they also fought bravely against yon Wadwos. To condemn them to the judgment of a mob would be a grave injustice.'

That brought another chorus of 'ayes' and 'nays'. Several of the women who were not being treated by Adhelina and strong enough to join the counsel were getting involved. The foremost among them, a lass of five and twenty summers, spoke up.

'These two,' – she gestured to where Anupe and Kyra stood, closely guarded by a dozen woodfolk – 'saved our lives. I'll not sit by and watch them condemned to hang. I say there should be no trial!'

More uproar followed.

'Who are you t'sey that, Gilda?' cried the woman who had called for a burning. 'They killed Baldo – Kenna saw it wi' her own eyes!'

'Baldo was askin' fer it!' yelled another woodlander. 'Kenna says she saw 'im attack Kyra.'

'And what about Robbo an' Derek?' asked the woman, quickly changing tack. 'Did they ask fer bein' killed by that foreign bitch too?'

'They were up fer rapin' 'em, not triallin' 'em,' retorted the other woodlander. 'Bad enough we've just seen dozens o' our fowk dishonoured by Woses, now our own menfowk are at it!'

The woodlanders fell back to ugly bickering. Madogan called again for silence but got none.

Adhelina pushed through the throng with Braxus at her side. Twin knives stabbed Torgun's heart: one of painful longing for the Lady Markward, the other of jealousy at seeing the Thraxian by her side.

'What is the meaning of this?' the Vorstlending damsel shouted above the din. 'Why this talk of hanging?'

Anupe glanced sidelong at Adhelina. She had barely reacted throughout the counsel, though Kyra looked scared. Adhelina's question was rewarded with a chorus of angry responses.

'Enough!' she cried. Something in her clear high voice got their attention. But then who wouldn't pay attention when someone like that was speaking to them? The damsel was marvellous, simply marvellous. Torgun felt hot blood coursing through his veins as she addressed the group.

'These lands,' – she stamped a booted foot on the rocky plateau for emphasis – 'stand on the Hyrkrainians south of the rivers Lyr and Hyr. That makes them property of the Eorl of Dulsinor, whose sole living heir I am! As such, I hold authority here!'

She swept the group with a stern gaze, daring anyone to gainsay her. None did.

'And I say there will be no trial!' she continued. 'There have been enough killings here, no more bloodshed! I have agreed to stay here and tend your sick – when they are fit to travel you shall take them back with you to the Argael. If these two women should elect to return with you, then what you do with them is your business – otherwise they are free to go. Is that understood?'

The angry shouting had subsided into discontented muttering.

Sir Braxus chose that moment to step forwards. 'I like you am a foreigner here,' he said, speaking slowly so the woodfolk could understand his accented Northlending. 'But I think you can see the justice in the Lady Markward's words. Heed them now as you heed your reason! We have just won a remarkable victory – why ruin it by fighting one another?'

The next rush of noise sounded generally approving. Adhelina glanced at him gratefully. Sir Torgun felt his cheeks flush. He was not given to intrigue, but even he could see he was in danger of being sidelined in a contest before it had begun.

And whilst he wasn't given to intrigue, he wasn't accustomed to losing either.

'If I might make a suggestion, my lady,' he said, stepping forwards and nodding courteously. He felt all eyes on him, but only noticed those of Adhelina and his rival.

'Of course,' she said, though she looked a little hesitant.

'Clearly these two women will not be safe if we leave them here with the woodfolk alone. With all due respect, my lady, after we leave you will be bereft of arms to enforce your word should something unfortunate occur.'

He hesitated. The dark mutterings from the woodfolk told him he had not spoken amiss.

'Go on,' pressed Adhelina. Feeling her eyes on him was like drinking a delicious Mercadian wine after days spent wandering the wilderness.

'In that case I suggest that yon ladies accompany us on our... venture. Though I disapprove of women taking up arms, they have both proved their valour and may be useful. And that way we can keep them safe from any harm.'

Anupe chose that moment to speak up. 'A Harijan needs no man to keep her safe.' She rested her hand on the pommel of her falchion meaningfully. No one had dared try to disarm her.

'Nonetheless,' persisted Sir Torgun. 'I think it would be better for all concerned if you both came with us. As the Lady Markward so rightly says, there has been enough bloodshed here. It will be best avoided if you join us, though I cannot promise our road is a safe one.'

Anupe glanced at Kyra before looking back at him and shrugging. 'I am not happy about this delay to my plans. What is in it for me?'

'Your safety,' replied Sir Torgun. 'Not even you can expect to defeat a hundred foes.' He wasn't used to acknowledging a woman's battle prowess. These were strange times indeed.

'If it helps to persuade you, I'll give you another reward when you get back,' sighed Adhelina.

'And my new business partner?' said Anupe, motioning towards Kyra. Adhelina rolled her eyes. 'She'll get her share too.'

Anupe looked at Kyra. The huntress nodded, though now she looked terrified. Torgun could hardly fault her for that – she had just been taken out of a melee and thrust into a duel.

'Well that settles it then,' said Adhelina. Torgun's heart beat faster as she favoured him with a gracious smile. 'My thanks for your help in this matter, sir knight.'

'Think nothing of it, my lady,' he replied sincerely, bowing again. He caught Sir Braxus looking at him. The handsome knight was still smiling, but ingenuous as he was even Sir Torgun could see that his eyes told a different story. Only his devotion to the Code of Chivalry stopped him indulging a feeling of pure, unbridled triumph. If this damned Thraxian wanted a war of wooing, he was going to get one.

⇥ CHAPTER XVIII ⇤

The Witch Hunter's Quarry

Adelko watched as the rain hardened, grateful for the shelter afforded by the shallow cave. The leaden skies rumbled as they released their burden; somewhere far off in the distance he heard a Gygant cry out. It put him in mind of his childhood when he used to climb the slopes of the Highlands, questing for a glimpse of the gargantuan race that still called the neighbouring mountains home.

He had reached the Hyrkrainians at last, though he was hundreds of miles south of Narvik, the village of his childhood. Back then it had seemed like an impossible dream; now it felt quotidian, another milestone on the adventurous path that events of the past year had set him on. Truly he was caught up in the grip of an immutable wyrd, a destiny he could neither completely fathom nor control: he prayed that whatever say in his future the Almighty had seen fit to grant him, it would be enough to preserve his life for a time, and his soul forever in the hereafter.

The kindling crackled as Vaskrian struck flint and tinder over it, the sparks giving birth to inchoate flames. After all he had seen in the past fortnight, Adelko would not have been surprised to see a Saraphus spring up out of it. On his seat by the entrance Horskram was muttering the Psalm of Abjuration, his eyes half closed as he softly mouthed the sacred words. Adelko hoped that would be enough to keep the fire natural.

The cave they had stopped in for the night was roughly shaped like a horseshoe. Running its length was a rocky bench jutting out of the wrinkled walls; some said it was a natural phenomenon that had made the cave popular with wayfarers, others claimed it had been chiselled out for use by such long ago.

Adelko huddled towards the fire, grateful for its growing warmth. The rain had started falling halfway through their day's journey up the pass, and his cloak and habit were thoroughly soaked.

He stifled a sneeze, feeling suddenly conscious of his physical frailty next to the hard men and women who shared the road with him.

Peering down at his copy of the *Holy Book*, he stared at the lines of the Psalm of Gramarye's Quenching. He was a quick study by anyone's standards, and confident of committing the words to memory by the time they reached the Warlock's Crown tomorrow at dusk. What he was less confident of was mustering anything like the necessary conviction to make those words of any use. But then he had always surpassed himself on such occasions: the demon Belaach in Rykken, the winged devil they had fought on the Brenning Wold and at Staerkvit, the spirits of air and fire they had tussled with more recently...

He was marked out for great things, or so the Earth Witch seemed to think. His own mentor, Horskram of Vilno, the most celebrated adept of his chapter, had hinted at as much. So what was there to fear?

He knew the answer to that question even as he asked it of himself. Immodesty, complacency, pride and vanity – young as he was, he knew that those notions would quickly get the best of him if he let them. It had already begun to dawn on him that it was precisely his lack of certitude that had got him this far.

Never take any victory for granted, he thought to himself. *Or it won't stay around for the taking.*

He shut his eyes tightly and refocused on the page, reciting the words in his head and opening his heart to the grace of the Redeemer.

✢ ✢ ✢

Another hour or two slid by and the rain showed no signs of softening, even after dark had stolen across the broken teeth of the land they now traversed. Vaskrian had built up the fire, filling the cave with warmth as the company sharpened swords, prepared bedrolls, and broke out rations. Adelko had taken his share of hard cheeses, honey, biscuit and goats milk and was just about to pick up the *Holy Book* again when Horskram cleared his voice and spoke.

'I think now would be a good time for me to tell you what I know about our foe,' he said. His voice was neutral, gentle almost, but Adelko's sixth sense told him his mentor was a roil of nervous emotion. 'I will also outline what powers we have at our disposal to counter his, and then a brief discussion of battle tactics would not go amiss before we go to bed.'

Adelko almost laughed. His mentor made it sound as if they were planning a tournament melee or hunting expedition, not an impending clash with a maniacal warlock holed up in a sorcerous ruin left by the most powerful race of wizards the world had ever known.

He knew better than to indulge the urge. The adept was scared, very scared, and doing his best to hide it so as not to dishearten the others.

'What kind of tactics does one employ against a pagan sorcerer?' asked Sir Aronn, his face screwing up as he looked askance at Horskram. Adhelina had reset his bandage, and he looked like an invalid with half his head swaddled in linen. Adelko hoped he was fitter for combat than that.

'I'll come to that in a minute,' replied Horskram, not seeming annoyed or perturbed by the interruption.

He's been preparing for this moment for years, Adelko realised as the adept continued: 'As some of you already know, I fought Andragorix at Roarkil in Thraxia several years ago, myself and one Belinos of Runcymede.'

'A dreadful place if all the tales be true,' put in Braxus. 'They say it's haunted with the shades of slaughtered soldiers.'

'I'll not deny it,' replied Horskram. 'You will recall the part Roarkil played in the loss of a Headstone fragment – it was the very thing we seek that led to the forest and fortress of that name becoming cursed in the first place.'

Sir Braxus nodded. 'Cadwyn's betrayal of Corann is well known among my people. He is not called the False Friend for nothing.'

Adelko caught Kyra and Anupe exchanging bemused glances. Horskram was speaking in Decorlangue, a language they didn't understand. Once again his wily mentor was indulging his penchant for secrecy. But that was hardly surprising.

'Thing we seek?' queried Aronn, looking to Torgun for an answer. 'All I know is that we're to protect you until you find and defeat this sorcerer.'

A pained looked crossed Sir Torgun's face. Adelko sensed the young knight wasn't nearly as comfortable with keeping secrets as his mentor.

'Forgive me, Sir Aronn,' he said. 'I was sworn to secrecy and told to tell you and the twins only what I thought you needed to know. There is more to this mission than at first seems, but for now you need to trust Horskram and listen to what he says.'

Aronn shook his head and took a pull on a wineskin, gesturing irately at the monk to continue.

'I will tell you of our encounter and do my best to explain the powers he marshalled against us, so that you have a good idea of what to expect. Adelko, I hope your Vorstlending isn't too rusty – you can translate for the benefit of yon women.'

Adelko permitted himself a wry smile. Now that he had got the need for secrecy out of the way, his mentor was inviting them to join the briefing.

'As we have gleaned from many a witch trial, every sorcerer learns from the Seven Schools of Magick,' said Horskram. 'Andragorix is versed in all of these in varying degrees. That he is a demonologist of growing powers we already know – he set demonic servitors to guard him at Roarkil, such as I will not describe here.'

The adept paused to make the sign and Adelko flinched as he felt a chill momentarily freeze his mentor's soul. 'However, I do not think he will send such against us, for reasons I'll come to. He also used Necromancy to send the remains of some of Cadwyn's dead soldiers to attack us. It was a horrid sight, watching as he bound their tormented shades to their skeletal bodies and sent them against us!'

His mentor paused and made the sign again. Once more Adelko had to suppress a smile. Horskram was indulging his storytelling histrionics again. If one hard question was asked of his soul at the gates of the Heavenly Halls, it would surely be of his vanity: Horskram could not help himself when he had an audience, he simply loved to tell a good story. Even if it was one that might be a prelude to their deaths.

'How many did he send?' asked Sir Braxus, clearly keen on keeping things practical.

'A good question,' allowed Horskram. 'He is not an accomplished necromancer, thank Reus, and should not be able to send more than ten reanimated corpses at us.'

'Only ten undead warriors,' said Braxus. 'Well that should even up the odds nicely, assuming he doesn't already have another garrison of beastmen waiting for us up there!'

'As I said, we'll come to tactics in a bit,' said Horskram, glancing at the Thraxian severely. 'After fighting our way past the skeletal swordsmen and demonic bodyguards we found him alone in his chamber. But I warn you, even bereft of such henchmen, Andragorix is no weakling in a straight fight. His knowledge of Alchemy has taught him to concoct distillations that give him unnatural strength and speed. But most deadly of all is his command of Thaumaturgy. You've already seen what he can do with elemental magic – well, expect more of that. Last time I fought him he sent bound Saraphi to fight us, and that was the death of poor Sir Belinos. He can also conjure Aethi and use those to harden the air around him in a protective shield, or to fly out of range.'

'Excuse me... "bound"?' Even when was translated, Anupe did not understand the word from its context.

'A sorcerer can choose to bind Elementi after he has summoned them,' explained Horskram, 'much as he can choose to bind demons – all that is needed is an inanimate host object. In our case it was a staff of silver and mahogany, a fair thing to look upon but when used for such foul – '

Anupe cut off both Horskram and Adelko – who was struggling to keep up with Horskram in his halting Vorstlending – with a wave of the hand. 'Yes, yes, I understand,' she said. 'I do not need a merchant's description of the item in question.'

Horskram allowed her a wry smile of his own. Adelko felt his spirits lighten a little. As always, it felt good to share a joke before going into danger.

'He may also try to use the School of Transformation to turn himself into a bird of flight or even a wreath of mist,' Horskram continued. 'But chances are he'll only use that if he feels the need to escape as he did last time.'

'What about us?' asked Kyra, looking terrified now. 'Won't he just transform us into... insects or somethin'?'

'So far as we know, the only warlock since the Elder Wizards well versed enough in Transformation to turn others into creatures against their will was Proteana, who troubled Antaeus on his voyages more than two thousand years ago.'

Adelko didn't bother translating that part. A simple 'no' sufficed to answer the superstitious woodlander's question.

'So let me see if I have this right,' queried Braxus, counting off on his fingers. 'You're taking us to fight a mad warlock who can fly, shoot fireballs at us, defend himself with an invisible magic shield, has the strength and speed to match the strongest knight, and can always transform himself into something conveniently fast or unassailable if by some miracle we do get the better of him. And that's leaving aside that he may be surrounded by a horde of Wadwos, a host of demons, and an elite bodyguard of undead warriors for good measure. You'll forgive me if I'm having second thoughts about this mission.'

His comments produced cracked smiles if not outright laughter. But then it was difficult to laugh at a joke when the punchline appeared to be their imminent and gruesome deaths by a variety of unnatural means.

'That brings me to what we can do to protect ourselves,' said Horskram, pointedly ignoring the Thraxian's attempts at humour. Reaching into his habit he produced the phial containing the blood of the Redeemer. Adelko made the sign, Torgun and Aronn quickly following suit, though Braxus and Vaskrian looked unimpressed and Kyra and Anupe simply baffled.

'This will protect us against any demons, save those that he binds to natural matter, so we shouldn't have to worry about any demonic servitors,' he said. 'Likewise any undead he sends to fight us should be given pause.'

'Well that takes care of his henchmen, barring the Wadwo horde,' said Braxus dryly. 'What about him though?'

'Andragorix is a fetishist of the Seven Princes of Perfidy,' explained Horskram. 'That means he considers himself the living embodiment of all the sins they represent, and as such the proximity of this relic will appal and sicken him. That should weaken his elan somewhat.'

Horskram anticipated the question before Anupe could ask it. 'A sorcerer's elan is his stock of psychic power, that which he draws upon to use magic. It is also worth bearing in mind that Andragorix's should also be strained by keeping a Wadwo army in thrall and whatever else he is planning on conjuring up.'

Sir Braxus nodded. 'Will it be enough to stop him from blasting us into oblivion or making himself invulnerable to attack?'

'Not on its own,' admitted Horskram. 'However, Adelko and I will channel the powers of the Redeemer – using the Psalm I recited at the Earth Witch's Girdle. His blood will amplify our prayers. If Reus smiles on our efforts, we should be able to neutralise his magic.'

Adelko felt a palpable sense of relief go through the company at that. Good news had been in short supply of late.

'However, I've a feeling he won't send much in the way of demonic agents to trouble us on our journey to the Warlock's Crown,' added Horskram.

'Why is that?' asked Sir Torgun.

'He's been yearning for this showdown for years,' replied the adept. 'I don't think he wants to put this duel off for much longer. Oh he won't make it easy for us once we reach the Crown, but he wants to be in our presence when he attacks us, so he can see me suffer first hand.'

'Sounds like a lovely individual,' quipped Braxus, though Adelko could sense the Thraxian hid foreboding behind his humour.

'So that brings us on to tactics,' said the adept. 'When we root him out Adelko and I will be chanting the Psalm. It's down to the six of you to take advantage of our efforts to press him. Under no circumstances allow him any respite! Andragorix will always seek to attack, whenever he can. Once you let him do that, his elan will run riot and he will destroy you and then us. So keep attacking! We'll do our best to neutralise his command over fire and air to give you the chance to do that. Kyra, I presume your arrow-tips are made from iron and not steel?'

Kyra blinked, looking surprised. 'Aye, master monk,' she said. 'Couldna afford steel ones!'

'No, that is a good thing. Sorcery likes not pure iron – that's why we always chain apprehended witches using shackles made of it. If you concentrate your fire on him, his wizardry will be less of a defence against it. Adelko and I have quarterstaves shod with iron for much the same reason, though I doubt we'll get involved in close combat – unless things really go ill with the rest of you.'

'Why didn't you tell us that when we were back at Salmor?' demanded Aronn angrily. 'Our swords are made of steel!'

'And have been since your forefathers relearned the secret of smelting it centuries ago,' put in Braxus, looking exasperated. 'What was Horskram supposed to do, have us look up a bladesmith and ask him to make us a clutch of swords our great-grandfathers wouldn't have been seen dead carrying?'

'Sir Braxus is right,' said Torgun mildly, though Adelko sensed his keen resentment for the Thraxian. 'We cannot expect Horskram to think of everything weeks in advance. Besides, as he says, a knight of your station wouldn't have carried such a crude weapon, never mind consented to use one. Nor would I.'

'I suppose we could always punch him instead,' muttered Aronn sarcastically. 'Our gauntlets are mailed in iron.'

'Enough!' snapped Horskram, betraying his tension. 'As I said, if we work together and stick to the plan, you won't need iron weapons to get past his shield – Adelko and I will neutralise it with prayer and you can give him a steel farewell to your hearts' content.'

'Assuming his potions of Wadwo-strength and the like don't have something to say in the matter,' said Braxus. 'Does he use any conventional weapons?'

'Not as far as I'm aware,' replied Horskram. 'But be prepared for anything. His powers of Demonology have grown, as has his command of elemental magic – he may have other surprises up his sleeve.'

'So that's our plan?' asked Aronn incredulously. 'We just march into his cursed stronghold, say a few prayers and hope that's enough for us to kill him?'

Horskram glared at him icily. 'Your reductionist remarks put said plan into rather an unfavourable light,' he said brittlely.

'Fie on this melancholy mood!' cried Torgun. 'I trust I do not boast when I say we have proved ourselves stout and valiant ere now – if we follow Horskram's advice and work together as he says we shall triumph over this fiend!'

Sir Braxus sneered and rolled his eyes at Vaskrian, who merely looked resigned and weary. Sir Torgun stared at the Thraxian coldly, his fists clenching.

Not for the first time, Adelko wished he could turn his sixth sense off. Bad feelings were running through the company like a sewer. Even Torgun had betrayed a hint of doubt behind his bold words.

The novice tried to think of something to say, something that would lift their spirits, but no words came. Turning to look gloomily out of the cave, he watched the night rains harden.

'Don't be afraid, we mean you no harm.'

Sir Torgun raised his hands to show they were empty. The terrified villagers huddled together, not knowing whether to believe him. Around them the wreck that had been their hamlet lay scattered across the side of the mountain. The corpses of its twenty-odd residents were crushed into its side, the huts where they had lived lying in piles of smashed wattle.

The night rains had done nothing to dispel the clouds, and a cold grey morning had greeted them as they continued their journey further up into the Hyrkrainians. The hamlet lay at the end of a trail leading off the pass. Horskram had wanted to continue without stopping, but Torgun wasn't about to leave innocents to die a second time.

Not that there were any lives to be saved. The four surviving villagers had escaped death, but the rest were beyond aid, ugly red smears against the green mountainside. The bodies had been crushed by some awful strength.

'Did Wadwos do this?' he asked gently, kneeling slowly before the foremost villager, a greybeard of fifty winters or so. The poor man shook his head. He stuttered, trying to speak and failing.

'They're too afraid to talk,' said the blond knight.

'Tell us something we don't know,' muttered Sir Braxus.

Resisting the urge to draw his sword on the Thraxian, Torgun ignored him and addressed Aronn. 'Do you have any wine left in your skin?'

The knight nodded reluctantly and passed it over.

'Here, have some of this,' said Torgun. 'There's enough left for a mouthful each.'

The greybeard accepted the skin gratefully and took a swig before passing it to the others: a bedraggled-looking woman of about five and thirty, another man around the same age and a lad of less than ten summers who was crying.

It seemed to do some good. The greybeard looked at him again. 'My thanks, sirrah,' he stammered. He spoke the same mishmash of Northlending and Vorstlending that all border folk used, though his accent was less strong than that of the woodfolk. All the same, he wasn't easy to follow in his terrified state, so Torgun beckoned Kyra over to translate.

'Says it 'appened four o' five nights ago,' she explained. 'It were rainin' and they could 'ear Gygants shoutin'. Didna think much o' it – Gygants dunna often venture from the higher ranges north o' here. But this time it were different – it got louder an' louder, then...'

The old man broke off, crying hysterically.

'Canna follow what he's sayin'...' said Kyra. 'Somethin' abowt losin' 'is whole family...'

'Ask one of the others,' said Horskram, stepping forwards and suddenly taking interest. 'This could be relevant.'

Sir Torgun spared the monk a reproachful glance. *Now it's relevant*, he thought. *Now they know something he considers useful, not when they were just strangers in need of help.*

He had respected the Argolian Order all his life, defending them vehemently from the accusations of witchcraft they had so unjustly incurred since the Purge, but the adept's seeming disregard for ordinary mortal concerns irked him.

The woman started to pick up the thread of the story, putting a comforting arm around the greybeard.

'Says it were dark, but they saw what looked like a man flyin' through the air,' said Kyra. 'He were carryin' somethin', a *cage* it looked like... Then they 'eard a great crashin' sound, got louder an' louder, along wi' the screamin' ...'

Kyra gaped as the woman finished her story. 'She says a Gygant came crashin' across the crest o' yonder peak,' she said, pointing to the next mountain along. 'It 'owled like it were... *sad?*' She interrupted the babbling woman to check she had heard correctly. 'Sad,' she confirmed.

'That isn't so strange,' said Horskram. 'Gygants have been sad since the Elder Wizards killed most of their race and enslaved half the rest. Tell her to go on.'

'The thing stopped givin' chase, the flyin' man or whatever it were disappeared...'

'Which direction?' asked Horskram.

'That way,' said Kyra, pointing to where the pass snaked up and around towards a higher belt of mountains. Where the Warlock's Crown lay waiting for them. Horskram anticipated reaching it by dusk: once they rounded the bend the villager had pointed to they should be able to see it.

'It turned around and spotted this 'amlet,' she said, her voice quiet now. 'Went into a rage and walked right up to it, smashed it to pieces, killed everyone except them. They've been too scared to move since then.'

Horskram frowned, rubbing his beard thoughtfully. 'Sounds as if Andragorix is provoking giants,' he said. 'The question is why?'

'What was in the cage?' asked Sir Braxus. 'Ask her if she saw.'

Kyra relayed the question but the peasants shook their heads. 'Says he was movin' too fast and it were too dark to see clearly. They're not even sure it were a cage he was carryin'.'

'What happened to the Gygant?' asked Horskram.

'Turned around and went back up to the higher ranges where it came from,' said Kyra.

'Well at least it reverted to type,' said Horskram. 'That means Andragorix hasn't learned how to enthral giants, not yet anyway.'

'We thank you for the information.' Fishing into his pouch the adept scooped out a handful of silver marks from the money supply King Freidheim had provided him with. He pressed the coins on the younger man. 'Take these and get yourselves to safety – there is nothing for you here any more, your crops are ruined, your livestock fled or killed. Follow the pass downwards until you reach our camp. You'll get food and shelter there.'

Sir Torgun felt anger stir in his breast. 'For pity's sake, Master Horskram, must you be so stark in your speech?' he demanded. 'These poor wretches hardly need their woes spelt out to them.'

The adept stared at him coldly. 'These "poor wretches", as you yourself so gently label them, are clearly in a state of shock,' he replied. 'If hard words are necessary to jolt them into saving themselves, then so be it. I have wandered among the hovels of the poor and disaffected for years, Sir Torgun, whilst you disported yourself at court and played at gilded tourneys. I don't need lectures from the likes of you on how to address afflicted peasants!'

Flinging his cloak over his shoulder irritably he turned back towards the pass. 'Let's tarry not, gentlemen,' he said. 'We've a mission to complete.'

Sir Torgun stared at the monk's back, not liking the feeling of cold hatred that seeped through him. He caught Sir Braxus looking at him.

'Something troubles you, sir knight?' he demanded, meeting his gaze.

'Nothing at all, sir knight,' replied Braxus, favouring him with a brittle smile before turning to follow Horskram back down the trail.

✠ ✠ ✠

The sun was low in the sky when they caught their first real-life view of the Warlock's Crown. It was much as it had looked in the Earth Witch's pool, only now the spectacle was underpinned by a lingering sense of evil.

Adelko recited the Psalm of Fortitude with greater fervour as he and Horskram took the company up towards the blasphemous edifice. If attacked by sorcery they would switch to the Psalm of Gramarye's Quenching: until then the priority was preserving their sanity.

Up ahead the pass forked. The left-hand fork continued through the mountains and would take them eventually into southern Thraxia. The other fork wound up the side of a mountain that terminated in a plateau; atop it the five broken shards pointed up and outwards at irregular angles. More evidence of the Elder Wizards and their peculiar asymmetrical architecture: it was impossible to discern what shape the entire building would have taken. Looking on the Warlock's Crown would have given Arclidius, the Golden Age founder of geometry, a headache: the Priest-Kings of Varya had cast their buildings from an alien die, an ancient and forgotten methodology that followed no mortal logic.

Adelko repeated the words that had sustained them back in Tintagael, hoping it would be enough to keep them from fleeing in terror.

The skies deepened as they approached the fork. Still chanting the psalm, they took the one leading up to their destination. Chill winds strafed them as they ascended; drawing his cloak more tightly around him Adelko wondered if the keening gusts would suddenly take unnatural life, but it was as Horskram had predicted. Andragorix appeared to be conserving his strength.

The feeling of evil began to grow stronger. Ravens circled overhead. Adelko forced himself not to think of the Northland superstitions, of Søren and his doom, when the ill-omened birds had pronounced it even as he reached for the very artefact whose fragments they now went to recover.

The psalm's words were a burning imprint in his psyche by the time they reached the plateau. The crater was vast, covering most of its surface, and the shards were gigantic, the lowest one being the height of several castles. Their stones seemed to change colour as he looked at them; sometimes they appeared to be hues he could not name or recognise. This close they could see that between the shards some vestiges of the rest of the structure had survived; these clung to the lip of the crater and were the height of several men in most places.

'How in Reus' name are we going to get in?' asked Sir Braxus, giving voice to Adelko's thoughts.

Horskram broke off from the psalm, motioning for Adelko to continue reciting. 'Andragorix may be able to fly, but his servants cannot. There must be a way, let's investigate. Don't stray too close to the walls! They are still redolent of the Elder Wizards' sorcery after all these centuries.'

Horskram resumed the psalm and they began walking around the vast perimeter. The clouds had dispersed somewhat during the afternoon and the sunset basked the plateau with its golden glow; but in the presence of the Warlock's Crown the light seemed to take on an unnatural radiance, absorbing the myriad colours of the blasted edifice. It was too bright and hurt his eyes.

He caught a flicker of movement as they approached the first of the shards. Two beastmen clutching pikes stood before what looked like a gigantic sucker protruding from the concave surface of the shard. There was no cover to be had on the barren rock, which looked to have been charred in several places: age-old testimony to the Wrath of the Unseen.

The beastmen had not seen them yet. Without breaking off from his recital, Horskram signalled to Kyra. Unslinging her bow she nocked an arrow, drew and released. A beastman fell in a quivering heap as the Wose's Bane took effect; the lady of Dulsinor had found time to prepare them some more before they set out. The other turned and reached out to touch the side of the entrance it guarded, if entrance it was. Something next to it lit up. A second shaft sprouted from the creature's back as Kyra shot it.

They moved swiftly over towards the shard. Both beastmen were dead by the time they reached it. Gazing up at the stupendous ruin they had guarded, Adelko gawped. The shard leaned over them menacingly, like the claw of a gigantic monster, blocking out the warped light of the setting sun and casting them in shadow.

Up close he could see the entrance was inscribed with hieratic symbols around the entirety of its lip: by now he knew well enough that this was the Sorcerer's Script. The entrance-way was the size of a castle gate. At its side a globe was buried in the alien rock of the shard: it pulsed slowly with a light that changed colour every time it did. A faint humming could be heard above the sound of his own voice as he muttered the Psalm of Fortitude in a voice that quavered. Somehow the sacred words seemed primitive now; he felt like a small child babbling in a grand hall of men.

The entrance was covered with a strange gelatinous substance that was black as night. The humming continued for a few more moments, then suddenly the substance dissolved. Before it was a chamber shaped like a lop-sided S that appeared to be made of some kind of black stone. At its far end was an irregular opening that he supposed was a window. The stone had stopped pulsing and gone dark, though another shaped like it only larger was set into the ceiling and shed a steady grey light on the room.

Still chanting, Horskram stepped across its threshold, motioning for them to follow. Adelko felt it first empathically as it touched Horskram's psyche, then directly as he crossed over himself: it was like stepping naked through an invisible waterfall, only it was cold to the soul not the body. He shuddered as he stepped up to join Horskram at the window.

As he did so it dawned on him that the chamber was not made of stone, but metal. What kind of metal was black?

'Ebonite,' muttered Sir Braxus. 'This room's made of *ebonite*.'

The others looked at him quizzically. 'There are deposits lying in hills on my father's lands,' the Thraxian explained. 'No other metal is like it. Black as night and harder than diamonds. So hard, no one knows how to smelt it.'

'Not since the Elder Wizards,' supplied Horskram, before adding: 'Come and look at this.'

The window looked like a lop-sided polygon. It was covered with a strange invisible substance, similar to the room's entrance but transparent. Adelko knew instinctively it wasn't the sheet glass he'd read about: that had been invented by artificers in the Empire some two centuries ago and was very rare in the Free Kingdoms. Reaching out to touch it he was scarcely surprised when it gave slightly, moving outwards before his fingers like a membrane.

'Don't touch anything!' cried Horskram sharply. 'I said come and *look*.'

The novice gingerly pulled back his hand. They had simultaneously broken off the Psalm, but he supposed that they had been reciting it for hours now: if that wasn't enough to keep them sane there wasn't much point going on with it.

Following his mentor's instructions more precisely he gazed at the view the peculiar window offered.

The crater was several hundred yards in diameter and topped a shaft that fell for at least the same distance. The lower levels originally counted five storeys, each one as high as those of the Watchtower of Tintagael: their broken remains jutted from the shaft's walls, giving it the look of a giant screw-thread. Roughly half of the lowest storey before the basement floor had survived the Wrath: Adelko guessed that Andragorix had holed himself up in there somewhere. The portion of basement floor exposed to the dying sunlight was littered with huge chunks of broken masonry, its bizarre stones glowing with the same shifting colours as the shards. At one end was a giant black grill set into the floor, presumably made from ebonite. He could make out two more humanoid figures standing at one end of it.

'It's a pretty enough view, but how do we get down?' asked Sir Braxus.

Adelko looked downwards, trying to follow the shaft wall directly below the room. He could see the shattered remains of the next storey jutting out from it, but nothing more. There were no other exits from the chamber.

'They must have a secret door somewhere,' said Horskram. 'Why else would they have been guarding it? Let's search.'

'Here,' said Anupe. 'Another stone, just like the one on the outside.'

The stone was exactly the same as its twin, directly opposite and set into the ebonite seamlessly. As a blacksmith's son, Adelko had to marvel at the craft of the Elder Wizards.

'Don't touch it,' said Horskram. 'It might shut the entrance and trap us.'

They searched the chamber but found nothing. The sun had set, but the vast ruin remained suffused in the strange light of the stones. No need to light a torch – Adelko felt strangely satisfied at that. A flaming brand in a place such as this would have felt too primitive somehow.

'Well it's either touch yon stone or continue with our tour of the perimeter,' said Braxus. His levity did little to conceal his nerves. Adelko could sense a palpable fear about the entire company.

Closing his eyes and muttering a quick prayer, Horskram touched the stone. Immediately it lit up and the black membranous substance reappeared. Horskram was about to touch it again when they felt the floor judder beneath them. Adelko felt a strange sense of weightlessness.

'It's... sinking!' he said.

Panic broke out. Drawing her falchion Anupe began hacking at the entrance, but the black portal turned her blade. Pulling her aside Sir Torgun hurled himself at it, only to be thrown back into Sir Aronn. Horskram began chanting the Psalm of Gramarye's Quenching. Kyra and Vaskrian stood stock still, terrified.

Adelko looked out of the window. They were moving quite quickly, passing through the next storey towards the floor of the ruin.

'Wait!' he cried, stepping over and grabbing Horskram's sleeve to break his concentration. 'Don't cancel it out! I think the spell is... well, taking us down to where we need to be.'

His mentor paused as if making up his mind, then nodded. 'Everyone be still!' he said. 'Get your weapons at the ready – let's see if Adelko has the right of it.'

The chamber descended to the lowest level and shuddered to a halt. With a hum the room started to turn on an invisible vertical axis. That provoked another panic, but Horskram told them all to stay calm and keep their wits about them. When the chamber stopped the entrance-way was facing into the shaft. Horskram touched the stone again and the black membrane vanished.

The sight it revealed took Adelko's breath away. The vast space they stepped into was lined with intricately sculpted friezes of demons and angels intertwined, punctuated at irregular intervals where walls would once have divided it into chambers. The ruined chunks of masonry were also carved with sculptures that looked to have once adorned swirling pillars, lopsided gables and irregular pediments that would have Arclidius turning in his grave. The sculpted demons cavorting with angels were unsettling enough, but there were other things too: depictions of men and women, tall and strong-limbed, with broad flat faces and strange-looking hair, wielding sophisticated tools he didn't recognise against the backdrop of stylised cityscapes whose buildings followed a bizarre structure. It wasn't like the crowded tenements of the lower levels of Strongholm, whose builders had strived but failed to achieve perfect angles... these ancient architects had deliberately pursued an alignment that made perfect sense to *them*. The hubris of it also struck him: a bygone culture that celebrated itself pathologically, even to the point of depicting monuments upon monuments. Not for nothing was Azathol one of the more prominently rendered demons. And yet there he was, hand in hand with his angelic opposite, Siona...

A noise startled him. He suddenly realised he had been wandering around the ruin for he knew not how long, enthralled by its eerie splendour. From somewhere distantly he heard the clash of arms. Turning disinterestedly he saw three knights fighting four Wadwos. Where was Kyra with her poisoned arrows, he wondered? There she was, staring at half a head from a gigantic statue. He couldn't tell who it was supposed to be. He couldn't blame her for looking at it, so much more interesting than a handful of armed –

'Adelko! Recover your wits!'

Horskram was shaking him roughly by the shoulder. Adelko blinked and stared into his keen eyes. Like sapphires they had seemed, when he'd first seen them all those years ago in Narvik...

'Adelko! The Psalm – this place is unmanning us with its magic. Now is the time!'

The novice shook his head to clear it, realising what his mentor was saying. He reached into his habit for the *Holy Book* but Horskram shook his head.

'You should have learned it by now,' he said. 'I need you to concentrate on the words themselves, not reading them. Your conviction must be absolute.'

Adelko nodded. This was what he had prepared for after all. Closing his eyes, he began reciting the Psalm of Gramarye's Quenching with the adept.

Loudly they chanted, shouting the sacred words up to the deepening heavens. Kyra blinked and stirred. The four Woses were the largest of their kind they had seen. Dressed in giant hauberks they wielded huge axes: the three knights were hard pressed. Kyra nocked and drew, her hands a blur. A Wose fell dying.

Vaskrian appeared from around a pile of broken stones, sword in hand. Anupe did likewise a few seconds later. Joining the fray they took the pressure off the knights long enough for Kyra to bring another low with a second shaft. A third turned and charged towards her. Holding her ground, she planted another arrow in its forehead moments before it reached her. The others cut the final one down, finishing it off with heavy strokes.

'What took you all so long?' asked Sir Braxus. 'Didn't you hear us charge yon beastmen?'

'Never mind that for now,' replied Horskram, risking breaking off the Psalm. 'We need to move quickly. There must be a way into the ruins.'

'There's an entrance over there,' said Sir Torgun. 'Two of them were guarding it.'

They picked their way through the warped masonry towards the surviving half of the lowest storey. Adelko caught the odd skeletal remains of warriors as they did: doubtless the grisly remnants of freebooters from a bygone age. The novice wondered at the greed that must have set them on such a doomed path.

The half of the lowest storey that had survived the Wrath was uneven and scored by a dozen broken walls jutting out of it at odd angles; a segment of it had fallen in altogether. But where there should have been a gap was a sheet of thick ice that sparkled in the light of emerging stars and the eerie glow of the ruins.

'More elemental magic,' said Horskram. 'We must use the psalm to neutralise it.'

A low rumbling sound distracted him. It was coming from below the grill.

'That's what the other two Wadwos were guarding,' said Sir Aronn. 'I'm not sure I want to know what it is.'

'Look!' cried Adelko. 'The ice barrier's disappearing!'

The barrier seemed to melt sideways into the ruined wall. From behind it stepped a tall figure, dressed in voluminous black robes and a cloak of the same colour covered with sigils of the Sorcerer's Script picked out in gold thread. A mop of unruly blond hair topped a cruelly handsome face. His left hand looked to be encased in a silver gauntlet of curious design.

'You didn't think I'd cower in my private chambers waiting for you to find me, did you?' he demanded as he advanced towards them. 'Ah, Brother Horskram, how I've longed for this moment!'

'I am only too happy to oblige you in this matter,' replied Horskram, keeping his voice calm and measured.

Andragorix stopped and raised his gauntleted hand. Adelko realised then it *was* his hand, fashioned entirely of silver. It moved with perfect dexterity. 'Perhaps I'll cut a few parts off you before I kill you – when you lie begging for mercy amid the slain corpses of your pathetic henchmen.'

'Enough talk, Andragorix,' answered the adept softly. 'This ends now.'

Without pausing Horskram launched into the Psalm of Gramarye's Quenching again. Adelko had already resumed reciting it. Pointing at Horskram with his silver hand, Andragorix muttered a few words, the fell syllables jarring horribly with the sacred litany. A torrent of red flame shot from his hand straight at the old monk. The fires wrapped around him... but the psalm worked a magic of its own and protected him.

Kyra nocked and drew. Her arrow flew towards Andragorix. He spat another arcane word and the air in front of him shimmered and condensed. The arrow's iron tip passed through it... but the sorcerous shield had slowed it enough, and the shaft bounced harmlessly off his robes.

The others charged him. Muttering another word Andragorix flew up into the air, landing on top of a chunk of masonry.

'Hardly fair odds I think!' he cried, then muttered again, raising both hands and gesturing upwards with his fingers. The skeletal remains of five adventurers suddenly stirred and rose up, clutching rusted weapons as they stalked towards them.

✣ ✣ ✣

A light shone from Sir Braxus. Glancing down he saw it was the brooch the Earth Witch had given him. The embossed hawk was now glowing with a blinding light. He heard Andragorix scream as the light exploded, and five silver hawks suddenly burst from the brooch and flew towards the undead warriors, descending on them with metallic screeches.

'Fair odds are overrated!' he yelled back at the warlock.

✣ ✣ ✣

Horskram and Adelko remained rooted to the spot, chanting the psalm. Andragorix rained fire on both of them, but the scarlet flames enveloped an invisible space around them. Horskram held the blood of the Redeemer aloft, its single drop curiously similar to the conflagration that threatened to consume them.

Adelko felt the warlock's power pushing against them, threatening to overcome their sanctity. Shutting out all thoughts of fear he focused on the words, basking in the grace of the Redeemer. All doubts that the Earth Witch had raised in him about the Creed were pushed aside; doubt was a luxury he could not afford now.

The skeletal warriors rolled across the floor as the silver hawks latched onto them, raking their bones as they slashed at them mechanically.

✣ ✣ ✣

Andragorix pushed with all his might. Visualising the symbol for fire, he commanded the Saraphi bound to his hand to attack the monks, enveloping them in a halo of red flames. He could sense their elan wavering before his onslaught, but the psalm would gather power over time and he had to act quickly. He kept the woodland peasant in the corner of his eye, waiting for her to fire again. Another woman was clambering up the chunk of masonry towards him, but he knew its eldritch stones and carvings would weaken her mind and slow her down.

The woodlander drew her bowstring back and released. Andragorix furrowed his brow: this next bit wouldn't be easy. While intensifying the Saraphi's attack on the monks he commanded the Aethi bound to his cloak, directing them towards the arrow. The potions he had swallowed allowed him to perceive everything as happening ten times more slowly: he saw the shaft coming towards him in slow motion, the air spirits curling around it...

Following his command, they spun the arrow around, pushing at its feathers and sending it back towards the shooter. The effort of commanding fire and air simultaneously with such intensity and precision nearly killed him, but it paid dividends: the Argolians were too busy focusing their elan on stopping him from burning them alive to neutralise his counter attack.

He felt a surge of pleasure as the woodlander took two steps backward and dropped her bow. Looking down with a shocked expression she registered the arrow buried in her sternum. She slumped to her knees and keeled over.

He had no time rejoice in his victory: the warrior woman was nearly on him now. Ceasing the attack on the monks he ordered the Aethi to gather him up, his robes billowing as he pirouetted through the air and landed agilely on the floor between the four swordsmen.

✣ ✣ ✣

Vaskrian gawped as Andragorix landed in their midst. In the blinking of an eye he swept a sword from its sheath. Its black blade was frosted over with tiny points of silvered light; it became a shimmering swirl as the warlock laid about him, fending off their attacks and going on the counter with a strength and speed that astonished him. Turning aside his blow and Braxus's in quick succession, he spun to face Torgun and Aronn. The blade seemed to move with a life of its own as he parried Torgun's thrust before knocking Sir Aronn's sword out of his hand.

Before Aronn realised what had happened Andragorix struck him down, shearing through the burly knight's mail coat, collarbone and sternum. Aronn fell to his knees as a gout of blood erupted from him, slumping back in the awkward pose of death.

Sir Torgun screamed a war-cry and launched himself at the warlock. The knight's strength and speed were a match for

Andragorix, who stepped back nimbly, fear written across his face. But fear turned to triumph as he caught Sir Torgun's blade with a fierce stroke, shearing through it a hand's breadth above the hilt. The warlock tried the same trick again, going on the counter with a lethal downwards stroke, but Sir Torgun saw it coming and hurled himself aside, rolling across the broken flagstones as Braxus and Vaskrian pressed him hard. Andragorix knocked their attacks aside as if they were children before countering. Vaskrian used footwork he never knew he had as they both retreated before the onslaught, breathing hard.

Grabbing up Aronn's sword, Torgun joined the three of them as they circled the sorcerer warily, not daring to close with him again.

'Stay separated,' he said. 'He'll cut us to ribbons if we attack him together.'

A scream fiercer than any Wadwo's ripped through the air. Anupe had seen Kyra's corpse and was bounding down the ruin she had climbed towards the warlock. But as she cleared the fallen monument something strange happened: her legs tottered and she fell to her knees gasping.

'Horskram might have warned you about not touching the stones the Elder Wizards wrought,' crowed Andragorix. 'They aren't very healthy for those unaccustomed to their magic!'

✥ ✥ ✥

Adelko muttered the psalm in a feverish voice. He was focusing hard on the words, but could not help notice what was happening. Aronn and Kyra lay dead, and Anupe was writhing on the floor having some kind of fit. Andragorix seemed possessed of a superhuman strength and speed, and was armed with an indestructible weapon to boot. The Psalm might turn his fire and weaken his force field, but even bereft of those he seemed invulnerable.

His hope was faltering when metallic screeches reminded him they were not alone. The silver hawks had got the best of the undead warriors, whose decayed weapons were of little use against their metallic feathers, tearing bones from sockets and skulls from vertebrae. The five birds now sped towards the warlock, who conjured up a force field to protect himself, swirling his cloak around him. But at least it distracted him enough to give the others some respite.

Closing his eyes and reattuning his psyche to Horskram's, the novice focused on the sacred words...

✛ ✛ ✛

From behind the swirling vortex of air spirits protecting him, Andragorix stared at his ten remaining opponents, half of them mortal, half not. He could feel the psalm's power growing, bolstered by the relic Horskram wielded. Its proximity sickened him; he could feel it sapping his elan and weakening his body, counteracting the effects of the potions. He couldn't hide behind his shield forever, but he wasn't sure his demonic blade would avail much against the conjured hawks. The Earth Witch's power coursed through them, spirits of nature bound to magic metal.

He furrowed his brow again. Time to change tack.

Raising his silver hand he visualised a stylised zigzag, dropping the shield as he summoned more Thaumaturgy to aid him. Opening his mouth he felt a pressure build inside his head. Energy coursed the length of his body. He spat hard. With a blinding crack, blue veins of electricity shot from his mouth, striking the silver hawks with jagged fingers and sending them skittering across the ruined precinct with screeches that set his teeth on edge.

The swordsmen hadn't attacked: they weren't sure if he had dropped his force field or not. Spitting on his blade, he sent a shock of electricity running up the length of it and renewed his onslaught.

✛ ✛ ✛

Andragorix dashed towards them, his body and blade wreathed in a crackling web of blue energy. Sir Torgun dodged out of the way, circling him frantically. He didn't normally go on the defensive, but this was no ordinary opponent. Keeping out of range of his sword wasn't much help though: energy coruscated the length of the sorcerer, intensifying before exploding towards him in a blinding bolt. Sir Torgun felt a shock course through him as his feet lifted off the ground just before he blacked out...

✛ ✛ ✛

Vaskrian watched as his hero went sailing through the air, carried by a blue bolt of lightning and landing in a crumpled heap ten yards away from where he had stood. The warlock must have used up his spell, for only a few stray strokes of energy flickered around him now. This was his chance. Dashing towards the sorcerer he raised his sword high to strike him down...

Andragorix spun and held up his silver hand. A torrent of fire shot from it. It wasn't as powerful as before but at close range it was enough to do damage – Vaskrian screamed as the crimson flames burned up his arm and a searing pain strafed the side of his face. He dropped his sword and slumped to the ground, agony exploding through him...

✢ ✢ ✢

Braxus came hard at the warlock, striking at his other side as he repelled Vaskrian with a blast of fire. The mage turned and deflected his blade, before riposting with a lethal thrust. Braxus gasped as he felt it slice through his side – a step slower and he would have been gutted like a pig. The wound burned with a strange frost. Ignoring it he struck at the sorcerer again. The Argolians were practically shouting the words now; he wasn't a religious man but something in them stirred him up. He was damned if he would die here, in this blasted godforsaken place: again and again he hewed at the sorcerer, driving him back towards the broken monument where Anupe had tried to attack him.

The warlock was starting to slow, though he was still very quick. His sword moved with a life of its own, but the strokes behind them were less mighty, the footwork less nimble. No more fire shot from the mage's silver hand, and the electricity had disappeared altogether. Was that a look of fear he saw on his face?

✢ ✢ ✢

Andragorix fell back before the enraged knight, sweat lashing off of him. He could feel his strength ebbing. He needed to kill this fool and deal with the monks quickly, before their cursed prayers neutralised all his magic.

A metallic screeching reminded him that wasn't his only problem. The birds had reanimated themselves: though their silver forms had been tarnished by his attack they were swooping down towards him again.

It was time to do something he had hoped wouldn't be necessary, but there was no alternative. Mouthing a command to the Aethi he flew up, circling around the crater before landing on top of the half-ruined storey that topped his complex of chambers.

The hawks pursued him mercilessly and he ordered the Aethi to shield him. He could sense the air spirits' power weakening: it wouldn't be long before they were useless to him.

Closing his eyes he mouthed a few syllables, envisaging a stylised gate opening and a bar being lifted off a great portal in quick succession. The vast ebonite grill slowly parted down the middle. He had not learned to control his captive – he had only captured it by temporarily shrinking it and putting it in a cage – but one more burst from his cloak should get him out of range of its demented attacks.

Andragorix smiled evilly as a gargantuan hand reached over the edge of the hole exposed by the receding grill.

He dropped his shield and the hawks descended on him. He sheared through the first with his demonic blade, before leaping backwards out of range of the others. His body was trembling with the effort now: his superhuman strength and agility were fading too.

✤ ✤ ✤

Sir Braxus turned in the direction of the rumbling sound. The vast grill was opening, parting into two halves as it slid into the floor. Something clutched at the lip of the pit it had sealed: Braxus gaped as it slowly hauled itself out.

The Gygant was humanoid in shape, but looked as though it had been fashioned from liquid rock; its vast knotted muscles moved supplely and yet somehow looked as solid as stone. Its face resembled a primitive statue of a man's, only one that was alive. Something like moss and lichen passed for its beard and hair.

Braxus trembled as it took a thundering step into the chamber: it was at the other side, but even from that distance it was obvious he reached no higher than its knee. The giant gave vent to a roar that shook the mighty ruin to its foundations; stray chips of stone fell from the shattered storeys, skittering across the floor hundreds of yards below.

The Gygant scanned the chamber. It seemed confused, though it was hard to tell from its chthonian features. Horskram and Adelko had broken off their psalm, and turned to stare wide-eyed at the gargantuan horror that now menaced them. The giant made the Golem they had fought look like a toy doll. Something in Braxus snapped as it turned its yellow eyes on him. They looked like two pools of molten lava, which for all he knew they were.

Sinking to his knees the knight mouthed a prayer, and hoped for a swift end.

✤ ✤ ✤

Adelko felt his faith drain out of him like lifeblood from a lethal wound as the colossus crashed towards them. No psalms that he knew of could ward off a Gygant, fashioned from the flesh of Aurgelmir, Father of Giants, of whose very body the earth was made. Making the sign he mouthed an ordinary prayer for succour – only a miracle could save them now.

The giant was lumbering towards Sir Braxus, obviously intending him as its first victim. The poor knight's will was broken, and he stared vacantly as his death closed on him with feet bigger than a man's torso.

Horskram sighed and shook his head. Stepping into the Gygant's path, he looked up at it and bellowed something in a language Adelko could not understand. The colossus paused and leaned down, cocking its head. It was disconcertingly man-like in its manner. Horskram repeated the foreign word he had yelled, before yelling some more in a voice grown hoarse with use.

The Gygant stared at him. Two great furrows of lichen slanted over the pools of molten lava. Was it *glaring* at him? Then it spoke, if you could call it that, the words reverberating around the cavernous shaft and shaking more residue from the walls.

Horskram yelled back at it some more. It knelt on one knee, bending its head closer to hear him.

Adelko was so focused on the bizarre conversation – not that he understood a word of it – that he almost forgot about the fight up on the roof. A final screech told him it was over: the last hawk fell, decapitated by Andragorix's night-black blade. But as the warlock limped over to the edge the novice saw that it was a dear-bought victory: his robes were torn in several places, and he was covered in his own blood.

The Gygant was looking from Horskram to Andragorix and shaking its head. Seeing the sorcerer approach it started to rise. Andragorix yelled something at it in the same tongue, his voice shrill and his face angry. Horskram was yelling too. The Gygant took a step towards Andragorix, then hesitated. It shook its head again. Turning, it bounded towards the wall, shaking the ground as it went.

'Did you think you were the only one who would ever bother learning the tongue of giants?' asked Horskram, gazing coldly up at the mage. 'It is a simple enough language to learn, though I grant you lessons are not easy to come by.'

Andragorix sneered. 'Let the cowardly brute run, I'll deal with it after I've finished with you! It's provided me with the distraction I needed to finish off that earth bitch's sorcerous thralls.'

Adelko's sixth sense put the lie to those words instantly: the warlock had clearly been hoping the Gygant would kill them for him in its fury. Whatever his mentor had said to it, he had evidently convinced it to let them be. The warlock was scared and his powers were greatly diminished. The Gygant began climbing out of the shaft, using the broken storeys as a ladder.

'Come down here and let's finish this off,' said Horskram. 'Enough chicanery – why don't we fight it out man to man? No more sorcery, no more psalms. Just you and me.'

'I don't see your merry band coming to much in the way of interference in any case,' laughed Andragorix.

Glancing around him Adelko saw it was true enough: Anupe appeared to have recovered from her fit, though she was moving slowly as she dragged herself to her feet. Sir Torgun lay dead or unconscious and Vaskrian writhed on the floor moaning and clutching at his face. Sir Braxus was staring off after the giant, still mouthing incoherent prayers. It seemed a strange time to find one's faith – or perhaps quite the contrary.

'I take it your novice knows well enough to stay out of this,' said Andragorix.

Without waiting for an answer he spat another word and his cloak furled up around him again, the symbols on it flaring into light. Rather than fly, all he could manage this time was a gust of air to settle him down on the floor gently. His powers had been sorely taxed by the psalm: it wouldn't wear off for a while so Horskram should be safe from his Thaumaturgy. Adelko half considered praying by himself, but his own psyche was badly drained and in any case he wasn't confident of being able to harness the psalm's power by himself.

Horskram drew his quarterstaff from his back in a swift fluid motion as Andragorix came at him with a feral snarl. His Alchemy was evidently still working some of its magic, and though he wasn't superhumanly fast he would still be a formidable foe. Adelko mouthed another prayer as the warlock closed on his mentor.

✣ ✣ ✣

Horskram clutched his staff in both hands, one end tilted towards Andragorix, his feet planted firmly apart in a defensive posture.

The warlock tore into him with a primal scream.

The next minute was a blur of motion as he absorbed the attack, parrying one blow after another as he stepped nimbly around Andragorix, soaking up his furious onslaught like shifting sands against a stormy tide. His quarterstaff rang across the blasted precinct, his arms juddering as Andragorix struck time and again with a strength that surpassed his slender body. The warlock was trying to shear through his quarterstaff, but good honest iron would turn any demon magic, denying his vorpal blade the chance to cleave it in twain: whatever else the warlock's powers ran to, smelting ebonite wasn't among them.

His spirit was weary with channelling the power of the Redeemer, but his body brimmed with vigour far exceeding his run of mortal years. His sixth sense anticipated every move the warlock made: as fast as he was, Horskram was a shade faster. A clinical battle rage burned in the old monk like a cold fire.

One of them would die tonight: let his soul rot in Purgatory for another killing if that was Reus' will.

At last he sensed Andragorix begin to tire. That was the moment he chose to counter attack. The warlock stepped back, ragged gasps dogging every footfall as Horskram enveloped him in a blurred maze of strikes and follow-ups, his feet moving in perfect synchronicity, always finding the right space beneath them. He followed up a blinding figure of eight that sent the mage's sword spinning from broken fingers with a pulverising sidewise swipe, twisting from the waist to get maximum power behind the blow. Andragorix gasped as his ribs cracked, spinning around with the force of the strike. A split second later Horskram reversed his staff, bringing the other end down on his clavicle with enough force to shatter it.

Andragorix slumped to the floor groaning, his silver hand scrabbling across the cracked flagstones as he struggled to keep himself from collapsing in a heap. He began to spit more words of magic but Horskram was ready, kicking him viciously in the gut and knocking the wind out of him before he could complete the spell. The warlock rolled over onto his back and the adept stepped in, placing the end of his staff against his larynx and applying pressure.

✤ ✤ ✤

Adelko watched as his mentor slowly began to crush his arch enemy's throat. He was dumbfounded. He had seen Horskram fight brigands, but what he had just witnessed was far beyond that. He had never seen anyone except Sir Torgun fight with that kind of controlled ferocity. There were few men who could make mortal combat look like a work of art, and his mentor was one of them.

Andragorix began choking. Adelko thought he was going to crush his throat and kill him there and then, but suddenly Horskram relented. Kneeling down on his chest before he could recover his breath for another spell, Horskram took the Redeemer's blood and placed it against the warlock's forehead. He began moaning and shuddering, his body convulsing spasmodically.

'Let's see you try any more magic while Palom's blood kisses thy cankered skin,' he said softly. 'I need answers before I send you to Gehenna. Where in yon chambers are the Headstone fragments? What sorcerous traps have you set around them?'

Andragorix moaned and writhed some more. Pulling back the phial Horskram grabbed him by the lapel of his robes, yanking his head up to face his.

'I'll spare you another touch if you answer swiftly. Where precisely are they and what traps have you laid?'

Andragorix began laughing. It was just as it had sounded the first time Adelko heard it, back in the Sea Wizard's chamber at Salmor Castle. It sickened him. Part of him wished his mentor would just kill the mad warlock now and be done with it.

'WHERE ARE THEY?' bellowed Horskram.

Andragorix stopped laughing for long enough to squeeze a few words out.

'They're quite safe... but not here.'

'Thou liest!' cried Horskram, applying the Redeemer's blood again.

The warlock howled and squirmed. 'NO!... Please, take it away, take it away... I'm not lying, I swear to thee!'

Horskram withdrew the phial again.

'If not here, then where?' he demanded.

'I can't... I can't tell you... I've been bonded...'

'Your service to the Author of All Evil is well known to me, poltroon,' sneered Horskram. 'Now tell me – '

'No... I don't mean bonded to Him, I mean ... aahh!'

The warlock started to shudder, as if straining against something. Adelko could sense some force stopping him from talking. Horskram's brow creased with consternation. Adelko's sixth sense was telling him the same thing as Horskram's.

Andragorix wasn't lying.

'He's been ensorcelled!' gasped Adelko as the realisation hit home. 'He's serving another warlock!'

'Who?' demanded Horskram, brandishing the Redeemer's blood.

'I'd tell you if I could...' said Andragorix, wincing with every word. 'Never... never meant for him to get the best of me... after all these years...' Looking up at the night skies, he muttered: 'I would have bested thee in the end.'

The warlock screwed up his eyes. Adelko sensed the controlling force recede, like pressure being lifted off something. 'Just get it over with, Horskram,' spat the mage, opening his eyes and grinning sickly. 'You've beaten me and won nothing. Yours is a hollow victory.'

'There'll be no death sentence until we find out who your master is,' said Horskram. 'Adelko, hold him down!'

Gingerly Adelko did as he was told, but there appeared to be little to fear: Andragorix was badly injured and his Alchemy had all but worn off. Taking the phial from around his neck Horskram placed it around the warlock's. He screamed horribly, but the monks tore a portion from Aronn's cloak and stuffed it in his mouth, binding it with another sliver.

'That should disable him until we work out what to do with him,' said Horskram, rising and moving away from the convulsing warlock. 'We'd best gather the others together, see about – '

'Where's Anupe?' Adelko interrupted, his sixth sense suddenly jangling. The warrior-woman had vanished.

They cast around, scanning the ruined precinct carefully. The Gygant had gone, leaving more debris in its wake. Kyra and Aronn lay dead, Torgun motionless. Adelko couldn't tell if he was breathing or not. Vaskrian was sobbing with pain and curled up in a ball on the cracked floor, while his master continued to stare and pray silently.

A noise came from behind the foot of a vast statue. In its heyday it would have been even bigger than the giant they had just faced. Horskram took up his quarterstaff and motioned for silence. Adelko drew his own shakily and they stepped cautiously towards the huge fragment.

Adelko's sixth sense flared at the same time as his mentor's. As one they turned to see Anupe, dashing over towards Andragorix from behind a chunk of broken wall, dirk in hand.

'No!' cried Horskram, rushing to intercept her. But it was too late. They had stepped away from the warlock, and a few seconds was all the swift Harijan needed. Whatever effect the magic of the stones had wrought upon her, it had been overturned by the primal forces of love and vengeance.

By the time Horskram restrained her she had stabbed Andragorix in the chest twice.

'You damned fool pagan!' he snarled, pulling her away from the dying warlock. 'We needed him alive!'

'He killed Kyra!' yelled the Harijan. 'He deserved to die!'

A pool of blood was forming around Andragorix as Adelko knelt beside him. He was close to death. Pulling the cloth from his mouth Adelko yanked the phial off his neck.

'A dying man is bonded to no one but Azrael,' said the novice frantically. 'You're free to talk – tell us who you serve!'

'He – ' began the mage, but blood trickled from his mouth as he coughed up the last of his life. His head slumped to one side, his eyes freezing over.

'Blasted idiot!' yelled Horskram, flinging the Harijan from him in disgust. 'Your perverted amorousness has cost us our mission!'

Anupe spat on the ground at his feet and stalked off towards Kyra's body. All was silent but for Vaskrian groaning. Horskram stood staring into the middle distance, his eyes registering nothing. Leaning on his quarterstaff he suddenly looked very weary.

A flutter of wings startled Adelko from his melancholy thoughts. He gazed up, half expecting to see more of the Earth Witch's silver hawks, but he saw nothing of the kind.

Perched on the roof, a lone raven stared at them with gleaming eyes, and let out a triumphant screech.

PART TWO

⤖ CHAPTER I ⤖

An Audience With Royalty

The old monk's face lengthened by inches as he read the parchment Sir Wolmar had given him. They were alone in the auditorium; the princeling stood in the broad shaft of sunlight admitted by the oculus and fidgeted impatiently. The sooner he was gone from this accursed place the better.

His three weeks at sea had been uneventful. A great pity: some ragtag remnants of Thule's rebel navy, or a Northland freesail or two, would have gone well to banish the boredom. At least they had made a space for him below decks of the carrack that had brought him to Rima; sleeping with the crew beneath the skies would have been an indignity past enduring.

The Grand Master of the Order of St Argo shook his head in consternation, his grey eyes never leaving the message Wolmar had crossed sea to bring him. The knight shifted his weight restlessly from one foot to the other.

He yearned for mortal combat. The fire that burned in him night and day would not be quenched. It had burned all the more hotly since his father had been slain. Lost to peasant scum as he lay dying, beaten by a traitor using pagan sorcery. Kill a thousand men in glory on the field, and the sting of that loss would never abate.

But at least killing would give him something to keep his mind occupied. It was his favourite past-time, and he was right good at it too.

And yet here he was, playing messenger boy for a king who could hardly find it in himself to show his nephew the respect he deserved. Despite everything he had done for Freidheim – avenging his brother and killing the leader of the uprising that had threatened to dethrone him.

Oh no, no thanks for Sir Wolmar! It was his hated rival, Sir Torgun, who got the King's blessing. Sir Torgun who got promotion. Sir Torgun who was probably even now being lauded by troubadours and knights and soldiers across the kingdom.

He knew his so-called fellow ravens called him many things. They called him unjust – but where was the justice in the way he'd been treated? They called him cruel – aye, he was where it was warranted, but then so was every knight. They called him vain – vain! What opportunity did they afford him to indulge in that sin? No glory for Wolmar: no, just opprobrium and cavilling, from men he'd proved himself superior to a dozen times and more. Tarlquist and Aronn and all the rest of them, prating on about a Code of Chivalry they scarcely understood.

None of his achievements mattered to the Order he'd served so loyally: all they cared to remember were the three poachers he'd killed earlier that year. Well, so what if he had? They had been dishonest, common, weak. Preying on their own verminous kind – not that he cared a jot about that, but what had bothered him was the smug look that villein had given him when he'd told him it wasn't a capital offence under the King's Law. How *dare* a common churl tell him, a prince of the blood royal, what the King's Law was and what wasn't?

He had deserved to die – yes, him and his two smirking cronies.

The Grand Master raised his eyes from the parchment and eyed him keenly. Sir Wolmar didn't care for the old monk's scrutiny. It reminded him of Horskram, only it seemed worse – more penetrating, in a less obvious kind of way.

'This is ill news indeed,' said Hannequin. 'In fact, the worst I have ever had the misfortune to receive during my tenure as Grand Master. What a pity Brother Horskram could not have delivered it in person.'

Wolmar caught his icy tone, but was too busy feeding on his outrage to revel in the thought of the friar getting upbraided by his superior.

'Yes indeed, a pity,' was all he said.

The Grand Master sharpened his gaze. He had a face that some would call kindly, but Wolmar knew better. The Argolians were a nest of vipers, little better than the wizards they claimed to fight. Why, they were practically wizards themselves! Hadn't the Purge established that much?

'You certainly don't have much to say for yourself,' said Hannequin. 'Given you're an emissary of royal blood, carrying a message of... such import.'

Wolmar gestured dismissively at the unfurled scroll in the Grand Master's hands. 'Yon parchment says it all,' he said. 'Beyond that, I'm to wait on your pleasure until you have decided on a course of action, then relay news of it back to mine uncle the King. Besides that I have other business to attend to in the capital.'

'I see.' Hannequin frowned and rested the parchment on his lap. Then he sighed deeply. 'I cannot pretend that this news does not leave me on the back foot. I must needs convene the Archmasters... we'll sanction a divination this coming Rest-day and see what we can learn.'

'And the King in Rima?' queried Wolmar, trying to take an interest in his mission. 'Will you tell him – or shall I be the one to do it? I bear a letter of introduction to his court, though His Majesty King Freidheim suggested you might want to inform him directly.'

Hannequin paused and rubbed his chin. He looked deeply perturbed. That pleased Wolmar – any suffering incurred by an Argolian was a good thing. All the more as it was their wretched intriguing that had brought him all the way out here in the first place.

'No, you may as well inform His Majesty if you have been given leave to do so,' said the monk. 'Tell him I will hold counsel with him on the matter as soon as he sees fit.'

The princeling knew enough of politics to realise that the Grand Master might not wish to divulge such details – but now he had no choice in the matter. He also knew enough of politics to understand that King Carolus III of Pangonia would not look kindly upon him for having informed the Argolian Order first about such a matter. But King Freidheim had been insistent on that point. Probably thanks to Horskram and his secretive meddling – Argolian vipers spreading their poison, clouding the judgement of great men like his uncle.

'Very well, I'll tell him when I see him,' said Sir Wolmar, dissembling his thoughts. He was about to excuse himself when the old monk said: 'Your business in Rima... does it involve His Supreme Holiness as well?'

The Grand Master was staring at him again, his face inscrutable in the bright sunlight that poured in through the oculus and the round windows of the hemi circular chamber.

How did he fathom that? Wolmar asked himself. As far as he knew, his father's message mentioned nothing about the Supreme Perfect. The princeling had also been charged with informing the head of the True Temple of Lorthar's imprisonment and the existence of the Redeemer's Blood in Strongholm. Lucrative pilgrimages would be arranged, the reliquary opened up to the Palomedian faithful after generations of secrecy: in return His Supreme Holiness would take no action over Lorthar's abrupt replacement.

Damned Argolians and their sorcerous sense – Hannequin was reading him like an open book. All the more reason to get away from this benighted place.

'His Majesty King Freidheim's other business is his own,' replied Sir Wolmar, meeting his gaze defiantly.

Hannequin nodded, as if making his mind up about something. 'Of course,' he said mildly, though Wolmar suspected his thoughts were anything but mild. 'I shall in any case have to inform His Supreme Holiness of this calamity, so you needn't bother dissembling when you meet him – although it would sound better if he heard it from me directly.'

Making a mental note to tell the Supreme Perfect of the Headstone thefts at the first opportunity, Wolmar nodded.

'It shall be as you say, Grand Master.'

'Your words are compliant, yet your soul speaks differently,' replied Hannequin, sounding weary. 'Well, I cannot compel you in this matter. And now if you would be so kind as to leave – I must speak with the senior brethren.'

Wolmar needed no further encouragement. Turning on his heel he strode from the chamber.

⁂

Striding through the antechamber of the inner sanctum and back out into the circular courtyard, Wolmar made his way over to the south-facing cloister he had entered by. This was one of four elongated buildings that joined the wall enclosing the inner courtyard to the outer walls that encompassed it in a much larger concentric circle.

Circles within circles within circles... The monastery was just like the minds of the monks who called it home: the Grand Priory of St Argo was by far the strangest building he had ever been in. Its bizarre layout confirmed all his suspicions about the Argolians.

At the entrance to the cloister Brother Abelard, the journeyman who had escorted him to the sanctum, was waiting.

'I trust your meeting with the Grand Master went as planned?' asked the monk, a bald man of about thirty summers.

'Yes thank you, just as planned,' replied Wolmar, without breaking stride as he marched into the cloister.

'I take it you have lodgings for the night in the city,' said the monk, struggling to keep up with the tall knight. 'Otherwise you are most welcome to – '

'No thanks,' sneered Wolmar. 'I'd sooner sup with the Fallen One than the likes of thee! No need to show me out, I know the way – good day!'

Leaving the monk spluttering in his wake, Wolmar walked past the monastic cells to either side of the cloister's colonnaded walkway, ignoring the other monks peering at him from their cells as he passed. Reaching the gatehouse on the perimeter wall, he took a side exit into one of the four outer courtyards. Novices were sparring on the clay under the stern tutelage of journeymen, but Wolmar paid them no heed as he headed over to the stables.

Without waiting for the monk on duty to assist him, he untethered his Farovian destrier and walked it back to the gatehouse. Years of serving in the Order had taught him self-sufficiency, and in any case he was damned if he'd linger here a moment longer than necessary.

'Come now, Svinnhest,' he muttered to the magnificent steed, in a voice that was soft for the first time that day, 'let's get thee gone from this strange place, before they do something to you!'

Leading Svinnhest out through the gatehouse, he took to the saddle and kicked him into a trot down the winding trail that had taken him up through hills to where the monastery sat on a promontory of rock overlooking Rima. He spared a glance for the Pangonian capital as he did. Though he was glad to be out of the monastery, he had mixed feelings about his next destination.

He had arrived in Rima that morning, sailing up the River Athos that spilled out into the Athan Estuary to feed the Bay of Biscayan. He hadn't had much time for sightseeing, but it seemed as splendid as the tales told: at least twice the size of Strongholm, its white stuccoed buildings betokened a rich city that did nothing to belie its origins under the fabled Chivalrous King Vasirius. That galled him somewhat. The Pangonians were widely regarded as the haughtiest of the Free Kingdoms, convinced of their innate superiority to all the other realms in Western Urovia. That such attitudes mirrored his own scarcely entered his mind.

Still, such places were liable to offer much in the way of diversion: especially to a prince of the blood royal carrying a letter of introduction to its reigning monarch.

Only a few stray ribbons of white cloud tarnished the perfect skies above. More southerly than his homeland, Pangonia was in the full bloom of high summer. That would mean tournaments and galas and other entertainments aplenty. The thought cheered him.

So the Pangonians reckoned they were better than everyone else did they? Perhaps they'd never had one of Northalde's finest to contend with – he'd soon show them the error of their ways!

Kicking his horse into a gallop he tore off down the trail, sending sprays of dust in his wake.

✢ ✢ ✢

Several hours later he was standing in the Palace of White Towers, choking on envy. As a king's grandson he was no stranger to great halls of men; his childhood had been spent between his uncle's royal residence at Strongholm and his mother Jorda's ancestral home in Vandheim. But neither his uncle's seat of power nor the splendid castle his mother had grown up in could rival the sheer grandeur that now enveloped him.

The palace had looked impressive enough from outside. Perched atop a broad hill in the northern quarter of the city, it was more elegant than its sister at Strongholm, its architects having given thought to pleasing the eye as well as defending a monarch, and its conical-topped turrets and finely-wrought corbelling made for a striking first view. It was also, he could not help but note, considerably larger than the palace he had called home for years before joining the White Valravyn.

All of that had been bad enough. But when the liveried palace guards had ushered him into the High Hall of Kings, his resentment had turned into outright mortification. For the Royal House of Ambelin ruled from a seat that could surely have no other rival in the Free Kingdoms.

Despite himself, Sir Wolmar took another long, lingering look about the hall that had done so much to stoke up his envy as Carolus read his letter of introduction. Like the Argolian inner sanctum it was circular, but not partitioned; it was colonnaded at regular intervals along its entire circumference with pillars of limestone, punctuated by large oblong windows that opened onto the courtyard. The front of each pillar had been sculpted to fashion a giant likeness of the original thirty knights of the Purple Garter, the greatest of King Vasirius' chivalry who had sat with him at the Crescent Table and helped rule the realm he had fought so hard to consolidate.

Each statue was twice the size of a normal man. Gazing on the graven images Wolmar could almost believe they really had been of such stature: he was new at court and yet he already fancied he recognised some of them, such was their legend. Sir Lancelyn of the

Pale Mountain, who slew the great dragon and was disfigured as a result, mightiest of all yet always sad and brooding; Sir Balian of the High Castle, who stormed and took the last great holding to defy Vasirius with just forty-seven knights; Sir Ugo the Giant-breaker, impossibly strong, who wrestled and overcame three Gygants, each one bigger than the last; Sir Alric the Pious, who saved the King himself from the curse of the White Blood Witch with a drop of the Redeemer's blood...

That last one reminded him of his own mission, and sent his gaze flickering back towards the King. But Carolus was either a slow reader, or liked to keep his guests waiting. Wolmar felt self-conscious, standing before the dais that stretched up towards the rear end of the hall's domed ceiling. The latter was lined with galleries fashioned of mahogany: Vasirius had seen fit to allow ordinary citizens to witness royal judgment, believing that a King should ultimately serve his people. The galleries were empty, and had been since his death at the Battle of Avalongne some two centuries ago: not even King Carolus the Pious, the well-intentioned dolt who had fathered the monarch he now waited upon, had seen fit to revive that ridiculous custom.

But if the galleries were empty, the court they overlooked was far from it: knights, ladies and other high-ranking nobles thronged the throneroom, chatting amongst themselves in their native Panglian as they moved to and fro across the marbled floor and selected sweetmeats proffered by servants from silver trays.

Come to think of it, Sir Wolmar had little reason to feel self-conscious; on the contrary he felt positively ignored. By the King, and his courtiers.

All but one, he noticed: he caught a tall handsome noble staring at him with keen black eyes. Something in that look gave him a thrill of pleasure, one that he suppressed immediately.

'So, your mission of state brings you here to see the heads of both the Argolian Order and our holy Mother Temple,' said the King, abruptly breaking his silence and addressing him in Decorlangue. 'Your uncle the King of the Northlendings bids me welcome you as a royal guest during your sojourn here – and yet divulges little details as to what this... religious business consists of.'

His voice sounded offhand, bored almost, and strangely at odds with the echoing hall that carried it through the splendid precinct. Yet the words were pointed enough: blood princes of realms rarely crossed seas to speak with clerical authorities. The richly dressed courtiers had stopped talking amongst themselves and suddenly taken an acute interest in their new arrival. The handsome noble was still staring at him.

Feeling self-conscious again, Sir Wolmar replied: 'The business you speak of shall be told to you at a better time, when there are not so many prying eyes.' He caught more than a few disapproving noises at his haughty words. Good, that would teach them to ignore him.

'You wish for a more private audience?' asked the King, his brow furrowing.

'The Grand Master says he will hold counsel with you and His Supreme Holiness on this matter,' said Wolmar. 'He shall tell you everything he knows then.'

The King held his gaze for a few moments. The Pangonian monarch was not yet forty, and seemed a far cry from Wolmar's uncle: a lean, spare man of middling height, with close-cropped sandy brown hair. His robes of office were brocaded black and surprisingly devoid of embellishment, cut neatly about his trim figure. The crown upon his brow was a rare beauty though, a compact circlet of gold fashioned to resemble mounted knights clashing, studded with rubies and emeralds.

But it was the seat he perched on that really drew Wolmar's eye. The Charred Throne they called it, in mind of the blackened skull of the Wyrm slain by Sir Lancelyn from which it was fashioned. The famed knight had brought back its head to commemorate his great victory; the eldritch creature's upper jaw formed the base of the throne. The top half of the reptilian skull had been hollowed out and covered with a convex basin of smooth stone to form the actual seat, but the sides were part of the dragon's skull – the monarch's arms rested on what must have been the creature's craggy brows.

In a much smaller and less impressive throne next to him lounged the Queen of Pangonia. Isolte the Fair certainly deserved her simple epithet, though her face could hardly be seen behind the elaborately carved fan she waved to keep the stifling heat at bay. She was dressed after the southern fashion, in maroon-coloured robes of samite bedecked with pearls and silver filigree that showed off her pleasing figure. Gazing on her lissom form Wolmar felt his loins stir again. They'd hang him for entertaining that desire too, albeit for different reasons.

'Very well,' said the King at last. 'I shall wait to hear from the Grand Master, seeing as your uncle saw fit to inform him first of the contents of his royal mind. In the meantime I shall have quarters arranged for you here at the palace. Sir Odo, see it done!'

From a chair on a lower part of the dais, a stout knight in early middle age rose and bowed stiffly. He was dressed in a purple tabard with a silver crescent and thirty stars, the age-old insignia of the Royal Garter. Several other knights dressed in the same regalia took up seats in that part of the dais too. One of them looked particularly well made. Sir Wolmar made a mental note to seek his provocation at the first opportunity – he looked to be a foe worth fighting.

Sir Odo descended the stairs of the dais to give orders to an old man of more than sixty winters, presumably his under-seneschal, who disappeared up a corridor leading to another wing of the palace. The knight shot him a dark glance as he returned to his place: clearly the haughty Pangonian did not like waiting on the pleasure of foreigners. Sir Wolmar favoured him with a sneering grin.

'In the meantime, I think you will need someone to show you around,' continued the King in the same bored voice. 'Lord Ivon, if you would be so kind as to acquaint the Northlending prince with the finer points of our customs... There is much for an outlander to learn about them.'

The same nobleman who had been appraising him favoured his king with a courteous half bow and approached Wolmar. The princeling felt a stirring of excitement again, one he struggled to master as the comely lord drew nearer.

'Lord Ivon, 23rd Margrave of Vichy and First Scion of the House of Laurelin, most delightedly at your service,' said the noble with a florid bow.

'Sir Wolmar, knight of the White Valravyn and scion of the House of Ingwin, at yours,' replied the Northlending, feeling suddenly awkward. He would scarcely own it even to himself, but faced with the Pangonian's graceful manners he felt like a landless vassal rather than a prince.

'Come,' said Lord Ivon, taking him gently by the upper arm. 'Let us mingle together. I'll introduce you to some people you should meet... and point out a few you would do well to avoid.'

The Margrave favoured him with a flashing smile, his white teeth catching the late afternoon sunlight. Ivon was taller than the average Pangonian, though that still placed him half a head shorter than Wolmar. Like the princeling Ivon wore his hair long and kept a neatly trimmed beard and moustache, though his tresses were raven-dark where Wolmar's were fiery. His cream-coloured doublet and hose, slashed with sky-blue silk, showed off a lean, athletic figure to rival his own.

Wolmar felt himself colour as the Margrave made contact with him, and hoped his cheeks weren't suddenly the colour of the rubies that dripped off the rings adorning his new host's fingers. He had struggled over the years to hide his less orthodox desires, knowing full well it meant expulsion from the Order and probable banishment from Strongholm if anyone ever found out. That or worse. He'd lain with as many wenches as he could to throw his father and the other knights he served with off the scent: not that he didn't enjoy women too, but getting them with child was tedious and caused problems of its own. Suppressing his yearnings for his fellow ravens had never been too difficult: frankly, he despised and looked down on most of them.

But the Margrave was by far the most attractive man he had ever set eyes on.

As Ivon led him into the throng of courtiers, Wolmar hoped his desire wasn't too obvious. The last thing he needed was to be exposed before the haughtiest bunch of nobles the Free Kingdoms could furnish while on a royal mission of emissary.

Lord Ivon steered him over to a group of richly dressed noblemen and women. They were standing close to the wall, near the statue of St Alric. That only made Wolmar feel more nervous as the Margrave began introducing him.

The princeling didn't bother to take in the names of the lesser courtiers, but made a point of memorising those of the higher-ranking nobles and noting their demeanours.

Lord Aravin, Margrave of Varangia, was a tall, well-muscled man of about thirty summers, dressed in a dark blue doublet and hose worked with silver thread and moonstones. A sapphire flashed from a ring he wore as he raised his hand to quaff from his goblet, sneering into his drink to show what he thought of the foreign princeling when Ivon introduced him.

Wolmar yearned to show Aravin what he thought of *him* in the lists – see how haughty the Pangonian would be spitting his own teeth into the soil.

Lord Kaye was scarcely less arrogant, but hid it better, giving a bow of welcome that was every bit as insincere as it was outwardly courteous. The Margrave of Quillon was dressed in black, though the embossed decorations on his clothes were set with tiny rubies and amethysts only visible at a close distance.

That says a lot, thought Wolmar, *wants to remind everyone he's rich, but doesn't want to shout too loudly about it either*. The secretive type, evidently.

Lord Rodger was a shocking sight. His clothes were of similar hue and cut to Ivon's, but there all similarity ended. They were dishevelled and stained with dark red patches that told of a man who loved his wine too well. Unlike the rest of the trim pack he ran with, he was portly and short of stature; he shovelled sweetmeats into his mouth from a proffered tray in an apparent effort to increase his girth even further.

Wolmar greeted him with a sneer of his own when Lord Ivon introduced them: he felt nothing but contempt for nobles who didn't keep themselves in shape as befitted members of the warrior class. But as the Margrave of Narbo, Lord Rodger was probably worth remembering.

'It's a pleasure to make your acquaintance,' said Rodger. 'We have oft heard tales of the Northlending chivalry, but we had no idea how wedded to the field you were... Is that armour comfortable? It's certainly a bold fashion statement.'

Ladies tittered behind their fans. Kaye and Aravin favoured Rodger's jibe with sneering laughs.

Wolmar felt rage rising. He wasn't used to being looked down upon, and tasting his own medicine was not an experience he relished.

'I hear much of your gilded tourneys,' he shot back. 'Perhaps my armour shall become me better at the melee, and you shall have the opportunity to show us your true mettle.'

He was expecting Rodger to be cowed or at least on the back foot. Instead he let a braying laugh off the leash as the ladies looked at each other and tittered again – only this time they didn't bother to conceal it behind their fans. Aravin looked at Kaye and rolled his eyes, the latter shaking his head.

Lord Ivon cleared his throat. 'My lord Wolmar, the custom of the melee was dispensed with in Pangonia some generations ago,' he said delicately. 'It's considered far too uncouth nowadays – jousting and pageantry are the main events at our tourneys.'

'Then perhaps I'll show you all what a Northlending can do in the jousts!' snapped Wolmar. But the remark was clumsy and he knew it: he'd just been outplayed by the Margrave and was now a laughing stock. His ears burned as Lord Rodger smirked and took a gulp of his wine.

'As to his dress sense,' said Lord Ivon, addressing his cronies in a firmer tone, 'Sir Wolmar can hardly be blamed for turning up in full caparison having just arrived after a long journey. And you should all treat our guest as an honoured one – foreigner or no, he is a prince of the blood royal.'

That raised a few eyebrows. 'You are related to the King of the Northlendings?' asked Aravin curtly, sounding interested if not entirely impressed.

'He's my uncle,' said Wolmar, sounding sullen and childlike. 'My great-great grandfather was King Thorsvald V, the Hero King, a rival to King Vasirius himself!'

He knew he'd said the wrong thing even as the words exited his mouth. Aravin snorted into his goblet. Rodger and Kaye added their laughter to the tittering of the ladies. 'Absurd contention,' muttered Aravin into his wine.

Wolmar was about to reply when Lord Ivon took his arm again. 'I think the good knight needs refreshment after his long journey. Here, Sir Wolmar,' – taking a goblet from a nearby servant he pressed it into the princeling's hand – 'drink up! Afterwards we'll see you to your quarters – your travelling things will no doubt be wending their way there as we speak.' He lowered his voice to a whisper. 'Should give you the chance to get into something more appropriate.'

Wolmar felt himself flush again, though not with anger this time. The Margrave's intimacy, however fleeting, excited him.

Lord Ivon led him away from the nobles. 'Try not to take their bait, Sir Wolmar,' he said gently. 'My crowd aren't accustomed to mixing with foreigners – but don't worry, I'll put in a good word for you!'

Wolmar scarcely had time to ask him why he would do that when the Margrave stopped to take another goblet of wine from a servant, nodding over towards another group of nobles loitering at the other side of the court as he did.

'Over there, the tall one – that's Lord Morvaine,' he said. 'He's a rival of mine and quite insufferable – if you think Lord Aravin is haughty try talking to him!'

'If he's as insulting as Lord Aravin there'll be more than words betwixt us,' snarled Wolmar. 'Or have you Pangonians abolished the duel of honour as well?'

'Well, we prefer to call it the duel of *chivalry*, but no,' replied Lord Ivon, smiling sweetly. 'But I see little need for any bloodletting between the pair of you. My advice is to steer clear of him, and his cronies… Unlike my lot, I won't be able to talk them around into showing you due respect I'm afraid.'

Wolmar turned to fix him with a stare. 'Why would you vouch for me? I thought Pangonians stuck together.'

Lord Ivon gave an expression of mock surprise that Wolmar could not help but find endearing. 'And Northlendings don't? But no – never mind all that! To answer your question, my King has commanded that I look after you, and I am loyal to my King.'

There seemed to be a world of subtexts in the Margrave's words, one that hid behind his impenetrable dark eyes. Wolmar took another sip of wine. It was every bit as good as it was supposed to be – the southerly Free Kingdoms were rightly celebrated for their fine vintages, and here he was in the richest of them, at its richest court. But as the fumes went to his head he wondered if intoxication was a good idea: he prided himself on being on the offensive at all times. This was, put simply, a new experience for him.

'I think I'll go to my chambers now,' he said. 'Change into clothes befitting a prince's son.' He underscored the last two words pointedly. Lord Ivon said nothing but responded with a nod. Doubtless it was intended to look deferential, but it wasn't quite convincing.

'A good idea, Sir Wolmar,' he said. 'Get out of your warrior's weeds and I shall see you for dinner presently. After that I'll point out a few more important people. Don't despair – we Pangonians are a difficult lot, but we're not so bad once you get to know us!'

'As if I cared,' sneered Wolmar, but the words sounded unconvincing in his own ears. Lord Ivon said nothing, remaining inscrutable as ever. With a frustrated sigh the princeling ordered the nearest servant to show him to his quarters.

✣ ✣ ✣

By early evening Wolmar was dressed in court clothes and sitting back from dinner, which had consisted of far too many courses, each far too small. Why all the fuss, he'd wondered, but he knew the answer. Pangonians showing off their wealth as usual.

At least he felt slightly more relaxed. He had rested at his chamber, a spacious enough affair in the western wing of the palace, before donning his best outfit: a white doublet and breeches made of satin and chased with black filigree picked out in silk. A few more goblets of Pangonian red from Armandy province had taken care of the rest. He could even sit next to Lord Ivon without flushing, though his desires had scarcely left him.

He made a mental note: when the time was right, he'd seek out one of the comely wenches that waited at table and a well-made lad from the stables. He'd have them both at once. That should satisfy his appetites and serve as some reward for the ordeal his mission now forced him to endure. He hoped they'd accept Northlending coin – for their service and their silence.

'So, to business,' said Lord Ivon, leaning over and whispering in his ear. 'I promised to point out a few other courtiers you'll want to know of.'

'What do I care?' said Wolmar. 'Reus willing I won't be here for long – in fact the sooner I'm on a ship back home the better!'

Several nearby nobles caught this remark and glanced at him. He was speaking Decorlangue, so everyone of note could understand him. Wolmar met the youngest noble's eyes with a cold stare. The noble averted his eyes after a few seconds.

Good, they hadn't failed to register that he was bigger and stronger than most of them.

'Perhaps you should lower your voice,' said Ivon quietly. 'Not everyone at court is quite the pushover in the lists you seem to think they are.'

'Did I say they were?' snapped Wolmar, the wine going to his head. 'On the contrary, I'd be only too glad to find out what the nobility of Pangonia is made of – if they fight as well as they talk they must be paladins indeed!'

This time the nobles sat nearby ignored him, although one or two ladies looked at him disapprovingly.

They were sitting at trestle tables arranged in a horseshoe shape in the feasting hall – unlike the King of Northalde, the Pangonian monarch had to dine in a different room, yet another indulgence. Wolmar and Ivon were seated at the section nearest to where the King sat with his family and highest officers of state: at least he'd been shown the proper respect as an honoured guest.

'Well, go on then,' he sighed, doing his best to relax into his stiff high-backed chair. Back home everyone barring the King and his family would have made do with a bench – but this lot had to have seats for everyone. He envied the luxury as much as he despised it.

'So, you've already met Sir Odo de Gorly,' continued Ivon, indicating the burly knight who had given him the dark look in the throneroom. 'He is Steward to the King. But don't be fooled by the homeliness of the title – he is responsible for all internal affairs of the realm and has eyes and ears everywhere.'

'I'm well acquainted with what it really means to be a seneschal, Lord Ivon,' said Wolmar. 'What about that fellow next to him with a face like an ox?'

'That is Sir Hugon, the Captain of the Knights of the Purple Garter. Not a man to cross – he serves as High Marshal and is castellan to the palace. That makes him head of the army in times of war.'

'My father held such office... before he died.' Wolmar stopped abruptly. 'Go on,' he pressed, keen to divert his painful thoughts. 'Who else should I challenge to a duel of chivalry?'

Lord Ivon looked at him peevishly.

'A jest, my lord,' sighed Wolmar. 'If I'm to be the butt of everyone else's jokes I should be allowed a few of my own, don't you think?'

Frowning, Lord Ivon continued: 'The knight next to him is Sir Aremis – he's tipped to succeed Hugon eventually. He's the best sword in the land.'

'I've already added him to my list,' said Wolmar, recognising the strong-looking knight he had been sizing up earlier. 'He looks to be a worthy opponent at least.'

'You might get more than you bargain for, knight of the White Valravyn,' cautioned Ivon, looking unusually serious.

Wolmar waved his goblet. 'Enough jokes then, seeing as they sit so ill with you. Who is the other Crescent Knight yonder, at the far end of the King's table?'

'That is Sir Alaric de Leon, bastard brother to the Margrave of Gorleon. The Margrave hates his brother for rising higher than him in the body politick... but the King knows a good Sea Marshal when he sees one. Gorleon is our westernmost province and long celebrated for its maritime tradition.'

Wolmar knocked back the rest of his wine. He cared not a fig for Gorleon's maritime tradition. 'So what about the rest of them? Your King's family table is rather small... pray don't tell me they've all had the misfortune to die.'

Ivon favoured him with another inscrutable look. 'The King has two living children. The eldest, Carolus the Younger, is but four and of a... sickly constitution. The youngest is princess Adeline and but a babe, so far too young in years to sit at table. Not even we are so formal.'

'What about that lass next to the Queen?' asked Wolmar, ignoring Ivon's attempts at deadpan humour. 'The plain-looking girl,' he added, unnecessarily.

'That is Lady Iveline, daughter of Prince Lothaire, the King's younger brother. He died the same year as His Majesty ascended the throne.'

Wolmar turned to look at Ivon, catching his tone. 'Both father and younger brother died in the same year, eh?' he offered. 'What a strange coincidence in time of peace.'

'How strange indeed,' returned Lord Ivon, his eyes sparkling in the brazier light.

'But in Pangonia, the eldest son inherits, just as in Northalde,' said Wolmar, measuring his words carefully.

'Indeed... Perhaps all the more reason to be pleased to have ambitious younger brothers out of the way.'

'How did they die? In separate incidents?'

'Oh no – they both perished seven years ago, when the royal pleasure barge caught fire on the Athos. It was quite the tragedy I assure you – His Majesty Carolus II was a dearly beloved liege.'

By some but no means by all, thought Wolmar, silently finishing the Margrave's sentence for him.

An awkward silence hung between them. Lord Ivon snuffed it out, motioning to the other side of the horseshoe. 'I already pointed out Lord Morvaine,' he said. 'The serious-looking fellow sat next to him is Lord Uthor the Younger, heir to the margravate of Aquitania.'

'What are they here for?' asked Wolmar.

'Same thing as usual,' replied Ivon, motioning for a serving wench to refill both their goblets. 'They want a repeal of the taxes the King has levied on all his domains.'

'Will they get what they want?'

'Unlikely, though Aquitania is the most powerful of the southern margravates, so technically that should give Lord Uthor some leverage... It's not really for me to speculate.'

Wolmar looked back at the Margrave. He had a feeling Ivon did a lot more than merely speculate.

'You are well informed, it seems,' he ventured. 'So what brings *you* to court? You seem over long in years to be enjoying its distractions.'

Ivon laughed at that, seemingly unruffled. 'I am five and thirty summers, that much is true,' he said. 'I have a wife and two children of my own, who get along perfectly well without me back in Vichy. And, to answer your implied question, no, I have not wearied in the least of Rima's *distractions*.'

The Margrave fixed Wolmar with a look that the princeling could have sworn mirrored his own desires, before taking a healthy swig of wine.

'He is by far the most accomplished debaucher among us,' said Lord Rodger, leaning in to interrupt their conversation. 'As no doubt you will come to know, Sir Wolmar. In fact, no man can rival His Lordship Ivon when it comes to drinking, carousing and... other appetites!'

Sir Wolmar looked from one lord to the other, not knowing what to say next, but Ivon merely smirked and raised his goblet in a mock toast. Lord Rodger continued: 'And speaking of carousing, the feasting is done, but now we shall disport ourselves with yet more drink while a dancing troupe from the Free City of Athina entertains us. Pray join us in our merrymaking, Sir Wolmar, if it please you.'

Lord Ivon favoured Wolmar with a wink. 'I said I'd put in a good word for you,' he whispered, grinning over his wine.

⸙ ⸙ ⸙

A few more goblets later and Wolmar found himself embroiled in a debauch. The dancers had come and gone but the troubadours had remained; the polite applause of the Riman court had given way to a riotous hubbub as the high-born proceeded to get royally drunk.

Not all had stayed: the King and Queen had disappeared from the feasting hall, along with most of the ladies. That left knights and lords free to grope the common serving wenches to their hearts' content – a desire many were giving free rein to. Several of the younger nobles were being sick in sputum bowls apparently set aside for that express purpose. Pangonian hauteur had given way to decadence, once again on a scale that put the royal court of his homeland in the shade.

Wolmar was on the point of approaching a dark-eyed wench who had been giving him the eye when Lord Ivon sidled up to him.

'Your goblet is empty, Sir Wolmar!' he exclaimed, throwing an arm around the knight. 'At the most opulent court in the Free Kingdoms, I can tell you, that simply *will not do*.' Barking an order he summoned another wench over to refill their cups, running an appreciative hand over her firm buttocks as she obeyed.

'Do you wish to lie with her?' he asked bluntly, though of course she would not understand Decorlangue.

'Not her – there's another over there I want,' slurred Wolmar, gesturing at the raven-haired beauty he'd been eyeing. 'And another over there…' He hiccoughed and shook his head. He usually held his drink well, but Pangonian wine was strong stuff.

Lord Ivon barked something else at the wench serving them and sent her off with a slap on the behind. Keeping his arm around the princeling, he led him over to a pillar in the corner of the rectangular hall.

'Yes, I believe you want her, and half the wenches here,' said the Margrave, leaning in close so Wolmar could smell the wine on his breath. 'And you can have her, or any of them, if you wish – as the King's honoured guest you shall not be refused anything.'

The Margrave leaned in closer. The music, its dulcet strains disrupted by ebrious shouting, sounded like a cacophony in

Wolmar's ears. The air had cooled to a pleasing balminess, brought in through the large bay windows lining the hall.

'But I believe there is something else you want, more than all the wenches in this room,' added the Margrave. His dark eyes burned with a black fire that seemed to snuff out the yellow flames of the braziers.

'What... what are you saying?' asked the princeling hesitantly.

'Do you know who my family are?' asked Ivon.

'No... you said you belong to the House of Laurelin...'

'An old and distinguished house,' nodded the Margrave, 'going back to Lotharion the Founder, First King of Pangonia. But that isn't who we are.' He paused to take a slurp of his wine.

'I don't understand.'

'Two hundred years ago, my ancestors fought on the side of King Vasirius and married into his family,' continued the Margrave. 'The Two Solons, we call them – Solon the Elder and Solon the Younger. Both had seats at the Crescent Table. The Elder was a founder member of the Purple Garter, and married a niece of the King. That makes Solon the Younger, and every one of his descendants, of royal blood going back to the Ruling House of Rius.'

Wolmar took another slug of wine. By the archangels, but these Pangonians loved to spout their heritage! Next to them he almost felt modest.

'And what does that signify?' he asked, trying to ignore the sudden redirection of his desire from the serving wenches.

'What that signifies,' said Lord Ivon. 'Is that like you, I am of royal blood.'

Still Wolmar didn't see the significance. 'And?'

'*And...*' the Margrave tossed his goblet aside, gently drawing Wolmar around to face him before putting his other arm around his waist. 'That means... we can do whatever we like.'

The Margrave stayed like that for a few moments, his arms encircling the princeling. Then a vulpine grin crossed his face as he pressed closer. The music swirled up to the pillared ceiling, its flurried notes reverberating and mingling with hoots and yells as high-born men and low-born women prepared to couple the night away. As the last of his inhibitions fled and he dropped his own goblet, Wolmar felt something inside him break, like a dammed-up river bursting into torrid life after years of being held in check.

Blissfully ignorant of the passions it had helped to stir up, the music continued to swirl madly about the high hall.

⊶ CHAPTER II ⊷

The Shield Queen's Hall

'Walmond has secured Varborg and invested it,' said the messenger. 'In addition to the three hundred men you left under his command, he has engaged five hundred freeswords that were at the port. That's eight hundred fighting men ready to repulse the Stormrider should he send a fleet to attack Jótlund.'

Guldebrand nodded, fidgeting with the new robes of state he'd had tailored to commemorate his remarkable victory three weeks ago. He was nervous: it was a victory that could be swiftly reversed, if he played his hand badly.

'And how are the berserkers?' asked the Thegn. 'Are they under control?' Of the warriors he had left behind in Jótlund, a third were fanatical devotees of the war god Tyrnor, who fought without armour or thought for life. They were fiercer than the levied shieldmen and even more skilled in battle than the noble seacarls, but they could be unpredictable.

'Eager for more slaughter as ever,' replied the messenger. 'But Walmond has them in check – you left behind one seacarl for every berserker, they'll keep an eye on them.'

'Good,' he said, taking a sip of wine. 'And what news from Utgard?' he asked, turning to his envoy Varra, a burly seacarl of forty winters covered in battle scars.

'Good news!' said Varra, grinning. 'Asmund has been cowed as predicted. He says he will make no intervention as long as you pledge not to raid his lands.'

'Excellent,' replied Guldebrand. 'Let him cower behind his walls at Hjalring for now. We shall soon demand tribute from him, when the next plan is hatched.' Turning to look at Ragnar, he said: 'White Eye, now is the time to tell us how your suit with Magnhilda has sped.'

He still wasn't comfortable with the idea of having a sorcerer as his right-hand man. But since he had left Walmond behind with most of his victorious warband to hold Jótlund, the position had been empty. And Ragnar had promised him great things.

His hand strayed habitually to the pomander he still wore as the wizard gave his report. Technically, he didn't need it any more – not since Ragnar had pronounced the incantation of Counter-Ensorcellment with his old understudy Radko witnessing – but all the same he had felt it best not to part with it. Just in case the wily mage tried anything underhand.

'I returned this morning,' said Ragnar in his cold voice. 'The Thegn of Scandia is at least willing to consider our offer of an alliance, backed by marriage.'

A hubbub of approving voices went up around the hall. Valholl, the seat Guldebrand had inherited from his father Gunnar less than two years ago, was filled with seacarls who had come to hear the news and take counsel for their next course of action. Guldebrand raised a hand for silence and the warlock continued.

'She wants to meet with us in person, at her seat in Utvalla, one moon hence,' he said. 'You are to bring a retinue with you numbering no more than a hundred men. She guarantees safe passage through her lands.'

Guldebrand nodded again. 'Very good, White Eye, send word to her again. I shall be there, with said retinue, at the next full moon.'

'I shall inform her in person,' said Ragnar.

A few discontented murmurings went up at that. Ragnar's ability to transform himself into a raven and deliver messages swiftly and safely was undeniably useful, but all the same his sorcerous ways made the men nervous. Guldebrand could not help but steal a sideways glance at Radko, who skulked nervously in the corner. The hedge wizard had best be right about Ragnar's counter charm being binding.

Still, he had his pomander to protect him, and Ragnar's former apprentice could renew the enchanted simples inside it whenever needed.

'Good,' said Guldebrand, not showing any of his misgivings. 'See it done.'

He half expected the warlock to transform himself on the spot and fly away, but the White Eye had enough sense at least to make a normal exit from the hall.

'Brega, come forwards,' said Guldebrand, beckoning to his next warrior. 'Let us have a tally of our battle strength.'

'Including the men you brought back with you from Jótlund, we have seven hundred warriors ready to sail west to bolster Walmond if need be,' said the broad-shouldered seacarl. 'In addition to that we've managed to commission another two hundred freesailors at Odense – we should hopefully be able to add a few more hired swords when the next merchantman pulls in from the Empire.'

The recent conquest of Jótlund had enriched him enough to be able to take on more freeswords than usual – that would be crucial to resisting Oldrik's numerically superior forces. That, and the proposed alliance with Magnhilda.

'And what of the Jarls Bjorg and Vilm?' pressed Guldebrand. 'I trust they are still loyal?'

It was a pointed question. The two lords who held lands from the Thegn of Kvenlund had served his father without question, but both had voiced doubts about his young and untested heir. He hoped his recent success had allayed those doubts.

Brega smiled. 'Both jarls have pledged their allegiance,' said the seacarl. 'They are mustering their leidangs even as we speak.'

Guldebrand took a long, satisfied pull on his wine. It was the same Pangonian vintage he'd brought back from Tjórhorn before they burned it to the ground. He watered it down so it wouldn't cloud his judgement, but even diluted it tasted a lot better than mead.

'Excellent,' he smirked. 'That's another five hundred warriors for our tally. Fourteen hundred total, with more to come when the next bunch of freeswords pulls in to Odense. And what of the Stormrider's forces?'

This question was directed at Asger, the oldest surviving member of his father's counsel. He had seen nigh on four score winters, and long forsaken court clothes and armour for a simple robe of dun brown, but he was hale enough for his advanced years. More importantly to Guldebrand, his mind was as keen as ever.

'At this stage, it's hard to tell,' said Asger. 'We know the Stormrider's leidang totals near three thousand, and besides that he has four loyal jarls commanding another two thousand fighting men between them. But...' – the old man raised his voice above the mutterings of consternation that suddenly rippled to the rafters – '... we don't know how many of those are at hand. The Stormrider has recommenced raiding the mainland, he didn't expect us to march in and take Jótlund. According to some of the traders I spoke to at Odense he has as many as a thousand reavers abroad.'

'That still leaves nearly four thousand men at his beck and call!' shouted one seacarl. 'Even counting Walmond's forces at Varborg that means he outnumbers us nearly two to one!'

'Which is why,' put in Guldebrand, raising a hand for silence again, 'this alliance with Magnhilda is so important. The Thegn of Scandia commands a thousand-strong leidang, and her jarls will have warriors of their own to contribute. And once we've secured an alliance, I'm sure that milksop Asmund can be threatened into sending us a few warriors of his own.'

'Fat lot of good that'll do!' yelled another warrior, earning a few jeers.

'Every bit counts in a war,' persisted Guldebrand. 'All told, we have the potential to even up the odds. And Magnhilda is a fierce general, one to rival the Stormrider himself they say.'

'Magnhilda is but a maiden!' shouted another seacarl.

'No, Magnhilda is a *shield*-maiden,' Guldebrand corrected him. 'A shieldmaiden who defeated two rival jarls in her lifetime to consolidate her realm. She is the first undisputed Thegn of Scandia in a generation. Woman or no, that is not an achievement to be ignored.'

'His Highness has the right of it,' said Asger. 'Magnhilda has proved herself a formidable foe, and that makes her a powerful ally.'

'*If* she consents to the marriage alliance we are proposing,' said Brega. 'I must confess, I cannot see why a proud woman like that would suborn herself to another Thegn.'

'Yes well, you leave me to worry about that,' said Guldebrand with a smile. Turning to the messenger he added: 'Get back to Varborg with all speed – tell Walmond I'll be sending a fleet five hundred strong to bolster his forces, there may be more depending on how we fare on other fronts.'

The messenger nodded and turned to leave.

'The rest of you get back to the war preparations. Asger, I'll leave you in charge of getting our ships ready at Odense. Brega and Varra, you're both coming with me – gather a hundred of our best seacarls, we're leaving tomorrow for Utvalla!'

Guldebrand finished his wine as he watched them leave, then stood to address the rest of his nobles. 'Well you know the situation, so be about your business!' he said. 'The future Magnate of the Frozen Principalities commands it!'

✣ ✣ ✣

The journey was a long one, for rather than choose to head directly north across the Vander Ranges and through the haunted Groenvelt, Guldebrand took his retinue north-east, skirting the crags and woods before striking back across the arable lands that marked the easternmost regions of the Principality he sought to ally to his own. Formed from three jarldoms, Scandia had been the largest of the principalities – until Guldebrand had taken over his neighbour's lands.

That, he hoped, should put the Thegn of Scandia in a more receptive mood to his suit.

That and the fact that to the west Oldrik was menacing her holdings. One thing Scandia lacked was secure access to the sea: its one port town, Ystad on the Vakka River, was being continually menaced by the Stormrider's forces. If Oldrik succeeded in annexing the town, he would have complete control of the western coast from the Vakka to the Var – the river that now formed a new border with his own lands.

Yes, the time was ripe for a new alliance. With Hardrada slain and his lands appropriated, Asmund cowed and out of the way in the far east, united he and Magnhilda had an opportunity to smash the Stormrider and assume complete mastery of the Frozen Wastes. That meant sharing power in a manner of speaking of course – but custom dictated that in marriage a man took precedence over his wife.

Naturally, that would make his suit harder to press.

For two days they had been skirting the Vkyr Wold, a high rough belt of hills that cradled the lake of the same name. Overhead the sky was cloudless and blue; winters were lethally harsh in the Wastes, but summers could be rewarding to those who survived the long cold season.

'There, I think I see it!' said Varra, pointing as they rode across scrubland.

Looking southwards, Guldebrand could make it out: a river emerging from the Vkyrs before bending sharply to the west, the Lidr that joined Lake Vkyr to the larger Lake Tor.

'We can't be too far now,' said Guldebrand. 'We should reach Halmstad by nightfall.'

A cheer went up from the column of men behind them. Magnhilda had kept her word, and they had been welcomed and feasted by seacarls loyal to the Thegn of Scandia during their journey – but the last time that had happened had been two nights ago. The men were saddlesore and eager for rest and food.

An hour later they drew level with the bend in the Lidr and began to follow it. The land ascended as they followed the river upstream; the waters of Lake Vkyr were fed by Lake Tor, which was set in a higher stretch of hills.

It was mid-afternoon when the river gave way to the Tor. Roughly shaped like a four-pointed star, sorcerers using the power of flight had long mapped it out. Guldebrand and his retinue drew level with its south-eastern tip, and now continued to skirt the lake, following a trail that hugged its lip. The glossy waters stretched for leagues to the south and west; they wouldn't be able to make out Utvalla until they reached the eastern side. That was where Halmstad was located, and where Ragnar would be waiting for them.

The thought of that made Guldebrand uneasy. Had he made a mistake accepting the priest's offer of alliance? The White Eye had been banished from Scandia – but that was before Magnhilda had taken over. As Guldebrand's emissary he had been tolerated, the banishment suspended if not entirely reversed.

But more to the point, he had been banished with good reason.

Rumours had been swirling among his seacarls. Ragnar was a warlock of the Left Hand Path, who had been expelled for practising blood magic – using a victim's lock of hair to inflict harm on them from a distance. Ragnar was in service to Logi, the Trickster God, whom the mainlanders called king of all devils, and had led Hardrada to a disastrous war in Northalde for reasons of his own. Ragnar worshipped demons, and would summon them up to possess strong men so they would do his bidding without question.

Guldebrand had heard all these stories and more. Yet the counter-charm seemed to be genuine, assuming Radko could be trusted, and he still had his pomander just in case… He felt his will was very much his own, and Ragnar's plans did seem solid. But whom did he really serve? He himself had made mention of a dark master…

Such uncomfortable thoughts were playing on Guldebrand's mind when Varra spoke and pointed again.

'Yes, yes, I can see it!' snapped the Thegn irritably. His thoughts had him feeling nervous and on edge.

The hills they were following turned north and dipped towards the lake. At its edge he could now make out Halmstad, its rectangular fenced homesteads an odd contrast with the erring design of nature that surrounded them. Smoke was already billowing from holes in the reed-thatched roofs of the logwood houses; the sun was low in the sky and even in summertime evenings by the lake would be chilly.

Following the glistening waters he could just make it out against the setting sun: Utvalla, the island hall that the woman he sought to marry called home. Despite himself a shiver went down his spine, and it had nothing to do with the chilling air. At this distance Utvalla was little more than a dark etching on the horizon; an unnatural break in the glassy panorama of deepening blue.

Unnatural, that was the word all right. Ragnar had given him an inkling as to the hall's eldritch foundations. Frankly, he didn't want to know any more.

He banished such thoughts as they picked their way down towards the town. A company of warriors was gathered by its outlying homesteads to greet them, loyal shieldmen led by a smaller group of seacarls.

Curt pleasantries were exchanged, and little more: Northlanders didn't bother to stand on ceremony like the effete mainlanders. Effete? No, that was a lie. There was nothing effete about the Northlendings, for all their priggish customs. Their distant cousins had thrashed them time and again, forcing them to the Treaty of Ryøskil like a whipped dog to the leash. Guldebrand clutched the bridle reins in angry fists as they rode towards the harbour. That was a trend he intended to reverse. Yes, he had to confess, Ragnar's plans fitted perfectly with his own ambitions, and that meant he had to trust him – for now.

His uncertain ally was waiting for them by the harbour jetty. Dressed in the same flowing sea-green robes, the scales that covered one half of his face caught the gloaming eerily. It was said the disfigurement had been a punishment inflicted on him by Sjórkunan himself, when the White Eye had dared to summon him. The Lord of Oceans had punished him for his temerity... but also granted him the power he craved, mastery of the oceans. Ragnar had paid for that gift with an eye, a high toll for such potent knowledge.

'Good e'en, Thegn Guldebrand,' said Ragnar in his flat voice. 'I trust your journey here was a safe one.'

'Safe... and dull,' replied the Thegn. 'We took the long way around – last time my father ventured through the Groenvelt he lost a good man to the Fays.'

'He was a foolish man to fall for faerie blandishments,' replied the Sea Wizard unsmiling. 'The Fays have ever delighted in setting traps for the unwary. Roska Hardfingers was reckless indeed to pursue the silver-skinned elk – it was hardly a natural quarry.'

Guldebrand gaped, his astonished expression matching the disconcerted mutterings of his nearby seacarls who had heard Ragnar's remarks.

'How could you know such a thing?' he gasped. 'That was six years ago – you weren't even there!'

'I see many things,' replied Ragnar, allowing an icy smile to creep across his asymmetrical face. 'Some near, some far. But come – this is no time for idle tittle-tattle. Our ship awaits.'

The wizard motioned towards a flat-bottomed ferry boat docked at the jetty. It was a fair size, equipped with thirty oars, but even so that would scarcely leave room for Guldebrand's hundred-strong retinue.

'You will not need all of your men,' said Ragnar when he voiced this complaint. 'The Thegn Magnhilda has given her oath that you will come to no harm on her lands. Take a dozen of your best men with you, and no more. Lodgings and food have been prepared for the rest here at Halmstad.'

Seeing the look of disquiet on Guldebrand's face, the warlock leaned in. 'You would do well to show trust at this juncture, Thegn of Kvenlund-Jótlund.'

The mage held him in his one blue eye. Guldebrand searched inwardly for some signs of enthrallment, but could detect none. His words seemed reasonable. They were here on a peaceful mission of emissary after all.

'Very well,' he said, turning to address his men. 'Varra and Brega, you will come with Ragnar and me. Pick ten others, everyone else stays here. Let us show the Thegn of Scandia that our intentions are genuine!'

He raised his voice as he uttered the last sentence, hoping to inspire confidence in his men. Even after his victory, he still felt a stubborn feeling of inadequacy that refused to go away; most of the seacarls in his company were twice his age. To his relief the men complied, though more than one shot a dark glance at Ragnar as they turned to follow their hosts into town.

Together with the rump of his retinue, Guldebrand stepped into the boat. At a command from the captain the ferry pulled away from the jetty. There was not enough wind for sailing and the men would have to row.

To the north the rugged hills were swathed with forests: the Torwood that provided Halmstad with its livelihood along with fishing from the lake. But Guldebrand fixed his gaze west as they scudded out across its calm waters, now turning a deep purple as the sun slipped below the Torwold. Larger it grew, Utvalla's silhouetted form rising up against the darkening skies to greet them. It appeared to be unremarkable enough: a squat two-storeyed fortress of ugly design. Northlanders were renowned for their shipwrighting, but the great castles and keeps of the mainland were unknown to them: save perhaps at Landarök, the walled city from where Oldrik Stormrider ruled his principality.

'You said it was built on the ruins of an older building?' he queried of Ragnar, succumbing to his curiosity.

'Much older,' replied the warlock, without turning to look at him. 'Utvalla was a seat of power for an ancient race that dwelt here thousands of years ago, long before the coming of our ancestors. The loremasters of Ancient Thalamy called them the Watchtowers of the Magi, outposts built by sorcerer-kings who ruled the world from Varya millennia ago. The Watchtower of Utvalla was their outpost here, in the Frozen Wastes.'

Guldebrand pulled his fur cloak more tightly around him. He was used to the cold, but this feeling was different somehow. 'Why come here?' he asked. 'You told me before that this Varya lies many leagues to the south. Our lands are cold, much of them barren and strewn with rock. Northlanders raid fairer coasts with kinder climes, nobody raids us!'

'Why seek to rule another principality, when one provides you with all the comforts you need?' countered Ragnar. 'Power is its own motive.'

The young Thegn pursed his lips. He hadn't thought of it like that before, but he supposed the priest had a point.

'So what happened... to this watchtower you speak of?'

'It was destroyed, long centuries ago. Only its foundations remained. For hundreds of years none would dare approach it. This very lake was cursed, its waters polluted by the magic its former owners had unleashed upon the world.'

Guldebrand shifted his feet uncomfortably on the deck, not liking the revelation.

'So... how did it become habitable again?' he asked.

'That is a mystery,' said Ragnar. 'Some say a mighty warlock, who lived during what the Thalamians refer to as the Golden Age, took up residence in Utvalla, banishing the demons and ghosts and lifting the curse that had lain about this place for so many aeons. Others say it was a holy man from Thalamy, by the name of Alysius, who did the cleansing.'

'Alysius?'

'A saint in the benighted faith of the Palomedians. Legend has it he came here to live out the rest of his days in exile, after being banished from the mainland. But nobody knows for sure.'

'And the foundations?' pressed Guldebrand, feeling suddenly enslaved by his curiosity. 'How far down do they go beneath the fortress?'

'Several levels,' replied Ragnar. 'Though that part of the building has long been sealed off, and many priests have put warding charms on the entrances, so none might venture down there.'

Ragnar turned to favour him with a one-eyed stare. His iris seemed to sparkle malevolently in the light of the lanterns hanging off the ship's masthead. 'Tis undoubtedly a good thing, Thegn Guldebrand – for who knows what fell secrets the ruins of the Elder Wizards keep?'

Guldebrand flinched away from his scrutiny. He had a feeling the warlock knew rather more about those secrets than he was telling.

✢ ✢ ✢

The island was shrouded in dusky darkness by the time they pulled onto the lone wharf connecting it to the outside world. A few other boats were berthed, mostly longships; the shields attached to their gunwales glinted in light from torches stuck into sconces in the walled enclosure separating the dock from the rest of the island. Craggy hills stretched up behind its rude crenellations, tapering into a summit crowned by Utvalla.

Perhaps it was Ragnar's tale telling that had him spooked, but Guldebrand could have sworn there was an aura of insidious evil coming from that place. The faces of the shieldmen who lined the walls, training crossbows on him and his men as they embarked, looked grim and unyielding in the torchlight, but there was a drawn and nervous air to them too that set his hackles rising.

Suppressing his fear he called out: 'Is this the best welcome the Thegn of Kvenlund-Jótlund will receive, after a journey of many leagues to pay visit to the Shield Queen of Scandia?'

His words sounded clumsy in his ears. He was just wishing he hadn't said them when Ragnar spoke.

'Our welcome is more royal than you think, Guldebrand Gunnarson – yonder comes Canute Mountainside to bid us well met.'

Focusing his eyes against the gloom Guldebrand saw it was true. The single gate in the walled enclosure was open, and through it now came Canute, accompanied by twenty seacarls, all well dressed in their best furs and wools.

Canute Mountainside, Magnhilda's cousin and champion, the man who had stood at her side and helped her win the Principality of Scandia. His reputation was legendary – perhaps even Walmond might quail before such a man.

Canute stepped into the uneven circle of light that undulated across the wharf.

'Magnhilda, Thegn of Scandia, bids you and your made men right welcome,' boomed the seacarl. He stood more than a head taller than the tallest Northlander there, and was built like an aurochs. His scarlet beard flowed to his waist and was plaited in two great braids. The finger bones of men he'd killed were woven into it. His arms were covered with scars from many battles – his arms, but not the rest of his body. It was said that was as close as men came to doing the great warrior any harm, before he crushed them like flies.

'The Thegn of Kvenlund-Jótlund and his made men are glad to be here,' replied Guldebrand, dispensing with formalities quickly and doing a good job – he hoped – of masking his intimidation.

'Good!' bellowed Canute. 'All is good! Come now, let us walk up to Utvalla – the Shield Queen awaits your arrival.'

Shield Queen – Magnhilda had earned the epithet for her stalwart defence during the years when her warband had been severely menaced and brought to the brink of destruction. But Guldebrand also suspected it had been a shrewd and deliberate choice: designed to give her favour with the lowly shieldmen, simple farmers who gave military service for land but held no title.

Without another word they all went through the gate, following the trail up towards Utvalla. Canute had only addressed Guldebrand, giving brief nods of acknowledgement to Varra and Brega – but had pointedly ignored Ragnar though he was standing right next to them. Guldebrand guessed the Shield Queen's temporary reversal of the wizard's banishment had not gone down well.

Up close the fortress looked even uglier than it did from a distance. Guldebrand hoped its mistress was more pleasing to the eye – he'd heard her praised as beautiful, but had met enough shieldmaidens to doubt that. They were mostly berserkers – female disciples of Tyrnor whose religion permitted them to abrogate customs that prevented women from fighting. At least the stone hall's builders had made some effort towards ornamentation, he reflected wryly as he looked at the crude statues flanking the entrance. The graven forms of Sjórkunan, Lord of Oceans, and Thoros, Bringer of Storms, looked down on the new arrivals with unimpressed neutrality. The Lord of Oceans clutched a trident similar to the one carried by Ragnar; the Bringer of Storms held his giant hammer aloft. Whenever he brought it down to strike Middangeard, thunder rolled across the firmament. Or so the priests claimed.

Another sculpted deity caught his eye, just above the crooked lintel: this was of a slender man, a cunning expression on his cruelly handsome face as he ran on winged feet. Logi, the Trickster God. That did not bode well. Rightly reviled as a devil throughout the

Frozen Wastes, he was commemorated by few. Perhaps the curse of
Utvalla had not been lifted entirely.

Thus it was with a sense of increased foreboding that Guldebrand
stepped into the hall. This was a large square room lit by soapstone
oil lamps hanging from hoops at all four corners and a great firepit
in the centre. It was crowded with seacarls crammed on long low
platforms lining the walls. There were also many women, dressed
in masculine garb like the men they ate with – shieldmaidens who
served their mistress as honour guard.

No dais had been erected, no table set apart, but he recognised
the woman he had come to marry immediately. She was sat in the
middle of the far row of tables, distinguished only by having a
chair to sit on. Magnhilda was certainly not unattractive, though
her outlandish appearance destroyed all semblance of femininity.
Nearly as tall as a man, her wiry frame was scantily covered with
a woollen jerkin, tight hose, with just a short cape of ermine and
deerskin boots to ward off the cold. The effect was more convenient
than erotic: as though the Thegn of Scandia dressed in anticipation
of the need for swift action at any time. She had a broad nose, thin
lips and a wide mouth. Most striking of all was her hair, a shock of
flaxen locks cut short that stuck out in all directions, giving her a
look of untamed wildness. About her knotted wrists were bracelets
of bronze and silver; no circlet graced her brows, but a torc of white
gold proclaimed her regal status.

'Guldebrand, Thegn of Kvenlund – *and* Jótlund – welcome at last
to my merry hall!' she cried, rising.

The playful smile on her lips echoed the one in her voice. She
sounded for all the Known World as though she were greeting
an acquaintance upon a chance meeting, not a prince who had
journeyed many leagues seek marriage alliance with her.

'Greetings, Thegn of Scandia, soon – I hope – to be Magna of
all the Frozen Wastes,' replied Guldebrand, using the line he had
rehearsed before leaving Valholl. He hoped he sounded suave, but
many of the assembled seacarls and berserkers clearly didn't think
so. Mutterings and frowns were exchanged. Did he hear the word
'beardless' mentioned once or twice? He felt his cheeks burn. He
would have to get rid of that epithet – even if it meant punishing its
use by death once he was Magnate.

But Magnhilda just laughed. 'Perhaps, Guldebrand Gunnarson –
we shall see! But first, you shall eat and drink with us! You and your
men have travelled long and hard to be with us this night, I shall

not have you go unfed – such important matters must be spoken of on a full stomach!'

Approving grunts from his seacarls showed what they thought of that. Canute motioned curtly for them to take up spaces left free on the benches at Magnhilda's table. A skald struck up a ditty, and soon the hall fell back to feasting as slaves brought fresh meat and mead.

As he quaffed his beer, Guldebrand felt himself relax slightly. It was good to be in a hall of men and music after their long journey: in fact Utvalla seemed surprisingly normal after all the fell tales he had heard about the place.

Magnhilda questioned him closely about his victory over Hardrada, but that was to be expected. Her manner was very informal, which helped to relax him more: she leaned back in her pinewood chair, one foot perched on the seat as she drank from a silver flagon. As he recounted his lightning raid across the Hrungnir he felt pride stirring in him, inflated by drink.

Meeting her steely grey eyes he felt something else stirring too: the Shield Queen was far from a classical Northland beauty, but she was attractive in her own way. Even without the prospect of a formidable alliance, the thought of sharing a bed with her pleased him more with every passing moment.

Out of the corner of his eye he caught Ragnar, sitting at a corner of their table, eating little and saying even less. The seacarls nearest to him did not try to coax him from his silence. At one point he caught Magnhilda glancing sidelong at the warlock, but her face gave nothing away.

✣ ✣ ✣

The slaves were clearing away the empty trenchers and pouring more mead when Magnhilda abruptly stood on her chair and called loudly for silence. The skald stopped playing his lyre and the chattering ceased. All heads turned to look at the Shield Queen as she hopped lightly over the table past Guldebrand and strode across the floor to stand before the firepit.

'Seacarls of Scandia and Kvenlund-Jótlund!' she called in her high clear voice. 'Men – *and* women – made strong in the eyes of Tyrnor! A great gathering of the finest of the Frozen Wastes!'

Magnhilda stifled the rising cheers with an impatient wave of her calloused hand. 'Let us not prevaricate – the noble Thegn of Kvenlund-Jótlund is here for one simple reason!'

She paused to allow a dramatic hush to fill the hall.

'He seeks marriage alliance, betwixt the two of us, that we might join forces and smash those of the Stormrider!'

This time not even the Shield Queen could stop the chorus of approval. Tankards were introduced to tables with hearty thumps as her seacarls and shieldmaidens roared their assent. They clearly liked the idea of conquest at least.

'*But*,' she added when the noise had died down. 'I did not spend the last ten years crushing men who stood in my way only to suborn myself lightly to another!'

This time most of the yells were female. Guldebrand wondered at the martial harridans, who looked as wild a bunch of women as any he'd ever seen.

'All right, all right,' Magnhilda went on, softening her voice to calm her shieldmaidens and placate her guests. 'Be sure that I mean no disrespect to the Thegn, whose recent prowess deserves praise.'

She turned slowly as she spoke now, as if daring all the listeners to meet her eyes.

'He may be young in years, but let no man or woman deny what he has achieved!' she cried. 'The icicles of blood fell like silver-red rain amidst the tumult of axes when he crossed the Hrungnir! Was it not so?'

'JA!'

'His forces stand ready to meet the Stormrider's surf horses, as they tear up the sail-road towards the lands he has taken! Is it not so?'

'JA!!'

Her voice went up a notch. 'But together, he and I shall raise an army by the sail-road and the plough-road, and we shall bring the spear din to his shores and break his ears! To Oldrik we will give the sleep of the sword, to his mead halls the bane of wood! His wave-swine we shall cut open on the skin of Valhalla, and give the feeders of ravens to the Lord of Oceans! Will it not be so?

'JAAAAAA!!!'

'On *two* conditions,' she shouted above the din. 'First, no marriage shall be consecrated until we stand victorious over the Stormrider's corpse! I shall not bind myself to a man until I am sure of what I am getting in return!'

Throats made hoarse by shouting roared to the rafters. The hall was a tumult of excitement. It was a feeling Guldebrand shared: her first condition was a fair one and he had anticipated it. All that mattered was that she allied her forces to his own. And it also meant that if he changed his mind after the war he could always refuse to go through with the marriage, depending on how weak the conflict had left her forces.

He was entirely unprepared for her second condition however.

'*Two*,' she yelled. 'I will not even consent to betroth myself to a man whose mettle I have not tested personally.'

Guldebrand blinked as she turned to look at him. 'Your deeds speak well of you, Guldebrand Gunnarson,' she said. 'But I shall never consent to marry a man who cannot best me in combat. So if you wish your suit to be granted, you must fight me now – to the first blood! If victory is yours, let us be betrothed henceforth in sight of men, women and gods. If not... there shall be no alliance.'

A confused silence fell abruptly on the hall. No one had expected this. Glancing over at Ragnar, Guldebrand could see even he looked taken aback. All eyes turned to the Thegn, staring across the heavy silence. This was his moment, and his alone. No one would or could advise him now.

Placing his tankard firmly on the table, he stood and met her gaze.

'The Thegn of Kvenlund-Jótlund accepts the Thegn of Scandia's challenge!' he declaimed. 'Let this hall now resonate with the yelling of Nurë's offspring!'

The next cheer could have reduced Utvalla to one storey by taking the roof off the rafters. Guldebrand allowed himself a slight smile of satisfaction. His courage had been tested, and he'd not been found wanting. He had found his eloquence at just the right time too – skalds personified swords as the children of the fire god, worshipped by all smiths. Two of Nurë's finest children were already being taken down off the walls, along with a couple of stout shields, when Magnhilda called for silence again.

'But stay!' she cried. 'In your lust to see a good fight, have you so soon forgotten who sits among us?' She pointed an accusing finger at Ragnar. 'The White Eye, banished till recently from these very lands!'

Boos and hisses went up from the hall.

'He shouldn't be here!' cried a berserker.

'He serves the Thegn of Kvenlund – neither of them should be here!' yelled a seacarl, getting more than a few murmurs of approval.

Magnhilda rounded on him.

'We shall not judge our honoured guest by the counsel he keeps!' she cried. Then a cunning look entered her eyes. 'Not so long as he shows willingness to bring his advisers to heel. I would not have it said I was brought low in single combat by the workings of a warlock.' She turned to address Ragnar directly. 'You are here only on my sufferance,' she said. 'As such, you shall obey my command or face banishment again from this hall!'

'And that command would be?' queried Ragnar icily.

'You shall consent to have your wrists bound in links of cold iron, to guarantee no sorcery is used to sway the outcome of this duel.'

Ragnar rose, looking genuinely perturbed and angry for the first time since Guldebrand had known him.

'I shall do no such thing,' he snarled.

'Then I hereby declare thee banished,' proclaimed the Shield Queen. 'Canute, eject this demonolator from my hall!'

If Canute was afraid he showed no signs of it. He rose to do his cousin's bidding, other warriors following suit.

'Wait!' cried Guldebrand. 'There is no need for such unseemly behaviour!' Turning to Ragnar he adopted a conciliatory tone. 'White Eye, thus far you have served me well and loyally. If you consent to do this, I hereby swear that whatever the outcome of this fight, you shall be freed of your shackles directly after.'

Ragnar said nothing. He seemed genuinely lost for words. Guldebrand leaned towards him. 'Now is the time to show some trust, Ragnar.' He could not help but smile as he parroted the mage's earlier words back at him.

Ragnar looked from Guldebrand to Magnhilda to Canute who stood ready to close on him, his hand on the hilt of a great axe he wore tucked into his girdle like a twig.

'What guarantee can the Thegn of Scandia give me?' he asked coldly.

'I swear to do exactly as the Thegn of Kvenlund-Jótlund has just said,' declared the Shield Queen solemnly. 'In sight of Tyrnor, Sjórkunan and Thoros who sees all from his airy palace in the skies.'

Ragnar gave the most barely perceptible of nods.

'Let's to it then!' cried Magnhilda, before turning to tell a slave to fetch the smith.

The hall erupted into raucous applause. More mead was served, the skald began playing again, and wagers were exchanged on the coming contest. Guldebrand could not help but overhear some of the nearest odds being shouted. None of them favoured him.

Ragnar had resumed his seat, an expression of cold fury carved across his face. Guldebrand didn't envy the smith his next job.

✢ ✢ ✢

Presently the terrified blacksmith had done his work, after taking two stoops of mead. Ragnar had sat stiff and motionless the whole while, his good eye looking as cloudy as his bad one.

Guldebrand and Magnhilda stood ten paces apart, both armed with sword and shield. He was wearing his mail byrnie, but she had availed herself of no armour. That came as little surprise – she had been a berserker before becoming a thegn after all. At least that gave him a slight advantage in terms of protection.

He sized up his opponent. Like any Northlander of his birth, he had learned to fight from a young age, but the Shield Queen was more than twice his age and had far more experience. She was strong for her sex, though he would probably have a natural advantage over her there. That just left raw skill at arms... and there her reputation preceded her.

'FIGHT!'

Canute bellowed the command. Magnhilda rushed at him, and within a few seconds Guldebrand knew her reputation was fully justified. They circled around the firepit, exchanging sword blows and shield barges, Magnhilda pressing him hard and forcing him onto the back foot immediately.

His father Gunnar had taught him there were only so many types of fighter. Men like Walmond and Canute relied on sheer strength to win the day; they were big hitters who overpowered their opponents with ferocity and aggressive swordplay. Others were more lithe, far from weak but likely to use dexterity and cunning, turning defence into attack. Both he and Magnhilda fell into the latter category, and should by rights cancel each other out. Going on that basis, it was likely to be a long and painful fight between them.

That just left one problem. Magnhilda was a far better fighter of their kind than he was, and Guldebrand knew it after less than a minute.

Hopping back lightly out of range to buy him a few precious seconds, Guldebrand tried desperately to think of some ploy that would avert a disastrous and humiliating defeat. She paused to let him have his respite, her face a fierce mask of concentration as she held her sword point towards him just above her shield. She was seemingly content to let him take the initiative.

His youthful impetuosity got the better of him, and he took the bait.

The ringing of sword on sword punctuated the ravening cries of the spectators as he chased her back around the firepit, the mead he'd drunk pouring out of him in torrents. At one point he thought he had her... but she dodged his thrust and came back at him ferociously, instantly reversing the cyclical dance as she came after him with her questing sword.

He felt himself beginning to tire, ever so slightly. He'd just had a long journey, and at sixteen summers had yet to grow into the fullness of his strength. Endurance now added its weight to the tally of superior skill and experience being thrown at him.

Guldebrand ducked a swipe. They were both pulling their blows so as to reduce the chances of lethality, and that gave him some chance: had it been a fight to the death he had no doubt whose shade would be seeking the Halls of Feasting and Fighting by now. Magnhilda followed up with a vicious shield barge: it caught him in the shoulder and jarred painfully, but fortunately didn't draw blood.

Staggering back, he raised his own target to fend off another deft strike, managing to get in a counter of his own that at least paused her onslaught. For the next half minute they stood rooted to the spot, trading blows...

Then she began to press him back again.

The myrmidons of Utvalla were on their feet by now, screaming for first blood. Again and again she struck and again he parried, dodged or blocked, stubbornly refusing to give up the fight as lost. His feet felt numb as he tottered back on them, his breath tearing from his chest in ragged gasps.

Just my luck, he thought as she pushed him back towards the wall, *bested by a female berserker in sight of dozens more.*

And then he realised how he could win.

Increasing his backwards strides so he moved well out of range of her attacks, he yelled: 'Is that the best you can do?! Magnhilda, Shield Queen! Berserker maiden of Scandia! You can't even beat a green youth of sixteen summers!'

Ignoring the jeers from the crowd he went on as she came at him: 'Perhaps *I* shouldn't see fit to marry *you!*'

It took all his strength and speed to fend off her next salvo of blows.

Disengaging himself again, he gasped: 'Why I think the Thegn of Scandia can't hold her mead! Look how she struggles!'

A few laughs mingled with the next chorus of jeers. Presumably many of the warriors thought he was going out with a burst of ironic humour.

But there was nothing funny about Guldebrand's intentions. He hadn't journeyed all this way to be made a laughing stock of. By all the storms of Thoros, but he *would* be king – by any means necessary.

He played his part for the next couple of passes, each time getting closer to being struck.

But it was starting to work. He could see rage rising in Magnhilda as he lashed her with one coarse jibe after another, maddeningly scrambling out of range before she could punish him for his temerity.

He couldn't keep that up forever of course – eventually he would tire and she would close him out, finishing him off.

But Guldebrand had no intention of keeping this up forever.

Wrenching himself back from her latest flurry of sword-strokes he cried at the top of his lungs so everybody could hear him: 'Why look – she doesn't even bear any real battle scars! The only slit she's got is the one between her legs!'

That was the final straw.

Magnhilda's eyes rolled into the back of her head, froth collecting at the corners of her mouth as the berserker rage took her. It normally required a battle for the Wrath of Tyrnor to possess one of his disciples, but relentlessly insulting her seemed to have done the trick.

The Thegn of Scandia gave vent to the kind of shriek that silences crowds in a split second. Charging across a hall stunned into silence she descended on him in a silver flurry, her blade seemingly in several places at once. First blood was out: in her enraged state she was now trying to kill him. He was about to take another gamble, to risk everything in the pursuit of power.

Guldebrand's shield splintered as she hacked at it furiously. He had a few seconds left to live: he would have to time his next move perfectly.

As she raised her sword to strike again, he let go of his own blade and launched himself at her, smashing his forehead into her nose as he sent them both tumbling to the ground. She writhed frenziedly, trying to shrug him off. This close she couldn't use her sword, but her berserker strength meant he wouldn't be able to hold her prone for longer than a few moments.

He felt as though he were wrestling with the Great World Serpent. Imminently he would be thrown across the hall and then hacked to bloody ribbons where he lay.

'First blood!' he screamed. 'FIRST BLOOD!'

With another piercing cry Magnhilda threw him off her. He landed painfully on his back several paces away. She rose, sword in hand, looming over him like the death goddess Hela – which to all intents and purposes for him she was.

From her nose a thick stream of red poured into her mouth.

'HOLD!' boomed Canute, stepping into the fighting area and motioning for several other seacarls to do likewise. 'Thegn Guldebrand has the right of it! Restrain the Shield Queen before she dishonours herself!'

It took Canute and half a dozen other strong men to disarm the shieldmaiden and restrain her. Presently she quivered into submission as the berserker rage left her. Her nose was still bleeding where Guldebrand had headbutted it.

'Mead for the Shield Queen!' thundered Canute. 'She needs a drink to revive her!'

Guldebrand made sure he had one himself. His gambit had paid off, but he was more surprised than exalted. On the field of battle berserker rage was a deadly thing, and one possessed warrior might cut down half a dozen or more before being slain. But in a carefully balanced fight to first blood, it was likely to prove a liability.

Or so he'd hoped – and so it had proved.

If Ragnar was impressed or pleased by the outcome, he showed no signs of it. Stepping forwards he held up his shackled wrists.

'The fight is done,' he said. 'Have your smith strike off these chains.'

Magnhilda, pressing a rag to her nose in between taking slurps of mead, glared at him. For half a second Guldebrand thought she was going to fly into another rage, but instead she nodded and motioned for the blacksmith to do his work.

'Well, Guldebrand Gunnarson,' she said, turning to face him. 'You have proved yourself a cunning foe, as well as a passable swordsman. There is a touch of Logi about you, methinks – but maybe that will prove useful.' She caught Canute's eye. Her champion had abided by the rules of the contest, but judging by the expression on his face he wasn't too pleased with Guldebrand's method of winning.

Let him sulk – he'd answer to Guldebrand before long.

'Ragnar,' she continued, 'you were a priest, before you took a darker road. Continue your return to the fold by witnessing this betrothal – Magnhilda the Shield Queen shall wed Guldebrand Gunnarson when Oldrik Stormrider feeds the eagles! Let us see the ceremony done here and now!'

'As you wish, Thegn of Scandia,' replied Ragnar, massaging his free wrists. He sounded as neutral as ever.

But that scarcely bothered Guldebrand. His heart soared as Ragnar declared them betrothed in sight of Godshome and mortalkind. He was one step closer to his dream of being Magnate. And once the Ice Thegns were united behind him, the real work would begin: the Known World would see a new Age of Reavers, the first since his ancestors had conquered the mainland seven hundred years ago.

A cawing sound caught his ear. He turned quickly, his heart in his mouth as he saw a black bird flying in through a window... But it was no raven, just a crow come to peck at scraps on the tables. Heaving an inward sigh of relief he turned back to face his newly betrothed.

She stared at him with cloud-coloured eyes, another playful smile on her lips.

⤛ CHAPTER III ⤜

Spared and Ensnared

'. . . **a**nd, due to lack of evidence, the tribunal finds you not guilty of high treason.'

Sir Vertrix heaved an inward sigh of relief. He found time to exchange grateful glances with Bryant and Regan before they were ushered from the Chamber of Justice by guards. The half dozen tribunes, none of them men he recognised, rose from the mahogany table from where they had just saved three good knights from going to the gallows. Not one betrayed a flicker of emotion at the judgment they had just pronounced.

More of Abrexta's thralls, thought Vertrix. *The question is: why did they spare us?*

Sir Lyall, captain of the guards, escorted them through the cramped corridors of the palace to a chamber in the guests' wing. Their walls were fashioned from interlocking branches, an eerie reminder of the Faerie Time when the Island Kings had ruled in Thraxia.

His bluff bearded face betrayed no expression as he said: 'You're to stay here until called for by the King.' Nodding towards the next door along, flanked by two men-at-arms, he added: 'Your squires are lodged in the room hard by. You may speak with them if you wish, but on no account are you to visit any other part of the palace without my say-so. I'll be posting guards on your door as well.'

'That's a fine way to treat three distinguished guests exonerated of groundless charges,' said Vertrix, trying his luck.

'Aye, it is,' returned Lyall, ignoring his irony. 'You've just been spared your lives. That's a sight more than most who go before the tribunal can say nowadays.'

If he had any feelings about that, the captain showed no sign of them.

'Good day to thee,' said Lyall courteously, clicking his spurs and striding off with the rest of his guard in tow – less two men who now lingered by the door to their room.

'Strange man,' murmured Regan as they entered it. 'Not seen him before at court.'

'Not strange – ensorcelled,' corrected Vertrix as he closed the door behind them. 'That'll be why you haven't seen him before. Anyone in authority whom she couldn't enthral has been replaced with someone she could.'

'Why hasn't she enthralled us?' asked Bryant, looking unusually nervous.

But Vertrix had no answer to that question. An Argolian might – but he'd seen none since arriving at Ongist, apart from the poor devil they'd executed at Market Circle.

'Come on,' he muttered, reaching for a jug of wine on the chamber's single table. 'Let's have a quick stoop before we go and tell our faithful squires we're safe and sound.'

His sarcasm did nothing to lighten his mood. Hopefully the wine would.

✢ ✢ ✢

The King's voice was stern and unyielding as he spoke. 'Northern Dréuth is lost – Tíerchán has defeated Lord Tarneogh and put his people to the sword,' he said. 'Your soon-to-be-erstwhile liege Lord Braun shall join him: more than half his knights have been slain or taken and the rest cower behind the walls of Gaellen. As for Lord Cael of Varrogh, he stands to share a similar fate. Word reached us yestere'en that the highlanders are marching through his lands, laying waste and burning as they go.'

'I cannot believe this news moves you not,' was all Sir Vertrix could say. The throneroom was all but empty – besides himself, the King, Regan and Bryant, the only occupants were the palace guards.

And, of course, Abrexta.

She sat beside the Seat of High Kings, coolly impassive. That she was fair there could be no doubt: her raven tresses fell to her supple waist, about which a girdle drew a robe of deep green velvet to her curving figure to pleasing effect. She was as tall as any Northlending beauty he had seen at the court of Strongholm, with pale skin. Her dark eyes looked right through him under lustrous eyelashes.

Wrenching his eyes from her he prayed she wouldn't try to ensorcell him. Her looks alone were enough to bewitch a man.

'No, the news does not move us,' replied the King firmly. 'Because we are going to do something about it.'

A flicker of hope dared to cross Vertrix's heart. 'You will march to war against them?'

'No, I shall invite them to peace,' said the King. 'In fact, I have already invited an emissary from the highland forces commanded by Slangá Mac Bryon to parlay.'

Vertrix's disapproval must have been written across his face, because the King eyed him coldly and said: 'You should be thankful I'm including you in our regal council, Vertrix – your reputation precedes you. Otherwise, the accusations against you might have been more readily believed.'

And who levelled those in the first place, as if I didn't know? thought the old knight.

'And why does Your Majesty confer such a boon upon me?' he asked. Might as well get to the truth of it if he could: he no longer cared for his life, it would perish along with everything he held dear in Gaellentir.

'Because the time has come for unity,' said Cadwy. 'We have put down numerous uprisings against our royal person here in Umbria. Tul Aeren complains of our new taxes, and rumours abound that it plans to lead the other regions of the south in rebellion. The realm needs a new cause, a real enemy to fight! You've seen the ships being built at harbour no doubt... Well, the time has come to reveal their purpose. Bring in my court! The King has an announcement to make.'

Like sheep to the fold, they filed in. They were for the most part knights and lords that held land in Umbria. All of its lands north of the Rundle were ruled directly by Cadwy; its southern reaches were parcelled out between a handful of barons.

Vertrix saw few faces that he recognised. These men had replaced the loyal nobles who had dared oppose their King's madness. How many of these new faces belonged to men who'd been ensorcelled, he wondered – and how many were simply toadies who knew when to knuckle under?

'I've summoned you all here to make an important announcement,' declared the King. He barely raised his voice, which sounded strangely neutral. 'For a while now rumours have been swirling about the capital – concerning the fleet under construction.'

He paused as if to let his words sink in, but there was scarcely a reaction. Some of the courtiers even looked bored – though it was clear their liege planned to tell them something of great import.

'Well, the rumours are true,' went on Cadwy, unabashed. 'A hundred war galleys our royal person has seen fit to commission

– even now I have sent agents abroad to solicit mariners from our erstwhile foe Cobia. For their excellence at sea shall be needed in this coming campaign.'

Even the subdued court could not help but react to that. Memories of the War of the Cobian Succession were still painful to any self-respecting Thraxian.

'Why solicit our implacable foes for help?' one noble dared to ask. 'Are our own mariners not good enough for the fleet Your Majesty is building?'

'Not for what we're planning, no,' answered the King bluntly. 'For we're going to take back the land from which our ancestors were so unjustly banished ages ago – we're going to war against the Westerlings! For that we'll need the best navy this realm has ever seen – and we'll need the finest army too. That's why I've sent word to all the southern barons – every lord south of Umbria shall commit an hundred knights and a like number each of archers and men-at-arms to the cause.'

'And what of the lands of the north?' one young knight dared to ask.

About time one of you showed an awareness of reality, thought Vertrix bitterly.

The King's face did not change as he turned to face the knight. 'The highland presence is a reality,' he said. 'Only Lord Cael of Varrogh holds back the armies of Slangá and Tíerchán. But fear not! For I have resolved to turn this pressing problem to our advantage – a thorn in our side shall be plucked forthwith, and pressed instead into the flanks of our age-old enemy. Let the emissaries be permitted to enter!'

The doors were thrown open and in walked four highland warriors. Favouring the throng with contemptuous sneers they approached the dais, pointedly refusing to take a knee and meeting the King's stare with defiance. They were dressed in the brightly coloured interlocking patterns of their clan and clad in furs and boiled leather. Rude weapons – axes, short swords and long knives – were clutched in their hands in further show of their complete indifference to courtly protocol.

Vertrix scowled as the tallest of them spoke up.

'Slangá Mac Bryon, conqueror o' the northern reaches, sends his greetings to ye, lowland king,' he said in thickly accented Thrax. His hair was tied back in a bun, his beard decorated with silver rings. Several of his teeth were missing, making his sneer all the uglier.

'Cadwy, First Man of the Ruling Royal Clan of Cierny, King of all the Thraxians, bids you welcome to his hall,' replied the monarch.

Was it his imagination or did the brigand's eye flicker momentarily towards Abrexta? The old knight felt his anxiety go up a notch – some dark conspiracy was afoot, of that much he felt certain.

'Well,' pressed the King. 'Here you are in my hall, granted safe passage by our terms of parlay. So out with it – say what you have come here to say.'

'I've nothin' tae say but this – Dréuth is oors, like it or no! Ye can send an army o' yer own tae fight it oot, or ye can come tae peace terms wi' us. It's the easy way or the hard way, yer royal majesty.'

The King turned to smile at Abrexta, who favoured him with a knowing smirk.

Oh you blasted fool, you think she's laughing with you not at you, thought Vertrix desperately. He knew what was coming next, but it still made him sick to hear it.

'You wish to settle the lands you have conquered,' the King went on. 'Without further dispute from our royal person. It shall be granted – on condition that you agree to ally yourselves with us.'

That seemed to take the messenger aback. 'Aye?' he managed presently. 'And what alliance are ye proposin'?'

'Firstly, our offer. All lands north of the holding of Varrogh shall be yours to do with as you wish, save for Port Grendel, which shall retain its status as a free cityport. In return I want the highland tribes to guarantee lowland merchants safe passage to and from it, for which you may of course exact a reasonable toll.'

The emissary raised an eyebrow, but did not interrupt the King as he went on: 'We are raising a fleet to attack your – nay, *our* – Westerling cousins. Kaluryn and Skulla shall be brought to heel, and Ongist shall rule a maritime empire that straddles the Tanagorm Sea and Tyrnian Straits.'

The four emissaries exchanged whistles and glances. If they had expected to hear this, they hid it well.

'I want the highlanders on board – literally,' the King continued. 'Slangá and Tíerchán are both to send a thousand of their finest screamers to join the invasion army. All things going well, it shall sail for the Island Realms on the autumn tides. Those men who join shall of course receive new lands in the Westerling Isles, as befits conquerors. In return for all of this you shall keep the lands you've conquered, but Varrogh you'll spare. You've enough as it is, and I need at least one buffer province betwixt my lands and yours for security.'

The emissaries exchanged glances again. Abrexta stared at them all with glittering eyes.

'That's... a fair offer,' the spokesman said at length.

'It's more than fair,' said the King. 'Did you really think I'd let you go on ravaging my hinterlands unchecked? No, you've done a sound job for me – those truculent northern lords are no better than their southern ilk, always using distance to keep my royal rule in abeyance! Their lands you shall keep without reprisal on our part, provided you play your part in the wars to come.'

'And what about Gaellentir?' pressed the highlander. 'We're at their gates but they're holdin' out – we've overrun the province, be a shame not tae... finish the job, if ye ken wha' I mean...'

'Gaellen is part of my offer,' clarified the King. 'Raze the castle, depose its liege – I care not, so long as you cease your hostilities against the crown thereafter and swear fealty to me as your leal sovereign.'

'This is madness!' cried Vertrix, stepping forwards. 'You cannot mean to abandon our homeland to a pagan savage like Slangá! Do you think these highlanders will really take part in your war against their own kin?'

'I don't see why not,' replied Cadwy, unperturbed. 'Kinship didn't stop our ancestors fighting the war that saw them banished to these shores in the first place.' Turning to face the highlanders, he added: 'Emissary, what say you? Think you that your leader would be tempted by our offer?'

The highland savage whispered briefly with his fellows before turning back and nodding: 'I'd say he'd be very interested indeed, sirrah.'

'Good,' said the King. 'Then get thee gone from my hall, and back to him with all due speed. I'll expect answers from him and Tíerchán by the next moon. And I trust your business in Gaellentir will be concluded by then – your energies will soon be needed elsewhere.'

Barely suppressing his look of surprise (if that wasn't just a sham), the emissary favoured the King with a curt half bow, before turning to exit the throneroom with his men.

'This is preposterous!' cried Vertrix, now addressing the courtiers. 'How can you...?! You cannot all support this mad venture? The Island Realms are bewitched, their lands long cursed by the very spirits they saw fit to meddle with in the first place!'

But the faces of the courtiers were mostly blank slates. Some did indeed look troubled, but if they agreed with Vertrix they dared not speak up.

'Our King's will be done,' said one, an ashen-faced man in middling years.

'We shall win glory for Thraxia and build an empire,' said another. He was younger, but Vertrix could see no excitement in the knight's glazed eyes as he spoke.

And then he realised it was hopeless. Abrexta had won.

Turning back to face the King he said helplessly: 'Are you resolved in this matter, Your Majesty?'

The King nodded. 'I am.'

Abrexta leaned forwards in her chair, her dark hair catching the light dully. 'Be of some cheer, sir knight,' she said. 'You have lost a home today, but gained a profitable place in a burgeoning new empire. Surrender the past! Give yourself up to a bright new future!'

He could feel her pressing at his will. She was so beautiful and powerful and... maybe she was right. Out of the corner of his eye he caught Bryant and Regan staring at her open-mouthed. Perhaps she was trying to enthral them too.

Closing his eyes he clenched his fists and thought of his beloved wife, Rihanna, dying amidst the fires of war...

He opened his eyes. 'I've seen the error of my ways, Your Majesty.' He took a knee and bowed his head, clinging painfully to the image of his wife and children burning and screaming as the walls of Gaellen castle tumbled about them. 'I was a fool to question the royal vision – thy will be done, in this as in all things.'

'Your service will be justly rewarded,' said the King. 'All who serve me shall share in the glories to come.'

'A grand command thou shalt have in the King's new army,' said Abrexta, her voice sounding sultry and breathless, as though she were whispering in his ear. He felt her pushing harder into him. He fixed his mind's eye on his family burning to death, as all he had ever held dear collapsed about them.

Vertrix felt a tear roll down his cheek.

'Your humble servant thanks thee,' he said in a voice that nearly choked.

'Good. Now get thee gone back to thy chambers, and prepare for a feast we shall give to celebrate the coming war.'

It was Abrexta who had spoken. She had not even bothered to keep up the pretence of the King being in command. Swiftly wiping the tear away Vertrix rose and beckoned for Bryant and Regan to follow him from the throneroom.

✠ ✠ ✠

Back in their chamber, Vertrix poured cups of wine for the three of them and stared out of the window. It overlooked the courtyard, but it was quiet save for the odd servant scurrying between the hall and kitchens: all the nobles would be preparing for supper.

'So what do we do now?' asked Sir Bryant at last. 'You can't mean to go along with this, Vertrix?'

'Aye, I mean to – for now,' replied the old knight, turning to face them. Bryant's face looked grave in the late afternoon sunlight. Regan was sitting on his cot and staring, holding his winecup in limp hands. 'We need to persuade the King – persuade *her* – that we're beaten,' Vertrix continued. 'Keep your friends close, keep your enemies closer...'

Bryant fixed him with a quizzical look. 'What exactly do you mean by that?'

'We're under guard here night and day,' said Vertrix. 'That means the only time we can get to her is at feast-times.'

'Get to her? What do you mean?'

But Vertrix was scarcely listening. He went on, as if talking to himself. 'We don't have access to any weapons, but our squires will need daggers at feast-times so they can cut our meat...'

'I don't like where this is going, Vertrix,' said Bryant. 'If you're proposing what I think you are... why, it's suicide!'

'It is.' Vertrix looked up and caught Bryant's eyes. 'But what choice do we have? Gaellen will fall – when that happens everything we've ever fought and lived for will be gone. I for one will not live out the rest of my days knowing I stood by and did nothing.'

Silence filled the room. Bryant remained locked in his gaze. Regan sat staring into his cup.

'All right,' said Bryant. 'Go on.'

'We need to do everything we can to convince Abrexta that we're under her spell – literally or otherwise,' said Vertrix. 'Offer suggestions about the invasion, try to set ourselves up as trusted advisers. She's made it clear she wants me to be part of this. So we play to her wishes! The more we succeed in doing that, the more likely we are to get a place close to her at table, as befits court favourites. Every yard we gain – and I mean that literally too – will be crucial. Once we're close enough we can do it. I'll be the one who strikes, the responsibility's mine. We'll need our squires to pass us their knives when I give the signal. Then it's down to you both to cause as much of a distraction as you can, give me a few precious seconds to get to her and...'

He passed a hand across his throat meaningfully.

Bryant looked at him sadly. 'They'll kill us all for this, you know that.'

'I'm as good as dead without Gaellentir and everything in it,' replied Vertrix. 'But no, it's our duty, Bryant, like it or not. It's what

Braxus would want us to do. In any case, we might just live through this, if we do it right.'

'How?' asked Bryant.

'Braxus and Lord Braun seem to think that a witch's spell won't survive the witch herself... That was the whole idea behind our planned rebellion in the first place. Assuming they're right, that means if I kill Abrexta quickly enough there's a chance Cadwy will come to his senses and call his guards off before they do us in.'

Bryant considered his words. 'It could work,' he said at last, nodding. 'It's a plan on a knife-edge, but it might just work. And if we can get ourselves a seat at the King's high table sooner rather than later we might just do it before Gaellen falls. Then we can have the King muster a relief army and put a stop to this madness once and for all.'

'Exactly,' replied Vertrix, his spirits slowly returning. 'So get the squires in here now, I'm going to brief them before we eat. We've no time to lose.'

Bryant nodded and left. Regan had raised his eyes from his cup and was staring at Vertrix.

'Well?' he asked sharply after the guards had closed the door behind Bryant. 'What say you? Not heard a peep out of you since we left the throneroom.'

Regan sighed heavily. 'It sounds like as desperate a plan for a palace coup as any I ever heard,' he said. 'But lacking a better alternative, I'd say I'm in.' With a wry smile he drained his cup.

Vertrix laid a calloused hand on the young knight's shoulder.

'That's the spirit,' he said. 'Be of some cheer, lad – Reus willing we might just live to see this through.'

✛ ✛ ✛

Regan heard the old knight's words as if from a distant speaker at the end of a long corridor.

Sounding like his old casual self was difficult; he felt as if his body were a puppet on strings, and he wasn't quite sure who was pulling them. Everything had changed since he'd entered the throneroom. She was so *beautiful*. He'd lain with many women, but every one of them had vanished from his mind the minute he had laid eyes on her.

Abrexta the Prescient – didn't that say it all? She *knew*, she *saw* – everything. How foolish of Vertrix to think he could oppose her, how foolish of anyone to think that! She was perfect in every way. Even her beauty was just a tawdry cover that hid the endless richness of the soul beneath. He felt something (was it her? he hoped so) controlling his every decision. It was a delicious feeling, one that had enveloped him like a warm shroud when she was talking to Vertrix. How nice not to have to think for oneself any more! To have every action, every thought, dictated by a higher power...

He wanted to thank her – ah, but that thought brought him pain! It reminded him he wasn't in her presence right now. He wanted her, full stop. Maybe she'd let him have her, if he did everything she told him.

That thought warmed him as he got up to prepare for the feast.

⊷ CHAPTER IV ⊷

A Dream Shattered

'Come on, drink up – you know it's good for you.' Adhelina practically forced the tincture down Hettie's throat.

But it really was for her own good. St Elenya's Root had worked wonders for some of the women in her care, women who'd suffered far worse than her friend had.

And on top of that, Hettie was a *noblewoman*. Adhelina was damned if she was going to watch her lady-in-waiting succumb to melancholia.

'There now,' she said, trying to sound soothing as Hettie grimaced the last of the potion down. 'You'll start to feel better again in a few minutes, you'll see.'

Hettie nodded dumbly, staring around the hospice with the eyes of a frightened deer. The tarpaulin roof did nothing to keep out the heat, and Adhelina was already beginning to sweat profusely. It was near noon and she had been up since dawn tending the sick and wounded. Woodfolk injured in the fighting had swelled the ranks of the ailing; it had been three days since Horskram and his motley band of heroes had left, and the hours had passed in a giddy blur. Not since her father's last war had she been so busy.

Looking at the wounded and sick, some of whom were weeping, Hettie's own eyes filled with tears. Her lower lip began to tremble.

'For heaven's sake!' cried Adhelina, grasping her friend by the shoulders and shaking her. 'I *know* it was horrible, but you're barely nineteen summers – you can't give up the rest of your life to despair!'

'I'm sorry, milady,' Hettie managed to mumble, snuffling back tears. 'I just... never thought we'd see such things...'

Adhelina's frustrated anger gave way to a tide of guilt. It was herself she was really angry with. Her mad dash for freedom had nearly got them killed, and brought anguish on her dearest companion.

But then men did that all the time – brought ruin on themselves and the ones they loved in pursuit of wealth, fame, glory. All she had sought was her own freedom.

Taking Hettie she rocked her gently, whispering things she hoped sounded soothing in her ear.

'I'm sorry t'interrupt ye milady, but ye'll want to see this.'

Adhelina turned and saw Madogan addressing her. She had treated him and his arm was healing well enough, though he'd be wearing a sling for weeks to come.

'See what?' she asked brusquely, letting go of Hettie.

The woodlander had several women with him. She did not recognise any of them.

'These are some o' the best healers from our communities – thought ye could use their 'elp.'

'You thought correctly,' she said, regretting her harsh tone. 'I've been rushed off my feet day and night. Are they familiar with all the herbs and poultices I've been using?'

Madogan cocked an eyebrow at that. 'Think ye'd be the best judge o' that milady', he said with a smile.

Adhelina flushed. 'Of course – why I'm so exhausted I'm barely thinking straight. Well now, women of the Argael, come with me and I'll show you the ropes...'

✣ ✣ ✣

An hour later Adhelina was taking the noon meal with Hettie, Madogan and other woodfolk. The women had proved able enough, and despite some language barriers she had managed to hand over her duties.

That was a relief and no mistake. As well as allowing her some respite, it meant she could plan the next stage of her journey. She had already decided to await the outcome of the friar's mission – if she understood correctly the death of this warlock should make the forests safe to travel through again. On top of that, Anupe would need to be paid for her extra services. Assuming she survived.

She might well offer her a third job if so, escorting her and Hettie to the coast. Events had taken them well out of their way, and Urring and Meerborg were roughly equal distances away. She still favoured the Northlending port, assuming the way through the Argael was safe enough to reach it. But there was the complication of the woodlander Kyra: Reus only knew what the Harijan's sapphic tastes would mean there. An extra travelling companion might slow them down. Then again, perhaps another sturdy female to have along might not be a bad idea...

She was just about to voice some of her thoughts to Madogan when she noticed another group of woodlanders had joined them in the clearing in the middle of the camp. About a dozen strong, they were all armed and ready for travel.

Madogan stood up and looked down at her. 'Well, milady, now ye've finished yer lunch, I think it's time we discussed something.'

Adhelina felt herself tense. She didn't like the way the woodlander was looking at her. Or the fact that he'd taken to his feet while she was still sitting. The rude manners of wild men took some getting used to.

'Indeed,' she replied, trying to keep her cool. 'Now that you have brought your own healers from the woods, I think it time we were thinking about leaving – but first I must needs wait for my – '

Madogan cut her off. 'Beggin' yer ladyship's pardon,' he interjected. 'But I'd say *leavin'* is abowt the sum o' it, though there'll be no *waitin'*.'

Adhelina glared at him. 'How dare you address me so? I am the heiress of Dulsinor, whose lands – '

'Aye,' Madogan cut her off again. 'Y'are. An' the heiress o' Dulsinor belongs in Graukolos, wi' her kith an' kin.'

'NO!' she rose to her feet, panic coursing through her as she grasped his meaning. 'You have no right – '

'On the contrary, yer ladyship,' interrupted Madogan, motioning for the armed woodfolk to come forwards, 'I've a duty to perform – if your father the lord o' these lands finds owt I had ye and let ye go, there'll be trouble fer us woodfowk. I've not fought a battle wi' beastmen only to bring an eorl down on our backs.'

'This is foolishness!' cried Adhelina as the group surrounded her and Hettie. 'My father would never do such a thing – the Argael forms no part of his holdings in any case!'

'Oh, I'd say that's a matter o' how ye look at it,' countered Madogan, smiling humourlessly. 'And since when have high lords ever respected borders anyway?'

'My father has never fought a war except in self-defence!' protested Adhelina. The woodfolk respected her station enough not to lay hands on her, but clearly there was no walking away from this situation. Hettie started to sob again.

'My father is a just man – you have no cause to fear any reprisals on his part!'

'In that case, ye shouldna be runnin' away from 'im in the first place,' said Madogan. 'A just man deserves to 'ave the things he owns returned to 'im.'

'No man owns me!' snarled Adhelina. But she knew the lie to her words even as she spoke them: out here in the wilderness men took what they wanted, just as they did in the high-walled cities and keeps.

'I can reward you richly if you let us go,' she said, desperately changing tack. 'I have jewelled rings, bracelets, pendants – a white gold circlet my father gave me...'

'Aye, I ken that right well,' said Madogan. 'Took liberty o' checkin' on all yer possessions when we were packin' 'em this morning.' He shook his head. 'Canna take the risk, I'm sorry Lady Markward.' Then he smiled again. 'Besides, yer father bein' a *just* man, I've no doubt he'll reward us richly fer bringin' ye back safe an' sound.'

He barked an order and another group of woodfolk brought up a string of ponies, saddled and ready. 'Everything's been prepared as ye can see,' said Madogan. 'I thank ye on behalf o' the woodfowk fer all ye've done, but now it's time fer you to leave.'

'And this is how you show your gratitude?' asked Adhelina disgustedly.

'World's no place fer gratitude,' said Madogan sadly. 'Be a sight better if it were, but it's not oors to make as we want it. Now come along, yer ladyship, I'd prefer it if ye came o' yer own free will – we've a lot o' respect fer ye, an' none o' the lads an' lasses rightly wants to lay 'ands on ye.'

Adhelina looked from Madogan to Hettie, to the grim faces of her forced new retinue, and saw it was hopeless. She suddenly felt dreadfully alone.

She had tried the powers and chances of the world of men, but for all her resilience and ingenuity men had bested her: not because they were cleverer or braver than she was, but because they played by rules they had set down long ago to suit themselves. Her father commanded a small army, even the threat of it was enough to move the hands of other men against her. Faced with such odds, what chance had she ever had of winning?

The heiress of Dulsinor felt her heart turn to lead as she took a step towards the waiting pony.

⤖ CHAPTER V ⤖

Of Sour Times

O nce the spectacle of Graukolos would have impressed him, but now all Adelko could find was a feeling of foreboding as they rode up through Merkstaed into the looming shadow of its eight towers. The skies that compassed its gargantuan frame were azure blue: it was early Balmonath and approaching high summer. The fast-flowing waters of the Graufluss sparkled in the sun's rays, and birds skittered to and fro above the burgeoning marketplace, hoping to pick up a scrap or two.

None of it could warm the chill of horror that had lain on his heart since the Warlock's Crown. It had been some two weeks since they left its cursed precinct, but everything he had witnessed there remained embedded in his mind like a poisoned arrow.

As they rode through the market square and out of the bustling town the novice muttered the Psalm of Spirit's Comforting for the umpteenth time that day.

He did not know which had been worse: the demonic friezes intertwined with angels (angels!) that had lined the asymmetric interior of the blasted ruin Andragorix had called home; the lingering aura of evil about the place; the putrefying stench of the hecatomb of corpses; the no less foul remains of some devilish consort they had found, looking like a half-melted skeleton with gobs of pus and flesh sloughing off it. And then there had been the all-too-human horror of the wretched lad they had found chained up in the mad mage's laboratory...

Perhaps that had been the worst of all, barely living evidence of the awfulness that mortalkind could visit on one another when caught up in the worship of Abaddon.

Or was the Fallen One just an excuse? The Earth Witch would probably have said as much. Were men wicked because they allowed themselves to be possessed by devils, or did they allow themselves to be possessed by devils because they were wicked in the first place?

Andragorix had made his choice. His mother's trapped spirit had said as much, just before the spell binding her to the ring he wore had expired, leaving her free to seek whatever fate awaited her on the Other Side.

Through all that horror – man and devil-made – they had searched, destroying everything they could: the grimoires, the scrolls, the paraphernalia. But no Headstone fragments. Together they had conducted a divination, used every psalm in the *Holy Book*. All to no avail. Andragorix had not, apparently, been lying: he did not have the fragments, nor the power to wield them.

Now they were at Graukolos, hoping to find another clue as to who did.

Vaskrian shifted uncomfortably in the saddle as they rode into the barbican so Horskram could state their business to the serjeant-at-arms guarding the outer ward.

By Reus, but he *hurt*. The woodland women had treated his burns during the week they had waited for their horses to be brought from the settlement they had saved from the outlaws. His arm was trussed up in a sling, and would be for at least a few more weeks, but it was his face that hurt most. Horskram had told him he should consider himself lucky; had they not had the Redeemer's blood to help them with their prayers, he would have been roasted alive just like poor Sir Belinos. One of the women treating him had told him he would be scarred for life.

Disfigured and out of action for the foreseeable future. Time was that would have left him crestfallen. Now, he just felt bitter. His fate was already sealed, if the Earth Witch told it true: he'd risk life and limb on one mad quest after the other, but no man would ever bestow title on him no matter how much he did to earn it. Once he would have put his faith in Braxus, the foreigner who had promised him much, to elevate him beyond his status if his deeds merited it. But since the Warlock's Crown his new guvnor had not been himself. Ashen-faced and withdrawn, the Thraxian simply stared into the middle distance, saying little and only when spoken to.

What did Sir Braxus have to feel so glum about, Vaskrian wondered. The Thraxian had escaped the worst of it: he wasn't scarred or maimed – or dead like poor Sir Aronn. Another funeral, for him and the woodland girl who had died fighting alongside them. He'd caught Sir Torgun and Anupe staring at Horskram darkly as the monk had given them both their Last Rites back at the camp.

There was bad blood brewing in the company all right.

The guards on the gate blew a note and the gates of the outer ward opened to admit them. Riding into it, Vaskrian glanced at the hurly-burly of the craftsmen's' stalls to his right. He looked up at the looming walls about him. The castle was huge: even bigger than Linden and Staerkvit. Adelko had said it was built by a stonemason inspired by wizards, or so the legend had it.

He didn't like the sound of that. He'd had enough of wizards and their doings to last a lifetime.

Half a dozen guards came to escort them through to the next ward. Across the yard from the craftsmen, ostlers emerged from the stables to take their horses.

Vaskrian dismounted, wincing all the way. At least they'd get some more rest while they were here. And he'd heard something about a wedding – involving the strange noblewoman who'd apparently been trying to escape her future spouse and been brought back while they were off trying to get themselves killed. Naturally, there'd be a tournament to celebrate.

Not that he'd be doing much there. Nor his guvnor, if he didn't pull himself together.

⁜ ⁜ ⁜

Torgun took a good long look around the courtyard. By Reus but it felt good to be back in a castle again, albeit a foreign one. Drinking in the neatly piled blocks of limestone, he inhaled deeply, banishing the memory of the Warlock's Crown. A stablehand took his horse from him; he felt a momentary twinge as the lad led his Farovian destrier away. It had been good to be reunited with Hilmir, to feel his mighty flanks beneath him again as they took the road to Merkstaed.

Merkstaed, and the castle that guarded it. Instead of urging Hilmir north, back towards his homeland, Torgun had chosen to steer him south, in the company of the monk who had become so disagreeable to him. His three best friends in the Order were dead, their lives spent on a mission that had proved only half successful. His duty was done: the King had given him the choice, whether to continue his adventures with Horskram after Andragorix was slain or return home to where he belonged.

So why was he here?

He knew the answer, even as the Eorl's soldiers escorted them towards the middle ward where their liege would receive them in the Great Hall.

He had not been able to get the winsome heiress of Dulsinor out of his mind since they had returned to the woodland camp to find her gone, spirited away by Madogan's men and back to the keep where she belonged. Even as they had buried Sir Aronn with full honours, her face had appeared before him, beautiful and proud as a morning sunrise. He had tried to force her away, fixing his eyes on Horskram as he intoned the Last Rites, replacing secret love with not-so-secret resentment.

To no avail.

The old monk had seemed surprised when Torgun told him he would continue his journey with them. Andragorix's sorcery had left him nursing burns on his chest, but the women had given him a salve for the pain and he'd soon got used to it. Doubtless the adept had expected him to ride off once the woodlanders brought them their horses and other supplies.

Instead he had calmly divested himself of his charred tabard and cloak, swapping the age-old insignia of the White Valravyn for the plain black surcoat of an errant.

It was an impossible love, and he knew it. Soon she would be married off to Lord Hengist, Herzog of Stornelund, soon to be Grand Herzog of Stornelund-Dulsinor. The Code of Chivalry's stipulations on romance didn't explicitly preclude a knight from having an affair with a married woman, so long as all the usual observances were made. But even an idealist like Torgun knew that such a powerful marriage alliance should not be interfered with.

Besides that, once the monk was done with his inspection of the castle, he would be off again, this time to Rima where he would report back to the Grand Master of his Order. Torgun would have no excuse for lingering at Graukolos.

He'd mulled that over time and again, but it made no difference. His heart was already beating faster as the guards escorted them through a second pair of double doors to the middle ward. The truth was, he would cross fire and flood for another chance to set eyes on Adhelina of Dulsinor.

✢ ✢ ✢

Braxus tried unsuccessfully to shake the cloud from his mind as they walked across the central courtyard towards the entrance to the Great Hall. The donjon loomed high above them; one of its turrets was covered with ivy, but he scarcely registered that or the clash of arms in the training yard.

Horskram had explained to him what had happened with the Gygant, how it had wanted to attack its captor but its natural fear of wizards had stopped it; how the old monk had persuaded it to let them live so they might be revenged on Andragorix on its behalf. It had been a close run thing, but eventually the Argolian had convinced it to leave them be.

Braxus had hoped that by understanding what had transpired he might be able to overcome the shame of his own fear, but thus it had not proved. Horskram had warned him that the very buildings of the Elder Wizards could wreak havoc with a man's mind. He had recited numerous psalms with his novice during their stay with the woodlanders and journey to Graukolos. They hadn't cured his melancholia, but at least he hadn't turned into a gibbering lunatic as other adventurers were said to have done after braving the ruins of the priest-kings.

The knight barely listened as the Eorl's chamberlain rattled off formalities before ushering them into the castle's triangular great hall. He had half hoped to catch another glimpse of the Eorl's daughter, now seemingly beyond his grasp. Hopefully that would cheer him up – he had thought about her many times during the journey to Graukolos, but all that did was intensify his shame. How could he possibly meet the lovely heiress's eye now? He had been tested, and found wanting. His poor squire, a man he was responsible for, was scarred for life. At least his sword arm should heal. The cut to Braxus' side was not deep and would heal too, though at nights it seemed to burn with a strange cold fire.

As they strode up the hall to meet their new host, Braxus tried to pull himself together. Perhaps he wasn't much of a knight errant, but he was still a lord's son.

✣ ✣ ✣

Sir Urist Stronghand surveyed the new arrivals as they drew to a halt before the Eorl's dais.

A mismatched band of companions... it was like something out of one of Baalric's lays, the sort written a couple of decades ago about a motley group of adventurers thrown together by improbable circumstances.

Here was a lay being played out in real life and no mistake. The monk was not unknown to him: Horskram had been a guest at Graukolos on a few occasions, stopping over on his way from one witch-hunt to another. The younger monk was evidently his novice.

Curious-looking fellow, with his chubby face and timid eyes: clearly not of noble stock, unlike his mentor. But then the Argolians judged the mettle of men differently to most mortals.

The two knights were clearly foreigners, judging by their dress: the Northlending was an impressive sight, towering over every other man in the room, though his strong features had a sorrowful cast to them. He was dressed in a sable tabard bereft of heraldic achievement, and carried no sword – bizarre, for such a well-made man must surely command some station in his homeland?

The handsome knight next to him looked even unhappier, though he was dressed better, in gilded mail and a surcoat bearing a stylised red wyvern coiled about a violet jewel on a verdant green background. He was flaxen-haired like the Northlending but of a lither build... a Thraxian or Cobian if Urist had to guess. His squire could be from anywhere – half his face was bandaged and his arm was in a sling.

But it was the sixth stranger who caught his eye. He was of slighter build than the Thraxian, and wore a hood brought low over his face. That wouldn't stand: court protocol demanded that all guests show their faces to the lord of the hall.

He was about to say something to this effect when Wilhelm spoke.

'So Brother Horskram returns to my hall, with a right ragtag band of freebooters in tow by the looks of it! I suppose you've heard about the theft, and want to conduct investigations.'

Horskram gave a courteous half-bow. Half, but not a full one, Urist noticed – these damned Argolians were notoriously dismissive of worldly rank and title.

'You are as direct as ever, Lord Wilhelm,' the monk said. 'And correct. Also, as you can see, my ragtag companions have seen some wear and tear – if they might have quarters and rest while my novice Adelko of Narvik and I conduct our investigation, I would be most grateful.'

'Of course!' boomed Wilhelm. 'Are we Vorstlendings not rightly renowned for our hospitality? Bed and board shall be given to your retinue without stint – but first I would know who my guests are.'

'Naturally,' replied Horskram, before rattling off introductions. When he got to the last one, a few gasps went up around the hall as the freebooter pulled back his – or rather her – hood.

'Anupe of the Harijan Isles seeks the favour of your hall,' said Horskram.

'She also seeks coin,' added the mercenary bluntly. 'I saved your daughter many times, during her bid for freedom.'

'How now?' cried the Eorl, fixing her with a look that might have melted frost. The monk was giving her a furious stare of his own: clearly this Anupe was not behaving as expected. But then what could one expect from a barbarian?

'Ah, forgive my companion's unguarded tongue,' interjected Horskram. 'If your lordship will permit me to explain, with fewer ears present...' He glanced meaningfully at the knights and ladies gathered in the frescoed hall.

The Eorl sighed and dismissed them with a wave of the hand. All that was left were the half dozen visitors, the Eorl, his seneschal Berthal and of course Urist himself.

'These are my most trusted advisers,' said Wilhelm. 'What I hear, they hear – my hall, my rules. Now out with it – I've a feeling you've been on one of your blasted missions again.'

Horskram cleared his throat and told them his tale. It wasn't a short one, and by the time he was done shadows were lengthening in the hall.

Urist didn't know what shocked him most – the story of Horskram's mission to root out Andragorix and recover the stolen stones, or the stab of pain that came to his heart when he learned that Sir Balthor was dead.

There had been little love lost between them, but for all his pomposity Sir Urist had admired the man. Now he was lying in a grave marked only by his sword on the northern foothills of the Eorldom, his life laid down trying to save the Lady Adhelina from an army of beastmen. At least it was a heroic death, one worthy of the knight Sir Balthor had thought he was.

He felt a flash of anger towards his liege's daughter – were it not for her headstrong wilfulness Sir Balthor would still be alive. The knight had been vain and boastful, but had not deserved to die. Urist made a mental note to have Baalric write a song in honour of his passing – that should please his shade as it gazed on the mortal vale from the Heavenly Halls.

'Well that is a grim tale and no mistake,' sighed the Eorl when Horskram was done. 'For all your efforts you're none the wiser as to who this thief is. You and your novice shall have the freedom of the Werecrypt – if it can furnish you with any clues, all to the better!'

He turned a beady eye on the Harijan next.

'As for you, tell me why I shouldn't have you clapped in irons pending execution for abetting the attempted escape of my daughter?'

Anupe stared back at him boldly. If she felt any fear she hid it well. 'I was in the employ of the Lady Adhelina,' she replied. 'It is not for a freesword to question her paymaster. I did what I was asked and expect to be paid for it. I had heard that the Markward family keeps its word.'

The Eorl stared at her. Berthal shot a sideways glance at Urist, who tensed at her insolence.

Just say the word my liege, he thought, *and I'll have half a dozen strong knights in here and a blacksmith in tow.*

An uncomfortable silence stretched across the next few moments.

If he gestures towards me, her life is over, thought Urist. *If he gestures towards Berthal, she's just enriched herself.*

The Eorl gestured towards Berthal.

'Pay her,' he said gruffly. 'Terms as agreed with my daughter. Time to draw a line under this infernal business.'

Urist could not resist breaking his silence. 'But, my lord, she – '

'I said pay her and be done with it,' said the Eorl firmly. 'The sight of this outlander sickens me, I'll not sully my walls with her pagan head.'

'My lord is gracious,' said Anupe, bowing low and deep. So far as Urist could tell, she wasn't being sarcastic.

'Yes, yes, carry tales of my generosity and justice back to whatever benighted bourne you came from,' said the Eorl dismissively. 'Berthal will accompany you and see your business settled, then you can thank me by getting out of Dulsinor with all due speed.'

The Harijan said no more at that and turned to leave with Berthal.

At least the savage knows when to shut up, thought Urist. He burned with resentment. This had not been a good day.

'The rest of you can go with him as well – he'll see you all quartered,' added Wilhelm. 'Then you can join us for supper. This horrid business aside, it's a joyous occasion. The Lanraks are coming to feast with us – in case you hadn't heard, there's a wedding back on.'

⚜ ⚜ ⚜

Adhelina sat by the window, staring despondently into the courtyard below. She had barely registered the arrival of the monk and his strange retinue a half hour ago. The two foreign knights who had seemed to show some interest in her were with him – not that that would avail her much now.

She looked around her chamber, once a riot of green, now bare and empty like the prison cell it had become. Her father had ordered all her things confiscated – there would be no more clever escapes. She wondered what had become of the guards she had doped; two different men now stood outside her door.

And just to make sure she didn't try anything again, she had Sir Ruttgur and Sir Agravine for constant company. Hettie had been packed off to Lothag monastery to be treated by the Marionites after her ordeal. She hoped they would do her some good, but she knew the real reason had been to separate them. At least her father had spared Hettie – Reus knew, she didn't deserve to be punished any more for her loyalty.

Ruttgur stood silent and stoical, but Agravine stared at her with sad and troubled eyes. He certainly wasn't flirting with her anymore – he hardly dared.

'The Lanraks will be arriving shortly,' the young knight ventured. 'You should think about getting ready for the feast. Shall I send for a lady-in-waiting?'

Adhelina turned her gaze pointedly back to the window. 'I care not,' she said sullenly. Yet again she felt incipient tears pushing themselves into the corners of her eyes.

Agravine's voice became earnest. 'My lady, you must shrug off this melancholy,' he urged, walking over to stand next to her. 'The future of Dulsinor is at stake.'

'We're lucky it still has a future,' muttered Ruttgur. 'It's a miracle the Lanraks didn't call off the wedding after this fiasco.'

'Hengist may be a fool, but his steward isn't,' shot back Agravine. 'Albercelsus understands as well as the Eorl that this alliance must take place.'

He knelt, trying and failing to catch Adhelina's weepy eyes. 'This situation... it isn't as bad as you think.'

Adhelina laughed bitterly. The handsome knight had always been so charming, when things were easier. Now he sounded clumsy of speech.

'There's no use trying to convince her,' said Ruttgur sourly. 'If her ladyship understood in the first place none of this would have happened.'

'Her ladyship needs to prepare for the feast – why don't you go and fetch her a lady to help her dress?' asked Agravine pointedly.

Sir Ruttgur gave a disgusted sneer but did as the knight suggested.

When he was out of the room Sir Agravine suddenly rediscovered his eloquence.

'My lady Adhelina, you are passing fair and keen of mind,' he said. 'Every man in the castle with an ounce of wit can see that. This is why I say that this situation is not so bad as you think.'

He surprised her by taking her hand. Her eyes met his.

'You simply must marry – a woman in your position has no other choice. And yes, the Herzog is a foul bedmate... but he needn't be your only one.'

Adhelina surprised herself by what she said next.

'Go on.'

'Lady Adhelina, I think I have made my feelings for you clear,' said Agravine. 'In a few days all the knights of Dulsinor and those the Lanraks have brought with them shall enter the lists. I would fain have your favour. Let me compete on your behalf – for your glory and honour!'

She had seen this coming but all the same she was a little shocked. She knew the Laws of Romance well enough, though they certainly didn't agree with the realities of politics.

'You are asking to become my paramour? Do you know what will happen when my father learns of this?'

'I do, and I care not,' replied Agravine. 'Set me as many tasks as you will, and I shall fulfil them – as an errant if need be.'

He must have read the anguish she felt on her face.

'Oh why so troubled, my lady?' he asked, leaning forwards with a half smile, his voice smooth and seductive. 'Adhelina, a damsel like you was not meant to go through this world without lovers! Take this loathsome man to your bedchamber, for it is your duty. And then do what every noblewoman in the Free Kingdoms has done since the time of King Vasirius, aye and probably before! Take on paramours, as many as you care for! If you consent to make me one of them – after you're married – I'll consider it an honour greater than any position at court!'

She did not doubt his sincerity. And he was right – what he was suggesting certainly wasn't unheard of. Besides, wasn't this what she had dreamed of all along, brave knights winning her favour? She just hadn't chosen to dwell on what happened to the damsels Gracius had written about before they embarked on their romantic love affairs – most of them were married, usually against their will.

She looked away. Yes she had been naïve, she supposed. Sir Agravine was doing his best to be romantic, but he was a realist too.

'At least consider my suit!' he said, sounding earnest again. He was obviously making a concerted effort to woo her. He probably had no intention of making her his only paramour – he clearly didn't expect to be hers.

And yet the thought of it pleased her. It was certainly preferable to that of marrying the Herzog.

'All right,' she said at length. 'I'll consider it.'

The door opened. Sir Ruttgur strode back in, a lady in tow.

Agravine got to his feet, making sure he didn't look too hasty.

'The Lanraks have arrived at the lists, their knights are settling in for the tourney,' announced Ruttgur. 'The Herzog and his retinue are making their way here to the castle, so you'd best be getting ready, my lady.'

Adhelina stood slowly. Her court clothes were in the next room. At least she'd get some time away from the menfolk while she prepared for the feast.

She caught Agravine's eye one last time as she made her way over to the side chamber. His expression looked impassive enough, but there was a gleam in his eyes that spoke volumes.

A thrill of excitement coursed through her. She had denied herself for so long, and Agravine was brave and comely. She held on to the feeling as she began to undress.

Perhaps there was life beyond marriage after all.

⊶ CHAPTER VI ⊷

A Tryst For New Lovers

Hannequin's face was grave as he gave his report. 'We conducted a divination at the Wytching Hour last night,' he said. 'We detected strong traces of sorcery across the Free Kingdoms. There appears to be a powerful concentration here, here and here...' The Grand Master placed Jedrez pieces on a map of Urovia to demonstrate his meaning. The first two pieces sat on Thraxia and Vorstlund. He placed the third piece on the edge of the map, where a stylised hand pointed downwards. 'There's someone at work in the Southlands too – whether the Pilgrim Kingdoms or the Sassanian Sultanates beyond, we can't be sure at this range.'

The King sighed and shifted in his seat, looking visibly bored. They were in a private audience chamber. Wolmar shared his boredom. He was heartily sick of all this talk of sorcerers.

'Are you able to be more specific?' asked Carolus. 'Do you know who exactly is responsible?'

Hannequin shook his head. 'We know of several powerful warlocks said to be operating across Urovia and Sassania, so those emanations could well be from them. Normally we'd be able to tie it to a more specific location but...' here Hannequin paused, his brow furrowed in consternation. '... it would appear somebody is using powerful blanketing magic. It's known by warlocks as counter-scrying and prevents us from divining exactly – '

Carolus cut him off. 'So in other words, some unknown mages are plotting to reunite an ancient artefact that could spell the end of the world – but you are unable to do anything about it.'

Hannequin frowned, not relishing the pointed remark. 'We need more time, Your Majesty,' he said. 'We shall gather our spiritual fortitude with prayers and fasting, then perhaps when Horskram arrives, he can join his elan to our efforts. He is gifted with – '

Carolus flicked a hand dismissively, snatching up the ebony pieces and tossing them back into a silvered mahogany box. 'Yes, yes, spare me the details, Grand Master. I have been apprised of enough already as it is. If you'll forgive me, I shan't concern myself with calamitous events that may or may not happen – especially when no culprits present themselves. I'll leave you to worry about that, just keep me informed.'

Hannequin seemed satisfied at that, though the man sitting opposite him evidently felt quite differently. Cyprian, the Supreme Perfect of the Creed, wore his seventy-odd years with a weathered sort of pride. His white beard flowed to his waist and looked just as ornamental as his bejewelled robes of office that shared its colour.

'If I may interject, Your Majesty,' said Cyprian. 'We have just now learned that the Argolians were keeping a cursed fragment of this anti-relic and let it go! I say charges of demonolatry and witchcraft should be reopened against the Order forthwith!'

Hannequin rolled his eyes to show what he thought of that.

Fortunately for him the King seemed of the same mind. 'As to having another Purge in my realm, I don't think I'll entertain that notion,' said Carolus. 'The last one wasn't too popular if I recall. No, let the Argolians make up for their gross oversight by investigating the matter further.'

'Your Majesty, this is most irregular!' protested the Supreme Perfect.

'I'll tell you what's irregular,' retorted the King. 'The fact that one of your senior clerics kept hidden the existence of a sacred relic of the Creed – be thankful that this Lorthar has been exposed. If I were you, I would divide your time between organising pilgrimages to Strongholm and giving thanks to the Almighty for this revelation.'

Cyprian favoured the King with a cold stare, but appeared mollified. 'It is indeed a blessing that the iniquity of Lorthar has been revealed – and that of the Northlending temple.' He turned his frosty eyes on Wolmar. The princeling could not help but flinch. The last thing he wanted was to offend the head of the Temple – Reus knew he had enough sins on his conscience as it was.

'Very well,' said the Supreme Perfect, his eyes not leaving Wolmar. 'I shall defer to your wishes in this matter – for now.'

'You have the crown's thanks for it,' replied the King cordially. 'Grand Master Hannequin, I have just vouched for you. I take it you shall repay my kindness by taking this matter in hand.'

'Thank you, Your Majesty,' replied Hannequin, looking grateful. 'Rest assured we shall conduct further divinations.'

Wolmar despised the Grand Master even more for his obsequious ways. He agreed with Cyprian – the Argolians should stand trial. But then he'd given up arguing that, nobody listened to him anyway.

'There is some good news as well,' Hannequin added. 'Our divination detected only trace elements of Left-Hand sorcery in the area of the Argael, whither our brother Horskram was bound. Perhaps that suggests he has been successful in rooting out the warlock Andragorix.'

'Perhaps it does,' said the King, looking even more bored. 'I care not. Matters of state are my business, I leave matters of magic to you and your ilk. Now if that is all, I believe I have a tournament to preside over. Good day.'

They all rose to leave the chamber. Wolmar felt his heart quicken at the mention of the Crescent Bridge Tourney. Lord Ivon had entered him at the last minute. There was a strict quota, and the flower of the kingdom's chivalry came from all over the realm to compete: Ivon had probably pulled a few strings to get him in.

That was good, Wolmar reflected as he marched back towards his quarters to arm himself. Today he'd show these haughty Pangonians some northern mettle.

✣ ✣ ✣

Sir Wolmar winced as the chirurgeon removed his armour to tend to his dislocated shoulder. Sir Aremis had sent him sailing over the crupper of his saddle, dashing his hopes of victory. Oh the shame of it – bested by a Pangonian in the third round of a prestigious tournament! At least the joust here was a formal event with no ransoms and he didn't have to forfeit his horse and armour. Losing a prized Farovian destrier to a foreigner would have been even more shameful.

Lord Ivon entered the tent. He was grinning urbanely, as though nothing much had happened. 'Well, never mind,' he said, spotting Wolmar's downcast expression. 'Sir Aremis is the top seed, you were unlucky being drawn against him so early. At least you managed to knock Kaye out in the first round – he'll have to show you more respect now.'

'I don't give a damn about Lord Kaye and what he thinks,' Wolmar shot back. 'I wanted to win!'

Lord Ivon stroked his head affectionately. Wolmar pulled away irritably, wincing again as an invisible lance stabbed his shoulder. He still didn't feel comfortable displaying unorthodox desires publicly.

The manners of this strange country were deeply unsettling – how could they be so formal and yet so candid?

'Ah, sweet prince, always wanting to win...' Ivon went on. 'Did you know some Sassanian mystic sects teach that one can learn more in defeat than in victory?'

'No, I didn't, and I don't give a damn – aaaargh!' Wolmar yelled as the chirurgeon pushed his shoulder back into place with an audible crack. He thanked him for it by lashing out and sending the man flying across the tent.

Ivon pursed his lips disapprovingly. 'Sir Wolmar, that was most unnecessary,' he said, watching impassively as the chirurgeon staggered to his feet clutching a bloody nose.

'No, it was entirely necessary,' said Wolmar venomously. Rising to his feet, he stalked past Ivon out of the tent. 'Have your squire pick up my armour, I'm in need of a drink.'

※ ※ ※

Sir Wolmar glowered at his platter. Several stoops of strong wine had not improved his spirits. Sir Aremis had been crowned champion of the joust, but losing to the eventual victor did not make him feel better about his defeat. The lists had been taken down and rows of trestle tables set up in their place. The summer night was balmy, meaning the celebration feast could be held outdoors.

'I've an idea,' said Lord Ivon, leaning in close so no one else would hear. 'I know of a lovely spot but half a day's ride from here. Let us go tomorrow, you and I – a break from the city will do you good, I trow.'

Wolmar sneered into his goblet. 'A lovers' tryst? We shouldn't keep indulging these effeminate desires, they clearly aren't doing my fighting prowess any good.'

'Yes, well as to that, there are other kinds of prowess one can cultivate,' replied Ivon.

Wolmar glanced at him. The Margrave's face was oddly neutral.

'What do you mean by that?' asked Wolmar, deciding it wasn't an innuendo.

Ivon replied by patting him gently on the shoulder. 'We'll set off tomorrow, at first light. I'll have the necessary arrangements made. Now if you'll excuse me, I have some mingling to do...'

He left Wolmar alone at the table, pondering the meaning of his words.

※ ※ ※

From the high hills they watched the last of the sun slip below the horizon. The green fields and meadows of the lands around Rima were bathed in a blanket of dusk, as was the River Athos that poured down towards the city, now reduced to a collection of twinkling lights off in the distance. To the north the hills rose gradually to meet the Orne ranges.

They were both naked beneath the blankets that swaddled them; up here at the hunting lodge Ivon had brought them to the air was chillier.

The Margrave let out a satisfied sigh. 'Did I not say the view was spectacular?' he asked.

'We have just such views in my country,' said Wolmar. 'Though yes, it is pleasing enough I suppose.'

'Always so defensive,' purred Ivon, refilling their cups. 'I was not inviting another debate on the relative merits of our countries.'

'I can hardly be faulted for that,' said Wolmar, taking the cup. 'Given the way your countrymen behave.'

'Let us not dwell on the manners of my countrymen,' said Ivon, sipping at his wine. 'I wanted to talk to you about something else.'

Wolmar glanced at him sidelong. Something in the Margrave's tone caught his attention.

'What?' he asked.

'As you know, I am held in high esteem because of my family's lineage, but I have also made myself indispensible to Carolus. You may recall I mentioned that Sir Odo has eyes and ears everywhere... But there are times when more than just spies are needed to carry out the business of state. That is where I come in.'

Ivon paused to sip his wine again.

'Go on,' said Wolmar, unsure what else to say.

'His Majesty has made himself unpopular for two reasons,' said Ivon. 'First, he is suspected of murdering his father to get to the throne sooner. Carolus II was a much loved monarch, as pious and honourable as the day is long. Many in our realm still grieve for him.'

Wolmar shrugged his shoulders. 'What of it? The affairs of your kingdom are of little interest to me – '

Ivon laid delicate fingers on the knight's lips. 'Let me finish. Second, and far more significant, are the high taxes he has levied since coming to power. Now, our King is a man of vision, you understand. He wants to make the realm truly great, not just the best of the Free Kingdoms. But many of his nobles are too self-seeking and near-sighted to realise this. Running a prosperous kingdom won't be enough – he needs to give them something they'll like.'

'Which is?'

Ivon smiled. Turning to point at the mountains, he said: 'Do you know what lies past yonder ranges?'

Wolmar wasn't used to travelling far and had to think a moment.

'Vorstlund...' he said, his voice trailing off as he suddenly grasped his lover's meaning.

'Precisely,' said Ivon. 'A rich realm, divided and leaderless – ripe for conquest! The King plans to invade, and I've been charged with drumming up support for the invasion. About half the barons have already agreed, the other half... may prove somewhat awkward.'

'I see,' said Wolmar. 'I thought a war would have appealed to any self-respecting baron.'

'You'd be surprised. Not all relish the idea of a war with our northern neighbour. Rhunia, Narvon and Orrin are proving intractable – they'll stay put, they're far more concerned about defending their borders from the Thalamians I'm afraid. And about half a dozen margraves despise the King so much they'll never agree to follow him to war, not even for the sake of plunder and glory.'

'Is Morvaine one of them?' asked Wolmar.

Ivon favoured him with a smug smile. 'Actually no, Morvaine agreed to the invasion some time ago – our enmity is based on purely personal issues. I seduced his sister last summer.'

'So what will happen with the barons who don't agree to invade?' asked Wolmar, choosing to ignore this revelation as something else occurred to him. 'What's to stop them trying to take the throne for themselves while the King is away fighting in Vorstlund?'

'That's the spirit, my sweet prince!' exclaimed Ivon. 'Now you're thinking! Yes, that is exactly what the King and I have fathomed... which is where His Supreme Holiness comes in.'

Wolmar blinked, nonplussed. 'Cyprian?'

'Oh yes, don't be fooled by the way Carolus talks to him – he and the King are in fact quite close. His Majesty was wise enough to exempt the Temple from his new taxes. In return His Supreme Holiness is going to declare a fresh crusade. You see, the margraves who hate the King most do so precisely because they are god-fearing men who respected Carolus the Elder. But when the Supreme Perfect declares the Fourth Pilgrim War they won't be able to resist the call – they'll be packed off to the Blessed Realm, leaving the King free to invade Vorstlund.'

'Very clever,' said Wolmar. 'Is that the real reason why Uthor the Younger is at court, to help broker another crusade?'

'Just so,' smiled Ivon. 'Although the taxes are a genuine issue in themselves.'

'So why are you telling me all of this?'

Ivon leaned in close and stroked his hair.

'My dear Sir Wolmar, as you may have noticed, I have taken a liking to thee... And I sense your rage and frustration. You have been overlooked all your life. When I look at you I see potential! I would have you join us - the King is an ambitious man, and will reward his allies well. You've already told me of your deeds of valour in your uncle's war - a pox on these gilded tourneys, you were made for sterner stuff!'

'What kind of sterner stuff do you have in mind?' asked Wolmar. He felt suspicious, but at the same time he was intrigued. The Margrave's words had piqued his pride.

Ivon smiled a sickly sweet smile.

'Why Sir Wolmar, I must confess it's been an absolute age since I donned armour and couched a lance... far more interesting things to do with one's time. Vichy has five hundred knights ready to do service at my command. You shall lead them into Vorstlund for me.'

Wolmar squinted at him, not quite believing it.

'You want me to be your marshal?'

'To begin with... and perhaps other positions shall open up later.'

Wolmar looked away, suddenly unable to meet his lover's eyes.

'I could not desert my country,' he faltered. 'I have sworn to defend it.'

'Aye, and what thanks did you get in return?' Ivon shot back. 'Sent hither like an errand boy. What business is it of yours to get involved in some sorcerous plot? You belong in the field I say!'

Wolmar turned and grabbed Ivon by the hair.

'How do you know of my mission?' he snarled. 'Speak now!'

'Ah... so hasty, my sweet prince,' winced Ivon. 'Did I not tell you just now I have the King's confidence? He tells me everything.'

Wolmar relaxed his grip. 'So you know about the Headstone fragments?'

A curious glint entered the Margrave's eyes. 'Oh yes... I took time to acquire my letters in my youth. I have read about them, enough to know that there are far older, darker powers in this world than you or I can fathom.'

'So the Argolians would have us believe,' said Wolmar, letting go of his lover. The new turn of conversation made him feel uncomfortable.

'I already told you that my house is intermingled with the royal blood of Rius, but we have many other stories, some glorious, some tragic, and some... strange.'

'Strange?'

'The ruling house of Rius is not the first time we Laurelins have married into royal blood. Centuries ago, when the kingdom was young, Tristande the Third Margrave of Vichy married the daughter of Aaron III. Ever afterwards he was known as the Bridal Cursed. His wife was Arawin the Benighted, and it was said that she learned pagan sorcery at the feet of her father, whom posterity now call the Bewitched.'

Wolmar gaped. 'You're saying one of the first kings of Pangonia was a warlock?'

'Just so,' replied Ivon with a sardonic smile. 'He lived a long life, but many about his court withered and died... including my ancestor Tristande. But not before Arawin had borne him a single son, Salomon, who inherited his title. He is said to have been taught the black arts by his mother... some even say he was carried off by the North Wind to the Other Side one moonless night, never to return.'

'I should have expected no less from Pangonians,' spat Wolmar. 'Thank Reus my own royal blood is not so tainted.'

'Yes,' said Ivon, caressing the princeling's cheek. 'You are indeed... fortunate. Such powers as the Elder Wizards wielded are not to be trifled with. And that is why I urge you to distance yourself from this business of the sorcerous fragments – you were made to fight foes of flesh and blood, Wolmar.'

Wolmar felt a shiver run down his spine. He had not told Ivon of the demon at Staerkvit. Even if he had wanted to, how did you broach such a subject?

Ivon let his hand run down Wolmar's back, soothingly stroking the knotted muscles.

'So tense, my sweet prince,' breathed the Margrave. 'You have witnessed such horrors, that I can see plainly. And losing your poor father on top of it all. No, you need a purpose – a worthy goal to set your sights on to banish this darkness from your mind.'

A barely suppressed shudder ran through Wolmar. The night suddenly felt very cold.

'I have seen... some terrible things,' he said.

'But you have done glorious things too,' said Ivon. 'And shall do yet more. Join with us, Sir Wolmar, and I promise the terrible things you have seen shall not seem so terrible any more.'

Wolmar felt powerless to resist as the Margrave gently drew his head down to rest in his lap. A great weariness was on him: all he wanted now was to sleep. As he drifted into unconsciousness he was dimly aware of Ivon murmuring words in a strange-sounding, alien tongue.

⊷ CHAPTER VII ⊷

The Warband Musters

'We've more than two and a half thousand fighting men at our disposal,' said Guldebrand. 'Not counting the five hundred we've sent to Ystad.'

A dozen war-lined faces peered at him as he went on outlining his battle plan. They belonged to some of the most powerful men and women in the Principalities. He could not afford to show any weakness.

He pointed to the map laid out on the tree stump and continued. 'I propose we divide the rest of our forces, send half across the Hror Ranges to attack Halgaard directly. The other half should cut through the Hrorwood and start pillaging the lands thereabout.'

Magnhilda raised an eyebrow. 'Pillaging? Why waste good men doing that? This is a war not a mainland raid.'

Guldebrand shook his head. 'No, we need to draw them out, provoke them. If we concentrate all our forces in a single pitched battle we risk losing everything on one throw of the dice. Not all of Oldrik's warriors will be mobilised – we kill as many shieldmen on their farms as we can, weaken his leidang and those of his jarls. So I say two forces.'

He moved a couple of chequers counters across the vellum to demonstrate his meaning.

'The first force takes Halgaard and commandeers the ships at the nearby river port of Umtsk to sail up the Holm towards Landarök. Meanwhile, the second force strikes north-west towards it, burning and slaying as they go. Both forces converge on the capital, like so – and we have Oldrik in a pincer. A crab's claw to crush him with!'

He glanced around the all-thing to see how his proposal was being received. Two weeks had passed since his duel with Magnhilda, and their combined forces were mustered. More than half a dozen jarls, Brega and Varra, the Mountainside, Magnhilda and Ragnar and several other champions were crowded under the awning. The sound of warriors drilling filtered in from the bustling camp that filled the plains around them.

'The original plan was simply to march on Halgaard,' rumbled Mountainside. 'But I like this change, it's bold and it's ruthless. I say we do it.'

'But how can you be so sure of Oldrik's deployments?' asked one jarl. 'What if he has all his leidangs mustered already?'

Guldebrand favoured him with a sly smile. The jarl was in service to Asmund – Ragnar had delivered him news of the alliance and the timid Thegn had quickly judged which way the wind was blowing.

'He doesn't,' said Guldebrand. 'This is where we have an advantage the Stormrider lacks – we have a spy who can fly! White Eye, now is the time for your latest report I think.'

Ragnar nodded curtly and pointed at the map with his trident. 'I have scoured all the lands of Gautlund. The Stormrider knows nothing of our alliance and is not expecting an attack. He has a thousand men under sail, heading towards Varborg to try and reverse our gains in Jótlund. He has despatched another jarl to deal with the men Magnhilda sent to Ystad a tenday ago.'

Mountainside whistled. 'So he took the bait then? Good, very good! Let the Stormrider waste five hundred men chasing our lads back across the Vakka, while we descend on him from the east. With any luck they'll come marching back to a conquered realm!'

'On top of that he has hundreds of men away on mainland raids,' continued Ragnar. 'By my estimates that leaves him with two thousand men. Five hundred are garrisoned at Halgaard under the command of Jarl Edgard. Another five hundred are in the lands south of the Røk and won't be on hand. That leaves a thousand stationed in Landarök and settled on the lands about it.'

Magnhilda smiled. 'Fifteen hundred men including Edgard,' she said, nodding enthusiastically. 'I begin to see your purpose, my betrothed. If we take Halgaard quickly we should be able to overwhelm Oldrik before any reinforcements arrive.'

'How will that be possible?' asked Brega. 'Halgaard is well situated, it commands a view of the Hrorpass – they'll see us coming for miles!'

'Not if I have anything to do with it,' said Ragnar. 'I shall put a glamour on the men who cross the Hrorpass. You will not be seen, until you are close enough to launch a surprise attack.'

Guldebrand's smile broadened. 'Useful to have a wizard in tow,' he said.

Several of the men including the Mountainside looked distinctly uneasy at that, but Guldebrand was quick to reassure them.

'Tis but illusion magick, friends,' he said. 'No harm will befall you!'

Magnhilda bit her lip. Several of the jarls and champions exchanged uncertain glances and one or two shook their heads.

'What guarantees do we have that this isn't some sorcerous trick?' said the Shield Queen, looking askance at Ragnar.

He returned her stare, his frosted eye catching the setting sun with a queer gleam. She held his cyclopean gaze unabashed. Guldebrand could have sworn something passed between them then, like a current of energy.

'I can offer you no guarantees,' said the mage coldly. 'You either choose to place trust in my powers, or you don't.'

'I say a pox on his powers!' cried another jarl, this one in service to Magnhilda. 'We are true-born Northlanders and should fight as such!'

A few throats showed what the men thought of that.

'Very well,' said Ragnar. 'Go marching down the Hrorpass without my protection. I guarantee you will find a host of armed men waiting for you at Halgaard. Other shieldmen on the lands below shall see you from miles away, and will mobilise. You will have a pitched battle with many lives lost on either side.'

'If that be Tyrnor's will, so be it!' cried a battle-scarred champion. 'Let the souls of the slain seek the Halls of Feasting and Fighting, as befits warriors who die in battle!'

'Enough!' cried Guldebrand, holding up a hand. 'I am fighting to consolidate a realm, and do you know why?'

He caught the eye of the jarl who had spoken, before turning to look everyone in the face in turn.

'Because this is just the beginning, my friends! Once Oldrik is slain, Magnhilda and I shall rule the Frozen Principalities! And then we shall bring together such an army as has not been seen since the time of Søren! Aye, the tumult of axes we shall bring in sea steeds across the sail road to the mainland, and take back the lands that dared sunder themselves from us! The Kingdom of Northalde we shall rule as ours, the race of northmen shall be reunited under our banner! Does this not appeal to you my friends?'

The myrmidons shrugged and suddenly looked bashful. He was thinking bigger than them, and they knew it.

'I still don't see why we need to use sorcerous trickery!' said the champion.

'Because to conquer the mainland we're going to need as many warriors as we can get, living and whole,' said Guldebrand. 'A fat lot of good we'll be if half of us are butchered in a costly civil war! For too long Northlander has turned on Northlander – in the days of Olav Ironhand it was not so! That is why we must strike quickly and decisively, best Oldrik as easily as we can – with the minimum of bloodshed. We take Halgaard, and we close in on Landarök. When he sees our superior numbers, he may even surrender to save his skin!'

Magnhilda frowned. 'I don't see Oldrik doing that,' she said. 'What's to stop him holding the walls until his reinforcements arrive?'

Guldebrand tapped the map. 'Because half our men will be assaulting him by river, remember? There are no walls where the Holm passes through the city. Once our men are inside, there's no way Oldrik's can hold us to a siege.'

The mutterings had turned to approval. The jarls and champions definitely liked his plan. Guldebrand felt his heart soar. By the time his sixteenth summer was over, he would rule all the Frozen Wastes.

Canute was looking at Magnhilda, his ugly face cracking a broad grin. 'By Thoros and Sjórkunan but the lad's plan is a good one,' he said.

'Well, betrothed,' said the Shield Queen, a smile on her own face now. 'It seems it was true what I said about you before – you really do have something of Logi about you. But your ambitions are worthy of Tyrnor.'

She held out her hand in the warrior's clasp and he took it. It was an odd gesture between a man and his future wife, but somehow it felt appropriate.

'Very well,' said Magnhilda. 'Let us deal with Oldrik as swiftly as we can, by fair means or foul, and consolidate our new kingdom. Then we'll bring such weather of weapons to the mainlanders as they have not seen in seven hundred years!'

The awning erupted in cheering. Guldebrand smiled, flushed with his success, and called loudly for mead. As he did he caught Ragnar's one good eye. The warlock did not join in the merriment, but merely stood stock still leaning on his trident.

In spite of himself, Guldebrand found his fingers reaching towards the pomander about his neck.

⊶ CHAPTER VIII ⊷

A Palace Coup

'All right, you all know what you've to do.'

The faces of his companions were set grim in the fading light. All except Regan's that was. The young knight worried Vertrix. He seemed like his old self, breezy and confident. And that was the problem: no one in their right mind should feel that way given what they were about to undertake.

Bryant nodded slowly. 'The plan is simple enough after all,' he said, speaking softly. The guards outside their door most likely wouldn't be able to hear them anyway, but it was best to be sure.

Vertrix turned to look at the others. Their squires were with them, all except Paidlin of course, who wouldn't have any pretext to be attending them on the eve of the feast. But the poor lad could have no part in their plan anyway, crippled as he was. Mulling over its chances of success, Vertrix reflected that perhaps that was for the best. At least one of them had a better than average chance of living out the day.

He met Regan's eyes last, holding them in his own as he asked him once more if he understood what was required of him.

'Well I'm still carrying an injury from the Northlending war,' said the knight, 'but Reus willing I'll be able to move quickly enough when the time comes.'

He sounded as confident as ever. Too confident. Vertrix's guts found a tighter knot for themselves as he forced himself to dissemble.

'All right, good,' he said, addressing all of them. 'Now let's be about it, lads. I believe we've a royal feast to prepare for.'

They dressed in silence, the absence of sound doing little for the old knight's nerves. It had taken him a fortnight to persuade Abrexta and the King that he had come round to their madcap plan to conquer the Westerling Isles. Tonight he'd be rewarded for his efforts with a place at the table adjacent to the King's. All his years of military experience had gone into winning that favour; if he could not expect to win their trust, at least he could prove himself indispensible and worthy of a more honourable position.

A knock on the door heralded the event they had prepared for. Taking a deep breath Vertrix called for their escort of guards to enter. Just as they did and the others turned to face them, he leaned in and whispered to Gormly: 'You know what to do if he can't be trusted.'

Gormly nodded, his bluff countenance betraying nothing, though he flicked a dark glance at Regan as they filed out of the room.

✠ ✠ ✠

Vertrix did his best to appear relaxed as they arrived at the hall. He could not afford to show his tension. He felt the witch's dark eyes on him as he took his seat. It still wasn't as close as he would like, but it would have to do. He forced himself to meet her gaze and nodded courteously. There was no presence in his mind: she wasn't trying to enthral him. That was a blessed relief.

Every yard counts, he told himself. Abrexta was sat twenty paces away. Two guards stood to attention behind her and Cadwy.

Regan and Bryant sat to either side of him. Their three squires took up position behind them. They'd rehearsed the plan endlessly, but timing and detail would be crucial to its success. The chance of that would be oh so slim, but they had to try...

He glanced sidelong at Regan as the court perfect intoned the standard prayer before meat. The young knight's face remained as casual as ever. Was he wrong to doubt him? A sudden pang of guilt crossed his breast. These were strange times indeed, when old comrades in arms mistrusted one another. A hundred plagues on the wretched sorceress who had made it so.

That thought only stiffened his resolve. He hoped he *was* wrong about Regan – but he couldn't take that chance.

Servants brought the first course. Roasted venison seasoned with nutmeg and pepper, precious spices brought from the hot Southlands. Gormly leaned forward to carve for his master. The court minstrels had begun playing a gentle ditty for the diners. Vertrix felt his heart quicken as his squire cut slices for him. Breaking off a crust of bread lined with chestnuts, Vertrix chewed on it and tried to look as though he were enjoying the food. Gormly began heaping slices on his trencher. When the third one was on, Vertrix nodded curtly.

Instead of stepping back behind him, Gormly passed him the dagger. Vertrix was already on his feet. Leaping across the table he felt every sinew in his old body strain. Forcing himself into a sprint he closed on the King and his paramour.

He risked slowing his pace for a quick glance back. Regan and Bryant were right behind him, daggers in hand, Gormly dogging their heels.

He had closed half the distance before anyone else had a chance to react. The King was staring at him, open-mouthed. Abrexta was on her feet.

'Kill him!' she cried.

The guards had stepped forward to protect their king, and exchanged confused glances, but Vertrix knew the order wasn't meant for them.

He turned again and saw Regan, his eyes glazing over as he raised his blade to strike. Then Gormly was on the young knight, throwing him to the floor as he wrestled the dagger from his grasp.

'Protect the King!' yelled Vertrix at the top of his lungs like a man gone wood. 'The King has been bewitched! Protect the King!'

He was just a few yards away from Abrexta now. He could see her beautiful face contorted in an ugly scowl as she mouthed the words of some spell...

He closed with her and grabbed her tresses, pulling her down over the table as he raised his dagger to strike. At that moment he felt a hand about his throat and a sharp stabbing pain exploded through his kidneys. His whole body went limp, his legs turning to jelly beneath him. The pain continued to spread up through his back as he felt something hard wrenched from it.

The hand let go of him and he sank to the floor.

Something dark and sticky pooled beneath him. Looking up he saw Bryant's face looking down at him, his eyes glazed and face expressionless. In his hand was a bloodied dagger. Vertrix struggled to sit up but could not. Bryant's face remained emotionless as he knelt and plunged his blade into Vertrix's throat. The old knight felt himself being sucked into a whirlpool of blood, it rose higher and higher as the life choked out of him...

✢ ✢ ✢

Abrexta felt herself stretched to breaking point. Beads of sweat stood out on her forehead. She could bear no more. She released the two knights from her thrall as Vertrix quivered into stillness before her. Bryant recoiled from the corpse, face going ashen as his senses returned to him.

'Seize these traitors!' she cried. The hall was a flurry of activity as knights and guards descended on Gormly, Regan and Bryant, who was screaming in anguish.

'Take them outside and hang them,' she commanded, recovering herself, though she felt like collapsing. It was a relief to have the two knights out of her control; she had stretched her powers to breaking point to enthral them on top of all the others.

The King had retreated behind his guards. She spared a sneer of contempt for him. He looked so pathetic, cowering in a corner: she longed for the day when she could finally be rid of him and rule directly in her own right.

The witch watched coolly as the five traitors were dragged from the hall. Looking at the corpse of Vertrix she smirked. Did he really think she could be so easily fooled? She could not hang them for treason without due cause – Vertrix had been too well respected, it was politically too risky. But now she had the pretext she needed to get rid of the troublesome northern knights. Another loose end neatly tied up.

'A very sad day,' said Sir Liant, the seneschal. 'I had thought Sir Vertrix a knight of some esteem.' Liant had been a landless knight until she got rid of his predecessor, who had been far too loyal and intransigent to enthral.

'I'll tell you what to think,' said Abrexta curtly. A corpulent drunk, Liant was barely fit for office, but he wasn't too much of a drain on her powers. In fact he barely needed enthralling at all. Palace affairs would have been a disorganised mess left in his hands, but fortunately the servants knew what they were about.

That thought amused her. How long had the preening nobility thought themselves indispensible to the nation? Once the new world order was ushered in, such vainglorious notions would be swept away. Men – *and* women – of real power would rule the earth, just as it had been on the Island Realms she would conquer next.

'Clean this away,' she said, motioning dismissively towards Vertrix's corpse. 'But keep his head, I want to see it hanging from the palace with the rest of his traitor friends.'

Men she had enthralled, bribed or cowed scrambled to obey. Within the hour the feast had resumed, King Cadwy timorously taking his seat again as servants poured him more wine.

'There now, my sweet king,' she purred in his ear. 'No need to affright yourself – another conspiracy against the royal person quashed.'

'But... Vertrix was an honourable man,' muttered the King, confusion written across his face. 'He wasn't like the others, he never coveted power. I don't understand...'

'These are dark times, and they bring dark inclinations with them,' she whispered, intensifying the image of a hand clutching a heart. She tried to ignore the nausea that washed over her as she stretched her elan again.

'Yes,' mumbled the King, 'dark times indeed. And what shall we do to make them brighter?'

As if on cue, the herald re-entered the room and bellowed: 'Your Majesty, an emissary from the highland clans seeks audience!'

Abrexta smiled at her lover. 'I think you are just about to have that question answered, my sweet. Pray bid the savage enter.'

Obediently the King did as he was told.

It was the same man who had led the first delegation of emissaries, only now he was alone. As well as an axe he carried a sack in his other hand.

'You disturb the royal person at feast-time,' declared the King, following Abrexta's mental script. 'Your news had best be good for the realm.'

The highland brigand's face cracked an ugly sneer. 'Aye, it's good news for ye, sirrah,' he said, before surprising them all by taking a knee. 'Slangá and Tíerchán like yer offer – a thousand o' their best men each they'll send ye, in return fer the lands ye've offered us.'

The enthralled and sycophants lost no time in cheering that, raising their goblets in a toast. Abrexta made a show of joining in, though the news hardly surprised her – she had been in contact with Cormic Death's Head on the matter already. Teaching one of his folk the rudiments of Scrying had been a good investment of time and effort.

'Let us all drink another toast,' she declared, rising. 'To our most munificent and valorous King Cadwy, the monarch who shall unite the Westerling peoples after two thousand years asunder! Lowlander and highlander, mainlander and islander – all shall find common kinship under his banner when this war is done!'

She fancied that the enthusiastic response was only partly down to her witcheries: her plans were ambitious, and had an appeal that even a sceptic could not deny.

'Aye, 'twill be a fine alliance,' cried the highlander. 'So long as yer majesty cleaves tae his part o' the bargain. But if he doesnae, know that the highland clans will be swift and merciless in exacting their revenge. For we stand in possession o' both the wards o' Daxor and Gaellentir, and *this* is what becomes o' those who oppose us.'

The savage opened the sack and tossed its contents into the midst of the tables. The first head was already in a state of decay, its eyes picked out. But the second was fresher, its identity unmistakeable to all who had met its former owner. Several gasps went up.

'Gaellentir fell a tenday ago,' said the highlander. 'We slaughtered every man in arms we found, including its master Lord Braun.' He met the King's eye and grinned fiercely. 'Ye can add the Lords of Gaellen and Daxtir tae yer collection o' heads on yon palace walls – consider it a reminder o' what happens tae those who cross highland folk.'

⊷ CHAPTER IX ⊶

The Trail Grows Cold

Stone effigies sprung to life, called from darkness by the light of Horskram's lantern. By now Adelko knew better than to flinch or shudder, though already he was thinking back to the top floor of the inner sanctum at Ulfang. The same lurking presence of evil was there, and a foul odour permeated the Werecrypt.

The tombs of the erstwhile lords of Graukolos stretched before them to either side; as Horskram guided them across the low vault Adelko could make out their names. Wilhelm Greybrow, father of the present-day Eorl; Urus the Strong, his father in turn; Alfric the Young... the names went on. Each of these tombs was crowned with the clenched fist of the Markward coat of arms. The tombs beyond those bore a different insignia: the heron of the House of Tal spread its petrified wings above more rude likenesses of the patrician lords of Dulsinor. There were a good deal more of these, he noticed: from the bygone days when Dulsinor had been a kingdom in its own right.

To Adelko they seemed much the same, king and eorl, Tal and Markward: in life they had all been doughty warrior chieftains glorified with title and castle. And nothing more than that. But then he was in a cynical mood, as he was more often these days.

Question everything... So the witch mistress of the Argael had bade him do. Now they were once more looking for a mystery warlock hell-bent on ruling entire kingdoms, provincial warlords seemed frankly trivial.

His sixth sense went up a notch as they reached a stone trapdoor set in the floor at the back of the vault, behind the row of tombs devoted to the seneschals of Graukolos. A great bronze ring was set into the middle of it.

'Well,' muttered Horskram. 'Whatever fell agent stole this fragment, it didn't use the door like a respectable visitor. I'll put a blessing on us and then you can help me to open this.'

Together they muttered the Psalms of Abjuration and Fortitude. Adelko felt the words channelling his psyche. Somehow they meant more to him now; he felt he understood them better than he had done three months ago. Together they heaved the heavy door open. He felt the lingering evil washing up over them in an invisible miasma.

More attuned to what was pure and holy; more sensitive to the wicked and profane. These were the fruits of spiritual growth.

Taking up the lantern again Horskram led them down a diagonal flight of stone steps. Now the feeling was different, no less horrible but more clearly identifiable: a demon's psychic spoor. That was one thing they hadn't detected in Andragorix's lair, though his scrolls and grimoires had contained depictions of the winged horror that had pursued them from Ulfang to Staerkvit.

'Why couldn't we sense a demonic presence at the Warlock's Crown, Master Horskram?' His own voice sounded curiously calm.

'Because he did not summon a demon to his presence,' said Horskram. 'He sent it to pursue us, so it never left its spoor in his quarters.'

'But there was something, coming from that... thing in his chamber. I could feel it.'

Horskram's lip curled in disgust. 'Aye, 'twas a Succubus – such fiends do not repel mortals but are designed to do exactly the opposite, inciting them to acts of depraved lust. Our Harijan friend would doubtless have approved.'

Adelko flushed, glad of the darkness. So that was why he had experienced altogether different sensations when they were investigating Andragorix's bedchamber. Clearly the servants of the Fallen One moved in diverse and mysterious ways.

The demonic spoor intensified as they stepped over to the other end of the cramped chamber. Adelko had seen enough of witchery and demonkind not to be surprised by the sight of what had been an iron casket now torn to shreds like a piece of parchment – and a gaping hole in the far wall.

'Something powerful enough to burrow through stone,' said Horskram, shaking his head as he reached for his phial of holy water. 'Join me in putting a blessing on this place. The heirs of Graukolos deserve better than to have such evil under their last resting place.'

'What do we do now?' asked Adelko once they were done. The aura of evil had diminished slightly, though it was still there.

Horskram nodded towards the hole. 'We follow its trail.'

This time Adelko's heart didn't sink, as it had done on so many other occasions: he had been expecting his mentor to say that.

Through the winding tunnel they made their way, both whispering psalms in the dark. The stench was enough to make him gag; he almost felt the mounds of fly-encrusted corpses outside Linden and Salmor would have been preferable to this preternatural reek.

The burrow-hole made its way steadily up towards the surface. In the light of Horskram's lantern Adelko could see the rock and earth had been hewn away in rough chunks. Had the demonic thief simply penetrated its way into the Werecrypt – or had it *eaten* its way down? The question made him feel queasier still.

On they scrambled and hours slipped by, with only their prayers and Horskram's light for company. When at last they emerged above ground Adelko thought he had forgotten the taste of fresh air.

He took it in gratefully as they looked around them. They were in a wood. The novice thought he caught a glimpse of an Aethus flittering between the branches. A few months ago that might have startled him or piqued his interest: now it just seemed mundane.

'We must be in the Glimmerholt,' said Horskram, looking around as he extinguished his lantern. 'Very clever... It only needed to emerge here and fly off under cover of darkness.'

'So it could fly as well?'

'Doubtless... a more powerful entity than the one that robbed Ulfang, a demon capable of shape shifting. Third Tier denizen most likely.'

'We didn't see anything like that in Andragorix's books,' said Adelko.

'No indeed – he wasn't capable of summoning anything powerful enough to burrow through stone, otherwise we would have been done for at Landebert's hut,' mused Horskram, rubbing his beard thoughtfully. 'Whoever he was serving kept him on a tight leash – he didn't want to give him too much knowledge.'

'So we're after another sorcerer – one even more powerful than Andragorix?'

'It would certainly appear so,' said Horskram, frowning as he inspected the circumference of the burrow hole before splashing some more holy water and intoning another prayer. 'Whoever it is, they've discovered some powerful Left-Hand magic, more potent than I thought in the first place.'

'The Earth Witch said something about that,' said Adelko as they began to make their way through the woods. 'But it wasn't Andragorix who had access to the Elder Wizards' texts.'

'No indeed,' said Horskram. 'He managed to summon up the horror that pursued us but that – and the Succubus – was the limit of his grasp of Demonology. His knowledge of Necromancy was also limited. Those are the two darkest of the Seven Schools, and our Order has worked hard to expunge every text that teaches them these past five hundred years.'

'Which is why such knowledge is hard to come by?'

'Precisely. But whoever enthralled Andragorix must have discovered the same grimoires as Ashokainan and Morwena presumably did.'

'If there's only one other Watchtower inhabited today, that means it's likely to be the Sassanian warlock you mentioned before.'

'His name is Abdel Sha'arza,' said Horskram. 'A black magician of some repute who dwells in the Watchtower of Leviathan, in the Abydos Ranges that separate the sultanates of Halepo and Nazharya.'

'So could it be him?'

'He is a possible suspect in our inquiry now,' said Horskram. 'But as I said before, world domination is not something Sha'arza has ever craved, though his soul is doubtless corrupted by his studies of the Left-Hand path. Perhaps his ambitions have grown with his thirst for power. And Cael is believed to have brought the final fragment to the Sassanian Sultanates, which places him most conveniently.'

'So... does that mean we're going to head south?' Adelko felt his pulse quicken at the thought. He had always longed to visit the Southlands, where loremasters were said to be wise beyond reckoning. Many Argolians travelled to the Pilgrim Kingdoms to share knowledge with the savants of the Faith, despite their different religions.

'It means we're heading to Rima, our original destination,' said Horskram firmly. 'We still need to consult Hannequin. Presumably he will have held a divination by now – we'll need to compare notes.'

'And what about Abrexta? Is she a suspect too?'

'Every warlock of repute is a suspect right now,' said the adept. 'But by all accounts Abrexta is an enchantress, not well versed in Demonology. I suspect she is another apprentice, as was Andragorix – but we shall see!'

The sun was setting by the time they emerged from the Glimmerholt. The eight turrets of Graukolos were etched against the skyline, a formidable silhouette beckoning them back. Adelko suddenly realised he was famished: the Eorl had said something about a celebration feast. On the other side of the Graufluss he could make out a camp of tents, pennants flying in the twilight breeze.

'I don't suppose we'll be going anywhere in the next few days with a tournament on,' he said, trying to sound light.

Horskram harrumphed testily. 'I have little doubt our chivalrous bodyguards have lost no time in entering themselves,' he said, pausing to relight his lantern. 'But the hinterlands of Vorstlund are lawless places, and we may need our trusty swords again. Be sure I shall take advantage of the interval to resume your tutelage – it's high time you caught up with your studies, young man!'

Adelko had to smile at that. Though the past few months had changed him, he felt that things between him and his mentor had normalised somewhat. For all their bickering, he still admired the adept immensely. And whatever the Earth Witch's prophecies had to say, he was still just a novice.

✜ ✜ ✜

The sun was vanishing by the time they struck the road leading to Graukolos. Just then they caught the sound of wings flapping: an eagle descended into their circle of light, flying around them once, twice. Something was clutched in its beak. It dropped the object on to the path and flew back into the deepening dusk with a shriek.

Horskram bent down to examine the item before picking it up. It was a leathern tube. Unbuckling it he emptied out a vellum scroll bound with a length of twine and opened it. A message was written on it in a spiky hand that Adelko did not recognise.

'The Ogham script of the Westerling Isles,' said Horskram. 'I think our ally from the Argael has something to tell us.'

Horskram read the message, then translated for Adelko's benefit:

Friar Horskram, I trust this finds you safe and well.

My thanks for your aid in ridding the world of Andragorix. If ever you pass this way again, the Girdle is yours to use as haven and sanctuary – for as long as it stands.

I wish I could repay you with better news, but my attempts at Scrying have borne little fruit; somebody somewhere is countering to great effect, and farseeing is difficult. As far as I can fathom, Abrexta is planning an invasion of the Island Realms: the northern wards have all been conquered or pacified and the Highlanders dance to her tune. And another power is stirring in the Far Southlands, but who or where exactly I could not divine.

And I sense another warlock operating, closer to home. If you intend to continue your journey to Rima, be on your guard! Something stirs in the Pangonian capital, someone powerful enough to blindside all the adepts of your Order. More than this I cannot tell.

These are complex times, when faeries aid mortalkind and witches and witch-hunters ally themselves to one another, so my advice to you is to expect the unexpected and trust no one.

I repeat, trust no one.

⊷ CHAPTER X ⊷

In Search of Prey

'A splendid day for hunting, quite simply marvellous!'
Lord Ivon squinted up into the cloudless sky, his handsome face creasing in the sun's strong rays. Wheeling his courser around to face the others he beamed. 'With a bit of luck we'll find ourselves a deer or two.'

Wolmar scowled as he took the saddle of his own horse. It was a piebald stallion the Margrave had lent him, but he felt little enthusiasm for the sport. As far as he was concerned, hunting was for petty vassals and those too weak or afraid to fight real foes.

Yet he increasingly found he could refuse his paramour nothing. Even now as their eyes met he felt a thrill course through his body. And it had only been a couple of hours since they had lain together that morning...

He caught Lord Kaye's eye as they nudged their horses into a canter, leaving the manor house where they had guested the previous night. The Margrave of Quillon had showed him grudging respect since the Crescent Bridge Tourney a week ago, though there was still no love lost between them.

Wolmar scowled at him and nudged his courser next to Ivon's. He didn't like to be apart from him. The trail they followed took them further up into the hills, past the hunting lodge where the pair of them had trysted a few nights ago.

He had been mulling over Ivon's proposal ever since, and knew not what to do. The idea had grown on him, he had to admit: serving as Marshal to a powerful baron from the most powerful of the Free Kingdoms promised fortune and glory. And what could he expect as an alternative in his homeland, where he was scorned, disliked and under-appreciated?

And yet... He was a prince of the House of Ingwin. Northalde was his native country. Something held him back from accepting Ivon's offer.

At any rate he still had time to make his mind up. That old fool Hannequin had not sent him any communication since their last meeting. Probably up to no good: secretive and suspicious, just like all

Argolians. But at least it meant he could linger in Rima a while longer, until Horskram turned up. The monk would give him the latest news of the mission and he could take that back to his uncle at Strongholm.

Or that was the excuse he gave himself for remaining.

They continued riding along a winding trail. As well as Kaye there was Aravin and Rodger, with their squires bringing up the rear leading sumpters laden with bows, arrows, spears, hunting knives and camping gear.

At the crest of the hills Wolmar could see their destination: the dark line of trees fronting the Arbevere.

'Prime hunting to be had!' said Lord Ivon. 'Tonight we'll feast well – the Arbevere is normally reserved exclusively for the King's privilege...'

'... but you enjoy the King's favour,' Wolmar finished for him dryly.

'Exactly!' said the Margrave, favouring him with a conspiratorial wink. 'Come now, look lively my dear nobles,' he barked, turning in the saddle to address the others. 'The game's afoot as they say!'

Kaye started to reply in Panglian but Ivon cut him off.

'In Decorlangue, *please*,' he said. 'You know how rude it is to speak in a tongue our guest has not mastered.'

Wolmar didn't bother to turn around, but he could guess the margraves were exchanging sneers. Typical Pangonians – expecting everyone else to learn their language.

'My head hurts,' offered Lord Rodger, now speaking in Decorlangue. 'Too much Armandy red last night.'

'Too much time spent debauching our host's daughter,' quipped Lord Aravin. 'Half the house could hear you.'

'She won't be marriageable now,' said Kaye. 'A vassal of the King gives us hospitality and thus you repay him.' His tone of voice suggested he couldn't care less, but then neither could Wolmar.

'Pah, he's only a landed knight, whilst we are lords of the realm,' scoffed Rodger. 'What do I care for the lesser nobility's opinion?'

The distinction baffled Sir Wolmar. 'In my homeland all men with titles are considered of noble birth... knights and barons share blue blood and may duel equally.'

'Your northern manners are as crude as your jousting technique,' said Lord Aravin, raising sniggers from Kaye and Rodger. 'No wonder Sir Aremis bested you in the third round.'

Wolmar brought his horse up and rounded angrily on the Margrave of Varangia. 'And I suppose he found you made of sterner stuff, did he?'

There was a dangerous glint in Lord Aravin's eyes as he answered. 'He didn't knock me off my horse – three tilts and I was still in the saddle.'

'He bested you on foot though didn't he?' snarled Wolmar. 'Put your clumsy swordplay to shame, the way I heard it told.'

Aravin's face hardened. 'At least I made it to the quarter finals – a respectable result given the Purple Garter were competing, and notably better than yours.'

'Oh aye?' shouted Wolmar. 'Shall we repair now to a place of our choosing and see who wields the better blade?'

Aravin was about to answer when Ivon moved his horse between them. 'My dear nobles, peace! Now is a time to seek sport with the beasts of the wood, not each other.'

Aravin remained unmoved. 'As to that, if the Northlending desires satisfaction, he may have it forthwith.'

Ivon's face lengthened. *'I said enough is enough! We are not here to fight one another like disgruntled tourney knights.'*

Something in his voice changed when he spoke: the timbre hardened and the words sounded deeper, more hollow somehow. Wolmar felt compelled to obey instantly. Aravin blanched and looked away. Rodger seemed confused, while Kaye simply frowned and shook his head as if to clear it.

'Forgive me Lord Ivon,' mumbled Aravin. 'I did not mean to speak out of turn.'

'I say while Sir Wolmar remains at court he is one of us,' said Ivon. His voice had returned to its usual affable tone, but Wolmar sensed that things were different somehow. 'I've vouched for him, and I won't have anyone gainsay that. You've all had your sport with the foreigner, now leave him be... I hope that's understood.'

The Pangonian lords looked from one to another before nodding. They were all high-born, but there was no doubt who was really in charge.

'Now come, come!' said Ivon, turning his courser again to follow the trail. 'There's fine hunting to be had, let us enjoy the day...'

Wolmar followed, feeling very peculiar indeed. Something told him he should be anxious, but instead all he felt was an odd tranquillity. That and an abiding adoration for his lover. His homeland was so far away... But Ivon was right here beside him. With one of its most powerful men to vouch for him, Pangonia seemed rich with opportunity.

He felt his loyalty to king and country fading.

✣ ✣ ✣

They spent the rest of the day in predictable fashion. Wolmar took part with as much enthusiasm as he could muster, helping Aravin chase down and kill a deer. Kaye felled another with the bow – he was clearly a better marksman than a jouster. Rodger managed to fall off his horse into a thicket, his contribution to the day's event.

Ivon seemed to do little, Wolmar noticed. He was always in the rear, yet there was never a sense that he was lagging behind. Rather the opposite... it felt as though he were orchestrating the whole day, to what end the princeling could not say.

At least it was cool in the Arbevere, Wolmar reflected as they made their way towards the spot they had designated for their camp. The late afternoon rays dappled through the verdant leaves as they pushed through the trees and into the clearing. Two of their squires had set up pavilions in anticipation of their arrival; the other pair led in the day's kill, strung across the sumpters.

The source of the Athos was not far from the clearing and poured from a cavernous rent in the high wooded hills overlooking it. The four Pangonians stripped and went to bathe in its waters. Another strange custom. Wolmar reluctantly followed suit and plunged into the icy waters. Pangonians were said to bathe once a month, whether they needed to or not. Wolmar didn't see the point – and he was sure he'd heard a physicker in Strongholm say bathing was bad for the constitution.

He had to admit though, the rushing torrent was exhilarating. He was shaking his red-gold locks and hauling himself out of the water when Ivon suddenly pulled him back in. A few seconds later Ivon was kissing him full on the lips.

He moves quickly for a man who doesn't engage in tourneys or hunting, Wolmar found time to think before baser thoughts overwhelmed him.

When it was over they pulled themselves from the river and lay together for a while beneath an ash tree, watching the stars wink into life above them. The others had returned to the camp.

'Have you had time to think over my proposal?' asked Ivon from where he sat cradled in Wolmar's lap.

'I have...' Wolmar hesitated. But what was there left to mull over? The Margrave loved him and had vouched for him, gainsaying some of the most powerful nobles in the land. Here he could look forward to a bright future. Back home he would always be in Torgun's shadow. And his late father's, come to think of it.

'I accept your offer,' he breathed, feeling the words carry across the gloaming. 'I accept your offer gladly.' It almost felt like somebody else were speaking. Something deep inside him screamed 'no', but he ignored it.

Ivon reached up to caress his cheek. 'I am so happy, my sweet,' he said softly. 'It would have been such a pity to send you back to Rima now and miss the rest of the night's entertainment.'

Wolmar stiffened, and not amorously. 'What do you mean?' he asked.

The Margrave got up. 'You'll soon see,' he said, smiling and offering the princeling his hand. 'Come, let's get back and join the others. I'm famished, darling!'

✛ ✛ ✛

The sun had set by the time Wolmar and Ivon rejoined the others. The squires were cooking the venison, having seasoned it with a bewildering variety of herbs and laid on a spread of cheeses and bread to go with the meat. Even in the wild, Pangonians insisted on eating well. Wolmar felt his stomach tighten as he caught the smell of meat: hunger was one appetite he had not satisfied today.

Rodger clearly did not have that problem, and was getting stuck into a wineskin to wash down the half a cheese he'd already guzzled. He had dressed again along with the others. He looked ridiculous in his green and brown hunting clothes, which were covered in crumbs and offset by the ripe red that now suffused his cheeks and nose. Wolmar wondered what he must look like in harness.

This is no man, he thought contemptuously. *I wonder he can even sit a horse.*

Presently they all sat down to eat, feasting from trenchers. The seasoned meat was delicious, and the wine was from the King's cellars and of the finest quality.

They seem to do everything better than us, Wolmar thought grudgingly. *I probably am better off serving here.*

Darkness was thickening about the fringes of the campfire when they had finished eating. The squires cleared away their trenchers and brought more wineskins.

Ivon paused to take a sip before languidly getting to his feet. He had drunk little throughout the evening.

'My dear nobles,' he said. 'We have disported ourselves admirably, but now the time has come to speak of business. You know why I have invited you here.'

The Pangonian lords exchanged uneasy glances.

'You would speak of this now... in Decorlangue?' queried Aravin, glancing at Wolmar meaningfully.

Ivon smiled thinly. 'As I said, the Northlending princeling is one of us. I have told him of the King's plan to invade Vorstlund and he has agreed to join the invasion.'

'What else does he know?' cried Aravin, his eyes bulging.

'Peace,' said Ivon, raising a hand. Aravin went quiet, like a dog brought to leash.

Rodger was looking confused again. 'I don't follow your meaning, Lord Ivon,' he said. 'I thought we had already agreed to take part in the invasion, what else is there to discuss?'

Wolmar was wondering the same thing.

Ignoring Rodger, Ivon turned to address Aravin and Kaye. 'My investigations are complete. His brother is the sort of man we are looking for – it's time to put the next phase of our plan into action.'

Kaye and Aravin exchanged uncertain glances. 'Here... now?' ventured Kaye. He motioned towards Wolmar. 'But what about him?'

Ivon took a step forward. Something in his gait became menacing. 'Do you doubt me now, worthy margraves, at the final hour?'

His voice had the same hollow timbre to it as before. The two lords shook their heads.

'We serve you in all things, Lord Ivon,' said Aravin.

'Excellent!' cried Ivon, clapping his hands together and pronouncing a harsh syllable.

Two things happened at once. The fire guttered and went out; and a cry went up from the edge of the clearing, followed by the sound of something heavy hitting the ground.

Wolmar sprang to his feet, hand instinctively reaching for his sword and finding only a hunting knife. Another strange word cut the night air, and the fire flared up again. Kaye and Aravin were standing to either side of Rodger, each holding one of his arms.

'What is the meaning of this?' cried the Margrave of Narbo. 'Unhand me at once!'

Lord Ivon stepped around the fire as the margraves hauled Rodger to his feet. There was anger in the corpulent lord's eyes now, poking through the bibulous glaze that suffused them.

'Lord Rodger de Narbo, I regret to inform you that you are a weakling,' said Ivon flatly. 'My plans extend far beyond the conquest of our crude northern neighbour, and I would fain have strong men at my side to execute them.'

Rodger began yelling for his squire.

'Oh, I'm sorry,' said Ivon. 'Your squire won't be coming to your rescue.' As if on cue three of the squires emerged into the circle of light, dragging the bloodied corpse of the fourth.

Lord Rodger gasped as he saw his dead squire. 'Why are you doing this?' he asked. 'Lord Ivon, I beseech you – '

'Unlike others of my brethren, I do not believe in wasting my elan enthralling weak-minded idiots,' said Ivon, as if explaining a lesson to a child. 'I prefer to focus my talents on men worthy of being controlled. I hear your younger brother is proving himself a fine squire, well suited to knighthood... and other things. I'm sure he'll be pleased to hear he's inheriting the margravate of Narbo.'

A stink reached Wolmar's nostrils. A wet pool was forming about Rodger's feet. 'But *I'm* the Margrave of Narbo!' he squealed. His voice was shaking with fear now. 'You can't do this! Please! I'll do anything! Whatever it is you have planned, I'll go along with it! I swear!'

Ivon's teeth flashed in the firelight as he bent down towards the struggling Margrave. 'What I have planned, my dear Narbo, is nothing less than the subjugation of the Free Kingdoms – a campaign to which I regret you are not invited.'

'No! NOOOO!' Rodger began kicking feebly, but Ivon sidestepped lightly. His movements seemed unnaturally quick.

'Oh don't worry,' said Ivon. 'I'm not going to kill you just yet. No, I have much more interesting plans for you...'

He barked an order to the squires in Panglian and they took Rodger's legs. Together with their masters they lifted the struggling Margrave up like a sack of suet. Neither the squires nor the margraves showed the slightest emotion as they obeyed Ivon's command. Turning to the fire he muttered some more words in the strange language and blew hard on the flames. The orange tongues rose and writhed together, forming a flaming ball that detached itself from the blaze and floated above them. He turned his dark eyes on Wolmar.

'Come, my sweet princeling,' he said. 'I want to show you some local history.'

Wolmar felt powerless to resist. What had been a subtle force on the penumbra of his consciousness was now a definite presence in his mind. It was as if by agreeing to serve the Margrave he had robbed himself of the will to refuse him anything.

They made their way up out of the clearing, towards the ridge of hills that straddled the crevice from where the Athos gushed. Etched against the moon Wolmar could see the silhouette of a curiously shaped stone. A sense of foreboding seeped into him, contending with the roil of emotions that already stirred his soul.

'I told you that my ancestors practised sorcery,' said Ivon, chatting urbanely as though they were still on a pleasure trip,

oblivious to Rodger's pitiful wailing as they carried him up a
trail through the wooded hills. 'It's said that Aaron the Bewitched
stumbled on the rock in his early youth. He placed his ear to the
strange stone and heard voices whispering to him. Some say this
is what inspired him to learn his craft. They also called him Aaron
the Deathless... long life his arts did grant him. Now that is a path
I would fain follow my ancestor down.'

✢ ✢ ✢

After half an hour they emerged from the trees to the summit of the
hills. The strange stone was about the size of a man and set on a
flat outcropping of rock that overlooked the Athos. An aura of evil
emanated from it. Wolmar felt the urge to flee but Ivon's magic kept
him rooted to the spot.

'Who can say what manner of edifice the Elder Wizards built
here?' asked Ivon, excitement in his voice. 'One of their legendary
watchtowers, perhaps? Or maybe a palace, or even a ruin of some
city – there are other stones like this one, dotted all over these hills.'
He raised his face to the bright heavens, staring at the stars and
sickle moon. 'Who can fathom what eldritch lore they learned when
they listened to the celestial music in times far gone?'

He turned to look Wolmar directly in the eye. The fireball burned
overhead, giving his face a demonic look. 'Long have I studied their
arts, and I shall have the answer to that question!'

'You!' gasped Wolmar, as realisation dawned on him. 'You're
the one who covets the Headstone!'

Ivon smiled again. 'The time is coming, Wolmar of Strongholm –
the King of Gehenna shall return to take his rightful place as ruler of
the Known World. The Master shall reward his servants as no mortal
monarch ever could – and all who oppose Him shall be bound in
fetters of burning brass! The pious and the holy shall taste the fate
of the anti-angels!'

Summoning up all his willpower, Wolmar jerked the knife from
his belt and advanced towards the Margrave. Pointing at him Ivon
closed his eyes and muttered a few more words. Their sound set his
teeth on edge, cutting across Rodger's screams as the others forced
him down onto the stone. Wolmar cried out as the knife turned into
a writhing serpent in his hand. As he let go of it Ivon muttered some
more words and Wolmar stopped dead in his tracks. At his feet
lay the knife. Had Ivon really transformed it, or was it just illusion
magic? He would never know.

Ivon opened his eyes and looked straight into Wolmar's soul. 'No hand shall you raise against me, Wolmar of Strongholm – no steel shall you wield to harm my person. So I have said in the Language of Magick, whose words bind the will as shackles restrain flesh!' Turning to address the third squire he muttered a question in Panglian. The squire nodded and together they walked off, leaving Wolmar motionless as the fireball followed its arcane master. By its light he could see a slain boar on the other side of the outcropping. One of its tusks had been hewn off but the kill was fresh. Nodding to himself in satisfaction after inspecting it, Ivon reached into the folds of his cloak and pulled out two objects. One was a small vial. The other was the boar's missing tusk. He walked over to where Aravin and Kaye still held Rodger fast against the stone. The Margrave of Narbo had stopped struggling, though his body quivered spasmodically.

'Try not to take this personally, Rodger,' said Ivon, unstopping the vial and swallowing its contents. 'But it's time you died in a hunting accident. I know... such a cliché! But a corpulent, dull-witted sot like you hardly warrants originality.'

Ivon's body seemed to ripple in the light. Cocking his head to one side he let out a satisfied sigh. 'I shall need the strength of a boar to simulate one,' he said, smiling evilly.

'NO!' screamed Rodger. 'I beg of thee! Spare my life and you can have all my lands!'

Ivon bent down closer and addressed the Margrave in a low voice. He was still speaking in Decorlangue, so Wolmar could understand. 'Oh, I don't need to rule your lands directly,' he said. 'That's not what I'm after tonight... In fact it's not even your life I really want. It's your soul I covet.'

Rodger's eyes widened. They looked fit to burst out of their sockets. The glaze had disappeared from them: sheer naked terror did wonders for sobriety.

'Oh don't be such a buffoon!' snapped Ivon. 'Did you really think it could end any other way? Body and soul, you've given yourself up to Creosoaneuryon and Satyrus – intemperance and lust have been your words of the day since you were old enough to drink and whore!'

Ivon raised the tusk high above his head. He was shouting now. 'The Princes of Perfidy yearn for you to join them in the City of Burning Brass! Age-old torments there await thee! Rich reward for the disciple who sends them what is rightfully theirs! Oh scions of Gehenna, receive now this sacrifice in the Wytching Hour – bolster my elan with anti-manna that I may serve thee even better!'

He switched to speaking in the Language of Magick, sounding now as though he were singing a horrid cadence. Wolmar felt his heart stop and his skin crawl; beads of sweat stood out on the faces of the other men as he chanted aloud in the fell tongue. The alien stanzas seemed to last forever, dragging across time and space with an awful slowness...

It almost seemed a mundane horror when Ivon stopped chanting and plunged the tusk deep into Rodger's chest just below the sternum, raking effortlessly down towards his groin with a wet tearing sound. The Margrave of Narbo screamed and screamed. Discarding the tusk Ivon plunged his hands into the rent, pulling out his intestines in a gushing spurt of blood. Kaye and Aravin let go of the quivering Margrave and plunged their own hands into the wound, covering themselves in gore made black by night as Ivon pulled Rodger's guts out, wrapping the gristly coils about him like a mantle.

Raising his arms the warlock gazed up at the dark skies, his body trembling as his darker gods rewarded him with unseen gifts. Rodger's screams subsided into choked moaning as his limbs convulsed horribly. The two squires let go of his legs and fell to the ground retching. Wolmar found himself doing the same, natural revulsion overcoming the unnatural power that held him spellbound.

Ivon laughed and sank to his knees, drinking eagerly from the fount of blood that had once been the Margrave of Narbo. Rodger quivered some more and then the stillness of death came on him. Looking up from a pool of his own vomit Wolmar saw the Margrave's eyes fixed sightlessly, his head turned to one side. He had seen many dead bodies: but there was an emptiness in those eyes that made all the corpses of the world look like hale men.

Raising his blood-drenched face to the heavens, Ivon grinned ghoulishly.

'A most satisfactory service,' he said, inverting the sign of the Wheel. Springing lightly to his feet, he uncoiled Rodger's innards and stuffed them back into his belly. Then he closed the eyes, moulding the grimace into a less horrified expression of death.

'There now,' said the Margrave, stepping back to survey his handiwork. 'A tragic death – killed during the chase! Just like my ancestor Perceval the Bold, he was killed by a stag you know... Now, my dear nobles, if I'm not mistaken, I think our trusty squires have prepared fresh hunting clothes for us. But first we should take another dip in the Athos, get rid of all this frightful blood...'

⫷ CHAPTER XI ⫸

Throwing Down the Gauntlet

Vaskrian felt his spirits rise as they entered the registration booth. The Marshal was sat behind a trestle table with another knight. Before him were a quill and inkpot, and scrolls indicating the names of various competitors. He stared coldly as Braxus approached.

'Name and lineage,' he said flatly in Decorlangue. Vaskrian remembered him from the feast last night. Evidently Sir Urist knew them for the foreigners they were.

'Sir Braxus of Gaellen, son and heir to Lord Braun, First Man of Clan Fitzrow.'

Urist continued to stare at him. 'You need to declare your noble birth as far back as your grandfather,' he said.

Vaskrian tensed slightly as Braxus met the knight's stare. The sight of the lovely heiress of Dulsinor in the great hall had brought his guvnor back to life somewhat, but he was still in an ill humour.

'Lord Morgan, First Man of Clan Fitzrow and father to Lord Braun,' he said icily. Holding his hand up he brandished his signet ring. 'Will you be wanting me to prove it? Or is the word of a foreign lord's son good enough?'

Urist held his defiant stare for a second or two, then looked away and ordered the other knight to mark Braxus down for the joust. 'Seeing as your deeds are not renowned in this land you'll enter the joust unseeded,' he said.

'What about the melee?' asked Braxus, ignoring the implicit slight.

Sir Urist shook his head. 'Special event, to commemorate the alliance of the Houses of Markward and Lanrak,' he said. 'Knights serving either house only. But if you wish, you are eligible to enter the duelling event, should you wish to press any rivalry in single combat, for love or blood.'

'Thank you,' said Sir Braxus. Vaskrian guessed his guvnor already had some ideas about whom he might challenge.

'You may pitch your tent on the south side of the enclosure, towards the riverside,' continued Urist. 'The jousts begin tomorrow at noon. May Ezekiel and Stygnos smile on you.'

Braxus bowed curtly and stalked from the tent.

Vaskrian's spirits remained buoyant as they emerged into the morning sunlight. What with his arm he wouldn't have been able to enter the melee anyhow. At least he'd get to cheer his guvnor on: one outlander rooting for another against the local talent. And what with everything they had been through, it would be good to do something normal for a change.

✢ ✢ ✢

Presently he had their pavilion set up and horses tethered and fed. Then he checked his master's harness. His hauberk still had a rent where Andragorix's black blade had sheared through the mail links. His sword was covered in dints and he only had a couple of jousting spears with blunted tips and hollow shafts. Chances are Braxus would need more than that if he couched half as well as he fought on foot. On top of that the bridle on his charger's reins was worn down and would need replacing.

Things to do, but that was good. He needed to keep busy, he reflected as he made his way through the tents towards the smithy. Across the Graufluss the turrets of Graukolos loomed, a spectacular backdrop for the coming tourney. Vaskrian felt glad of its presence: it made him feel safe.

He hadn't been the same since their mission, but then none of them had. He was certainly more pious: whenever recollection of the strange stones and horrid friezes of the Warlock's Crown threatened to overwhelm him, the memory of the monks chanting pulled him back from the brink. He drank more now, and gloomy moods came upon him more often.

Forcing himself back into the present, he glanced at the variegated pennants with their coats of arms as he passed them by: four lines in gules on a quartered yellow field, an ermine tincture of black and white diagonal stripes, a couchant leopard and a black dagger on a partitioned green and orange field... He didn't recognise any of the armouries, but then he was far from home.

Time was, that would have set him musing on his own coat of arms, but he'd long given up on that aspiration. The words of Earth Witch haunted him just as much as the things he'd seen at the Warlock's Crown.

By the time he reached the smithy's tent he was in a melancholy mood. His arm and face were sore and itchy, and he still got an occasional twinge in his side from where he'd cracked his ribs at Staerkvit. But at least the cut he'd got in the fight against the outlaws had healed up. Something to be thankful for he supposed.

Fie on Horskram and his damned adventures! What had they brought him but a miserable fate?

'Dinted sword,' he muttered, putting the blade down on a table near the forge and fishing in his sabretache for some coins.

The bladesmith shook his head at the proffered coins. Vaskrian cursed as he realised he was only carrying Northlending currency. A shouted exchange followed, with neither party understanding the other: Vaskrian's Decorlangue was rudimentary and the smith's was non-existent. Eventually the matter was settled with much gesticulating and loud talk. Leaving the blade, Vaskrian stomped off to get hoodwinked by the moneychanger.

Presently he was back, having been cheated just as expected. A Northlending sovereign was a sight bigger than a Vorstlending regum and worth twenty marks as opposed to a dozen – but that hadn't stopped the moneychanger giving him just twelve silver pieces. 'I do you favour, no interest!' the money man had insisted in broken Decorlangue. Vaskrian had been sorely tempted to leave him with broken teeth to match, but thought better of it. At least his guvnor wouldn't notice – no self-respecting noble ever handled money.

He was paying the smith when a welcome face appeared.

'Sir Torgun,' he said, favouring the tall knight with a half bow. 'It's good to see you ... I take it you've registered for the joust then?'

'Well met, Vaskrian – of course.'

Torgun smiled, but his eyes looked sad and troubled. Vaskrian had caught him staring at Lady Adhelina throughout the feast. When the Eorl had stood up to toast the future couple a pained look had crossed his rugged features. His guvnor hadn't looked too pleased either. Vaskrian could understand why. Hengist made for a pitiful sight all right – another useless blueblood who just happened to be from the right crib. Apparently he'd entered the joust. That would be an entertaining sight – the Herzog had been so drunk he could barely stand, never mind sit a horse.

'Don't suppose I'll be up to much,' said the squire, trying to sound cheerful as he indicated his bandaged arm. 'But at least I'll get to watch you and Sir Braxus compete.'

Torgun's face clouded. There was no love lost between the two knights at the best of times – now by the looks of things they had a courtly love rivalry brewing. That would complicate things further and no mistake. Not that either of them would have much joy of the heiress of Dulsinor. It all seemed a bit pointless to Vaskrian – the Laws of Romance was the one part of the Code of Chivalry he'd never really understood.

Sir Torgun stepped over to the smithy and dumped his cloven sword on the table. Fishing into his sabretache he surprised Vaskrian by pulling out a handful of silver marks and tossing them next to it.

'I thought knights didn't handle money!' blurted Vaskrian, forgetting himself.

Torgun turned to him and smiled wanly. 'Unless they're errants,' he said. 'I have no squire, remember?'

'Oh, right,' said Vaskrian, feeling suddenly foolish.

The smith was gawping at the bastard blade, wondering who or what had chopped it in half. That brought another memory flooding back into Vaskrian's mind, of swords that cut through steel like butter.

He shuddered. Torgun placed a hand on his shoulder. 'Vaskrian? Are you well?' he asked, looking genuinely concerned.

The squire felt himself flushing beneath his burns. 'Quite well, Sir Torgun,' he said quickly, wanting to put on a brave face in front of his hero. 'Why aren't you wearing the White Valravyn any more?' he asked, eager to change the subject.

Sir Torgun shook his head. 'I no longer serve the Order – my orders were to accompany you as far as... the warlock. Now I serve under my own auspices, though I would prefer not to display my family crest.'

Vaskrian nodded. 'I suppose the friar Horskram's secrecy is rubbing off on all of us,' he said.

Torgun frowned. 'Aye, Vaskrian, perhaps you're right. Well, I shall see you tonight at the feast of honour – all the knights tilting tomorrow will be there.'

'See you there,' said Vaskrian, his heart lightening a little at the thought as they exited the tent. Without another word the knight turned on his heel and strode away, spurs jingling. Suppressing a sigh Vaskrian went to see about a new bridle and some more jousting spears.

✣ ✣ ✣

Having finished carving for his guvnor, Vaskrian retired with a curt bow and walked back down the length of trestle tables to where the other squires sat. His stomach was rumbling but his appetite was keener for more spectacle, and not the one currently on offer. The dwarf balancing on a small pony's back continued to juggle knives with a flourish, while a group of troubadours played on.

That was all well and good, but after feasting the herald would call on competing knights to seek the favours of their ladies. There were quite a few winsome damsels, though none as beautiful as Adhelina of Dulsinor, who sat crowned with white gold in a richly embroidered white gown.

She looked as unhappy as ever, Vaskrian reflected as he took his seat. At least her future husband seemed to be stinting on the wine for once, perhaps in anticipation of the joust. Taking in the Herzog's awkward frame he doubted whether sobriety would make much difference. The blueblood might be rich and powerful, but when it came to tourneys he had first-round knockout written all over him.

When the eating was done (in no short time – these Vorstlendings loved to feast all right), the music stopped. A fat jester dressed in motley and bells with a big straw hat had just been entertaining the knights and ladies. Vaskrian didn't understand a word of it, but judging by their laughter the fool was funny. To all except the Herzog, he noticed, who scowled throughout the whole performance.

Of Adelko and Horskram there was no sign. They'd gone burrowing around beneath the castle on Argolian business. The squire felt a chill thinking about it. Helping himself to more ale he downed another stoop.

The sun was sinking behind the castle as the knights stood one by one and declared their lady loves, or the lady whose favour they sought. One or two of the prettier damsels even had two suitors pledge their swords – but the Laws of Romance allowed for such. It was all part of a good tournament, a bit of pageantry before the real fighting started.

Then a handsome knight got up and walked into the middle of the tables. Walking directly up to where Adhelina was sitting, he knelt before her, announcing her name and laying his sword across the grass. Several gasps had gone up around the green: evidently this had not been expected. The herald, pausing only for a brief moment, declared his name: Sir Agravine.

Vaskrian's eyes flicked towards the Herzog. Hengist was staring at the knight with a look that he presumably wished could kill. Next to him his steward, a flint-faced man with a cold demeanour, looked singularly unimpressed. The father of the bride didn't look too happy either, although the squire noticed that his daughter didn't seem surprised.

Vaskrian held his breath as she rose to her feet and walked around the table towards the young knight.

⊹ ⊹ ⊹

Reaching into the folds of her dress Adhelina produced a silk scarf she had prepared, and leaning down she fastened this around Sir Agravine's arm.

'Adhelina of Dulsinor accepts Sir Agravine, bachelor of Graukolos, as her favoured knight,' she told the stunned assembly. 'In accordance with the Laws of Romance, as stipulated by the Code of Chivalry.'

She shot her father a triumphant glance, before turning it towards Hengist, his seneschal Albercelsus, and his sisters Festilia and Griselle. Hengist's lickspittles Reghar and Hangrit glared at her insolently, bibulous and loutish as ever. She barely spared them a look, they weren't worth it. But she had eyes for the Herzog's mother Lady Berta, who stared at her with undisguised hatred. Adhelina drank it in, savouring her spite like a draft of Armandy red.

The herald stammered out the declaration. 'The Lady Markward accepts Sir Agravine, bachelor of Graukolos, as her tourney champion.' No one applauded. Though not forbidden, what she had just done was highly irregular under the circumstances. And everyone there knew it.

Sir Agravine favoured Adhelina with a cool smile and one last bow before picking up his sword and turning to resume his place at table. Her father's eyes bored into his back like spears. The young knight stood to lose his place at court for this, but she supposed love made men do foolish things.

No more knights rose to declare their paramours. Agravine had left his pledge till last, presumably for dramatic effect.

In this he was destined to be upstaged.

'I am Sir Torgun of Vandheim, errant of Northalde and lately knight of the White Valravyn.' He made the declamation in the high speech of Ancient Thalamy; its icy formality froze the returning chatter about the feast tables. Stepping into the rectangular space between them the Northlending knight walked directly up to Adhelina, never taking his eyes off her.

I barely know him, she thought. *Surely he doesn't mean to...*

Kneeling before her and unsheathing his blade in one fluid motion, Sir Torgun declared for all to hear: 'I would fain have your favour, Adhelina of Dulsinor. A second champion you shall have, if it please you.'

'And a third.'

All eyes shifted again to the new speaker. Torgun's face darkened as Sir Braxus stepped into the space. 'Lady Markward, Sir Braxus of Gaellen, errant of Thraxia, seeks your favour in the coming joust.' Advancing to stand beside his rival he took a knee and unsheathed his own blade. 'My sword is yours, if Luviah wills it so.'

'Stygnos I shall invoke on your behalf, my lady!' declaimed Torgun, not wishing to be outdone on piety.

'May Virtus grant me fortitude in the lists in your service!' responded Braxus.

'And may Ushira smile on you both,' said Adhelina, trying to sound gracious as she did her best to placate them.

But her mind was awhirl. Sir Agravine she had expected. This she had not. Catching the young knight's impassive stare she recalled his words to her earlier: *A lady like you should have many suitors.*

And then her choice was clear. After all, why not? There was nothing forbidding it. Favouring her father and the Lanraks with a smug glance she turned back to address the two kneeling knights.

'Lady Adhelina of Dulsinor accepts both champions, and consents to give them her favour,' she said. 'Three bold knights shall fight for her honour!'

'You have no favours to bestow on them.'

It was Albercelsus who spoke, silencing the uncertain applause. His voice was cold and measured. Adhelina felt the tension rise another notch.

'A lady may give whatever token of her favour she pleases,' she replied. Beckoning to a squire for a dagger she cut off two strands of her strawberry hair, giving one to each knight. Clearing his throat the herald declared them both her champions.

Her father got to his feet. 'That's enough chivalry for one evening,' he said, his voice ominous like distant thunder. 'More wine and song, I say! Let us drink to the coming contest!'

The assembled nobles followed suit, some with obvious relief, although judging by the hubbub that started up Adhelina guessed she had given them plenty to gossip about. Her two new champions had returned to their seats. They were sat together in the section for foreign visitors, though they pointedly ignored one another. Not far from them a burly knight with a bushy black beard chuckled to himself and slurped on his stoop.

Adhelina returned to her own seat. Her father did not look at her as he growled: 'Well, I suppose you're very pleased with yourself. Enjoy your last bit of freedom while you can – you won't get another opportunity to make mischief.'

She chose not to dignify that with a response. Besides, she was beyond caring about what her father thought. Flicking a sidelong glance at Hengist and Albercelsus she half expected them to say something, but both men were staring into the middle distance, tight-lipped. Her future husband fiddled with his goblet but did not drink.

✣ ✣ ✣

Horskram stood by the window, pinching the bridge of his nose tightly as the Eorl relayed the unwelcome news.

'You and your blasted knights errant, Horskram,' Wilhelm finished. 'I give you the freedom of my castle to conduct your investigations, and this is how you repay me! As if my fool of a daughter hadn't caused me enough trouble as it is!'

The adept turned from contemplating the torchlit courtyard below and walked back to the low walnut table. He didn't usually drink much, but he felt he needed one now. Picking up his cup he took a deep long draught. He and Adelko had arrived back at the castle well after sunset. His limbs were stiff and sore.

'Well at least you won't have to punish Sir Agravine,' said Horskram dryly. 'Now you've got two of the best knights in the Free Kingdoms lining up to chastise him in the lists.'

Wilhelm made a disgusted noise before draining his own cup. 'The Code forbids me from chastising him myself,' he said, looking moodily around his solar. 'But that won't stop me giving him his marching orders when the tournament's over. She'll have three errants suiting her by next Rest-day!'

'Assuming they're all still alive by then,' said Horskram, seating himself opposite the Eorl. 'There's a challenge event after the joust... I sense the hand of Zolthoth and Invidia at work, dividing ally against ally.' He made the sign. His sixth sense was jangling unpleasantly. This tournament would bring trouble, he knew that much.

The Stonefist snorted into his cup. 'I thought it was good old Luviah at play – oh the things brave knights will do for love! Well, they'll have no joy of my daughter – whatever else they might be thinking. I'll not have this alliance wrecked for the blasted Code of Chivalry! I should never have indulged her unnatural passion for those bloody books!'

'At least your daughter is alive,' Horskram reminded him.

'Aye – thanks to you!'

'And the very same knights who now compete for her favour... the ways of the Unseen are strange, are they not?'

Wilhelm harrumphed. 'And speaking of which... how did your travails speed, or do I even want to know?'

Horskram sighed and sat back, trying to ease the tension in his muscles. 'Truth to tell, there is little more that we can say. Andragorix was not the mastermind, of that I am now certain. I thought at first it might have been a parting gambit, a way of throwing us off the scent just to spite us, but no – we really are dealing with another sorcerer, and one far better versed in Demonology.'

'I thought Andragorix was supposed to be the deadliest demonologist of our age?'

'Not quite – there is another, reputedly far more powerful, though he reportedly keeps to himself and lives in Sassania. But it's possible someone else has acquired the power to conjure greater demons... I must get to Rima and consult Hannequin, see what he has learned.'

'Well you aren't leaving just yet – I forbid you from departing my hall, not until you take your blasted foreign knights with you!'

Horskram favoured him with a dark glance over the brim of his cup. Technically the Eorl was well within his rights, though his behaviour seemed churlish.

'There will be no need for such ordinances,' he said.

Wilhelm looked apologetic. 'I just don't want any lovelorn romantic knights hanging around Graukolos, I'm sure you understand. My daughter is hard enough to control as it is!'

'No, in any case I may well still need their help,' sighed Horskram. 'I presume Upper and Lower Thulia are as restive as ever? When was the last time they weren't at war with one another?'

'When Upper Thulia was at war with me,' said the Eorl ruefully, refilling his cup.

'That's what I thought... I'll wait a few days in the hope that I have some kind of bodyguard left intact by the time your tourney is over. After all we've been through, I don't need to take any more risks travelling without protection.'

'Ach, Horskram, you didn't think I'd fail to repay you for rescuing my daughter did you?' said Wilhelm, trying to sound affable. 'Once the tournament is over I'll send a company of knights to take you as far as Westenlund. I suppose I owe those blasted errants of yours that much at least!'

'I'm sure they'll be lining up to thank you,' said Horskram sarcastically.

He drained his cup. It had been a long day. Yet for all their labours they still had no idea who they were hunting.

⊹ CHAPTER XII ⊹

When Brave Knights Tilt

Adelko wandered through the maze of tents, feeling slightly bewildered. Being at a tournament was the sort of thing he used to dream about back in Narvik. Only now, after everything he had been through, a tourney seemed almost mundane; he felt more relieved than excited, though the riot of colours afforded by the banners and pennons was certainly pleasing to the eye. Likewise the smell of charring meat as the squires prepared hearty breakfasts for the competing knights was not unpleasant. The sound of troubadours mingling with the whickering of horses completed the welcome assault on his senses. It took his mind off more troubling matters.

At last he spotted the coat of arms he was looking for. Making his way over to Sir Braxus' pavilion he saw Vaskrian struggling with a roasted joint of meat, trying with his one good hand to get it off the spit and on to a platter for carving. His master was running through a series of manoeuvres, his sword swishing through the air as he danced in time to its flashing blade. He moved swiftly despite his hauberk.

'Adelko!' called Vaskrian, seeing him approach. 'Just in the nick of time! Be a good chap and help me.'

The novice did so, secretly hoping he would get a slice of beef and some crusty bread and cheese for his efforts. He had risen just before dawn and left the castle before Horskram could awake and forbid him from attending the joust.

'Here we go,' said Vaskrian after they had prepared breakfast. 'Some mild ale to wash it down – nothing too strong cos the guvnor's got a big day ahead of him.'

Adelko glanced sidelong at Sir Braxus as he munched on his breakfast. The Thraxian did not appear to be in good cheer. A distant look was in his eyes, but there was yearning and anger behind them – Adelko's sixth sense told him what his own eyes could not. He felt an all too familiar tingling at the back of his mind.

No good would come of this tourney. A spectacle he had dreamed of seeing his entire childhood, and now it was here it filled him with foreboding.

But then wasn't that just the sum of things in a life of adventuring?

✢ ✢ ✢

The bleachers had been set up on the edge of the camp just next to the feasting area. Before them the lists had been measured out, their boundaries marked by ribbons tied to posts bearing standards depicting the gauntleted fist of Markward. Beyond that a much larger area was demarcated for the melee, the main event of the tournament.

The Lanraks and Markwards had taken their seats in the bleachers together with their retinues. Behind them the waters of the Graufluss made sparkling ripples of light as they caught the sun; across the river loomed the cyclopean stones of the castle.

Drinking in the vista Adelko felt himself relax slightly, and something akin to excitement began to creep in around his feeling of foreboding. The Warlock's Crown suddenly seemed far away, and his old sense of adventure began to return. Perhaps he was misreading his sixth sense. He hoped so.

A herald dressed in the Markward livery stepped onto a podium at the edge of the lists and raised his arms for silence. A gaggling crowd of common folk had gathered on the other side to watch the spectacle, their clamouring punctuated by the sound of hawkers selling meat on sticks, ale, honey cakes and fruit. Rare treats for the peasant folk: gazing on them from the quarter reserved for knights and their squires, Adelko recalled his own childhood before Ulfang. The plains of Vorstlund were fertile, its climate kind: that probably meant its yeomen got to eat such things several times a year. In this they were luckier than most of their kind.

'Ladies and noblemen, welcome!' cried the herald in a stentorian voice. 'And what a fine day for jousting it is! Haven't we got a treat in store for you...'

The herald spoke slowly enough for Adelko to follow his Vorstlending, but he wouldn't be needing it to follow a tourney with Vaskrian around.

'So I'll tell you what you need to know,' said the squire enthusiastically. 'A hundred knights have entered from Dulsinor and Stornelund each, plus another fifty-six places reserved for outlanders. So that'll be eight rounds of knockout altogether. You get three tilts in each round, if no one's been unhorsed by then the combatants have to dismount and fight it out hand to hand...'

Adelko smiled ruefully as his friend went on in a fever of excitement. He wasn't sure he wouldn't rather have listened to the herald, but it was good to see the squire more like his old self.

✣ ✣ ✣

The novice watched with mixed feelings as the jousting got under way. It certainly wasn't as horrendous as a full-blown war, but not all the bouts were bloodless affairs. The Marionite monks from Lothag monastery had set up their own tent for chirurgery, and their assistants were soon busy fielding injured knights from the lists on stretchers. There was even one fatality: a hapless bachelor from the Herzog's retinue broke his neck in a fall.

'It happens,' said Vaskrian with a shrug as Adelko looked on aghast. 'To be honest that blueblood had no place being in the lists, sitting a horse like that. His saddle wasn't on high enough, left himself wide open to getting hit in the chest.' The squire shook his head, as though it were the most obvious thing in the world.

'Don't worry, his family can claim a weregeld,' Vaskrian continued, seeing the crestfallen look on Adelko's face. 'That usually means the winner gives them back his opponent's horse and armour free of charge, instead of keeping or selling them. Settles the debt. That's why he won't be happy about killing his man – see, we've got rules to discourage knights from getting carried away. We're not barbarians, you know.'

'Erm, right, I see. No of course not...'

'I see Vaskrian is explaining the wonderful fairness of chivalrous sporting events,' said Horskram dryly, surprising Adelko both with his sudden appearance and by the fact that he was holding a cup of wine.

'Master Horskram, I didn't think – '

'I'd enjoy the fun of the fair?' his mentor finished for him. 'On the contrary Adelko, I used to participate in tourneys – pray allow an old man to reminisce over his lost youth once in a while.'

The adept took a sip from his cup. Adelko could never tell if he was joking on such occasions. At least he wasn't dragging him away – although having just witnessed another death he wondered if that would have been such a bad thing after all.

✣ ✣ ✣

It was approaching mid-afternoon by the time the first round was over. They had witnessed more than a hundred jousts, though most of them had been over quite quickly. Only a handful had resulted in hand-to-hand combat. That had got the crowd really excited, though Adelko could barely watch; it reminded him of the war in Northalde. At least there weren't any more deaths thanks to blunted weapons, though one knight had his arm broken with an audible crack.

'Good job we've got Marionites about,' commented Vaskrian as he tightened the crupper on his master's charger. 'Chances are he'd lose that arm otherwise.'

'Why on earth do they do it?' asked Adelko. 'Fight when there isn't a war on?'

'For the glory!' said Vaskrian. 'Haven't I taught you anything? Also, it keeps a knight fresh – for when a real war comes along. How do you think Torgun and that lot got so good at fighting in peacetime? Arresting poachers?'

'That's why you do it? So you can *practise being in a war*?' Adelko shook his head in astonishment and looked from Vaskrian to his mentor.

'Though it pains me to admit it, there is some method to the madness,' allowed Horskram.

'Well now I've heard it all,' said Adelko, shaking his head again and heading over to the wine stall. He'd need a cup himself before the second round got under way. Knights were quite mad, he'd decided.

✢ ✢ ✢

'Touch! And Sir Braxus of Gaellen advances to the third round! And poor Sir Gunther of Vorstbrau will just have to wait till next year for glory at the Graufluss Bridge Tourney!'

This time the cheers were a lot louder. Foreigners weren't always popular at tournaments, but Braxus felt he was winning the crowd over. Bowing with a flourish in the saddle, he dismounted in one easy motion and helped Gunther up off the ground. The experienced vassal of the Eorl had been a top seed and a clear favourite to win their bout. This victory would make an impression on the rest of the knights in the draw.

That was good: send out a message.

Pulling off his great helm, Braxus smiled and waved and blew kisses at the damsels. He made sure he caught Adhelina's eye. If his heart hadn't already been pounding it would have beaten even faster. A smile played on her lips as she applauded her champion, though few of the nobles sat near her were smiling.

'And next up, we have another errant championing the Lady Adhelina! Put your hands together for Sir Torgun of Vandheim, knight of Northalde!'

Cheers and hoots went up in equal measure. Torgun had already made an impression in his first round – not least of all on his hapless opponent, whom he had sent to the infirmary for an extended spell.

'Unbeaten in his own country,' the herald went on. 'Can anyone unhorse him here today? Sir Ruttgur, bachelor of Graukolos, will certainly be hoping he can!'

Braxus felt his mood cloud as he strode out of the lists, Vaskrian carrying his spear and leading his charger. He certainly didn't envy Ruttgur: as one of the Eorl's better knights he was seeded, but as an unranked outsider Torgun was a dangerous floater.

So was Braxus come to think of it. He wondered when they would clash. He needed to focus on this next bout, Torgun was a legend in the lists but everyone had a weakness, no matter how good they were...

Whatever weakness Torgun might have, Ruttgur failed to find it. The Northlending sent him toppling from his horse at the first pass.

'Sir Torgun for the third round! And the outlanders are certainly making an impression here today!'

Cheers mingled with some gasps – Sir Ruttgur had been a local favourite to progress deep into the event.

Vaskrian came up and yelled excitedly in his ear. 'That's two sets of armour and two chargers you've netted, Sir Braxus – you'll be able to sell those back to the knights you bested for a pretty penny!'

'Aye,' said Braxus, only half listening. He wasn't really concerned with spoil – as a lord's heir he hardly lacked for money. In fact there was only one thing here he really wanted... and she was currently smiling at Sir Torgun, just the way she had smiled at him. The Northlending saluted with his lance before urging his Farovian destrier from the lists.

'Next up, Hengist III, 16th Herzog of Stornelund, lord of Hockburg Keep!'

This time the cheers sounded forced. By some miracle (or was it down to baser means?) the future lord of Dulsinor had managed to overcome his first-round opponent, at the third tilt. His next opponent looked to be made of sterner stuff though: a stocky, barrel-chested knight spurred his dun-coloured charger into the lists.

'And we have ourselves a black knight!' cried the herald. 'Whence he comes, no one but himself knows... Only once he is vanquished will he reveal his true identity!'

Whoops and cheers went up at that. Black knights were popular at tourneys; they added an air of mystery, not least because more often than not they turned out to be people of high status.

'He could be a lord in his own right,' Vaskrian was explaining to Adelko.

'Why would he choose to hide that?' asked the novice.

'Not everyone wants to be recognised as a man of privilege,' put in Braxus, nodding pointedly towards Hengist. 'Some lords believe it more chivalrous to pose as an ordinary knight, so as not to discourage fair competition.'

'Couch!' cried the herald. Both knights lowered their lances. Hengist was clearly distinguishable by his coat of arms, a coiled serpent in argent on an escutcheon purpure, but the other knight had only a black cloth over his kite. His face was invisible beneath his helm.

The herald looked to Wilhelm, who nodded curtly.

'Tilt!'

The knights thundered towards each other. The black knight was about the same height as Hengist but considerably bigger. His war saddle was set a little higher, making it harder to balance but giving him more leverage from which to strike.

Always a sign of an experienced jouster, thought Braxus.

It was experience that paid off. The two crashed together but the black knight caught Hengist square in the chest as his own spear glanced harmlessly off his shield. The jousting lance shivered to pieces but the impact sent the Herzog hurtling from the saddle. His humiliation was completed as his leg remained caught in the stirrup, resulting in his being dragged from the lists by his stampeding horse. A couple of commoners were ridden down before his squires got the perturbed stallion under control.

'How do you survive that kind of fall?' gawped Adelko as the crowd erupted into undisguised raptures. The pampered Herzog was clearly no match for the black knight in terms of popularity either.

'Every knight wears a gambeson under his mail,' Vaskrian explained. 'It provides padding, you see. They also wear a linen hood under the coif – together with a good head of hair that stops head injuries if you're lucky.'

'Though as I recall the Lord Storne lacks the latter defence,' quipped Braxus.

In the event, Hengist had suffered little more than wounded pride. Disentangling himself from the stirrup he got up and pushed past his squires, stomping off towards the wine booth reserved for the nobility. His conqueror was making a meal of his victory, wheeling his steed around to face the bleachers and the crowd in turn and nodding his helm in cumbersome acknowledgement.

'Well he's not the most graceful of jousters, but he's effective enough,' said Braxus, accepting a cup of watered wine from Vaskrian. It was approaching late afternoon and the intense summer heat was starting to cool pleasantly. For the first time since the Warlock's Crown, he felt his spirits rise.

✠ ✠ ✠

The second round matches came to a close with a crashing of armour as another knight was brought low to the soil. Vaskrian let out a satisfied sigh. It had been a good day. His guvnor was safely through to the next day of jousting. He'd helped Sir Braxus out of his armour; all that remained was to give his harness a quick check, then he could relax and get drunk.

'Ladies, noblemen and commoners!' cried the herald, his voice hoarse with shouting. 'It's taken nigh on two hundred bouts, but we've separated the hedge knights from the true challengers! Tomorrow at noon I'll see you again for the third round... and that's where it gets *really* interesting!'

'Well how did you find it, Adelko?' said Vaskrian as he checked his guvnor's hauberk and gambeson for dints and scratches. He'd had them repaired before the tourney and it had cost another handful of marks. Not that money was an issue now Braxus was winning forfeits, but getting them fixed again would be a pain.

'Um, it was all right,' ventured the novice.

'It was more than all right,' insisted the squire. 'This is the best I've felt since... well, you know.' His guvnor's hauberk was fine, as he'd hoped it would be – but then last time he'd checked, knights didn't use magicked blades that cleaved through mail like a knife through butter.

'I suppose it was, um, quite entertaining,' said Adelko. 'And you're right, it felt good to do something normal at least... if you can really call this normal.'

'Well compared to what you lot do in a day's work, I'd say it is, Adelko.'

'Yes, you've probably got a point there,' Adelko had to allow. 'Though I'm not sure it's any less dangerous.'

'Come on,' Vaskrian clapped him on the shoulder. 'Look lively and fetch us a couple more stoops of wine. I should be done in a bit – then we can get busy drinking!'

The novice grinned. 'I can agree with you there,' he said, and bounded off towards the stall.

Adelko groaned into consciousness about an hour after dawn. His head was thumping. He and Vaskrian had got royally drunk after supper; he had somehow persuaded Horskram that he needed to remain in the camp to help the injured squire with his duties.

'Look lively, Adelko,' said Vaskrian, poking his head around the tent flap. He was three summers older and had a better head for the stuff. 'I'll need you to help me cook up the guvnor's breakfast for him.'

Grinning, Vaskrian waved a piece of raw meat in his face. Lurching to his feet, Adelko pushed past him as he stumbled from the tent to be sick.

About an hour before noon Adhelina took her seat in the bleachers next to her father. Hengist sat on the other side of her. Perhaps it was a pity he hadn't made it to the next round after all: now she had to sit next to him. Down the end of her row of seats she could make out Hettie. She had insisted that her friend be released from Lothag for a few days to see the event. It might do some good for the Melancholy Sickness. Her father had finally relented as she pestered him over the feasting boards relentlessly, though relations between the two of them were at breaking point.

As the sixty-four remaining knights began crowding into the competitors' stalls with their horses and squires she felt herself tensing. At last she could bear it no longer.

'I shall sit with Hettie,' she blurted. 'She shouldn't be alone.'

She half expected her father to put his broad foot down, but he didn't.

What happened next was even more surprising.

'Pray have her take my seat,' said Lord Storne, rising and moving away. 'I would not see my betrothed parted from her dear companion.'

His scratchy voice sounded oddly neutral. The Herzog did not make eye contact as he shuffled down the aisle away from her, giving her no chance to read his expression. She caught Albercelsus' gaze as she watched Hengist move away. The seneschal stared back at her but said nothing.

Torgun rechecked his equipment as the third round got under way. He made sure the flanchards and crupper were secure on his destrier and tightened the stirrup leathers. Taking his great helm from where he had slung it across the cantle of his saddle, he put it on and waited to be called. Normally he disliked restricting his vision, but he felt the occasion warranted the extra protection. Jousting lances, being hollow, broke more easily but good knights had been known to die from a splinter through the eye. He didn't relish an ignominious death.

But more than that, he realised as he mounted, it enabled him to block out the others. He knew he shouldn't resent Braxus – it was unchivalrous. But he could not help his feelings. And every time he looked at Adhelina he felt his heart clench sickeningly. He had never felt like this before. Not even with Princess Hjala.

To win the day he must be fully focused – just as he had been at all the other tournaments he'd won. Taking his shield and spear from the rack provided for errants, he kicked his horse gently towards the lists in anticipation of his next clash.

His next couple of bouts seemed to fly by. Both knights jousted well, and it was an honour to vanquish them. The last one had a broken collarbone by the looks of things. He was a vassal of the Herzog, a seeded jouster and well respected. Torgun made a mental note to visit him in the infirmary later. He'd give him back his armour and horse too; he wasn't interested in booty.

'Sir Torgun for the fifth round!' cried the herald. 'And who will he meet in the last sixteen? Grab a bite, and buy an ale – but don't go too far! Because we're going to find out who he's facing after this next bout!'

Yanking off his helm, Torgun pulled Hilmir up at the edge of the lists. Forcing himself not to look at Adhelina, he concentrated on sizing up his two possible next opponents.

'Sir Hangrit Foolhardy and Sir Aethelwald of Gothia!'

Studying them as they urged their stallions into the lists, he had the measure of them almost immediately. Hangrit was obviously a court favourite, one of Lord Storne's hangers-on. That gave him the kind of swaggering confidence that could win the day against lesser knights, but would see him come up short against more experienced fighters.

Sir Aethelwald was an experienced fighter. A grizzled and scarred veteran, he hailed from the southern provinces of Vorstlund and probably did the tournament circuit regularly for a living. He was in it for prize money, forfeits and ransoms: not a chivalrous knight by any means, but a foe to be respected nonetheless.

Watching Sir Hangrit prance into the lists, waving overconfidently to the crowd as though the bout were already won, Sir Torgun saw spectators in the bleachers placing bets behind him.

He never presumed anything in matters martial, but he had a strong feeling which would turn out to be the winning wager.

Another knight nearby shouted loudly as Sir Hangrit couched. Reghar his name was. Just as boorish as his friend, the pair of them had spent most of last few nights quaffing wine. That hadn't done Reghar much good and he had gone down in the second round.

'Go on Hangrit, send the southerner packing!' yelled Reghar, pausing only to slurp more wine.

Torgun shook his head. Such boorish behaviour! Men like that gave knighthood a bad name. He silently prayed for Ezekiel to favour Sir Aethelwald. Give him a worthy opponent for his next round.

As it turned out, his prayers weren't needed. Aethelwald toppled Hangrit at the first pass, catching him square on the fess point of his shield and sending him clean over the cantle and into the churned mud. Reghar cursed loudly, dashing his cup to the ground. As Hangrit picked himself up and limped off the lists, his friend yelled for more wine.

Torgun forced himself to remain calm. If the drunken oaf kept this behaviour up, he'd find himself busy in the duelling event. He didn't like to sit in judgement, but the man's behaviour was scarcely tolerable.

As the herald called a ten-minute pause before the next round, he glanced at Adhelina. His heart skipped a beat as he locked eyes with her.

✣ ✣ ✣

Adhelina felt a confused roil of emotions as Sir Torgun looked at her. She truly had not expected anything like this. Their horrible adventures in the forest had happened so quickly; she'd barely had time even to register the two knights, except to be grateful to them for helping to save her.

Could they really both be in love with her?

Another dream of her youth coming true, she reflected bitterly: chivalrous knights competing for her favour. But despite what Agravine had said, she wasn't so sure she would get much joy of her paramours. Not if her father could help it, she wouldn't. And then there was Albercelsus... Adhelina didn't trust him.

She would have to fight for every inch of freedom she could get, of that she felt sure.

At least Hengist wasn't anywhere near her now: he was down in the stalls getting drunk as usual. Perhaps that was why he had offered his seat to Hettie, to give him the excuse he needed. But since when had the Herzog needed excuses to indulge himself?

Pulling her eyes away from Torgun's hot-eyed stare she focused her attention on Hettie.

'It is quite the contest, is it not Hettie?' she asked, forcing herself to sound cheerful.

'Yes,' replied Hettie, staring off into the middle distance. 'They joust well.' Her voice sounded disembodied. Perhaps she needed the ministrations of an Argolian not a Marionite – she might as well have been possessed.

'Hettie, do try to cheer up!' Adhelina pleaded. 'Now more than ever I need you here, present!'

'What do you expect?' growled her father. 'You embroil her in a madcap misadventure and wonder why your best friend has lost her wits? Perhaps now you understand the value of duty! This would never have happened if you'd stayed put and done as you were told.'

Adhelina felt her rage rising and forced herself to take a step back from her anger. Perhaps her father was right, she thought, her bitterness deepening. She had risked their lives and sanity, and in the end nothing had changed. Less than a week from now, after the tourney was done, she would marry Hengist.

She felt her father tense as Sir Agravine nudged his charger into the lists. All three knights who sought her favour were still in the tournament; the man who would wed her was long gone. Didn't that just say it all?

Perhaps Hengist wouldn't care who she dallied with as long she bore him an heir. But to do that she'd have to... She shuddered and closed her legs involuntarily. The thought of it still sickened her.

She tore her mind from her bleak future as the herald remounted the podium.

'Ladies, noblemen and commoners!' he yelled. 'I hope you've all refreshed yourselves! And now Sir Agravine, bachelor of Graukolos, and Sir Otto, bachelor of Hockburg, will compete for a place in the quarter finals!'

The herald swayed slightly as he spoke, his face flushed and sweaty beneath the late afternoon sun. Adhelina guessed he'd had a few refreshments himself. The crowd were in full flow by now, their raucous yelling drowning out the polite ripple of applause from the bleachers. Down in the stalls the knights were evenly divided in their affections, with the Lanraks and the Markwards each cheering on their man.

'Couch!'

For the umpteenth time lances went down.

'Tilt!' cried the herald, forgetting to get the nod of approval from the Eorl. Formalities tended to diminish as the day wore on and the officials got drunker.

At the first pass both knights smashed their lances, neither one unhorsing the other. Rearming for the second tilt, they thundered together again. Agravine's spear glanced off Otto's shoulder as Otto caught him in the chest. He teetered backwards, dropping his lance. Adhelina rose, her heart in her mouth – but at the last second Agravine grasped the pommel of his saddle and heaved himself back into it before bringing his horse up short.

An excited hubbub went around the crowd. Most bouts were over after one or two passes. There had only been a couple fought on foot that day.

The two knights squared off again for the final pass. The herald gave the command and they crashed together once more. This time they both flew off the saddle, landing in the mud amid the broken splinters of their lances.

Their squires came and armed them. Agravine chose a sword while Otto opted for a mace. The two rashed together furiously, but Otto had been injured in the fall and was limping. It was no hard matter for Agravine to outfoot him and bring him low with a swipe to the back of his good leg. As Otto sprawled in the mud, Agravine placed his blunted sword point against the aventail of his bascinet where it guarded the throat, a symbolic gesture of victory in a bout for love.

'Touch!' cried the herald, slurring his speech. 'Sir Agravine does it for the host team! And the House of Markward has the first knight in the quarter finals!'

Cheers and applause erupted. Her father remained seated, pointedly refusing to join in. Looking past him to Albercelsus, Adhelina saw the Steward of Hockburg staring coldly at Agravine. That only made her clap more loudly. She smiled and waved at her paramour, flirtatiously blowing him a kiss.

'Wine!' she cried to a nearby servant. 'And one for my lady-in-waiting too!' If this was to be her last bit of freedom, she would bloody well enjoy it.

The contest was moving swiftly now as the draw whittled down to the real contenders. Torgun was up next, and made light work of Aethelwald. Even had he not been her champion, Adhelina would have applauded him: she had grown up watching tourneys and his jousting technique was flawless. Before the Northlending even a seasoned campaigner like Aethelwald looked ordinary.

If he was the victor that would mean he would be ahead of the other two in her favour. But Torgun was an outlander, and would have no reason to linger after the tournament was done. Most likely her father would banish all three of them anyway. She tried not to dwell on that as the herald ushered in the next bout.

'And now we have our quarter-final line-up!' cried the herald a few bouts later. Sir Adso Bastardson was the last knight in: the stern-faced Marshal of Hockburg was of middling years and middling girth, but still knew how to couch. Down in the stalls she saw Hengist ranting drunkenly: 'That's my marshal! That's my marshal! One of the best! One of the best, I say!'

Was she really about to marry this man?

She turned to look at her father, but he seemed to be pointedly ignoring the drunken Herzog, who was linking arms with Hangrit and Reghar. His sisters Festilia and Griselle weren't much better, yelling boisterously as they wagered on the winners of the next round.

'I wasn't aware that ladies ought to place wagers,' she said loudly, so Albercelsus would hear. He ignored her, but Berthal leaned up from the row below them and nudged his fellow steward in the knee. 'That reminds me,' said Berthal. 'I believe you bet me ten regums against Sir Agravine making the quarters…'

The old steward winked at Adhelina as Albercelsus tossed him a purse with a muttered curse.

Her father called for more wine in an irritable voice.

'Oh yes father, an excellent idea,' said Adhelina. 'More wine for Hettie and me too! Hettie will have another goblet, won't you Hettie!?' She had fairly torn through her last drink. Her head felt light. It was not an unwelcome feeling.

'Why not?' said Hettie, evidently thinking much the same. 'My nerves could do with it.' She sounded more like her old self, but Adhelina noticed her hand trembled as she took the proffered cup.

The damsel pushed her troubled thoughts away as she focused on the remaining field.

There were half a dozen knights besides Adso and Agravine left: both her other paramours had made it through, along with Urist, who seemed to be enjoying a late summer in his tourneying career like Adso. That left a sleek-looking tournament veteran from Westenlund, a burly vassal of Stornelund, and the black knight, who had left his last opponent nursing a broken shoulder and a dislocated leg in the infirmary. The herald appeared to take ghoulish delight in enumerating the jousters' injuries, but that was part of his duty after all.

Adhelina made a mental note to help the Marionites later. Provided she didn't get too drunk.

'My honourable – and not so honourable – friends!' bellowed the herald, to hoots and jeers. 'And now we come to the business end of the tournament! Eight brave knights remain – but only one shall be crowned champion of the Graufluss Bridge Tourney! A purse of a hundred gold regums and a Westlun stallion awaits the victor!'

Grunts of approval went up at that. Doubtless the charger was the more prized reward – the white horses were foaled on the southern plains of Westenlund and very rare.

'For our first quarter final bout, show some appreciation for Sir Hugo of High Wharram and the black knight!'

'Who do you think he is?' murmured Adhelina as she did her best to relax back into her seat. The wine was helping, but she'd have the drinking sickness come morning at this rate.

'Possibly a minor baron from one of the border provinces between Westenlund and Aslund,' said her father. 'Perhaps we'll find out soon – Sir Hugo couches a decent lance.'

A decent lance wasn't enough, in the event. Three passes went by without either knight dislodging the other.

'Dismount and choose your weapons!' cried the herald.

Hugo opted for a morning star and shield while the black knight took up a two-handed war axe. He was hugely strong and wielded the thing like a toy, but for a while Hugo kept him at bay with great sweeps of the spiked ball and chain.

'He moves quickly for a man his size,' commented Adhelina.

'Too quickly for Hugo,' muttered her father. 'I don't think your man's going to be in this tournament for much longer.' This last comment was aimed at Albercelsus.

'I fear you may be right,' the seneschal conceded. 'At least I didn't wager any coin on this bout.'

It would have been money lost if so. Biding his time the black knight waited for Sir Hugo to attack again. Ducking the blow aimed at his head he stepped in, stabbing forwards with the toe hooks of the axe blades. It was an unexpected move and caught the vassal completely off guard. He staggered back with a cry as the blow caught him square in the chest, flailing desperately with his shield as he let go of his morning star. Taking another step forwards the black knight raised the axe high above his head and brought it crashing down on Hugo's helm. The metal crumpled beneath the force of the strike and Hugo sank to his knees with a pitiful groan. He keeled over sideways and did not get up.

'Touch!' cried the herald. 'And the black knight bests one of Stornelund's finest to advance to the semi finals!'

Cheers erupted as two lay brothers dressed in white overalls dashed over with a stretcher to carry Sir Hugo from the lists.

Holding his axe over his head the black knight turned a full circle in triumph. It reminded Adhelina of reading about the fighting pits of the Thalamian Empire. She supposed every era had to have its blood sports.

'He's not the prettiest to look at but he fights well,' remarked the Eorl. 'If he isn't too high-born for service I've a good mind to recruit him.'

'I was thinking much the same,' replied Albercelsus dryly.

Hearing this Adhelina glanced over at her future spouse. As the present lord of Hockburg Keep it should have been Hengist doing the recruiting. But Hengist wasn't even paying attention to the tournament any more. Down in the stalls she could see him with Hangrit and Reghar, shouting and laughing boisterously as they groped a serving wench.

✢ ✢ ✢

Sir Braxus took the proffered spear from Vaskrian and prepared to be called. His heart was thumping in his chest as he looked down the oblong of churned mud at his next opponent. Sir Adso Bastardson was half brother to the Herzog and the illegitimate son of his father Henrich. The purple plume on his helm marked him out as a distinguished knight, a man of high achievement.

He spurred his horse into the lists at the herald's call. How had he got this far? He hadn't fought a tourney for more than two years – with the highlanders a constant threat there simply hadn't been any need to hold one. He was a veteran of skirmishes, surprise attacks fought at close quarters in unexpected circumstances. Tourney knights fought best in the open field when there were rules. The closest he'd got to that was taking part in the civil war of the Northlendings. Perhaps that had benefited him, he reflected as he couched his spear.

Sir Adso was tall for a Vorstlending, and built more like a Northlending. That meant he presented a higher target and would be easier to hit – but it also gave him a better position from which to strike.

Braxus measured his breathing, which sounded loudly in the confines of his helm. A bead of sweat ran into his eye as the herald shouted the command to tilt.

Spurring his horse forwards he felt its hooves thundering as the spectacle of the armoured knight before him grew larger and larger... The Lanrak crest on his shield loomed across his limited field of vision as the distance between them vanished.

Braxus tunnelled his vision, focusing on the honour point of Adso's shield. He pulled his heater in across his torso at the last second – he'd watched Adso's last couple of bouts and he tended to favour the chest strike.

Adso's lance caught his shield a glancing blow, but not enough to turn him in the saddle. Braxus' spear caught him dead centre in his, with enough force to twist him around, wrenching his lower back into the cantle and lifting his left leg clear of the stirrup. Braxus thundered past him, bringing his charger wheeling around. The cheers of the crowd told him his gambit had paid off. Adso lay sprawled in the mud, his steed rearing madly.

'Siiiiiiiiir Braxus of GAELLEN! And the Thraxian is into the semi-finals!'

This time Braxus did not bother to take off his helm, contenting himself with a lap of honour around the lists before retiring. Perhaps it was premature, but he was in high spirits. This was just what he had needed after the terrors he had witnessed. Something to put courage back into his bones. If only his father could see him now!

The herald's call brought him back to reality.

'Sir Agravine, bachelor of Graukolos, versus Sir Torgun, errant of Northalde!'

So now we come to it, Braxus thought feverishly as he handed his helm and spear to Vaskrian. *Let's find out who's really worthy to court her.*

He caught the look in his squire's eyes as he struggled one-armed with his helm and spear. He knew how much Vaskrian admired his compatriot. The expression on the youth's scarred face wasn't encouraging.

Come on, study him Reus dammit! Everyone's got a weakness...

If Sir Torgun had one, he hid it well. Agravine couched a fine lance, but the Northlending sent him flying over his crupper at the first tilt. The crowd erupted into an ecstatic frenzy of applause. There was no denying the foreigner had won over the home crowd.

Braxus felt a cold bitterness creeping through his guts as Torgun humbly acknowledged the crowd before exiting the lists with an effortless grace and dignity.

He barely registered the last quarter-final bout. Sir Urist managed to best the tourney veteran from Westenlund at the final pass. He didn't look so sleek after that, limping off the lists with his multi-coloured plume spattered with mud and his purpure and sable tabard torn in two by Urist's questing spear.

The herald declared a fifteen-minute pause to allow the remaining four knights to refresh themselves and prepare for the semi-final bouts. Braxus would be paired with Urist next, though that concerned him far less than what lay after.

Concentrate dammit, he berated himself. *One step at a time...*

He had studied Urist in the previous couple of rounds. The Marshal of Graukolos jousted well, but at well over forty winters he was clearly a fading force.

The black knight and Sir Torgun were the first to take the lists. Saluting each other, they lowered their lances at the herald's command and tilted.

The two thundered together with a roaring crash at the first pass, exploding together in a shower of wooden chips as both their spears shattered.

'Another tilt it is, folks!' cried the herald, struggling to be heard above the rabid crowd. It was hard to tell which of the two knights was the most popular.

They couched again and waited for the command. Again it came, and again the two of them smashed together, their shields cracking with the force but neither of them budging.

'Like an unstoppable force against an immovable object,' said Braxus.

'Nah, Sir Torgun'll have him at the next pass, sirrah, you'll see,' replied Vaskrian.

Braxus turned and glared down at him from the saddle. The squire blushed as he realised to whom he was talking. Adelko and Horskram exchanged wry smiles.

'Well we'll soon find out, won't we?' Braxus snapped.

Unluckily for him Vaskrian was proved right. Torgun caught the black knight at the third pass, disguising his strike until the last moment before catching him in the midriff. The black knight rolled head over heels off his horse's crupper, sliding down its hind quarters to land sitting upright in the dirt.

'And the black knight falls!' cried the herald amidst cheers laced with booing. 'And will he now kindly reveal himself?'

Staggering to his feet the knight obliged, pulling off his helm and bowing courteously towards the bleachers.

Braxus had half expected to see a lord of men met with gasps, but instead the nobles laughed as they registered the knight's bushy black beard and twinkling eyes.

'It's Sir Wrackwulf of Bringenheim,' muttered one knight standing close by. 'Trust him to pull a caper like this.'

'He's no lord of men, I take it,' said Braxus.

'No,' said the knight. 'He's another errant – does the tournament circuit every year. We'd had word he wasn't coming this year due to dysentery. This is probably his idea of a joke.'

'Sir Wrackwulf!' cried the herald, warming to the theme. 'You've led us all a merry dance – but now it's time for you to call the tune to a halt! Make way there for our next competitors: Sir Braxus of Gaellen, and our very own Sir Urist, Marshal of GRAUUUUUUKOLOS!'

The cheers intensified as the home favourite urged his horse into the lists. Braxus felt his surroundings fall away from him. He felt strangely mechanical, as though he were witnessing the spectacle from afar, communicating with his physical self across a great distance. Once more spears were couched. Once again the order was given to tilt.

In the blinking of an eye it was over.

Sir Braxus was wheeling his steaming charger around, pulling tightly on the reins as it churned up more soil beneath its iron-shod hooves. Sir Urist was lying flat on his back in the mud, the wind knocked out of him. In his other hand Braxus clutched a broken lance.

The cheers of the crowd lifted his spirits high up into the wispy clouds to nestle against the sun. He was in the final!

'A half hour pause, most honourable sirrahs,' cried the herald. 'I think we all need to catch our breath back after that excitement! So grab yourselves a drink – but don't go far, because after the break we have our final to look forward to... Sir Braxus of Gaellen, versus Sir Torgun of VAAAAAANDHEIM!!!'

Thunderous cheers. Braxus felt his spirits return to earth with a thump as he realised what lay ahead. He almost wished he was back at the Warlock's Crown with the Gygant. For truly his love rival was a giant among men.

'Any tips?' he asked Agravine glumly at the wine stall.

The handsome Vorstlending shook his head miserably. 'Don't joust against Sir Torgun,' was all he said, before stalking off to drown his sorrows.

Taking his own cup, Sir Braxus sat down on the benches to think while he drank. Vaskrian busied himself preparing his charger and weapons for the next bout. Glancing across the stalls he saw Torgun methodically preparing his own harness. He looked so calm and self assured. Braxus hated him for that. From where he was sat he could not see the bleachers. He was grateful for that – surely Adhelina's heart must be moving towards Torgun? With all the top seeds gone the Northlending was the clear favourite to win.

Braxus took another sip as he eyed Torgun's powerful frame. He'd fought alongside him for weeks, surely there must be some chink in his armour? None that he could recall, and if possible the young knight jousted even better than he fought on foot. He seemed to become one with his horse; he had heard that as part of their training knights of the White Valravyn were required to sleep with their destriers in the stables, to bond them closer to the animal.

He was up against the perfect gentle knight, the kind troubadours sang stories about. The question was: what was he going to do about it?

Presently the herald called for them to take the saddle and enter the lists. Putting on his helm and taking his spear from Vaskrian he ambled slowly into them, playing for time.

It was then that he remembered something Vertrix had told him, long ago when he squired for him. *If you can't beat a foe in a head-on fight, change the direction of attack. Out-think your enemy, and victory is nearly always assured.*

But such advice was all well and good in the field, when different terrain and tactics could be employed to devastating effect. This was a tourney joust, fought under formal rules of engagement. What could he change, and how?

Gazing through the eye slit of his helm he saw Torgun at the other end of the lists, a formidable sight atop his mighty dappled charger.

'Couch!'

And then the answer came to him.

At the last second he reversed his grip, couching his spear over-arm. He heard a few muffled gasps and grunts of surprise through his helm. No one in the Free Kingdoms jousted over-arm: the style was particular to the heathen Sassanians and the Imperial cavalry. But Braxus had been a keen hunter since his early youth, when he'd chased deer and boar across the wooded hills of his homeland. The over-arm grip came naturally to him.

'Tilt!'

Braxus felt his heart racing in time to his horse's hooves as they gobbled up the distance between them. This was his only chance and he knew it: a knight as good as Torgun would only be surprised by the change-up for a few precious seconds. It was now or never.

Torgun varied his strikes and tilted in a way that made it impossible to predict which way he would go. Braxus would simply have to choose an area to defend with his heater and hope Ushira smiled on him. He held his shield across his chest, bringing it up at the last split-second to protect his face. Head shots were the hardest to pull off with a lance strike, and the most dangerous.

But Torgun was no ordinary knight, and this was personal.

The *thunk* of metal on wood told him he had guessed correctly. Braxus hardly dared to look as he drove the point of his own spear down hard against the middle chief of Torgun's kite, slamming the rim against his helm. The downwards angle of the strike caught the Northlending completely off kilter, sending him reeling backwards in the saddle. Sir Braxus tore past him and spun his horse around. Sir Torgun was teetering against the cantle, both legs torn free of the stirrups as his destrier reared and neighed.

For an agonising second Braxus thought he was going to recover his balance... But then Torgun slipped off his horse, limbs flailing wildly as he landed in the mud.

The crowd lapsed into stunned silence. Everyone there, noble and commoner alike, knew they had just witnessed something special.

And then the sound of clapping came from the bleachers. It was Adhelina, applauding her favourite champion. Gradually the sound was mirrored by the Lanraks and other Markwards; applause spread through the bleachers and down into the stalls, thickening into roars of adulation as it flowed across the crowd.

But only when the herald announced it did it truly sink in. Sir Braxus was jousting champion of the Graufluss Bridge Tourney.

⊷ CHAPTER XIII ⊶

Blood on the Horizon

G uldebrand ran lightly from one homestead to the next, torching them as he went. The crucified men and women shrieked pitifully as they died slowly in sight of their burning homes.

But the Thegn had no pity for victims of war. He was fighting for a greater good, of that he felt surer with every passing day. His warband had broken cover of the Hrorwood a week ago: this was the umpteenth village they had razed on their march to the capital. In what had been its centre Brega and Varra were finishing off the executions, beheading the handful of shieldmen who had surrendered.

'May their spirits find the Halls of Feasting and Fighting beneath the Sea of Valhalla,' said Guldebrand as the last headless corpse slumped to the ground. 'Brega, how many does that make?'

Brega scratched his beard, with the air of a horse trader counting stock. 'By my reckoning these make three hundred and seventeen shieldmen we've killed since we broke cover of the woods,' he said.

'Three hundred and *nineteen*,' corrected Varra, wrenching his axe from the spurting neck of another shieldman. 'You can't count, Brega.'

'At least I know how to behead a man,' countered Brega. 'Look at that one, he's still alive for Tyrnor's sake.'

Varra looked down at the twitching warrior and shrugged. 'My axe is blunted with all this toil,' he said. 'He'll bleed out soon enough and find his way to the Lord of Oceans, don't you worry.' Gazing at the two dozen slaughtered warriors he grunted approvingly. 'Fought well and bravely this lot.'

'By now word of our depredations will have spread,' said Guldebrand. 'This is probably the last inhabited settlement we'll find between here and Landarök. The rest will have fallen back to the city if they've any sense. Regroup the boys, a quick bite and some mead, then we press on.'

Not all the slaves had been nailed to crosses. The wailing of women among the long grass told Guldebrand that ravishings were under way.

'Ho there, lads!' he cried, striding among them. 'Get your ruttings done quickly and cut their throats when you've finished – we've a city to take!'

Cheers went up at that. One slave woman had broken free and was running for dear life. Poor thing, she'd been ravished by Haga Longshaft and could barely run. Pulling an axe from his belt Guldebrand hurled it. It pirouetted through the air and buried itself in her back. She fell with a cry and did not get up again.

'Fetch my axe Haga!' cried Guldebrand. 'Lord of Oceans, do I have to clean up your mess for you? Come on the rest of you, eat and gather your strength – we should be hearing from Magnhilda's lot any time now.'

✣ ✣ ✣

They had just finished eating their fill of slaughtered bullock when Ragnar appeared on the horizon.

'Are you sure it's him?' asked Brega, following Guldebrand's line of sight. Against the cloudy sky he could just make out a raven.

'Ja, it's him,' said Guldebrand. 'I know him by instinct these days.'

The raven drew nearer, descended and appeared to merge into the wet skies, pregnant with a coming squall. The mage's mortal form coalesced before them.

'Good e'en,' said Ragnar curtly, ignoring the gasps of the superstitious warriors. 'My magic was successful. The Shield Queen's warband has taken Halgaard and razed Umtsk.'

'To the point as always,' grinned Guldebrand. 'I hope she didn't raze the longships at harbour as well.'

Ragnar shook his head, ignoring his attempt at humour. 'Her forces are sailing up the Holm towards Landarök and will arrive in two days. I see your work has sped well too.' The warlock looked around at the butchered bodies and burning shacks without emotion.

'We're still nigh on five hundred,' replied Guldebrand smugly. 'We did encounter a mustered leidang at the last town but they were barely a hundred strong. We've killed more than three hundred of Oldrik's shieldmen. My plan worked.'

'The Stormrider is on the back foot, but expect him to react swiftly now he is ware of you,' said Ragnar unsmiling. 'He will have sent word down south and his leidang will be mustering south of the

Røk and hard on your heels. You'll need to strike Landarök quickly before his reinforcements arrive.'

Guldebrand laughed. 'Have no fear, White Eye,' he said. 'By my reckoning we are not more a day's march from Aurgelmir's Tooth. We'll meet up with the jarls Bjorg and Vilm there, then we'll march on Landarök. We should get there around the same time as Magnhilda and the Mountainside.'

'I shall fly south now, to see how Walmond fares at Varborg,' said Ragnar. The warlock's form shimmered again, and a raven flew south across the desolate moorlands.

A crack and a rumble announced the arrival of rain. The sudden downpour washed the smell of blood from Guldebrand's nostrils. The crucified men and children shrieked and groaned, their torment amplified as rainwater lashed their punctured wrists and feet.

'What are you lot complaining about?' yelled Guldebrand. 'A good drink of water might see you live another day if you're lucky!'

He got a few laughs at that. A good leader should always know how to joke with the men.

Skulling the rest of his mead the Thegn stood to address his warband. 'All right, you've had your fighting, your ravishing and your feasting,' he yelled. 'Now let's get back on the warpath – we've at least three hours before sunset and I mean to cover some ground!'

☩ ☩ ☩

It was past noon the following day when they reached Aurgelmir's Tooth. It looked like a giant's molar, stuck into the hard unyielding ground. Guldebrand couldn't say if it really had anything to do with the legendary father of the Gygants, but it was a fine landmark to pick for a meeting spot.

Bjorg and Vilm were waiting for him by the gnarled rock with their warbands, just as Ragnar had said they would be. The storm clouds had cleared since the day before and he greeted his jarls under bright skies.

'Ach, Guldebrand,' said Bjorg, his tattooed head doing little to hide his broad grin. 'We have left a sea of wounds behind us! The sleep of the sword my men brought to more than a hundred brave shieldmen.' Bjorg was very tall even for a Northlander, with lean wiry limbs like knotted ropes.

'And let it not be said that I have slept on my sword,' put in Vilm. 'I left the blood ember burning on the necks of a like number of warriors.' Vilm's hair was corn yellow, his beard cut in a short square that went well with his stocky frame.

'Good,' said Guldebrand. 'Together with our efforts that makes five hundred shieldmen loyal to Oldrik who now feed the ravens.'

Impulsively he leapt up on to the large rock and drew his sword. Sweeping his gaze across his leidang he pointed at the firmament with his blade.

'Hear me, o feeders of the eagle!' he cried. 'Now we march north, to bring weather of weapons to Landarök! Like the breaker of trees we shall bear down upon their walls! A bloody harvest we'll reap with the wound-hoe! Oldrik shall not live to see another season, for soon the skies shall be washed with his blood! What say ye, shieldmen and seacarls and berserkers? Who shall be crowned Magnate of the Frozen Wastes?'

Guldebrand felt his father's blood course through his veins as a thousand throats roared his name.

⊷ CHAPTER XIV ⊷

Of Duelling Hearts

A dhelina watched with trepidation as the two knights approached the wooden dais. Her father stood beside her, still and silent. He had evidently resolved on keeping his feelings to himself for now.

'The runner up of this year's Graufluss Bridge Tourney, Sir Torgun of Vandheim!' cried the herald. The assembled knights, squires and ladies applauded. Many of the former wore bandages under their court clothes; at least a dozen fighting men were still laid up at the Marionite tent. And would be for some time.

Sir Torgun stepped forward with a wave of acknowledgement and kneeled before the makeshift podium that topped the dais. Adhelina placed a laurel wreath upon his brows as the Eorl took up a purse of jingling coins and a gilt-pommelled dagger sheathed in a dark leather scabbard set with amethysts.

'Fifty gold regums and this fine dirk to our runner-up!' proclaimed the herald.

The high-born audience clapped again as Torgun held the dagger aloft for all to see. If he felt chagrin at losing the final he showed no signs of it, smiling bashfully as though it were his first tourney.

He is modest as befits a true knight, thought Adhelina. *How unlike so many of my father's.*

She realised with a surge of guilt that she was thinking of Sir Balthor. The braggart who had laid down his life to save her. She let the thought die as the herald called out again.

'And now, ladies and noblemen... this year's champion, Sir Braxus of Gaellen!'

The applause was a little louder, but not much. The commoners loved a winner, but the local knighthood could be counted on to allow parochial envy to dull their appreciation of the better man. The common folk had descended on Merkstaed hours ago to continue their revels at its three inns. Thinking on her adventures there she suppressed a shiver. Where was Anupe now, she wondered? Probably on the road to Meerborg if she had any sense.

She eyed Braxus as he kneeled before her. That rakish smile, the sparkling eyes... He reminded her a lot of Agravine. But Braxus had proved himself the worthier champion. Not only that, he had other talents too. She had heard him play and sing back at the camp, there was more to him than just a ladies' man.

And yet, a ladies' man he clearly was.

As she put the victor's wreath garlanded with white roses on his head she surprised herself with the realisation that she did not care. It wasn't likely to happen anyway, she might as well indulge in a bit more fantasising.

'A hundred gold regums, and a Westlun stallion for the victor!' announced the herald. Adhelina had the distinct impression the applause was for the fine white horse, led by a squire into the space between tables.

'And now a few words from our brave champion,' said the Eorl, his voice dangerously neutral. Unbidden, Adhelina's eyes swept across to the table reserved for the Lanraks. Hengist was nowhere to be seen, nor Reghar and Hangrit – doubtless they were roistering among the peasantry in town. But Albercelsus was there, along with the Herzog's sisters and Sir Adso. At least the Marshal had the decency to applaud; the others just stared stonily, as though bored by the spectacle.

'I thank you,' said Braxus, courteously addressing the assembly in his lilting Decorlangue. 'For your warm hospitality, so rightly famed across the Free Kingdoms! And your generosity does not go unmarked either!'

More applause, sprinkled with a few 'ayes'. The Thraxian could charm the tusks off a boar: even the rivalrous knights of Stornelund and Dulsinor were starting to warm to him. As for the ladies, clearly most had already made up their minds about him. Taking in their hot-eyed stares, Adhelina could not help but feel proud that such a comely knight would joust in her name.

'So impressed am I with said generosity that I shall return it in kind!' continued Braxus. 'Every Vorstlending I bested shall have his horse and armour returned free of charge!'

It was a bold gesture. Few would be so generous; even chivalrous knights prized their spoil. Cheers went up and goblets were drained to the Thraxian's health.

'And I hope you will forgive me if I keep this mighty stallion in reserve – now I have a steed the like of which I have coveted for many a year.'

A few frowns met that statement. But Adhelina was far more interested in Torgun's reaction. His face darkened instantly.

'A Farovian destrier is as fine a steed as any knight could wish for,' said Braxus, meeting the tall knight's black stare.

Why are you provoking him you idiot? Adhelina thought. *Can't you see when you've won?*

Torgun took a deep breath as if to master his growing anger. Addressing her father he said: 'My lord, if the runner-up might have a word?'

'Of course,' said Wilhelm, motioning for him to speak freely. Adhelina glared at the Eorl. She knew him well enough to realise he had anticipated this situation.

Sir Torgun rarely raised his voice, but this time he spoke a shade louder. Everyone listened.

'Sir Braxus of Gaellen, you jousted well and truly deserve to be champion. Your methods are unorthodox, but no one can dispute the strength of your right arm. Or the cunning with which you use it.'

Silence fell. Torgun's words, though polite, had a pointed sting to them.

Braxus smiled thinly.

'My humble apologies, sir knight,' he replied. 'It must be difficult to taste defeat for the first time. 'Tis a greater test of one's chivalry than victory, they say.'

'Indeed,' returned Torgun, keeping his composure. 'And let it never be said that I was found wanting. You bested me fairly, and with like sincerity will I now ask this boon of you.'

Braxus raised an eyebrow. Silence persisted.

'Seven brave knights I bested before falling to thee,' said Torgun, sounding ever more formal. 'One I have returned his harness to, as recompense for the excessive injuries I dealt him. The rest I shall sell back to their owners, as per the rules of the contest. Every coin I raise from such proceeds I shall give you, if only you will return my horse and armour.'

Braxus smiled and shook his head. 'Your armour I will return to you gratis,' he replied. 'But as for the Farovian, not all the gold in the Pilgrim Kingdoms would part me from him. I have longed for such a steed and I will not be denied!'

Adhelina was shocked. Generally vanquished knights were permitted the opportunity to buy back their harness, though the Code wasn't strict on that point. There was real spite in the Thraxian's voice now.

Torgun blanched, his eyes freezing over with cold rage. 'That horse has a name, and it is Hilmir,' he said, measuring his words. 'Three years have we been bonded, man and beast. Such a bond can rarely be broken.'

Braxus laughed hollowly. 'Well then, I shall enjoy rising to the challenge – and if I don't succeed, I have a fine horse here waiting to bear me!' He gestured towards the white stallion.

Sir Torgun started to say something in his own tongue, then caught himself. Adhelina knew it was far from complimentary. She caught her father's eye, willing him to intervene. But the Eorl simply watched the two knights, a half smile playing on his lips.

'Sir Braxus, I am not a worldly man, but I believe my winnings amount to well over a hundred regums in value,' continued Sir Torgun. 'This together with my prize money I shall give you, if only you will return my horse.'

'It isn't your horse any more,' said Braxus. 'I suggest you retain a charger from your winnings.'

From the corner of her eye Adhelina caught a look of disgust on Horskram's face, though he hardly seemed surprised. Next to him his novice gawped, looking perplexed and troubled.

Sir Torgun said no more but bowed curtly and withdrew, stalking off towards the camp.

The Eorl cleared his throat and called for Baalric. 'Play us a ditty there! The prize-giving is done, now it's time to feast and make merry!'

'Why didn't you say something?' Adhelina hissed as they sat down to eat.

'I'm quite sure no words on my part were necessary,' Wilhelm replied, nonchalantly breaking off a chunk of bread and popping it in his mouth. 'All is going just as I had expected,' he added, reaching for his goblet.

Adhelina did not need to ponder those words over long, for presently Torgun returned. He was carrying something in his hand. As he drew level with the tables she saw it was a mail gauntlet.

She felt her heart sink as the Northlending strode up to where Braxus was sitting. Baalric stopped playing as Torgun threw it down on his trencher.

'I trust my meaning is plain enough,' he said loudly. 'I believe the challenge event takes place the day after tomorrow, and I would fain have satisfaction.'

Braxus rose, drew his dagger and drove it into the table.

'Satisfaction you shall have, Torgun of Vandheim,' he said coldly. If he felt any fear he gave no show of it. Torgun towered a head higher than him, his powerful frame dwarfing the Thraxian's. And yet Adhelina had seen him best the Northlending that very day...

Torgun gave another curt bow before walking calmly to his place at table. The Eorl motioned for Baalric to play and ordered more wine. Adhelina looked at him with scorn.

'You contrived this,' she accused him.

'Hardly,' he sneered. 'Those rakehell foreigners could be counted on to provide us with more sport. Once they've put each other in the infirmary I'll only have to deal with that dolt Agravine.'

'They are brave knights all three!' Adhelina protested. 'Far better men than the one you've chosen for me.'

Wilhelm turned towards her. His breath smelled of wine as he leaned in close. 'Even now, you still don't understand do you? I don't give a fig what kind of man the Lord Storne is – as long as he *is* Lord Storne! You don't get to marry for love, you are an Eorl's daughter.'

'And did you obey the same law when you married my mother?' asked Adhelina.

Her father glared at her, but she wasn't done yet.

'I wonder did you love your darling daughter, or was it her mother's image you saw? Perhaps that explains why you can't bear to see me married to a man I actually care about. It's your way of punishing me for not being her.'

The tirade was unfair, and she regretted it directly it exited her mouth. Her father said nothing, but stared at her with bulging eyes. He stayed like that, frozen, for a few moments. Then he turned and beckoned to a page boy.

'My daughter has had over much fresh air and wine today,' he said. 'Send for an escort to take her back to the castle. Her lady-in-waiting shall also need one, to return to Lothag.'

The page scurried off to obey. Wilhelm sat back and drained another goblet.

Adhelina swept a restless glance across the feast she was being dismissed from. None of the men who had borne her favour looked happy. Torgun and Braxus sat a few pews away from each other, staring sullenly at their trenchers and making little talk. Agravine looked flushed from too much wine, and glowered at his rivals with resentment.

So much for living in a romance.

✤ ✤ ✤

Vaskrian sat at table feeling heartsick. The squires' fare was good and hearty, almost as appetising as the board reserved for the nobles uptable, but he had no stomach for it. Two men he admired more than anyone were at daggers drawn. In two days' time one or both of them could be dead.

'And all for a woman,' he muttered, pushing gravy around his trencher aimlessly with a hunk of bread. The horse was an excuse, even he could see that. His master's love rivalry with his hero had turned mutual dislike into hatred. He felt sure the Code of Chivalry would be better off without the Laws of Romance. Glancing across the green he caught Horskram's eye. The dour adept scarcely looked more happy. For once, he suspected, they were in complete agreement.

'There goes your bodyguard, Master Horskram,' Vaskrian muttered, catching Adelko's glance and sharing a frown with his friend.

'Why so glum, lad?'

He turned to look at the speaker, who was addressing him in his own tongue. Vaskrian was sat at the higher end of the squires' table, just next to the table reserved for errants and other poor knights. He recognised him immediately. Sir Wrackwulf, the black knight. This close he could see his nose was bent and broken. His mouth flashed a grin that showed several of his teeth were missing.

'An old wound, but a defining one!' he chuckled, seeing the squire staring at his ugly features. 'Took a mace in the face at the Tower Castle Tourney in Lundheim. First and last time I ever entered a melee without a great helm!'

'You jousted well at the tournament,' said Vaskrian, not knowing what else to say.

The burly knight raised his tankard and took a hearty slug. 'Not well enough to carry the day, but you can't win 'em all, eh?'

'One day I hope I'll win a tourney,' said Vaskrian, then let his voice trail off. That was the old Vaskrian, full of hopes and ambition. Why fool himself now?

'You don't look so sure of yourself,' said Wrackwulf, spearing a shred of venison with his dagger. 'Your master couches an excellent lance, a tad unusual but he gets the job done!'

'He'll need to fight even better on foot and no mistake,' said Vaskrian. 'Sir Torgun is the best swordsman... well, in Northalde at least. Probably the Free Kingdoms.'

'Hmm, I know him well enough,' said Wrackwulf. 'Bested me at Saltcaste, and Linden the following year. Doubt if he remembers. Sir Torgun's victories are not easily counted.'

'So you've travelled amongst my countrymen, then?'

'Travelled the whole of the Free Kingdoms,' said Wrackwulf, in between mouthfuls. 'Been playing the tourney circuit since I won my spurs. I usually do better in the melee – I won Linden ten years ago, but that'll be before your time. I also won the Crescent Bridge Tourney in Rima.'

'Really? They have the best of the best there don't they? I heard Sir Azelin won it five times in a row!'

'Aye, he did... I won after he went off on crusade. Best thing that ever happened to my career that. Reus be praised but piety's a wonderful thing!'

The jovial knight drained his tankard. Vaskrian had to smile. Sir Wrackwulf was flippant and impious, but clearly a good man to drink with.

And by Reus did he need a drink.

'I suppose you'll be headed to Linden next then?' he asked. 'Seeing as outlanders can't compete in the melee here this year?'

Wrackwulf frowned. 'Aye, I'll have to break my nag to make the entry quota on time,' he said. 'Fie on this blasted wedding, politics is never good for tourneys!'

'You've a tenday by my reckoning,' said Vaskrian, feeling a sudden pang of homesickness. 'Though don't expect to find the castle as you left it.' He told Wrackwulf of the civil war.

'Aye, I'd heard as much,' said the Vorstlending. 'Well you've seen a fair bit of action by the sounds of it – and that's only judging by the parts you've told me!'

The knight grinned, his eyes twinkling over his bushy black beard.

'You're... perceptive,' said Vaskrian lamely.

'An errant has to be, if he expects to live long in the wilderness,' replied Wrackwulf. 'A Northlending turns up at Graukolos squiring for a Thraxian in the company of the finest knight the White Valravyn can boast... well, there's a tale there to be sure! Not to mention the two Argolians and those strange burns you bear.'

Vaskrian touched his congealed cheek self-consciously. At least the ale did a good job of dulling the pain.

'Ach, forgive me lad,' said Wrackwulf. 'No harm intended, no offence meant! Your business is your own – all I'm after is a drinking companion for tonight.'

That caught Vaskrian off guard. 'But... why me? I'm just a squire. You've all these knights...'

'What this lot?' said Wrackwulf, motioning towards the other errants sat about the board. 'I've known these old sworders for years! You never get anything more interesting out of them than what tourneys they've fought in, what tavern wenches they've bedded, and where they'll be off to next! That's why I make an effort to learn languages besides Decorlangue – you meet so many more interesting people!'

'But... I thought knights aren't supposed to mix with squires and common folk,' said Vaskrian.

Wrackwulf snorted. 'Landless, lordless knights like us don't get treated much better,' he said. 'They aren't too bad here, but you should see what they're like in Pangonia.'

Vaskrian's heart sank. Their next destination. The last thing he needed now was the prospect of more snobbery.

'Well I'll drink with you gladly,' he said, keen to do something to raise his spirits. 'I suppose you'll be wanting to hear the parts of my story that I didn't tell.' The drink was starting to loosen his tongue.

The knight refilled both their tankards and winked at him. 'Well, some of it at least – if you can manage.'

Vaskrian paused. He knew Horskram was particular about secrecy. Having said that, Wrackwulf *was* good company, and the ale was flowing freely...

Even if he left out half of it, that still left him plenty of tales to tell.

✣ ✣ ✣

Away from the din of the night-time revel, Sir Torgun sat alone before his pavilion, idly running a whetstone up and down his sword. He had soon lost interest in the feast after Adhelina was sent away.

Adhelina. Just the thought of her name brought a tightness to his gut. The burns on his chest had not fully healed, but next to the inner pain he now bore they were nothing.

Hadn't he loved a girl called Hjala once? Or had he ever loved her at all? It was impossible to tell. He had heard that some men and women were capable of loving more than one paramour, in different ways, but Torgun felt sure he wasn't among them.

Adhelina. He wished he could be with her now, back at the castle, holding her in his arms, protecting her...

She clearly loathed the man she must marry. No wonder. Hengist was an oaf, a drunken churl who barely knew how to sit a horse. But Torgun came from a high house himself, and understood all too well the duties that entailed. He also knew the effect politicking and intrigue had on a man's honour. He could challenge the Thraxian, a man of high birth but far from home on errantry: challenge Hengist and he would depute another knight to fight in his place. And another after that, and another.

'Win or lose she'll be wed to that cur,' he snarled at his blade. Driving it into the turf Torgun raised his eyes to the uncaring heavens. 'O Luviah, thou hast speared my heart,' he cried bitterly.

For the truth was bitter. The Eorl of Graukolos would bid them leave once the tourney was done; no man in his position could afford to have three swains on his doorstep and risk wrecking a political alliance so valuable. Even Torgun understood that. His older brother Toros would do the same thing – because he had to as a lord of men.

And Wilhelm Stonefist was a lord of men.

'At least I'll get Hilmir back, Ezekiel willing,' he muttered to himself. But even as he said the words, he knew the ostensible reason for their pending duel was only half the story. His Farovian meant a lot to him and the Thraxian had behaved churlishly, but really Adhelina was the cause. He longed to see himself triumphant before her eyes, just as Braxus had been.

Then a horrible thought came to him. Was he bitter about losing?

Getting to his feet he began pacing frantically around his sword. No, that kind of sentiment went against everything he stood for! Surely he could accept one defeat after all the victories he had savoured?

But why did it have to be in front of *her*? Why couldn't he have lost any other joust? Why had the Unseen chosen here and now to test him? He knew the answer directly he had asked the question. This *was* the test.

Falling to his knees, he grasped the hilt of his sword and mouthed a prayer to Virtus.

✢ ✢ ✢

Plucking his lyre delicately, Braxus had little trouble sounding convincing as he sang *The Ballad of Lancelyn and Isoud*. An old favourite throughout the Free Kingdoms, it celebrated the great knight's love for the queen he could never wed. Troubadours and loremasters told that Isoud had been married off to the corrupt and cowardly King Markus of Thalamy, which had nearly driven Lancelyn mad.

It was a feeling Braxus was coming painfully to know: being in love with someone unobtainable was enough to drive a man to distraction. Especially when she was to be wed to a man just like King Markus.

And he *was* in love. He felt surer of that with every passing moment that pained him due to her absence. Adhelina of Dulsinor, at once so sweet and so bitter to him. He could not get her out of his mind.

'Do you know any more songs by Guillarme de Leon?' asked one knight. 'It has been an age since I was in my homeland, and I yearn for its songs!'

He was a young errant from Pangonia, less haughty and more affable than most of his countrymen. Braxus could not recall his name; he'd had a few stoops of wine.

'Certainly,' he said. 'How about Guillarme's *Lay of the Spider Queen…*'

The knight clapped enthusiastically as he broke into the staccato tune, which told the story of the eponymous villainess's demonic servants that troubled Sir Malagaunce of Triste before he slew her.

The knights applauded when he had finished. 'Guillarme's evocation of that era is impressive given that King Vasirius died more than half a hundred years before he was born,' said one of them. It was Sir Wrackwulf of Bringenheim, the lordless knight Vaskrian had befriended during the feast.

He's no fool, this one, thought Braxus. *Best to keep him close.*

'Aye, 'tis often the way,' he smiled, taking a cup of wine from a serving wench. 'The poets that tell the tales live long after the heroes they sing of! I hear it's much the same with scripture.'

Horskram frowned at that. 'I would not have you speak so lightly of the *Holy Book*,' he said.

'Why do you linger here then, to trouble us worldly men of the sword?' Braxus shot back. 'Can't you leave us in peace to carouse? Keeping an eye on your novice, I suppose!'

The adept harrumphed as he quaffed his wine. For a man who rarely drank he held it well enough. 'That is exactly what I am doing,' he conceded, prompting a blush from Adelko.

'No need Master Horskram,' he slurred. 'I'm fine.'

A few laughs showed what the assembled company thought of that statement.

There were a good few dozen of them left, scattered about the green in two or three groups of drinkers. Most of the knights serving the Lanraks and Markwards had retired to the castle, gone to seek pleasure in Merkstaed, or decided on an early night ahead of the melee preparations. The outlanders including the tourney regulars had remained at the feasting tables to drink and sing the night away.

Ordinarily Braxus would have felt elated, and had an eye for the wenches who remained to serve them. But as it was he had a feeling of trepidation.

What had he just done?

Just thrown away your advantage, he thought, answering his own question as he idly fingered an instrumental piece. *You'll get thrashed and she'll see it all.*

But what did it matter in any case? Assuming he lived they would be on their way soon, off with Horskram to Rima. After that he would take ship home, to whatever pitiful state Thraxia was in. He could only hope his father had held out against the highlanders, that the King of the Northlendings would remain good to his word and send help...

He knew that was unlikely. Freidheim was a man of honour, but he was also a king. He had to put his own realm first.

Braxus felt his spirits sink lower with every dirge-like note. A hopeless quest and a hopeless romance, his inheritance hanging by a thread and his father's disappointment to look forward to – what was the point of living?

Another knight, a scarred veteran from Thalamy, strode up and nudged him none too gently in the shoulder.

'Play something more cheerful, for Reus' sake! It feels like we're at a bloody funeral!'

Braxus glared at the grizzled errant and considered challenging him. Then he thought better of it. He'd need all his strength for his duel with Torgun.

'Alright, dammit,' he muttered, before breaking into Maegellin's *Five Fine Horses*.

✠ ✠ ✠

For the third time that afternoon, Horskram thumped his fist down on the table and swore.

'I said the third person singular present subjunctive!' he yelled. 'How in the Known World do you expect to fare in Pangonia if you speak their tongue like an illiterate peasant?'

'I speak it well enough to get by, don't I?' Adelko sniped. There was a time when he wouldn't have dared answer his mentor back. But with the heightening of his sixth sense came strange new emotions that he struggled to control. Or maybe it was just part of growing up: he had just turned fifteen summers after all.

Horskram glared at him. 'It would help if you hadn't spent half the night carousing,' he said gruffly. 'I should never have indulged you, but after the horrors of our journey...'

'Most of the nobles speak Decorlangue anyway,' Adelko persisted. 'I'll be alright.'

'And you may find yourself conversing with those less well-born,' Horskram countered. 'Fail to master its native tongue, and a foreign country will always remain a closed book, Adelko.'

He sighed and took a sip of his cows milk. Adelko followed suit reluctantly. It didn't taste the same as the goats milk he'd been raised on. Besides that his stomach felt queasy. Perhaps Horskram was right about overdoing it on the wine and ale.

Gazing longingly out of the castle window at the sunlit fields below he asked: 'Will we even be staying that long in Rima?'

'For my part, I don't know,' said Horskram. 'It all depends on what Hannequin determines our next course of action to be. As for you, I have involved you enough in this business as it is. It's high time you resumed your studies.'

Adelko's feelings upon hearing that were mixed, but not entirely unexpected. His sixth sense told him that much was in the offing. But beyond that he felt something else lay ahead... and he doubted it was a good thing.

'Your year with me is drawing to a close,' continued Horskram, staring out of the window. His mind was clearly elsewhere; probably he sensed the same as Adelko. 'You've seen far more than I ever intended. The time is coming when you must take what you have learned and channel it into the rest of your training.'

'Will I be assigned a place at Rima?' the novice asked. At least the prospect of studying at the Order's headquarters took the sting out of concluding his adventures.

'Aye, more than likely,' conceded Horskram. 'If you behave! No, you have earned that much at least.'

His mentor was looking at him now. It was the same steely blue look he had given him years ago in Narvik. Adelko was surprised to feel a tingle running down his spine.

'Am I... special in some way, Master Horskram?' He was even more surprised at his own question. It smacked of temerity, though he instinctively felt it was the right one to ask.

'Only time will tell,' was all his mentor would say on the matter. 'For now, content yourself with knowing that I deem the Grand High Monastery to be the best place to continue your tutelage.'

Horskram fell to brooding silence. That made Adelko feel only more anxious, so he pressed him for more conversation.

'It's not going to end well tomorrow is it? Between Braxus and Torgun I mean.' As if to confirm the notion, his sixth sense flared momentarily.

'I doubt it,' replied Horskram. 'But our mission to find Andragorix is done and our brave knights must needs return to their countries. Once this ridiculous business over the heiress of Dulsinor is brought to whatever bloody conclusion the Almighty wills. They both have enough problems to contend with back home, Reus knows.'

'Won't we need their protection? For the journey to Rima?'

Horskram shook his head. 'The Eorl has agreed to provide us with an armed escort as far as the borders of Westenlund after the tourney is finished. We'll take ship from the port of Westerburg to Rima. Braxus will accompany us as far as the free city, from where he'll be able to sail back to Thraxia. Torgun's route home is simplest if he retraces his steps. Of course that's assuming they're both in one piece after tomorrow's foolishness.'

'Braxus fights well, but I don't think he has much chance against a knight like Sir Torgun,' said Adelko.

'I think you're right,' sighed Horskram. 'And I wouldn't put it past Sir Torgun to detour on his way home to seek a fool's revenge on the Earth Witch for the Chequered Twins.'

Adelko felt his sixth sense flare again: he had been thinking much the same.

'I have this horrible feeling,' he said. 'Last night I saw Azrael in my dreams.'

He was half expecting his mentor to rebuke him for drinking too much wine. Instead he just stared at him.

'The Angel of Death watches all of us,' he said.

✢ ✢ ✢

Adhelina watched with a tight feeling in her chest as the knights filed back into the stalls next to the lists. The noon skies were overcast. She shifted uncomfortably in the cloying heat, the stench of bodies packed in the bleachers clogging her nostrils. Next to her Hettie sat and fidgeted. At least she seemed a bit more receptive to her surroundings; little by little, she had to hope, her friend was recovering.

To the other side sat her father, a cup of wine in one hand, the Duellers' Baton in the other. The knights took weapons from their squires as minstrels belted out a martial tune. There had been several challenges registered ahead of the duelling event. Sir Urist had thoughtfully left Torgun and Braxus last on the itinerary. High drama for the gaggle of townsfolk and peasants who had gathered to watch. More agony for her.

Once again the herald took to the podium, looking flushed as ever with drink. 'Ladies, noblemen and the rest of you ne'er do wells!' he cried. 'And today brings us to the duelling! Personal contests – for honour, for chivalry, for justice! Witness skill at arms on foot as brave knights fight hand to hand, some for love and some for blood! I hope you're ready for a spectacle...'

On and on the herald went, making a meal of it. Adhelina felt her guts twist. This was just the sort of thing Gracius and Guillarme had made their name recounting: knights fighting for love. Except this wasn't about love any more, if it ever had been. Adhelina wasn't the root cause of their animosity, but she was the catalyst: their rivalrous feelings had proved the breaking point between them, and now two knights who had fought side by side to save her would seek to kill each other in her name.

The herald called out the names of the first two combatants. Two of her father's vassals settling a land dispute, they had agreed to fight with swords to first blood. A couple of minutes saw the matter resolved: one knight was sent packing to the Marionite tent with blood streaming down his face, and several acres the poorer.

Adhelina glanced about the bleachers as the crowd called out in eager anticipation of the next bout. Her future husband was nowhere to be seen; he had been unusually temperate at the feast last night, drinking only a few stoops before sloping off with Reghar and Hangrit. His steward Albercelsus was also absent, along with the Herzog's sisters.

'Did the Lanraks decide not to grace us with their presence this afternoon?' she asked her father, without turning to look at him. 'I would have thought my betrothed would be interested to see how his rivals would fare.'

'His Grace is doubtless plotting tactics ahead of the melee,' replied her father, unsmiling. 'I think he hopes to win renown in your eyes after his dismal efforts in the joust.'

Adhelina snorted to show what she thought of that notion.

'Your other swain Agravine will also be making preparations for similar reasons, I trow. It'll be his last chance to distinguish himself in your eyes, and the last time he fights under the Markward banner.'

'Banishing him is a churlish thing to do – he is well within the Laws of Romance, as you know,' said Adhelina bitterly.

'He is in breach of loyalty to his liege is what he is,' snapped her father. 'He's lucky I've decided to keep him on till the end of the tournament. Perhaps I'll assign him to Horskram's honour guard – he can see that damned Thraxian off too.'

'I doubt Sir Braxus will be in fit condition to move after today,' put in Sir Urist. 'He is a valiant knight, but Sir Torgun is clearly the better fighter.'

'The better fighter who lost their joust,' Adhelina reminded him.

'A chance affair my lady,' said Urist. 'I doubt unorthodox tactics will avail him much in a sword bout.'

Adhelina frowned, lapsing into moody silence as her father waved the baton and got the next duel under way. She liked both her paramours for different reasons, and the thought of them hurting one another brought her little pleasure.

The next two duellists began circling each other. This was a fight in earnest, between a lordless tourney knight from Upper Thulia who had accused another errant from Pangonia of cheating at dice. The two rashed together for a while before the Pangonian caught the Vorstlending a bone-crunching mace blow to the knee just below his hauberk. The knight slumped to the ground screaming as his kneecap exploded in a shower of red and white. Adhelina winced as the Pangonian discarded his mace, pulling a poignard from his belt and driving it into his foe's neck under his aventail as he writhed in the dirt.

The next couple of bouts were for love, younger knights from the Lanrak and Markward hosts eager to prove their worth and mettle. One ended with a knight being disarmed and the second was called quits by mutual assent after both parties were too exhausted to fight on any further.

'And next, Sir Wrackwulf of Bringenheim challenges Sir Carlus of Bezantia!'

Braxus and Vaskrian shouted encouragement as Wrackwulf strode into the lists, clutching an axe in one hand and a spiked mace in the other. His Thalamian antagonist squared off against him, his scarred face glowering beneath his bascinet.

'Sir Carlus, you have accused Sir Wrackwulf of being incapable of holding a tune while under the influence of strong wine!' declaimed the herald. 'Sir Wrackwulf contests that his baritone is passing fair, to which you gave him the lie. As you have called him a liar you have slurred his honour, for which he would fain have satisfaction! Sir Carlus, do you recant your accusation?'

'I do not,' growled Carlus. 'Yon knight can scarce sing better than a castrated wolf. Therefore I say he lieth!'

'Very well, honour will be decided by the sword!' cried the herald above the ripple of laughter. 'By your leave, my lord!'

Wilhelm brought down the baton, and the knights launched themselves at one another.

Sir Carlus was a wiry man who moved like a snake, his sword darting and weaving as he probed at Wrackwulf's guard. But the burly knight moved surprisingly well for his girth, always keeping his torso out of reach while riposting sporadically. For a few minutes they continued like that, their breath coming in ragged gasps as they took turns to circle around each other.

Presently both knights disengaged, breaking off for a draft of ale to refresh themselves. The herald looked again to Wilhelm, who brought the rod down once more.

That was the moment Wrackwulf chose to take things up a notch.

Carlus fell back before the sudden onslaught, struggling to fend off alternate blows as Wrackwulf struck at him with axe and mace, his arms lethal cartwheels of steel. The Thalamian brought his heater up to parry another thunderous axe blow: this one caught it dead centre, right in the nombril point, splitting it in two. Wrackwulf swung his mace in a follow-up strike; the Thalamian brought up his sword to fend off the expected blow to the head.

But Wrackwulf wasn't aiming for his head.

His second blow smashed past the cloven pieces of Carlus' damaged heater. Adhelina supposed his gauntlet saved him from losing a hand, but the yell that exploded from the knight's lips was instructive as he staggered back in the churning soil, his shield arm hanging limply.

The Thalamian tried a desperate counter-swipe with his sword, but Wrackwulf circled agilely around him and renewed the attack. The injured knight struggled to keep up, but with one weapon against two it was only a matter of time before Wrackwulf found his way past his guard: the Thalamian screamed as the Vorstlending buried his axe in his face. Wrenching the blade free he watched calmly as Carlus fell back in a swoon, a deep cut across his nosebone crowning a torrent of blood.

'Honour has been satisfied!' declaimed the herald, as a pair of lay brothers rushed on to the field carrying a stretcher. 'Sir Wrackwulf of Bringenheim's baritone is as fine a voice as any in the Free Kingdoms!'

Wrackwulf raised both his weapons in a salute, turning to face the bleachers and grinning a snaggle-toothed grin. She could only applaud with the others. The southlander was certainly quite the showman.

The herald soon dampened her high spirits.

'And finally, Sir Torgun of Vandheim challenges Sir Braxus of Gaellen!'

The crowd erupted as Adhelina reached for her goblet. Hettie glanced nervously at her. At least the spectacle was bringing her friend back into the world of the living.

'Sir Torgun craves the opportunity to buy back his steed from his vanquisher,' said the herald, pressing on with the formalities. 'The which Sir Braxus has denied him. The Northlending knight considers this a slur upon his honour, for which he will have satisfaction! Sir Braxus, wilt thou relent and return Sir Torgun's steed to him for due recompense?'

Silence descended on the crowd as the Thraxian did not reply. As if on cue the clouds overhead rumbled, brooding giants giving birth to a summer squall.

After what seemed an age, Sir Braxus spoke.

'The Northlending is welcome to have his horse back... if he bests me in combat.'

The resulting cheer drowned out the sound of incipient rain. Adhelina drained her goblet and exchanged a fraught look with Hettie. The commoners were going to get what they had come for.

The herald looked to her father and once more Wilhelm let fall the baton.

Both knights were armed with sword and shield and dressed in hauberks, though neither had bothered with great helm, bascinet or coif. This would be as much a battle of wits and reaction as strength or sword skill – peripheral vision was paramount. Though the signal had been given, neither one moved, each daring the other to set the bout in motion.

Reaching across Adhelina found Hettie's hand and grasped it. Her friend's fingers felt reassuringly warm in her own.

⸎ ⸎ ⸎

Down in the stalls Adelko tensed as he watched the knights square off against one another. His sixth sense was jangling. But what could he do? This was mortal combat betwixt mortal men; an Argolian had little place here. He glanced at his mentor as he pulled up his cowl against the rain. Horskram sipped from his winecup, his face set grim.

The crowd let out a roar as Torgun launched himself at Braxus, breaking the stillness. The novice caught a familiar hooded figure, standing still in the midst of the raging mob. He had no time to ponder that as the clash of steel on steel cut across the pattering of rain: Sir Torgun's onslaught drove Sir Braxus to the edge of the lists before the Thraxian got in his first riposte.

The novice watched heart in mouth as Sir Braxus countered. He moved faster than Adelko had ever seen him move, his sword a grey blur as he jabbed and hacked at Torgun's guard: up, down, left and right. Three times they rashed shields together; the third time Braxus got the worst of it, staggering backwards before Torgun's superior strength. The Northlending gave him no respite, renewing the offensive with a speed and strength that could only be described as astonishing.

Adelko had hoped that the two would be more evenly matched: maybe with the rain they might wear each other down, and call a draw just like the younger knights had done. But after a few minutes it was already apparent who had the upper hand. Braxus moved as fast as any knight Adelko had seen, and was gifted with a dextrous hand and quick mind. The problem was, Torgun moved just as quickly, fought at least as well and had twice the strength of the lithe Thraxian. It was only a matter of time before he overwhelmed him.

Round the lists they went, the rain hardening as the baying of the crowd reached an ugly pitch. Again and again Torgun barged and slashed, hewing chips off Braxus' shield as the Thraxian struggled to riposte. These became less frequent as he began to tire, the mud pulling at his boots and his hauberk looking heavier by the second. Torgun seemed to have an endless store of energy; not once did the settled expression on his face change, while Braxus gasped for dear life, sweat mingling with rain as it soaked his hair.

As a last gambit the Thraxian tried a feint, pulling up his sword from Torgun's lower torso in a disengage thrust targeting his armpit. It was a lightning stroke and a clever move... but the Northlending effortlessly anticipated, reversing his own blade so it caught Braxus' sword in the hilt of his own.

With a graceful twist of his huge forearm, Sir Torgun wrenched the blade from Sir Braxus' grasp, sending it flying into the mud. With a roar Braxus tried an overhead shield barge, but Torgun knocked it aside with an outwards swipe of his own kite. The knights were too close together for a sword strike, so Torgun stepped in and slammed his sword pommel into Braxus's forehead. The Thraxian sank to his knees with a moan, blood streaming down his face as he slumped backwards to lie prone in the bubbling soil. Torgun towered over him, his face still calm as he placed a foot on the Thraxian's chest and levelled the point of his blade down towards his throat.

'And the Thraxian has been outfought, outwitted and outfooted!' cried the herald above the screaming crowd and driving rain. 'Now, will he spare his opponent, or send him packing to the halls of Azrael?'

Adelko felt his sixth sense spike as the herald mentioned the Angel of Death. It seemed to him then that Torgun had taken on the shape of the Lord of Azhoanarn, looming over his fallen foe with great black wings that blocked out the light. He'd seen those wings before...

The Thraxian tensed, waiting for the death stroke. Adelko knew from what Vaskrian had told him that his life was forfeit. He had lost a duel of honour fought in earnest; according to the Code, Torgun could kill him with impunity. Glancing at the squire he saw the anguish in his friend's face. Horskram stood rigid, a look of profound distaste etched across his aquiline features.

Torgun stood like that for several long moments, his boot resting on Braxus' heaving chest, his sword tip tickling his unarmoured throat. His face remained impassive, though his eyes seemed to burn with an unquenchable fire.

The Northlending pulled up his sword. Stepping off the Thraxian, he sheathed it.

'Honour has been satisfied,' he said. 'I reclaim my horse in lieu of ransom money. All debts between us are discharged.' Without another word the knight turned and walked towards where Hilmir stood, whickering and stamping in the stalls.

Adelko's sixth sense flared. Turning he saw Braxus hauling himself upright, discarding his shield as he pulled a dirk from his boot. His features were contorted with rage.

'Vaskrian, stop him!' he cried.

The squire was over the fence and into the lists in the blinking of an eye. Dashing through the mud he interposed himself between the knights, holding his hands aloft.

'Don't do it, Sir Braxus!' he begged.

'Get out my way, you churl!' roared the knight.

'I can't let you do it, guvnor, I'm sorry,' faltered the squire. 'He bested you in a fair fight.'

By then the element of surprise was lost in any case. Torgun had turned around, alerted by the renewed jeering of the crowd. Seeing Braxus clutching the dagger and raging at his squire, he sneered and shook his head. Without a backwards glance he exited the lists and went to tend his horse.

'All right, all right,' yelled the herald over the baying mob. 'That's your lot, you bloodthirsty scoundrels! Sir Torgun of

Vandheim bests Sir Braxus of Gaellen in single combat and spares his life! A more chivalrous knight you could not hope to find in all the Free Kingdoms! Go get yourselves another ale, and drink a toast to Sir Torgun of Vandheim. TORGUN OF VAAAAANDHEIM!'

Raucous cheers went up as the placated peasants went to feed their other coarse habits. Adelko looked at Braxus standing in the rain and mud, a stricken expression on his face. He felt a stab of pity. He could sense the Thraxian's turmoil: all his heroism of the previous days was undone, and he knew it. The dashing knight had lost the duel on every level.

It was only when the lists had been cleared and the bleachers were emptying that Adelko realised his sixth sense was still jangling.

⇀ CHAPTER XV ⇌

A State Funeral

'Mortal man's flame burneth but a short time, and is beset on all sides by the darkness of the grave...' Cyprian's crisp voice echoed about the chilly precinct of the Supreme Temple as he intoned the Last Rites.

Wolmar stared at Rodger's corpse on the gold-filigreed bier. The Royal Embalmer had done his work well, stitching up the grievous wound that had killed him during his tragic hunting accident, and the Margrave of Narbo was certainly getting a splendid funeral. Four columns of marble pillars stretched from each side of the limestone dais they stood on, one for each of the Redeemer's limbs. On the mosaic floor a richly detailed depiction of scenes from Palom's life culminating in his ultimate sacrifice at Tyrannos completed the rendition. The entire circumference of the vast chamber was crammed with alcoves covered in gold leaf, each one containing a life-size statue of every saint and avatar in the Creed. Lining the gallery above were whitestone renditions of the Unseen; all the archangels and angels who had fought alongside the Almighty in the Battle for Heaven and Earth at the Dawn of Time.

Once the sight might have put Wolmar in awe; now it just sickened him. He was bound to a servant of the King of Gehenna: the very man who stood next to him now, his hands clasped together in pious devotion. The same man whose bed he had shared last night, in a passionate clinch the temple perfects would line up to condemn as sinful.

Conflicted did not begin to describe his state of mind. Tortured would have been nearer the mark. Yet every time he went to scream out the truth, an invisible hand clasped itself around his throat, choking the words from him before he could utter them.

The Supreme Perfect completed the rite, reverentially making the sign of the Wheel. He followed suit, feeling a hypocrite. He wondered how Ivon could even set foot in a temple, never mind pretend to mourn the very man he had sacrificed to Abaddon.

He had never been a godly man, Wolmar reflected as the assembled nobles took turns to pay their last respects. He had killed, sometimes without mercy or regard to age; he had fornicated and been arrogant and slandered those he envied. Yet he had always held himself loyal to his kin, and brave in the face of danger. He had always believed that between the fury of battle and the stillness of the grave there would be time to repent one's sins, so he could seek the Afterlife with a clear conscience.

That opportunity was fading fast. He was in thrall to a man who had given up his soul to the Fallen Angel, and he would fall into darkness with him.

Unless he could work out a way to break the spell.

'He was a jovial fellow and a noble,' Sir Hugon was saying. 'He shall be sorely missed...' If the captain of the Purple Garter was at all insincere he gave no sign of it. Next to take up the thread was Sir Odo. 'He always kept the kitchens busy with demands for wine and food...' That got a chuckle: at least the Royal Seneschal was being honest. The margraves of Morvaine and Aquitania were next to speak. Their words were spare and cold; their court rivalry with Narbo was well known and there was little point in dissembling.

Then it was Ivon's turn.

Clearing his throat, he spoke softly in a fruity voice. 'He was my boon companion, my partner in crime as it were. Unto his very end we disported together...' His voice seemed to catch. 'I had more words to say, but now I find myself quite unable – oh how responsible I feel! If only I hadn't taken him hunting!' The Margrave of Vichy completed a masterful performance by sobbing into a sky blue handkerchief bordered at the hem with topaz stones.

'Peace, Vichy!' said Queen Isolte, turning in a bravura performance of her own. 'You must not blame yourself for the will of Reus!' Wolmar wondered bitterly if the words were actually being fed to her directly by Ivon. The King's wife was yet another of his thralls: how his lover had delighted in telling him so the previous night.

'Thank you, my Queen,' Ivon snuffled. 'I shall try to console myself with your kind words.'

While she consoles herself with the thought that you haven't told her husband about her affair with Sir Hugon yet, thought Wolmar dryly. Now that his silence was ensured with sorcery, the Margrave seemed to delight in telling him of his plans. Queen Isolte had been brokering an alliance with the King of Thalamy, who also harboured ambitions in Vorstlund.

While Ivon simpered on, Wolmar's mind drifted back to that morning in his suite at the palace.

✣ ✣ ✣

It had been sunny, light streaming in through the high arched window of Ivon's bedchamber. The Margrave had arisen early to dress, summoning his valet Gasper to help him select an outfit for the funeral.

'What do you think of this bliaud?' he asked, turning so Wolmar could see the finely ornamented white gown. It was studded with sapphires and moonstones, though the cut seemed strange for a man to wear.

'You look like you're about to take holy orders at a rich temple,' said the princeling acidly. 'What do you care for my opinion anyway?' he added sullenly. Witnessing Rodger's sacrifice and the realisation that his paramour was a warlock had diminished his feelings of adoration, though he still found it hard to refuse him anything.

The Margrave pouted. 'Of course I still value your opinion... Just as long as it doesn't conflict with my plans for domination of the Free Kingdoms.'

He laughed as Wolmar started. 'Oh don't worry about Gasper, he's deaf as a quintain post, poor thing.' Ivon motioned for the valet to remove the item of clothing. 'It's a funeral not a pleasure trip,' he continued. 'One should look somewhat... religious for a service in the seat of our Holy Mother Temple should one not?'

'I wonder a dastard like you is able to stand a place of holy sanctuary,' said Wolmar, his lip curling.

'Ah, found our piety have we?' said the Margrave, slipping out of the bliaud. 'Well as it happens, a trip to the temple *does* sicken me. But the King of Gehenna rewards his faithful servants with fortitude beyond reckoning.'

Wolmar lay back on the four-poster bed, gazing up at the canopy in despair. Never in his worst nightmares had he expected to come to this. A death on the battlefield held no fears for him, but this...

'Ye Almighty, why don't you just kill me and have done with it?' he said desperately.

'And waste all that vigour and potential?' said Ivon, running a lascivious tongue across his lips as he stepped into a black brocade cainsil with dagged sleeves picked out in purple. 'Ah now that's *much* better,' he said, turning to survey his reflection in the body-length silver mirror. 'Yes, it bespeaks of solemnity and sorrow, with just a hint of appropriate piety,' he said, nodding at Gasper to show his approval. 'Now I think the dark blue chausses will go well with that...' He pointed at the pantaloons hanging on the wooden rack.

'Kill you? Oh no,' he continued. 'You, my dear Wolmar, are going to taste glory on the battlefield for many years to come. As one of my marshals you shall help me to consolidate the new world order.'

'One of demonolatry and sacrifice such as you had me witness the other night?' snarled the princeling. He had scarcely liked Rodger, but no man deserved that.

'The Master's teachings are not for the faint of heart,' said Ivon, a hint of steel entering his voice as he stepped into the chausses and allowed Gasper to belt a girdle around the pantaloons and cainsil. 'In any case, first things first. Vorstlund must be conquered, then the King must be deposed and his children disposed of. After that I will assume the throne with the support of the nobles who've agreed to back me in return for... certain concessions. So there'll be plenty of fighting to be done.'

Wolmar got up and helped himself to watered wine from a silver ewer. 'I can hardly wait,' he said, wishing the wine were undiluted.

The Margrave favoured him with a frustrated moue. 'Oh do *try* to sound excited,' he said. 'I would have thought you'd be delighted at the prospect of slaughtering enemies and looting castles to your heart's content!'

'Not against my own free will,' spat Wolmar. 'And not at risk of perdition of my soul!' Knocking back the contents of the goblet he slammed it down on the mahogany table.

'Oh my, but you really are quite the pious one,' sighed Ivon. 'Who'd have known? I could always send you off on crusade with Lord Uthor and the southern nobles. Though I'd really prefer to keep you – '

'I want to fight for my country!' yelled Wolmar. 'I'm a knight of the White Valravyn, sworn to protect Northalde! That means something!' He had rediscovered his loyalty in the past few days, though that wasn't enough to break the enchantment.

'I'm afraid that won't be possible,' said Ivon, his face darkening. 'You are bound to a much larger fate now. The old kings and their countries won't exist for much longer – the sooner you accept that the easier it will go for you.'

Picking up the goblet Wolmar hurled it across the room in frustrated rage. It rang loudly off a sconce on the far wall. Gasper went on with his work, oblivious, helping the Margrave into a black pair of pointed shoes fashioned of deerskin leather.

'And I think this chapperon will go well...' Ivon motioned towards the black velvet cape, worked with agates set in bizarre swirling patterns. 'Our Sassanian friends certainly know their gemwork,' he added approvingly as his valet fastened it around his neck. 'You know you really mustn't throw temper tantrums, Wolmar darling – what will our neighbouring guests think? Now... Ah, yes, perfect... What think you, my sweet prince?'

'I think you look like a Left-Hand magician hell bent on taking over the Known World,' said Wolmar sarcastically.

He wasn't entirely surprised when Ivon burst into laughter. 'How very sardonic of you,' purred the Margrave. 'Why yes, so I do! And all this time, right under their noses – the dolts never suspecting until it's too late...'

He turned from the mirror to look at Wolmar. A crooked smile played across his lips, an expression halfway between lust and triumph on his face.

'Now, I think it's time we dressed you, my sweetling. Come here, I've the perfect doublet and breeches for you...'

⁜ ⁜ ⁜

Wolmar felt Ivon nudging him in the elbow, bringing him back to the echoing temple. It was his turn to speak. All the other nobles including Aravin and Kaye had had their say. Wolmar cleared his throat, conscious of his thickly accented Decorlangue as he said: 'I knew him but short time. He made me feel welcome as a lord of men should. May his soul rest in peace.'

Aravin and Kaye looked at each other and smirked. The King was last to speak, in accordance with custom.

'He served the Ruling House of Ambelin well and loyally, as his ancestors have done since the days of the Fourth Royal War. House Oraunt of Narbo has lost a faithful scion.'

Carolus nodded at Cyprian, who made the sign again. Everyone followed suit. Glancing sidelong at Ivon, Wolmar caught his hand as he brought it down to his chest. The fingers were curled rather than splayed in the proper sign of devotion. He didn't have time to see if Aravin and Kaye had done the same.

Nor Morvaine come to that... he was part of the planned invasion of Vorstlund, but was he part of Ivon's coup plot? And if so, did he know who Ivon really served? Vichy's scheming seemed to operate on a multitude of levels.

Pallbearers dressed in gowns of white samite covered with red scapulars took up the bier, taking it from the dais down marble steps towards the red carpeted walkway leading back to the temple entrance. Courtiers lined the aisles flanking the nave, throwing white roses down as the pallbearers passed. The household of Ambelin followed solemnly.

The Knights of the Purple Garter were standing outside, flanking the temple gates. They drew their swords in a formal salute as the pallbearers passed by, slowly descending broad stairs that perambulated the temple in ever increasing circles down to the flagstoned plaza of Temple Square below. There the common folk of Rima had gathered to watch the procession.

All this for a fat oaf who could barely couch a lance, thought Wolmar as they descended the sun-drenched stairs. *Perhaps Ivon has a point about sweeping away the old order.*

Glancing sidelong at his lover he noticed how pale and drawn he was. Perhaps the King of Gehenna's fortitude only went so far.

Temple Square was set atop the southernmost of the five hills surrounding Rima; the procession would take them through the heart of the city to Regus Square on the other side of it where the Palace of White Towers was. There Lord Rodger's body would be laid in waiting for collection by a retinue from Narbo, who would bear it back to his ancestral seat in Castle Beaumure.

As they passed along the Way of Kings, Rima's main thoroughfare, Wolmar picked up more than a few discontented jeers from the townsfolk lining the street. Guards prevented anyone from approaching, but some of the freemen were even daring to shout.

'What's that all about?' he whispered to Ivon, feeling his bare knowledge of Panglian again.

'They're protesting the King's latest raft of taxes,' Ivon whispered back. 'Wait until they see what he plans to spend them on! The commoners won't benefit much from a war, but it'll keep his nobles and the rich merchant houses happy.'

'Merchants?'

'Oh yes... Somebody has to provide supplies for an invading army. The merchants will be only too happy to take the King's coin.'

'And then the King recompenses the nobles he's taxed after taking Vorstlund, by giving them new lands. Keeps the knights and lords in check, which ensures the common folk don't make any trouble.'

'You understand perfectly,' purred Ivon. 'Not for nothing are you a prince's son! But this will be only the beginning – our pending war with the Vorstlendings is but one exchange of Jedrez pieces, as it were.'

Wolmar felt the sweat pouring down his back in the high summer heat. He noticed the colour had returned to Ivon's face. It was drawing towards Gildmonath – or Aotus as they called it down south – and he could smell the stink of townsfolk as they clogged the meaner mudcaked streets leading off the Way of Kings. The white stuccoed buildings reflected the scorching sun with a blinding glare.

'What about the Thalamians? Do they know about your plans?'

'The King of Thalamy is proving... most amenable,' replied Ivon. 'He'll agree to the invasion of Vorstlund, have no fear of that. The lovely Isolte is our point of contact there – having her in Sir Hugon's bed will also help us to keep the Purple Garter on side once the thing is done.'

'Well you've thought of everything, haven't you?' said Wolmar.

'One does try,' replied Ivon smugly.

They were drawing towards Trader's Circle. The main public arena of Rima, of a size with Regus Square, it was crammed with market stalls festooned with brightly coloured awnings and street hawkers loudly proclaiming their wares.

'And what about... the stones?' Wolmar asked, keeping his voice low. Even now he hoped to fish some vital information from the Margrave, something he could take back to his King in Northalde. Should he ever chance to escape.

'Oh ho!' said the Margrave, smiling thinly. 'So that's what you're after! You let me worry about such things, Wolmar, they are not to be trifled with by the unversed... What think you of our splendid city? Is it not a proud testament to the Chivalrous King's legacy?'

'I thought King Vasirius was humble, as befits a true knight,' Wolmar shot back, irritated at being caught out. 'Hard to believe a city could become so splendid in such a short space of time.'

Ivon chuckled. 'Ah, so that's your line of attack!' he said. 'Well, yes, Strongholm is the more ancient capital of the two... But not the more ancient city, I'm afraid.'

Wolmar looked at him quizzically.

'Rima was expanded by Vasirius into its present magnificent form, but it existed long before him, and Strongholm for that matter. It was founded by the Ancient Thalamians as a base for their Iron Legions, after they conquered Upper Vallia.'

'Upper Vallia?'

'The name given to what are now the northern provinces of Pangonia. From there the Thalamians launched their next campaign, conquering Lower Vallia to the south. After that it was only a matter of time before they took Occitania, which today comprises the western margravates.'

'Yes, yes, and so three kingdoms became one,' said Wolmar impatiently. 'It was the same with Northalde, and all the rest of the Free Kingdoms – go back five hundred years and most of them were fragmented just like Vorstlund.'

'Indeed, my sweet prince, but I think you are missing the point,' said Ivon. 'So three petty kingdoms become united under the Imperial Banner of Ancient Thalamy, only to fall again to petty squabbling after the collapse of that empire... A few centuries pass, and eventually the three kingdoms become one again, this time under the Ruling House of Rius and King Lotharion the Unifier. Thus was born the Kingdom of Pangonia. And yet... still we fall short of the Thalamian Empire – we are but one kingdom of six, if you count Vorstlund. And that's before we even get on to the rest of Urovia, or Sassania for that matter.'

Wolmar glanced sidelong at him. They were in the thick of Trader's Circle now. The deafening clamour enveloped them as the crescent knights, now mounted on jet black destriers, fell in to either side of the procession.

'What is your point?' he asked, risking raising his voice slightly to be heard above the din.

'My point, darling Wolmar, is that we of the Silver Age still lag far behind our Golden Age forebears. Save perhaps for our imperial cousins beyond the Great White Mountains, we lack consolidation. At its peak the Thalamian Empire comprised half the Free Kingdoms, much of northern Sassania, and the lower half of the Urovian New Empire... Now that is consolidation!'

Ivon slammed his fist into his hand to demonstrate his point. They were walking two abreast so no one else saw him do it.

'And you're saying we need to consolidate, to get to where our ancestors were?'

'My dear Wolmar, I am saying we need to get to where our ancestors were *and beyond*. You have heard tales no doubt of a Platinum Age, when the sorcerer-kings of Seneca ruled the Known World?'

'I've heard enough to know that they were blasphemous and rightly punished for their iniquity.' *As you will be*, he added silently.

The Margrave laughed. 'You are so righteous today! But yes, you are correct in a manner of speaking... Though some have foretold a second coming, when the true master of the world shall return to rule his birthright.'

Wolmar felt a chill go down his spine. It contrasted oddly with the sweltering heat as they pushed from Trader's Circle back on to the Way of Kings.

'You really mean to do it, don't you?' he asked, looking beyond the knights and soldiers at the common townsfolk and envying their ignorance. 'You think the entire Known World can be ruled under one banner.'

'Why not?' said Ivon. 'It has been done before. And we shall have plenty of aid, never fear!'

The Margrave patted him gently on the shoulder as they began to ascend the hill towards the palace. A sharp sound suddenly rang out above the hubbub. Glancing back at Trader's Circle, Wolmar caught sight of an ironmonger loudly clattering pots together as he tried to make a sale.

And that was when the idea hit him.

⇢ CHAPTER XVI ⇤

When Houses Clash

'I've put another dose of Linfrick's Node on and mixed it with some Vella's Kiss,' said Adhelina as she finished winding on the fresh bandage. 'You're young and strong and you're healing up nicely. Your shoulder and your ribs have fully mended too – you should be thankful, Vaskrian. I've seen good knights die of less.'

The squire felt a pang of youthful longing as the heiress of Dulsinor caught him in her green eyes. He suppressed the desire immediately. That was the last thing the present situation needed – a lusty squire in the mix. But then, what red-blooded male wouldn't conceive a liking for the gorgeous Vorstlending noblewoman? Not that she'd ever look at him that way, he reflected bitterly.

'Thank you ma'am,' he managed to mumble. Despite the poultice his arm still ached as he awkwardly pulled on his jerkin. A Marionite lay brother helped him; the monks in the tent were busy tending the latest raft of injured knights. Sir Carlus was still groaning pitifully after they had been forced to amputate his nose. At least Wrackwulf's blow had left him alive: the Thalamian's bascinet must have caught part of the axe blade, reducing the impact and saving his life.

'You didn't have to help me,' Vaskrian added, doing his best to sound gallant. 'I mean, with all your troubles recently...' His voice trailed off and he flushed, suddenly feeling foolish.

Adhelina smiled. 'Think nothing of it, Vaskrian of Gaellen,' she said, refastening the sling around his arm. 'It does me good to get out of the castle confines. And besides, I have my chaperon right here to keep an eye on me.'

She motioned ruefully towards where Sir Ruttgur stood at the entrance to the tent, ready to escort her back to the castle. 'Though no doubt I'll be needed back here before long – the melee is by far the most injury-laden event of a tourney.'

'No need to remind me of that!' grinned Vaskrian. 'At least they'll be fighting for love, though a blunted blade can still do a tidy bit of damage.'

'Now you're telling me something I already know,' said Adhelina, grinning back at him. 'Well, you'd better get back to your master.'

'Of course,' said Vaskrian, getting off the wooden bench. 'What shall I tell him...?' His voice trailed off again.

Adhelina frowned, gazing out of the tent at the light drizzle. The squall of two days ago had not cleared the skies, and the camp now sweltered in a muggy heat as it went about its business.

'Just tell him to take care of himself for now,' she said after a few moments. 'I understand why he did what he did... I just need some time, that's all.'

She shook her head as if to clear it, then looked at the squire with sad eyes. 'Oh Vaskrian, why fool ourselves?' she said. 'After the melee is finished three days hence my father will send all of you packing.' She sighed. 'It was never meant to be, I'm just a pawn in a Jedrez game.'

Darting forwards she impulsively kissed him on his unburnt cheek, making it flush even deeper. 'Give him that, from me. I doubt we'll see much of each other after the tourney's over.'

Lifting her skirts she turned and left with Sir Ruttgur.

Vaskrian watched her go with mixed emotions. Was she more relieved than anything else? Perhaps having three brave knights for paramours was too much to handle.

What did it concern him one way or another, he wondered as he stepped out into the rain. He was just a squire to a dejected liege, his fate fixed by the words of a woods witch.

✢ ✢ ✢

His dejected liege hadn't budged an inch. He was sat in the porch of their pavilion, moodily swigging from the wineskin Vaskrian had purchased for him that morning.

'Adhelina sends you... a kiss,' he began awkwardly. He thought he knew what Adhelina wanted him to say, but how to say it?

'That's nice,' Braxus deadpanned, staring into the hardening rain. 'The heiress of Dulsinor and Stornelund is kind-hearted to take pity on dishonoured knights.'

'It's not as bad as all that,' ventured the squire, stepping into the porch and sitting down next to his guvnor. 'You're still champion of the joust, no one can take that away from you.' *It's an honour I'd give anything for you ungrateful sot*, he added mentally.

'Ah but in the chivalry game, you're only as good as your last result,' said the Thraxian bitterly. 'Anyway, it's all irrelevant isn't it? That's what she wants you to tell me.'

Vaskrian's eyes found the grass. 'More or less I think, sire. Her marriage is inevitable. The Eorl's keeping us here only out of courtesy, if I'm any judge. Once the melee's done he means to banish us. Torgun and Agravine too.'

Braxus nodded and took another slug. 'I thought as much. Well let's not linger any longer than we have to! When does Friar Horskram leave? We'll go with him as far as Port Westerburg. From there we'll take ship back to Thraxia.'

Vaskrian nodded. He had been expecting this. 'I spoke to Adelko last night, sire – he says Horskram will wait till the end of the tourney. The Eorl's promised him an honour guard as far as the border of Westenlund – the lands between here and there aren't too safe.'

Time was when that would have thrilled him – the prospect of more skirmishing. As it was he just felt flat and weary. Not that he could fight worth a tinker's damn with his arm all trussed up anyway, Adhelina had said to give it another fortnight of rest before using it again.

Braxus must have read his thoughts. 'Very well, we'll wait it out until the tournament's done,' he said glumly. 'I don't reckon on our chances against roving robber knights or brigands with you crippled and no one else besides Horskram and myself who can fight. Anyway, another few days will give me time to recover.'

Vaskrian stared after him quizzically as the knight rose and stumbled back into the tent. 'But you don't have any recent injuries apart from the cut to your head, and that's not too serious.'

Braxus laughed bitterly as he threw himself down on his pallet. 'That isn't the kind of recovery I was talking about.' He waved his squire away with the wineskin. 'Go and find something else to do,' he said. 'I release you from your duties today. I want to drink, alone.'

That was all the encouragement Vaskrian needed. Seizing up his cloak, he threw it around himself and stepped back out into the rain. Let his guvnor sulk into his wine, if that was his will. The ale tent for the commoners should be open – that would have to do for now. Trudging through the muddy camp, he reflected that perhaps the Earth Witch's prophecy wasn't such a terrible blow after all. It seemed that all the knights he knew ended up dead or miserable.

✣ ✣ ✣

The sun was peering out from behind the clouds as Adelko made his way down from Graukolos towards Merkstaed. His limbs ached. Horskram had finished their morning lessons in Panglian with the surprise and unwelcome announcement that they would spend the afternoon working on combat technique.

The novice could understand why. Leagues of lawless terrain lay between them and Westerburg, it made sense to focus on his fighting skills. At least training with Horskram wasn't as torturous as it had been under Udo back at Ulfang – the adept seemed far more patient with him, saving his jibes for their more cerebral exercises.

'Your quarterstaff technique is passable, but you'll really need to develop your footwork at Rima,' was all he had said after an exhausting two hours in the middle ward. No knights were in the training ground with them, having deserted the castle for the battlefield marked out for the melee.

Adelko could see it as he followed the path into town. Each camp to either side of it centred on a ring of trestle tables: feasting and plotting seemed to happen concurrently. Perhaps strong ale helped one dream up more devilish battle tactics, Adelko reflected wryly. Looking at the rival swarms of armoured knights and their squires, smiths and cooks, he wondered at the ways of mortal men. He still couldn't get his head around it. A mock battle, fought for *fun*. Or to keep one's skills sharp, if Vaskrian was to be believed... Adelko just hoped it wouldn't be as horrid as a real war. At least they'd be fighting with blunted weapons, or so the squire had assured him.

It was Vaskrian he hoped to find. He'd probably be at the ale tent in the main camp with the commoners – outlanders wouldn't be allowed into the melee field as they weren't taking part. As he skirted the bustling town towards the bridge crossing the Graufluss he wondered about his sparring bout with Horskram. He had half expected to see the adept pull off the same series of dazzling moves he had used against Andragorix, but no: the older monk's fighting had been sure and steady, nothing to dismiss but nothing like what he had seen. Adelko had felt his confidence growing during their practice – curious, considering he'd improved very little during their journey. But for all his amateurishness, he had felt an assurance that hadn't been there before. As though progress were *possible*.

A gaggle of commoners was already thronging the green before the ale tent when he arrived. Pushing himself through the reeking crowd, he spied Vaskrian and was just making his way over to him when he felt a hand tugging at his sleeve.

He whirled, mentally cursing the lazy impulse that had impelled him to leave his quarterstaff in his room when he'd gone to eat in the castle kitchens. He tensed – then relaxed as he recognised the tanned foreign face peering at him beneath a hood.

'Anupe!' he said. 'What are you doing here? I thought I saw you in the crowd two days ago – but shouldn't you be...?'

The Harijan grinned, raising a finger to her lips as she drew him gently to one side, away from the throng. 'Banished? Yes, this is true. I think soon I will not be the only one, yes?' She glanced sidelong at where Vaskrian was gesticulating with his tankard and talking animatedly to a serving wench. He seemed well in his cups.

'I think the Eorl means to send us all far away once the melee's done,' Adelko confessed. 'But why are you still here?'

'Ah, why indeed?' replied Anupe, shaking her head as if baffled by that herself. 'In my land we are not used to seeing women treated so... I think Adhelina of Dulsinor deserves a better fate.'

Adelko's eyes widened. 'You don't seriously mean...?'

'Listen,' persisted Anupe. 'She is the closest thing to a strong woman I have seen in this cursed country. I will not see her married to that... buffoon. You are friendly with the squire. Get him to talk to his master. And talk to the other knight. They both love her, and will do anything to help. We must arrange to meet, all of us, to make a plan to rescue her.'

'Why me?' asked Adelko. 'Why not ask them yourself?'

Anupe paused to look at him, a twinkle in her eye. 'People *like* you, Adelko of Narvik,' she said. 'I am not sure why, but they do. They will listen to you. Now, go and talk to the squire, and find the other knight. Meet me here at sunset and tell me what you have arranged.'

'Why should I help you?' asked Adelko uncertainly. 'The business of the Markwards is none of ours and Master Horskram is already furious enough with you as it is. If he finds out I've been – '

'You will do it because you are *good*, Adelko of Narvik. Kyra said she sensed much goodness in you...' A spasm of pain crossed the Harijan's face. 'You will do the right thing, of this I am sure.'

Without another word Anupe loped off between the tents, leaving Adelko to ponder her words. Suppressing a sigh he turned back towards Vaskrian, who seemed to be making headway with his wench despite being crippled and scarred.

The squire was going to absolutely *love* this one.

✠ ✠ ✠

'It might just work.' Sir Braxus frowned at the makeshift plan of attack they had mocked up in his tent. 'With most of the Eorl's knights in the field or watching and the rest off tourneying elsewhere, he should only have a few soldiers standing guard. If we act swiftly we can overpower them and be gone with the damsels right soon. They won't have a chance to react.'

Sir Torgun frowned. His rugged face looked deeply troubled. 'I like not this plan,' he said. 'It smacks of dishonour to whisk a high lord's daughter away like this.'

'And yet here you are, in my pavilion, discussing it,' said Braxus. 'I note my squire did not spend over long persuading you join us.'

Vaskrian winced inwardly as Torgun favoured his guvnor with a sour sneer. 'After your conduct in the lists, I wouldn't expect you to have any scruples,' he said. 'I fought by your side in the Argael and beyond, but now I see you and I are cut from different cloths.'

Anupe glanced quizzically at Adelko, who quickly translated from Northlending to Vorstlending so she could understand. Braxus and Torgun fell to bickering in Decorlangue as he did.

It made the squire's head hurt. This was degenerating into a babbling mess and no mistake. But that's what came of taking up with foreigners and going abroad, he supposed.

The Harijan shouted them all down, pointing at the crude map of the area she had sketched on a scrap of vellum. Adelko translated for her so everyone could understand.

'She says she's done a scout of the perimeter. The battlefield is actually a series of wooded dells that slope down to form a natural basin of open fields. The Lanraks are camped over the far side, but the Markwards are at the near end here... That's where the Eorl and his daughter will be. Anupe saw servants putting up a large awning this afternoon so they can watch the fight in the shade.'

Anupe pointed to the edge of the fields and went on speaking. 'If we hide our horses ready and saddled here beyond this copse of trees,' said Adelko, translating, 'that's only a short distance from where the Eorl and his retinue will be. Ride swiftly and you'll be on them before they know what's hit them.'

'I'm not killing the guards,' said Torgun. 'Loyal men don't deserve to be butchered.'

'You don't have to kill them,' translated Adelko. 'Just ride them down or incapacitate them. The main thing is to get Adhelina and Hettie back to the copse. Vaskrian will have horses ready for them to mount and you can all beat a retreat.'

'This plan may just about be feasible, but it's still insane,' said Braxus. 'We'll have two companies of knights on our backs from here to Westenlund.'

'I doubt they'll pursue us far into Upper Thulia,' put in Torgun. 'An armed escort is one thing, but the Eorl of those lands would consider two armies crossing into his territory as an act of war.'

'Good point,' allowed Braxus grudgingly. 'Well I still think it's madness, but a brave knight will do anything for love!'

A fey light was in his eyes. Vaskrian knew all too well how desperate his master was to redeem himself in Adhelina's eyes. Not to mention creating a chance for those same eyes to see him again after the melee was done.

But Torgun shook his head. 'I love Adhelina as much as you, but to do this to a nobleman who has treated us as honoured guests...'

Vaskrian had to feel for his hero. Despite his loyalty to Sir Braxus, he couldn't deny Sir Torgun was the better knight. But love was love, as the troubadours liked to sing.

The Northlending stepped away towards the tent entrance, peering out into the balmy night. Sounds of revelry filtered through the turgid air. The celebrations were at their most frenzied in the run-up to the melee, and Vorstlendings drank copiously by anyone's standards.

'All right,' said Torgun, turning around at last. Vaskrian could see anguish written across his face in an ugly hand. 'But only on condition that none of the Eorl's men or his retinue are seriously harmed.'

'Agreed,' said Braxus. Anupe nodded at Adelko to indicate her assent.

'Well I'd better be getting back,' said the novice nervously. 'Horskram will be wondering where I've got to.'

'Here,' said Braxus, tossing him his wineskin. 'Take a few mouthfuls, flush that fresh face of yours. That way he won't get suspicious.'

Adelko nodded and took a few swigs. Braxus eyed him keenly. 'You think Horskram will throw his lot in with us?' he asked Adelko. 'For old times' sake, as it were.'

Adelko shook his head sadly as he passed the wineskin to Vaskrian. 'I doubt it,' he said. 'We won't be joining you. Not unless we catch up with you, but you won't want to see us then. Chances are we'll be riding with the knights the Eorl sends after you.'

Braxus laughed at that. 'Of course! For security on the roads. Well, thank you for your help, Adelko of Narvik, and I wish you well. It has been emotional.'

'There's another couple of days left before the melee,' said Adelko. 'Hopefully I'll get a chance to drink a stoop with you before then.'

Torgun shook his head. 'That cannot be,' he said. 'If this plan is to work, we must to all intents and purposes be gone from Graukolos tomorrow, before dawn. We can lie in wait in yon copse of trees – they'll provide us with cover so we can't be seen from the castle.'

Vaskrian felt a stab of sorrow as Adelko bade them farewell. Fate had kept them on the road together for so many weeks, but now it looked as though they would finally be parted.

'So long, Adelko,' he said as he took his young friend in an awkward one-armed embrace just outside the tent. 'I kept you safe on the road, just like the Earth Witch said, eh? But I suppose you're getting tough enough to look after yourself nowadays. Besides, you'll have the Eorl's knights for protection.'

'If they aren't too busy tearing up the highway after you,' replied the novice glumly. 'Look after yourself, Vaskrian.' He paused, then added: 'And don't set too much by the words of a sorceress either. Prophecies can be misleading.'

Something in the self-assured way he said that caught Vaskrian's attention. 'How did you know I was thinking about...?'

Adelko shrugged. 'I just know things sometimes,' he replied. Then his face grew serious again. 'This idea of Anupe's, I know she means well but...'

'... it's going to get us into trouble,' the squire finished for him. 'I know – I don't need your special sense or whatever you call it to fathom that much. Don't worry, I'll look after these crazy bluebloods – I mean prophecy or no it's what I do, right?'

The novice nodded and smiled, then pulled up his cowl and stepped from the porch. Another light drizzle had begun to fall. A brief wave and he was off, trudging through tents back towards the castle.

Vaskrian sighed as he watched him go. Curious goggle-eyed fellow – unlike any youth he'd ever known. Strange how he missed him already.

✣ ✣ ✣

'I've missed the boat for Linden,' said Wrackwulf, scratching his bushy black beard. 'Took me longer than I thought to sell on the armour and horses I won. I'll never make the entry signing now.'

Vaskrian eyed him quizzically. 'Didn't the knights you bested want to buy them back?'

'Nay,' replied the Vorstlending. 'One of them lost most of his coin at dice, another was too poor to buy his harness back. Had to go into town and sell the horses at Merkstaed. Managed to flog the hauberks to a smithy, but a wretched price I had for them! Got well and truly swyved!'

Vaskrian made a sympathetic noise and took another slug on his tankard. They were drinking outside the beer tent. There were still plenty of commoners and poorer knights out roistering, despite the lateness of the hour.

'So where will you go next?' asked the squire. He liked drinking with Sir Wrackwulf – he was the one cheerful knight he knew, now that the Chequered Twins were dead. And making small talk helped to take his mind off their mad rescue attempt.

'Think I'll head to Dunkelsicht – the Eorl of Upper Thulia holds a tourney there on the 1st of every Gildmonath. It's not so far from here – a few of the other freelancers are heading that way. The Blattholt isn't too safe nowadays, but let's see how our highwaymen friends fare against a party of knights!'

Vaskrian murmured his assent, dissembling nervously.

Wrackwulf patted his bulging money pouch contentedly. 'Well it's been a good tourneying season so far,' he said. 'I've a fair purse of regums and marks to show for it, despite that coxcomb of a smith doing his best to bugger me like a catamite! A pity you and your friends insist on leaving so early tomorrow – it would have been nice to ride with you. But then I expect we'll catch up with you on the road!'

'Aye,' said Vaskrian, feeling his nerves tighten. 'Chances are my guvnor will want to enter the same tourney.' It was a hasty cover story they had prepared – plenty of foreigners could be found doing the tourney rounds in summertime.

'See that he does!' said Wrackwulf. 'I'd welcome the chance to have a crack at him in the lists – see if I can't get one over on the champion of Graufluss!'

'So... you still think him worthy? After his duel against Sir Torgun I mean?'

The burly knight shrugged. 'Of course, he fights well enough doesn't he? I've been on the circuit long enough to know the Code of Chivalry goes out the window when a knight's blood is up. We can't be perfect gentlemen all the time.'

'Try telling that to Sir Torgun,' said Vaskrian.

'Well, perhaps he hasn't been challenged enough yet – I wouldn't mind another crack at him either, if he comes to Dunkelsicht!'

'Perhaps he will,' mumbled Vaskrian. He hated all this lying. Wrackwulf seemed an ingenuous fellow; besides that, good squires were supposed to be honest.

Wrackwulf took another slug of ale. 'At any rate, I look forward to another chance to sing with Sir Braxus – plays a passing fine lyre, that one.'

For the second time, Vaskrian was forced to dissimulate. Wrackwulf's singing voice wasn't as bad as Sir Carlus had claimed, but he'd heard better. Draining his flagon he motioned towards the counter. 'Fancy another?' He couldn't get too drunk the day before their rescue attempt – but he also had to keep up appearances for the plan to work. And the Vorstlendings didn't half brew a good drop of ale.

'Aye, why not?' beamed the freelancer. 'Not as if we have to worry about getting any work done tomorrow, eh?'

Vaskrian muttered something in the affirmative before turning quickly to order another round.

✢ ✢ ✢

Hettie woke to a soft touch on her shoulder. One of the Marionite brothers was there, as always, proffering her a cup of tea infused with St Elenya's Root. Sitting up in bed she sipped the bitter brew.

At least her sleep had not been disturbed by nightmares, she reflected gratefully as she blinked herself into full wakefulness. That was the second or third night running her hideous dreams had subsided. Perhaps Adhelina was right and the tournament spectacle was doing her some good. It was violent – but at least it was a familiar kind of violence. Not like the white-faced horrors who had come so close to dishonouring them both. For the umpteenth time, she shuddered at the thought.

The Marionite bowed and withdrew from her room. She did not know his name and the brothers seldom spoke if at all. By virtue of her high status she had been given a cramped little cell to herself; most of the other patients were housed together in the main infirmary. Brother Aethelwold, the Abbot and the only monk whose name she knew, made sure she mingled with the other patients in the herb garden daily. Keeping company with others and the sunlight were good for her melancholy, he insisted.

And she got precious little sun in her chamber. Only a narrow slit high up in the wall permitted any light, and she shivered in the cold dawn as she pulled herself out of bed and dressed. Taking up the cup she drained it before heading over to the refectory.

This was a long low oblong room, dimly lit by more slits. There were two rows of trestle tables: one for the lay brothers and patients and another for the ordained monks. Sitting down to a simple breakfast of gruel and weak wine, she reflected for the thousandth time on the course of events that had brought her here.

There were things she had seen that she would never be able to confront. She had realised that much, tossing and turning in her bed at night as she relived their captivity in the darkness of the Wytching Hour. The spectacle of a woman, her distended belly splitting apart, her pitiful shrieks drowning out the wailing of the newborn monstrosity her captors had forced upon her... Thank Reus the beastmen had seen fit to do their ravishing elsewhere, she felt sure such a spectacle would have driven her mad.

She started as she felt another touch on her shoulder. She was clutching her spoon tightly, revulsion spilling from her with every ragged breath. Her bowl lay upended on the table before her, its contents spilling onto the stone floor. Several of the other patients and lay brothers sitting near her had moved up the benches away from her.

She looked up into the kindly bearded face of Prior Aethelwold.

'All is well Hettie,' he said softly. 'Come with me to the gardens. Some fresh air will do you good.'

Presently they were sitting on a stone bench. Hettie stared at the chrysanthemums and dandelions and tried to soak up some of the calmness emitted by the bushes and shrubs and trees. Sat next to her Aethelwold looked at her sympathetically. Her hand was in his; the celibate septuagenarian could take such a liberty without seeming inappropriate. Hettie trusted him.

'You may not be capable of believing this right now, but your condition is improving,' he said, fixing her with his soft grey eyes. 'In a week's time I shall discharge you from our care. It is time you went back to your life, Hettie Freihertz.'

'What life?' asked Hettie sorrowfully. 'Even if I do recover, I doubt Wilhelm will want me back, not after I helped milady to...' Her voice trailed off. Even now she couldn't bear to recount their misadventures.

Fortunately the Abbot knew all too well what had transpired. Not even the recondite monks could have missed the biggest story in town for a generation.

'The Stonefist is a more forgiving man than his epithet suggests,' he said. 'And your lifelong companionship with Adhelina will not count for nothing, even now.' He placed another gentle hand on her shoulder and turned her slowly to look at him. 'Hettie, you are stronger than you give yourself credit for,' he said, his voice becoming serious. 'Given the horrors you've had to endure, the swiftness of your recovery is remarkable. In order to deal with what lies ahead, you must learn to believe in your own resourcefulness.'

Hettie fought back incipient tears. 'Fat lot of good my resourcefulness has done us of late,' she snuffled. 'First I get sick on the road and delay us, then when the beastmen attacked us in the woods I succumbed to panic, and ever since I've...' She broke off as the monk's words finally sank in. 'What do you mean "to deal with what lies ahead"?' she asked, peering at the abbot askance.

Aethelwold smiled avuncularly. 'The Order of St Marius has ever been a humble one, devoted to the healing arts of both mind and body,' he said. 'But we would scarce be able to heal either if we didn't spend time nourishing the spirit as well. Our aptitude in that area falls short of our Argolian brethren, but sometimes the Almighty permits me a glimpse of the future. Just a small one here and there.'

Hettie felt unsure of what to say to that. 'Go on,' she said after a few moments of silence punctuated by birdsong and buzzing.

'You have featured in my dreams of late, aye and your mistress too,' said the Abbot, letting go of Hettie and turning to stare at a small cluster of cypress trees in the corner of the garden's walled enclosure. 'You have both been caught up in a larger destiny, what the farseers of the northern lands call a wyrd. The parts you both have to play may be small, but they will be significant.'

'But our adventures are over,' protested Hettie. 'We're bound to the castle now, probably for life. I don't see how we can influence anything any more.'

The Abbot did not take his eyes away from the trees as he answered. 'No, you don't see, not right now. Only the Almighty sees all. Not even Azrael, against whom my Order toils night and day, has the gift of perfect farsight. Long ago, an enlightened man, whom some say was more than mortal, posited that time does not exist. It is only mortal ken that makes it seem so – past, present and future. But in reality everything that ever has been and ever will be simply *is* – happening since always, now and forever. Only Reus sees this with perfect clarity, and not even the Unseen share His complete vision.'

Hettie frowned. The old prior was starting to sound like Adhelina when she got carried away talking about her books. But it was better than thinking about her horrid ordeal.

'So what's your point?' she asked.

The prior laughed. 'Must there always be a point? But no, if there is, it is to say that you can't see yourself completely because your perception is restricted by time – you have powers that you have yet to discover in yourself, that only time will reveal. Your mistress too, I trow.'

'Powers? What kind of powers?' Now she was feeling anxious again. She didn't care much for this kind of talk.

'Oh they may be quite mundane – I'm not saying you're going to become a witch, so don't worry!' The Abbot chuckled. 'Just don't be so quick to dismiss yourself because of what you have been through recently. The whole story of who you are is far from told.'

The old monk rose slowly to his feet. 'Well, I'd better be getting back to the rest of my patients, morning rounds and all that. Ah Reus, but my knees are stiff! The one thing we Marionites don't know how to cure is old age. But that too is part of the Almighty's plan, I suppose. I bid you good day, Hettie. I believe your escort will arrive shortly.'

'Escort? What for?'

Aethewold looked over his shoulder as he walked away. 'Have you forgotten? It's the final day of the tournament. Adhelina wishes for your presence at the melee, and once again her father has acquiesced to her wishes. I told you he is more forgiving than he seems.'

With another wry chuckle the Abbot disappeared back inside the monastery, leaving Hettie to mull his words over in the company of the songbirds and the fruit flies.

✣ ✣ ✣

Adhelina smiled warmly at Hettie as she dismounted. Her knightly escort lost no time in nudging their steeds over towards the Markward camp to join the melee. It was but two hours away: over by the awning reserved for the noble spectators the heralds were ready with signal flags and trumpets.

'Hettie, I'm glad they let you out again,' she said, embracing her friend. 'The weather's cleared up and it's a fine day to be out! How is old Aethelwold treating you?'

'Well as ever,' said Hettie, then looked at her curiously. 'What's got into you? It's only been three days since we saw each other, and you act as if it's been a lifetime!'

It certainly felt that way to Adhelina, what with all the carry-on. Sir Agravine had tried to catch her eye repeatedly at feast-times, though she had been unable to bring herself to acknowledge him. He would soon be banished and that would make it a hopeless romance. Perhaps tales of his deeds done in her name across the realm would filter back to her, but like Lancelyn and Isoud it would be a distant love, one never consummated.

Much the same could be said of her other two paramours: they had left early yesterday, without so much as a farewell.

Or perhaps there would be no deeds, no long-distance love affairs. Perhaps the passions of chivalrous knights were more fickle than the courtly romances told.

And perhaps it would be easier for everyone that way.

Adhelina did her best to quell her sad thoughts as she watched Agravine buckle on his armour with the other knights who had been picked to represent Graukolos. He still carried her favour, tied to the lance he would use in the first charge. He had made sure of being in the vanguard, to try and make up for falling short in the joust. But glory wouldn't do his suit much good now.

'Adhelina? Oh but you're miles away!'

'I'm sorry Hettie,' said the damsel. 'A lot to think about, that's all. You seem well, anyhow... or better at any rate.'

Hettie nodded, almost looking cheerful. 'I think so milady,' she said. 'I have started to feel more like my old self this past week or so. I don't suppose I'll ever fully recover, but if your father agrees to take me back into service then...' She glanced meaningfully over to where Wilhelm was sat next to Albercelsus and Berthal. He was already drinking, but then the melee was a grand event and only came to Dulsinor once a year. Behind them men at arms from both houses stood, sweltering in the rising heat.

Adhelina took Hettie's hands in her own. 'I'm sure we'll work something out,' she said. 'After all as Grand Duchess I'm bound to wield some influence! Just steer clear of him for now.'

Hettie nodded docilely and allowed Adhelina to lead her over to where tables and chairs had been set up beneath the awning. Of the rest of the Lanrak retinue there was no sign: Sir Adso, her future husband and his hangers-on would be in their camp on the other side of the field. That just left the ladies of the house, but they were running late as usual.

'I'm afraid the Lady Berta will not be joining us,' said Berthal when she quizzed him on the subject. 'Taken ill with the gout. Her daughters are staying with her in Merkstaed while she recovers.'

'Merkstaed? Why aren't they in the castle?' asked Adhelina.

'Her Grace was taken ill during a shopping expedition,' said Berthal, tugging at his wispy white beard. 'Some fine baubles she was interested in purchasing I believe.'

Adhelina wondered wryly if she'd had an eye for the brooch Hettie had sold for her. Back when her escape had been an exciting possibility. Ignoring her gloomy thoughts she asked: 'Where exactly is she staying? One of the inns?'

'I believe so, milady.'

Adhelina allowed herself a slight smile of satisfaction. That would be a painful experience for the haughty old harridan – sojourning at an inn like a common traveller.

'I'm sure she's loving that,' was what she contented herself with saying.

Presently the knights were ready to deploy. Those on her side had divided themselves up into three contingents. Sir Urist took the vanguard of fifty, taking up position in a wedge-shaped formation on a stretch of green surrounded by hills and wooded dells. One group of twenty-five knights led by Sir Ruttgur had crested a hill to her right, using the cover of trees to lie in wait. The third group were being held in reserve, flanking the vanguard's rear left.

Craning her neck she peered beyond the gauntleted fist of the Markward standard, her eyes questing for the Lanrak banner. The field sloped a little, giving her some vantage. They had grouped themselves in standard formation at the other end of the green, a vanguard of fifty knights flanked by two battalions of twenty-five apiece.

Putting all their eggs in one basket, she reflected. She knew enough of battle tactics to spot a bold strategy. The uneven ground favoured the home team, which explained in part Sir Adso's decision to field all his men: if the Markwards pushed through with extra momentum there would be two flanks ready to cover them. That said, holding no one in reserve and planning no ambushes amounted to a risky throw of the dice.

Noon approached. The sun crept up towards its zenith; a wash of gold painted the cobalt skies, with the odd dash of white cloud here and there. Gradually the awning filled up: castle retainers, older knights who had come to watch relatives compete, and wives and betrothed and paramours. Before long there were well over a hundred people present, sipping wine and eating sweetmeats and placing wagers. Beyond the section reserved for the nobility the commoners crowded, eagerly jostling one another to get a good view.

Adhelina felt herself start to relax. Tourneys were generally non-lethal, but there were always one or two deaths: perhaps Hengist would be among them. She sipped at her goblet of Armandy red and savoured the thought. Next to her Hettie still fidgeted, but she undeniably looked better than she had done in weeks. Slowly, her spirits started to rise.

Then the herald took to the stands and called for silence. At least he was sober today, Adhelina reflected wryly.

'Ladies and noblemen... and the rest of you churls, welcome! Today marks the climax of this year's Graufluss Bridge Tourney, we hope you've had a fine time! Now prepare to be thrilled one last time, as the Markwards take on the Lanraks! Two great houses, soon to be joined forever, shall pit their wits and skill against one another in the field!'

The herald stepped down and his colleague blew a series of notes on a silver clarion. A deathly silence descended across the field. Even the common folk knew better than to break with this custom. The silence hung in the air for a few moments more and then her father lowered his baton.

The note came, a single piercing sound to rend the silence.

With a roar spurs were joined to flanks as both vanguards couched and charged. Adhelina stood up to get a better view. The Markwards thundered towards the Lanraks, a hundred spines bristling towards one another as the two hosts drew nearer. Besides the Lanrak vanguard rode the two flanks, swords drawn, their blades glinting in the sunlight...

'They're going to try a pincer manoeuvre,' said Adhelina. As if hearing her, the herald blew another succession of notes. The reserve began galloping towards the anticipated fray.

'What's Sir Urist playing at?' muttered Adhelina. 'They're going to surround our boys – he should deploy Sir Ruttgur as well!' From where they were it would be short work to ride down the hills. It would mean breaking cover and losing the element of surprise, but what was the point in keeping them back? The Lanraks had anticipated perfectly – sometimes the simplest strategies were the best.

She caught a flicker of movement to her left just as the vanguards met in the middle of the field. Three riders emerged from where a copse of trees overlooked a deep wooded dell. They were galloping hell for leather towards them.

Cries from some of the nobles under the awning turned her attention back to the melee. She had watched dozens of tourneys, and straight away she could tell something wasn't right. Many knights on either side had been unhorsed. Too many on the Markward side were not getting up. Now the enemy flanks were closing, swords raised high to strike as the Lanraks completed their pincer movement...

Another toot on the clarion. The ambuscade began pelting down towards the melee, led by Sir Ruttgur. The Lanrak flanks had closed on the Markward vanguard. Swords slashing in the bright sun. Red splashes as some found chinks in armour.

'Ye Almighty,' cried Adhelina, clutching Hettie. 'They're using real weapons!'

As if on cue another bugle sounded. This one was coming from Graukolos.

'That's a warning from the castle!' cried Adhelina. 'We're under attack. This is no melee, it's an invasion!'

Her father had clearly realised the same thing. He was on his feet, drawing his dagger and bellowing orders. The Lanrak guards had drawn swords and cut down half the Markward men at arms before they could react. Albercelsus was up too, dagger in hand. He moved fast for a man of his years. The remainder of Wilhelm's bodyguard formed a ring around him and Berthal while the Lanrak soldiers pressed them. Albercelsus fell back behind the soldiers – then his eyes caught Adhelina. A murderous look entered them as he stalked towards her.

✢ ✢ ✢

From the castle battlements, Adelko watched as a company of knights came tearing across the countryside to the east. There had to be at least two hundred, the coiled wyvern of the Lanraks writhing on the winds before them. Small wonder his sixth sense had been jangling all morning: the new Stornelending arrivals evidently did not mean well.

He was still out of breath after their headlong dash up myriad flights of stairs from the private chapel to the curtain wall overlooking the river and camp beyond. Horskram had insisted that they spend their last day at Graukolos in prayers of thankfulness: clearly his mentor felt some need to atone for their sins in watching the tournament. Now fate had brought him another much worse conflict – watching Lanrak knights butcher their Markward rivals was a sickening spectacle. So much for the rules of chivalry and fair play.

'What do we do now?' he asked.

'We leave right soon is what we do,' said Horskram. 'I'll not tarry here a moment longer – our mission is more important than watching the continuation of Vorstlending politics by other means! We'll just have to take our chances on the road without an escort.'

Brigmore strode up the walkway towards them. The captain of the guards looked worried and perplexed. Clearly he had not been expecting to be on active duty today. 'We'll be closing the gates in the next half hour, that's enough time for the townsfolk to get up here if they want sanctuary,' he said. 'You have till that long to make your decision – you stay with us or take your chances abroad.'

'We'll take our chances, thank you,' said Horskram, pushing past him. 'Adelko, come along! Our trusty steeds await us in yon stables – good thing I asked you to prepare our saddlebags first thing this morning!'

Adelko hurried after him. He didn't dare say anything about the others: Horskram had barely noticed them when they had broken from under cover of the trees just beyond the river. He could only hope that they succeeded in their rescue attempt before the rest of the Stornelendings arrived.

They made their way down narrow flights of stairs towards the ground level; men at arms and crossbowmen were scrambling for position across the gargantuan keep, busy ants in a hive of activity. Dashing through the gatehouse into the middle ward they passed soldiers and the odd household knight on duty emerging from the barracks and armoury. A throng of terrified craftsmen was pouring in through the second gatehouse, their stalls in the outer ward forgotten.

With some difficulty the two monks pushed past them, emerging into the ward and heading for the stables. Several trembling merchants were there too, mounting their horses hurriedly. Their forked beards waved almost comically as they hastened to beat a retreat.

Taking their steeds from the flustered ostler the monks mounted and rode out into the barbican, pausing only to refill their waterskins from the well in the outer ward tower. Emerging onto the crest of the hill they could see a swarm of commoners and townsfolk engulfing the trail leading from Merkstaed.

'We'll have to ride around them,' said Horskram. 'We can rejoin the road further south.'

They were just about to spur their horses down the hill when they heard another bugle blast from the walls. A few seconds later they saw what had prompted it: another company of knights, riding from the south. These were on their side of the river, and heading towards Merkstaed.

'They must have crossed the Graufluss further upstream,' said Horskram, indulging in a string of impious obscenities. 'We'll have to ride cross country, make for the Glimmerholt! We can hide there and make our way south once night falls.'

Without another word they spurred their horses downhill. As they did Adelko mouthed a prayer for his erstwhile comrades, wondering if he would ever see them again.

✤ ✤ ✤

Adhelina risked a glance around her. There was no sign of the incoming forces yet, but some of the Stornelending knights from the melee had broken off and were coming towards them. At least half of the Markward knights were down, dead, dying or wounded. She caught a glimpse of a broken lance buried point first in the sward, a silken scarf fluttering forlornly from its shaft... Then more Lanrak knights pulled into view, cutting off her vision. Panicked commoners were running in all directions. The Lanraks rode some of them down as they swept across the field towards the awning.

Adhelina returned her eyes to Albercelsus as he advanced. She felt her courage fail her. No weapon, she needed a weapon dammit...

In a flash the steward was on her. He raised his dagger to strike. With an instinct born of desperation she grasped his wrist. He was old, giving her a chance to grapple with him, but she had no inkling of how to fight. Suddenly she was on her back, her life flashing before her eyes as the seneschal wrenched his arm free and raised the dagger again...

A flash of movement behind him and Albercelsus fell forwards, landing in a heap beside her. Blood trickled through his thinning grey hair. Looking up again she saw Hettie, clutching the chair she had been sitting on in trembling hands. Albercelsus groaned and struggled to pick himself up, scrabbling for his blade. Hettie's face was a mask of fury as she raised the chair again, bringing it crashing down on his outstretched arm. He howled as it snapped audibly. Hettie raised the chair to strike again...

Thundering hooves all around. Armoured knights were carving a swathe through the nobles, cutting down greybeards, women, youths. Screams and blood and fear filled the air.

A shadow fell across Adhelina. She looked up, expecting to see the Angel of Death in the form of a man on horseback.

What she saw was Anupe.

The Harijan was mounted on a swift courser, a bloodied falchion in her hand. Next to her a charger reared and whinnied and a knight writhed on the ground, screaming and clutching a spurting fingerless hand.

'Get up behind me!' cried the Harijan. 'Get up now if you want to live!'

Adhelina hesitated. 'What about Hettie?' she cried.

'We've got her,' said a familiar voice behind her. It was Sir Braxus. Next to him Sir Torgun was holding off three Stornelending knights single handed. A flash of silver and red. Make that two Stornelending knights.

Two more knights were hurtling towards them. Without a second thought Adhelina scrambled up behind Anupe. The two Lanraks were on them as the Harijan wheeled her horse back around towards the copse. Ducking a sword swipe from the first knight she lashed out at the second, opening up his calf from knee to ankle below his hauberk before he could attack. He screamed and dropped his blade as a gout of red erupted from his leg. In a flash she brought the point of her falchion back towards the first knight, ramming it into his mouth. He could barely muster a cry as he tilted backwards in the saddle, choking on his own blood.

Adhelina took advantage of the brief respite to look behind her. Hettie was in the saddle behind Braxus. Torgun had despatched his last knight. But that wasn't what caught her eye as Anupe kicked their horse into a gallop. What she saw would remain fixed in her mind forever, and her life would never be the same again.

The spectacle receded as they thundered away, but it was no less horrible for all that. The Lanrak guards had cut down the remainder of the Markward men at arms. Berthal lay on the ground groaning, blood forming growing pools across his brocade robes of office. They had her father surrounded. Roaring like an angry bear he came at one of them, stabbing him in the face while using a chair to barge another to the floor. But half a dozen men was too many even for Wilhelm. She saw their swords rise and fall... The Eorl of Graukolos fell, blood spurting from many wounds.

Adhelina gave vent to a scream of anguish as they hacked her father to pieces.

As if mocking her plaintive cry, the green hills to the east of the fields were suddenly covered in a ripple of shining silver. As the Lanrak host poured down towards the dwindling Markward knights, cutting down fleeing civilians high born and low, Adhelina realised with a grim certainty that she would finally have her freedom.

For by the time the Lanraks were finished with their treachery, the house of Markward would not exist.

PART THREE

⊷ CHAPTER I ⊷

The Warrior-King's Passing

'He will not live out the year.' The chirurgeon's words fell like a tombstone across the silence of the antechamber. Despite the sun streaming through the high-arched windows, Princess Hjala felt cold.

'I am sorry, Your Highness,' the chirurgeon went on, 'But the Sweating Sickness is a grievous malady even unto the young. For one so advanced in years as His Majesty...' The greybeard's voice trailed off. He looked increasingly anxious. Hjala understood why. Placing a hand on his bony shoulder she did her best to reassure him.

'Have no fear, Yurik,' she said in a subdued voice. 'I know you've done all you can. It's just after everything we've been through this year, I had not expected... this.'

Yurik nodded kindly. 'Rest assured we will do everything we can to ease his passing. For now it's best to let him rest.'

The chirurgeon was already bowing and retreating as he spoke. Hjala let him go and walked over to stare out of a window at the sun-strafed streets of Strongholm and dappled surf of the Strang Estuary beyond. Her home city was normally a beautiful sight at this time of year, but now all she felt was sorrow. Soon she would have a beloved father to add to the watery ghosts of her drowned children.

She was not long alone with her thoughts. A couple of minutes later the door opened and Lord Ulnor entered, his cane clacking on the flagstones.

She did not turn from the window as he drew level with her.

'Well?' was all he said.

'The sickness is in full bloom,' she replied, still staring out of the window. 'My father shall not see another spring, if the chirurgeon is to be believed.'

'I am right sad to hear it,' said Ulnor. 'His Majesty's passing shall be a grief to all the nation.'

She did not doubt the sincerity of the seneschal's words. Lord Ulnor was loyal to a fault. But behind the sincere condolences there was another angle. There always was with men of power.

The steward allowed a few moments of respectable silence to pass before he confirmed her apprehension.

'Price Thorsvald has returned,' he said. 'He reports growing numbers of freesailors and seacarls on the Wyvern, plundering ships. It's only a matter of time before they raid the mainland – '

'Must we talk of this now?' She could not keep the irritation out of her voice.

'Yes, we must,' replied the seneschal implacably. 'Your brother the Sealord's warnings are not to be ignored – something is stirring in the Frozen Principalities, that much is clear.'

'I will see Prince Thorsvald directly,' said Hjala. 'I am sure I will hear his tidings in person then.'

'Your Highness, the realm is in jeopardy,' persisted Ulnor. 'We've barely pacified the southern provinces, the new jarls we've instated already have their hands full finishing off outlaws from Thule's levy and putting down uprisings from disinherited younger sons – '

'I know that,' snapped Hjala. 'I was there when we planned the campaign to put down the Young Pretender, in case you've forgotten.'

She didn't care for the steward's patronising tone, loyal as he was. But then she was only a woman, she reflected with bitter irony, how could she be expected to keep such complex affairs of state in her head?

'What's your point anyway?' she asked. 'You might as well out with it now, if it can't wait.' She already knew what it was, but wanted to see how Ulnor went about raising it. You could tell a lot about a person's agenda by the way they broached things. Years at court had taught her that much.

'If what you have just told me is true, that means the King is officially incapacitated – from today,' said Ulnor. 'No man in the final stages of the Sweating Sickness can be relied upon to discharge his office of state. Under Northlending law that means we have a fortnight from today to name a regent, to rule in His Majesty's stead until he passes or recovers. During that time I am acting regent. We must convene a royal council to discuss the matter and confirm the nominee as soon as possible.'

For the first time, Hjala turned to look at him. The seneschal's frosty eyes gave little away as ever, though she could fathom him well enough.

'*The nominee*?' she said sharply. 'Or *candidates* perhaps... For surely you don't mean...'

Ulnor did not blink as he said: 'He is the rightful heir to the throne, Your Highness.'

Yes, that was Ulnor. Loyal to a fault.

'Lord Ulnor, even at the best of times, my brother is hardly yet fit for rule. He is brash, impetuous, why even in this most recent war he showed himself to be – '

'Your Highness, he is the *heir*,' repeated Ulnor, more sternly now.

'Lord Ulnor, need I remind you that Prince Wolfram has not yet recovered from his injuries? Why only two nights ago he fell into one of his rages!'

Her brother had not been himself since taking the arrow wound at Linden. Though his body had healed well enough – less one eye and the bridge of his nose – his mind had been corrupted. Yurik had said something about a splinter entering his brain, whatever that was supposed to mean.

She didn't know much about chirurgeon's talk, but she did know one thing. Her brother was too unstable to rule.

'He is not like that all the time,' insisted the seneschal. 'And when he is, there are trusted advisers he can count on to guide him.'

And no tourney prize for guessing who those might be, thought Hjala sourly. Men of power. Always pursuing an angle. Even the loyal ones like Ulnor.

'And when he isn't, is he fit to lead us at a time like this?' she pressed, trying a different tack of her own. 'My brother spent his years hunting, hawking and tourneying – he knows nothing of how to rule a realm in times of trouble!'

Ulnor's face hardened. 'And I suppose you do?' he asked pointedly. 'Like it or not, your brother will be King soon enough. Better to get him accustomed to his royal duties now.'

Hjala shook her head. Technically what Ulnor said made sense, but all her instincts told her it was the wrong move. 'Not yet, he needs more time to recover – and learn what it means to be a king. Throwing him in the watery deeps won't help – '

A spasm of pain crossed her breast as she unwittingly brought back the ghosts of her children. Ulnor took advantage of her discomfort to ram his point home.

'I am calling a royal council to decide the matter. I'll need to send to Staerkvit for Sir Toric, so you've a couple of days to come to your senses.'

Without another word the steward turned to leave, his walking stick clacking as he exited the room.

✢ ✢ ✢

'Well what did you expect?' said Lady Walsa, pausing to nibble daintily on a sweetmeat. 'Ulnor's always been obsessive about controlling all that goes on in the palace. You know full well what he's like.'

Hjala let a frustrated sigh off the leash as she sipped wine from a silver goblet. But not even a vintage white shipped all the way from Aquitania could soothe her troubled mind. It wasn't just palace politics that troubled her. She missed Torgun. Memories of their last night together washed across her mind... She could feel his hot embrace, strong yet gentle. It brought her a different kind of pain, a longing that was all the more tantalising because she knew it might one day be fulfilled.

'My brother isn't fit to rule the kingdom,' she said, staring absently at her favourite tapestry. It depicted a gallant knight slaying a Wyrm and had adorned the far wall of her room since she was a child. But the dragons were all dead, and her gallant knight was off who knew where trying to save the world.

'Well of course he's not,' snapped her aunt. 'Wolfram has about as much sense in him as a brained hare. Too much fatherly indulgence and not enough scripture, if you ask me. If only Brother Horskram were here to knock some sense into him.'

Walsa gazed wistfully out of the window as she sipped her wine.

So that's who she's been thinking about while I've been pining for Torgun, thought Hjala with some amusement. Her aunt had not been noted for chastity in her youth: who could say how pure her reverence for the mysterious monk was? Horskram might be celibate, but he was handsome enough for a man his age.

'What are you smirking at?' cawed Walsa, catching her eye.

'Oh nothing,' replied the princess, wiping the tell-tale smile off her face. 'Anyway, more to the point, what do we do? As nearest relative to the King, I'll get a vote on who serves as regent. That's assuming Wolfram consents to have his name put forward.'

'Oh he will, don't you worry,' said her aunt. 'As proud as the day is long, that one.' She was about to launch into one of her tirades when what Hjala had just said registered. 'Wait, how does that make you the nearest blood relative? Have you forgotten your other brother...'

She trailed off, her eyes widening as she finally grasped Hjala's meaning.

'Ah, so that's your game,' she said. 'You want to nominate Prince Thorsvald!'

'He's a lot more sensible than Wolfram,' ventured Hjala. 'And would never put his own contumely above the needs of the realm. He served with honour during the uprising, keeping Thule's fleet at bay – why even now he continues to defend us from northland reavers, while Wolfram rants and raves and plays at dice and prepares for the Strang Bay Tourney!'

Tournaments. The realm had just had a real war, but that wouldn't stop the local chivalry engaging in a mock one at the drop of a lance.

'Yes, but that doesn't change the fact that he's the younger son,' said Walsa. 'Even allowing for the vagaries of the law, it would be most irregular. Sets a bad precedent, putting a younger sibling on the throne.'

'It wouldn't be forever,' pressed Hjala. 'Just long enough to give Wolfram more time to recover, while father...' Her voice trailed off. She drained her goblet, willing the musky wine to banish away her sorrow.

'Yes, it is a dreadful thing this illness of your father's,' sighed Walsa. 'It's funny, I always thought he'd meet his end in the field, or on horseback at least. Northalde won't be the same without him. Rulers like that don't come along too often.'

'That is precisely what I am afraid of,' said Hjala, reaching for the wine jug. 'That's why we have to put Thorsvald on the throne, at least buy Wolfram – and the realm – more time to recover.'

'What makes you think he'll get any better?'

'If he doesn't get better then chances are he'll get worse. If his condition degenerates, not even succession purists like Ulnor will be able to deny that my brother is unfit for office.'

Lady Walsa gawped at her. It was amusing to see her crusty aunt look thus – she was seldom surprised at anything. 'You really have been thinking this through – how unflinching you are! A true scion of our house.' Walsa raised her goblet in a half-toast.

'I've only ever wanted what is best for the house of Ingwin – and the realm it rules.'

'Well even if you're right, you'll have a job persuading your candidate,' said Walsa. 'Thorsvald is a second son to his core – loyal, dutiful, and humble too.'

'That's why I'm sure he would make a good king,' replied Hjala. 'There will be five of us on the council – myself, Lord Ulnor, Sir Toric as head of the Valravyn, Visigard as Marshal of Strongholm, and the head of the Temple... I even forget his name.'

'Cuthbert of Leirvik,' supplied Walsa. 'Complete non-entity, small wonder you should forget his name. I daresay he can be plied either way.'

Hjala put down her goblet. She needed to think straight. 'Visigard will vote with Ulnor, he doesn't have the intelligence to see sense above tradition. Sir Toric I'm less sure of... Had it been Freidhoff there would have been no chance of getting that vote, he was always a stickler for form. But Toric is unquantifiable... with him on the council we might just have a chance.'

Walsa nodded slowly over her goblet. 'Yes, if you can get Cuthbert and Toric on board you could put Thorsvald on the throne, at least until your father passes. If Wolfram is officially declared mad by then you'll need another vote to decide who serves as regent until his son Freidhrim comes of age...'

'... but by then my younger brother will have hopefully established himself as a steady pair of hands,' Hjala finished for her. 'And Prince Freidhrim is but eight summers old. He has six years before he comes of age.'

'That gives Thorsvald the time he needs to prepare his nephew for the throne. Time enough to steer the realm through whatever crisis awaits.'

Hjala could not resist another sip of wine. She had to admit planning the future of her realm was exciting. Behind that was a sense of shame though – she could not deny that part of her hoped her older brother did not recover. But the good of the realm outweighed the good of one man – even its heir apparent.

'No, the more I think about it, the more I share your enthusiasm,' said Walsa. 'It's about time we women had more say in the affairs of state in any case.'

'So you'll help me?' Hjala felt her spirits rise. She had hoped to gain her aunt's support.

'Of course I'll help you,' said Walsa with mock irritation. 'Now that poor Freidheim lies on his deathbed it's fair to say we've got more sense between us than the rest of the menfolk in the palace put together.'

'I'd hoped you felt that way,' beamed Hjala. 'A toast then – to wise women!'

'To wise women,' replied Walsa, clinking goblets with her. 'So when will you broach the matter with Thorsvald?'

'This evening,' replied Hjala. 'I want to hear what he has to say about the Northland reavers in any case. If we're going to manipulate the succession in the name of the realm, we'd best learn more about the dangers it faces.'

✤ ✤ ✤

Thorsvald was in his bedchamber playing with his son Linnaeus when Hjala entered. Over by the window sat his wife, Princess Lif. A dark-haired slip of a girl with little to say, and little to her merit, other than her pallid beauty and blood ties to the House of Hjalfaste – her uncle was Lord Kelmor of Salmorlund. Hjala had never had much time for her. Weak-minded women were bad for the cause: they only encouraged the menfolk to clutch the reins of power more tightly.

'Hjala, sister dearest!' boomed Prince Thorsvald, rising to take her in a brotherly embrace. Tall and lean and hard-muscled, he smelled of the sea as always, salt and brine tanging in her nostrils as he took her in a crushing embrace. His long red locks reeked of the stuff; even on land he was never away from the sea. His chambers were directly above the throneroom and overlooked the harbour; her people's ancestral love of the waves roared in his bosom with the force of a tidal wave. A coral effigy of the un-angel Sjórkunan was fixed above his bed; it had stood there since he had come of age, in defiance of the Temple who had accused him of paganism and idolatry. Never was there a man more fit to be Sealord than Thorsvald.

That was why it pained his sister to do what she had to do next.

'Aunt Hjala! Aunt Hjala!' Linnaeus pulled excitedly at her skirts. The boy was barely three summers, and still excited by his powers of speech and walking.

Hjala picked up the lad and kissed him affectionately on the forehead. Already he had a mass of flaxen curls just like his father. Lif walked over from the window and took the boy from Hjala, smiling wanly. Hjala returned the smile perfunctorily. She still didn't think much of her, but she would do well enough as a bearer of her brother's children. Assuming she could squeeze any more out of that skinny frame of hers.

'Come sit with me!' said her brother excitedly. He was seven years younger than her. He had always looked up to her as a small boy, when she had taken him about the castle on mock adventures, holding him high above her head and pretending to make him fly like an eagle. But he had loved it best when she took him down to the Strang Estuary, so he could be close to his beloved sea.

He offered her a goblet of wine, which she refused. She had drunk enough that afternoon with her aunt.

'So tell me how have you been?' he asked when they were sat by another window. His wife had disappeared into the next room with Linnaeus. That was good – she could speak frankly.

'Never mind about me,' she countered. 'You'll have heard about father – well, it's as bad as they say.'

Thorsvald's face darkened. 'Lord Ulnor told me this afternoon,' he said. 'There's to be a council.'

Hjala nodded. 'I want to talk about that in a minute,' she said. 'But first I want to hear from you – how speed things at sea?'

Her brother sighed. 'Well enough – for now. The last of Thule's fleet have disbanded. Half of them were pirates recruited out of Port Urring. Now we've secured it, most of them have given up the cause as lost. The rest of the rebel fleet – Saltcaste's vassals – have surrendered in return for a general amnesty.'

'That's good,' said Hjala. 'I have a feeling we're going to need them.'

Her brother nodded. 'You always were the clever one,' he said ruefully. 'How I wish you were wrong in this case... The threat from the Northlanders is growing. A tenday ago we intercepted a dozen longships.'

'Freesailors?'

The Sealord shook his head. 'Seacarls, serving Oldrik Stormrider. We luffed up to them on a starboard wind and fought them to a man. I lost seventeen good men, but finally we had the best of them. We managed to take a few prisoner. Questioned them with iron and fire. Our northern cousins are as hardy as any, but one of the younger ones finally broke and told us what we needed to know. They'd been preying on shipping in the Wyvern but their next destination was the mainland. They're getting bolder, Hjala – this is just the first taste. They know all about the civil war thanks to Hardrada's involvement – they know we're preoccupied, weakened.'

'That's why we have to – '

But her brother wasn't done yet. He continued: 'The last reaver also told us that Hardrada's neighbour has taken advantage of his weakened position to raid his lands. The Thegn of Kvenlund is said to be an ambitious man – a young ruler anxious to make his mark. Chances are the Thegn of Jótlund won't be the only one sending ships south-west before long.'

Hjala took a brief moment to digest the news. That only made her plan more urgent. She looked her brother square in the eyes.

'Thorsvald, we need strong leadership.'

Her brother nodded. 'Aye, the council. We need to get Wolfram appointed as regent right soon, when Sir Toric arrives we'll take a vote – '

Hjala reached out and put her hand on her brother's. 'That isn't strong leadership, brother, and you know it. Wolfram is still sick. He hasn't fully recovered from his injury and I'm not sure he ever will. He has fits of apoplexy. He cannot rule.'

Thorsvald stared at her, a shocked expression on his ingenuous face. 'But... Freidhrim is just a boy, he can't...'

'I'm not talking about Freidhrim. I'm talking about you.'

Her brother shook his head and started to protest, but Hjala cut him off.

'I need you to consent to be nominee for regent,' she said. 'Do that and I'm entitled to sit on the council. You'll get my vote. After that we need just two more to put you on the throne.'

'I can't, my duty lies at sea! And I'm the younger son, it's unheard of...'

'But not against Northlending law,' pressed Hjala. 'The chirurgeon has given our father a few months to live. That's time enough to see if Wolfram recovers more fully.'

'I don't want to be regent!' Thorsvald protested. 'I am not made for the cares of state.'

'Yes, you are,' persisted Hjala. 'You are loyal and cautious, not only courageous but a man who puts others before himself. You would make an excellent king.'

The word that exited her mouth unbidden shocked her as much as it did her brother.

'Hjala, you're speaking treason!'

She shook her head, inwardly cursing herself for having had too much Aquitanian white. 'Oh, king, regent... call it what you will. You should lead us in this time of trouble, not Wolfram! He nearly lost us Linden, all because he was too busy playing at war to fight a real one! With Freidhoff gone and our father dying who do we have left to rule the realm?'

'Ulnor is a wise man,' ventured her brother. 'He can be trusted to guide Prince Wolfram.'

'Can he? Ulnor is a schemer, always has been. He'll run things to his benefit and convince himself that he is serving the realm by manipulating Wolfram. But he'll be the power behind the throne. I would have Northalde ruled by the House of Ingwin, its rightful owners, not a scion of the House of Canwolde!'

Thorsvald frowned. 'It sounds to me as though you are more concerned with the fortunes of our house than the realm, sister,' he said sternly.

That gave her pause for thought. 'Aye, perhaps I am,' she conceded. 'Or perhaps I truly believe that the two are one and the same.' She was squeezing her brother's hand now. 'Thorsvald, while you were away at sea, a secret council was held... concerning the cause of the war, and another much larger matter. If half of what I heard was true, then all the Free Kingdoms and beyond are going to face a threat that transcends all the petty wars of mortal men. That's why Northalde is going to need a strong ruler, the strongest we can find.'

Her brother looked at her askance. 'Sister, are you well? Now you're sounding like a farseer.'

The princess bit her lip. This was the part she had the most misgivings about. Her father had sworn them all to secrecy. But her brother was blood royalty, if he hadn't been at sea he would have been included in the secret council. And besides that, her father was dying.

Taking a deep breath, Hjala made her decision.

'You must keep what I'm going to tell you an absolute secret...'

✤ ✤ ✤

When she was done Thorsvald leaned back in his chair and drained his goblet. It was a lot for him to take in. His life had been simple and worldly. Up until now.

'There's far more at stake here than house politics,' said Hjala. 'We can't afford to take any chances with the succession. Once he's installed on the throne Wolfram has absolute power – not even Ulnor would be able to keep him in check if he's minded not to heed his counsel.'

Thorsvald stared out of the window at his beloved ships and harbour and the rolling waves beyond, slowly being absorbed by the darkening skies. Anguish buckled his proud face. Wolfram looked more like their father, but Thorsvald had inherited the lineaments of their mother, as elegant a woman as any who sat a throne. Hjala hoped Weirhilda would have done likewise in her position.

'All right,' he said at length, turning back to look at her. 'I'll stand for regent – but only until our father recovers or passes. After that... well it depends on how things speed with Wolfram.'

Hjala felt her tension give way to relief. She had hoped he would say that – it would make his candidature look more sympathetic, less self-interested.

'Thank you brother,' she breathed softly, reaching out to take his hand again. 'I know how hard this is for you. The realm owes you a debt.'

Thorsvald said nothing, just smiled weakly before turning to look out at the dark waves again. She followed his gaze as they sat in silence, listening to the distant sound of the sea above the evening clamour of the city. Somewhere beyond the vanishing horizon an invading army was gathering.

⊷ CHAPTER II ⊷

An Invasion Stalled

Abrexta forced herself to remain calm as the Lord Treasurer gave his unwelcome news. Dressed in fustian robes of office and standing nearly a head shorter than average, Caratacus was an unprepossessing sight – but she knew better. As he finished giving his report she visualised a hand clutching a heart inside a cage, but her Enchantment was weak and lacked power: she was sorely overstretched.

At least she did not have to ensorcell him fully; a light suggestion would do. Caratacus was the type of man who lived to serve the crown. He would follow his King unto death, even if that king happened to be enthralled by a witch.

'And cannot you chastise them? Why not hang a few as an example to the rest?'

Caratacus shook his head. 'The shipwrights' guild has ever been solid,' said the treasurer. 'They will not resume work on the fleet until they get the wages promised them. Shipwrights are hard to come by – if you start killing them you won't get your fleet built. And as I have just endeavoured to explain, that cannot happen until the tax revenue is in. It would help if the southern wards agreed to pay their share.'

'Yes, well you leave me to worry about the southern wards,' snapped the sorceress. The reports south of the Fern river were growing more disturbing: Garro, Fythe, Penllyn and Tul Aeren had now united in a flat refusal to heed the call to war. Worse still, the rumours of a planned uprising had been thickening about this already unwelcome news, and a full-blown southern rebellion against the crown now seemed likely.

'The treasury's coffers are all but empty,' pressed Caratacus. 'Had the taxes you levied earlier this year not been spent in idle dissipation – '

'How dare you question the will of the King?' she rounded on him in a fury, rising from her seat. Then she remembered that same king was next door in an entranced slumber and lowered her voice. 'The King's

Fold shall spend as it sees fit,' she continued, forcing herself to look out of a window to calm herself. The harbour was just visible: she could see the skeletal galleys, bereft of the ants she needed to complete them. 'I thought the last tax levy was enough to cover their wages in any case.'

'It should have been,' replied the treasurer implacably. 'But corruption is rife since you got rid of my inspectors and replaced them with men ill suited to the office. Might I suggest in future you vet their replacements more thoroughly?'

Abrexta shut her eyes, silently wishing she had done a more thorough job of enthralling the treasurer instead. But some men were more resistant than others to her Enchantment, especially those such as Caratacus who did not desire her.

'We need to levy more taxes, on the nobles who have already paid and the townsfolk from here to Port Craek,' she said at length.

She turned back to see how the treasurer was receiving her new order. He had a shock of red hair that was still rich for a man of fifty winters, though his skin was pock-marked by an old disease. He disgusted her, but such mortals were useful after their own fashion.

'I doubt even the most loyal nobles will be able to stomach more payments,' he said, making sure to keep his voice neutral. 'And they need money to outfit their contributions to the invasion army.'

'Very well then, put your tax collectors under investigation,' she said. 'If you suspect them of embezzling revenue I want them brought to justice immediately.'

The treasurer blinked, surprise registering for the first time in his hazel eyes. 'You would give me power of attorney in this matter?'

'Yes, yes, and all the resources you need – just get me that blasted coin! I want those churls paid and back working on the fleet as soon as possible!'

'It shall be as you say,' said Caratacus, bowing and withdrawing.

She poured herself some wine as he withdrew from the antechamber. Things were not going according to plan. Gildmonath was just a few days away; at this rate the fleet would not be ready to sail on the autumn tides come Ripanmonath. Not only that, but the Highlanders were dragging their feet. Too busy plundering and ravaging the lands they had conquered to muster their own contribution to the army. The pirate kings of Cobia were also a problem. The men she needed to navigate and captain ships had refused the crown's standing offer, and as it was that would empty what was left of the royal coffers.

She took an angry gulp of wine as she stared at the stinking city she had been forced to call home these past two years. Even with half its notables ensorcelled, a realm was not easy to rule. Forcing herself to relax, Abrexta drained her goblet, taking a pinch of Tyrnor's Foil with it. She would need the extra strength, for she had a report of her own to make.

For the third time Abrexta visualised a hawk, an ear, and an eye in succession, breathing gently on the silver mirror she kept on her dressing table. Behind her Cadwy snored, his breathing weighted by the light spell she had placed on him. Ignoring the sound and forcing herself to concentrate, she let herself reach out, questing for Andragorix...

Nothing. Once again only darkness answered her call.

Sitting back in her cherry wood chair she exhaled a long slow breath. This wasn't good. With Andragorix eliminated the chain of command changed. That meant reporting directly to... No, she couldn't think about that, not yet. Gathering her elan for another attempt at Scrying, she visualised the symbols again, attuning herself to another warlock's psyche. She hadn't communed with him before and it required more effort; she would have to let a few thralls go for now.

A few leagues away a couple of vassals in Umbria suddenly stopped what they were doing and wondered why they had spent the past year serving a pagan enchantress who didn't have the realm's best interests at heart.

No matter, she would re-enthral them when she was done.

The room was dark, with heavy brocade curtains drawn across the windows; only light from tallow candles on the mahogany dressing table spilled across the dark. From a censer she had hung from the ceiling the scent of incense, brought from the Pilgrim Kingdoms at considerable expense, filtered through the air borne on tendrils of smoke. It helped her achieve the necessary mindset.

At last she felt something. The mirror began to swirl before her, adding an unnatural light to the flickering candles. The King moaned softly in bed but she ignored him.

Gradually the features of an old man took shape. His beard and moustache seemed to glint with hoarfrost; one of his eyes was like a cloud.

'Ragnar of the Frozen Wastes, we meet at last,' she murmured.

'Abrexta the Prescient, if my Scrying doesn't deceive me,' he replied. 'Your reputation precedes you. The will of kings bends to thy incanted word.'

'And the four winds gather at your invoked command.' Protocol required accomplished sorcerers meeting to acknowledge one another's power: neither wanted to provoke an uncertain ally.

'What moves you to make direct contact?' asked Ragnar. 'I was under the impression we both reported to the same master.'

'That master is no longer potent. The seventh sense heeds not his elan.'

Ragnar's face darkened briefly, his icy mask of composure breaking. 'You are quite sure?'

'As sure as the seventh sense can render an adept practitioner. His elan moves not through the cosmic interstices that separate and join the two worlds.'

Ragnar frowned. 'I had wondered why he had not reached out of late,' he said. The mage paused a few moments, then added: 'We must proceed as planned. If we know that something has befallen Andragorix, doubtless the Master does too. I have no doubt he shall reach out to us individually, when the time is right.'

'Proceed as planned?' Abrexta spat. 'I was promised an undead army and a Gygant to crush the southern provinces, who even now seek to move against me! How am I supposed to invade the Westerling Isles with a rebellious army at my back?'

'I too had hoped for better luck with my own civil war,' replied Ragnar impassively. 'Plans change. The war for both worlds will not be won without setbacks. Do what our kind do best and improvise.'

'That is easy for you to say.'

'Nothing worth achieving is ever easy. I have my own difficulties to contend with.'

'That's all you have to say?'

'No, as a matter of fact I can probably tell you who is responsible for eliminating Andragorix. A monk who goes by the name of Horskram, an age-old foe of his. 'Twas his meddling that helped the Northlending King put down my rebellion. If someone has written Andragorix's ruin, chances are it will be him.'

'This is your idea of help?'

Ragnar smiled thinly. 'I thought you might derive some comfort from knowing we share the same foe. Doubtless the Master shall deal with him in time.'

'And in the meantime I have a near impossible task on my hands! I've to keep half a kingdom pacified and fend off the other half while planning an invasion of the druid islands.'

'I'm sure the Master is aware of your difficulties and will make contact directly. For now I would look on this as a blessing in disguise – Andragorix was an unstable master at best.'

'But his power was indisputable – we are greatly weakened without it.'

'You forget that the Master whom we ultimately serve is more powerful than all of us put together. We report directly to him now. Look on this as an opportunity for personal advancement – but woe betide you if he finds you wanting! If I were you, I'd spend less time complaining and focus on a contingency plan.'

Ragnar muttered the closing sequence and the mirror faded back to normal, leaving her alone in the flickering candlelight. Leaning back she shut her eyes tightly. She felt drained. She almost forgot to re-enthral the two knights, she was that tired.

Improvise. Contingency plans. Yes, she needed to think her way out of this situation, but not right now. Her lithe body trembled as she stood and walked over to the bed. Without bothering to undress, she pulled back the silk sheets and climbed into the four-poster bed next to the king she commanded.

She needed to sleep, to regather her strength. With any luck the seventh sense would guide her as she dreamed, help her plan her next move. Within seconds she was fast asleep.

⇥ CHAPTER III ⇤

Of Birds and Men

Wolmar watched with little interest as the falcon lanced across the skies and turned a graceful arc, before plummeting towards its prey. The pheasant gave a dismal screech as the blue-grey raptor eviscerated it in mid-air, yanking its entrails from its cloven belly.

'Oh splendid!' cried Ivon, holding aloft his buckskin glove and beaming as Kaye and Aravin applauded. 'What did I tell you? A fine day for falconry, no? Aotus is on us, and a fine summer month it is for sport!'

They were on the hills south of Rima and the sky was a perfect cloudless blue. Not that it did anything to raise Wolmar's spirits.

'Wolmar, darling!' chided the Margrave. 'Not enjoying the spectacle? Falconry is the sport of kings – it's high time you learned!'

'Really,' said Wolmar. At least the Margrave's bewitchment hadn't robbed him of his sarcasm.

'The loremasters say it was introduced to Urovia by the Muradis,' continued Ivon unabashed, 'when they conquered Mercadia in the time of King Lotharion – why it's been with us since Pangonia was young!'

'I knew there was a reason why I disliked it,' muttered the princeling.

'So obstinate!' laughed Ivon, as Aravin pulled on his gauntlet and stepped up to release his own falcon. Across the top of a copse on the next hill a couple more pheasants could be seen swooping to and fro. Ivon's falcon was winging its way back; he held up his gauntlet and caught it.

'That's a good boy!' he said, refastening the creature to the glove. It peered skittishly from Wolmar to Ivon, its eyes looking almost comical beneath its hood.

'You see, you misunderstand the point of falconry,' said Ivon. 'Or hawking as you call it in your vulgar language. It isn't about catching the prey – it's the relationship between bird and master that makes it such a special distraction.'

'I'm bored,' Wolmar deadpanned. 'Can we go and do something interesting?'

'Oh Wolmar,' said Ivon, pouting. 'I am trying to tell you something interesting, if you'd only listen...' His black eyes suddenly became intent and feral. 'You see, the falcon is not like a horse or hound – it does not love its master. It *serves* him, out of loyalty motivated by self-interest. I train the falcon and reward it with food, and it learns not to desert its master – it chooses to be bound rather than free. And why? Because I have shown that it can expect a greater reward through being bound.' To demonstrate his meaning, Ivon took a piece of raw meat from a leather bag. The falcon fed greedily.

'Do you see?' said Ivon. 'I have instilled loyalty in the falcon by appealing to its greed – even to the point where it is willing to forsake its freedom. And *that* is the lesson – greed trumps freedom, always! You can learn much about the ways of men by studying the animal kingdom, Wolmar.'

'If that is true, why bother ensorcelling me?'

Ivon grinned a vulpine grin. 'Some birds are wilder than others. A little extra incentive is needed – in the first instance. But in time I shall not need to enthral you – when you see for yourself how great the reward I promise is.'

'We'll see.' Wolmar did his best to keep his thoughts suppressed. He wasn't sure if the warlock could read minds, but he didn't want to take the risk. He had to appear to be coming round to the warlock's plan for his own to work...

Fortunately the need for dissembling wasn't immediate. As Aravin released his falcon Ivon looked past Wolmar, shading his eyes.

'Ah very good,' he said. 'Here comes Rodger's younger brother, right on time.'

A rider was approaching from the direction of the Crescent Bridge, galloping towards them across the plains that rose gently to meet the hills.

'Ah the young,' smirked Ivon. 'Always in such a rush! Unbefitting a noble, but he's young and will learn... Aravin! Kaye! Look lively there! It's time to receive the new Margrave of Narbo.'

The flushed youth who dismounted from a piebald palfrey could not have been more different from his late brother. Though but sixteen summers, Clovis was well made: stocky and muscular. He wasn't the handsomest of men, but a keen manliness was in his mien. He would make a good knight.

Or a good thrall, thought Wolmar as Ivon favoured him with a courteous bow.

'Clovis, welcome!' he said, leading the youth over to where their squires had pitched an awning. Sweetmeats and wine were laid out upon a thick rug of ermine. 'And may I be the first among us to say how dreadfully sorry I am about your poor brother. His tragic loss grieves the depths of my very soul.'

Or would if you hadn't sold it to the Fallen One, thought Wolmar as the other margraves offered their false condolences.

'Let us not prevaricate,' replied the youth bluntly. 'My brother was weak and lecherous, over fond of wine and women. He was bound to come to a bad end eventually.'

'Your Lordship is most direct of speech,' said Ivon, exchanging amused glances with Kaye and Aravin as they accepted wine from their squires. Their duty discharged, the squires left the five nobles alone under the awning.

'Clovis, you have been direct with us, and I shall deem it a point of honour to repay your frankness in kind,' said Ivon, studying the youth over the rim of his goblet. 'Your late brother – Reus bless his soul! – may have appeared a drunken sot to many, but he was party to some pressing affairs of state.'

That appeared to catch the young noble's attention. 'I see,' he said. His voice was neutral, but his eyes told a different story. Hooked, like a fish on a reel. Or perhaps one of Ivon's trained falcons.

'You have just arrived at court and cannot be expected to know all its goings on.' Ivon handed the young noble a goblet. 'So allow me to supply you with the requisite information. The King means to take us to war next year – for too long now have we allowed our unrefined northern neighbours to lounge uncontested beyond the Orne Ranges. A new age is dawning, and Carolus means for all who follow him to share in its glory!'

'So you want my knights to join an invasion of Vorstlund?' The youth certainly did not mince his words.

'Quite,' allowed Ivon. 'As you will doubtless know, not all the margraves are favourably disposed towards their king. If the planned invasion is to succeed, he needs to know who his friends are.'

Clovis nodded, thoughtfully sluicing wine around his mouth before swallowing. 'I am not my brother,' he said. 'If there is to be a war, I would glory in the chance to serve my king, not shy away from battle like a coward.'

'Ah, eloquently put,' smirked Ivon. 'I knew we could count on you, Your Lordship – I have heard much about you that is promising.'

'Before I came by my title I was squiring for a vassal of my father's. He says I couch a lance as well as any dubbed knight after but two years' training. Before that I was a page of course, but that didn't stop me from practising – '

Ivon raised a bejewelled hand. 'Yes, yes... I am well aware of your credentials, Lord Clovis. I have no doubt that you shall be useful in the field.'

Clovis glared suspiciously at Ivon. 'Is that why you've brought me out here? Why does this come from you and not His Majesty?'

'I speak for the King in such matters,' said Ivon. 'He personally requested that I solicit your opinion. One other thing I would ask of you... How speed your devotions?'

The young noble blinked. 'My what?'

'Your devotions,' repeated Ivon. 'Are you a devout man? Do you pray on Rest-days, as a good Palomedian should?'

Clovis looked as puzzled as Wolmar felt. 'I do service as a noble should. What of it?'

Ivon raised his eyes to the heavens, as if scouring the horizon for more pheasants. 'If I were to tell you that another crusade is possible, and that the southern barons were moved to take the Wheel, where would your heart's desire lie?'

The youth did not hesitate. 'My first loyalty is to king and country, always,' he said sincerely.

Ivon raised his goblet in a half toast, looking at the lordling and beaming again. 'Excellent! Lord Clovis, I think you and I are going to get along marvellously! Now pray, if you'll indulge me, show us your skill at falconry just once before we finish our lunch and go back to the city...'

✢ ✢ ✢

'Of course the boy is a complete dolt and quite malleable,' explained Ivon, running his fingers up and down Wolmar's muscled torso. Only a couple of weeks ago the sensation would have thrilled the princeling; now it was all he could do to conceal his revulsion. He had to keep dissembling, play the game...

'So why all the questions and fair speech?' asked Wolmar.

'I had to be sure which way his youthful choler would spur him,' said the Margrave. 'Some young gallants take it into their heads to go crusading. A fine trick of the Arch Deceiver's the Pilgrim Wars have been, but we'll need all the swords we can get if the invasion of Vorstlund is to be successful.'

Wolmar gawped, sitting bolt upright and nearly banging his head on the canopy. 'Did you just say what I think you did?' he exclaimed.

'Oh yes,' replied Ivon with a devilish grin. 'Tis said among sorcerers' circles that it was the work of the Seven Princes – one of them possessed the Vizier who advised the Sultan to banish pilgrims of the Creed from Ushalayim, while the other possessed the Supreme Perfect who sanctioned the First Pilgrim War in retaliation. Once it got started it was really quite easy – most rulers were only too glad to get truculent knights and barons out from under their noses, and a foreign war was the perfect way to do it. In fact that's exactly the purpose the next Pilgrim War will serve. Here, let me show you...'

Hopping lightly out of bed, Ivon strode over to his desk and opened a drawer. Rummaging around he pulled out a parchment scroll tied with a ribbon and brought it back over to the bed. Unravelling this he thrust it under Wolmar's nose.

'A map of my fair kingdom,' said Ivon. 'Pangonia's polity is complex, as you can see. You remember I told you how it used to be three provinces of the Thalamian Empire? Well that still holds to some extent – we may be a unified kingdom, but each region has its own identity. Now as we've already established, the next Pilgrim War will take care of the southern margraves of Lower Vallia. They have a tradition of crusading that goes back to the First Pilgrim War.'

'Why not get the lords of Lower Vallia to go along with your plot? If they hate the King and his taxes so much.'

Ivon shook his head. 'I've been observing them for some time. The Lower Vallians may despise the King – but not enough to depose him. They prefer to keep him weak, but they would stop short of an outright rebellion. And they're hardly well disposed towards me either – I'm known as an ungodly man and they won't countenance the idea of having me as king. No, best to have them out of the way in the Pilgrim Kingdoms... I have allies there who can deal with them in good time.'

He pointed further up the map. 'Here we have Upper Vallia, that's all the provinces surrounding the capital. They're the loyalist hardliners, they'll be the most difficult to persuade, except Valacia that is.'

'Valacia? Isn't that where Hugon is from?'

'Well remembered my sweet – but it's his older brother you need to be thinking of... You'll have heard of Sir Azelin?'

Wolmar stifled a yawn. 'Slew the last of the Wyrms, went off on crusade, said by some to be a reincarnated avatar of St Alred the Pious.'

'My, you have been paying attention!' exclaimed Ivon. 'He joined the Knights Bethler to be precise, a religious order of warrior-monks charged with defending the Pilgrim Kingdoms. Said to be the fiercest fighters in the world. Also very, very rich. One of the Order's rules states that any knight joining – be he landless and poor or titled and rich – must donate all his possessions to it. So... Valacia has been held in escrow by the Bethlers ever since Sir Azelin joined them.'

'Which puts Valacia on board for another crusade.'

'Exactly. It also gives me extra leverage over Sir Hugon – he'll get Valacia for himself as long as he accepts me as king. Together with Isolte keeping his loins warm that should ensure his loyalty.'

'What about the rest of Upper Vallia?'

'Well Narbo is taken care of thanks to young Clovis – I don't think I'll tell him about our coup just yet though. I want time to observe him, see what kind of idiot he proves to be. As for Morvaine, he hates me but is ambitious and has no love for the King either. I've offered him my old lands in Vichy once the thing is done. It's a convenient enough transaction after all – they neighbour his own.'

'That's why Morvaine is at court... you've been meeting him in private! The King thinks he's still mulling over the invasion plan.'

'Wolmar, I think you are finally beginning to understand Pangonian politics.' Ivon beamed at him again, his lips crooking a sinister smile.

'So what about the last two margravates in Upper Vallia? Gorlivere and Verrun?'

'They are loyalists to the bone and won't be turned. But we'll take care of them once the invasion of Vorstlund is done. They can die defending their precious king.'

'And that just leaves...'

'The peninsula – Occitania. It was the last to hold out against the Thalamians of old and nothing much has changed. They are rebellious to a fault and thus the easiest to turn – they resent the King's taxes more than anyone else. That's where Aravin and Kaye have proved most useful – Varangia and Quillon are in the heart of the western provinces. Over time they've managed to persuade the rest of the Occitanian barons that I'll reverse the King's taxes and grant them autonomous status once I'm on the throne.'

'Are they your thralls too?' Wolmar could not keep the bitterness out of his voice.

'To some extent,' said Ivon. 'I caught them young when they arrived at court years ago. I have initiated them into some of the mysteries of the Left-Hand Path. Such power is very persuasive over men's minds.'

'So they prefer to be captives, like your precious falcons,' said Wolmar.

Ivon grinned. 'Indeed. Aravin and Kaye are my closest allies, my acolytes if you will. I have bound them body and soul to the King of Gehenna. Only they of all the margraves know our true plan, and the rewards it shall bring. The rest are just pawns.'

Wolmar scanned the map again. 'And what about the border provinces, to the east?'

'As I said before, Narvon, Rhunia and Orrin are too preoccupied with their skirmishes with barons across the border in Thalamy to get involved with the invasion, but they might come round once the Thalamians are invested in Vorstlund with our forces. Even if they don't, they won't be strong enough on their own to oppose us.'

Wolmar looked at the map once more, counting territories.

'That's thirteen barons, including you, behind the invasion of Vorstlund... In my country that's an unlucky number.'

'Oh really? Perhaps it will be unlucky for the Vorstlendings then. Or the King that leads them into battle.'

Springing to his feet the Margrave rolled up the map and put it back in the drawer.

'Why not simply enthral Carolus himself and have done with it? Be much more straightforward than all this skulduggery.'

'Ah, would that it were so easy,' mused Ivon, pouring himself some wine. 'I may have succeeded in blindsiding him, but Carolus is no fool. He is a man of strong will, unlike some other rulers I could mention...' He turned and caught the princeling in his dark eyes again. 'But then you'd know all about resisting Enchantment wouldn't you, my sweet Wolmar?'

The knight felt his heart leap into his mouth.

'Oh I've got you under my thrall for now,' the Margrave continued, sipping at his wine. 'But I am wise enough to know the limits of power. Your vanity and pride are weaknesses, but it was your lust that clinched it. That was how I was able to enthral you, but I don't need to read minds to sense how... your feelings for me have waned.'

The warlock actually looked sad when he said this. Wolmar felt himself relax – at least he didn't suspect him of anything more specific than wanting to break his spell.

'Resist my magick all you like,' Ivon went on. 'It will take you weeks to break free of my glamour, like a captive with a rusty file sawing through his chains. But by then it will be too late to make any difference. For I shall not seek to control you forever, Wolmar. Unlike some of my brethren, I don't like relying over much on my powers of Enchantment. There are other ways to command mortalkind.'

Wolmar felt his hackles rise. 'What do you mean, other ways?'

Ivon gestured with his goblet at the darkening skies outside. 'You will be initiated at the next full moon. After that you shall serve me of your own free will – once you have had a taste of the True King's power you will not think twice about doing so.'

The Margrave walked slowly over to him. 'And once that is done...' He leaned down to kiss him full on the lips. 'We shall rule in Rima together.'

Ivon put down the goblet and cupped Wolmar's chin gently. 'I was being sincere when I said I'd taken a liking to you. I sense a powerful spirit in you, Wolmar of Strongholm.'

'Your confidence in me is... flattering,' Wolmar managed. His mind was spinning. Forcing himself to play along, he reclined on the bed and let the naked Margrave straddle him.

The next full moon was less than a tenday away: he needed to get to the smithy right soon, and put his plan into action.

⭐ CHAPTER IV ⭐

A Road Rejoined

They broke cover from the Glimmerholt at dawn. Only when the two monks were a few leagues south of it did the spectacle of war become visible to the north-east: Merkstaed was burning. Beyond it the turrets of Graukolos were just visible, defiantly intact against the skyline.

'They'll be investing it now,' said Horskram as they paused to feed their horses and take mouthfuls of water. 'Hopefully that should keep the Lanraks preoccupied.'

'Do you think they'll send men after us?' asked Adelko. It felt strange to be on the road again, once more the hunted.

'Us? Unlikely – they'll be far too busy laying siege to Graukolos and eliminating Markward's knights wherever they find them to care about a pair of Argolian friars.'

'Of course, Master Horskram,' stuttered Adelko. 'A foolish question.' He had been thinking more of his erstwhile companions when he asked it. He hoped his mentor wouldn't catch on.

Trying to dissemble someone with the sixth sense was never a good idea.

'You're not thinking of us though are you?' Horskram asked, turning beady eyes on his novice. 'I thought I saw a familiar coat of arms down there on the tourneying field... speak! What do you know that I don't?'

Sighing inwardly and preparing himself for yet another scolding, Adelko confessed all he knew.

'Pah, I should have known those idiot swordslingers would try something stupid,' spat the adept. 'And how very like you to go along with their reckless tomfoolery! I shouldn't be surprised by now – heavens Adelko, you are by far the most rebellious novice I've ever trained! If it weren't for your obvious psychic and intellectual talents, I'd have long cast you into the wilderness!'

'I trust I haven't been without my uses so far,' the novice managed to stammer back, though he could not meet his mentor's eyes.

'And quell that blasted pride this instant!' yelled the old monk. 'Most unbecoming a fledgling – which you still are by the way – of the Order! Hush now, let me think a minute.'

It seemed a long minute to Adelko. Presently his mentor spoke again.

'Well, there's little doubt the Herzog will send a party to recapture Adhelina and eliminate the others,' he said. 'I can only fathom that Hengist deemed a war preferable to marrying someone who had dishonoured him so... I doubt Albercelsus would have counselled this, he's far too cautious.'

Adelko cared not a jot whose idea the surprise invasion had been. 'What are we going to do to help our friends?' he asked. 'We can't just leave them to be butchered by the Lanraks!'

Horskram turned his sapphire eyes on Adelko again, only now they had the hardness of diamonds. 'Need I remind you, Adelko of Narvik, that our first loyalty is to our mission. We needs must get to Rima – we've delayed long enough as it is!'

'But the way south is fraught with brigands – you said as much yourself! If we can catch Vaskrian and the others we'll be safer travelling in numbers. Surely the Lanraks won't pursue them beyond Dulsinor's borders – not if they've a war to fight.'

'I wouldn't be so sure of that,' said Horskram. 'Presumably Hengist's plan depends on there being no incumbent left in Dulsinor. He must mean to wipe out the entire Markward lineage and parlay with Brigmore, convince him to give up the castle without a fight.'

The monk paused again, deep in thought.

'All right, we'll try to find them if we can,' he said. Adelko felt his heart surge. 'But no heroics!' he added, catching the look on his face. 'Chances are they've decided to go cross-country, reduces the chance of meeting anyone on the south road who might recognise Adhelina and detain them.'

'But what about vassals of the Eorl?' queried Adelko. 'They hold lands from Wilhelm and might just as easily recognise her.'

'A fair point, but I should think they will be too busy mustering to notice. No, both routes are risky but I think our gallant friends would most likely ride across country. Very likely the Lanraks sent to despatch them will do likewise... The chance of plunder will sway them as much as their orders, and knights are a bloodthirsty lot in times of war.' He nodded towards the horizon. 'We keep riding cross country for now – we can make the Blattwood from the north-west, where it meets the foothills of the Hyrkrainians. From there we can skirt the woods until we reach the road.'

Adelko could see the last of the ranges as they tumbled down towards the plains of Dulsinor, just a faint sketch encroaching on the horizon.

'Let's not tarry,' said Horskram. 'Without a road it's two days of hard riding to reach the forest.'

Without another word he spurred his horse into a gallop. Following suit, Adelko mouthed a quick prayer of thankfulness. Reus willing, he'd see his friends again. Hopefully alive and in one piece.

✢ ✢ ✢

It was early the following morning when they came across a sight Adelko had hoped never to see again. The burned village and hewn corpses put him in mind of the ravages of Thule's knights earlier that year. On a hill overlooking the lands around the village the shell of what had been a manor house still smouldered. Once again the killers had given no thought to age or sex. The novice felt his stomach churn as they dismounted to inspect the blood-spattered villagers.

Horskram made the sign as he finished intoning a prayer. 'Looks like I was right about the Lanraks sending knights after our intrepid idiot friends at any rate – there are too many hoofmarks for just half a dozen.'

'I shouldn't think our friends would do a thing like this in any case, Master Horskram,' replied Adelko, although he had seen enough of the world by now to wonder how true that was.

They were about to remount when they heard a groaning sound. It was coming from a barn. A trail of blood led from the village through its open door. The marauding knights had not bothered to burn it down. Investigating they found a villein coughing up blood, his chemise soaked scarlet where a spear had pierced his breast.

'The spear tip is still lodged inside the wound,' muttered Horskram after a cursory examination. 'Probably what stopped him bleeding to death, though his end cannot be far away.' Bending closer to the peasant he addressed him in Vorstlending. 'When were you attacked? How many of them?'

Horskram watered the bondsman's mouth with some water. He coughed and spluttered. 'About a dozen knights... came on us out o' nowhere yesterday afternoon... They wanted to ask us questions but the lord o' the manor insisted on fightin'... Loyal to a fault... Said Lanraks had no business bein' on his lands... We tried to 'elp the master but we're jus' ordinary common folk... They butchered us all...'

'For your loss I truly grieve,' said Horskram, more gently now. 'I can but pray for your soul to ease its passing through Azhoanarn – can you tell me what questions they asked?'

The peasant coughed up another torrent of blood. '... Said they were after two damsels... hkk... an' a party o' foreign freeswords... hkk... we saw just such an hour or so afore the knights came... but they didn't stop...' The bondsman's voice trailed off as he coughed up more dredges of red. Horskram intoned another prayer, pressing his circifix against the man's forehead as he hacked up the last of his life.

'We've no time to bury them,' said Horskram as they returned to their horses. 'The folk of Dulsinor will have to look to their own.'

By now Adelko knew enough of war not to protest, though he still felt queasy. 'Is that why they slaughtered the villagers?' he asked as they retook the saddle.

'By the sounds of it the vassal who owns these lands really was loyal to a fault,' said Horskram, taking the reins. 'Had he been less so, the Lanraks might have spared his domains. At least their bloody deed will have given our friends a chance to extend their lead on them. Butchering peasants takes time.'

As they kicked their horses into a gallop again Adelko hoped the next vassal would be a bit more compliant. Despite everything he'd seen, he still wasn't used to war. That was a good thing, he supposed.

✤ ✤ ✤

Dusk was creeping across the plains as they crested a hill to get a better view of the land they had spent the day fleeing across. Squinting, Vaskrian could make out a blaze of light on the horizon.

That'll be the demesne we passed this afternoon, he thought ruefully. He felt sorry for the innocents who got caught up in a war, but war was war for all that: a chance of glory and spoil for the knights, death and privation for the commoners. He supposed he was somewhere in between.

At least his squiring job had got easier, he reflected as they set up a rudimentary camp for the night. His days of leading a laden sumpter were long gone: daring rescues of damsels meant speed took precedence over everything. His guvnor now had to ride in full harness on a charger and tough it out like Sir Torgun did.

Neither knight had exchanged a word, but they were still rivals alright: you could see it in the way they jockeyed for Adhelina's attention, each one doing his utmost to make sure she was comfortable. Not that she had much of an eye for either of them right now.

But who could fault her for that? Vaskrian had seen it all unfold from the copse, itching to get involved and cursing his arm all the way. So the Eorl of Markward was dead – a shame that, he'd seemed alright as barons went. But she shouldn't go weeping like that: she was better off than a lot of poor buggers he'd seen bite the dust.

He winced as he rose to gather wood for a fire. His arm ached from riding all day – not exactly the rest Adhelina had advised for it but still, knightly fortitude and all that. Even if he'd never get to be a knight he could still try to act like one.

Anupe came and laid a hand on his shoulder as he was awkwardly breaking branches off a lone laurel that topped the hill. She shook her head, saying something in Vorstlending.

'She says not to make a fire,' translated Adhelina, wiping her eyes. 'Best not to attract attention.'

'But our pursuers are busy burning villages,' said Vaskrian, motioning towards the horizon. 'Doubt they'll go much further tonight.'

'Even so, we shouldn't take that chance,' put in Braxus. 'Leave it be, Vaskrian, we'll sup on cold meats and cheeses – is there any wine to warm us?'

'Fair enough, sire,' said Vaskrian. 'Night's not too cold at this time of year anyway. Managed to pack a wineskin too...' Walking over to his horse he pulled it from his saddle bag and handed it to Braxus.

'We'll post a watch just in case,' said Torgun. 'The night skies are clear but they'll be riding by torchlight, so we should get to see them if they catch up with us.'

'Good,' replied Braxus curtly. 'Vaskrian, you take first watch.'

Sighing inwardly the squire sat down to a plain supper under starlight. At least he'd get a few mouthfuls of wine to set him up for the night.

His watch passed uneventfully. Once or twice he saw flickering lights off in the distance, accompanied by the low rumble of distant horses, but they were headed north. Markward vassals most likely, riding to relieve Graukolos. It felt strange to be riding away from a battle. If only the Vorstlendings knew they were riding straight past their new liege. Funny old game, adventuring.

✠ ✠ ✠

Adelko's heart slumped just as his gorge rose when they came upon the next ruined village. Slaughtered peasants lay scattered about their burned-out wattle huts. Nearby two slain knights lay sprawled in the mud, flies clustered about their wounds as an opportunistic crow pecked out their eyes.

Horskram stooped to examine them. 'These weren't Lanraks,' he said. 'Most likely father and son, the lord of the manor and his lucky heir.'

'What makes you so sure?' asked Adelko, ignoring his sardonic humour.

'Coat of arms,' said Horskram, pointing to the triple-coloured escutcheon on the older knight's rent tabard. 'It matches the one on yonder banner.' Adelko looked to where Horskram was pointing. A flag blazoned red, white and blue lay on a broken shaft before the smoking manor house that overlooked the village. 'Whoever's in charge of the knights pursuing our friends is taking every chance he can to wipe out knights loyal to Dulsinor.'

'But why slaughter the peasants too?' Even now, after everything he had seen, Adelko could not bring himself to accept the realities of conflict. It seemed so brutal and senseless.

'Every able man slaughtered is one less man to serve as a conscript, or support the Markwards with toil in the event of a prolonged war,' replied Horskram.

'But the women... the children?' Adelko gestured expansively at the four score dead bodies. 'Thule's knights did the same thing, back in Northalde... Why did they have to kill them as well?'

'To terrorise the population,' replied Horskram, more sadly than anything else. 'It all adds up over time – war is as much an endurance test as it is a battle of wits and skill. The more people you kill, the more likely you are to end up the eventual victor. Or so the received wisdom has it.'

'That can't be right,' protested the novice.

'I am not saying it is,' sighed Horskram. 'But that is how many knights and lords believe war should be conducted. In truth I think some do such things simply because they enjoy it. The rest – cause, methodology, justification – is an excuse.'

Adelko mulled over his mentor's words while he said a quick prayer over the mutilated bodies. Something occurred to him.

'Did you fight like that?' he dared to ask as they remounted. 'When you were a knight I mean?'

'I fought for different reasons,' replied Horskram. 'But in the end those reasons brought me to blood and guilt, just the same. As I told you outside Strongholm, I have repented my sins. Now let us be gone – the Blattwood is but a few hours away. At least one good has come of this travesty – our quarry's bloodthirsty behaviour should mean our companions have gained some distance on them.'

Horskram said no more and spurred his horse on again. As Adelko followed in his wake he had a vision of his mentor, covered in mail with the sign of the Wheel on his tabard, slaughtering peasants in some distant land in the name of the Almighty.

That thought filled him with more horror than all the things he had seen on his travels.

✢ ✢ ✢

The skies were a deepening purple by the time they reached the Blattwood. Horskram took them in an easterly direction now, skirting the trees as they made their way towards the highway. Gazing across the green fields and well-tilled lands they had passed through, Adelko felt pity for the prosperous people of Dulsinor. He had read of Vorstlund back at Ulfang: many of its lands were rich and arable, and its peasantry lived as well as the yeomanry in the King's Dominions.

Judging by what he had seen, they wouldn't be living well for much longer.

War. It seemed to be coming on all the lands they passed through. For one mad instant he had a fancy that it was them bringing the spectre of desolation wherever they went. He thought back to his vision in the Earth Witch's realm, of the black angel. Azrael's words came back to him with a chilling clarity.

All shall meet me in the end.

Was it true, he wondered: did the Lord of Azhoanarn ride at their backs? The unpleasant thought blanketed him like a shroud as they rode through the gloaming towards the road.

✢ ✢ ✢

Adelko awoke to find Horskram nudging him with his boot. His mentor proffered him a skin of water and an oatcake with a slab of hard cheese. For an instant he thought they were back in the Brekawood in Northalde, his adventures just beginning... But no, they were in another forest in another country. The air was rich and alive with summer smells, but the clearing off the road where they had bedded down was much like any other he had been in, the birds and bees no different.

It was he who had changed.

As he ate his breakfast hurriedly he found himself wishing that wasn't the case. He had come so far and learned so much, and yet he felt jaded. Where before his spirits would have risen at the thought of more lands to explore, now they felt as weary as his aching limbs.

He needn't have feared, for things soon became interesting again.

They had been riding along the road for a couple of hours when they heard voices up ahead. Slowing their horses to an amble, they rounded a bend in the road... A tell-tale glint of armour had Horskram raising his hand, motioning for him to stop.

Following his mentor's lead, Adelko dismounted and led his horse off the road. Tethering them to an ash the two monks crept through the woods towards the sound of voices up ahead. Beyond that they could now hear the Graufluss wending its way steadily from the Hyrkrainian foothills to the west. Gingerly they moved through the thinning line of trees, until they could see a cleared area around the road where it crossed a triple-arched bridge of stone fording the river. To one side of the clearing a tent was pitched. Adelko recognised the coat of arms at the same time as he recognised Sir Wrackwulf, the Vorstlending freelancer who had distinguished himself at Graukolos.

But what really grabbed his attention were the dozen swords pointing at Wrackwulf. All but one of the knights clutching them bore the emblem of Lanrak on their surcoats and shields. The other appeared to be the leader, judging by his personalised coat of arms.

'Well, well,' said Horskram. 'I might have known. A vert stag on a sable chief with two gauntleted fists clutching a chain in argent on an azure base.'

Adelko blinked. Vaskrian had taught him the basics of heraldry, but it wasn't a strong point.

'Sir Hangrit Foolhardy,' clarified Horskram. 'That rakehell has been causing trouble since he was old enough to wield a flagon. Small wonder the Stonefist's yeomanry found no mercy.'

Adelko strained his ears to follow the exchange in Vorstlending above the roaring of the river.

'... on the Herzog's business,' Hangrit was saying. 'As such I recommend you stand aside forthwith.'

'I am not a man to interfere with His Grace's business,' answered Wrackwulf. He was dressed in his hauberk and leaning on a large warhammer, looking unruffled. 'Nevertheless, we stand on the border of Dulsinor and Upper Thulia. In accordance with the common law of Vorstlund, a knight of the realm who pitches his tent at any such crossing is permitted duelling rights, for ransom.' The bushy-bearded knight grinned, showing his crooked yellow teeth. 'And as you can see, I am well acquainted with the law.'

A couple of Lanrak knights sneered and nudged their horses forwards menacingly. Wrackwulf spun the hammer up into a fighting stance.

'Ride me down if you wish,' he said, raising his voice. 'But don't forget you're about to enter demesnes belonging to the House of Ürl. I don't think the Eorl of Upper Thulia would be pleased to learn you have violated his laws – especially if you plan on bringing armed Lanraks into his territory without his say-so. For something tells me you aren't planning on entering the tourney at Dunkelsicht... A great shame I might add, a jouster of your calibre will be sorely missed.'

The rotund knight's eyes sparkled as he favoured Hangrit with another grin to accompany the sarcastic jibe. The rakehell glowered back at him, but ordered the two knights to halt.

'All right, Wrackwulf, have it your way,' he spat. 'Sir Gunthor! Get down off your charger and clear this jumped-up freesword out of my path.'

Sir Gunthor complied cheerfully. A bull-necked man about a head taller than Wrackwulf, he looked well able for the task in hand. Sir Wrackwulf did not move as the knight bore down on him, kite held across his chest and the point of his blade extended towards his face.

Adelko had seen many evenly matched fights on his travels. This was not to be one of them. At the last moment Wrackwulf sidestepped, his graceful movements oddly contrasting his stocky bulk. Bringing his warhammer around in a whirling arc as Gunthor lunged past him, he caught him square in the back of his head. Gunthor's bascinet saved him from being brained, but the knight went down like a sack of oatmeal as a resounding clang from the blow sent a flock of woodgulls careening from the branches overhead.

'Far too eager,' commented Wrackwulf, resting the hammer over a broad shoulder and twirling his moustaches thoughtfully. 'He might as well have sent a town crier telling me he was going to try a charge and lunge! Oh well, never mind – I'm sure he's learned a valuable lesson, assuming my blow hasn't robbed him of his wits!'

Hangrit cursed loudly. 'All right, Wrackwulf, you've had your bit of fun,' he snarled. He barked an order to two more knights to get Gunthor back on his horse. Wrackwulf cleared his throat pointedly.

'I think you are forgetting the law again,' said the freelancer. 'That's *my* horse and *my* armour now... Old Gunthor will just have to ride pillion, or head back to Hockburg on foot.'

Hangrit nudged his horse forwards until he was towering over the knight. 'I think,' he said, leaning over the pommel of his saddle, 'you are forgetting that I command a dozen knights, while you stand alone. You're well liked on the tourney circuit, Wrackwulf, and for that reason alone I've indulged you thus far. I'd take it *very* kindly if you didn't abuse my generosity.'

Hangrit nodded and the other Lanraks moved forwards. Their swords were still pointing at Wrackwulf, who looked from one knight to the next in slow succession. Adelko held his breath.

'I see,' said Wrackwulf after an uncomfortable silence. 'How sad the traditions of our forefathers are no longer regarded. Still,' – with a sigh he stepped aside off the road – 'at least you were decent enough to let me give your fellow a lesson in duelling. You'll forgive me if I don't wish you well.'

'I care not a jot what you wish,' sneered Hangrit. Gunthor was just coming to his senses. They paused long enough to get the groggy knight back on his horse, before leaving without a backwards glance. Wrackwulf's eyes fired invisible crossbow bolts into Hangrit's back until they vanished beyond the trees on the other side of the river.

'I think now would be a good time for reintroductions,' said Horskram.

Wrackwulf betrayed no surprise as they emerged from the trees. 'Thought you might be along presently,' he said, placing his warhammer back among the assortment of weapons he carried on his sumpter. 'Saw your friends yesterday. They told me about the ambush. Bad business, but then the Lanraks always were too big for their spurs. Should have seen it coming really – fat chance a jumped-up little sot like Hengist would stand for it, his future bride causing a scandal like that.'

'Sir Wrackwulf, did they say where they were headed?' Horskram pressed.

'Aye, as far away from Dulsinor as possible!' replied the knight. 'Their plan is to take the south road through Upper Thulia and try to get to Westenlund. The Prince of that realm is too powerful to trifle with – they should be safe to take a ship from Westerburg once they get there. I said I'd try and delay any Lanraks as best I could – the Stonefist always made me feel welcome at Graukolos, and I'm right sorry to hear of his death. Never could stand Hengist, nor his uppity seneschal.'

A light entered Horskram's eyes. 'We could use a strong right arm on the road. Would you come with us? A chance to be avenged on Hangrit for denying you your ransom…'

Wrackwulf scratched his beard thoughtfully. 'Coming with you would mean missing the tourney at Dunkelsicht,' he mused. 'And I'm in good form right now. 'Twould be a shame to miss another chance of spoil.'

Horskram licked his lips. 'Wrackwulf, I am a senior monk of the Order, and our business takes us to Rima. Our headquarters there is both wealthy and powerful. If you elect to come with us, I can make it worth your while.'

'Well I suppose a stint of freeswording wouldn't go amiss,' said Wrackwulf. 'Don't suppose there's any chance of an advance though? Just in case – heaven forefend! – my new employer should meet Azrael upon the road, you see...'

With a wry smile Horskram reached for his purse and pulled some coins from the money the King had given him at Strongholm. Adelko caught the glint of gold as he pressed them into Wrackwulf's hand.

'Five Northlending sovereigns up front – as a gesture of goodwill,' he said.

'Foreign coin, eh?' mulled the knight. 'I'll get swyved by the moneychanger when we get to Westerburg – you know what the exchange rates are like nowadays...'

Horskram sighed and reached into his pouch again. 'Another sovereign then – to cover said swyving.'

Wrackwulf burst into a fit of stentorian laughter. 'Brother Horskram, I think I'm going to enjoy working for you very much!'

'That's *Master* Horskram to you, sirrah,' replied the irascible monk. 'Give us a minute to fetch our horses, and we'll be on our way.'

'Do we really need him?' Adelko queried as they went to fetch their steeds. 'I mean if the others are only half a day ahead of us...'

'I've no idea whether they'll get out of Upper Thulia alive,' replied Horskram bluntly. 'And whilst we may not be embroiled with Hengist's knights we could still fall prey to highwaymen – and after our last lesson I don't fancy your chances in a straight fight, Adelko of Narvik.'

Adelko paused, then made up his mind to speak it. 'But, after the way you fought against Andragorix... surely you could – '

'The way of the hierophant is not to be used lightly,' said Horskram curtly. 'Enough of your prattling and questions now! We ride with the freelancer. Our first responsibility is to get to Rima in one piece – if we can aid our madcap friends without jeopardising that, all well and good. If not, they'll just have to fend for themselves.'

Adelko knew well enough by now not to push his mentor. But he noted the new word the adept had let slip.

Hierophant. That would be worth looking up when they got to the Grand Monastery in Rima. Of that he felt sure.

⊶ CHAPTER V ⊷

A Brawl Beneath The Rafters

Dawn gifted the fields a meagre light from turgid skies as they roused themselves to a snatched breakfast. Vaskrian moved his stiff limbs and yawned. He had posted the last watch, but the night had passed uneventfully on the southern fringes of the Blattwood. At least now they were in Upper Thulia they wouldn't have to worry about avoiding knights answering the call of Graukolos.

Gazing upon the rolling plains as he untethered Yorro and fed him some oats, Vaskrian reflected that the farmsteads dotted about them looked unkempt compared with those of the land they had left behind. The hamlets were more crooked: as were the peasants who now emerged to toil the rest of the day away.

Not that it bothered him much. After all, you couldn't expect foreigners to look after their yeomanry, not like the King of Northalde did back home, or the lords of Efrilund who were loyal to his law. That Dulsinor's peasantry had seemed just as prosperous scarcely crossed his mind. The squire had to admit, for all that he loved errantry, he was starting to feel just a touch homesick.

Sir Braxus called curtly for his breakfast. Vaskrian went over to serve him while the bluebloods gathered around and discussed what to do next in Decorlangue. He'd picked up the basics here and there – learning it had been part of his ambition to become a knight after all – but he'd never really had the opportunity to master it.

And maybe he might just need it after all... hadn't Adelko suggested that the Earth Witch's words weren't to be trusted? A kernel of hope kindled in his breast.

He suppressed it instantly. Hope was a dangerous thing.

The heiress of Dulsinor was speaking animatedly, shaking her head as she pointed to where the road forked. Anupe looked just as nonplussed as Vaskrian.

Typical: the bluebloods speak over us as if we aren't even here, thought the squire resentfully.

Presently Braxus filled him in while Adhelina did the same for Anupe.

'The right-hand track leads to Dunkelsicht, where the Eorl of Upper Thulia has his seat,' explained the knight. 'We'll need to take the other road through the crossroads town of Volfburg and thence to another castle called Turstein. It guards the road taking us to Lower Thulia.'

'Why all the debate then?' queried Vaskrian as they finished their breakfast and began packing up. 'The choice seems obvious to me.'

'There's a risk we get spotted and questioned by the garrison at Turstein,' answered Braxus. 'Even if we don't, the road takes us between moorlands and fenlands and it's prey to highwaymen and robber knights. But my lady love believes we'll have fewer of the latter what with the tournament at Dunkelsicht – which is why we don't want to take the other road, it goes right through it. Too many people there who might recognise her or ask questions.'

His guvnor said no more, but bustled over to help Adhelina into the saddle just as Sir Torgun did likewise. Watching the two knights he revered scowling at one another as they competed for the heiress's attention, Vaskrian felt his heart sink. Never mind outlaws and garrisons – at this rate they were likely to kill each other.

He caught Hettie's eye as she mounted next to her mistress. Not bad at all that one, with her oval face and winsome eyes. Not as beautiful as Adhelina, but maybe not as unobtainable either...

Hettie averted her eyes with a frown. With a sigh Vaskrian took the saddle, wincing as he jostled his injured arm. The sun rose steadily behind a stifling blanket of cloud as they made their way along the road towards Volfburg. It was rutted and potholed in several places, with pools of dirty rainwater obligingly placed there by the heavens to slow their way.

'Can't we just strike out cross country?' Vaskrian complained as they navigated a difficult stretch.

'Look there,' said Braxus, pointing towards a sturdy-looking manor house not far off the road. 'I think the vassal who lives in yonder homestead might have something to say about a bunch of foreigners trespassing on his lands, no? Upper Thulia isn't at war like Dulsinor – no distractions to take advantage of.'

'But what about the knights chasing us?' asked Vaskrian, ignoring his master's sarcasm. 'At this rate they'll be on us right soon.'

'Not if Wrackwulf succeeds in delaying them,' replied the Thraxian. 'And besides that I think our Lanrak friends got sidetracked by the prospect of plunder and slaughter. We've a good head start on them.'

Vaskrian bit his lip at that. His master sounded foolishly optimistic. But then love did strange things to men's minds. Vaskrian caught him gazing longingly at Adhelina as she nudged her steed through the churned mud that passed for a road. Sir Torgun was on the other side of her. The two knights caught each other's eyes and glared at one another.

Sighing exasperatedly, Vaskrian pushed Yorro through the last of the muddy water. Decorum meant riding behind the knights: a pity, as it meant having to look at the sorry spectacle. He still didn't understand the Laws of Romance. Why get killed over a woman? But then even King Vasirius had been laid low by his love for Queen Mallisande, fighting a war against the Margrave of Gorleon for her hand in marriage. Several of his best men had succumbed to the same mad lovesickness, if the troubadours told it true. Sir Balian and Sir Dwalian had been brothers, renowned knights who held sieges at the Crescent Table. They had ended up killing each other in a futile duel of honour to decide who loved Mallisande the best.

Vaskrian hoped that was one piece of history that wouldn't repeat itself.

✥ ✥ ✥

Presently the heavens opened, gifting them with yet more rain. At least it gave them an excuse to pull their hoods over the heads – they didn't pass more than the odd itinerant craftsmen and a few peddlers that afternoon, but there was always the chance somebody of noble blood might recognise Adhelina.

'Most of the high-born folk of Upper Thulia should be at Dunkelsicht for the tourney,' said Adhelina when he raised the matter. 'Another good reason for taking the south road.'

It wasn't too long before they came across a good reason for not taking it.

Topping the crest of a hill as the rain eased off they saw four corpses impaled on wooden stakes. Unlike executions in Northalde, the bodies hadn't been tarred: half-skeletal mouths gaped at them beneath eye-sockets long pecked clean. The rotting remains filled the torrid air around them with a cloying stink.

'A most cruel punishment,' said Adhelina. 'My father would never have sanctioned it.' Her voice choked and she burst into tears, adding their water to the steady patter of rain on her face. Hettie nudged her horse closer to her mistress, trying to comfort her and irritably waving away the two knights as they tried to attend her.

'What crime had they committed?' Vaskrian asked her, but she ignored him.

'Banditry most like,' put in Braxus. 'That means we should keep moving, these aren't good lands in which to linger.'

'For once I agree with Sir Braxus,' said Torgun. 'Let us begone from this accursed spot. The Lady Markward is right, the punishment was cruel and unnecessary. Our King would not have sanctioned such either – a simple hanging would have sufficed.'

The Northlending put gilded spurs to his horse's flanks, splashing downhill. Without another word the others followed.

Vaskrian felt his mood sinking as he descended the hill. If it hadn't been for his arm he would have heartily wished for the Lanraks to catch up with them. A good fight would have done wonders to lighten his flagging spirits, but as it was he'd probably just make one more corpse. The road mercifully improved, and they spent the rest of the day at a gallop, greedily eating up the leagues that lay between them and Volfburg. They stopped at sunset to eat and water their horses at a stream. The sound of a lone wolf howling came across the darkening fields. The bluebloods held another conference and decided to press on through the night. Vaskrian dutifully unpacked the torches he'd thought to bring. Somebody had to think about the practicalities of a mission after all. Not that he'd get any thanks for it.

He was struggling one-armed to get the tapers out and cursed as he nearly dropped them.

'Here, let me help.'

He turned, half-expecting Anupe... But she didn't speak his tongue.

'You speak Northlending?' he gawped as Hettie took the torches from him.

'Don't look so surprised,' she said, without meeting his eye. 'My mistress taught me many things at Graukolos. When we were growing up together... before all this.'

'You speak it well,' said the squire, doing his best to sound charming.

'Save your flattery for the town wenches,' Hettie told him. 'Now show me where you keep your tinderbox – we need to get these things lit...'

They had just lit a couple of torches when they heard another sound. A couple more wolves had answered the lone call, but this was something else. A distant rumbling. Peering north Vaskrian saw the pinpricks of flickering lights.

'The Lanraks!' cried Braxus, giving voice to his thought. 'They're using the darkness to ride cross country!'

In a blaze of motion they all retook the saddle. Anupe took a torch and rode up ahead, while Hettie took the other.

'We can't risk riding on the road at night,' said Vaskrian. 'There might be more potholes and we don't want our horses to get lamed.'

'He's right,' said Braxus. 'But we can follow the road by torchlight. The Lanraks must be doing the same. Hurry! They're gaining on us!'

They rode hard for another couple of hours. The land dipped again, dropping away from tended demesnes into rough wilderness, forcing them to circumnavigate. By the time they rejoined tilled fields the moon was high in the sky. Turning Vaskrian peered intently into the darkness, searching for the tell-tale points of light.

Nothing. Then...

'They're on the other side of the wilderness I think – I can see their lights!'

Their tired steeds whinnied disparagingly as they wheeled them around for another hard ride. Steam from their flanks rose up into the night. The clouds had parted, gifting them with summer stars to help light their way. As they rode across the furrowed countryside Vaskrian could see further lights to the south. He felt the tension in his tired body ease as he realised these ones were stationary. As they pushed their horses towards them, the twinkling lights of Volfburg beckoned them towards its welcoming warmth.

✣ ✣ ✣

It was possible to see the Lanrak knights in the distance by the light of their torches, glinting off armour as they made their way across the night-shrouded fields. Horskram had even dared to light his lantern, though he kept it half shuttered.

Presently the Lanraks stopped moving, before veering off to the right, their torches suddenly disappearing.

'They've probably hit a patch of wilderness, which should be about right by my reckoning,' muttered Horskram.

'You've travelled often in these lands?' asked Wrackwulf.

'I've travelled often in many lands,' replied Horskram. 'Let's follow them.'

'Why don't we take the road?' asked Adelko. 'Surely we can travel more quickly?'

'You don't know Thulian roads,' said his mentor. 'Maintenance is not the Eorl's strong point. No, in any case, we can't afford to lose sight of the Lanraks. They'll need to stop and rest their horses eventually... And my guess is they won't be seeking lodgings at Volfburg. Come!'

Even without Wrackwulf's sumpter, the going was painfully slow. The freelancer had sold it along with half his weapons and supplies to a peddler on the outskirts of the Blattwood. The delighted vagabond had got the goods for a fraction of their true worth; Horskram had recompensed the knight with Freidheim's coin worth double that (making everyone a winner at the King of Northalde's expense, as Wrackwulf had cheerfully remarked). But navigating overgrown dells and thickets by light of moon, stars and lantern did not make for easy travelling, and Adelko felt as exhausted as his whickering horse sounded when they finally dragged themselves from the thorny embrace of wild lands back onto tended fields. Up ahead they could see a fire.

'The Lanraks are camping the rest of the night away,' breathed Horskram. 'Their steeds will be exhausted... Chargers are fine for bearing armoured men into battle, but not made for stamina unless they're Farovians... Let's keep moving!'

'I don't think our horses have much energy left themselves,' protested Adelko, though in truth it was his own aching muscles he was thinking of.

'If we skirt around the knights we can make for Volfburg,' said Horskram. 'We'll probably get there just before dawn. We can get a room at the inn there after curfew finishes.'

Mention of a warm bed and a hearth swept away Adelko's misgivings. He had thoroughly enjoyed his stay at Graukolos, and already missed the castle's comforts.

The only objection came from Wrackwulf.

'I'd fain pay them a surprise visit while they sleep,' he grinned, running a gauntleted thumb along the edge of his axe.

'And they'd fain make you welcome with many blades,' retorted Horskram. 'You'll get your chance of revenge, sir knight, but now is not the time.'

'It was just a thought,' smiled the freelancer as they moved off into the darkness.

✛ ✛ ✛

For the umpteenth time Anupe banged on the worm-eaten boards of the taproom door. Vaskrian picked idly at the stinging scabs on his face. There were still patrons up drinking; you could tell by the light seeping through cracks in the ramshackle building's wooden facade and the sound of drunken singing coming from inside.

The innkeeper evidently didn't want to let anybody in after curfew. That was normal for a town, and Volfburg looked pretty much like any normal town. It reminded him of Kaupstad, the last time he'd stayed at an inn. The place where he'd met Adelko and their strange adventures had begun.

This time the Harijan's efforts were rewarded with the sound of shuffling and a muffled voice yelling. He didn't understand the words but he reckoned he understood 'clear off and get lost' in any language. Looking down the crooked street that fought for space between hotchpotch wooden houses with rudely thatched rooves, he wondered when the watch would be turning up.

Anupe yelled back at the person inside and a heated exchange took place. With a restless sigh Adhelina dismounted and stepped over to the door, gently but firmly moving the Harijan aside. It wasn't seemly for nobles to get involved in common squabbles, all the more so when said nobles were travelling incognito, but needs must Vaskrian supposed.

In a high clear voice she said something that sounded commanding and imperious. A few seconds later the bolt was drawn and the door flung open. A wizened hunchback of a man stood in the doorway, weak light from tapers doing little for his uncomely frame. His jowls drooped to either side of his face like a dog's, and his eyes were watered with one ale too many.

Adhelina had her hood drawn up over her face, but she still knew how to strike a pose. Good job they had thought to pack cloaks for the damsels: she was still dressed in long sequined samite skirts, hardly fit for travelling. She had torn off the bottom part to get more freedom of movement; hopefully the innkeeper wouldn't look too closely at his new unwelcome guests.

Fortunately he didn't: Adhelina obviously knew how to invoke her nobility without giving away who she was. 'He says to come in and hurry up about it before the watch make any trouble,' she said. 'I suggest we do as he says.'

A bleary eyed stable boy was fetched to see to their horses. Vaskrian sidled into the common room and sized up its contents. There were three knights sitting in a corner, up late drinking and dicing. Probably heading over to Dunkelsicht, though he didn't know the country well enough to say where from. Apart from that there was just the usual assortment of riffraff dotted about the place: some drinking, some trying to sleep next to the hearth, and more than a couple passed out in a stupor.

Peddlers, artisans, mendicants and pilgrims... they all looked alike on the wrong end of a few skinfuls. The stench of beer, sweat and boiled meat was welcome to his nostrils: it reminded him of castle life. Civilisation, you might say.

'Don't suppose there's any chance of a stoop?' he asked his guvnor.

'Maybe,' replied Braxus. 'I have to see to my lady love first.'

Vaskrian swallowed his next remark and watched the two knights get flustered around Adhelina yet again. He would need an ale just for watching that. He glanced sidelong at Anupe but the Harijan was muttering something to Hettie beneath her hood.

We look a right suspicious bunch, he thought to himself ruefully. *You'd have to be as blind as Yareth the Predictor not to notice us.*

Much as he hated to admit it, they could have used Horskram. He would have known what to do, maybe even kept them out of trouble. Although come to think of it the old monk had led them into it as often as not. He glanced over at the knights in the corner, but they were intent on playing dice and ignored the new arrivals. Just as well.

Hettie was talking to the innkeeper, who had retreated back behind the rude board that passed for a counter. The unfortunate fellow yelled something in Vorstlending at a bent-backed crone whom Vaskrian took to be his wife. She yelled back at him and spat on the rushes, before beckoning politely for the damsels to follow her upstairs.

The squire was watching this exchange with a wry smile, and just thinking about renewing his suggestion of a flagon or two, when he heard a banging on the door.

✛ ✛ ✛

Hettie turned at the sound. Heavens, what next? She had just negotiated a couple of rooms and a cold supper; things had started to look a little more civilised. The innkeeper's wife turned from the stairwell and shuffled over to answer the door. Hettie sighed inwardly. Sleep and food would just have to wait a bit longer.

'Oo is it?' barked the innkeeper's wife. 'It's after curfew – go away!'

'We know that full well, for it's us that keeps the curfew,' came the reply. 'Open up and let us in!'

Hettie felt her nerves go taut as a lyre string. They had barely settled after everything she had been through – then the Lanraks had murdered her liege, and nearly her and Adhelina. She could still feel the chair in her hands after using it to club Albercelsus...

She fought to master her rising panic as the mistress of the inn threw the door open. 'We've 'ad complaints 'bout banging from yer neighbours,' said the head of the watch, bustling in self-importantly with three constables in tow. They were a shabby lot, dressed in rough brigandines and wearing short swords at their belts. Clearly no match for their hardened escort, but what if they called for more men? Or got the knights dicing and drinking involved?

All these thoughts and more ran through Hettie's mind as the head watchman stepped up to them.

'Well now, what have we here?' he queried, looking them up and down. 'Outlanders by look of it. Come now, sirrahs, what's yer business makin' a racket at this time o' night?'

'We're respectable travellers from the north,' said Adhelina, in icily regal tones. 'And we don't take kindly to being questioned by commoners.'

Her manner had the watch captain on the back foot. For a moment Hettie thought he would turn and stalk back out into the night...

'I see,' he said. 'Right strange, high-born ladies supping at an inn. What with Turstein Castle bein' just down the road and all.'

Hettie decided to get involved. The watchman was peering at her mistress, trying to discern her features in the dancing light of the tapers. She ought to distract him.

'We were delayed by rain on the roads,' said Hettie, using her haughty voice. 'So we decided to stop here instead. These are our bodyguards,' she added, gesturing at the others.

The captain looked sidelong at the four hooded figures whose hands were suddenly much closer to their sword hilts than before.

'I see...' he said again. 'Strange that high-born folk such as yerselves would use foreign freeswords as bodyguards. Where in the north be ye from?'

Adhelina took up the thread. 'We're from Freiburg,' she said. 'A relative of mine has taken poorly in Westenlund. I'm travelling to see her.'

Hettie had to think a minute. Freiburg was a minor barony, its lands nestling just west of the Great White Mountains on the northern reaches of Ostveld. It made sense that they would be using the road through Thulia to get to Westenlund... The watch captain looked just about satisfied with that answer. He seemed on the point of ordering his men out the door when she heard the jingling of spurs behind her.

Turning she saw one of the knights had got up from the table in the corner.

'Good evening,' he said, proffering a courteous half bow. 'Sir
Lors of Micklenburg, at your service. I could not help but overhear
your conversation. My comrades and I have come from Ostveld.
We're on our way to Dunkelsicht for the tournament. Curious that
we did not see you on the east road...'

Sir Lors eyed them keenly. He was tall and broad-shouldered,
an elaborately curved pair of mustachios after the fashion of the
eastern Vorstlendings crowning a handsome face. 'I was fortunate
enough to guest at the baronet of Freiburg's castle last summer,
and met all his household,' the knight continued. 'If you would but
remove your hoods it would be seemly to reacquaint ourselves with
one another.'

Hettie held her breath. Nobody moved, except the two other
Ostvelding knights, who slowly rose from the table and stalked
over to join Sir Lors. Everybody else in the taproom who was still
conscious now watched the scene unfolding before them.

Then it came, a tortured whining. The sound of a blade slowly
being drawn from a scabbard. Anupe brandished her falchion, its
wicked edge catching the torchlight.

'I think you ask too many questions,' said the Harijan.

Sir Lors stared at the hooded freesword. His composed
expression had not changed, but his hazel eyes had hardened.
Without taking his eyes off her he slowly unsheathed his own sword.

'That is an unmannerly remark for a foreign churl to make to a
vassal of the House of Kaarl,' he said in a voice that was dangerously
calm. 'I suggest you apologise now.'

His two companions added naked steel of their own to emphasise
the suggestion, prompting Vaskrian, Torgun and Braxus to bring
their own blades to the gathering. The four watchmen followed suit,
probably more for fear of being left out than anything else: they
already knew they were in over their heads.

'We don't want any trouble,' said Torgun, addressing the
Ostvelding knights in Decorlangue. 'Put up your blades and let us
go about our business, no one need get hurt. Reus knows we've seen
enough bloodshed of late.'

Lors turned cool eyes on the lofty knight. 'And who might you
be, sirrah?' he replied. His tone had suddenly become formal. He
clearly realised he was dealing with a fellow nobleman.

Pulling back his hood Torgun shook out his flaxen locks. 'Sir
Torgun of Vandheim, knight errant and lately commander of the
White Valravyn, at your service.'

That gave Sir Lors pause for thought. 'Sir Torgun,' he said, nodding courteously. 'Your reputation precedes you. I had the honour of seeing you joust at the Glade Ring Tourney in Saltcaste two summers ago... Pray what brings you so far from your native land?'

Torgun was just about to reply when the sound of trotting horses came filtering in through the open door. The landlord had been slowly edging away back towards the counter, but now he darted over to close it.

'You there!' came a cry from outside. 'Hold that door if you value your life!'

The landlord froze. The horses had pulled up, Hettie could hear them whickering just outside. She had lived long enough in a castle to recognise the sound of jingling armour as their riders dismounted.

'The Lanraks!' she said, turning to look at Adhelina.

'What's this about Lanraks?' asked Sir Lors sharply.

'Enough games.' Adhelina pulled down her hood. 'Sir, we have deceived you,' she said bluntly. 'I am Adhelina of Dulsinor, and this is my lady-in-waiting, Hettie Freihertz. We are refugees from a war that has killed my father and driven me from my ancestral home.'

Sir Lors gawped at that, just as four more knights strode in through the door. All wore Lanrak colours and carried drawn swords. The lead one was a beefy, bull-necked fellow with a rude bandage around his head. He looked to be in similarly rude spirits for all that.

'We're bachelors in service to the Herzog of Stornelund,' he declaimed. 'Soon to be ruler of Dulsinor as well. These damsels are traitresses to their liege and must return with us to face trial and punishment.'

Torgun and Braxus had taken up fighting stances along with Vaskrian, and joined Anupe to stand between the Stornelendings and the damsels.

'A bold claim, sir knight,' said Lors. 'And yet even if it be true, I believe we stand on lands belonging to the House of Ürl... Which means you have no more authority here than we do.'

The bull-necked knight sneered at that. 'So whose authority do we answer to? These riffraff watchmen? Don't make me laugh.'

He spared a vicious glance for the captain of the watch. The churl's poorly kept blade quivered in his hand and he said nothing. Clearly the House of Ürl would have to forego its authority for the nonce.

One of the Ostveldings stepped forward and whispered something in Lors's ear. He had a mop of brown hair and an ugly face made all the worse by the scar that bifurcated it; Hettie felt sure she recognised him. Sir Lors looked at his fellow and frowned. He seemed troubled by what the other knight had said.

The bull-necked knight waited patiently for a few moments more, then said: 'Come on, no need to draw this out – we've twice our number again just out of town. Give up the damsels and there'll be no need for bloodshed. That goes for you lot too.' The last remark was aimed at their protectors. Presumably the Stornelending bruiser had mistaken them for freeswords, loyal only to coin.

'Just a moment,' said the scarred knight. 'I'd say we've just as much claim to the damsels as you do, seeing as how we're all on neutral territory.'

The bull-necked knight glared at him. 'And who might you be?'

'Sir Ugo of Veidt,' replied the scarred knight. 'As it happens I've been following the Lanraks and their recent plans with great interest... I take it the wedding didn't work out as planned then.' Sir Ugo's face was creased in two directions now as he smirked nastily. Hettie felt her nerves tighten to breaking point.

Of course, she thought. *He was part of the emissary that tried to persuade Wilhelm to cancel the wedding this spring – the last thing the Ostveldings want is to let us go!*

Adhelina had clearly realised much the same. 'The wedding was a hoax,' she said quickly, addressing Ugo and Lors. 'The Lanraks never intended it to go ahead – 'twas merely a ruse to get my father to lower his guard so they could murder his best knights, him, and myself before laying claim to Dulsinor.'

'Oh the wedding was genuine,' put in bull-neck. 'Only Hengist wouldn't consent to wed anyone who'd dishonoured his house by trying to flee her nuptials. So your father's blood is on your own hands, my lady.'

Adhelina blenched at the knight's cruel words. She looked as though she had just been run through.

'What matter is it who caused what?' cried Hettie, picking up where her mistress had left off. 'The point is that the Houses of Markward and Lanrak are now at war. Think on it Sir Ugo, your liege opposed the alliance on the grounds of the Treaty of Lorvost – no one family should become all-powerful in Vorstlund. If you let the Lanraks take us, you're allowing that to happen!'

Both knights considered that.

'She's right,' said Ugo. 'That's why we can't let the Lanraks take Her Ladyship. Better to take the damsels back with us to Ostveld. Our liege will reward us greatly for such a service.'

Lors seemed to make his mind up. 'Sir Ugo has the right of it,' he said, addressing bull-neck. 'We're taking them back with us – something tells me your eight friends aren't close enough to put the odds in your favour. For only a fool would ride into a foreign town near a castle with a dozen armed men at his back.'

Bull-neck scowled. 'All right then, sirrahs, if it's a melee you're after, let's have at it!'

Torgun was already lunging at him as he spoke. In a second the room was awhirl with flashing steel as all hell broke loose.

A four-way tavern brawl was always going to be a good way of starting a general panic. Hettie found herself lying under the counter clutching her mistress as patrons ran pell-mell, trying to exit a taproom that had suddenly become crowded with highly trained men in armour doing their level best to kill each other.

By the time the stampede had ended, two watchmen lay on the floor bleeding their lives into the rushes as bullneck sat against the wall, screaming as he watched blood pump from the stump of sword-arm Torgun had left him with. The third Ostvelding was also down, wailing as an arc of red spurted from a gash where his eye had been. The rest were involved in a messy tangle of blades. The innkeeper had left with the mass exodus, which had included the watch captain screaming blue murder.

'They'll have half the town on us!' she yelled at her mistress. 'We have to get out of here now!'

'We can't just leave on our own!' Adhelina shouted back.

Hettie looked at the antagonists, trying to fathom who was fighting whom. She saw Vaskrian, wildly waving his dirk left-handed, but in his state he was little more than a distraction. Unexpectedly she felt her heart clench at the thought of his dying or getting hurt.

She had no time to reflect on the emotion as Sir Torgun cut down another Lanrak and Anupe sidestepped a lunge from Sir Ugo, slicing open the back of his neck and bringing him crashing to the floor in a limp heap. Sir Lors yelled in pain as Sir Braxus struck him just below the knee: tottering back on one leg the knight crumpled to the ground. The two remaining Lanraks backed out of the door before bolting for their horses.

'After them!' cried Braxus. 'We can't let them warn the others!'

Anupe was one step ahead of him. Drawing her dirk, she bounded over corpses to the doorway and flung it. A cry followed by a crumpling sound told of the trueness of her aim. Sir Torgun shoved past her and ran out of the door, instinctively apologising as he did. Well technically the Harijan was still a woman, Hettie supposed.

Sir Braxus had his sword point at Lors's throat. 'Don't move an inch if you wish to move again,' he said gruffly. The injured knight froze obediently. 'All right,' said Braxus. 'I'll not kill a knight in cold blood if I can help it. Vaskrian, watch over him.' The squire moved to obey. Lors was still bleeding profusely. 'He'll bleed out if I don't help him,' said Adhelina, getting to her feet. 'I need some cloth to bind his wound and his comrade's – find the innkeeper's wife, I'm sure I saw her cowering in a corner somewhere.'

'But the captain of the watch is probably raising a hue and cry,' said Hettie. 'And one of the Lanraks got away by the looks of things.'

'All the more reason not to strike out cross country in the dead of night,' said Adhelina. 'I say we take our chances with the rest of the watch and try to save a life.'

'Aye, you're right my love,' said Braxus, nodding deferentially. 'Truly your intelligence is exceeded only by your beauty – '

'Enough,' said Adhelina, raising her hand. 'Save the courtly loveplay for a better time, Sir Braxus – perhaps you should see about helping Sir Torgun hunt down the last Lanrak.'

The sound of mighty hooves tearing up the highway told them Northalde's greatest knight had that task firmly in hand. Looking sheepish, Braxus turned to help Hettie up.

I notice he only notices me when my mistress is accounted for, she thought resentfully. Part of her wondered why Vaskrian hadn't come to help her. *Because he's busy doing as he's told and guarding Sir Lors you idiot,* she berated herself. *And anyway, why should you care either way?*

A pitiful groaning provided her with a welcome distraction from her awkward thoughts. The bull-necked knight had expired, bleeding away the last of his life. Hettie had no pity for him. She knew a chivalrous knight when she saw one, and he wasn't it.

A scrabbling sound alerted her to the innkeeper's wife, trying to sneak towards the door.

'You, churl,' said Hettie, grabbing her. 'We need cloth from the bedsheets or anything else you have, and some water in a bowl. Hurry! Two knights' lives are at stake.'

'I'm no churl but a freewoman of the town,' retorted the crone, yanking her sleeve free. 'I'll see to it, but there'll be hell to pay when the watch come back, mark my words!'

Hell wasn't how Hettie would have put it after all she'd seen, but new problems presented themselves soon enough. Her mistress was busy patching up the Ostveldings by the time the innkeeper returned with the captain, a dozen watchmen and a score of sturdy town dwellers in tow.

'All right, we know you're still in there,' said the captain in a timorous voice. 'We've an escort ready to take ye to Turstein and we're far more in numbers, so don't make any more trouble!'

Braxus stepped towards the entrance, bloodied sword in hand. Anupe clutched her dripping falchion as she took up position on the other side of the doorway.

'Lady Freihertz,' he said. 'You speak their tongue... what are they saying?'

'They're inviting us to enjoy the hospitality of the castle dungeons,' said Hettie. 'They say they overmatch us in numbers.'

Braxus spared the mob a dismissive glance. 'Tell them numbers don't always make for victory. They've seen what we can do – we'll cut them to ribbons if they try and take us.'

Hettie did her best to translate diplomatically: 'We've got enough trained swordsmen to make life short for the first of you that come in through that door.' She added to Braxus in Decorlangue: 'There's only two of you that can fight and more than thirty of them – even when Torgun comes back that's odds of ten to one!'

'They still have to come at us through the door,' said Braxus. 'Let them try it.'

That gave Hettie another idea. 'We're of noble blood,' she yelled, stepping up to the doorway. 'If commoners raise a hand against us in peacetime... you know the law! Thulia isn't at war – that means the Eorl will have to respect it and punish you all!'

That gave the mob pause for thought.

'All right,' came the answer at last. This was an elderly man dressed in a sumptuous nightgown. She took him for one of the rich burghers of Volfburg, which prospered from trade thanks to its crossroads location. 'We don't want any more trouble. Just pack up your things and be gone!'

'My mistress is tending two knights of Ostveld who were injured in the brawl,' replied Hettie. 'Give her leave to finish and we'll be on our way.'

'What about Torgun?' asked Adhelina, looking up from the binding she had just wrapped around Lors's calf. 'And there's other Lanrak knights out there waiting for us!'

'What choice do we have milady?' asked Hettie. 'We can't stay here – they'll send for knights from the castle! Then we'll have to submit.'

'She's right,' said Braxus. 'We'll have to take our chances, hope Sir Torgun got to the last one and stopped him warning the others.' Even now the Thraxian couldn't resist underscoring the Northlending's name with hatred.

They waited in tense silence while Adhelina saw to the knight with a missing eye. He had passed out, making her job easier.

'There,' she said, rising at last. 'I've done what I could for both of them, but without my herbs – '

She was interrupted by the sound of galloping. Sir Torgun rode into the circle of light from torches carried by the mob, which scattered before his Farovian's hooves.

'Leave them be!' cried Braxus, 'we've agreed a truce!'

Torgun sneered at him. 'Think you that I would condescend to strike poor churls, Sir Braxus? Even for a knight of your calibre, that is low.'

Braxus flinched and seemed about to step out of the inn, but Hettie laid a hand gently on his arm. 'Please, Sir Braxus, now isn't the time,' she said, hoping it would be enough to bring him to his senses. Fortunately it was. 'Did you get the other Lanrak?' he managed to ask.

'Aye,' replied Torgun. 'Hilmir is not only swifter and stronger than other horses, he has an instinct that will not be stayed by dead of night – '

Braxus waved him away disgustedly. 'Spare me the catalogue of yon horse's merits,' he said. 'I feel his loss keenly enough as it is! All I need is the sum of your actions.'

'Another Lanrak seeks the Judgment of Azrael,' supplied Torgun.

'Good,' said Hettie. 'We've just negotiated a truce with the townsfolk here. They don't want any more trouble – we've to get out of town now though.'

Sir Torgun frowned at the mob. 'Running from such commoners is unseemly,' he said. 'Tell them we shall stay the night here and be on our way in the morning.'

'Are you wise?' cried Sir Braxus. 'If we stay here any longer they'll have the half the garrison from Turstein on us!'

'As to that,' replied Torgun, dismounting, 'a knight does not flee a mob of peasants. How sad that you need reminding of that.'

Braxus was about to say something but held back, his face reddening. Torgun began making his way through the mob, leading his horse towards the stables. One or two of the men muttered, but none dared touch him as he moved among them.

'That idiot will be the death of us one day,' said Braxus, finally finding words.

Anupe and Vaskrian were gazing at them in bafflement: the entire exchange had taken place in Decorlangue. The Harijan shook her head as Hettie translated. 'This is no time for chivalrous – how do you say it? – antics.'

'No, it isn't,' sighed Hettie. 'But knights will be knights, I suppose.'

✣ ✣ ✣

Sunrise was about an hour away when Adelko finally saw the lights of what he hoped was Volfburg. They had rejoined the road a few leagues north of the town. As they were approaching the outskirts Wrackwulf suddenly pulled his horse up short.

'Give me that torch,' he said. 'I think I saw something glinting off the highway.'

Adelko complied and they nudged their steeds over towards it. A hewn corpse of a man in armour, cut down by two fierce strokes. A whickering sound caught their attention. On the other side of a ploughed field a charger stood riderless, obediently waiting for a master who would never take the saddle again.

Horskram shone his own torch over the dead knight. 'One of the Lanraks, judging by the tabard,' he said. 'And I don't know many knights strong enough to cut through a mail byrnie – I think our old friend Torgun has been distinguishing himself again.'

'I can cut a man through his byrnie,' offered Wrackwulf cheerfully. 'Tends to happen when I'm using my double-handed war axe...' His voice trailed off as Horskram fixed him with a sour look. 'Ahem,' he said. 'So, it looks as though your comrades passed this way then.'

'Let's get into town,' said the adept. 'I've a feeling it won't be sleeping, despite the hour.'

It wasn't. A crowd of townsfolk were gathered around an inn just off the central square. Horskram had whiled away the moonlit journey telling Adelko all he needed to know about Volfburg. It was a market town of some two thousand souls, mostly tanners and fullers who worked side by side with the dyers who made a prosperous living from the woad trade; besides that were traders who profited from the weekly horse market in the nearby town of Turstein. The proximity of a castle had left them confident enough to live without walls, although perhaps they were regretting that now.

For outside the inn were piled half a dozen corpses: he saw one middle-aged woman weeping over the youngest, a lad of no more than sixteen summers, a levied constable by the looks of things. Adelko murmured a prayer for his soul and wondered how much more of Azrael's ruin he would have to see before his adventures were at an end.

The townsfolk met the new arrivals with timorous stares. Several of the nearest watchmen levelled rusty spears in their direction, but Horskram paid them no mind.

'Good morrow,' said the adept. 'Horskram of Vilno, adept of Ulfang, greets thee.'

The mutterings that greeted the monk sounded more relieved than anything. Evidently the townsfolk recognised him. Adelko had to marvel: they had travelled hundreds of miles and still his mentor could count on being known wherever he went.

'Good morrow to you, Horskram,' said one of the town elders, a wealthy looking man about the monk's age. 'Though in truth it's hardly a good one, under present circumstances.'

'I can see that, Aelfred,' replied Horskram, nodding towards the corpses. 'You've had some troublemakers by the looks of things.'

'We've had to send someone to the castle,' replied Aelfred. 'Robber knights kicking up a storm – a host of them are still holed up in the inn. We offered them a chance to leave, but one of them wouldn't stand for it apparently.'

'I see,' said Horskram, exchanging a wry glance with Wrackwulf. 'And this "host" as you put it, was led by...?'

'Tall well-made chap, a northerner if I'm any judge,' replied Aelfred. 'Or he's the one that refused to leave, from what I can gather. Doesn't speak the language.'

'Hmm,' said Horskram. 'Blond fellow? Rides a dappled grey stallion, eighteen hands high?'

'That's the one!' barked Aelfred. 'You know him?'

'I do indeed,' replied Horskram. 'He was lately in my service.'

A few outraged yelps went up at that. With some difficulty Aelfred silenced the crowd. 'Let Master Horskram speak!' he cried. 'He's helped us out enough times – it was only last summer he banished the evil spirits inside of Gretta.'

'Thank you,' said Horskram cordially. 'And how does Gretta, incidentally?'

'She died, last winter,' said Aelfred. 'Still it was a clean death at least, thanks to you.'

Horskram cleared his throat. If he felt embarrassed at his faux pas he showed no sign of it. 'My condolences,' he said. 'May the prophet's peace be upon her spirit. If you'll just let me and my companions through, I can have yon outlanders out of Volfburg come dawn. Is that agreeable to you?'

As one the townsfolk nodded. Clearly it was very agreeable.

'Excellent,' said Horskram, dismounting. 'If you'll excuse us now, we'll have a word with our friends inside. Adelko, come along! Sir Wrackwulf will stay here and mind our horses.'

✢ ✢ ✢

'Have you taken complete leave of your senses!?' Horskram stared about him in bewilderment before levelling his stern gaze on Torgun. 'I leave you to your own devices for a week, and you concoct a hare-brained plan to abduct one of the most powerful women in Vorstlund – a few weeks after we rescue her! And not content with that, you get into a lethal brawl in the middle of the largest town in Upper Thulia!'

The common room was a wreck. Smashed tables, overturned barstools and cracked flagons vied for space on the floor with smears and pools of red where the slain had fallen and been dragged outside. Adelko sighed inwardly. Maybe Horskram had a point about taking up with killers after all. Were these really the sorts of friends he wanted?

Suddenly he thought of his old cronies, Arik and Hargus and Yalba, back at the monastery. Yalba! To think he'd once felt intimidated by his oafish friend.

Sir Torgun met Horskram's stare defiantly. 'I fail to see how we could have done otherwise,' he said. 'We saved Her Ladyship from certain death. As for the Ostveldings, you speak of abducting the damsels? That is just what they were about to do when we stopped them! A chivalrous knight would have done no less.'

'And the dead watchmen?' said Horskram. 'Was that a chivalrous thing to do too?'

Torgun averted his eyes. 'That was... regrettable,' he conceded. 'I for one struck no common man down.'

Braxus spoke up. 'They were in over their heads,' he said. 'We couldn't even tell you who killed them. Commoners have no business getting in the way of knights going about theirs.'

'Eloquently put,' sneered Horskram. 'Nonetheless your "knightly business" as you put it has stirred up the wrath of Upper Thulia. Now there'll be plenty more knights, coming from Turstein to apprehend you even as we speak.'

'We know that full well!' said Braxus. 'We wanted to leave, but somebody's sense of honour got in the way.'

Torgun stared at Braxus coldly. 'Yes?' snapped the Thraxian. 'Something bothers thee, sir knight?'

The two of them were about to square off against one another when Horskram stepped between them. 'ENOUGH!' he roared. 'I've a good mind to leave the pair of you to face the Eorl's justice! Peace now, let me think a minute.'

Adelko exchanged a wry glance with Vaskrian while Horskram ordered the innkeeper's wife to pour him a cup of ale. He had to admit, it felt good to see his friend again, even if he was trouble. Two wounded knights lay slumped against the wall. One of them was groaning pitifully but the other was fully conscious and alert. He felt his sixth sense tingling. They would have to plan their next move carefully.

Clearly his mentor was thinking much the same.

'We can't take the south road, that's obvious enough,' he said. 'There'll be knights upon us and the rest of the Lanraks might decide to circumvent the town and lie in wait for us there. We must take the west road.'

'But that'll take us straight to Dunkelsicht,' protested Adhelina. 'You heard what yon Ostveldings tried to do! The House of Ürl was opposed to our alliance of houses too – most likely he'll kidnap me and hold me for an Eorl's ransom!'

'Yes, I'm aware of that,' snapped Horskram testily. 'Let me finish, Reus dammit. We take the west road ten miles out – it meets with another heading to Turstein. At that point we get off the road and strike directly south, make straight for the Draugmoors.'

Adelko's heart sank. The name of the place alone told him what dangers that route would offer. He thought immediately of Tintagael.

'Are you mad?' gaped Adhelina. 'Those moors are haunted! The Draug Kings suffer none to pass through their realm and emerge... not in this world at any rate.'

'In case it had escaped your notice,' said Horskram in a brittle voice. 'I am an ordained adept of the Argolian Order, and as such I don't need a lecture from a damsel on the perils of the Other Side!' Adhelina shot him a peeved glance, but he ignored her. 'No, it's our only option,' he continued. 'If we can find the Draugfluss river we can follow it out of the Draugmoors. That will lead us straight to Heilag monastery, established by my order to stop sorcery leaking into the Westenfluss. From Heilag we can cross over into Lower Thulia – the Herzog there has no love for his northern neighbour, we'll have no trouble from Ürl soldiers on his lands.'

'And what about the Lanraks?' queried Braxus, although his tone suggested he was considering Horskram's plan.

'I doubt they'll get much further once the Eorl of Upper Thulia finds out about them,' said Horskram. 'Their last chance will be to catch us as we leave Volfburg – so if we take the west road now we should be able to shake them off for good.'

Adhelina still looked unconvinced. 'I know of Heilag monastery,' she said. 'They say even its monks won't venture on to the Draugmoors they guard – and with good reason! What makes you so sure you can lead us through them safely?'

Horskram produced the Redeemer's blood. It caught the torchlight in a blaze of red-gold that seemed to fill the room with warmth. Adelko felt a beatific peace descend over him. His sixth sense stopped tingling.

'Behold, the blood of Palom, True Prophet, broken on the Wheel in mortal form for our salvation!' cried Horskram dramatically. 'His grace shall be our guiding light!'

Torgun dropped a knee to the rushes and made the sign. Even Braxus did likewise, albeit more hesitantly. Vaskrian glanced at them and followed suit awkwardly. Anupe slouched by the doorway, looking bored. Perhaps she wouldn't be when Adhelina told her what was going on.

At any rate the damsel seemed impressed. 'You are full of surprises, Master Horskram,' she said, gently making the sign. 'Well, it would seem providence has put us on the same road. I'll trust your judgement, for now.'

'Excellent,' said Horskram, putting the relic away and draining the last of his flagon. 'Now let's be moving along! We've less than an hour before dawn – we'll need as much of a head start as we can get on our pursuers.'

With a flurry of activity they scrambled to obey.

'I hope your guvnor knows what he's doing,' Vaskrian whispered to Adelko as they hurried out of the inn. 'I don't speak Decorlangue too well, but it sounds like he's leading us into another mess!'

'Be of some cheer,' replied Adelko. 'He's steered us right so far, hasn't he?'

'Try telling that to Sir Branas,' said Vaskrian, before sloping off to the stables.

Adelko felt a pang of guilt as he watched his friend go. *Or Sir Aronn, or the Chequered Twins, or Kyra*, he thought disconsolately.

The townsfolk muttered darkly as they rode out by the west road, but did nothing to stop them leaving.

'Where are we going?' asked Wrackwulf, looking perplexed.

'Um, I'll explain it to you as we go,' hedged Adelko.

Dawn broke at their backs as they thundered up the highway. As the sun reached for the company with infant fingers, Adelko wondered how long it would be before the Draugmoors deprived them of its light.

⊷ CHAPTER VI ⊷

A City Under Siege

With a triumphant roar Guldebrand's leidang poured over the outer walls of Landarök. The inner wall of timber and turf was burning in several places. Magnhilda and Canute had done their work well.

But then that was what happened when a battle plan worked, thought Guldebrand as he led his men across the ditch towards a smoking gap in the wall. Magnhilda's forces had commandeered twenty warships and sailed down the Holm to storm the city. Sped by Ragnar's sorceries, they had arrived there in half the normal time; Guldebrand had crested the high hills overlooking the river to see a thousand warriors pour into the city, clashing with Oldrik's shrinking forces in a vicious street battle.

That was a fight he was keen to join. Striding across smouldering planks into the city outskirts, he roared a command to his men. 'Make for the harbour! Kill any fighting man you find but don't waste time raiding houses! We're going to cut the serpent's head off at its neck!'

Ragnar had told him all he needed to know. The Stormrider and what was left of his leidang were retreating back towards the centre for a last stand. Two jarls were with him: Canute had one of these pinned in the northern half of the city, Magnhilda was closing down the second in the south. That left Guldebrand to take care of Oldrik.

He and his men dashed along the narrow boarded walkways running between tenements of houses. Some of them were burning, while warriors could be seen butchering families and ravishing women in courtyards joining the houses to the streets. They were running through the south of Landarök now – clearly the jarls serving Magnhilda were not showing much in the way of restraint.

'Stay with me!' he bellowed back at the line of men following him. 'There'll be plenty of time for looting and ravishing once we've taken the Stormrider's head!'

Varra turned to repeat his command. The streets of Landarök were built in crisscross fashion; Brega could be seen in the next street parallel to them, leading a company of men towards the centre. He hoped Bjorg and Vilm would be doing likewise. They were so close to victory now – everything depended on discipline. He knew from Ragnar's report that he outnumbered the Stormrider two to one: he couldn't afford to lose men to looting now.

They passed skirmishing warriors in the streets amid screaming civilians running to and fro. This far into the thick of it he couldn't even tell friend from foe. Best to leave them to sort it out themselves.

As they reached the city centre the wooden buildings gave way to stone ones. Crossbow bolts zinged from a top window, one whistling past Guldebrand's head and another burying itself in Varra's throat. Oh well, he'd been loyal to a fault and helped him get this far.

'Ryghar, take ten men and storm that house!' he ordered a seacarl, ignoring Varra's death throes. Ryghar nodded and took a detachment of shieldmen across the courtyard towards the house. 'The rest of you with me!' cried Guldebrand. 'Keep your shields up, chances are there are more of them holed up in this part of town!'

From here the walkways dipped, sloping down to meet the river's edge. By the time they burst into the main square adjoining the south harbour, Guldebrand had lost several more men to snipers and sent another few dozen to clear the buildings housing them.

All such thoughts vanished from his mind as he sized up his final foe. A shieldwall several scores strong awaited their arrival. Behind them longships burned, sending ugly grey columns to the cobalt skies as warriors fought and died on the wharf before them.

Guldebrand returned his attention to the shieldwall. It retained formation, inviting him to attack. Swords and axes bristled behind a hotchpotch curtain of hide and oak.

'Prepare to charge!' cried Guldebrand at the men who poured into the enclosure behind him. 'Formations NOW!'

His warriors obediently scurried into position, forming five companies each a hundred strong. More and more fighters were flooding in, led by Brega, Bjorg and Vilm.

'OLDRIK!' he roared, pointing at the shield wall with his sword, slick with the blood of seacarls who had died on his blade. They had fought hard for half a day before finally breaching the outer walls: after today he would need prove himself no longer.

'OLDRIK!' he bellowed again, so he could be heard above the crackling of burning boats and the clash of arms. 'It's OVER! I outnumber thee two to one! Step forwards and kneel, and I shall spare your life. The Magnate of the Frozen Wastes commands it!'

Silence greeted his surly challenge. Guldebrand felt his men shifting tetchily behind him as the rest of his forces finished taking up position.

'I've three leidangs to your one,' said Guldebrand. 'Even now my allies subdue your jarls. You can't win this fight.' He knew from Ragnar's report that another force loyal to Oldrik would be hastening towards the city from the south. But by the time it reached the burning walls of Landarök the battle would be over.

He knew it, Oldrik knew it.

After another awkward silence a gap appeared in the shieldwall. Through it stepped a tall, lean man, with dark wiry hair and a scar that ran from his right eye down his cheek before disappearing into his mustachios. At five and forty winters, Oldrik Stormrider was haler than many a man of advancing years. He was dressed in boiled leathers and furs of ermine, and many gold rings decorated his brawny arms. Despite the situation he moved with a grace and confidence borne of years of command. Across his back were two single-headed axes. Hjalmbitr and Lindbrotna, men had nicknamed them, the Helm-biter and Shield-breaker. Together they were known as the Twin Furies.

'Guldebrand the Beardless,' he said flatly, in a voice that betrayed no emotion. 'You have presumed to bring the blood ember to my city, engirdling it with bane of wood. Weather of weapons has turned its headwinds against me. I crave only a flame farewell.'

Guldebrand took in a breath of air made warm and dusty by the burning of ships. The Stormrider's meaning was unmistakable.

'An honourable death you shall have, by my troth!' he roared. 'Single combat it is then! Logi's seed and spoil of the sword to the victor – battle sweat and sleep of the axe to him that loses!'

'My lord, do not this thing!' growled Brega behind him. 'The Stormrider's prowess is legendary – we have not seen a breaker of rings his like since Hrolf reigned as Magnate!'

King Hrolf was exactly who Guldebrand was trying to follow. 'Two hundred years have passed since Hrolf tasted the sleep of the sword and the last Ice Kingdom fell,' he declaimed loudly so everyone could hear. 'Fitting then that his successor should slay the man judged his equal!'

Gasps went up on either side at that. Though his victories were remarkable, few would say Guldebrand had proven himself equal to the great heroes of old. Today he would change that forever.

'Come now,' he said, stepping forwards and limbering up. 'Let us decide this.'

Oldrik gave a compliant grin as he stepped into the space between warbands, unslinging the Twin Furies in one fluid motion and whirling them around for good measure.

Guldebrand stopped moving and crouched in a fighting stance, sword and shield stock still as he waited for his antagonist to attack.

Once again he was up against a superior opponent. Only this time it was no first-blood fight, but a death-duel of honour to decide who would rule. His mind flashed back briefly to his last conversation with Ragnar, the night before they had arrived to storm Landarök. The White Eye had offered to daub his body with strange marks in the language sorcerers used, marks that would make him as impervious to blade and blow as the ocean itself. Guldebrand had refused. How could he trust a banished Left-Hand warlock to lay such magick on him? He would not be controlled so easily.

As Oldrik circled around him, he wondered briefly if that had been the right choice. Perhaps giving up a sure victory by force of numbers was a mistake... but something deep in his marrow told him this was his day.

He did not doubt that even as the Stormrider launched his first devastating attack.

Guldebrand stepped back as two whirlwinds of steel whistled about him, searching for a gap in his defences. Guldebrand offered none. Blow for blow he met the Stormrider, answering Helmbiter and Shieldbreaker with his sword and target; an unearthly speed and strength seemed to possess him, a cold battle-fury that channelled berserker rage with none of its recklessness. Oldrik's stoical features allowed a flicker of surprise as his youthful antagonist matched his striking, parrying and riposting again and again before launching a counter attack of his own.

No cheers went up from either side: a death duel to decide the outcome of a war was met with grim silence. No wagers would be made on the outcome of this fight. None but the fate of a future kingdom.

Of all this Guldebrand thought little as he felt his body move with a lithe swiftness seemingly of its own accord. He felt rather than saw his feet move in perfect time to Oldrik's; he sensed rather than heard the clang of steel on steel and the thunk of blade on oak as his notched sword and ravaged shield saved him from one lethal blow after another. He seemed only to see his foeman's eyes now, dark pits surrounded by two swirling vortices it was his destiny to still forever.

A whining screech. Shieldbreaker buried itself in the rim of his target and stayed lodged there. A split second later and he caught Helmbiter's haft in the guard of his sword. The two men stayed locked together like that for a split second... did he see or sense a raven as it fluttered overhead? Whose doom would it pronounce?

With a roar Guldebrand lashed out with his foot, catching the Thegn square in the midriff. Oldrik huffed and doubled up as the wind went out of him. As he did, Guldebrand made two outwards circular motions with his arms. An incredible strength seemed to possess them; the Twin Furies were prised remorselessly from Oldrik's grasp as he fell to the ground.

Guldebrand stood over him, breathing heavily. He felt a presence at his back: in his mind's eye he saw Hela, Queen of the Dead, spread her dark wings across them both. Shieldbreaker remained buried in the rim of his target, which was one blow away from being splintered into fragments; Helmbiter lay on the ground where it had fallen.

Calmly he dropped his sword and pulled Shieldbreaker free of the mangled target, letting it slip off his arm. Without taking his eyes off his opponent he bent to pick up Helmbiter. The axes felt smooth and well-balanced in his hands. Some said both blades had been inscribed with the Sorcerer's Script to give them more puissance, but Guldebrand paid no heed to such tales.

Oldrik had recovered enough to pull himself upright, though he was still winded from the kick, which might have come from an angry stallion. With a dismissive air Guldebrand kicked his sword over to the Thegn of Gautlund.

'Pick up my sword. Let's finish this like made men.'

The words sounded as if they were coming from somewhere else. Oldrik obeyed, though he still moved gingerly.

'Recover your breath. I'll give you a flame farewell as befits a warrior of your station.' Guldebrand couldn't even say for sure if it was him speaking. He felt as though the blood pumping through his veins was flowing outside his skin, drowning his body in a cascading torrent of battle sweat.

At last Oldrik jerked himself upright, falling back into a fighting stance as he clutched the sword Guldebrand had given him. No fear was in his eyes, only a look of resignation.

Guldebrand lopped off half the hand that held the sword at the first pass. A second swipe from the other axe clove deep into Oldrik's hip. Guldebrand yanked the blade free, and Oldrik gasped as he slumped to the dark earth, his lifeblood seeping down towards the hungry worms that called it home.

Through the roaring in his ears Guldebrand was aware that his foe had conveniently fallen into a kneeling position. Gently he rested Shieldbreaker and Helmbiter to either side of Oldrik's neck. The erstwhile Thegn of Gautlund looked up at him with glazed eyes that no longer looked upon Middangeard, but quested for the Halls of Feasting and Fighting.

Raising both the axes high above his head, Guldebrand screamed primally as he brought them back down to exactly where they had been a second ago. Oldrik's head shot off his body, a wedge-shaped portion of his neck following it on a tide of gore.

A great groan went up from behind the shield wall. A few moments later dull thunks and clattering followed as the Stormrider's leidang disarmed.

'It is over,' said Guldebrand in a weary voice. 'Secure the harbour and take these warriors prisoner. None are to be harmed or mistreated.'

Turning around to check his orders were being followed, he wasn't entirely surprised to see Ragnar, an inscrutable smile playing on his lips. As always in those situations he felt distinctly uneasy, but he was too tired and jubilant to care.

He nodded towards the regal corpse he had just made. 'Have a funeral pyre built, I want him cremated with full honours. He earned his flame farewell.'

Ragnar nodded and sloped off to do his bidding. Guldebrand's strange battle rage was ebbing out of him and he felt exhausted. Still clutching the Twin Furies he surveyed the burning city he had won. With news of the Stormrider's death in single combat his jarls would have to surrender; Magnhilda and Canute would bring any dissenters to a bloody heel.

He could taste Oldrik's blood where it had sprayed across his face and lips, could smell its delicious tang in his nostrils. That gave him a bit of strength he needed. Raising his eyes to the firmament he laughed.

As if on cue, Brega cried: 'All hail Guldebrand Stormbreaker, magnate-in-waiting of the Frozen Wastes!'

Guldebrand shut his eyes and exulted as hundreds of men called him by his new name. The beardless boy had become a king.

⇒ CHAPTER VII ⇒

Where Dead Kings Walk

By the time Horskram took the company off the road Volfburg lay a dozen miles behind; apart from the odd trader and vagabond they had seen no one else. Another couple of hours saw them riding hard through fields and orchards, giving the hamlets and manor houses they passed a wide berth, before the adept finally called a halt.

Adelko groaned as he eased himself off his horse. He was feeding him some oats when Vaskrian wandered over.

'So – another madcap mission with the legendary friar Horskram,' he said. 'And what fell dangers is the good Argolian leading us into this time, eh?'

The novice grimaced, and not because of the stale well water he sipped from his gourd.

'If only you knew how appropriate your gallows humour is,' he sighed. His mentor had told him what to expect in the Draugmoors when they'd stopped to navigate another potholed stretch of road, although he'd been chary of letting the others know. But that was typical of the secretive old monk.

Vaskrian shrugged his shoulders. 'I've been scarred by witch-fire and lost two guvnors to war and quest – and nearly a third to boot for the sake of a woman,' he said, a queer light entering his eyes. 'Whatever's coming next, I'm ready for it!'

Adelko sized his friend up. Maybe he really was, come to think of it. The squire had always looked tough enough, but when they'd met there had been a rawness to him that wasn't there now. Scarred and trussed up in a sling, it was more than the physical injuries he'd sustained: there was a darkness to his mien that hadn't been there before.

'You know what?' he handed Vaskrian the gourd. 'I actually believe you.'

The squire was about to reply when Horskram interrupted them. 'Five minutes,' he barked. 'Then we're back in the saddle again.'

'He still likes to let everyone know who's in charge,' muttered Vaskrian, taking a swig and handing back the gourd.

'That's Master Horskram for you,' grinned Adelko. 'Wouldn't be the same any other way.'

✛ ✛ ✛

As they neared the moorlands, Adelko reflected on what Horskram had told him. There had only been time for snatched conversation as they steered their horses through another ruined patch of road, but he'd gleaned enough to know the Draugmoors weren't much safer than Tintagael.

'They were corrupted as Tintagael was by the presence of one of the Elder Wizards' watchtowers,' his mentor had told him. 'The Codices of Zhorrah kept by the priest caste of Sendhé tell of a myriad such edifices, dotted about Urovia and Sassania. This one must have watched over all of Vorstlund, before the Breaking of the World when its lands were called by another name long forgotten.'

The Sendhéan texts Horskram quoted spoke of ancient burial mounds of warrior-kings who had served the Elder Wizards as vassals. 'Whether they were of a lineage predating the Elder Wizards, or of the Varyan race itself or a mixture of the two, is not known,' the adept had continued. 'But what the sages do agree upon is that the sorceries of the Witch Kings gradually polluted the moorlands about the tower as they gave themselves up to the worship of Abaddon. After Ma'amun's attempt to summon him brought down the Breaking, a great silence fell upon those lands as the First Age of Darkness swept across the realms they had once ruled.'

But during those thousand years, things in the barrows had stirred.

'What kind of things?' asked Adelko. 'You mean Gaunts?' A shiver tickled his spine as he recalled his own encounter with the dreadful ghost in Tintagael.

'In a manner of speaking, only much more dangerous and malign,' replied Horskram. 'In truth we don't know enough about them. Written accounts of the Draugmoors are in short supply. You see, the wildernesses of Gothia – the old name given to the southern reaches of Vorstlund – were never civilised until King Aslun the Younger undertook a great clearing project some five hundred years ago, cutting down the forests to make room for arable land. Until then not even the Thalamians could subjugate it, and the fate of the Great Lost Legion is well documented by Ibid, the Empire's greatest historian and loremaster.'

Adelko nodded as they picked their way through a muddy bog that had eaten up the road. He had read Ibid's account of the disastrous expedition from Tyrannos some three hundred years before the coming of Palom. It had cemented once and for all a political certainty: the Thalamian Empire met its northern limit at the Orne Ranges.

'In those days the Breitrand covered most of Gothia, and as well as the barbarian tribes it was the haunt of Fays and Wadwos,' his mentor went on. 'Most scholars including Ibid believe that it was here that the Lost Legion met its end. But some sages claim that a portion of it survived their depredations... pushing farther north, the surviving legionaires came upon a ghastly moorland, topped by a broken tower. And having survived the Faerie Kindred and the beastfolk, the remaining soldiers fled into the moorlands, only to succumb to tall grey-faced kings who stank of the grave and wielded great swords of black iron... All but one, who fled back into the forest. Somehow he made his way back south, the legend goes, persuading a barbarian chieftain to give him safe conduct back to the Empire.'

'Why would the Gothians spare his life?' asked Adelko.

'According to the same legend, the legionnaire promised to spread tales of the terrors beyond the Orne Ranges, to discourage any further attempts at conquest. And thus he did upon his return to Tyrannos, according to written records cited by loremasters. And of all the half-mad soldier's tales, none were more frightening than those of what he had witnessed on the Draugmoors.'

'Cheering to know you're leading us by another safe path, Master Horskram,' said Adelko wryly.

'The blood of the Redeemer should be enough to protect us,' replied Horskram, though the novice wasn't completely reassured. 'The rest of what we know about the Draugmoors comes from the usual fireside tales, handed down from mother to child in the wildernesses of Vorstlund, and few dare venture there nowadays. The last folk known to do so were adventurers who lived in the time of Aethel, last of the House of Bede, in the days when Vorstlund was a united kingdom. They sought the fabled treasures thought to lie in the watchtower and the barrow mounds of the Draug Kings. The King's Annals begun by Eadred the Learned some two centuries before that chronicle the old kingdom's history and include their tale. Of the original party only two freebooters returned. One of them had his mind broken forever by his ordeal, the other withered away from a strange sickness and never revealed what he had seen.'

'That doesn't sound encouraging, Master Horskram,' sighed Adelko.

Horskram favoured his novice with a sardonic smile. 'I have led you into many situations that were not encouraging,' he said. 'Yet here we are, another step closer to Rima.'

'Another muddy step,' moaned Adelko as his horse splashed through the pool. At least the mud didn't show up on his brown habit.

'Not many more of those, I trow,' said Horskram. 'Look, firm road up yonder! Time to kick our nags into a gallop and put some more leagues between us and our pursuers.'

'I thought you said the Lanraks probably won't try to pursue us any further?' asked Adelko.

'The Lanraks, no,' replied the monk. 'They're on thin ice as it is, chasing us through hostile territory. It's the knights from Turstein I'm worried about. When the Ostveldings tell them who we are they'll chase us through the entire eorldom if it means a chance of capturing Wilhelm's daughter. Taking us through the Draugmoors is our best chance of getting out of Upper Thulia.'

They had struck up a gallop after that and not spoken since, leaving Adelko to wonder if hostile knights were really more dangerous than what lay ahead.

⁘ ⁘ ⁘

That was a question Adelko would soon have answered. As grey dells wreathed in mist steadily encroached against the pale horizon, he steeled himself for yet another test of his psychic fortitude. As with the trees of Tintagael, the eldritch moorlands seemed to draw the light from the skies into them, suffusing the hills and valleys with an unearthly sheen. As they drew closer to the Draugmoors he felt rather than heard the ghostly voices pushing at the penumbra of his sixth sense. They were different from those he had experienced in the cursed forest, less numerous but more malignant.

Something occurred to him. 'When we were in the Warlock's Crown, it felt evil but I didn't hear so many... entities,' he said to Horskram as they stopped for one final rest before entering the moorlands. 'Why is that?'

'The Warlock's Crown was under a sorcerer's control,' replied Horskram. 'Andragorix kept the entities in check. Also, it is not thought the Warlock's Crown was a watchtower – originally it was most probably a prison colony for the Gygants whom the Elder Wizards enslaved. As such its sorceries were not quite as potent. Judging by his paraphernalia, Andragorix had yet to obtain power enough to master the magicks of a watchtower.'

'But there is one sorcerer alive today who can?' ventured Adelko. 'The one who lives in the Sultanates.' His sixth sense told him it was best not to name Abdel Sha'arza right now, though he was hungry for more information about the Sassanian warlock.

'Indeed, but I will not speak of him here,' said Horskram, confirming his instinct. 'It is time we began reciting the Psalm of Fortitude.' Turning in the saddle he addressed the others. 'Same procedure as the Warlock's Crown,' he said. 'Stay in formation, and focus on our words if you value your sanity!'

Sir Wrackwulf frowned. 'I still don't think this is a good idea,' he protested. 'And I've never been one for scripture, master monk. I say we turn about and take our chances with the Eorl's knights.'

Most of the company clearly agreed. Horskram wheeled his courser around to face them. Drawing the Redeemer's blood out he held it aloft. The ghostly light from the moors suddenly seemed a little fainter, and the chill of the twilight hour abated slightly. 'The sword shall avail us nothing against an eorldom of men!' he cried. 'It is in this that you must place your trust – the blood of the Redeemer, sent to save our souls from perdition!'

The company still did not look entirely convinced. Horskram motioned towards Adhelina. 'Would you give this lady up to captivity, having fought so hard to rescue her? For such is the risk you run, if you heed not my counsel.'

Braxus and Torgun exchanged frowns, both sharing the same sentiment for once. Adhelina spoke up. She looked pale and drawn, but Adelko sensed her courage had not left her. 'If Master Horskram says the Draugmoors are our best chance of escape, I say we follow him,' she said.

Sir Torgun looked more than a little disgruntled at that. Adelko sensed he still carried sorrow for his dead brothers in arms and didn't trust Horskram one jot. But that feeling struggled with the love he bore for the damsel.

In the end love won out: the tall knight nodded and said no more. Sir Braxus shook his head in disgust and shrugged his shoulders resignedly.

'Good,' said Horskram, just a hint of smugness entering his voice. 'That settles that then. Remember, do not stray from the path I lead you on! Stay within the light of Palom's blood, and heed the words of the *Holy Book*. The Redeemer shall be our succour.'

Without another word Horskram turned his horse again towards the moors. Adelko mulled over the ways of men as they followed him. Girls. He still couldn't quite see what all the fuss was about.

✣ ✣ ✣

The cold mists wreathed themselves about the company as they penetrated the Draugmoors. Instantly the fading sunlight was transformed into diffracted beams that seemed to turn those mists into something thick and tangible; Adelko had the feeling of moving slowly through thick tar. The words of the Psalm of Fortitude sounded muffled in his ears as he chanted them with Horskram: '… a crooked path … darkened vale… not falter… soul corrupted…'

The sound winked in and out, confusing his senses as he nudged his horse between the hills. The sedge atop them shared the flinty colour of the skies, now faintly illuminated by a shrouded sun.

'…wings of Morphonus… my shield… Oneira… my dreams…'

Gradually the ghostly voices that whispered in his head receded; he felt a calmness infuse his spirit as the crimson circle of light emanating from the glass phial about Horskram's neck grew stronger, driving back ghostly tendrils that threatened to engulf them. A profound warmth washed over him, and he was smiling as he recited the next verse of the psalm, which sounded clearer now:

> The Betrayer's words shall stick in his mouth
> For the manna of the archangels shall be my balm
> Against the poisoned words of his perfidy!

Glancing behind him without breaking off the psalm he saw his companions riding as if in a trance, sitting stock still in the saddle. Beyond them the hills and valleys receded into shapelessness, banished into darkness by the light of Palom's blood.

> The Almighty hears the prayers of strong and weak
> The archangels shall give them the wings to fly
> And though the road be broken it shall not hinder them!

On they went, repeating the psalm as they had done all the way up to the Warlock's Crown. Adelko fell into a meditative state. He felt the Redeemer's benign presence; yet he felt his pain also. The words of the Earth Witch came back to him, telling him to question everything… He could still feel the dark voices trying to penetrate his inner sanctity, to profane his serenity with spiteful words. What tongue they spoke he could not say; all he knew was that they did not mean him well.

The mists began to darken, deepening into a grey that bordered on black. The sun vanished, choked into extinction by the preternatural fog that held them in a cloying embrace. Only the circle of crimson kept them from being swallowed up by the cursed moors that now sought to tear them from the mortal world. A foul odour began to permeate the dead air: the charnel stench of decay.

Changing tack in response, Horskram began reciting a different psalm. Adelko didn't know it by heart, though he had read it before. The Psalm of Death's Lingering, the adepts called it.

'Ma'alfecnu'ur, prince of decay,' declaimed Horskram in his sonorous voice, 'Thine foetid raiment shall not clothe the one who walks in the path of the Archangels! Thy corruption shall turn and feed upon itself before the bright eyes of the Seven Seraphim! Begone, foul canker! Trouble the flesh and spirits of the living no more! In the name of Virtus, I command it! In the name of Stygnos, I command it! The Redeemer's power I invoke, He that defied the grave to seek the blessed bourne of the Unseen shall shield me now! IT IS THE POWER OF THE REDEEMER THAT COMPELS THEE!'

The light from Palom's blood flared, growing brighter. Adelko felt the voices recede and a joyous wellbeing returned; the noisome smell of rotting flesh ebbed away and the fog about them lightened somewhat. High overhead the sun made its presence felt again, and although it was but a pale imitation of summer he was glad of its stifled rays. Horskram went on repeating the psalm as their horses whickered nervously beneath them. Had it not been for their sacred protection Adelko could well believe their steeds would have been driven mad. After a while the novice had memorised the psalm and joined his voice to Horskram's. They continued reciting in unison for some time. Glancing back at the others Adelko saw that their trance-like state had not lifted, though their faces seemed less pallid and drawn now.

It was only when the sun was disappearing behind a horizon they rode towards but could not see that a question occurred to him. He was reluctant to risk breaking off the litany to ask Horskram, but there was no need in any case: by now their sixth senses were attuned to one another and the adept knew his question.

'We must trust to the Redeemer and Reus Almighty to guide us through our prayers,' said Horskram softly, risking breaking off the psalm. 'Once the sun goes down, Palom's blood is the only thing that will keep the stygian night of the Draugmoors at bay.'

His mentor's melodramatic turn of phrase did little to reassure Adelko. 'But don't we run the risk of getting lost? Just like we did in Tintagael?'

'This won't be the first time I've attempted to enter and leave the Draugmoors alive.'

'Really? You never said... What happened?'

'It was many years ago,' said the adept. 'Some fool son of a craftsman at Turstein took it into his head to flee the town and seek a life of adventure. Before long he got lost in the wilderness and stumbled into the Draugmoors. I was charged with rescuing the lad.'

'And...? Did you find him?'

Horskram pursed his lips as they rode along. 'I did in the end, but it was a close-run thing. Luckily some villeins working the fields not far from the moors had seen the lad enter them. I was on horseback so I managed to catch up with him not too far in. He'd only been on the moors for a few hours, but already he'd seen enough to drive him half mad with terror. I managed to calm him down with the Psalms of Fortitude and Spirit's Comforting. Then I took him on my horse and prayed for deliverance. The Almighty answered my prayers and we managed to retrace our steps and get out in time.'

'Well that doesn't sound so bad,' ventured Adelko. 'And now we have Palom's blood, there's even more chance that Reus will hear our prayers.'

'That is what I am hoping,' said Horskram. 'We need to find the source of the Draugfluss so we can follow it to Heilag. The only problem with that plan is it means travelling into the heart of the moorlands – according to maps sketched by apprehended warlocks, it starts some leagues south of the watchtowers' ruins.'

Adelko was quick to pick up the thread. '... which means the Draug Kings' barrows won't be far away.'

'Indeed,' confirmed Horskram. 'Not ideal, but then since when has anything ever be-'

His voice trailed off as they came upon the first sign of the Draugmoors' hideous rulers. The light of Palom's blood revealed the bones of several men and horses. All had been scrupulously picked clean.

Adelko shuddered and made the sign, repeating the psalm again as they passed through the hecatomb. Somehow the sight of white skeletons and glaring eye sockets was more horrible than the butchered peasants he had seen up north. The remains appeared to reach for them with ivory fingers frozen in the paralysis of death. The novice half expected them to come to life, as the skeletons had done at the Warlock's Crown. The thought of that comforted him though: it reminded him they had been through much worse than this.

He voiced that thought to Horskram.

'Don't get too complacent, Adelko of Narvik,' he admonished. 'Their dead victims may not harm us, but the power of the Draug Kings is not to be dismissed! Andragorix himself might have quailed before them.'

That statement instilled a healthy respect into Adelko. 'Let's pray we don't meet them then,' he said.

'Indeed,' replied Horskram.

Adelko didn't need his sixth sense to tell him their prayers would not be answered. Hard experience told him as much.

✣ ✣ ✣

The sun had long vanished, swallowed up by the mortal vale, and a sere cold had settled in, stealing into the rocky crooks and hollows they now wandered through. Adelko had no idea what time it was when something caught his eye.

Shivering into his cloak, he squinted and could make out a peculiar looking creature. It took a few moments of scrutiny before he could pair it with pictures he had seen in books at Ulfang.

'A cat...' he mouthed softly. 'Look Horskram, its fur is all grey, just like the fog...'

Grabbing his sleeve Horskram called a halt. Like automatons, their companions obeyed, looking about them with bewildered expressions. The cat continued to stare at them from where it perched on a rock halfway up a hill, its eyes a strange blue colour.

'Draugs have the ability to shapeshift,' hissed Horskram. 'We're being spied on.'

No sooner had he said that than the cat darted off the rock, disappearing into the darkness.

'Well that's quite literally the cat out of the bag,' muttered the adept. 'They know we're here now.'

'What do we do?' asked Adelko. Their comrades remained seemingly oblivious.

'We've no choice but to press on,' said Horskram. 'Put our trust in the Redeemer to guide us to the river. Keep the Draugfluss ever in your thoughts as we pray, Adelko! Otherwise as like as not we'll be meeting more draugar before long.'

'What about if we just stay put?' suggested the novice. 'Wait until dawn. At least we get some sunlight here, not like in Tintagael.'

Horskram shook his head. 'We've just been spotted by a draug – if we stay here we'll have a host of them upon us long before sunrise. No, we press on! Faith alone must be our guide now!'

Perhaps the Earth Witch had shaken that faith, or perhaps it was Adelko's sixth sense that told him Horskram's choice would only lead them into greater danger: whatever the cause, he felt a sense of foreboding grow steadily as they chanted their way between hills that now seemed wrought half of shadow. Even the Redeemer's blood seemed to offer less cheer, its scarlet hue limning the black fog and giving it a perversely hellish look. On the penumbra of this ghastly chiaroscuro the sloping sides of cragged dells loomed, their creviced surfaces grinning soullessly at them as they meandered they way across the moors. It was as if the very land itself were hostile to them, and cursed their intention ever to leave it behind.

After what seemed like hours but could have been minutes, Adelko broke off the psalm. He was on the point of saying what he previously had not dared to when Horskram did it for him.

'We're lost,' said the adept grimly. 'Only a madman would call the crooked path we have wandered a straight line.'

Adelko was mulling over whether a muttered 'told you so' would be appropriate or constructive when they heard something. The sound of stones being dislodged and rattling down a hillside.

'Up over there!' whispered Horskram, pointing to their right beyond the circle of light. Reaching into his habit he pulled out his circifix and held it aloft so that it caught the full glare of the Redeemer's blood. The silver shone brilliantly, extending the light.

'Hellspawn show thyself!' bellowed Horskram. 'By the grace of the Redeemer let thy lucubrations of wickedness be exposed!'

A silhouetted shape appeared on the edge of their halo. It was humanoid, though its limbs appeared elongated and disfigured. Presented with the blinding rood it collapsed on the side of the hill. It started whimpering, then began to weep.

'Ye Almighty!' breathed Horskram. 'That is no denizen of the Other Side, but mortalkind sure as we are!' He shone his circifix in Torgun's eyes. The knight blinked and shook his head, as though awakening from a reverie.

'Where are we?' he asked sleepily.

'Never mind your foolish questions,' snapped Horskram. 'I've a heroic task for you, sir knight. On yonder hill is a mortal man. Bring him down to us – I need to stay here and maintain our aura of protection.'

Sir Torgun frowned at the old monk, but did as he bade him. Dismounting he clambered up the hill towards where the frightened figure huddled. It screamed and thrashed as the knight dragged him down the hill.

The others were coming to their senses when Torgun deposited the wailing figure in a heap on the ground between their horses.

Adelko peered at him in the silvery-red light. He was a tall gangly man in early middling years; his blunt features, large hands and rude woollen clothing told of a labourer, probably itinerant and seeking work over the summer. What fey moon had led him here, the novice wondered.

The hapless wanderer stopped writhing around long enough for Adelko to make him out more distinctly. He wasn't disfigured after all – that must have been a trick of the light – but Adelko noted the man's hair, which was white as the driven snow. Besides hoary old age, only a direct confrontation with the Other Side could do that to a mortal.

'Oh no, oh no, oh no, OH NO...! Wulbert will be quiet yes, he'll be very quiet! He won't tell a soul, no, only leave him be, oh leave him be...!'

The man called Wulbert continued his ranting, mostly repeating the same words and punctuating them with pathetic moaning.

Horskram recited the Psalm of Spirit's Comforting, holding his circifix aloft while presenting the Redeemer's blood. Adelko joined in with the psalm. He felt pity for Wulbert, who had been driven mad by draugar by the looks of things.

Their prayers had the desired effect, and gradually the man's gibbering subsided. He stared up at them with terrified eyes, his body shivering. But slowly a vestige of sanity returned to him.

'They killed them all...' he gasped. 'The blue-eyed kings killed them all... They tore out poor Ulrick's heart before mine eyes... They ate... *they ate*...'

Turning over the labourer wretched, but nothing came up. Taking a wineskin from his saddle bag Torgun proffered it. The labourer gazed at it stupidly, as though he had been presented with some long lost treasure. Then, slowly and gingerly, he took the skin and gulped back mouthfuls.

'Tastes good,' he hissed. 'Oh tastes *so good*... So long since Wulbert tasted wine! Oh thankee sir knight, thankee, thankee!'

Sir Torgun glanced quizzically at Horskram. Wulbert was speaking Vorstlending.

'Yon labouring man finds your wine passing fine,' translated Horskram. Turning to Wulbert he addressed him. 'The words of the Redeemer and Kaia's bounty have fortified your spirits, now speak! Tell us what happened to you.'

Wulbert grimaced, as though the memories conjured by Horskram's question pained him. But at last he managed to gasp out his sorry tale.

'A dozen of us there were, travelling to Dunkelsicht for to seek work in the Eorl's demesnes,' he said, taking another swig. 'But attacked by highwaymen we were, on the road from Turstein – four of us managed to escape, and we fled into the moors. Lost our way in the fog we soon did, and then the night came... They took us one by one... Poor Otho was the first, they cut him to pieces with their huge black blades... The rest of us ran and wandered we knew not how long. At last, when we could go no further, we fell asleep where we were. When we awoke...'

He paused and started to shudder again. 'When we awoke... they'd returned Otho to us. Only gutted he'd been, like a wild animal! And parts of him were missing, the fleshy parts... Oh Reus Almighty, I'll never forget what they did to his face... HIS FACE!'

Wulbert screamed and lapsed back into gibbering insanity. Clearly the power of the Redeemer's words and Pangonian wine only went so far.

'Yon wretch has been driven mad by his torment,' said Horskram, not unkindly. 'I fear his mind will never recover, even if we do get him out of this godforsaken place.' He quickly related Wulbert's story to the others.

'Why did they spare him?' asked Braxus.

'For sport,' replied Horskram, his lip curling. 'Like many denizens of the Other Side, draugar delight in tormenting their victims. As like as not they forwent the opportunity to feast on his flesh so they could keep him alive for entertainment.'

'How long do you think he has been here?' asked Torgun.

'Probably longer than you think,' interjected Adhelina. 'His manner of speech is old-fashioned... greybeards I knew in childhood spoke thus.'

Adelko felt his heart sink. 'That means time is playing tricks on us again,' he said. 'Just like in Tintagael.'

Adhelina looked at him quizzically.

'Never mind,' said Horskram quickly. 'Let's take him with us, see if he recovers his wits again and can tell us anything more. We haven't a moment to spare – the sooner we find the Draugfluss the better.'

Wulbert's ears pricked up and a queer light entered his watery eyes. 'Draugfluss?' he said. 'The river you mean, yes? Oh by all the heavens, sirrah, that river I can find for you, oh yes indeed for Wulbert knows where it is!'

Horskram looked at him askance. 'How so?' he barked. 'And if you know where it is, why have you not left the Draugmoors of your own accord?'

Wulbert shook his head frantically and started to sob. 'Oh no, no, no, NO!!! They won't let me, no... Only to partake of its waters, you see. They say if I try to leave, come for me they will, just like the others...!'

His sobbing overtook him. Adelko felt his sympathy deepen. But beneath pity his sixth sense was flaring. Wulbert wasn't telling them everything.

Horskram was sensing much the same. 'Stop hiding the truth from those who would help you,' he snapped. 'Think you that an Argolian is easily deceived? Speak the contents of your mind, Wulbert, or we'll leave you here as we found you.'

'No, NO!' the peasant reached up, scrabbling at Horskram's stirrup with long, emaciated fingers. Adelko wondered how long it was since the man had eaten. 'Don't leave me here,' he whimpered. 'Don't leave me here with *them*. Please...! More than I could bear it is!'

'Alright,' said Horskram, his tone softening. 'We won't abandon you, Wulbert, just tell us what you know.'

The peasant stopped pawing at Horskram's boot and slumped to the ground on all fours. He started drooling and whining into the hard soil.

'We can't take him with us,' said Wrackwulf. 'Yon man's mind is clearly gone, prayers or no. The best thing we can do now is put him out of his misery.' He moved his hand meaningfully towards his axe.

'No!' said Horskram sternly. 'There'll be no killing of innocents on my watch, even if life is a misery to them.' Turning back to the peasant he said: 'Wulbert! Some of my companions would fain leave you here, or else put you out of your misery. I want to help you, but only if you help us. In Reus' name tell us what you know!'

Wulbert looked up at Horskram. There was a tortured look in his eyes now, one that went beyond mere terror. 'They kept Wulbert alive,' he whispered. 'The grey-faced kings let him drink of their waters... and eat... they let him *eat*...'

Adelko felt his stomach churn as he suddenly realised how Wulbert had survived in the Draugmoors.

Adhelina and Hettie made disgusted noises as the same realisation dawned on them. Horskram looked down at Wulbert with revulsion as he collapsed into a sobbing heap. Wrackwulf looked at Horskram as if to say *I told you so* and began dismounting.

'What are you doing?' demanded Horskram as the knight unslung his axe.

'Ending his pain is what I'm doing,' replied Wrackwulf, raising the axe. 'This villein has lived long enough methinks.'

'Stay your hand!' cried Horskram. His voice seemed to echo off the sides of the dell they were in. Adelko shivered as he fancied he heard something in the distance. On the edge of his hearing, it was too faint to be identifiable.

Wrackwulf paused, axe in hand, glaring up at Horskram. Torgun took a step forward, interposing himself between Wulbert and the freelancer.

'Leave him be,' said Torgun. 'He's suffered enough as it is.'

'Yon villein is a flesh-eating ghoul, fit for naught but swift death!' insisted Wrackwulf. 'We cannot leave him alive, for pity's sake!'

'No soul is beyond redemption whilst it lingers in the mortal vale, as the Redeemer sayeth,' said Horskram. 'While he remains alive he has the chance to atone for his crimes, gross as they are.'

Turning again to the labourer he said: 'Hear that, Wulbert? Your crimes are not unforgivable. Guide us to the river and the Almighty who sees all shall pardon your sins.'

A glimmer of hope entered Wulbert's eyes. 'If Wulbert takes you to the river, you will bear him abroad with you?' He seemed uncertain and far from trusting.

'See this?' said Horskram, brandishing the Redeemer's blood. 'This is a sacred relic, one of the greatest of the Creed. Its power should be enough to protect us from the draug kings... but we need your guidance. Help us and I promise we shall give you succour.'

Adelko felt his stomach twist. He'd heard Horskram's promises of sanctuary and forgiveness all too often. He suddenly remembered Ulla the hedge witch being dragged off to the dungeons in Salmor.

Whatever the novice's misgivings, Wulbert seemed convinced at last. 'Oh very good, very good, thankee, thankee master monk!' The peasant reached up and pawed gratefully at Horskram's boot.

'Enough of your unctuousness!' snapped Horskram, barely concealing his contempt. 'We've tarried long enough, now let's be off! You lead the way, Wulbert. And we'll be staying in the saddle, so don't even think about trying to run off!'

Wulbert gave fulsome assurances to the contrary before bounding off into the nacreous mists, like an enthusiastic dog let off the leash.

'Do you really think we can trust him?' whispered Adelko as they followed him. His sixth sense had not subsided.

'After Reus knows how long in this accursed bourne, I doubt it,' muttered Horskram. 'Yon villein has been turned into a plaything of the draugar... As like as not he regards them as his keepers now.'

'So why follow him?'

'At least there's a chance our prayers and the prospect of escape might break their hold over him long enough to get us to the river. The alternative is we wander at will, hoping to chance upon the Draugfluss ourselves.'

Adelko couldn't resist his next remark. 'Was entering the Draugmoors really a good idea, Master Horskram? It seems no better than fleeing into Tintagael.'

'Entering Tintagael proved to be our saviour, much as I hate to give credit to the Faerie Kings,' Horskram reminded him. 'The road to redemption takes many a twist into dark hollows, as the Redeemer sayeth.'

The novice frowned. Palom's reference to dark hollows was eerily appropriate to their current predicament. 'You think... we were meant to come here?' Adelko thought of fate and destiny, the powers the Earth Witch had claimed to channel.

'Possibly,' replied Horskram. 'Some say all men's actions are preordained, guided by His will to further an ultimate purpose only He can fathom. Others claim free will as the Almighty's greatest gift to mortalkind. Like most of our Order I incline towards the latter view. It is up to us to make the decisions we feel to be correct at any given time. I make my choices, and hope I have been guided towards the best solution by Palom's grace.'

Adelko thought about that for a bit. 'But didn't the loremaster Sallust of Hierapolis say that free will is an illusion... Men are only free to choose the actions that occur to them...'

'... because the will is always bound to make a choice,' Horskram finished for him. 'Even doing nothing is itself a choice.' The adept spared his novice an impressed look. 'I had no idea you'd read any of the Thalamian philosophers,' he said. 'Clearly you've not just used your spare time in the library to read Gracius and Maegellin.'

'I've always loved reading,' said Adelko simply. 'Well, ever since you gave me my first book at Narvik.' Mention of his home village usually brought pangs of homesickness, but this time all he felt was a faint longing. Far stronger was the desire to sit in Ulfang's library again, to be immersed in the musty smell of its books. He hoped Heilag had a sizeable library. The Grand High Monastery at Rima would – but that still seemed like a long way away.

'Anyway, what was your point?' asked Horskram.

'Well... If we're only free to choose the actions that occur to us, and we were made by the Almighty, then surely He decides what those actions might be. Why make bad choices occur to us if He only wants the best for us?'

Horskram mulled that over as they ambled on after Wulbert, who was scrambling over rocks as he led them into the darkling valley.

'You are not just speaking of choices that are erroneous, but morally wrong as well,' he said at length.

Question everything.

'Yes...' faltered Adelko. 'If free will is the freedom to choose from ideas that occur to us, why make bad or wicked ideas occur to us at all?'

'Tis Abaddon, not Reus, who puts such ideas in men's minds,' said Horskram. 'Don't forget the Author of All Evil had a hand in our making, when he was foremost among the archangels.'

Adelko wasn't about to give up on his argument that easily. 'But Abaddon is an emanation of the Almighty,' he persisted. 'Just as the Seven Princes of Perfidy are emanations of the Seven Seraphim. Reus created him... and if Abaddon is responsible for all evil, then that means Reus is either not omniscient, or He is but...'

The novice left his thought unspoken, not daring to voice it.

Horskram surprised him by picking up the slack. 'Or else He *is* omniscient but does not always have mortalkind's best interests at heart. That is what you mean to say?'

'Yes, Master Horskram.'

Adelko barely managed to get the words out. Even just thinking them made him feel guilty. The Order had taken him in and given him a way of life beyond his wildest dreams: who was he to question the motives of Reus? And yet the question had been invited by his own thinking, pursuing the very ideas that occurred to him.

Horskram surprised him again with the candour of his next statement. 'Adelko, I do believe you are beginning to grapple with the very question that has plagued me for decades. Should you chance upon an answer to it, be sure to let your old mentor know.'

Flashing his novice a wry glance, Horskram steered his horse in front of him. Another discourse over. Yet more unanswered questions.

Adelko blinked and shook his head to clear it. He was beginning to wonder whether horseshoes might not have been such a bad choice of living after all. They were certainly less baffling than books. Had it been the Redeemer's grace or Abaddon's pride that had moved him to pick the latter? Or both?

His ensuing reverie was a painful one.

✣ ✣ ✣

On and on Wulbert took them, always hovering on the fringe of their circle of light. They seemed to meander for hours, yet the sun did not rise. Adelko barely had the energy left to mutter the psalm, and more than once caught himself nodding in the saddle. At last, mercifully, Horskram called a halt. The others had slipped back into their trance-like state; Horskram revived Anupe and Vaskrian with a muttered prayer.

'We need to rest,' he said curtly. 'You two are on first watch – keep an eye on our guide and make sure he doesn't slip off!'

But the adept need not have worried. Wulbert had curled up on the side of a hill and was already fast asleep.

It wasn't long before Adelko joined him.

His sleep was disturbed by frightful dreams. Only this time he could barely remember them upon waking: a black angel had come to him over and over and asked him to make a choice... hosts of armoured men swarmed to the call of arms... and at the head of the foremost rode a one-eyed general, fierce and proud and stern. Lastly of all he glimpsed a strange fat man dressed in brightly coloured exotic clothing... he winked over elaborate mustachios at the novice, smiling in the manner of a friend, yet on his shoulder a demon perched...

Adelko roused himself from his pallet. His body was covered in a light sweat that was already freezing over. Shivering he got up and walked around. The fog had not abated. The company had arranged their horses in a circle around themselves. Even if they had dared to light a fire, there were no trees from which to make one. At least they had the light of the Redeemer: Horskram slept on his back, the phial around his neck emitting its soft yet comforting radiance.

Vaskrian and Anupe were still on watch. The Harijan's eyes were fixed on Wulbert, who appeared blissfully untroubled in his sleep. Perhaps that was the only peace he ever knew, Adelko reflected sadly.

'I hope we find this river soon,' Vaskrian muttered as Adelko drew level with him. 'We're running low on water.'

Adelko didn't like to think about drinking from a river cursed by sorcery.

'What time is it?' he asked.

'No idea,' replied Vaskrian. 'Still no sign of the sun. I imagine we'll be on our way soon enough. Horskram said to wake him when we get tired.'

The squire seemed calm enough. Adelko supposed they had the Redeemer to thank for that much at least, though uncomfortable questions about his faith lingered. He was about to offer to go on watch next when Anupe yelled.

Turning he saw the Harijan lurching back, a shocked look on her face. Looking at the ground Adelko saw why. A long thin arm, its grey muscles knotted and tinged with blue, was reaching up out of the ground, the fingers of a gaunt hand clamped around her calf.

In a flash her blade was out. Its razor edge sliced off the hand at the wrist; the rest of the arm disappeared back below the ground. The hand remained clutching Anupe's leg. The Harijan cried out as its fingers dug deep into her flesh. Vaskrian dashed over and tried to prise it free but an unearthly strength was in the thing. Adelko was about to recite the Psalm of Banishing when he saw there was no need. The hand was beginning to dissolve; patches of decay appeared across its cadaverous skin, growing and clumping together. The bones of the land seemed to groan in pain as the hand opened, releasing the Harijan and falling to the dank earth. In the blinking of an eye it had disappeared, swallowed up by the dark soil.

Horskram stirred from his sleep and sat upright, blinking into wakefulness. Vaskrian tended to Anupe while Adelko brought his mentor up to speed.

'Looks as though our draugar friends weren't chary of trying their luck,' he said. 'But the Redeemer's power is not to be trifled with!' The adept made the sign before bustling over to have a look at Anupe. Her flesh was badly bruised just below the knee, but the skin hadn't been punctured. 'That is a good thing,' said Horskram. 'No chance of the wound becoming infected by draugar poison.' The adept intoned a quick prayer over it.

'It came at me from the ground,' breathed the Harijan. 'What manner of devil does that?'

'Draugs can move through stone and earth as well as shapeshift,' Horskram explained. 'As like as not this was the same one that was spying on us earlier, or another one alerted by it. Well, our unwelcoming hosts know we are here for certain – but at least they know we enjoy the Redeemer's protection too! Wake the others – it's high time we found that river.'

Something caught Adelko's eye as they were preparing to strike camp. Bending down he picked it up gingerly. It was a bracelet, presumably worn by the thing that had tried to attack them. With a shock of revulsion he realised it was made of human knucklebones. Horskram threw him a piercing glance as he dropped the horrid ornament.

'Best not to toy with the keepsakes of the Draug Kings,' he said. 'Remember they were mortal men once, just as you and I.'

Adelko could not resist a sidelong glance at Wulbert, already skulking on the fringes of the Redeemer's light as he waited for the others. The novice could have sworn the wretch felt less comfortable within its aegis, preferring the darkness without. His sixth sense had not left off from jangling, but that was hardly surprising given where they were. All the same, he kept his gaze fixed uneasily on the labourer as he led them off once more.

✣ ✣ ✣

After a while the moorlands began steadily to rise. That made sense at least, the source of the river must be higher up. Adelko began to register desiccated plants and shrubs; they looked almost to have been petrified, and offered no cheer to the blasted iron landscape that now held them in its clutches. Whenever the Redeemer's light fell on these, they sloughed pitifully away into ashes, as though Palom's blood were putting them out of their misery. The novice yearned to be out of these tortured lands; with the others in a trancelike state, he had only the psalms and his mentor's sonorous voice to distract him.

As such his heart leapt for joy when he heard the unmistakeable rushing of a river. Wulbert turned back and favoured them with an enthusiastic wave of the hand, before scampering over the crest of the valley pass they had been following and disappearing into the fog.

'I still don't trust him,' said Horskram. Turning his horse around he muttered the Psalm of Reawakening, bringing the others out of their induced reverie.

'We've reached the river but we need to be on our guard,' he said. 'Weapons at the ready, just in case!'

'I thought weapons would avail us little against the rulers of these lands,' muttered Braxus darkly. But he drew his sword nonetheless.

'Blades won't be much use against them,' conceded Horskram. 'But we don't know what dangers await us – best to be prepared for all contingencies. Stay within the light at all times!'

The company prepared itself, keeping the damsels in the middle. Horskram and Adelko rode out in front, with Torgun and Braxus flanking and Vaskrian, Wrackwulf and Anupe bringing up the rear. Nudging their steeds over the rise, they gazed down upon a strangely welcome sight.

The waters of the Draugfluss carved a slate-coloured rift through a great valley, larger than any they had passed through. The source was a gaping chasm that yawned starkly above its fast-flowing waters. The ground before them fell at sharp angles towards the riverside; Wulbert was clambering lithely across rock and scree to get to it, and could be glimpsed through patchy rents that had appeared in the fog.

Dismounting, they gingerly led their horses down towards the river. The going was not easy for their steeds, and they had to take a zigzag route. By the time they reached Wulbert he had drunk his fill, and was perched atop a rock, singing a tune contentedly.

'See, told you Wulbert would bring you here,' he beamed, looking happy for the first time since Adelko had met him. 'Now you brave adventurers can rest and drink! Then you can take Wulbert with you when you leave, yes?'

'Your service to us will not go unrewarded,' Horskram promised. Stepping over to the river he eyed its leaden waters distastefully. Bringing out his circifix he intoned the Psalm of Cleansing and Consecration. As he closed the prayer, he reached down and touched the river with the rood.

Three things happened at once. The fog hanging in thick tendrils over the river retreated as smoke before a keen wind, and its waters nearest the monk took on a silvery sheen, as though reflecting the brightest sun. But it was the third thing that caught Adelko's attention. A low rumbling sound reverberated from the hills that loomed about them. With a shock the novice realised it sounded like voices. Deep voices crying out in profound anger.

The fighters in their group clutched weapons more tightly, casting about them fearfully. Wulbert fell off the rock with a tortured scream and began convulsing, tearing clumps of white hair from his head. Horskram backed away from the river and brandished his circifix and the Redeemer's blood.

'Everyone stay in formation!' he cried. 'Keep within the circle of light, no matter what!'

The fog continued to recede, rolling back from both sides of the river and clambering up the sides of the valley. The skies above remained the colour of granite, but far, far above the tenebrous clouds Adelko fancied he could make out the faintest glimmer of sunlight.

'Remount!' yelled Horskram. 'We're taking up too much room as we are! Everyone get inside the circle!'

The party scrambled to obey his orders, but their horses were skittish and chary of being ridden. By the time they had all managed to get back in the saddle the fog had rolled back entirely, revealing the valley.

Adelko felt a chill of horror ice his bones as he realised it was not lined with hills. On both sides of the river as far the eye could see stretched barrows, each one sealed fast with a stone slab covered in strange sigils. No, not strange any more, but all too familiar. Memories of Andragorix's lair and the Abbot's inner sanctum came flooding back to him as he recognised the hieratic language of magick.

Horskram turned on Wulbert with a snarl. 'You faithless cur! We offer you a chance of succour and you lead us straight to the Draug Kings!'

Wulbert had stopped his convulsions and was huddled up against the rock he had been sitting on. Without taking his head out of his hands he snivelled: 'Wulbert didn't lie – led you to the river he did! But the grey kings see everything, everything...!'

The wretch was just outside the circle of light.

'Never mind that for now,' said Horskram, relenting. 'Get up and come over here.'

But Wulbert had no ears for the adept now. 'C-can't,' he moaned. 'Blue-eyed lords see all... punish me they will...'

'WULBERT!' cried Horskram. 'Get over here now! Only the power of the Redeemer can save you!'

'Master Horskram, look!' cried Adelko, drawing his attention back to the barrows. From around the sides of the slabs a thin mist was beginning to emanate. Unlike the fog, it was of a grey-blue sheen and diaphanous; Adelko fancied he could see right through it.

'Of course the Draug Kings would guard the only route out of their realm,' muttered Horskram. 'I should have known better!'

But it was past time for self-recriminations. The mists began to coalesce in front of the barrows. Ghostly forms could now be discerned, inchoate shapes of humanoid figures that stood taller than the tallest man. The low rumbling cry continued unabated as the draugar condensed into awful reality; with horror Adelko realised it was a chorus of unearthly voices, venting their anger in unison.

The voices ceased just as their unnatural owners finished taking form.

Several dozen figures looked down on them from either side of the valley. Each one was clothed in strange armour, fashioned of interlocking plates that were black as charcoal yet tinged with a silvery sheen. It surpassed even the complexity of the Thalamian harnesses Adelko had seen drawings of at Ulfang: the pauldrons were a series of carapaced spiked plates, giving the draugar the appearance of having wings; their vambraces were likewise of a baroque design that hurt the eye with its peculiar symmetry.

Next to him Vaskrian gasped. Adelko sensed his friend was awestruck by the frightening beauty of their arms. Each king wielded a great sword fashioned from the same silvery black metal; on the fullers of each blade the sorcerer's script danced, its spidery engravings burning with a resentful orange light.

But it was their owners who really took the novice's breath away. Tall and proud they stood, though their grey skin was pulled taut over their faces, obscuring their mortal provenance; their contours were tinged a ghastly blue, and deep in their sockets ancient eyes flickered with a relentless white fire. Upon their eldritch brows were set crowns of tarnished silver that resembled a hotchpotch of swords and other blades.

High and proud the Elder Ones built their towers/And just as high walked those who served them in their glory!

With a start Adelko realised the draugar were not speaking: the words were disembodied. They were perfectly comprehensible to him, and yet he could not tell for all the world which language they addressed him in. The effect was profoundly unsettling.

The Priest-Kings taught their craft to those deemed wisest/Princes who served them in life and beyond!

Adelko glanced at his companions to see if they understood, but he could glean nothing from their entranced faces. They were barely moving.

With sword and spell we carved out distant empires/Wherein mortalkind was bound in blissful bondage!
The Unseen hearkened to our call in forms both fair and foul/All shared in plenty yet none were free!
The balance was disrupted and the World Order fell to ruin/Leaving naught but draugar in their howes where princes once did sport!

At last Horskram spoke up. 'Spare us these elegiac lamentations for the bygone days of your wicked reign,' he sneered. 'Your punishment was justly deserved after you and your arcane masters turned to deviltry. The Almighty Himself declared your civilisation wanting, oppressive and unfree as it was, and sent the angels down upon thy halls with righteous wrath!'

Adelko sensed his mentor had entered into a psychic duel with the Draug Kings. He spoke in Decorlangue, the language of the Redeemer; the novice could feel him channelling his elan.

Blessed in His eyes were all our halls for many years/Yet there was another to whom we learned better allegiance!

The King of this world and the next unrightly deposed/The time fast approacheth when He shall take up his brass sceptre!

Then all shall quail before us as the seas roil red and gold/The rivers shall run with liquid fire that purifies as it burns!

'Enough of your blaspheming cant!' snarled Horskram, brandishing his circifix and the Redeemer's blood. 'Into your bourne have we strayed, and out of it we shall emerge, whole and unharmed! You know what power it is that I wield – obstruct us at your peril!'

The disembodied voices started laughing in unison. Experienced though he was, Adelko felt the hairs on the back of his neck turn to pins and needles as the fell sound reverberated through the valley. Wulbert whimpered, curling himself up into an ever tighter ball of trembling flesh.

The Five shall summon back the Seven and the One/The Master and Disciple and Descendant will join forces!

The Draug Kings shall stir from their barrows to reclaim their realm/ Our black swords will cast long shadows across the lands of the earth!

None who oppose us shall go unscourged/The flesh shall be torn from the bones of our enemies!

The draugar started laughing again. With a shock Adelko suddenly realised that he recognised the undead kings... But where from?

Then it hit him. *Of course, his dream...* Which of the hosts had it been? He shut his eyes tightly, trying to focus above the laughing as he struggled to recall his earlier vision.

He was dimly aware of Horskram shouting.

'What is this unholy trinity thou speakest of?! Tell us more – by the Redeemer's grace I command it!'

The laughter died off, but the next words felt rather than sounded cruelly mocking:

Your profane magicks cannot compel us in our realm/The which shall presently extend over all the peoples of the earth!
A gift of prophecy have we given thee for thy power/Now take it back to thy benighted mortal bourne!
But as you speed take one last parting gift from draugar lords/A taste of the splendour of dark kingdoms to come!

A horrible hissing sound filled the air. Opening his eyes Adelko saw that the undead princes had opened their mouths, and from their distended maws a black smoke billowed. Down the hills on either side of the river it rolled towards them, blotting out all in its wake. The draugar vanished behind two undulating curtains of blackness that crept down steadily towards them in a horrid pincer movement. A stench filled the air, like before only many times worse. Adelko doubled over in the saddle and began retching. He was dimly aware of the others doing the same. Just before the tidal wave of smoke rolled over them he saw Wulbert shrieking as it consumed him...

Somewhere in the deepest dark a red light flared. By it he saw the vague outlines of his companions, their horses rearing and panicking. He felt his own steed buck and jolt; instinctively he pulled at the reins, digging his heels into its flanks as he struggled to stay in the saddle. He felt sheer naked terror slide cold fingers through his guts, pulling at his entrails with supernatural strength.

Forcing himself to concentrate he began mouthing the Psalm of Fortitude. He felt the syllables float from his mouth to be swallowed up by a hollow silence, but somewhere in the void they resonated with similar words spoken by another... Adelko dimly recognised the Psalm of Spirit's Comforting. Somehow the two psalms were intertwining, augmenting one another. He felt rather than saw the light of the Redeemer flaring brightly...

✤ ✤ ✤

He blinked as wan light pushed against his eyes. Sitting up he saw he was still in the saddle; somehow he had managed to stay mounted. Around him he saw his companions coming to in the same bewildered fashion. The putrid black fumes had gone; so had the fog. Overhead a weak sun pressed against thick clouds. Gazing up at the sides of the valley he saw the Draug Kings had vanished. Their barrows still remained, the sigils on their stones glowering softly. With a trembling hand he made the sign, mouthing a thankful prayer.

Something else caught his eye. Over by the rock Wulbert had slumped against, the blackened silhouette of a humanoid figure was sketched against the hard ground.

✠ ✠ ✠

It took them a while to recover. A subdued air lingered over the group, a funereal aura that was not easily abated. They risked a quick drink from the Draugfluss, whose waters nearest them had at least retained some of the sparkle Horskram's blessing had brought them. Then they followed the river west.

It was not long before they had an inkling as to the draugar's parting gift.

Vaskrian was the first to demonstrate symptoms, coughing and shivering. His skin had acquired a greyish pallor and the whites of his eyes took on a bluish tinge. The damsels were next, followed by the knights and Anupe.

'Draugbreath,' muttered Horskram as they stopped to rest and eat. 'A sickness of the spirit that corrupts both mind and body.'

Adelko glanced over at his comrades. They could barely force down enough food to make it worthwhile; one or two heaved up the contents of their stomachs immediately.

'I thought the Redeemer's blood and our prayers should have been enough to protect us?' hissed Adelko. He struggled to master his rising anger. Once again his mentor had led his friends into grave danger on a pretence of protection.

'Well they were certainly enough to protect you and me,' said Horskram tartly. 'But then we are seasoned members of the Order... The others have not such natural defences.'

Adelko was too upset to register the compliment implicit in being called 'seasoned'. 'But what will happen to them?' he demanded. 'You said we'd keep them safe!'

'I said the Redeemer's blood would protect us from the draugar, and so it proved,' said Horskram. 'Had we not enjoyed His protection our fate would have been the same as Wulbert's.' The adept made the sign, but that only made Adelko angrier.

'So it's better this way is it?' he snapped. 'They don't get disintegrated, they just die slowly of a horrible sickness instead!'

'Heavens, lower your voice!' Horskram snapped. 'I didn't say their cause was hopeless. We should reach Heilag monastery in a

day or two if we keep following the river. Our brethren there should
be able to treat them.'

'Well I certainly hope so,' said Adelko pettishly. 'It's not fair to
keep risking other people's lives like this.'

Horskram flashed his novice another piercing look. 'Isn't it? And
didn't you do just that at Salmor when you bade those brave knights
charge at trees? War is war, Adelko, and that means risks must be
taken – often with the lives of others. You of all people should fully
appreciate that by now.'

Adelko was about to give a sarcastic response when a sudden
realisation hit him, borne on his sixth sense.

'Wait... It wasn't by accident that you led us into the Draugmoors,
was it? You knew the Lanraks and other knights chasing us would
give you the perfect excuse... You planned to take this route all
along, didn't you?'

Horskram raised an eyebrow. 'Astute as ever, Adelko... You are
not quite right in this instance, but still you ask a good question! To
answer it truthfully, no – I did not intend for us to encounter the barrow
kings directly. My prime motivation was to get us out of Upper Thulia
safely, as I said. But after the Fays of Tintagael, I had an inkling that
some of our enemy's future generals might have advice should my
original plan to avoid them go awry... So I resolved to leave it in the
Redeemer's hands. Once we became lost, I began to suspect it was indeed
the Almighty's will that we meet the Draug Kings, for good or ill... and
thus have things transpired! We have been gifted with another dark
prophecy, and must ponder its words at length to see what we can glean.'

'But... how did you know the Draug Kings would talk?'

'Little is known about draugar for certain,' replied his mentor. 'But
one common tradition has it that they are compelled to give prophecy
to those who can withstand them. According to this theory they are
frustrated by their powerlessness in the mortal vale, and will seek to
torment those they cannot defeat within their realm with glimpses
of a darker future. Now, that's enough questioning until we reach the
monastery – let's be getting along, while our sick friends are still fit to ride!'

Horskram got up from the boulder they had been sitting on and
barked a curt order, leaving Adelko to wonder if wars were ever
worth taking sides in at all.

⤛ CHAPTER VIII ⤜

A Spell Broken

The weaponsmith looked at Wolmar as though he had just asked to be slapped in the face. He felt like doing just that to the snobby master craftsman. Pangonians, insufferable to the core – even their commoners were haughty.

'You wish me to make you a sword from pure iron?'

He repeated the words in Decorlangue, slowly and incredulously. At least Wolmar had found a bladesmith conversant in the common tongue of the high-born. But then the palace armoury was likely to have nobles from all over the Free Kingdoms coming to stay and needing blades and other harness repaired.

'No, not a sword, a dagger,' repeated Wolmar patiently. 'About so long...' He held his hands apart to demonstrate the length.

The bladesmith licked his lips. 'Many centuries have passed since your ancestors relearned the secret of steel from the ancients,' he said. 'Why would you want such a primitive weapon?'

The smith looked mocking now. Wolmar resisted the urge to strike him on the spot. He couldn't cause a scene. He was already lucky to have distracted his squire – surely a spy paid or enthralled by Ivon – long enough to give him the chance to visit the armoury. He could only pray the fireside tales his governess had told him as a boy would prove true...

'A chivalrous pledge to an amor, if you must know,' Wolmar lied. 'I swore to my lady love that I would fight my next three duels with a dagger made of crude iron.'

The princeling felt secretly proud of himself for coming up with such a tale: outlandish deeds were not uncommon among knights devoted to the Code of Chivalry. Sir Lancelyn himself had pledged to fight for a year with one eye closed. Apparently that hadn't stopped the legendary knight killing all his opponents.

The smith smiled indulgently, his demeanour changing at once. 'Ah, love is love, as we say in Pangonia,' he said. 'Now I understand!

Pray forgive me, sir knight, I did not think the Code of Chivalry was so popular in the northern kingdoms.'

No of course you wouldn't, you ignorant dolt, thought Wolmar.

'Your opinions are of no concern to me,' he snapped. 'I am a prince of the realm and expect to be served without foolish questions.'

'A hundred apologies,' said the armourer, bowing curtly. 'When will you be needing the blade?'

'I'm to fight a duel of chivalry tomorrow,' Wolmar lied again.

'Ah, I regret to say I have many prestigious patrons in need of – '

Wolmar cut him off by placing a gold sovereign on the work bench next to him. The coin caught the sunlight streaming in through the nearest window. The armourer smiled, reaching out and pocketing the coin before his busy team of craftsmen could notice it. There were half a dozen of them in the large rectangular room, working on a variety of blades, helms and hauberks.

'It shall be ready by sunset,' smiled the smith, running a hand casually through his sooty white hair.

'Good,' said Wolmar. 'I would send my squire to pick it up, but the wretch has taken ill with the Runny Sickness. I'll just have to come by again myself.' He did a good job of putting on the air of a haughty princeling incensed by his circumstances. 'And one last thing,' he added. 'Tell no one of this transaction. I'd rather people didn't know what I'm doing… In truth I fain wish I had promised Her Ladyship some other task.'

The smith smiled again. 'Love is love, sir knight! It makes even the highest born do strange and foolish things.'

Impertinent cur – clearly his status as master bladesmith to the King had given him ideas above his station. Wolmar swallowed the urge to backhand the commoner and stalked out of the armoury.

He felt an unseen weight pressing down on him as he made his way through corridors decorated with ornate tapestries and teeming with busy servants. He could feel the enchantment Ivon had put on him, trying to quash his natural impetuosity; several times he had to fight the urge to go back to the armoury and cancel the job he had just ordered.

Likewise as he approached his quarters he felt the keen desire to throw himself at Ivon's feet and confess his plan well up inside him. He clenched his fists so hard the fingernails dug into his palms.

Sweeping into his rooms he found them empty. So Ivon was still busy consulting with the King. That was a good thing. Probably planning the next stage of the invasion of Vorstlund. The Supreme Perfect had arrived at court this morning as well, that probably meant the next Pilgrim War would be discussed too.

Ivon and his nefarious scheming... Well he wouldn't be part of his plans for much longer. No matter the cost.

Wolmar helped himself to a goblet of wine and gazed fretfully across the palace grounds. The wing he was staying in overlooked a series of walled gardens, but the riot of colours offered him little in the way of comfort.

Reus damn it, but where was Horskram? Much as he hated to admit it, the old monk's arrival might help. Not that he would be able to confess what he knew – Ivon's spell prevented him from divulging his diabolical plans to anyone. But at least Horskram would recognise Wolmar and want to question him – the adept's sorcerous powers might enable him to divine what Wolmar knew without his having to tell him.

His next sip of wine tasted bitter. A pretty pass things had come to, wishing for an Argolian's help! He supposed there was Hannequin too... but the Grand Master hadn't paid him much attention, treating him as little more than a messenger, and he hadn't met him again since Ivon had enthralled him. His lover had made sure of that.

Wolmar emptied the contents of his cup. No, a pox on the Argolians – for all he knew they could be in league with Ivon, he wouldn't put it past them. He couldn't afford to trust anyone. And that meant going ahead with his plan. And that meant...

His sad reverie was interrupted by the door opening. In stepped his squire. A diffident, chinless stripling: poor material for knighthood, perfect material for a spy.

'Well, did you see to it that my horse is receiving the special care it deserves?' he snapped, putting on his act again. 'Yon Farovian is worth ten Pangonian destriers!' It wasn't much of an act come to think of it – he would have behaved no differently where his horse was concerned in any case.

The squire gave no indication of what he was thinking as he replied calmly: 'Yes, Your Highness, your horse is being kept in the finest wing of the royal stables. I saw to it personally.'

Yes, I'll wager you did what with your connections, thought Wolmar acidly.

'Good,' he said, turning back to gaze out of the window. 'Now pour me another cup of wine.'

✣ ✣ ✣

Wolmar was finishing his last sword bout as the sun slipped down beyond the white walls enclosing the palace grounds. The practice yard was located just next to the armoury, as one would expect:

he was perfectly positioned to pick up his special order. All he needed now was to get that damned prying squire out of the way.

He looked down at the knight he had just knocked into the dirt. He was one of the ordinary palace knights and not a member of the prestigious Crescent Table. A pity that, but at least he was Pangonian. He favoured his beaten opponent with a mocking sneer before beckoning curtly to his squire.

'Bertrand, come here!' The squire ran up dutifully. 'You're to go to Lord Ivon's chambers and tell him I want to meet him down here right away.'

The squire looked surprised. 'But, sire... you need help with your armour – '

'I served in the White Valravyn for years,' Wolmar reminded him sternly. 'And we make do without squires, like the true errants of old. Now do as you're told and go and fetch His Lordship.'

Bertrand could do little but obey. He might serve Ivon, but he had to defer outwardly to his betters. That of course was what Wolmar was counting on. Ivon's chambers were on the other side of the palace. That should give him the time he needed.

He waited until Bertrand was out of sight, then headed straight for the armoury.

✣ ✣ ✣

Ivon had not yet arrived by the time he returned to the training grounds. Excellent – everything was going to plan. He felt the rude blade pressed against his flesh where he had hidden it beneath his girdle and undertunic.

A wave of sorrow rolled over him as he contemplated what he must do next. How easy it would be, to succumb fully to Ivon's enchantment and go along with his plans...

He shook his head to clear it, clenching and unclenching his fists. In his mind's eye he pictured the double unicorn insignia of Ingwin. He would not betray his countrymen; nor would he condemn his soul to eternal perdition. No ensorcellment would ever make him perjure those things – not if he could help it anyway.

He paced the yard, watching his lengthening shadow as it swayed unsteadily in the fading light. A roil of emotions was tearing its way through his guts. Anger, guilt, despair, determination: all vied for a slice of his troubled soul.

'Wolmar! Darling! You look ever so worked up – been practising over much in the yard, Bertrand tells me...'

The princeling looked up, fixing the lover he had learned to despise with a venomous glare.

Ivon pouted. He was dressed like a dandy as usual: his sequinned doublet and hose caught stray slashes of dying sunlight and seemed to mock the dimming skies with their cobalt hues.

'Oh Wolmar, if looks could kill...! And you're still dressed to kill too, quite literally. Night is almost on us and it will soon be time to feast... Can't have you turning up to dine in full armour now can we?'

Wolmar pushed the Margrave away, preventing him from kissing him.

'Don't patronise me,' he snarled. 'You may have' – he felt the enchantment tighten around him like an invisible noose – '... influenced me, but I will not be your plaything any longer...' He struggled to get more words out. He could feel the warlock tightening his grip. Desperately he forced his mind to focus on the Margrave and not his plan.

Fortunately Ivon seemed more intent on other things. 'Ah but that is where you are wrong, sweetling,' he said, his tone catching a shade of the encroaching dusk as he reached out to caress Wolmar's cheek. 'You are soon to be mine, body *and* soul...'

He winked towards the dark blue skies and lowered his voice to a sibilant whisper. 'Full moon is nearly upon us! Tomorrow at the Wytching Hour you shall be initiated... Then all of this will seem but as a frightful dream... Bertrand!' Turning to the squire he snapped his fingers. 'I think Sir Wolmar needs help with his armour – we've some important guests at the palace tonight including His Supreme Holiness, it would be *criminal* not to attend in timely fashion...'

✣ ✣ ✣

Back in his chambers Wolmar sent Bertrand packing after he had laid out his clothing on the bed. Taking the iron dagger out, he placed it under his mattress. Not the best hiding place, but he was a knight not a sneak thief. Besides, that way it was handy. If Ivon decided to spend the night with him in his chambers... All he would need to do is break the enchantment for a few precious seconds...

He felt the weight press down on him, followed by the urge to run in search of his lover and tell him everything. Forcing his attention to the clothes on top of the bed, he began to dress for dinner.

✣ ✣ ✣

He need not have worried about keeping his mind distracted from his true intentions at feasting time, for Ivon had plenty of things to talk about.

'See that one there, next to the Supreme Perfect?' he asked Wolmar, surreptitiously pointing towards the spare pale man dressed in a white kirtle. His head was shaven and his pinched face showed little emotion. His economy of movements betrayed a martial man, though he resembled a Marionite monk in his simple garb.

'Another distinguished guest?' asked Wolmar cynically.

'Oh *very* distinguished,' replied Ivon seriously. 'That man is Sir Godfrey, Master of the preceptory of the Bethler Order here in Rima. Those estimable warrior-monks have made themselves indispensable to any crusade – doubtless his presence here means Cyprian means to make good on his pledge to declare another Pilgrim War.'

'When will it be declared?' asked Wolmar, feigning interest.

'Soon, don't you worry!' grinned Ivon, patting him on the shoulder. But he said no more on the matter.

'I notice your great rival Morvaine isn't here,' said Wolmar, keen to keep himself as preoccupied as possible. He still feared succumbing to his lover's magic and telling him everything if he dwelt too much on his plan.

'That is because Lord Morvaine has got what he came to court for – the war in Vorstlund is a certainty. His job now will be to persuade the rest of the Occitanian barons to sign up... and join my little coup afterwards. He thinks we'll be putting him on the throne once that's done, but of course my plans are quite different...'

Breaking off from his whispered conversation he addressed Aravin and Kaye loudly. 'My lords, such fine weather cannot possibly be allowed to go to waste – what think you both of another hunting trip? Tomorrow perhaps?'

Aravin betrayed the hint of a grin as he replied: 'Why, I was just thinking the same thing. I'll have my squire make the necessary preparations.'

Kaye murmured his assent, catching Wolmar a meaningful glance. The princeling feigned resignation, dropping his eyes to his silver trencher.

'Ah what a life of ease and comfort we lead,' sighed Ivon, beckoning for more wine. 'You'd think we were in the Heavenly Halls, when all that falls to us is to disport and make merry...'

Taking a deep draught of wine Wolmar forced himself to think of the White Valrayvn, the insignia he had worn and served for so long. He felt tears welling up behind his eyes, and blinked hard to keep them in check.

One way or another, soon it would all be over.

✠ ✠ ✠

Back in his chambers, Wolmar paced again frenetically. Glancing out of the window he caught the silvery moon, nearly fully waxed. Was it his imagination or did it seem to mock him somehow?

He hadn't expected Ivon to leave him directly after the feast. Not for the first time, anxiety lanced his pounding heart. Did the Margrave suspect him? No, he reminded himself yet again, he had muttered something about needing to prepare himself for tomorrow night's ceremony. Wolmar barely suppressed a shudder. He didn't like to think what blasphemous arcana the warlock was revising in his own suite right now.

So his initial plan was out. A pity. Bringing an end to the depraved mage's life during their lovemaking, he would have liked that. But the more he thought on it, the less likely it seemed that such an attempt would have worked. Ivon had already hinted that their liaison had made him more susceptible to ensorcellment: small chance then of breaking it while they were engaged in an amorous clinch.

Again he felt the yearning seeping through his pores... He could just take the dagger and go now to Ivon's chambers, tell him everything... Wolmar pressed his hands to his temples, trying in vain to crush the point of sharpening pain coalescing in the middle of his skull. A whispering voice seemed to call to him, telling him to give it up as lost...

With a groan the princeling slumped to the carpeted floor, hunching over as Ivon's magic fought to overthrow the last vestiges of his will. He could only pray the warlock was too engaged in his preparations to notice the struggle; forcing himself to stand with a gasp he stepped over to the garderobe and flung open its cedar door. Rifling through the court finery Ivon had furnished him with, he found what he was looking for: his old surcoat, emblazoned with the crest of the White Valravyn. It seemed so long since he had worn it.

Pulling it free he wrapped it around his head and shoulders, inhaling the musty wool like a dying man gasping for breath. He forced himself to think of his homeland, his father... even his brethren in the Order seemed a welcome thought now. He pictured the high grey walls of Strongholm, the banner of Ingwin fluttering in the strong sea breeze...

Falling onto the bed he wept into the tabard, torn with longing for a home he would probably never see again.

✤ ✤ ✤

He awoke to the sound of knocking. Sitting up on the bed he glanced out of the window, suffused with the rosy tinge of dawn. Springing off it he discarded the surcoat, reached under the mattress and found the iron dagger.

Again the knocking, a little louder this time.

'I'm coming, Reus dammit!'

He slid the blade back beneath his undertunic, binding it in place with a length of twine he had secured for that purpose. It felt cold and hard against his skin; the feeling reassured him.

The door opened and in stepped Bertrand.

'I told you never to enter without my say so!' snarled Wolmar.

'And Lord Ivon told you to be ready to leave at dawn,' replied the squire coldly. 'You're not even dressed.'

All pretence of deference was gone. The princeling met the squire's defiant gaze and resisted the urge to throttle him.

'Well help me by fetching out my hunting clothes then,' he barked, swallowing his pride for the umpteenth time.

The squire shut the door behind him and did as he was told. When he had laid out the clothes Wolmar began to dress. He was just pulling on his hose when the squire picked up the jerkin and went to put it on him.

'I said I always dress myself!' shouted Wolmar, conveniently concealing his rising fear behind genuine anger.

'And I say we are running late,' replied Bertrand implacably. He had a completely different air about him now, like a long-suffering servant about to trump his master. The squire reached over to grab Wolmar's undertunic. 'You don't need this, it's going to be hot – ' Wolmar pushed him away but it was too late: the squire had hold of the tunic and he pulled on it as he staggered back. The linen tore, exposing a glint of metal. Bertrand's eyes widened as he registered what it was.

Wolmar didn't even think about his next move. Stepping forward he slammed an uppercut into the squire's chin, knocking a tooth out as he sent him sprawling back against the bed. Grabbing him by his lank mop of hair, the knight smashed his head into the oak headboard several times. He felt a tremble of satisfaction run the length of his body as the squire slumped senseless and bleeding to the ground.

Bending down Wolmar checked him. He had a vicious cut to the head and a bloody mouth but he was still breathing. Not dead then. The princeling was on the point of pulling out his dagger and cutting the stripling's throat when he thought better of it. Ivon might notice if one of his thralls suddenly died, and he'd have some explaining to do as it was.

Shoving Bertrand under the bed he finished dressing quickly, first changing into a fresh undertunic. The sun's rays were hardening through the window as he exited his bedchamber.

✣ ✣ ✣

The others were waiting for him outside in the courtyard. Ivon narrowed his eyes as Wolmar approached. The princeling took a deep breath and focused.

'Where is Bertrand?' he asked suspiciously.

I just knocked him unconscious after he discovered my attempt to foil your plans. Those words were on the point of exiting his mouth but somehow Wolmar found the willpower not to utter them.

'I've no idea,' he replied levelly. 'I had to fetch a courser from the royal stables myself. I assumed you had him running another errand.' Just for good measure he underscored the final word with contempt.

Ivon eyed him darkly. Aravin and Kaye and their squires barely spared him a glance. They seemed far away. Just as well.

'I sent him over to your chambers just before dawn,' he said. The Margrave's eyes continued to search him. He could feel his will bending his own...

It was useless to struggle.

'I knocked him unconscious,' sighed Wolmar.

That got the other lords' attention.

'What?' gaped Ivon. Wolmar had to relish the look of outrage and surprise on his face.

'He keeps trying to dress me,' said Wolmar. 'I've told him I don't know how many times that a knight of the White Valravyn dresses himself, but did he listen? I lost my temper and gave him a beating. It was high time the youth learned his manners.'

Aravin and Kaye exchanged glances. They seemed more amused than anything.

'That youth happens to be my second cousin!' snapped Ivon. 'Where is he now?'

'Sleeping off his injuries in my bedchamber,' replied Wolmar, telling the perfect truth. 'I'm sure he'll recover in time... and perhaps learn to treat princes of the blood royal with more respect in future.'

'Bah, I should never have entrusted him with keeping an eye on you,' sneered Ivon. 'Always was an overweening little troglodyte, that one. You do a favour for one of the family and this is what comes of it...' He rolled his eyes melodramatically. 'Very well, we'll just have to manage without him. I won't be needing anyone to keep an eye on you after tonight in any case. Right! Let's be off then, noblemen. We've a long day ahead of us and we need to make a start.'

Without another word, the margraves turned their coursers towards the palace gates. Wolmar allowed a slow sigh of relief to escape his lips as he followed. The iron blade still felt cool and hard against his skin.

✣ ✣ ✣

It was another hot day, and before long Wolmar felt the sweat coagulating beneath his woollen hunting clothes. They rode hard the whole morning, and the blazing sun was approaching its zenith when they found the cool comfort of the Arbevere. Ivon did not stop there, but took them further up into the wooded hills. It was obvious where they were going long before they reached the clearing overlooking the source of the Athos.

Barely a word had been spoken during their journey. Ivon barked a curt command at their squires and the three youths laid out a spread. It looked for all the world as though they were just another party of nobles enjoying a pleasure trip, but Wolmar's entrails failed to unknot themselves as he sat down to eat.

Despite his natural hunger after hours in the saddle, he had little appetite for the wine, cheeses and sweetmeats. He forced himself to eat abundantly anyway: he would need all the energy he could summon if his plan was to work.

Afterwards he went over to the riverbank to relieve himself. Ivon did not bother to send a squire with him, but merely issued a stern command not to run off. He felt the words bind him like shackles: his plan really had little chance of fully succeeding. But then he had known that all along. He drank in the forest sounds and smells as he emptied his bowels, wondering if this really was the last time he would experience the natural world's pleasing embrace. He had never had much time for such appreciation: funny how it came to him so poignantly now.

He returned to the clearing to find the remainder of the food packed away. The squires were busy unpacking something else from their horses' saddle bags, what looked like bundles of linen.

Ivon stood and stared at him. His voice was bereft of all emotion as he ordered him to undress.

Wolmar felt panic churn upwards from the base of his stomach as he struggled to disobey the command. Forcing himself to think of his homeland and the White Valravyn slowed down the process somewhat, but eventually his fingers complied. To his surprise he saw Kaye and Aravin were also beginning to strip.

He pulled off his cloak and riding boots, before taking off his hose and tunic and chausses. He was down to his undertunic and breeches. Slowly he began to pull the latter off... The iron dagger pressed against his sweaty skin, slipping down his body slightly. The twine held it, but its point was just above the hem of his tunic. He tried to resist following the command literally, but Ivon's words were like a binding law to him.

He shut his eyes tightly as he grasped his tunic...

'All right, that's enough. It gets chilly up there at night and I won't have you shivering in sight of the Master's servants like a timorous peasant. Put this on next.' Ivon's voice was still strangely flat.

A squire came over and proffered him a bundle of white linen. Taking it he saw it was a kirtle, oddly reminiscent of that the Bethler commander had worn at dinner. He was too busy feeling relieved to ponder that as he slipped it over his head and shoulders. The squire handed him a girdle and he tightened it at the waist, just above the concealed dagger.

'Good, now sit down,' commanded Ivon. 'We've quite a wait before the others arrive. If I were you I'd concentrate on preparing your mind for what's to come. Not lightly should mortal men look on one of the faces of their true maker.'

Wolmar could scarcely begin to ponder the cryptic nature of Ivon's words. His mind was concentrating all right, but not on what the warlock hoped.

Aravin and Kaye were getting into similar gowns, only theirs were black as night. The three squires followed suit. Only Ivon remained dressed in his hunting clothes, looking curiously mundane as he sat on a rock. But there was nothing mundane about the strange words he mouthed silently to himself, nor his eyes as they rolled back up into their sockets.

Wolmar glanced at the sun. It must be around three hours after noon. *Wait before the others arrive.* He should have known the warlock would have more members in his arcane cult. Perhaps now was the best time to strike, before more people arrived, while Ivon was in a trance. He tried to order himself to get off the rock, to dash over to Ivon and stab the life from him... But his limbs remained rooted in place.

There was only one way his plan might work.

Once again he cast his mind back to the secret council at Strongholm, and their interrogation of the monk Horskram at Staerkvit. From what he had gleaned, warlocks could only concentrate on so many magical tasks at once; take on too much and their powers became overstretched and weakened. He had to pray that whatever ghastly conjuration Ivon planned for tonight, it would be enough to loosen his grip on him: he had long been regarded as one of the swiftest swordsmen in his kingdom, all it would take was a few seconds...

When he was sure the others weren't looking, he slipped a hand into his kirtle and felt the dagger. It was an unusual place to keep a weapon but he was confident that wouldn't slow him down too much. Glancing back at Ivon he saw him muttering the strange syllables. Rehearsing a spell, surely... Then he felt the weight pressing down on him. He kept his hand inside the gown, struggling with the urge to reveal the dagger and beg the Margrave's forgiveness. Screwing his eyes shut he burned the image of the Valravyn into his mind, and with agonising slowness the urge subsided.

He was breathing heavily when he withdrew his empty hand.

✣ ✣ ✣

Presently Ivon ceased his silent recital. Getting up he walked over to Wolmar and gently brushed delicate fingers through his hair.

'I think it is time you rested ahead of your ordeal,' he said in the same neutral tone. 'Initiation into the rites of the Master are not easily borne.' He murmured a few syllables in the hateful tongue of magick. At first their sound set Wolmar's teeth on edge, but the feeling was replaced almost immediately by a pleasant sensation of ease and comfort. The princeling saw his lover's eyes fill his vision, two dark pools of night that grew to swallow him up...

✣ ✣ ✣

... he awoke to the sound of an owl hooting. Sitting up on the rock where he had fallen asleep he glanced around fitfully. Evening shadows were painting the clearing with long, tenebrous fingers; Aravin and Kaye and the three squires were sat at five points around where the fire had been the night they sacrificed Rodger. They appeared to be in a similar state to Ivon, their eyes half shut and murmuring softly to themselves. Of the warlock himself there was no sign.

No sooner did the thought of running occur to him than he felt the weight return. Shutting his eyes and taking a deep breath he thought of his house's banner and the insignia of the Valravyn.

A sound alerted him to a figure approaching through the gloaming, from the path up to the plateau where the eldritch stone lay. It was Ivon, only now he was dressed in a manner befitting the head of a coven of witches. Sorcerous sigils writhed in a faint orange glow upon rich robes of purple velvet; about his neck was an amulet of crystal, its five points mocking the four limbs of the Redeemer. He wore white silken gloves, above which bejewelled rings flashed with an unnatural luminosity in the fading twilight.

The five acolytes stopped chanting as he stepped up to address them in Panglian. As one they stood up. Walking over to their saddle bags they reached inside and each produced a hollowed-out goat's head. Wolmar felt his hackles rise as they put on the diabolical masks. Ivon beckoned to the princeling and he followed him obediently towards the trail, like a lamb to the slaughter.

✠ ✠ ✠

The Wytching Hour was fast approaching by the time they reached the plateau of rock where Rodger had breathed his last. The balmy summer night did little to abate Wolmar's rising tension. If the presence of manifest evil had been acute before, it was palpable now. On the far side of the rocky shelf was a boulder. Ivon barked something in Panglian and two of the acolytes went and rolled it over, revealing a great hollow beneath. Wolmar felt his gorge rise as they dragged a whimpering figure from its lightless depths: the bound and gagged form of a girl dressed in naught but a dirty shift. Wolmar fixed his eyes on her as they brought her back to the cursed stone and forced her down on to it. She could not have been older than fourteen summers.

'The serfs won't long miss a daughter of theirs,' said Ivon coldly. 'Most of them are fated to die of disease and ill usage as befits their lot – but this waif shall join the King of All in glory tonight!'

Wolmar made to curse the depraved warlock, but no words came from his clenching throat. Ivon pulled a phial from his robes and nodded towards one of his acolytes; Wolmar couldn't tell which of them beneath the goat head. The acolyte pulled the gag from the girl's mouth and Ivon poured the phial's contents into it before she could start screaming.

In moments the potion took effect and the girl stopped struggling and went limp. No sleep spell this – her eyes remained open but glazed over. Reaching down Ivon tore the shift off her, leaving her nubile form exposed upon the stone, which seemed to burn at the edges with a lustful red light.

A more natural yellow flickering caught Wolmar's eye. Glancing back down towards the clearing far below, he saw faint points of wavering torchlight.

'The others are here,' said Ivon. 'All is going according to plan.'

Wolmar watched as the acolytes set up braziers at five points around the stone. By their light he could see a pentangle had been scored with silvery dust around it, each of its points terminating in one of the braziers. Ivon began to walk around the circle, muttering softly in the language of magick. Wolmar shuddered with every syllable. Instinctively he moved a hand to where the iron dagger lay pressed against his midriff.

The silver dust seemed to glow faintly in the dark now, the pentangle it sketched taking on a lucent definition eerily reminiscent of the natural light of the stars above. It was only then that he noticed he had been placed inside the pentacle, within one of its triangular points.

Gradually the other members of Ivon's cult began to arrive. Who they were he would never know, for all were dressed in black robes and goat head masks. They carried torches and filed silently onto the plateau, forming a thickening circle about the pentacle as Ivon continued to perambulate it, chanting in the fell tongue of sorcery.

Wolmar's heart sank as they encircled him. There were at least fifty of them, staring at him through shadowy sockets. Escape was impossible. All that remained was one last superhuman effort of will – at least he would go down fighting.

Night had reached its zenith by the time Ivon ceased his preparations. Stepping into the middle of the circle he stood before the glowing stone, which made the drugged girl draped across it look like a harlot from hell.

Inverting the sign of the Wheel, the warlock addressed his blasphemous congregation in Decorlangue. 'Lords and ladies, from castle and temple, manor and monastery have I chosen thee! The Hour of All's Ending approacheth, and the King of Gehenna shall soon return to reclaim His birthright! That which was stripped away from Him at the Dawn of Time, during the Battle for Heaven and Earth, shall be restored to Abaddon, and his true servants shall share in His glory!'

The warlock paused. Wolmar half expected the diabolical flock to cheer, but all were deathly silent.

Ivon continued: 'Our numbers have grown steadily, both those of us here deemed strong enough to be privy to the Master's darkest arcana, and those who will serve us, knowingly or otherwise. Soon the antiquated realms of mortalkind shall be swept away, the Synod of Priest-Kings that once ruled the Known World shall rise again – through us, and others like us! Sorcerers shall rule the Known World once more, and all shall be fettered in blissful bondage!'

Again he paused; again a quiet as still as the grave met his words. Only the crepitant fires of the braziers could be heard above the rising wind.

The Margrave who would be master of the world turned to face Wolmar. 'Tonight we gather, brothers and sisters, to welcome another member to our illustrious fold – Sir Wolmar of Strongholm, who came to us a prince of mortal blood royal... Tonight, if he prove strong enough to pass his initiation, he shall emerge a scion of a new world order! Wolmar, kneel!'

The princeling did as commanded. No point in trying to fight Ivon now, while he was out of striking range. Best to bide his time.

The congregation at last broke its silence, and began to chant in a strange tongue. At first Wolmar assumed it was the language of magick, but he quickly realised it was something else: at once strangely familiar and yet completely outlandish.

He had little time to ponder that as Ivon addressed him again. 'Wolmar of Strongholm, thou hast been chosen to receive the rites! Molaach, Receiver of Souls and Seneschal to Abaddon in his city of burning brass, shall I implore on thine own behalf! From the Second Tier shall he be moved to make a reckoning of thine animus! Wolmar of Strongholm, earthly power such as you have never known shall be yours in recompense! Your soul shall be ripped from thy heart and broiled in a casket of fire – dost thou consent?'

Wolmar could barely stop the words escaping his lips. 'I do consent,' he gasped in Decorlangue. He kept the image of the White Valravyn and the standard of Ingwin burned in his mind: the two merged and blended, a white raven circling above two unicorns that danced and reared...

If he could retain some of his willpower for just long enough...

Ivon turned to face the girl. Her glazed eyes stared up into the night. Was she aware of what was happening to her? Wolmar prayed she wasn't: not even he could be so cruel as to wish otherwise.

Raising his eyes to the heavens, Ivon cried aloud in the language of magick. Wolmar could not fathom its meaning, though he heard the name 'Molaach' repeated over and over again. Around him the chanting swelled as the dark disciples raised their voices. Though not eldritch like the sorcerous tongue, there was something undeniably profane about the language they spoke.

Wolmar could only watch as Ivon pulled the hapless girl's legs apart. Opening his robes he exposed his sex. His erstwhile lover was fully engorged, just as he had seen him on many a hot night in the palace at Rima. That seemed a thousand years ago now.

Holding the girl firmly by her supple waist the warlock entered her. The chanting reached a fevered pitch as Ivon violated her, all the while crying aloud in the language of magick. Reaching into the upper folds of his robe without breaking off his copulation, Ivon produced a kris-shaped dagger, its wavy blade seeming to undulate with a malignity of its own.

Wolmar had done many questionable deeds in his life, but this was beyond the pail of anything he had ever witnessed. He felt his last meal come up in a burning torrent as Ivon climaxed inside the prostrate girl, uttering the last syllable of his spell and plunging the knife deep into her heart. His frenzied thrusting slowed as her lifeblood pumped across his exposed torso, her body quivering into lifelessness as he slumped over her dead form with an ecstatic sigh. The congregation did not cease its chanting, though a euphoric tone now suffused the rising voices.

Withdrawing from the corpse, Ivon stood and raised his arms. His white-gloved hands and wilting member were slick with fresh warm blood.

'Molaach, a soul I give thee in bondage, borne on a tide of blood and seed! Now take a second soul, given willingly by one who would serve thee in life!'

The warlock began to back away out of the pentangle, genuflecting as he did. Wolmar realised it was now or never. Forcing himself to stand, he pulled the iron dagger from his kirtle. Ivon's eyes widened as he registered the glint of metal. The chanting wavered as some of the acolytes noticed it too.

'Do not break off the chant!' he cried. 'We must not be discovered!'

Turning back to face Wolmar he said in a low even voice: 'Put that down.'

Wolmar felt the weight pressing him from all sides. Gritting his teeth, he forced himself to think only of a white raven circling a pair of unicorns.

Slowly and painfully he took a step towards the mage. The circle continued chanting, though the euphoria had left it.

Ivon repeated the command. Again Wolmar took a step forwards, though every movement was agony. His fingers, clenched feverishly around the dagger's hilt, felt as though a Wadwo were trying to prise them apart.

Anger crossed the warlock's face and he barked a few syllables in the language of magick. It was the same incantation he had used before to turn Wolmar's steel blade into a serpent. But this time nothing happened.

'Very clever,' breathed Ivon. 'Pure iron. Your resourcefulness does you credit.'

Again Wolmar took a step forwards. The weight was almost unbearable now. He could feel Ivon fighting him. Beads of sweat stood out on the mage's forehead, dripping down his face to mingle with the girl's blood spattered across his midriff. But behind the force he could sense there was a weakness. He had guessed rightly – his lover had been left drained by his spell-casting. His plan was working!

Only he had not reckoned on what purpose the spell had served. A flaring light from the stone informed him.

Turning to look he saw the girl's corpse rise off it. Where but a moment ago blood had gushed from a mortal wound now red fires sputtered; her eyes burned with flames as black as the night skies.

Ivon scurried out of the pentacle as the girl's form lurched towards Wolmar. Her lithe body shifted and cracked as she did, the limbs distending and contorting horribly as she grew in stature. Her drooling mouth opened and an impossibly long tongue snaked out, as if tasting the air between them. Her skin had taken on the reddish hue of the stone.

Ivon addressed the demon now, speaking in the language of magick. The dead girl's form spat out some words in a cracked voice. To Wolmar it felt like there were aeons of hatred in it. A hint of desperation entered Ivon's voice as he yelled back at the demon he called Molaach.

Switching back to Decorlangue he barked: 'Wolmar, kneel before thy true master! Do not spurn a second-tier Lord of Gehenna, or he shall consume thy body as well as thy soul!'

Even now Wolmar felt the enormous pressure on his will. As well as Ivon's power of suggestion, he now had mortal terror of a ravening demon to compel him. And the warlock had taken advantage of the distraction to back away out of range. The acolytes remained an unbroken circle around him, though their chanting was now suffused with fear.

There was only one option. There had only ever been one option.

Turning from Ivon he looked upon the demon called Molaach, as it beckoned towards him with fingers that bent back on themselves and cracked hideously.

'Releassss the iron... come... and... kissss me...' It was using Decorlangue to speak to him; there was a susurration to the demon's speech that made Wolmar feel nauseous. He retched up bile as he registered the lop-sided grin on the peasant girl's face, now horribly twisted.

'Do as he says!' shrieked Ivon. 'Embrace Molaach and become one of us! Or go straight to Gehenna and burn there forever!'

Shutting his eyes Wolmar clutched the dagger in both hands and raised it high above his head. 'Oh Reus, forgive me,' he managed to utter, before plunging the blade deep into his chest.

The pain that lanced through him was almost welcome as he slumped to his knees with a gasp. He was dimly aware of the congregation breaking up as the demon gave vent to a roar of primordial rage. Falling onto his side, he saw Ivon presenting his amulet as he yelled another incantation. The demon had warped the girl's body even more in its rage; it looked like a gigantic four-legged spider as it stalked towards him. Ignoring the iron blade lodged in his chest Wolmar dug his fingers into the rocky ground and began pulling himself towards the edge of the pentangle with the last of his strength. By now he was beyond all pain; his only thought was to get his body out of the demon's clutches so he could die a clean death.

He was peripherally aware that Ivon was still standing just outside the pentagram, casting another spell. The demon's host body was now suffused with fires that changed colour; its form seemed to grow long and diaphanous, its undulating contours swallowed up by a shadow that grew steadily from out of the flaming miasma where its heart had been...

With a strangled cry Wolmar reached the edge of the pentacle just as Ivon mouthed the last of the spell. The demon seemed to collapse in on itself in a ball of darkness and guttering light. The braziers went out all at once, plunging the plateau into starlit gloom. Wolmar felt a searing pain in his chest grow and spread throughout his body, a welcome numbness following hard on its heels. A deep sadness rippled through him...

Then he felt no more.

⊷ CHAPTER IX ⊷

Unwelcome Tidings

The brawny highlander leaned back in the creaking chair. It was made of oak, but barely looked strong enough to support his weight. Wiping greasy fingers unceremoniously on his fur cloak, he gave vent to a satisfied belch.

Abrexta distastefully eyed the ravaged remains of boar he had chomped his way through. To most lowlanders, Cormic Mac Brennan was a fearsome sight, all the more so given the ugly scar that appeared to give him a perpetual rictus grin, but she simply found the highland general uncouth and distasteful to look upon. The allies the Moon Goddess commanded her to make... Reminding herself that it was for the greater good, she pressed him again for answers.

'So, when you've finished your ravaging, your ravishing and your burning – when all the "essentials of conquest" as you so eloquently put it are done – when do you think the lords Tíerchán and Slangá will be ready to send me their warriors?'

A fortnight had passed since her conversation with Ragnar. He was not the only warlock she had communed with during that time, and her last scrying had given her good reason to expedite her plans. The Master was not someone who tolerated failure.

All of this and more went through her mind as Cormic took another slurp of mead. She almost regretted having chosen to grant him private audience in her personal antechamber, but she needed to be alone with him.

'As I've just told ye,' he breezed, licking froth from his scarred mouth. 'There's nae cause for concern, yer ladyship. Two thousand o' our finest screamers ye'll have by month's end.'

'But that takes us to the eve of Ripanmonath and the beginning of autumn,' said Abrexta, reaching irritably for her goblet. 'You know full well how early winter sets in on the seas that surround the Westerling Isles – in all probability that will mean delaying the invasion until spring!'

'Aye, lassie, it will,' conceded Cormic, who seemed to be paying more attention to the mead than her. 'But I couldnae help but notice that yer fleet's no' exactly close tae bein' finished. Canny set sail withoot them in any case...'

She wished she could enthral him, or better still, set fire to his ermine cloak and braided beard. But that was out of the question while she was this taxed. He stared at her across his silver tankard, his dark eyes meeting hers. A naked savagery was in those eyes, one that well matched the necklace of cured tongues he wore: keepsakes from his many victories. The Cormic Death's Head had become a thing of legend.

But that was exactly why she needed him. His kind of brute strength, animal cunning and ruthless savagery would make him a formidable ally.

'The dock workers are being appeased,' she said. 'The shipwrights are due to go back to work after this Restday. It's true they've delayed things, though we should hopefully have a hundred ships ready to set sail by the end of Ripanmonath.'

Cormic shook his head. 'That'll be too late,' he said, emptying his tankard and beckoning towards a page boy for a refill. 'By Blakmonath the seas'll be too rough tae sail... So ye're looking at a spring invasion in any case.' His rictus broadened as he took another slurp. 'That'll be bonny, the lads are tired after all the fechtin' we've been daein' of late – be good tae rest up an' celebrate the Year's End in style.'

Abrexta fought to keep her temper. 'Then why are you even here?' she barked.

'Show of good faith,' replied the highland chief. 'By sendin' me doon here, Slangá's demonstratin' that he's loyal tae the crown... Ah've plenty tae keep me busy up north but he deemed it important. Still, I have tae say, it's no' been a bad trip all in all. Yer meat an' mead's passin' fine, and ah love what ye've done wi' the palace decorations.'

Cormic was referring to the corpses of Vertrix and the other rebels she'd had eviscerated and strung up above the gates. Yet another example of what happened to those who dared defy her. But she wasn't in the mood for flattery.

'Yes well, regardless of whether it's a spring invasion or not,' she said, 'I'll be wanting you and your men down here by end of Ripanmonath. You'll need to be present for planning the invasion in any case.'

'Aye, aye, dinnae worry, yer ladyship,' replied the highlander. 'I'm fully lookin' forward tae enjoyin' the king's hospitality over winter.

Just ye make sure my lads have bonny lodgings – they've become quite accustomed to such since they took Daxor and Gaellentir.'

'Yes, I've heard all about the orgy of rapine and slaughter your "lads" have been indulging in since we gave you the north,' said Abrexta. 'I do hope you've left some of the original inhabitants alive.'

'Aye, that we have,' Cormic assured her. 'Enough tae see tae oor needs, anyway...' He grinned again, revealing a cluster of silver teeth.

Abrexta hid her revulsion. She knew exactly what kind of needs the womenfolk of Daxor and Gaellentir would be serving. When the new order was imposed women would no longer be the thralls of men, not under her rule at least. The Moon Goddess demanded it.

'Well, don't forget that lands need to be ruled after they've been conquered,' she contented herself with saying. 'You'll need peasants to work it... until my kind are able to bend nature to our will again, as it was in far-gone times.'

For the first time during their audience the highlander looked perturbed. 'Aye, well... I'll leave matters o' religion tae you, o' course...'

He still looked distinctly uneasy. Abrexta shook her head inwardly. In the long centuries that had passed since the Westerling clans ruled in north-west Urovia, even those descended from their stock had forgotten the ways of the druids and priestesses, succumbing to superstitious fear of magic. She would fain see those days at an end – even if it meant serving a Left-Hand warlock. That thought brought back fears of her own as she rose to usher the highland chieftain out of her chambers.

But she had no time to ponder the dark master that Kaia had willed her to serve. Caratacus was her next visitor – she hoped he had better news.

Fortunately he did.

'The Shipwrights' Guild has accepted our offer,' he confirmed. 'Work on the fleet will recommence next week.'

'Excellent,' she said. 'And the coin to pay them?'

The treasurer nodded contentedly. 'My investigations were swift and thorough. Several dozen talents of gold have been recovered and five men have been hanged for embezzling the Royal Fold. I've replaced them with men more suited to the office.'

And doubtless more inclined to doubt my rule, the sorceress thought disparagingly, though it was a necessary sacrifice.

'Good. And how speed things with the Cobians?'

'Now that we have more coin and are in the process of collecting taxes we should be able to persuade them,' said Caratacus. 'In all likelihood we'll have a fleet of officers assembled in Ongist by early Ripanmonath.'

'Cormic assures me that Tíerchán and Slangá will have their warriors posted here in the capital by that time. So we'll be ready to plan in earnest by then – what of supplies for the journey?'

'All victualing is proceeding as planned,' replied Caratacus. 'The invasion fleet should be ready by Blakmonath.' He hesitated. 'In all probability that will mean delaying until – '

'Yes, I know,' said Abrexta, cutting him off irately. 'Well there's naught else we can do about it – we'll just have to sail with the spring tides. At least that will give us time to train our forces for the coming war. Have you given any thought as to where we'll house the highlanders?'

'Lands without the capital are being made ready for them.' The treasurer's tone betrayed his misgivings.

'I'll see to it that a guard is posted about their camp over winter,' said Abrexta, correctly reading his concerns. 'See to it that they don't run amok.'

'As you say, your ladyship,' replied Caratacus, favouring her with a half bow. If he still had any misgivings he didn't show them. Just as well, because –

Her train of thought was interrupted by a banging at the door.

'Enter,' she said, wondering who dared disrupt her private audience.

A flustered courtier entered. Another of her thralls, she could not even remember his name.

'What is it?' she asked, noting the expression on the young knight's face.

'We've just had messengers arrive... from the south,' he faltered. 'They are asking to speak to His Majesty the King.'

'Cadwy is away on a hunting trip,' she informed him curtly. These days it was simpler just to keep the King out of the way by distracting his attention with useless sports. 'You may address me in his stead.'

'The messengers come from Port Craek,' he said. 'It's about the southern wards.' His voice trailed off hesitantly, in the manner of one afraid to give bad news.

She didn't need farseeing to divine what was coming next.

'Out with it,' she said, gesturing impatiently.

'Garro, Penllyn and Tul Aeren have declared war,' stammered the knight. 'They are marshalling their armies and plan to march on Garth imminently.'

'And what of Fythe?' The courtier had not mentioned the southernmost province of Thraxia.

'The lord of Fythe has his hands full coping with border raids from Cobia – he won't be taking part in the rebellion, but he won't be joining us either. Some good news at least, my lady.'

Abrexta scowled. Some, but not much. The three provinces combined would be able to field a sizeable army. And now Andragorix wouldn't be sending her any help, she would have to deal with it herself. That would mean a civil war to fight on land before any invasion of the Island Realms.

'Leave me, both of you,' she said. 'Caratacus – speak to these messengers yourself and glean all you can from them. Then come and make your report to me.'

Without another word both men bowed and left.

Suppressing a sigh of trepidation she turned towards the bedchamber, where her polished silver mirror and incense brazier awaited. It was time to make another report of her own. The Master would want to hear this news at once, bad as it was.

⊷ CHAPTER X ⊷

A Regency Disputed

'I put myself forward as candidate for regent.'

A shocked silence greeted Prince Thorsvald as he stepped from the throng of courtiers and drew level with his brother. Prince Wolfram stared at him, mingled disbelief and rage fighting for a place in his one good eye. His younger brother could barely meet it; Hjala winced as she registered the pain in his face. Ulnor was staring at her with a barely tamed anger of his own from where he sat as acting regent on the Pine Throne.

A hubbub began to brew among the elegantly dressed men and women in the high hall. Ulnor banged down his staff of office for silence.

'ENOUGH!' he roared when the chattering failed to subside. 'This is a crucial matter of state, not some gallery at a performance.' The noise subsided reluctantly. Fixing Thorsvald with a keen stare the seneschal addressed him. 'Your Highness, are you quite sure this is what you want?'

Pained though he was, Thorsvald did not hesitate to answer. 'I am, my lord. With all due respect my brother has yet to recover fully from his wounds. As such, it behoves me to rule as regent in his place, but temporarily, until he has had more time to heal.'

'YOU DARE!' yelled Wolfram, barely containing himself. 'I will be the judge of whether I am WELL ENOUGH TO RULE!'

Hjala closed her eyes. For an instant it looked as though Wolfram were going to have one of his fits on the spot. She supposed that might decide the matter in her favour, though the last thing the realm needed was to have its future ruler show such weakness.

As if sensing this Wolfram moderated his speech, though not without difficulty. 'Who put you up to this, brother?' he demanded, taking a step towards Thorsvald. 'Always I have loved you, treated you as an equal – now this is how you repay me? Oh, base treachery!'

'Aye, treachery!' cried one knight, a hanger-on of Wolfram's. 'He bides his time, then strikes when he sees a chance to take the throne! Don't trust him!'

'Aye,' cried another. 'Wolfram is our future king, not his child brother!'

Hjala bit her lip nervously. For all his faults Wolfram was immensely popular, loved by noble and commoner alike. This was not going to be easy.

Ulnor banged down his staff again. 'I said SILENCE!' he roared, his voice reverberating around the hall. Hjala fancied even the Giantslayer's Gift trembled at his voice. 'There will be no running commentary while we discuss MATTERS OF STATE!'

Credit to Ulnor, he would have due protocol, even though he obviously sympathised with Wolfram's supporters.

'I bear no treason in my heart towards thee,' said Thorsvald sincerely, finally managing to meet his older brother's burning stare. 'Nor do I covet what is rightfully yours. But brother, the realm is in grave danger – only yesterday did you hear my latest tidings! Before that you were... indisposed. The king's own chirurgeon has recommended further rest – it is to preserve your very reign that I would not have you jeopardising it by returning to duty too soon.'

'A likely story, I am sure,' sneered Wolfram. 'Someone has put you up to this, for what fell purpose I know not.' He looked about the throneroom, as if daring anyone to step forward. No one did, though Hjala flinched as his eye passed her by. Of course, her hotheaded brother would never credit a mere woman with coming up with a scheme like this.

Ulnor sighed. 'Well, if you're determined in this matter, Prince Thorsvald, I've no choice but to proceed accordingly.'

Looking over to where the royal scrivener sat behind a cramped desk in the corner, he declaimed: 'Amanuensis of the court, note it duly – Prince Thorsvald of the House of Ingwin presents himself as candidate for Regent until His Majesty King Freidheim II should recover from his malady or seek the Judgment of Azrael. A vote of council will be held at the next moon to decide which of the two candidates shall be selected. Votes to be held by Lord Toric of Runstadt, High Commander of the White Valravyn; His High Holiness Cuthbert of our most sacred True Temple; Lord Visigard, head of palace security; and myself, Lord Ulnor, seneschal of the realm. Final vote to be held by nearest of royal kin to the present incumbent, King Freidheim, which in the absence of candidates Prince Wolfram and Prince Thorsvald...' – he shot a glance at Hjala that had a bodkin-like quality to it – '... is Her Royal Highness, Princess Hjala of the House of Ingwin. Myself, Lord Ulnor, to serve as acting regent until said council has convened and made its decision. This matter being now settled, court is hereby dismissed.'

The seneschal banged his staff once on the dais. Hjala had a feeling he wished the flagstoned floor was her head.

Next to her Visigard was muttering, loudly enough for her to hear him. 'A younger son standing for regent, most irregular, most irregular indeed...! What on earth has got into his Royal Highness?' The hoary old raven plucked at his sideburns disapprovingly, oblivious to her part in the whole thing.

Well, there was no doubt which way his vote would be going.

Doing her best to be surreptitious, Hjala left the hall swiftly. The last thing she needed right now was to be accosted by her brother Wolfram, or Lord Ulnor for that matter. The game was afoot: now all that remained was to hunt it.

It was time to seek out her aunt Walsa, and see how her morning visit to the Temple had gone.

✤ ✤ ✤

In his room overlooking the citadel, Lord Ulnor paced fretfully. He was far from a young man and the effort tired him, but his nerves demanded it. That wilful strumpet would be the death of him – and the realm. This was what came of allowing a woman into the affairs of men, he thought ruefully as he turned and gazed out at the clustered streets below him. The city he loved more than any place on earth had returned to normal since the war's end. The refugees had been a problem: some had starved while others had been hanged after taking to thieving to feed themselves. But since then most had been resettled. He had no doubt the outcome was better than it would have been if Thule had won the war.

But now he was faced with an altogether different kind of problem. The line of succession could not be broken, of that he felt certain. True, Wolfram had his flaws, but he was the rightful heir and immensely popular. Under his careful tutelage, he felt sure the prince would blossom into a worthy successor to his father.

And why shouldn't he influence the throne when Freidheim was gone? Better him than a woman, with no practical experience of the affairs of state.

Yet that was surely what would come to pass should Hjala succeed in putting her younger brother on the throne. The two younger siblings had always been close: that would shut him out of the Regent's confidence. And should Wolfram's condition worsen during that time, Thorsvald's tenure might stretch into years until his nephew Freidhrim came of age... By which time Ulnor would be long gone.

No, it was unthinkable. He had not served the realm body and soul all these years to see its care snatched from him in the twilight of his life. Something had to be done.

That Hjala had her allies at court he knew all too well. His eyes and ears kept him informed of all the things his own keen judgement had not already revealed. The princess's long-standing affair with Sir Torgun had brought her close to men who served the White Valravyn. Visigard, loyal dolt that he was, could be trusted to stick to protocol, but Toric... He might be swayed by his best knight's paramour. And as for the Temple... His High Holiness Cuthbert appeared pliant enough, but where had Lady Walsa been during the hearing? It wasn't like that interfering old busybody to miss out on court intrigue of any kind.

A knock on his door heralded an answer to that question.

A page opened the door and in came a stableboy. Well, that was his official job: his unofficial duties entailed keeping track of who left the palace and reporting anything unusual to Ulnor.

'Well boy,' said Ulnor, not entirely unkindly. 'Have you news for me that will earn you a silver or two?'

'Yes, milord,' said the raggedy boy, managing a half bow. 'I b'lieve so, milord. The Lady Walsa took a horse this mornin', milord.'

'I see,' replied Ulnor. 'Was it a palfrey or a courser?'

'Twas a palfrey, milord,' said the boy. 'Meanin' Her Highness wasn't planning on venturing out of the city, milord.'

'Thank you, I know full well what her choice of steed indicates. Have you anything else to report?'

'Yes, milord. She returned an hour after noon, milord. Looked very satisfied and sure of herself if I may say so, milord.'

'You may,' replied Ulnor crisply. 'Every detail is important. And did her horse's hooves have little muck or much muck on them?'

The stablehand paused for a second or two, reflecting. Then he said: 'I believe they had little muck on 'em, milord.'

'Thank you boy, your services have been most useful.' Reaching into a box on his desk he pulled out two marks and tossed them over. The boy caught them expertly and tucked the shining pieces into his coarse jerkin.

'Not a word of this to anybody, as per usual,' Ulnor said sternly.

'Yes, milord, I mean no, milord – thank you, milord,' he stuttered, managing another half bow before exiting the room.

Ulnor felt his chest tighten as he returned to his pacing. A short visit, probably within the confines of the less dirty citadel, most likely meant one thing: Lady Walsa was using her influence with the Temple to pull a few strings.

Blasted women. They did so love to scheme and plot against the menfolk.

Well we'll soon see about that, he thought.

After a few more turns about his room, he barked an order to the page boy outside. The youth opened the door, wearing his most obedient face.

'Fetch my cloak,' he ordered. The page scurried across the chamber to obey.

He would need it where he was going: it was cold in the dungeons, and it was time he made a little visit of his own.

⁜ ⁜ ⁜

Prince Thorsvald stared out at his beloved sea, but not even its sparkling rills could assuage his anxiety. Once again he shook his head, absent-mindedly fingering the goblet of untouched wine in his hand.

'I already told you I don't like politics – temple politics even less!' he said, turning back to face the two women.

Lady Walsa was as implacable as ever. 'Yes well, I'm afraid that's just what you'll have to get used to if you're to be Regent,' she said. 'His High Holiness Cuthbert is more malleable than most, but he isn't a complete milksop. I've been organising donations to the Temple regularly since Brother Horskram cured me, so I've got quite a bit of leverage there, but even so he won't help us for nothing.'

Hjala watched her aunt work over the Sealord. He looked so confused, tormented even: part of her hated herself for putting her brother in this position, but she knew it had to be done.

'Aunt Walsa is right, brother,' she said softly. 'And Cuthbert's request is a reasonable one. Already he has received three petitions from the Supreme Perfect to send the Redeemer's blood to the head of the True Temple in Rima. Our father promised he would vouch for the Northlending branch of the Temple, and now our father lies sick and incapacitated. All his High Holiness requires is a guarantee that you will back his claim that the relic remain here and pilgrimage routes to Strongholm be opened up.'

'It will be a good policy for the realm in any case,' put in Walsa. 'Think of all those revenues the crown will get from wealthy Pangonian pilgrims.' She paused to make the sign. 'Not to mention prestige in the eyes of our father the Almighty.'

Hjala had to suppress a wry smile. Her aunt had always seemed sincere in her devotion to the Creed since Horskram banished the Ifrit that possessed her – but she had learned the value of money from a much earlier age.

Her brother sighed and turned from the window, draining his goblet in one go. 'All right, tell His High Holiness that if elected as Regent I will undertake to vouchsafe all Northlending claims to the relic's being kept here in Strongholm. Cuthbert has my word that my father's intended policy in this matter will be carried out.'

Hjala and her aunt exchanged triumphant smiles. 'Excellent,' said Walsa. 'I'll let His High Holiness know directly. You can count on his vote at the council next moon.'

Hjala felt a sense of relief. It had been a sound stratagem: Wolfram was well known in his disregard for the Temple, and had even expressed a grudging admiration for the Pangonians on a few occasions. As Regent, his chances of angering a powerful king whose country he admired for its martial spirit would have been less than sure. That was just one example of why Thorsvald would make a better ruler: as much as he purported to hate politics, he was far more capable of seeing the bigger picture than his narrow-minded brother.

She caught herself, realising where her thinking was leading her once again. Reus' teeth, was she really wishing for Wolfram not to recover? It was true she had never been as close to him as she was to Thorsvald. From a young age, their older sibling had made clear that he regarded himself as different, the heir to the throne. Not that he had been unkind or even haughty towards them... just somewhat aloof. Maybe that was enough to prevent her having too many qualms about intriguing against him, but it wasn't enough to despise him. Despite believing that she was acting for the good of the realm, Hjala felt a gnawing sense of guilt. Her older brother must despise her now.

Pushing the unwelcome thoughts aside, she bade her aunt a cordial farewell as she left to see word delivered to Cuthbert.

When she was gone Thorsvald refilled their goblets. There were no page boys on hand to serve them – with Ulnor in charge of the palace spies it was best to keep things as secret as they could. They had even made sure his wife and children were away on a pleasure trip out of town.

'So what about Toric?' asked Thorsvald. 'Do you really think you can sway him?'

'You leave me to worry about the High Commander,' replied Hjala, sipping thoughtfully from her goblet. 'Sir Torgun introduced me to him, back when we were... He's a bluff, stern character, but I think he liked me all the same. And like any good raven he's absolutely loyal to the crown. Reus willing he can be made to see the sense in this – as you were.'

Her brother's pained expression did little to encourage her. Even now, with everything in motion, he remained conflicted.

'Oh Thorsvald, this must be,' she insisted. 'After everything I told you the other evening...'

Her brother raised a calloused hand. 'Yes, yes... I know that,' he muttered, still not meeting her eye. 'It's just a lot to take in – a mad warlock bent on subjugating the Free Kingdoms, and we don't even know for certain where he is or with whom he is allied... Normal wars I can understand, but this...'

'Have faith, brother,' said Hjala. 'The monk Horskram is both learned and resourceful, and with Sir Torgun at his side, his victory must be assured.'

Now it was her turn to feel pained. She missed the earnest knight, heart and soul. Part of her wished they had not rekindled their romance on the eve of his parting. Life seemed to be relentlessly cruel: it visited misfortune and misery on one so often, then it dropped a boon into one's lap unexpectedly... only to pluck it away again, leaving the fresh pain of a new loss to cope with.

Slugging back her wine she conquered her thoughts. They were brooding and weak, unbefitting a princess of the house of Ingwin. Stepping closer to her brother she took him gently by the shoulders and met his eyes.

'It is not for us to choose what fortunes the Almighty visits upon us,' she said, her voice hushed yet strong. 'We do what we must, and that is all.'

Thorsvald stared back at her before nodding. 'Of course you are right, dear sister,' he replied. 'Please forgive my frailty, I shall endeavour to grow into the role the Unseen have assigned me.'

She kissed him gently on the forehead, standing on her toes to do so.

'There now,' she smiled. 'That is more like it – scions of the House of Ingwin are we! Now, I'd better see about Lord Toric, and hope my female charms can weave some magic of their own.'

'Last I heard the High Commander was still down south, pacifying the conquered territories.'

'I'm sure the scions of the Efrilunders and the King's Dominions our father settled on the rebel provinces will be only too ready to take such matters in their own hands,' replied Hjala wryly. 'I doubt the King's Justice will stretch into his newly extended dominions for long.'

'I'll see to it that it does if I'm elected,' said Thorsvald. 'Even if it means extending the White Valravyn's charter.'

She cupped her brother's rugged cheek affectionately. 'I'll be sure to mention that to Toric when he arrives at court,' she said knowingly.

At last her brother managed a half smile. 'I suppose one could get used to being Regent,' he offered tentatively.

Her own smile broadened. 'I've no doubt that you will,' she said. 'How long until he arrives?'

'Ulnor will have sent word directly that he's summoned to a council of state,' said Hjala, her smile dropping into a frown. 'That means the Lord Seneschal has stolen a march on us, so to speak – doubtless his message will stress the urgency of keeping the line of succession intact.'

'So what will you do?' Her brother's face became anxious again.

'I will bide my time for now,' replied Hjala. 'Toric won't get here for a few days and from what I know of him he is a sensible, prudent man – he won't make up his mind about whom to back until he's had a chance to get the lie of the land. Wolfram may be popular with the regular chivalry, but many in the White Valravyn feel he was remiss in his duties, caught tilting when he was badly needed in a real war. I think the head of the Order can be persuaded to take our side – the ravens prize loyalty above all, and yours is peerless within the realm.'

Her brother actually had the grace to blush slightly. 'You do me too much kindness, sister,' he said. 'I but serve the realm.'

'That is exactly what a good raven would say,' replied Hjala. 'Now if you'll excuse me, I'll away to my chambers. I need to be alone to think a while. In the meantime, don't talk to anyone about what we're doing, not even your wife understand?'

Her brother smiled again. 'Now you chide me, just as you used to when we played games about the palace!'

'It's for your own good,' she replied tartly, 'now as it was back then. Good day to you, brother.'

Kissing him lightly, on the cheek this time, she swept from the chamber. Turning once from the doorway she saw her brother had returned to looking out at the lashing waves of the Strang Estuary. The brooding expression was back on his face.

Suppressing a sigh, she closed the door behind her.

⊷ CHAPTER XI ⊷

In Search Of Succour

'The damsels should be fully recovered in a couple of days – but as for the others, such tainted souls cannot so easily be cured of the Draugbreath.'

Brother Johann's face was like a granite sculpture in the firelight as he addressed Horskram. The Abbot of Heilag Monastery was as stern a patrician as any in their Order. He had rather too much of Lorthar about him, inflexible in his thinking: it surprised the adept he was an Argolian, never mind a prior trusted with a key outpost.

Horskram had never liked him, and was sure the feeling was mutual.

'Really Brother Horskram, bringing women and men of the sword into this hallowed precinct!' he said for the umpteenth time. 'We've enough to contend with daily what with warding off the evil that pours from the Draugfluss without – '

'Yes, yes,' Horskram cut him off, raising a tanned hand in acknowledgement. 'I am well aware of your misgivings, Brother Johann. Suffice to say that I am forever in your debt and shall be gone with my unwelcome ragtag band right soon. Just tell me what the prognosis is for the others.'

'The prayers of this chapter have done somewhat to allay the psychic illness that afflicts them,' said Johann, assuming a matter-of-fact tone. 'But without further help they will wither soon enough. Their skins shall fall from their flesh, which shall weaken by the day as their souls pass over into the shadow world of the Other Side... A week or two from now they'll begin coughing up blood as their entrails collapse beneath the draugar's curse – '

'For heaven's sake!' thundered Horskram, losing his temper. 'I meant how long do they have before the curse does irreversible damage! I don't need a ghoulish enumeration of the symptoms that will destroy them!'

Johann's face remained unyielding as he replied: 'Thanks to our efforts, I'd give them a fortnight at most.'

'Well that settles it,' said Horskram irritably. 'We had best be on our way – only such power as we have pooled at our headquarters can save them if what you say is true.'

'Yes, well,' sniffed the Abbot. 'I've no doubt that Rima could summon a greater elan than we here at Heilag can muster – though I for one am not sure such killers deserve succour.'

'You have no idea of the debt mortalkind owes those killers,' snapped Horskram. It felt strange to be defending the very warriors he had warned Adelko against taking up with, but it was true nonetheless: without their aid his mission would surely have faltered by now.

'Yes, I have no idea,' Johann was saying, 'because you refuse to tell me anything! Four nights since you and your rakehell band tore out of the moors seeking sanctuary, and naught but a secret mission have I heard you tell of.'

'Well if Hannequin acts on my news as I expect him to, you'll find out soon enough,' said the adept, secretly glad that Johann's sixth sense wasn't as acute as Prior Aedric's. Had the Abbot of Ørthang reached any conclusions about Belaach's prophecy, he wondered? He had asked him to send word to Rima should he do so, though their headquarters still seemed a long way away.

'We need to get to Westerburg as soon as possible, see about getting berths on a ship to Rima,' said Horskram, giving voice to just some of his thoughts. 'Reus knows but we've delayed enough as it is.'

To make matters worse the Draugmoors had played tricks with time just as Tintagael had: though it had felt like a journey of a few days to follow the Draugfluss out of the moorlands, a couple of weeks had passed in the mortal vale.

'Remind me again, what date is it?' asked Horskram.

'Tomorrow will be the 14th of Gildmonath,' replied the Abbot.

'Right, we'll leave on the 16th then, said Horskram. 'Two more days should give you enough time to finish treating the others?'

'As much as we can with the craft we here possess,' replied Johann pompously.

'Very well,' said Horskram, rising to leave the inner sanctum. The round window overlooked Heilag's precinct and the view it gave caught the adept's eye as he rose, giving him pause. It was night and a few clusters of journeymen and novices were leaving the cloisters, having finished their lucubrations. Heilag was built around a bridge that straddled the Draugfluss: the cursed river entered and exited via its circular compound walls, bifurcating the courtyard. The cloisters ran in colonnaded covered walkways around the circumference of the wall on one side of the river, centring on the library; on the other side were the refectory, kitchen, storehouses and sleeping quarters. The sanctum was located in the top floor of a tower that crowned the bridge. He could hear the sound of monks softly chanting scripture in the chapel below, channelling the Redeemer's words to keep the terrible magicks of the Draugmoors in their place.

From the Abbot's private chambers he could look across the crenellations of the wall towards the cursed moorlands. They had mercifully been swallowed up by the darkened firmament, but that didn't mean the adept couldn't sense their lingering evil. Another ordeal the Redeemer had seen fit to deliver them from.

'He is a terrible fighter you know,' said the Abbot, disturbing his reverie. 'Why you place such importance on your novice I have no idea.'

Horskram didn't know whether to scowl or chuckle at that remark. What with their location by the Draugmoors and on the borders of two incessantly warring baronies, the monks of Heilag placed more emphasis on martial skills than most.

'As I have said to others of our Order before, his talents lie elsewhere,' replied the adept, without turning around from the window. 'But rest assured, the monks at Rima shall see to it that his weaknesses are improved upon as well.'

'Let us hope so,' said Johann. 'For your sake.'

Something in the remark struck Horskram as odd. Turning to face the surly abbot he looked at him askance. 'What do you mean by that exactly?' he queried. His sixth sense had not flared, though in proximity to steadfast evil it was continually alerted anyway.

Johann's face betrayed just a flicker of regret. But the mask was back on as he said: 'I mean to say that you have put a lot of faith in the lad's significance. Not lightly do we herald the coming of a hierophant, and it's your reputation on the line if you turn out to be wrong.' Before Horskram could interject he went on: 'Oh you may not make me privy to your secrets, Brother Horskram, but I've served the Order long enough to know when some devilry is in the offing. We've had to double our prayers in the past few months to keep Lymphi from overrunning the Draugfluss... The Rent Between Worlds is growing wider by the day.'

Horskram's eyes narrowed. 'Well, you let me worry about my reputation,' he said. 'And keep your mind on stemming the Draugfluss. Doubtless you'll learn everything you need to know from the Grand Master, in due time.'

'Oh I've no doubt but that he'll inform me, when he deems fit to do so,' replied the Abbot. He seemed about to say more, but held his peace.

Bidding the prior a curt goodnight, Horskram left his chambers, wondering at the meaning of his strange manner.

✣ ✣ ✣

Hettie gazed upon the sleeping form of Vaskrian. His face was lit by a shaft of moonlight streaming in through a window of the chapel. He looked wan and sickly, but even so she had to admit she found him handsome, in a rakish sort of way. Even his burns seemed to add to that rakishness, somehow.

She had been unable to sleep for a couple of hours, and had only the continual chanting of the monks for company. One of them walked over to sprinkle them ritualistically with holy water, as he had done an hour or so ago. He continued to chant the litany as he did.

They had been given pallets by the sacristy: the Argolians had explained that the proximity of its relics would render their prayers more potent. Horskram had warned them all to make no mention of the Redeemer's blood, but if it was such a potent relic to be worth all that secrecy, Hettie wondered why it hadn't been enough to protect them. Her mistress Adhelina had voiced that thought, but Horskram had sternly replied that the curative powers of the Creed were not an exact science. Whatever that was supposed to mean.

Still, she had undeniably felt better since arriving at the monastery. Their journey through the moors had passed in a horrid haze, during which her troubled thoughts had returned to plague her as she recalled the ordeal with the Woses. Now that too seemed like a fading nightmare, as did the awful spectral kings she remembered seeing...

Had all of that really happened? Best to remain unsure: some things weren't worth knowing.

She glanced at her mistress. Her face looked peaceful in the silver moonlight; it had a healthier pallor than the previous night.

The same could not be said of the rest of their companions, apart from the chubby novice Adelko, who seemed to have fared well enough along with his mentor. Returning her gaze to Vaskrian she inwardly berated herself for entertaining any feelings for him: now was hardly the time for romance. And besides that he was a commoner, and a foreigner to boot.

And yet... perhaps now was precisely the time to entertain such feelings. For after all the dangers they had endured, who could deny that life was fragile? Their homeland was overrun, her past lay in tatters. Why not enjoy herself while she could?

She felt herself flush at the thought. She hadn't had much experience with men, growing up in the strict patrician order of castle life there hadn't been much opportunity... She had stolen a kiss or two from a visiting tourney knight three summers ago; at sixteen summers she'd thought it the most blissful experience ever. Of course her swain had wanted to take it further, and she had been tempted – but fear of being shunned if she let him and got found out had stopped her.

He had left the day after, the tournament finished, to seek other conquests elsewhere. That had made her bitter at the time, but she soon got over it – a girl had to be pragmatic in a world like this. And that same pragmatism had told her a poor landless knight's daughter was unlikely to be married off any time soon. That meant a world without conjugal love, so she might as well get used to it.

And used to it she had become. Not for her Adhelina's flights of fancy about paramours and love affairs and chivalrous suitors. But now, with the world she knew swept away by the seas of unruly fortune, none of those considerations seemed to matter much any more.

Returning her eyes to the sleeping squire she felt the flush spread from her cheeks down her neck and across the rest of her body. Let the Argolians pray for her sins: a girl had to have some small pleasures in life.

✠ ✠ ✠

Adelko tossed and turned on his pallet. His bruises still ached. Brother Severus, in charge of combat training at Heilag, was just as unyielding as Udo had been at Ulfang. Perhaps it was to show the novices that no favouritism would be given to visiting friars. Or maybe Horskram had had a quiet word with the muscular journeyman, instructing him to spare his charge nothing.

Whatever the reason, Adelko had found the last four days every bit as torturous as their benighted journey across the Draugmoors. At least it was refreshing to have more worldly reasons to feel pained, he reflected ruefully as he sat up wincing. He had been housed with Horskram in a cramped cell in the journeymen's quarters. His contact with other novices had been limited outside of lessons, and though several had praised his command of scripture, few had proffered any words of real friendship.

The novices here weren't so keen to hear tales of the outside world, unlike his old comrades at Ulfang. But then many of them were from more illustrious backgrounds: the sons of noble families who had travelled before being indentured to the Order. Besides that, their proximity to the Draugmoors gave them plenty of opportunity to witness denizens of the Other Side. Both those things gave them a certain pride.

Perhaps their standoffishness was for the best anyhow, Adelko reflected as he got up and walked over to the window: there seemed little point in trying to make friends here, for soon they would be off again. And it made Horskram's usual secrecy rule easier to abide by.

Gazing at the dusky courtyard, Adelko wondered what the future held in store for him.

The damsels had recovered from the curse of the draugar, but the others had fared less well. That meant they would have to get to Rima right soon, travelling by sea from Westerburg. The thought filled him with excitement and trepidation. Until this year he had never even seen the waves: soon he would voyage across them. And once at the Pangonian capital, he would be released from Horskram's service and assigned to Grand Master Hannequin.

That prospect also churned up mixed feelings. To study at the feet of the Order's most learned monks was a great honour, yet it seemed like an age since he had been seconded to Horskram. They hadn't always agreed, but he had become bonded to the crabby old adept, who was almost a second father to him now. The thought of not being at his side filled Adelko with sadness. His life of adventuring would be at an end too – for the time being anyway. Though part of him yearned for a return to the security of monastery regimen, Adelko knew he would miss the road.

He watched the water sprites dance across the river towards the bridge before the prayers of the monks turned them back, and felt his trepidation grow. The sour-faced prior of Heilag clearly didn't think much of him, but his mentor seemed convinced he was marked by destiny – as did the Earth Witch.

Adelko didn't like to think of himself as exceptional: it was unbefitting a pious monk and hardly in his nature. All he had ever yearned for was an unusual life, but beyond that he'd never considered whether he actually deserved such. Horskram seemed to think he did, while pointing out the sacrifices involved. At barely fifteen summers he had intervened in wars, survived skirmishes, and fought warlocks and shades and demonkind.

Horskram had been right: he was caught up in events larger than himself. A wyrd was on him, just as the Faerie Kings had implied at Tintagael. And yet, even now, he could scarcely credit the idea that he might be a tool of the Almighty.

Who was that person really? What was he becoming?

His sixth sense continued to jangle as he watched the Lymphi turn and swim up against the current, their watery bodies writhing in displeasure as they clawed their way back towards the Draugmoors.

Questions. Always so many questions.

✢ ✢ ✢

Adhelina awoke early to find a monk sprinkling her with holy water. Waking before time had been nothing new to her of late: it was a tell-tale sign of the Melancholy Sickness.

And she had reasons aplenty to be melancholy.

She shut her eyes against the encroaching dawn, trying to focus on the Argolians' prayers instead of the visions of her butchered father that strafed her mind. Their strange journey through the Draugmoors seemed but a distant dream now; her grief was all too real.

Her fault. All her fault.

If not for her headstrong plan to flee her wedding, the Lanraks would probably have gone through with the marriage alliance. She knew Hengist well enough to realise his pride had been mortally insulted; he would never agree to marry a woman who had spurned him so publicly. And so he had opted for war instead. Because of her, Adhelina's father lay dead and so did many of her countrymen. Subjects who would have looked to her for guidance and protection.

She felt tears push themselves between her eyelids and stream down her cheeks. She was distracted from her sorrow by a gentle touch on the shoulder. Opening her eyes she saw Hettie, looking anxious in the pale light.

'Milady, sit up and talk to me,' she urged softly. 'It is not good to be alone with one's pain – believe me, I know that all too well!'

With some effort Adhelina sat upright. 'You're up early,' she said, wiping the tears away.

'I couldn't sleep. But soon it will be time to break our fast. Yon Argolians may not suffer us to eat with them, but they proffer a tidy spread at least.'

Adhelina smiled at her friend, grateful for her attempts to cheer her up.

'Oh Hettie!' she exclaimed. 'I don't know what I'd do without you here. And you saved me from Albercelsus... I don't believe I've even thanked you.'

Hettie blushed a little. 'Think naught on that, milady, it was all he deserved – why, I hope I cracked his brains!'

Adhelina could not help laughing. 'Hettie, it's the skull that cracks, not the brains within – but yes, I hope so too!'

Her lady-in-waiting was still staring at her. 'A pity you don't have any of that stuff you gave to me when I was ill – that Elenya's Root.'

Adhelina sighed. 'All my herbs are in my medicine pouch back... back at Graukolos.' She could hardly bear to call the besieged castle she had fled twice home. She bit her lip as a new problem occurred to her. 'As is all my jewellery. Hettie, we've no coin. Even if we do get to Rima, we're going to have our work cut out for us just surviving.'

'But you're somebody important,' Hettie insisted. 'Indeed, you are now the Eorla of Dulsinor – its rightful ruler. Surely the King will treat you as an honoured guest, even if you are in exile!'

'Yes but that all depends on politics,' said Adhelina. 'Carolus may choose to take the Lanraks' side – or he may simply not care either way.'

'Well if the latter proves true, I'm sure he would extend every courtesy to a high-born noblewoman.'

'Possibly... But in that case he will almost certainly refuse to let us leave his court. Most likely he would keep me close, in case he should ever need me as bargaining tool. Don't you see Hettie? After all we've suffered, I'll just be in a man's power all over again!'

'So what are you suggesting? You can't mean – '

'My original plan was to get to the Empire,' said Adhelina. 'Admittedly via Rima is a roundabout way to go, but we could take ship across the Sundering Sea... sail to Khronos in Nacia, that's the south-western tip of the Empire. It's a longer journey than I'd planned, but it's doable.'

Hettie looked aghast. 'In heaven's name, Adhelina, we've just been through all the horrors of this world and the next! We nearly died and lost our souls to the Other Side, we've lost everything we ever had – and yet you talk of more misadventures! Can't we just settle down in Rima and make the best of whatever life we have left?'

Hettie's plea brought renewed stabs of pain to Adhelina's heart. Her yearning for freedom had already cost them so much, and yet to falter now... Somehow that would make all their sacrifice seem in vain.

'No,' she said, her voice hardening. 'A well-kept slave to a king at his court, I won't have it Hettie! That's precisely the kind of life I've spent months trying to avoid. We'll travel with the others, as soon as they've recovered. When we get to Rima we'll branch out on our own. Anupe will probably come with us anyway, so it's not like we won't have any protection.'

'I doubt she'll want to protect us now there's no coin in it for her,' said Hettie. 'And besides...' – she glanced meaningfully at the Harijan, who coughed and shivered on her pallet – 'Our foreign friend doesn't seem to be doing so well... Who's to say she'll even survive the trip to Rima? And even if she does, you said it yourself – we've no money! How will we live?'

'You're forgetting I have two brave knights who are madly in love with me,' said Adhelina. 'I doubt my paramours will let me starve. Why they might even be persuaded to come with us!'

Hettie rolled her eyes. 'This planned excursion is getting more fanciful by the second! You're starting to sound like one of your romances!'

Adhelina had to laugh at that. 'Hettie, think on everything we've experienced of late – all the dangers you've just pointed out! Has it not occurred to you that we're already living a romance, albeit a ghastly one? Troubadours will make songs out of everything we've endured, mark my words!'

Her friend sighed, but had to acknowledge the point. 'All right,' she said resignedly. 'But can I just add that your swains aren't faring too well either?'

Adhelina pursed her lips. Casting her eyes across the two knights, she had to concede Hettie had a point of her own. Both men, normally so strong and healthy, looked weak and sickly. Even mighty Torgun's movements seemed crepuscular, while Braxus coughed fitfully and stared blankly most of the time. It pained her to see them in such a way. Even with her herbs, she would be powerless to help with this kind of malady.

But seeing them so vulnerable somehow intensified her feelings for them. They were both so different, yet she had come to see the good in each of them. How indeed would one choose between such suitors?

She banished the question from her mind. This was no time for indulging in courtly love.

'Well, *we* seem to have recovered,' said Adhelina. 'We can only pray that the monks are able to heal our saviours as well, given enough time.'

The thought of time made her more anxious. She had gleaned enough from Horskram to learn they had passed a fortnight on the moors, however strange that seemed. At least that meant their trail had gone cold – no more Lanraks chasing them. But word of the war up north must have spread by now: it wouldn't be long before word of their escape got out too. That would mean opportunistic freeswords on the lookout for runaway damsels.

At this rate, Adhelina didn't fancy their chances of getting even as far as Rima with naught but five sick bodyguards and a pair of monks to protect them. As the Argolians brought them their breakfast she welcomed the distraction from her troubling thoughts. But when she began to eat, it was with a subdued appetite.

⊶ CHAPTER XII ⊷

Another Close Shave

A delko looked ruefully at his companions as they assembled in the courtyard. His Argolian brethren had done what they could, yet they were a sorry sight for all that. Sir Torgun and the rest of them moved sluggishly, crawling up into the saddle and huddling into their cloaks as though it were a bitter winter morning. The splendid sunrise that painted the brown stones of Heilag rosy red put the lie to that notion.

At a nod from Horskram the journeymen on duty opened the south gate, allowing them to enter Lower Thulia for the first time. Adelko supposed they were out of danger for the nonce, but that would quickly change if they met any trouble on the road. Their trusty swords looked as though they would struggle to draw a blade, never mind wield one.

'Are you sure this is a good idea, Master Horskram?' he asked as they nudged their steeds through the gatehouse and on to the track leading back to the main road. Johann had not bothered to see them off, but that was hardly surprising given the prior's surly arrogance.

'We have little choice,' replied Horskram, more wearily than anything else. 'The curse has been slowed, enough to get our trusty swords to Rima alive – if we don't dawdle! But lose too much time and they will surely die.'

'And you think our brethren in Rima will fare any better?' The thought of losing all his comrades appalled him.

'You know not the power of the monastery that the High Circle presides over,' explained Horskram. 'The kind of elan that our senior chapter can summon should be enough to lift the curse altogether – on top of that I can join my prayers to theirs and we can use the Redeemer's blood.'

'Why didn't you do that here?'

'Because that would have meant telling Johann I have it in my possession. I don't trust him – I never have. The man is ambitious and self-seeking. He applied for a pew on the High Circle once, but was voted down. Also he has always resented my status as a hierophant. He wouldn't have let me join my elan to his precious chapter, even had I offered to do so. His vanity would not stand for it.'

'So he'd risk the lives of our friends... At least you have good reason when you do it, Master Horskram.' Overstepping the mark, Adelko expected a rebuke. Instead the adept favoured him with a sardonic smile.

'Yes, Adelko, I do not risk the lives of others without good cause – thank you for noticing. Anyway, now you know what kind of man Johann is.'

Adelko pondered that. How many men like Johann held senior positions within the Order? The High Circle comprised the six Archmasters and Grand Master, one for each of the Seven Acolytes or the Seven Seraphim, depending on how you interpreted it. But beyond that he knew little of the powerful men who would soon enter his life.

Enter his life if he preserved it as far as Rima that was.

✣ ✣ ✣

An hour later they joined the main road. Over to the west a grim-looking keep loomed, its single turret glaring at them over a rude-looking bailey that crowned a sparse motte. It looked unremarkable save for the white standard that flew atop its battlements. To his surprise Adelko saw the sign of the Wheel, daubed on it in blood-red.

'Bethler holding,' replied his mentor when he quizzed him about it. 'Most of their lands are scattered across the Southern Kingdoms and the Blessed Realm, but they have one or two castles this far north as well.'

Adelko shifted uncomfortably in his habit. The sun was barely up but he felt hot. He didn't feel so far north.

'Why would they bother with holdings here?' he queried. 'I thought the Bethlers were tasked with defending the Pilgrim Kingdoms?'

'They are,' replied Horskram. 'But it doesn't hurt them to have property. Helps to fund the Order. In fact the Most Holy Order of the Sacred Bethel is the wealthiest organisation in the Free Kingdoms. The Bethlers also function as moneylenders throughout western Urovia and beyond.'

That shocked Adelko. 'But I thought usury was a sin! Surely they of all people...'

Horskram favoured him with another grim smile. 'It is indeed a sin,' he said. 'That is why they do not charge interest on loans as such. They call it an "administrative fee" instead.'

The novice had little to say to that. Truly the ways of mortalkind were strange.

Up ahead the crooked wooden buildings of a town built around the road were becoming visible.

'Tamsweg,' supplied Horskram. 'Not much to say about it really. About a thousand souls, mostly artisans and traders. They enjoy the Bethlers' patronage and protection.'

'How does the Herzog of Lower Thulia feel about that?'

'None too pleased, but even a lord of men dares not cross the Bethlers. And to be fair, their presence here has reduced the internecine skirmishes that used to plague the area. The barons of Upper and Lower Thulia have seldom found cause not to quarrel.'

Horskram's dry humour did nothing to alleviate the distress Adelko felt at the thought of more peasants being butchered. He wondered how the folk of Dulsinor were faring up north. The two baronies would have been at war for close on a month now.

They passed Tamsweg as it was coming to life and soon left it behind. The roads in Lower Thulia were somewhat better kept, but even so the going was slow, and Adelko found little to cheer him in the miserable hovels and crooked hamlets they passed. The peasantry down here looked scarcely better fed than the others he had seen recently.

'Remember what I told you about each lord being a king in his own right,' Horskram reminded him when he voiced his thoughts. 'Some treat their bondsmen little better than slaves, others like Freidheim or the late Stonefist view them as servants who should be well kept. If you think this is bad, wait until we get to Pangonia! The serfs there are the most wretched of the lot, save perhaps the Wolding peasantry and those of the Kingdom of Thalamy.'

'But I thought Pangonia was the richest of the Free Kingdoms!'

'It is – rich for those who own it.'

A sudden thought occurred to Adelko. 'Then why do we call ourselves the Free Kingdoms?' Strange that the question had never occurred to him before. It was all to easy to take a name for granted when one had grown up with it.

Horskram laughed sardonically. 'Because we abolished slavery centuries ago – in keeping with the Redeemer's teachings. Abolished it in theory, that is.'

Horskram said nothing more, and Adelko had no appetite to press him further. At least it wasn't raining, though the southern heat would take some getting used to.

✠ ✠ ✠

The setting sun was painting the wheat fields a lemon yellow when they saw a roadside inn.

'We'll stop here for the night,' said Horskram. 'I know the innkeeper.'

Despite Horskram's reassurance, Adelko felt uneasy. His sixth sense had started up again. He glanced behind him but saw little to ease him. The damsels rode at the rear: between them their five bodyguards slouched in the saddle as they ambled along like lost sheep.

'I sense something...' faltered the novice. 'Can you feel it?'

Horskram nodded, frowning. 'Yes, I can. But we need to get our sick patients indoors. Those suffering the curse of Draugbreath should not be left exposed to the night – it will only worsen their illness.'

The inn consisted of a main building three storeys high with a few outhouses including the stables around it. These buildings formed a rough courtyard around the main entrance. The ostler greeted them with a shocked expression as they entered. No wonder: their comrades' stricken faces were nearly white as snow: it must have looked for all the world as though five spectres had ridden up seeking lodgings.

'Don't be troubled by my friends' unfortunate appearance, Varek,' said Horskram, tossing the lad a silver piece. 'Charges of mine, I'll take full responsibility.'

'Sorry, Master Horskram,' stammered the stableboy, pocketing the coin. His right arm and leg were each shorter than the left, giving him a lopsided gait. 'Almost didn't recognise you, sirrah – haven't seen you around here in a long while.'

'I see you've grown in the interim,' said the adept kindly. 'It's good to know Ecbert has been feeding you properly.'

'Why so he has,' said the cripple with an inane grin. The smile suddenly dropped. 'We've 'ad some rough types here though of late – includin' tonight. War's broken out up north and there's a lot of freeswords on the move.'

'Indeed?' was all Horskram said to that. Dismounting he handed the reins to Varek. The boy limped off with his horse as Adelko eased himself gratefully from the saddle.

Adhelina and Hettie approached Horskram after dismounting themselves. The damsels had pulled up their hoods, but that only made them look more suspicious given the clement weather. Meanwhile the others stared off into space, as though not knowing what to do.

'I think you can all get off your horses now,' Horskram said pointedly. Adelko groaned inwardly as he watched the brave fighters slough off their steeds like rancid butter from a churn.

'Is this a good idea?' hissed Adhelina. 'You heard what yon stableboy said – if there's freeswords in there, chances are they might recognise me!'

'Well you'd better keep your hoods on then,' said Horskram. Turning on his heel he stalked towards the door of the inn. Adelko exchanged a brief glance with Adhelina and shrugged his shoulders amiably. She shook her head but followed the monks inside, pulling her hood down further.

The taproom was the reeking mess Adelko had come to expect at an inn. The front windows were open, allowing the dying light to penetrate. The layout was different from the inn he'd seen in Northalde: two rows of trestle tables ran along either side of a long narrow room. In one corner at the far end was the counter; adjoining this was the entrance to a side room where he could just make out stacks of barrels. In the other corner a flight of stairs went up. At the centre of the room was a firepit, which evidently had not seen much use lately. A handful of travelling labourers had taken up seats by the windows, but most of the noise was coming from the freeswords clustered by the table nearest the counter.

Adelko felt the men peering at them as they approached the back of the room. A couple of lanterns hanging on hooks gave just enough light to see by. Horskram ignored the mercenaries and rapped his knuckles on the counter. A portly man about a head shorter than the adept appeared from the barrel room.

'Why Master Horskram!' the innkeeper exclaimed. 'Haven't seen you in a long while – it's always good to have an Argolian under our roof.'

'Why's that?' called out a rough voice. 'Evil spirits got into yer ale? Better not 'ave, seein' as we be drinkin' it.'

The freeswords laughed unpleasantly at their comrade's joke. Ecbert glanced nervously at the mercenaries before continuing: 'Well, you'll be wanting a stoop I shouldn't wonder... Been busy off travelling, I expect! Suppose you've just come from Heilag. And how is Prior Johann?'

Adelko felt his sixth sense go up a notch. The conversation was forced, the innkeeper clearly frightened. The freeswords had ceased all banter and were now staring at them. The novice felt his gut tighten as he registered them sizing up his companions. One of them was scrutinising the damsels. This was not going to end well.

Horskram kept his cool, making small talk with Ecbert while the innkeeper snapped his fingers at a tavern wench serving the labourers. She gave the adept a brief nod of greeting as she went into the storeroom to fill some flagons. Adelko supposed she must be the innkeeper's daughter. He could sense she was anxious too.

'How many ales will ye be wanting?' queried Ecbert, looking dubiously at their companions.

'Just the two,' replied Horskram. 'For myself and my novice here.'

'Ah right ye are,' said the innkeeper, trying to sound cheerful. 'We've got a good drop of Maglun's Pride just arrived this morning...' He motioned irritably at his daughter to hurry up.

'Maglun's *ride*, if you get a wench drunk enough on it,' quipped another freesword. More nasty laughter. A couple of the freeswords leered at the innkeeper's daughter as she put two full tankards on the counter.

'Rolf, you've got an ear for bard's song,' said another freesword. 'Tell me about that lay again, the one about the first king of Vorstlund.' It was the mercenary who had been looking at Adhelina and Hettie. His voice was somewhat more refined. His corn yellow hair was neatly kept, his beard and moustache finely trimmed. Evidently the leader.

'That would be the *Lay of Aslun's Gift*, sirrah,' replied the mercenary called Rolf.

'Ah yes, that's the one,' replied the leader. 'Tell me again, what's it about?'

Risking another furtive glance at the freeswords, Adelko saw one or two exchange knowing winks. There were seven of them altogether, dressed in shabby brigandines. All wore stout swords.

'It's the story of how King Aslun brought all the other eight lords to heel,' said Rolf. 'One by one, he made 'em an offer they couldn't refuse.'

'And remind me, Rolf, who was the last baron to hold out?'

'Ah that would've been Oberon, Last King of Dulsenar,' said the freesword. 'The Wise, they called him... See, he could've held out for years, seein' as he had Graukolos for his seat. But he saw the folly in it, fightin' a war that was already lost. So he surrendered the keep, an' King Aslun let him keep his demesnes... so long as he recognised his rule.'

The novice felt Adhelina stiffen next to him. Horskram stopped sipping at his tankard and slowly put it down on the counter.

'And that was when Aslun founded the House of Cuthraed, if I remember rightly?' the leader went on.

'Aye, sirrah, that it was,' said Rolf. 'An' the Cuthraeds ruled the kingdom for many a long year after that. As for the House of Tal, wot ruled in Dulsenar, they held on there for another couple hundred years, I've heard it told.'

'Ah yes, that's it,' said the leader amiably. 'But they didn't last forever now did they?'

'Oh no,' replied Rolf. 'Poor old Dhaelen, wot the troubadours call the Unfortunate, he angered King Aethel the Oak Hearted, wot stripped him of his title. Then he was killed by Ranveldt Longyear, who replaced him as Eorl and founded the House of Markward.'

'Ah yes, *Markward*, of course... Now they're due for *their* reckoning by the sounds of it. Isn't it funny how history repeats itself, Rolf?'

'Aye,' smirked Rolf. 'That it is, sirrah, that it is. Way I've heard it, the Markwards are all dead... All save the Stonefist's daughter.'

'Indeed,' replied the leader, leaning back against the wall and loosening his sword in its scabbard. 'But I've heard she was rescued by a ragtag band of outlanders and fled south. Wonder where in the Known World she could be, eh?'

'No idea, sirrah,' grinned Rolf, slowly starting to rise with the other freeswords.

'Alright now,' said the leader, addressing Horskram. 'There's more than half a dozen of us and none of your swords looks overly well. Yon damsels are ours. Don't put up a fight and we'll make this quick and painless for the rest of you.'

There was a flurry of movement towards the exit as the labourers abruptly decided to call an end to their evening's drinking.

Horskram squared off against the freeswords, unsheathing his quarterstaff. 'Striking down a man of the cloth is counted among the most grievous of sins,' he said, sounding almost cordial. 'I'd think twice about trying to kill us, lest you favour burning in Gehenna for eternity.'

The blond leader smiled affably. 'With respect, master monk, I suspect we're already hellbound... I far prefer to concentrate on the pleasures of *this* life, and a tidy sum I'll have in return for your heads. I've heard the Lanraks are a most generous house, to those that serve their interests.'

Without moving from the spot Horskram incanted a verse from the Psalm of Fortitude. Adelko could feel him channelling his conviction, putting all his psychic strength into the words. The mercenaries exchanged baffled looks; they were ignorant of Decorlangue.

But the words must have stirred their stricken companions, for suddenly they fumbled for their weapons, shifting awkwardly into something resembling a fighting stance. The blond leader yelled a command: as one the freeswords kicked over the tables and drew swords. Cursing inwardly, Adelko drew his quarterstaff, trying to ignore his legs, which suddenly felt like jelly.

The damsels backed away with the innkeeper and his daughter as the freeswords launched themselves over the tables. They were matched perfectly in numbers, but a glance at his ashen-faced comrades was enough to tell Adelko the outcome: they would be cut down like corn stalks imminently.

He had just parried the first couple of strokes and was backing away and saying his final prayers when he heard whinnying and shouting from the courtyard outside. The fleeing labourers had left the door open: the sounds coming from it grew louder. A few moments later two tall figures burst into the common room. They were dressed in mail hauberks and helms and carried drawn greatswords. They looked like knights but were dressed in simple white tabards.

'Cease fighting, in the name of the Lord Almighty!'

The command came from a third man who had entered just behind the knights. He was an old man, something over fifty and dressed in a white kirtle. He lacked the stature of the other two but his stentorian voice carried a weighty authority. His head was shorn save for a crown of grey hair, and his beard was cut square across his chin.

The mercenaries put up their swords. Their leader glanced sidelong at the three newcomers. He seemed confused as he said: 'What's the meaning of this? Can't fighting men go about their business?'

'Not when that business entails spilling blood in a public house,' answered the greybeard sternly. 'This road passes through lands owned by the Holy Order of the Bethel of our Saviour – as such we enforce the law here. You are in violation of that law. Now sheathe your swords, all of you.'

The blond freesword sneered. 'Since when? The Bethlers enforce the law in the Blessed Realm, not the Free Kingdoms. These lands are ruled by the Alt-Ürls.'

'The Bethlers own more land in the Free Kingdoms than any of its barons – including the Herzog of Lower Thulia,' replied the Bethler unsmiling. 'Now sheathe your swords – I won't ask again.' He spared a stern blue-eyed glance for Horskram. 'That goes for your bodyguards too, Argolian, if such they be.'

Horskram paused a moment, then seemed to make up his mind. In a low but clear voice he gave the order. The Bethlers stared at them in bafflement as they struggled to return weapons to scabbards.

Adelko flicked his gaze back to the freeswords. The blond leader still had not given the order, and the novice could sense he was perplexed about something.

'We don't want trouble with the Bethlers,' he said at last, motioning for his men to sheathe their swords and doing the same. 'Just tell me one thing – where have you come from?'

The Bethler glared at him suspiciously. 'I don't see how that is any business of yours, rakehell,' he said.

'Ach, we'll be on our way,' said the freesword captain, adopting a conciliatory tone. 'I'm a vassal's bastard son – so I've some blue blood in my veins. You'll do me the honour at least of telling me which direction to avoid taking next!'

That seemed to mollify the old warrior-monk. 'If you must know, we've just come from Regensburg,' he said gruffly.

The blond mercenary nodded, as though that made sense. 'Well perhaps that explains things,' he said, though he looked deeply unsatisfied.

'I have no idea what you mean by that,' said the Bethler. 'But if you are thinking of heading south only to cause further trouble when we're gone, I would advise against it.' He held the freesword's gaze to underscore his meaning.

The captain met his eyes for a few seconds, then shrugged his shoulders. 'Have it your way,' he said, sounding affable again despite the expression on his face. Turning to his men he added: 'Alright lads, let's be having you! We'll just have to pass up this opportunity for another one. Back to Tamsweg it is then – and from there we'll head north, see what the fortunes of war bring us!'

The freeswords left the inn boisterously, though Adelko noticed they gave the Bethler knights a wide berth.

When they were gone the innkeeper scurried over to bolt the door after them, calling for his daughter to clear up the mess and right the tables. The old Bethler waved him away curtly when he proffered his thanks. 'Just bring us stoops of your finest ale,' he said. The three of them had taken up seats where the mercenaries had been. He motioned for the two monks to join them. The damsels were sitting a couple of tables up with their bodyguards, who had lapsed back into their morbid state.

The Bethler looked them over suspiciously as he addressed Horskram. 'Well, friar, now is the time for introductions I believe. I am Brother Sir Guthrum of the preceptory of Tamsweg.' He returned his keen eyes to the adept's face. Clearly he expected an answer.

'I am Horskram of Vilno, adept of the Argolian Order, from Ulfang chapter in Northalde. This is my novice, Adelko of Narvik. Yon damsels are travelling in our care, as are these warriors who have come down with a spiritual sickness. I have been charged with taking them to our headquarters in Rima for healing.'

Ecbert's daughter had just set fresh ale on the table before them. Sir Guthrum licked the froth from his bearded lips before replying. 'I see. And what, pray tell, is the exact nature of this "spiritual sickness"?'

Adelko felt his sixth sense start up again. He knew little of the Bethlers, but recalled that the Argolians had never endorsed the Pilgrim Wars. That alone would be enough to earn their enmity, if everything he had heard about the fanatical order was true. Next to Guthrum the two knights quaffed their beer and said nothing. Did they ever speak, the novice wondered.

'The five warriors you see were recruited by myself to help in a witch hunt,' replied Horskram. 'We apprehended her in a cabin on the fringes of the Draugmoors. We believe she had been drawing her power from the cursed magic that stems from the ruined Watchtower of the Elder Wizards.'

All three Bethlers followed Horskram in making the sign.

'We were able to overcome her magic with prayers, and my trusty swords slew her along with several knights she had bewitched into serving her,' Horskram said, continuing his dissimulation. 'As she lay dying, she invoked her foul demon-gods and put the curse of Ma'alfecnu'ur on my companions.'

They all made the sign dutifully again at the mention of the demonic avatar of decay and corruption. Adelko felt all the worse for knowing it was a pack of lies, but Horskram went on: 'Not even our prayers were enough to overcome her last spell – though myself and my novice resisted it, our comrades were not so lucky. They are now wasting away psychically, and only the prayers of my Order in Rima can save them. We took them back to Heilag, whence I had originally been assigned the mission, but it is a small chapter and much of its elan is already spent stemming the tide of evil that flows from the Draugfluss.'

'That is a black evil, well expunged!' cried Guthrum, slamming his empty tankard down on the table. 'What a pity you could not bring her to death by the fire, as befits all pagan witches! But what of yon damsels? How did they come to be in your company?' The keen light had returned to his eyes. Adelko could sense some kind of counter intuition at work in the old warrior-monk. Could it be that the Bethlers cultivated a sixth sense of their own, given their renowned piety and devotion? His mentor had better tread carefully if so.

'Yon damsels had been put under a spell by the sorceress we slew,' dissembled Horskram. 'They are from Westenlund, and we will return them to their castle on the way to Rima.'

'I see,' said Guthrum, clicking his fingers for more ale. Adelko now knew where the expression 'to drink like a Bethler' came from. And he'd thought the Argolians were bad. Even the most religious orders needed a vice, he supposed.

Guthrum's eyes narrowed as he went on talking. 'The Bethlers have always admired the service the Argolians do against the works of the Author of All Evil,' he said. 'What a pity your Order does not see the wisdom in supporting the Pilgrim Wars.' His voice had hardened.

'Our order has ever believed that the fight against the Fallen One is of a spiritual nature,' replied the adept diplomatically. 'It is not for us to give an opinion on the wars of men.'

Guthrum's eyes blazed. 'And yet we fight on behalf of the Almighty! For only by His grace could the First Pilgrim War ever have succeeded – when with but ten thousand soldiers of Palom we retook the Holy City!'

The warrior-monk's zeal was palpable. The Bethler knights paused from their drinking to make the sign again.

'The accomplishments of the crusaders and the Bethlers who guard the Blessed Realm they conquered are widely and justly praised,' said Horskram, almost sounding unctuous now. 'They surely need no further approbation from a humble friar such as myself.'

Guthrum frowned at that. 'Yes well, you Argolians have ever been a slippery lot,' he muttered, taking another swig. 'Very well, you seem to have your own matters in hand at least. Just tell me one more thing – how did yon freeswords come to trouble you?'

Horskram paused to take a sip of ale before answering. 'Freeswords have ever been a troublesome lot,' he said, trying to sound casual. 'My guess is they saw two monks and a pair of damsels accompanied by naught but sick bodyguards, and sought to kill us for sport and plunder. Even with the efforts of the Bethlers, these are lawless times.'

'They are indeed,' sniffed Guthrum. 'About time we had another crusade, if you ask me – that should get the robber knights out of the Free Kingdoms, give them a righteous outlet for their violent spirits.'

'Indeed,' said Horskram. 'And may I ask what brings you to the road?'

'Business,' replied the Bethler. 'I have just concluded a loan agreement on behalf of my Order with some merchants at Regensburg. We'll need every bit of coin we can get if there's to be another Pilgrim War.'

Horskram raised an eyebrow. 'You really think there will be another one soon?'

'Oh yes,' replied Guthrum. 'We've heard that the King of Pangonia and the Supreme Perfect are planning to declare it. About time too, as I said.'

The adept said nothing more, but Adelko sensed the news troubled him.

The Bethlers finished their stoops and rose. 'And now if you'll excuse us, we've had a long day's ride and I need to make sure our squires have seen to our horses before turning in for the night. If I were you, I'd get to Westenlund with all haste – the Prince rules there with an even hand, and the roads are a lot safer.'

'That is what I am counting on,' replied Horskram, bidding the Bethler a cordial good night.

When they had left, the adept breathed a sigh of relief and drained his flagon. 'Right, we'd better see about getting some rest ourselves,' he said. 'With that shambling lot in tow it'll take us the whole of tomorrow to get to Regensburg.'

Adelko could not help but feel disappointed. Their latest encounter had left a lot of unanswered questions.

'Who were those freeswords?' he asked. 'How did they recognise us so easily?'

'That was just what I was asking myself while I was spinning fairy tales for that zealous idiot,' replied Horskram. 'But it'll keep for now. Time to arrange supper and a room I think.'

Adelko decided that right now, food and sleep were just as welcome as questions and answers. As his mentor rose to speak to Ecbert, he looked across the room at his companions. The damsels were speaking in low voices and looked frightened. The other five sat slumped against the wall, staring at the table with glassy eyes as they shivered against the encroaching night.

⊷ CHAPTER XIII ⊷

A Wedding Of Reavers

Raucous cheering greeted Guldebrand as he ascended the raised wooden platform overlooking the feasting tables. His bride was waiting for him, standing beside the priest in his glaucous robes. The magnate-in-waiting grinned at the assembled seacarls as they raised drinking horns in yet another toast to their new ruler.

The wedding feast had lasted with scarcely a pause for the past five days: now it was time to crown the celebration. After that a few more days of feasting would follow, before sobering-up time. Then he himself would be crowned in Landarök. Turning from the rows of warriors, he looked down at the city he now owned. From the cliff top where they were celebrating he had a perfect view of the Sea of Valhalla, its foaming waves matched by the deepening blue of early evening skies. To either side of the platform burning braziers filled with incense banished darkness and cold alike, filling his nostrils with an intoxicating scent.

He felt intoxicated enough as it was, even though he had made sure to stint on the wine and mead in the past couple of days. Tonight he would consummate his marriage vows: he wanted to be in fine form for that. He'd had a couple of town girls brought to him on the night of their victory over Oldrik, but he'd stinted on women too since then. Again, he wanted to give the best of himself to his new bride.

Taking her in, he thought her worth every effort. Dressed in a sky-blue woollen gown that hugged her lithe figure, she looked savagely beautiful; a pair of electrum oval brooches held the garment in place, and between them she wore a silver pendant set with an amber stone the size of a duck's egg. Her wild hair was hidden by a silk head-dress of purest white, fastened with a circlet of worked gold set with garnets. Around her slender neck was a close-fitting gold ring made from plaited strands; similar rings encircled her bare wiry arms.

He could not wait to get her back to the palace, strip all that finery off her a piece at a time, and hold her naked in his arms. It would be worth a thousand ravishings and more.

She smiled back at him as he beamed at her, the broad mouth he had come to love doing nothing to abate his desire. The priest raised his hands for silence. Slaves came and laid platters of fresh meat and refilled cups one last time before retreating into the shadows. A hush fell over the thousands-strong assembly, and the priest began to intone the rites of brudhlaup.

'We are gathered here, in sight of the Lord of Oceans, to join together these two children of Aurgelmir, who fathered the race of Gygants that once ruled the earth whence all men sprung,' the priest intoned. 'Does anyone here find fault?'

'NAY!'

'Magnhilda, Thegn of Scandia, consents to be bound to Guldebrand, Thegn of Kvenlund, Thegn of Jótlund, and soon to be Magnate of all the Principalities, and he undertakes to make her his girl of the houses. Does anyone here find fault?'

'NAY!'

'It is well. Guldebrand, take Magnhilda's hand betwixt thine own and repeat after me: "I, Guldebrand Gunnarson, in sight of Thoros, wielder of lightning, king of the firmament who sees all, take Magnhilda as lawful wife."'

Solemnly, Guldebrand repeated the vow.

The priest turned to Magnhilda. 'Magnhilda, repeat after me, "I, Magnhilda, Shield Queen of Utvalla, in sight of Kaia, bringer of bounty, earth mother who gives life to all, take Guldebrand as lawful husband."'

Steadily, Magnhilda repeated the words. The broad smile was still on her face, and her eyes sparkled in the firelight.

'Guldebrand, repeat after me: "I swear in sight of the gods to treasure Magnhilda, my girl of the houses, to render unto her all the spoils of the sail road to look after as she sees fit."'

Again Guldebrand repeated the words. It seemed strange investing her with the power of a housewife, given her status as shieldmaiden, but the marriage traditions of his people did not vary.

'Magnhilda, repeat after me: "I swear in sight of the gods to be a loyal wife to Guldebrand, to render unto him all my chattels as bride price, and to take care of all his estate in his absence."'

Slowly Magnhilda repeated the words. If the Shield Queen felt any resentment at uttering them she did not show it.

The priest raised his voice as he intoned the final words of the ceremony. 'In sight of the Great North Wind, sent by the Sky Eagle's wings to sweep the sail road and the plough road, I proclaim thee man and wife. Guldebrand Gunnarson, cleave unto thy bride!'

Hoots and cheers erupted as Guldebrand took his wife in a firm embrace. Her salty tongue tasted of the sea; he felt his loins stir beneath his rich woollen hose.

As he turned to face the cheering warriors he caught sight of Ragnar, lurking on the edge of the circle of light. The saturnine warlock had not been much present during the feast, though Guldebrand could hardly say he was unhappy about that. He felt an unwelcome tension coiling in his gut. The warlock seemed to stare at him with his one good eye for the briefest of seconds... then he was gone, vanished into the shadows whence he came.

✤ ✤ ✤

Guldebrand's men were still cheering when they carried him up the ramp and through the gate into the courtyard of the palace. As they had borne him through the streets of his capital city, he had found time amidst the euphoria to note that most of its stone buildings were intact. That was good: the less time and energy spent rebuilding Landarök, the sooner he could concentrate on raising a national army. Many of the wooden buildings of the outer city had been burned, but they could be replaced easily enough. Likewise, most of the city's ten thousand souls had been spared the depredations of conquest, save of course for the obligatory ravishings. That was good too: he would need a loyal population in the coming years of war.

All thoughts of future conquest vanished as his men carried him into the great hall and set him down. Another party had arrived ahead of him, bringing the bride in first as custom dictated. Magnhilda was there already, shieldmaidens enthusiastically divesting her of jewellery and outer garments. And he had so been looking forward to doing that himself.

The berserker women stood back from her now, giving him a view of his wife. She was dressed only in her linen chemise that came down to her thighs. He felt desire welling up in him again as his seacarls began to strip him of his cloak, brooch and tunic. Brega had been with him every step of the way, leading in the singing, a tankard never leaving his hand. Loyal Brega... He would see him made a jarl for his services.

Soon he was dressed only in his underbreeches and shirt. The rough flagstones felt oddly pleasant beneath his bare feet.

'AND NOW,' bellowed Brega. 'TO THE BEDCHAMBER WITH THEM!'

More raucous yelling. The gathered men and women swept them both up again and began carrying them up the rude stone stairs towards the wing of the palace where they would lie as man and wife. The palace was centuries old, having been built by Olav Ironhand, and at three storeys it was higher than ten men – easily the tallest building in the Principalities.

The consummation party arrived at the top floor and brought them into a chamber that was surprisingly small and intimate. Well, Northlanders weren't known for their grandiose architecture. Perhaps he'd take up residence in the palace at Strongholm, once he'd crushed the Northlendings.

The bed looked grand enough, fashioned of pine and coated with sheets of white satin imported from the Empire, and shrouded with gossamer hangings. The men and women set them down on either side of it.

'My king and queen,' said Brega, giving a florid bow and nearly spilling his drink. 'Now is the time to leave you to celebrate your wedding… We've left a pitcher of wine and cups for you, just in case you need some refreshments!' The burly seacarl winked and backed out of the room. He was the last to leave and shut the oak door behind him.

Glancing over towards the side of the bed, Guldebrand saw the silver pitcher filled to the brim with wine. He hoped it was that Pangonian red he'd become so fond of. Although right now drink wasn't what he wanted.

Turning to look at his wife, he smirked and said the words he had longed to say all day.

'Magnhilda, my sweetest! Alone at last.'

Within seconds they were both naked. With a shock Guldebrand realised he was still wearing the pomander that Radko had given him. He was wondering whether to take it off when Magnhilda pulled him to her.

'Kiss me, my love,' she whispered, her voice hot and breathy in his ear. He complied gleefully, lying on top of her as she moved her long legs open to accommodate him. Now he was inside her, his senses exploding with pleasure as he gyrated on her and in her. She wrapped her legs and arms around him tightly and began to moan loudly. He forced himself to focus, not wanting it to be over too soon. The pomander bounced between them, obstructing their lovemaking maddeningly. With a fierce grunt he tore it from his neck, flinging it across the room. She cried out as he thrust himself into her with renewed savagery. He felt her fingers digging deep into his back. It was almost painful but it was a pain he enjoyed. They rolled together madly on the bed, caught up in the lustful play of love.

He felt his wife tighten her grip on him. Now he couldn't move properly; he felt his rhythm slow as she crushed him to her. Her body felt hard and angular against his. She was murmuring in her love throes now. Glancing at her face he saw her eyes were rolled up into the back of her head. He tried to renew his amorous strokes, but found he could not move. Magnhilda held him to her in a vice-like grip.

And that was when he realised she wasn't murmuring in Norric.

The words came tumbling from her mouth now, sounding harsh and hateful, alien to the ear. He felt his manhood wilting inside her. Panic rose as he found he could not move: an unearthly strength seemed to possess his wife as she went on murmuring, her voice gradually rising until it sounded like she was chanting.

He felt his will drip away, like the last drops of blood from a death blow. As it did he stopped writhing, letting his body go limp as she continued to hold it tightly to hers. How much better not to struggle, just to lie here in his lady love's arms...

Magnhilda stopped chanting. Relaxing her grip on him, she said in an icy voice: 'Get off me.'

He complied instantly. Disobedience was unthinkable.

Sitting up she tidied her hair before pulling on her shirt. Motioning towards the pitcher she ordered him: 'Drink.'

He watched, powerless, as his hands poured a cup of wine. It was indeed the Pangonian vintage he loved so much, though now it tasted bitter on his tongue as he swallowed it.

'Pour me a cup,' she said in the same brusque tone. 'This needs to look good.'

He obeyed and then poured himself another cup at her command. 'Keep drinking,' she told him. 'Keep drinking until I tell you to stop.'

His head was swimming by the time he had finished his sixth cup. 'Good,' said Magnhilda. 'Now go over to yon window and open the shutters. Take the pitcher and your cup with you.'

He complied, feeling the cool night air rush in as he opened the shutters. The window looked down onto the city of Landarök; its twinkling lights seemed to mirror the stars above. How beautiful they looked... Down in the streets he could hear singing and carousing, as the citizens celebrated a royal wedding.

'Now turn around and sit on the lintel,' Magnhilda commanded. 'Put the pitcher down on it beside you... That's it. Don't let go of your cup. Yes, perfect.'

She drew closer to him so that her face was an inch or two away from his. Her eyes looked dark and merciless as she stared at him and smiled. 'My dearest Guldebrand,' she breathed, her voice as soft as silk. 'Did you really think I would consent to be ruled by a beardless milksop like you?' Her broad mouth tightened in an evil smile. He could feel the sea breeze stroking his back with fingers that carried the chill of the grave.

'Now lean back, my love,' she whispered. 'Hela is waiting to catch thee in the next world.'

Guldebrand did not start screaming until he was halfway down.

✣ ✣ ✣

High above the palace a raven turned, banking down towards an open window on the top floor. Its keen predator's eyes discerned the crumpled naked figure that lay bleeding in the courtyard. Pushing away thoughts of feasting, the raven flew in through the window and pictured a stylised bird, an egg splitting in two, and a humanoid figure.

Ragnar coalesced in the bedchamber and looked around the empty room.

'I'm over here, brother,' said a voice from behind a partition cloth. 'Just making water after drinking too much wine. In a minute I shall return to the room, and find that my husband has suffered a tragic accident on his wedding night.'

'So my Thaumaturgy gave you the strength you needed to overpower him?' asked Ragnar coolly.

Magnhilda appeared from behind the cloth, pulling down her undershirt. 'I already told you it would not have been necessary for me to overcome that boy,' she said. 'Though I'm sure he could not have triumphed over the Stormrider without your help. Still, I should thank you for teaching me the rudiments of Enchantment when we were young. That proved most useful.'

'It was my pleasure, sister,' replied Ragnar. 'Though our father did not thank me for it.' Even now the mage found it hard to keep the bitterness out of his voice.

His half-sister approached him and stroked his scaly cheek. 'He should have thought about that before he fathered a bastard son on a witch,' she said. 'And I am sorry not to have been able to accept you back into his hall.'

'It was necessary for the plan to work,' replied the warlock. 'Things will be different now.'

She smiled up at him. He had no doubt she loved him. 'Indeed, brother, things will be different. Thanks to the laws of our land I now inherit everything – including Guldebrand's claim to the throne.'

'You know there will be some opposition nonetheless,' Ragnar reminded her.

'There will,' she acknowledged, taking her cup and pouring herself some wine. 'But we shall overcome it. Brega, Bjorg and Vilm shall find themselves alone. With all the other jarls and thegns behind me, what choice will they have but to recognise my claim? We've just fought a war to unite the principalities… And united they shall be, under my rule.'

She took a triumphant sip of wine.

'Magnhilda, Magna of the Frozen Wastes,' intoned Ragnar. 'Even your name presaged your destiny. The Farseers of Norn predicted as much.'

His half-sister frowned at that. 'Yes, well, I never was as religious as you, brother… What if Hardrada had been successful on the mainland? Guldebrand might never have taken the opportunity to raid his lands and tilt the balance of power in the Principalities.'

'No, I think he would have regardless – he was ever overweening and ambitious. And I had his father Gunnar Longspear poisoned at just the right time. A sixteen-year-old does not make for a wise Thegn.'

Magnhilda smirked at that. 'No indeed – but what if Hardrada had returned to Jótlund and defeated Guldebrand?'

Ragnar smiled back. 'Then we would have found a way to manipulate him instead. The destination would have been the same, only the route would have differed. We are all of us caught up in wyrd – part of something larger than any of us. You and I shall sit at the top tier of a new world order, sister.'

Magnhilda laughed and drained her goblet. 'If you say so, Ragnar… We'll see about new world orders. For now I am content to reign as queen of the Frozen Wastes – and lead my people to victory on the mainland. Together we shall build an empire of northmen such as the world has never seen.'

Ragnar kept his thoughts to himself. His half-sister could not know how small her dreams seemed to him.

'Well, I had best be off,' said the mage. 'You, I believe, have a hue and cry to raise.'

Muttering the words of a Transformation spell, he pictured the three symbols in reverse. A few seconds later a raven was flying from the window of the palace, as a woman leaned out of it and began screaming.

⇥ CHAPTER XIV ⇤

A Hard Road For Sick Wayfarers

If Regensburg had anything to offer the curious traveller, Adelko wasn't about to find out on this occasion. No sooner had they reached the bustling city of five thousand souls than Horskram sought lodgings with a well-to-do master craftsman he knew. At first the prosperous furniture maker looked none too pleased at being woken up in the dead of night by two Argolians and five sworders who looked to have been possessed by Abaddon; but Horskram placated him by suggesting they spend the night in his stables – and with a timely reminder that it was but three summers since he had saved his daughter from possession.

And how was the lovely Analise faring these days? Enjoying the life of a virtuous Palomedian maiden? To his credit, the craftsman's eyes had only narrowed briefly before he agreed to take them in.

He need not have worried in any case, for come first light they were off again, threading their way through narrow cobbled streets and back onto the road (by now it seemed a lifelong companion to Adelko). The proximity of the Herzog's seat meant Regensburg did without walls, trusting its security to the towering pentagonal keep that watched it like a hawk from a high motte on the city's outskirts. Banderoles bearing the Alt-Ürl coat of arms, a gules stag on an ermine fur, fluttered in the morning breeze atop its turrets. After all their misadventures, Adelko half expected a sortie of knights to sally forth from the bailey gatehouse. When they saw the velvet sheen of the Breitrand catching the mid-morning sunlight, the novice allowed himself a sigh of relief. If the Bethler's words proved true, the rest of their journey should be safe from here.

'I know the forester who keeps this stretch of the Breitrand,' said Horskram as they followed the highway into the woods. 'He has the Prince of Westenlund's authority, so he'll put us up for the night. Heaven help the poor poacher caught hunting deer here though!'

'What happens if they are?' asked Adelko, though he had a sinking feeling he knew the answer.

'The poacher loses the hand that released the arrow or wielded the knife is what,' replied Horskram. 'But there now! Prince Leopold isn't the worst of rulers, not by a long chalk.'

Adelko had seen enough of the world's rulers by now not to disagree.

Sparing a backwards glance for their companions, he felt his sixth sense tingle. If possible they looked even paler. Vaskrian was coughing up blood regularly now. He caught Hettie looking at the squire with a concerned expression, but he sensed there was more than just concern in her right now.

He blushed and looked away. Girls. Such strange creatures, when you thought about it.

'What are we going to tell this forester?' he asked Horskram. 'About our friends, I mean?'

The adept sighed. 'I do wish for my sake at least you would not call them such,' he said. 'But you leave me to worry about Yorik. He owes me a favour just like yon craftsman... And we won't be imposing on him long either.'

Adelko could sense the urgency behind Horskram's words. He reckoned now was as good a time as any to get some more answers.

'So... those freeswords back at the inn knew we were coming, didn't they?'

'I know well enough by now not to be surprised at your acuity, Adelko of Narvik,' replied Horskram. 'Indeed – they must have been given a description to spot us that quickly. The question is...'

'... who gave it to them?'

'Indeed. We were badly delayed on the Draugmoors. That is time for our trail to grow cold and the Lanraks to give up the chase and return north to the war...'

'... but it's also time enough to send word south to any roving freeswords. Two damsels travelling with foreign knights are none other than the heiress of Dulsinor...'

'... and a rich reward to the man who brings her back. Bodyguards expendable.'

They rode on in silence for a while.

'It sounds like a neat explanation, Master Horskram,' ventured Adelko at last. 'Perhaps... too neat.'

'Much as I was thinking,' replied the adept. 'Go on.'

Even now, his mentor was testing him.

'Well, for starters it seemed as if the freeswords knew about our comrades being cursed. Which means they must have got the message after we left the Draugmoors.'

'Very good. Go on.'

'And... I sensed their leader was confused about something. Almost as though he wasn't expecting the Bethlers to turn up when they did.'

'Exactly. And why would that be?'

'That could only mean...' Adelko's voice trailed off as it hit him. 'You surely don't think the Bethlers were involved somehow?'

'I am certainly not saying I am sure that is the case,' said Horskram, measuring his words. 'But the freesword captain's confusion, which I sensed also, does seem bizarre.'

'But why would the Bethlers stop the freeswords if that was the case?'

'Keep thinking, Adelko – make it a habit not an exercise. Brother Sir Guthrum told us himself he was coming back from Regensburg, in the other direction from the preceptory.'

'... which means he couldn't have known if the Bethlers in his own chapter had commissioned hired killers to find us.'

'Exactly.'

Adelko could sense his mentor was not completely satisfied with this explanation however.

'But you said yourself the Bethler Order is the richest in the Free Kingdoms – why would they bother to hire men to kill us and take the damsels back for coin?'

'You're right, that doesn't quite add up. Although it's possible they might have intended to use Adhelina as leverage against the Markwards and Lanraks in their coming crusade,' said Horskram, keeping his voice low. 'But you are missing a step in any case – even if it was the Bethlers who were involved, how did they come to know about us?'

'Well, the only people who did know – ' Adelko almost pulled his horse up short. 'No... it's not possible!'

'Oh it's possible,' sighed Horskram. 'But thankfully not certain, not until we have eliminated all other avenues of inquiry anyway. Still, it gives us something to cogitate on, wouldn't you say?'

Horskram lapsed back into his customary silence, leaving Adelko to mull over the unsettling thought. Even after everything they had been through, it had never seriously occurred to him that there could be a traitor within their own Order.

Then the Earth Witch's message came back to him.

Trust no one.

✠ ✠ ✠

The forester's lodge was cramped and smelly. Adhelina was wise enough to realise that this was the life she had chosen, and not to resent her circumstances too much.

Besides, she had far more to be despondent about. Grief for her father's death remained lodged in her heart like a deep wound, guilt adding to the pain like a splinter. Next to that feeling the suspicious looks she and Hettie received from the forester's wife scarcely bothered her.

Now on top of that, there was another painful loss on the cards. She had insisted on going with Horskram when he went to the stables to give their bodyguard a blessing against the coming night. They had looked even more ghastly in the moonlight as he sprinkled holy water on them; Adhelina could have sworn they were almost translucent.

'I told you earthly ministrations are of no use,' the friar had told her sternly. 'Even if you had your herb pouch with you, it would be of little use against such a sickness.'

They had arrived at the forester's cabin an hour before sunset, giving Adhelina time to gather herbs, but even so she was far short of the supply she had left at Graukolos. So much that was precious to her, gone... At least Hettie was still with her, though she hadn't found much time to show her gratitude. That made her feel even more guilty.

It pained her to see brave fighters to whom she owed her life fading away, passing over to the Other Side. And she was powerless to help them. Anupe hugged herself, rocking back and forth and singing a strange song in her own tongue. Braxus stared vacantly, while Torgun slumped against the stable walls looking sullenly at the ground. Poor Vaskrian was coughing frightfully now, and as for Wrackwulf he simply lay down flat, his eyes tight shut as though in the grip of some febrile nightmare. All shivered spasmodically, though the summer nights were balmy.

Her eyes lingered on Torgun and Braxus. She could not deny their love suits had stirred up some feelings within her. And yet there had been little time to play any games of romance: far too many real dangers to go inventing challenges for bold knights.

Adhelina sighed heavily and shifted uncomfortably on the cot the forester's wife had prepared for her in the cabin. She was a roil of emotions. Reaching into her purse she pulled out some Silverweed and chewed upon it. Better to brew it in a tea, but right now she'd settle for what she could get.

When she was sure Horskram wasn't looking, she turned to Hettie lying next to her and nudged her. The old friar was sitting at the other end of the room with his novice, talking to the forester. Adhelina got the feeling he was trying to keep the crusty old gamekeeper occupied, so he wouldn't ask about his bizarre guests.

'What is it?' hissed Hettie. 'I'm trying to sleep, milady... hard enough to do with all their chitter-chattering.'

Clearly her best friend was unhappy, to talk to her so. Or perhaps she no longer commanded deference, she reflected gloomily.

'Well I'm sorry to bother you,' replied Adhelina tartly. 'I'm only trying to help... I found some Silverweed in the forest. It works better in a tea of course, but if you chew it there's still some effect.'

Hettie propped herself up on her elbow, suddenly looking interested. 'Silverweed? Isn't that the stuff you used to make when we were girls? Made us giddy as headless chickens.'

Adhelina grinned, feeling almost cheerful for the first time in weeks. 'That's the one! It won't be strong enough to do that if we just chew it, but should help us... relax.'

Hettie paused for a second or two. 'Oh go on, then,' she said, returning the grin. 'One leaf won't hurt.'

✠ ✠ ✠

Adelko was struggling to stay awake. His mentor and the forester were making incessant small talk and none of it was of any interest. That was probably a good thing, he reflected: it was a relief to be in peaceful lands. The forester barely seemed to register news of the war in Dulsinor, only muttering that such unruly behaviour was typical of northern folk.

A giggling sound stopped him nodding off. Glancing over he could make out the two damsels, huddling together and sharing some joke. The forester caught it too and raised an eyebrow at Horskram. Hettie whispered something to Adhelina and she burst out laughing, before remembering herself and stifling her mirth.

Horskram looked at the pair of them, then back at the forester and shrugged his shoulders. 'Too much excitement,' he suggested. 'They have been through quite an ordeal. The sooner I get them back to their castle the better.'

The forester shook his head and took another sip of ale.

✠ ✠ ✠

The well-tended pastures dotted with cows and sheep made Hettie feel homesick: Westenlund looked every bit as prosperous as Dulsinor. Or as prosperous as it had been. The thought of her countrymen fighting and dying was too much to bear on top of homesickness, yet she could not shake the thought. She had half a mind to beg another leaf of Silverweed from her mistress. Last night had been the most fun she'd had in ages.

Adhelina seemed scarcely less troubled, gazing across the lands they rode through with a troubled mien. At least they were able to travel more quickly now: Prince Leopold kept his roads well, and there was nary a pothole to be seen. Good, the sooner they were out of this pleasant land the better: she didn't like being reminded of a home she would probably never see again. Not that the prospect of a sea journey appealed much either. She had only ever seen it once, on a pleasure trip to Meerborg shortly after coming of age. How exciting the bustling cityport had seemed back then, full of sights and sounds and smells – though not all of them had been wholesome. By all accounts Westerburg was even bigger, perhaps twice the size of its northern rival. Hettie couldn't summon much in the way of excitement, but at least a city's streets or a ship's deck wouldn't remind her of her ravaged homeland.

'The peasantry are well kept here as you can see,' said Horskram, as if reading her thoughts. 'Prince Leopold has a reputation for ruthlessness against those who cross him, but he believes in looking after his subjects. Makes them less likely to revolt, you see.'

'I read that it used to be different,' ventured Adhelina. 'Before the Red Plague. My great grandfather Urus the Strong was married to a Drüler. By all accounts they were insufferable – as haughty and arrogant as the day was long. Why, after the Partition Wars they even insisted on keeping the title "prince"! And all because Aelle was the last king of Vorstlund!'

'You are well read, Lady Dulsinor,' replied the adept with a nod of approval, oblivious to the spasm of pain that mention of home brought to Adhelina's face. 'You are correct – the Red Plague changed many things. Loremasters say it killed a third of the population of the Free Kingdoms – more than half in some parts. In those places it made farmers such a rarity that the survivors were able to negotiate better conditions, elevating themselves from serfs to freemen. That happened here and in your homeland, and many parts of Northalde too.'

The monk paused, as if deciding whether to continue. Then he added: 'Some even say the Red Plague was divine punishment, brought back by rats infesting crusader ships – for making bloody war on the Sassanians in the Redeemer's name.'

Horskram made the sign. Hettie didn't see what he was getting so pious about. As far as she was concerned, all wars seemed fairly unholy. Palomedians were supposed to respect life and be pacifists, as the Redeemer himself had done. Then again, not even the prophet had been perfect in that respect.

'But the Redeemer was a soldier, wasn't he?' she asked, daring to voice her thoughts. 'Oh, I know he renounced the sword eventually, but the *Holy Book* says he spent years leading a rebel army of deserted legionnaires against the Thalamian Empire.'

Hettie felt a patch of hot scarlet reach her ears as Horskram looked at her with surprise.

'My, my,' said Horskram, raising an eyebrow. 'Two well-educated damsels! The Redeemer evidently sent us to save you with good reason.'

Hettie couldn't tell if he was joking or not.

'I made sure she was taught well,' said Adhelina, beaming at Hettie. 'I had to have someone in the castle I could talk to about all the books in my father's library!'

Hettie smiled back at her mistress bashfully. The conversation felt awkward to her, but she was happy to see Adhelina in better spirits.

'Yes, it is a good point anyway,' resumed Horskram. 'All too many unscrupulous men of power have seen fit to use Palom's early life to justify bloodshed.'

'Even so, why does your Order not support the Pilgrim Wars?' asked Adhelina. 'It's a holy cause... Surely it's different if you're fighting against heathens to keep pilgrimage routes to Ushalayim open? I read that's how the crusades started... the Sultan wouldn't let Palomedians into the city unless they paid exorbitant tariffs.'

'That is a very idealistic way of looking at the Pilgrim Wars,' said Horskram. Hettie could see from the dark expression on his face that the subject displeased him. 'There are certain theories about how the crusades really started, which I shall not detail here. But suffice to say we Argolians do not see the validity in seeking conflict in Palom's name... even if pilgrimage routes are at stake.'

'And I thought the Argolians had a reputation for secrecy,' smirked Adhelina ironically.

Horskram frowned at that, but stubbornly held his peace.

'Master Horskram, something's wrong!'

It was Adelko, who had been bringing up the rear and shepherding their sick bodyguards along the road.

Turning Hettie saw the six of them were lagging far behind. They had been riding at a brisk trot and hadn't noticed. Their horses were neighing and stomping; a couple looked as though they were about to rear and throw their riders.

Hettie could see why. The hot sun seemed almost to shine straight through the once-hale warriors. She shivered involuntarily and made the sign. Horskram cursed and nudged his own steed back down the road for a closer look. Sprinkling them with holy water, he intoned a prayer. Only when he produced the relic he wore around his neck and touched each of them with it did they show any signs of improving. Their pallor seemed to lighten and Vaskrian's cough subsided. Hettie almost cursed herself for the relief that flushed through her when that happened.

'I've managed to abate the illness somewhat,' said Horskram. 'But we've no time to lose! With every minute they are slipping further towards the Other Side. No member of the animal kingdom will suffer them in this condition.'

Hettie gulped nervously. Perhaps this sort of thing was meat and drink to an Argolian, but she'd had quite enough of supernatural scares. To last something in the region of a lifetime.

'So what do we do?' asked Adhelina. Both monks were ushering the five warriors off their horses. 'It'll take far longer to reach the cityport if they're walking.'

'Well observed,' replied the old monk sarcastically. Hettie felt sure that was no way to talk to a lady, even a disinherited one; she was about to say so, but her friend shot her a glance and shook her head.

'Travelling at this rate we've another three days on the road,' continued the adept, oblivious. 'I'm friendly with some vassals in these parts, we'll just have to impose on them.'

'Won't that mean unwanted questions?' asked Adelko.

'It will,' conceded Horskram. 'But frankly I'm past caring about that now. The sooner we get to Rima and pass this mission over to Hannequin's oversight, the better I shall like it. Keep bringing up the rear, Adelko! See that our friends don't lose their blasted horses!'

Retaking the saddle he nudged his steed into motion again. Hettie sighed as she and Adhelina did likewise, sparing a furtive glance for the squire as he stumbled along the road like a blind man.

⊷ CHAPTER XV ⊷

A Throne Secured

Sir Toric's granite face never gave away too much, but Hjala could sense his scepticism. 'So you say he might extend the Valravyn's charter if he becomes Regent?' asked the commander. 'And where, if you don't mind my asking, would the resources come from?'

Princess Hjala waved her hand dismissively. 'Oh, these are but details – as you know full well,' she said.

Her glance lighted uneasily on her mahogany dressing table, and the shards of broken mirror lying on it. It had been imported from the Empire at considerable expense, but she'd broken it the other day by accident. She'd heard that some mystics believed breaking a mirror was bad luck; Hjala used to think it just a superstitious metaphor for not breaking costly items, but now she wasn't so sure.

'Well?' she said, turning to look at the High Commander, who was deep in thought. He was dressed in mail and tabard despite being at court. The candlelight in her room reflected off his shiny bald pate, making it look as though he had turned up at her chambers in a helm too. The knight tapped his broad fingers on the pommel of his sword, his eyes narrowing as he continued to mull over her proposal.

He had arrived that afternoon, almost a week later than expected. Apparently the new lords of the Southern Dominions had needed a bit of pacifying themselves, and Toric had stayed behind to prevent a bloodbath in Saltcaste.

'I'm considering your proposal,' he said laconically.

'Well at least let me know what form that consideration is taking.' She hated being kept in the dark.

The raven remained silent for a few moments more, then he said: 'I can see how putting Thorsvald on the throne as regent might be a wise thing to do. The news we are getting from the Sealord and other sources is that the Northlanders are uniting – we're not sure who it is yet, but it would appear they will soon have a Magnate for the first time in generations. It's also rumoured that the Sea Wizard is involved. Very likely we'll have an invasion next spring – perhaps sooner if that accursed warlock meddles with the elements.'

Hjala's windows were open despite the lateness of the hour. Autumn arrived early this far north, and already the air had a chilly tinge to it. Walking over to the window she brought the translucent bone panes together and fastened them.

'So what are your misgivings?' she asked, turning to look at him.

'As leader of the White Valravyn and High Marshal of the country's forces, I must weigh two considerations,' replied Toric. 'Loyalty to the crown, and the security of the realm. Currently it feels as though the two are in conflict.'

Hjala sensed her opportunity. 'Oh, Lord Toric, then you *do* admit that putting Wolfram on the throne would endanger Northalde – even if he is the rightful heir!'

Toric's cheekbones sharpened. That was the closest he came to showing inner turmoil, she supposed.

'I have heard that His Highness's condition is… unstable. But here's the thing – we've just fought a short but brutal war to see off another pretender. Administering the peace is always more difficult, and so it's proving. If we abrogate the line of succession – and whatever the law says that's how it'll look – we're sending a message to all the disinherited squires and pages down south. We're saying, "the crown we just fought so hard to protect lies askew".'

He held her gaze, allowing his words to sink in.

Hjala considered them. Perhaps he had a point. 'But surely we can unite against a common foe,' she said. 'Those squires can be readily pressed into service against the invaders, a chance to redeem their tarnished family names!'

Toric put his tongue in his cheek and nodded slowly. 'Yes… I can see how that kind of message could be delivered to some effect.'

Hjala sensed she had him; now she closed in for the kill.

'Toric, if we don't unite behind an able leader, there'll be no kingdom left to have another civil war in! How many experienced seacarls and berserkers do you think a new Magnate will bring at his back? If we have to fight it out with the southrons again after we've sent the Northlanders packing, then so be it – but I will *not* sacrifice my kingdom to lineal propriety and my older brother's whims!'

Toric bunched up his face. Hjala almost swore she could hear a grindstone at work.

'All right,' he said at last. 'You'll have my vote next week. But I want that charter extended. Ezekiel knows we'll need the White Valravyn's powers augmented if we're to come through this.'

Hjala could have hugged him. Restraining her ebullience, she said: 'Thank you, Lord Toric. Thank you for seeing sense on this matter.'

The bull-necked knight refused to meet her eye. 'Don't make me regret it,' he said gruffly. 'Now, if you'll excuse me, I've been busy all day and I'm famished. I'll away to the kitchens before bedtime.'

'No need, I'll have a page boy bring you supper,' said the princess, showing him out.

'Don't suppose you've heard from Sir Torgun?' he asked her on the point of leaving. 'Last we heard down south, he and the others stayed a couple of nights at Ørthang before pressing on for the Argael. But that was three months ago.'

Mention of her paramour made her heart jolt. 'Then you know more than I do,' she said sadly. 'I pray for him every day. The others too.'

Toric nodded curtly and bade her good night. The pain lingered in her breast as she closed the door behind him. Her brave goodly knight errant – wandering the wildernesses of the world trying to save it. She supposed it was his wyrd, to do such great deeds. All the same, she missed him. Did he think of her every day too, she wondered?

✢ ✢ ✢

'Well, we're poised for victory!'

Lady Walsa raised her goblet in an impromptu toast to Thorsvald, who was nervously fidgeting in his new court clothes. He looked distinctly uncomfortable in his cobalt silk garnache lined with beaver fur, gold-buckled girdle and black hose decorated with silver lace. His pointed chausses were really quite fetching Hjala thought, though she knew her brother would far prefer to be in his usual breeches and chemise.

But her aunt had insisted that if he was running for Regent, he must look the part. She was probably right, although the princess had to pity Thorsvald just a little.

'I think any such toast is premature,' he said, pointedly refusing to pick up his goblet from the marble table. They had gathered in Walsa's suite of chambers for a last-moment confabulation. Though really there was nothing left to discuss.

'I believe there is nothing left to worry about,' said Hjala, trying to reassure her brother. She took a sip of her Mercadian dry white. It was a delicious vintage that tasted of the exotic lemons that grew in that southerly kingdom, and matched the zest of her spirits.

Today at noon they would assemble in the throneroom. All five council members would declare which of the two candidates they had picked. As long as Cuthbert and Toric held good to their pledges, hers would be the deciding vote.

Her final misgivings had been swept away by Wolfram's latest fit: two days ago he had been brought back to the palace raving, after falling into an apoplexy on his way to the Strang Bay tourney. Thank Reus he had only just left the palace. His courtiers had thrown a cloak over him to obscure his identity. Fortunately there had only been one or two bystanders in the citadel, with most of the nobility being down on the plains to watch the jousting. They had been bribed into silence, although she couldn't help but wonder whether Ulnor was taking more drastic measures into consideration.

Perhaps that would be enough to make the hoary old seneschal finally see sense. She doubted it somehow: men and their vanities, they could never be counted on to do the sensible thing.

Meanwhile her poor father's condition had worsened. Yurik was now saying it would be a miracle if he lasted out the rest of the year, never mind the winter. There had been no further news from the Frozen Principalities, but she knew time was pressing. The sooner they had Thorsvald safely on the throne the better. Even if he only got to rule for a few months before Freidheim passed, that would be enough for Wolfram's condition to worsen... Then everyone would have to see the sense in keeping on his younger brother.

'Hjala! Dearest, but you're miles away... are you quite all right?'

Hjala brought her attention back into the room, smiling at her aunt. 'I'm fine,' she said. 'Just... there's been so much to think about lately.'

'Yes there certainly has,' said Walsa, with just a hint of smugness. 'But we've dealt with it marvellously. And don't you worry about young Cuthbert, he's quite amenable. When I told him of our promise to shore up his position against that horrible Supreme Perfect in Rima, why he positively drooled!'

'Auntie!' Hjala admonished. 'As a woman of the Creed, aren't you supposed to look up to His Supreme Holiness as Reus' deputy on earth?'

Walsa sniffed. 'A Pangonian? The Almighty's right hand? Why certainly not – I've never met this Cyprian, but I'm sure he isn't half the man Friar Horskram is...' The feisty old dame took another mouthful of wine. There was definitely a glint in her eye that was not borne of zeal. Hjala exchanged a glance with Thorsvald. She could tell her brother was trying not to laugh.

But some shared humour was a good thing. Reus knew, they all needed it as much as the wine right now.

A knock at the door announced the moment they had all been anticipating. Hjala ignored the butterflies in her stomach as her aunt bade them enter: a clutch of raven knights come to escort them to the throneroom.

Falling into step among them, Hjala forced herself to concentrate as they took her along the echoing corridor lined with furs and tapestries. She didn't dare look at the latter – she didn't want her eye to chance on some tale of the Ingwins that might presage doom of any kind. Getting involved in politics had made her decidedly superstitious.

✢ ✢ ✢

Every noble of any importance was gathered in the throneroom. The antechamber was crowded with commoners: word of the election had got out and even proximity to the grand event was considered worth clawing out a space for. The sash windows that looked onto the harbour showed leaden skies and wet sails and streets: not even the rain had dissuaded them from coming out.

All such thoughts vanished from her mind as they drew level with the dais on which the throne rested. Before it an oval table of cedar had been set up, with five sieges around it. Ulnor was there already, standing to one side of the table. Next to him stood Lord Visigard and Prince Wolfram. Her brother had recovered from his latest fit, but the look he shot at Hjala and Thorsvald was filled with feral hatred. She didn't like to think what he might have done had she failed to win over Cuthbert and Toric. Neither of them had arrived yet, which didn't help her nerves any.

Walking up the stairs of the dais, she took her position on the other side of the table with her brother. Walsa whispered a last word of encouragement before joining the front of the throng of courtiers. Above it all loomed the Giantslayer's Gift, its vast eye sockets staring dispassionately down at the unfolding spectacle.

Minutes dragged past. The excited hubbub of courtiers did little to calm her. Presently the herald announced the arrival of Lord Toric. Hjala felt her nerves settle a little. She shot a sidelong glance at Ulnor as the High Commander jingled his way up to the dais. He was still dressed in full battle armour, save for his helm.

Ulnor's stony demeanour gave nothing away. As Toric took his place behind his designated seat, an under-seneschal ushered the two candidates to stand before the Pine Throne. Neither brother looked at the other; both men stared ahead into the middle distance and tried to look as regal as possible. Wolfram was dressed in a similar fashion to Thorsvald, only his chosen colours were cream and white. On a marble plinth off to the side she caught a silver circlet fashioned to resemble Seakindred and war galleys, set with a single blue topaz: the Regent's crown. She drew in a tight breath and forced it out slowly.

The hubbub seemed to raise itself a notch. It was impossible to tell with the overcast weather, but surely it must be noon by now? Hjala shot a nervous glance at her aunt, who raised her eyebrows. The princess was on the point of asking the under-seneschal where on earth Cuthbert was when the herald declaimed: 'All make way for His High Holiness, Lorthar, Arch Perfect of Strongholm!'

Hjala gawped as the familiar figure swept into the throneroom. He looked a lot more emaciated than the last time she had seen him, but everything else was the same: the regal finery, the staff of office, the confident manner. The zealous look that burned in his eyes.

She shot a furious glance at Ulnor. He met her gaze, and this time a thin smile crept up his craggy features.

'What is the meaning of this?' she barked. 'Lorthar was attainted of treason and stripped of office!'

'Charges which I was entitled to reverse as acting regent,' replied Ulnor coolly. 'On further consideration, it was found that the accusations levelled against him were... unfounded.'

'This is in direct contravention of my father's own decree!' she yelled. 'How could you?'

'Doubtless His Majesty's illness was already upon him when he imprisoned His High Holiness,' replied Ulnor, unable to keep the smugness from his tone. 'Freidheim was a great monarch, but even the greatest are vulnerable to fault, particularly in their last days.'

'And what about the war he won that saved all our necks in his last days!?' cried Hjala as Lorthar took up his position at the table. 'Have you forgotten about that?'

But Ulnor did not reply. The under-seneschal called for silence and formally declared the reason for the assembly.

The words disappeared behind a torrent of rage and despair. All her wily politicking had come to naught. She had been outplayed from the start by a man who held a deck of cards stacked in his favour.

The vote proceeded, though she knew it was now a farce. As Lorthar cast the deciding vote in favour of Wolfram she caught the perfect smiling at Ulnor. Oh, he had earned his freedom well... She spared a glance for the two princes standing behind them. Wolfram was smirking triumphantly, a savage look in his eyes. Her brother was inscrutable: he simply stood and stared ahead, his face pale and taut.

The coronation proceeded swiftly. Being only for a regency it wasn't a long ceremony; when it was done, Wolfram stepped up to the edge of the dais and raised his hands for silence from the applauding nobles. Many young knights were cheering and it took a while for them to settle down.

'My Northlending brothers – and sisters!' said Wolfram. 'It is with great gladness on this happy day that I accept the crown of Regent! I promise to serve thee all, and the realm too, as it faces glorious new challenges in the coming months!'

More cheers erupted. Hjala felt a core of sickness growing in the pit of her stomach.

'By land we have been assailed,' continued the Regent. 'Now by sea a new danger comes – the Northlanders have ever been covetous of our status and our wealth!'

The cheering intensified, some of the supporters hooting at the mention of their barbarian cousins. The under-seneschal banged down his staff for silence.

'And I say – LET THEM COME!' roared Wolfram, to tumultuous approval. 'They shall not find us unprepared! For we shall gather our armies from the four corners of this kingdom – the which we have but lately defended from treasonous rebels – and together we shall make a fist to SMITE THEM WITH!'

Wolfram shook his fist for effect. Hjala felt her sickness ebb slightly. It was undeniably a good speech – an honourable tribute to their father's charisma. Had she misjudged him? Would the boy prince finally become a king and a man?

Wolfram raised his hand again for silence. 'But while we are speaking of TREASON...' He turned a jackal eye on his sister. Hjala felt her blood run cold. 'Mine own *sister* sought to put my younger brother on the throne instead of me, its rightful heir! IS THIS MEET?'

The cheering soured immediately into boos and jeering. Hjala felt her sickness return. Her brother rounded on her and Thorsvald. 'Should the rightful Regent of Northalde stand for such base TREACHERY!?' Wolfram took a step towards her. 'NAY! I say – ' He stopped in his tracks. His one good eye was twitching spasmodically. His fist remained clenched. 'I say...' he repeated, in a weaker voice. 'I say... suh-say...'

The Regent's body started spasming. He fell to one knee, still struggling to finish his sentence.

Not even Hjala could have predicted what happened next. Ulnor motioned to the under-seneschal, who immediately ordered guards to escort the Regent from the throneroom. She was expecting him to address the assembly, to proffer some feeble excuse for her brother's illness.

Instead it was Lorthar who stepped up to address the crowd.

'My lords and ladies, hearken to me now!' His voice was less loud than Wolfram's, but it carried such conviction that it cut across the muttering nobles. 'This is no ordinary affliction! This is a *sign*, I tell thee!'

The throng hushed. All eyes including Hjala's were now fixed on Lorthar.

'In ages past, when the Redeemer made war on the Thalamians for the souls of mortalkind, the *Holy Book* tells us he was gifted by the Almighty with prophecy! And this gift he passed down, upon his death, to one of his Seven Acolytes.'

The Arch Perfect paused to let his words sink in, and they did. A man did not rise to such a position in the Temple without becoming a skilled orator.

Lorthar went on: 'Twas St Athanasius, who wept when they broke his soulfather on the Wheel in Tyrannos, that received this gift. And the Redeemer said unto him, "let thine eyes be touched with the gift of farseeing whenever they shed tears; let the futures of men be seen in their glistening drops".'

The hush had turned deathly. The Northlending nobility were as godless as any in the Free Kingdoms, but a good story wasn't lost on them. Hjala knew this one from her visits to Temple on Restdays – but why in the Known World was Lorthar bringing it up now?

She soon had the answer to that question.

'And the scriptures tell of St Athanasius' many prophecies – including one that I shall recite to you here and now.' The pompous perfect paused and drew himself up to stand even taller. '"Mighty forces shall sweep the lands of men in the Last Hour of Judgment/ Great armies shall war for the kingdoms of the earth/ But all shall fall before the One-Eyed General."'

Lorthar pointed at Wolfram, being escorted towards the double doors leading out of the throneroom. He was convulsing horribly, a nasty juddering sound escaping his lips.

'Such is our Regent!' cried the Arch Perfect. 'Touched by the Almighty Himself! Sent to us by the Unseen to aid us in our darkest hour! BEHOLD, THE ONE-EYED GENERAL BEFORE WHOM ALL SHALL FALL!'

The throneroom doors were flung open just as Lorthar finished declaiming. Outside a gaggle of dirty-faced commoners pressed forwards. The palace guards just about managed to interpose their halberds after Wolfram passed through.

Springing down the stairs Lorthar marched up the horsehair carpet, repeating his last words over and over again as he strode into the antechamber after the Regent. By the time he had disappeared upstairs with Wolfram and his guards some of the common folk were even repeating them.

As the bemused nobles filed out of the throneroom jabbering excitedly, Ulnor turned and favoured Hjala with a triumphant glance.

'You engineered this entire charade from start to finish, didn't you?' she said venomously.

Ulnor shrugged. 'I am a secular man of state,' he replied. 'It is not for me to gainsay our highest religious authority in matters of holy prophecy.'

Thorsvald remained rooted to the spot, unable to take in what had just happened. Visigard looked at the ground, unwilling to meet anybody's eye.

'No good will come of this, Ulnor,' Hjala assured him. 'Wolfram is constitutionally unfit to rule. We both know it.'

Ulnor smiled. 'Then we shall have to trust that the Almighty provides His chosen one with advisers to steer the realm through the challenges awaiting it.'

Without another word the seneschal turned and began walking down the stairs, his cane clacking rhythmically.

The throneroom was emptying, but Lady Walsa had remained behind. She approached Hjala.

'Well this is a fine mess, and no mistake,' she said. 'We've just been outplayed by a schemer and a fraud. We'd best away to my rooms – all of us. At least your brother's fit gives us a chance to get you and Thorsvald out of the city. Judging by his last coherent words, I don't think Strongholm will be very safe for either of you for much longer.'

Hjala did not reply. She stood watching as the throneroom continued to empty, until just the three of them were left. She suddenly wished she were with Torgun: wherever he was right now, it had to be better than here.

Above the throne that had caused so much tumult, the Giantslayer's Gift continued to stare down at them, a gargantuan grin on its fleshless lips.

⊷ CHAPTER XVI ⊷

The Final Stretch

'If you think I'm taking that lot on board my ship, you've been fighting phantoms in the wilderness over long!' The sea captain spat on the wharf for emphasis. Shaking his head he ran thick fingers through his grizzled beard as he added: 'I've a fine cargo of trade from Port Craek. I didn't just run the gauntlet of the Pirate Straits to lose my ship to a curse!'

'We don't fight phantoms,' said Horskram pedantically. 'We exorcise them. And I can assure you, captain, that yon men are nothing of the kind.'

The captain had beady black eyes which became even smaller as he screwed up his fat face. 'Avast your protestations,' he growled. 'You said yourself they'd been cursed by a witch! That's just as bad in my reckoning.'

Horskram sighed, fighting to keep his exasperation in check. Pangonians. Insufferable to the core – always thought they knew better. But the captain was still here talking to him. He didn't need his sixth sense to tell him a deal could be struck.

'I've already offered you my assurances as a sworn brother of my Order that these men will not bring any calamity on the *Red Jerfalcon* while aboard her. And I've offered you double the going rate for berths.'

'Ah I see,' sneered the captain. 'So in other words everything's all fair and above board is it? Well let me tell you this, friar – I know the world, see? And I've heard it told that you Argolians are naught better than witches yourselves. Now why don't you go about and leave me to get on with my job, eh?'

Behind the captain his crew were busy loading barrels and crates and chests on to the deck of the ship, a sturdy looking hulk whose canvas sails fluttered in the late afternoon breeze. The captain intended to sail with the evening tide: it was convince him now or wait another few precious days. Most of the other ships at Westerburg's harbour were fishing vessels and wouldn't be heading to Rima. More to the point, the *Jerfalcon* was the only ship at port large enough to take their horses.

'I'll pay you triple,' said Horskram, meeting the sailor's eye.

'Oh and a fat lot of good that'll do me, sirrah, when we all go under to the Seakindred's Locker.' But a light had entered those gimlet eyes.

'Might I intervene?'

Adhelina stepped up to join the conversation. The damsels had used their couple of days in the cityport to spend the King's coin well, purchasing new clothing to complement the snatched belongings they had brought with them from Graukolos. Though still dressed for a long journey she looked every inch the noblewoman now, a fine shawl wrapped around her head.

'Captain, I don't believe I know your name,' she said, addressing the mariner in fluent Panglian.

'Abrehan, ma'am,' he said, managing a half bow. 'At your service.' Pangonians might be rude, but they knew when to defer to their betters.

'A pleasure,' replied Adhelina. 'Now there's no way you could know this, but my lady-in-waiting and I have been through quite a *frightful* experience. We're from Asberg and my family is related to the House of Hessé. You *do* know who the Hessés are don't you, captain?'

The captain muttered something but Adhelina cut him off. 'That's right – they rule all of Aslund. In fact my father is a personal retainer to Eorl Aethelbald, and as a man of the world, I'm sure you know he controls all the trade routes that pass through Asberg to this very port.' She pointed a slender white finger downwards for emphasis. The captain looked somewhat perplexed.

'So my father is a *very* influential man,' Adhelina went on. She gestured towards the three knights sitting slumped over their horses. 'Yon knights are three of his finest swords, whom he sent with this learned friar to rescue me and my lady-in-waiting. The witch that kidnapped us managed to magick them before they put an end to her, as you've probably gathered. But my father would fain not see his most heroic bachelors die of such a curse. In fact he'd be *very* angry if he learned that happened.'

Adhelina paused briefly, favouring the captain with a dazzling smile. 'So angry, in fact, that he might just put in a word with the Eorl, who might just send word to the Prince of Westenlund.

And when that happens, His Highness *might just* send word to the merchant houses here in Westerburg, asking them to revoke the *Jerfalcon*'s docking licence.'

Adhelina continued to smile sweetly, fixing the captain with eyes that sparkled in the lowering sun.

'This is outrageous!' spluttered Abrehan. 'You're threatening me!'

'No,' replied Adhelina, her voice hardening. 'I'm offering you an *excellent* opportunity – a chance to take on nine extra passengers at double the rate, while gaining the Eorl of Aslund's undying gratitude and keeping your trading privileges in Westerburg.'

The captain's fat face flushed red. 'Double? He just said triple!' He motioned towards Horskram, who could not hold back the amused smile that now played on his lips.

Adhelina cocked her head coquettishly. 'Oh no, captain, I definitely heard him say *double*. Isn't that what you said, master monk?'

Horskram cleared his throat. He didn't normally like to go back on his word, but the captain was a greedy coxcomb and he supposed Adhelina had a point to make.

'Oh yes, yes indeed,' he said affably. 'I apologise if it sounded like triple. It is a while since I used my Panglian.' The monk favoured the captain with a smile of his own.

'Fie on all blasted foreigners!' snarled Abrehan, spitting again. 'All right then – but I'll be wanting payment up front, if you please.'

'Certainly,' beamed Adhelina. 'Master Horskram, I trust you will attend to business…'

Horskram favoured her with a deferential nod. 'With pleasure,' he purred.

✤ ✤ ✤

With some trepidation Adelko ushered their stricken charges on board. It wasn't just the suspicious glances of the crew that made him nervous, but the prospect of his first boat trip too. As he helped Anupe, last in line, up the gangplank he felt the *Jerfalcon* lurch slightly. It reminded him of the horrible moving room they had used to enter the Warlock's Crown. At least that abnormal journey had lasted barely a minute; Horskram had told him they could expect a sea voyage lasting several days. His feet found the deck unsteadily.

One of the bigger mariners had stopped what he was doing to stare at the Harijan. She had enough presence of mind left to travel with her hood up, but she clearly had the air of an outlander. But then sailors should be used to seeing foreigners… The sailor returned to working on his rigging, just as the captain bellowed at him: 'Look lively there! I want that shroud fixed afore we set sail!' Striding across the deck, Abrehan singled out another sailor, a hapless looking lad of about ten summers struggling with a large chest.

'What are you doing there!? I said lash down those chests to the larboard side! *Larboard* not starboard! *Port* side, dammit! You think I'd ask a barnacle like you to lug heavy loads across the main deck?'

Horskram drew level with Adelko as the flustered lad began dragging the chest back to port side.

'Good to see our captain runs a tight ship,' he said dryly.

Adelko couldn't help but share his amusement. 'He reminds me of our old friend at Ulfang... Sholto used to call his underlings barnacles.' Thinking on the old quartermaster who begrudgingly got their journey off to a start months ago felt strange.

'Well let us pray Abrehan's eyesight is better than Sholto's – otherwise we're in for another misadventure!'

Before Adelko could reply the captain rounded on them. 'You see the trouble you've caused me?' he moaned. 'I've to keep half the bloody cargo above board to make room for you and your blasted horses!'

'You are being paid handsomely for the inconvenience,' Horskram reminded him.

'Aye, handsomely enough,' spat the captain, no doubt remembering the hard bargain Adhelina had driven. The two ladies had descended below decks. Adelko supposed they were already commandeering the lion's share of whatever miserable space their coin had purchased. 'Just keep yon staring loons out of my way, and I'll thank you kindly for it.'

'Rest assured,' said Horskram, turning to go below decks and motioning for the loons to follow him. 'We'll keep a close eye on them.'

As Adelko brought up the rear again, he half expected at least one of their cursed comrades to fall down the stairs. But docile as sheep they consented to be led into the hold. Horskram's prayers and the Redeemer's blood seemed to have kept the worst at bay, though they were eating less every day, and Anupe and Braxus had joined Vaskrian in coughing up blood. None of the vassals they had stayed with on their journey to Westerburg would have them in their manor houses, and it had taken Horskram's reputation and a lot of old favours called in just to get a space in the stables.

Just before he went below decks, Adelko turned to get a last look at the bustling cityport. If anything it was slightly bigger than Strongholm, though its walls weren't quite as high. These enclosed the city proper in a semi-circle, with the rest being defended by a barbican that overlooked the Bay of Belfarling along the length of the harbour. Out of the corner of his eye he caught the Prince's castle; built on high cliffs overlooking the bay, its gleaming white walls matched their chalky surfaces. Westerburg had been granted a free charter after the Partition Wars, but that hadn't stopped the wealthy Drülers from retaining their ancient seat. As the dying sun caught the whitewashed houses, the novice reflected on how little time he'd had to explore his new surroundings. But he supposed there would be time aplenty to soak up fresh environs when they got to Rima.

With a sigh he pulled his eyes away from the city and descended the stairs. As he did the ship lurched again. This time he felt incipient nausea uncoil itself within his entrails.

Adelko had a sinking feeling he was going to like ships about as much as he did horseshoes.

✣ ✣ ✣

Several days later and the sinking feeling had not left him. It stayed with Adelko as he staggered above decks and lurched towards the gunwale, leaning over its side to be sick. He coughed up the last dregs of bile miserably, watching the gooey tendrils get swallowed up by the rolling waves.

'Consider yourself lucky – the Athan Estuary is calm at this time of year.' His mentor had joined him at the gunwale, though his words provided little in the way of comfort.

'How much longer must we endure this, Master Horskram?' he asked in a small voice. He almost felt he would rather be back on the Draugmoors or inside the Warlock's Crown fighting supernatural horrors.

'Not much longer, Adelko,' replied his mentor. 'Look what the morning brings us – the Pangonian coast. We'll be sailing up the Athos by sunset.'

Following Horskram's outstretched finger he saw it. Pangonia. No longer just a word, its high cliffs chalked a rugged line of ivory across the wine-dark seas. He felt a strange sense of elation run through him, assuaging his seasickness. After months of gruelling adventure, they were finally within sight of their goal.

But hard on the heels of that feeling came one of foreboding. He didn't need his sixth sense to tell him things would be anything but straightforward at Rima.

As if reading his mind, Horskram said: 'You'll have to gather yourself together, Adelko of Narvik. Soon you'll be under

Hannequin's tutelage. I warn you, though wise he is a stern taskmaster. You'll have to bring all the experience you've gained to bear if you're to succeed in the next stage of your journey.'

The adept's words were weighty with implied meaning: Adelko knew they were not intended to be literal. Forcing himself to stand upright, he gripped the rail and took in lungfuls of fresh tangy air. At least the salty breeze did something to revive him.

'I know, Master Horskram,' he said, trying to sound brave. 'But after everything we've been through this past year, I think I'm ready.' He paused, then added: 'Thank you.'

Horskram raised an eyebrow, though Adelko sensed he understood his meaning.

'For taking me with you,' the novice clarified anyway. 'It's been a dangerous journey, but I think it's taught me many things.' He faltered, unsure if he'd said the right thing.

Horskram nodded slowly, favouring him with a rare kindly smile. 'I hope if nothing else you have learned to appreciate the responsibility that comes with power – of all kinds.'

Adelko returned the smile guardedly, not feeling too much cause for levity. 'I believe I have,' he said, hoping that was true.

He paused, unsure whether to say what he wanted to next. Making up his mind, he added: 'Come what may... I'll miss you, Master Horskram.'

The adept's candid reply surprised him.

'And I you, Adelko of Narvik. And I you.'

They said nothing more after that, but remained staring out to sea, watching the coastline thicken on the horizon.

GLOSSARY OF NAMES

Here follows an overview of some of the more common names relating to legends, geography, history, religion, magic and supernatural entities that feature in this book. It is not intended to be exhaustive but may be used as a reference to guide the reader.

Abaddon Foremost among demonkind; led the revolt against **Reus** and the loyal angels and **archangels** during the Battle for Heaven and Earth at the Dawn of Time. Was condemned to languish in the Kingdom of **Gehenna** on the **Other Side**, but has been influential in the affairs of mortalkind ever since. Corrupted **Ma'amun**, foremost among the **Elder Wizards** of **Varya**, by teaching him the **Left Hand Path** of sorcery. Also known as the Fallen One, the Dark Angel, the Author of Evil, and the King of Gehenna in **Urovia**; known as Sha'itan, Loth, **Logi** and the Cloven Hoofed God in other cultures.

Acolytes Palomedes' seven closest advisers and disciples who afterwards were instrumental in spreading the **Creed** – a religion based on his teachings and life examples – throughout **Urovia**. Generally heralded as bringing spiritual salvation to benighted peoples, though dissenters argue that their teachings were flawed interpretations of the **Redeemer**'s beliefs and practices.

Alric Most holy of the knights of the **Purple Garter**; saved King **Vasirius** from the curse of the White Blood Witch using a drop of the Redeemer's blood.

Alysius One of the Seven **Acolytes** of **Palomedes** the **Redeemer**; brought a phial containing His blood to the shores of **Northalde** shortly after the prophet's execution in Tyrannos.

Ambelin Ruling royal house of the Kingdom of **Pangonia**. Its present incumbent is Carolus III, a scheming and self-serving monarch who has alienated many of his barons with high taxes since ascending the Charred Throne. Ambelin has held power for more than a hundred years since it emerged victorious from the Fourth War of the Royal Succession, fought after the reign of King **Vasirius** was brought to an end at the **Battle of Avalongne**.

Ancient Thalamy   Also known as the Thalamian Empire, a
    Golden Age hegemony that straddled the Sundering Sea and
    incorporated the modern kingdoms of Thalamy, **Pangonia**,
    Mercadia, the southern reaches of the **Urovian New Empire**
    and northern **Sassania**, lasting for several centuries until its
    destruction by Wulfric of Gothia.

Antaeus   Legendary mariner and adventurer belonging to
    the **Golden Age**, said by some to have been the son of the
    archangel Aqualcus, worshipped as a god in pagan times
    before the coming of the Faith and the **Creed**. Hailed from
    Ancient Thalamy in the Era of Warring City-States before the
    empire was consolidated. His exploits against **Gygants**, Ifriti,
    Seakindred, **Wyrms**, **Wadwos**, warlocks and other supernatural
    foes are celebrated in song and poetry throughout **Urovia**.

Anti-angels   Demonkind or evil spirits; angels who sided with
    Abaddon in the Battle for Heaven and Earth at the Dawn of Time.

Archangels   Most powerful of the angels who stayed loyal to **Reus**;
    foremost among them are the **Seven Seraphim**.

Archdemons   Most powerful of demonkind along with **Abaddon**
    himself; foremost among them are the seven **Princes of Perfidy**.

Argael   A large stretch of primeval forest straddling the border
    between **Northalde** and **Vorstlund**. Long the haunt of **Wadwos**,
    it was formerly much bigger until the rise of the **Free Kingdoms**
    saw much of it pared back. Its centremost part is rumoured to
    be the enchanted lair of the Earth Witch, a right-hand sorceress
    of fearsome repute.

Argolian Order   Founded by Saint Argo five hundred years ago,
    this learned order of monks and friars is tasked with fighting
    evil spirits and hunting down witches and warlocks throughout
    the **Free Kingdoms** and **Pilgrim Kingdoms**. It is also celebrated
    for its learning.

Ashokainan   A legendary left-hand wizard who reputedly lived
    for hundreds of years until **Søren** slew him seven centuries ago.
    One of the most powerful warlocks to walk the Known World
    since the demise of the Priest-Kings of **Varya**.

Avatar   A collective name intended to summarise a complex
    terminology that covers all supernatural entities regarded as
    a manifestation of **Reus Almighty** (i.e. a direct extension of
    His being). This includes **archangels**, angels and their demonic
    opposites; the word is also commonly used to describe such
    entities sent to earth in mortal form to guide mankind for

good or ill. The term can also be used to describe a saint who is rewarded for a virtuous life by being exalted to the ranks of the **Unseen** upon death. Most religious scholars across the Faith and **Creed** agree that the **Two Prophets** fall into the former category of avatar (i.e. that they were angels or archangels sent to earth to help mortalkind), though some cleave to the second interpretation (that they were mortals rewarded in the Afterlife for their service to mankind).

Azrael The Angel of Death, tasked by **Reus** with judging the souls of the dead, determining whether they go to **Gehenna** or the **Heavenly Halls**. Known by many different names across cultures throughout history, including Orcus, Osirian, Mortis, Mahatsu and Imraan.

Battle of Avalongne Decisive battle fought a century and a half ago that brought about the end of King **Vasirius** and his reign. Even though his forces were victorious, it ultimately proved a pyrrhic victory as most of the Knights of the **Purple Garter** and his loyal nobles were slain; this created a power vacuum that prompted the Fourth War of the Royal Succession. For this reason the Battle of Avalongne is still mourned by loremasters and troubadours alike as heralding the end of the halcyon era of Vasirius' just rule.

Blessed Realm Common name given to the **Pilgrim Kingdoms**.

Breaking of the World Cataclysm visited on the Known World by **Reus** and the **Archangels** five thousand years ago as punishment for **Ma'amun**'s attempt to open the gates of **Gehenna** at the behest of his master **Abaddon**. Resulted in the destruction of the **Varyan** civilisation and substantially altered the geography of the **Urovian** and **Sassanian** continents. Ushered in the **First Age of Darkness**, during which nearly all the vast learning of the Varyan Empire was lost.

Cael A learned youth from the **Island Realms** tasked with taking the fourth fragment of the **Headstone of Ma'amun** to **Sassania** after it was broken by **Søren**. Disappeared with the fragment centuries ago, though since rumoured to have become one of the undead, wandering the deserts of the hot southlands.

Cierny Ruling royal clan that holds the throne in **Thraxia**. Current incumbent is Cadwy, a weak ruler widely rumoured to have been ensorcelled by the witch Abrexta the Prescient.

Creed Monotheistic religion founded by the **acolytes** of **Palomedes**, one of the **Two Prophets**, who opposed the tyranny of the

Thalamian Empire. It falls into two mainstream churches: the Orthodox Temple in the **Urovian New Empire** and the **True Temple** in Western **Urovia** and the **Pilgrim Kingdoms**.

Draugar   Undead race of warlock kings who are believed to have served the **Elder Wizards** as vassals. It is not known if they were themselves **Varyans**, subject peoples who were rewarded with great power by the Elder Wizards for their service, or a mixture of the two. Draugar are reputed to occupy certain remote areas, including the Draugmoors in central **Vorstlund** and the Valley of the Barrow Kings in the **Westerling Isles**, and have numerous powers including shapeshifting and draugbreath, a curse that afflicts victims with the preternatural Rotting Sickness.

Dulsinor   Lands in northern **Vorstlund** ruled by the House of Markward, current incumbent Eorl Wilhelm Stonefist. The Eorldom is one of nine principal states that compose the Vorstlending realm.

Elder Wizards   Ancient race of warlocks who ruled over the Known World from their island homeland of **Varya** for a thousand years until the **Breaking of the World**. Foremost among them was **Ma'amun**, who became corrupted by **Abaddon** after he learned the **Left-Hand Path** of black magic at his feet. Also known as the Priest-Kings of Varya and the Magi.

Elementi   Race of spirits belonging to the **Other Side** corresponding to the four elements: Terrus (earth), Aethi (air), Saraphi (fire) and Lymphi (water).

Faith   Principal and monotheistic religion of **Sassania** based on the teachings of the Prophet Sha'abat, who preceded the coming of **Palomedes** by several generations. Unlike Palomedes, Sha'abat was never a warrior and always counselled peaceful resolution of conflict wherever possible. However, this has not prevented adherents of the Faith from making war in his name.

First Age of Darkness   A thousand-year period of backwardness and strife directly succeeding the **Breaking of the World**; few civilisations if any flourished during this bleak era.

First Clarion   Marked the Dawn of Time and the creation of the Universe by **Reus Almighty**, who set his angels to work creating the galaxies, solar systems and planets thereafter. Scholars dispute over what timeframe this occurred, with estimates varying between a few hundred years to aeons in mortal reckoning.

Free Kingdoms   Collective name given to the six principal realms of Western Urovia: **Northalde**, **Thraxia**, **Pangonia**, **Vorstlund**, Mercadia and Thalamy. The epithet 'free' comes from the fact that slavery was abolished throughout these realms with the coming of the **Creed** – although serfdom and other types of feudal bondage still persist.

Frozen Principalities Name given to a string of petty kingdoms belonging to the **Northlanders**, barbarian tribes who still worship angels and demons as gods and cling to their age-old customs. Also known as the Frozen Wastes, these lands are ruled over by the Ice Thegns and their seacarls – fierce warriors who pledge fealty to their liegelords.

Gaellentir Stretch of lands in northern **Thraxia** ruled over by Clan Fitzrow, the present head of house being Lord Braun of Gaellen. The Ward of Gaellentir has been hard pressed by highland rebels for some time, who threaten its very existence.

Gautlund Most powerful of the five Frozen Principalities, not least because of its command of the Sea of Valhalla and the rich opportunities this provides for trade and plunder. Ruled by Oldrik Stormrider, the foremost **Northland** chieftain of his age.

Gehenna The island prison on the **Other Side** to which **Abaddon** and his demonic followers were banished by **Reus** after the Battle for Heaven and Earth was lost. At its heart lies the City of Burning Brass, divided into Five Tiers – the first and highest of these is reserved for **Abaddon** himself, the **Seven Princes of Perfidy** and other **archdemons**.

Golden Age New era of civilisation that flourished after the end of the **First Age of Darkness** some four thousand years ago and lasted for three millennia. During this time the civilisations of Sendhé and Ancient Thalamy flourished; much lore was relearned or rediscovered, though the glory of mortalkind never attained that achieved during the apogee of the preceding **Platinum Age**.

Golem Animating spirit that must be summoned and bound to a statue or manikin fashioned from earth, clay, wood or stone that has been inscribed with the **Sorcerer's Script**. The creature is then able to wreak havoc at the command of the sorcerer who has conjured it, though a Golem cannot always be easily controlled. Its one weakness is music: the spirit animating a Golem cannot abide rhythm or melody.

Gracius Pangonian poet whose works primarily celebrate the Age of High Chivalry under King **Vasirius** and the exploits of the original knights of the **Purple Garter**.

Grand High Monastery Informal name given to the headquarters of the **Argolian** Order just outside Rima in **Pangonia**. Its proper

name is the Most Revered Priory of St Argo, and it is the first
chapter of the Order founded by the saint of that name five
hundred years ago.

Great World Serpent   The first of **Reus Almighty**'s sentient
creations along with Aurgelmir the Titan. Fathered the race of
Wyrms with Hydrae the Many Headed (whom **Søren** slew on
his Seventh and final Deed). According to legend, the Great
World Serpent's body was used to create the world when Reus
crushed him and Aurgelmir together to stop them destroying
the Universe with their constant fighting. The same legend
states that the World Serpent lies coiled at the centre of the
earth, surrounded by the flesh of Aurgelmir; should he ever be
woken from his slumber the Known World will fall apart and
be destroyed. As such, the Great World Serpent is also referred
to as He Who Must Not Be Disturbed, particularly among the
Northlanders of the **Frozen Principalities**.

Gygant   A race of giants, believed to be **Reus'** first attempts to
fashion mortalkind from the rock and clay of the earth (itself
created from Aurgelmir the Titan, who is thus also known
as the Father of Giants). Many times larger than their human
descendants, though extremely violent and stupid, Gygants
terrorised early human settlements until the **Elder Wizards**
slew most of them and enslaved the rest. Today there are only
believed to be a handful left alive, mostly in remote mountain
retreats far away from mortalkind.

Headstone of Ma'amun   Tablet of incalculable power wrought by
Ma'amun five thousand years ago; inscribed with hieroglyphic
writing said to represent additions he made to the Sorcerer's
Script under the tutelage of **Abaddon.** It is said to contain the
power to break the hold placed on the Fallen One by **Reus** and
summon him and his followers back to the mortal vale. It is not
clear whether Ma'amun sought to control Abaddon or serve him,
and as such whether the Headstone will enable its user to bind
him to his or her will.

Heavenly Halls   The Kingdom of **Reus**, where the **Seven Seraphim**
sit at his side and the rest of the **archangels** and angels dwell.
The most splendid of the island realms of the **Other Side**, where
the souls of those judged fit by **Azrael** are sent to reside until
the Hour of All's Ending and Judgment Day.

Hierophant   A member of the **Argolian** Order who has attained
exceptional psychic powers, outstripping those of even the most

accomplished adepts. In this era there are thought to be three: Horskram of Vilno; Hannequin, current Grand Master of the Order; and Malthus of Montrevellyn, who left Rima years ago on a secret mission and is rumoured to have sought audience with the Fays of **Tintagael** before vanishing into the uttermost north.

Ingwin   Ruling royal house of the Kingdom of **Northalde**; current incumbent is Freidheim II. Coat of arms is two rearing white unicorns facing each other on a purple background.

Island Realms or Westerling Isles   Series of islands, the two principal ones being Kaluryn and Skulla, ruled over by the Marcher Lords and Druids, lying in the Great Western Ocean. The most westerly known civilisation, the Island Realms cling steadfastly to their ancient beliefs, having been visited by Kaia the Moon Goddess during the **First Age of Darkness** and taught the **Right Hand Path** of magick lost to man when the **Varyan** Empire was destroyed at the **Breaking of the World**. Also known as Druidsbourne and the Islands of World's Ending.

Jótlund   Lands of south-west Frozen Principalities ruled over by Hardrada, subsequently conquered by Guldebrand, thegn of the neighbouring realm of **Kvenlund**.

King's Dominions   Stretch of rich lands between **Efrilund** to the north and the Southern Provinces ruled directly by the **Northlending** King. Here royal law is strongest; consequently this is the wealthiest and most stable part of **Northalde**.

King's Fold   Northern half of Umbria in **Thraxia**, ruled directly by the Royal Clan **Cierny**. The rest of the ward is parcelled about between several barons.

Kvenlund   Southernmost mainland principality of the Frozen Wastes; ruled over by Guldebrand the Beardless, an ambitious and cunning thegn of tender years.

Lancelyn   Greatest of the Knights of the **Purple Garter**, most renowned for slaying the Great Wyrm Anglaurang in the time of King **Vasirius**. The latter's skull he brought back to court at Rima, where it was used to fashion the Charred Throne on which the Pangonian king sits to this day. His life was tragic and brooding, marred by madness brought on by his impossible love for the beautiful Isoud, who was married to the cowardly King Markus of Thalamy, and cut short when he died at the **Battle of Avalongne**.

Laurelin   Ruling house of Vichy, a prosperous margravate close to the heart of **Pangonia**. Its present incumbent, Lord Ivon, is a wily politicker of notoriously dissolute appetites, often connected to intrigue at the court of King Carolus. The House of Laurelin is one of the oldest and most prestigious in the kingdom, and has ties to the Ruling House of Rius from the time of King **Vasirius**. Some of its elder scions are also rumoured to have practised sorcery.

Left Hand Path   Black magic, derived from the teachings of **Abaddon** to **Ma'amun** more than five thousand years ago. Comprises Necromancy and Demonology, the two **Schools of Magick** most closely aligned to the Left Hand Path. However, some sorcerers who practise left-hand magic claim it is not necessarily wholly evil of itself, for instance those who use it to ask the dead for advice.

Logi   Name given by **Northlanders** to **Abaddon**, reviled by them as a trickster god.

Lower Thulia   One of the nine major baronies in **Vorstlund**, the Dukedom is perhaps the most powerful in the realm along with the Principality of **Westenlund** and the Dukedom of **Stornelund**. It is ruled by the House of Alt-Ürl.

Lower Vallia   Old name given to the southern margravates of **Pangonia**, of which Aquitania is the most powerful. Its inhabitants have a distinctive identity and are on the whole more zealous in the **Creed**. As such they have a proud tradition of crusading and have contributed many knights and soldiers to the **Pilgrim Wars**.

Ma'amun   Most powerful of the **Elder Wizards**, became corrupted by **Abaddon**, who taught him the **Left Hand Path** and encouraged him to extend his powers. Ma'amun was slain along with all the other Magi at the **Breaking of the World**, when the **Unseen** punished him for perverting the Gift of Magick and daring to challenge the Laws of Reus. His shade is believed to be trapped in **Gehenna**, where he languishes in the City of Burning Brass ruled by his erstwhile teacher along with all the other souls of the damned.

Maegellin   **Thraxian** bard who lived three centuries ago; widely held to be the greatest poet and songsmith of the **Silver Age**, surpassing even the classical poets of the **Golden Age**. Most noted works include *The Tales of Antaeus the Mariner* and *The Seven Deeds of Søren*.

Morwena   Beloved of **Søren**; a sorceress of fearsome repute who hailed from the **Island Realms**. Ensorcelled the great hero and sent him on his Seven Deeds, which were ultimately purposed to recover the **Headstone of Ma'amun** from the Forbidden City on the Island of **Varya**. Slain by Søren after she spurned him on completion of his Final Deed, in which he brought the Headstone from Varya to the Island Realms.

Northalde   One of the **Free Kingdoms**, settled by Northland reavers from the **Frozen Principalities** seven hundred years ago. Has undergone something of a revival under the reign of Freidheim II since its power diminished from its zenith more than a century ago under the reign of the Hero King Thorsvald. Comprises the lands north of the Argael and west of the Hyrkrainian mountains that divide the north-west peninsular of Western **Urovia** between it and the kingdom of **Thraxia**. **Northlendings** are famed for their skill in warfare, horsemanship, shipwrighting, armoury and castle-building.

Northlander   Inhabitant of the **Frozen Principalities**, whose ancestors founded the mainland colonies that would eventually become the Kingdom of **Northalde**. Northland raiders also settled the coasts further south and many Vorstlendings trace their ancestry back to the Principalities too.

Northlending   Inhabitant of the Kingdom of **Northalde** in north-western **Urovia**; not to be confused with **Northlander**, an inhabitant of the **Frozen Principalities**.

Occitania   Western peninsula of **Pangonia** comprising more than half a dozen margravates. Occitanians are fiercely independent and have historically caused the crown trouble. Its foremost powers are probably Gorleon, noted for its maritime tradition, and Armandy province, also widely celebrated for the quality of its wine.

Other Side   Collective name given to all the dwelling places of spirits, **elementi**, fays, demons, angels and **Reus Almighty** Himself. Said to be an endless sea of vapour punctuated by islands, including the **Heavenly Halls**, **Gehenna**, and the Place of Judgment where **Azrael** dwells. All supernatural beings hail from the Other Side, and this is consequently where warlocks of all bents derive their powers using the Language of Magick and the Sorcerer's Script.

Palomedes   Second of the **Two Prophets**; inspired the **Creed**, the major religion of **Urovia**. Born to a soldier in Ushalayim about a thousand years ago in what is now the **Pilgrim Kingdoms**. Initially intended to follow his father into the Thalamian Legions but began hearing the Voice of **Reus** shortly after coming of age at fourteen. Resolved to use

his martial skills to lead a revolution against the tyrannical Thalamian
Empire and acquired a great following, but later forsook the sword
and led his supporters in a campaign of passive resistance. Was
finally apprehended by the Thalamians after being betrayed by his
former lieutenant Antiochus the Red-Handed, taken to Tyrannos and
broken on the **Wheel** at the Emperor's command. Also known by his
abbreviated name, Palom, and his most common epithet, the **Redeemer**.

Pangonia   Most powerful of the **Free Kingdoms**, though its
influence has waned somewhat since its apogee under the
Chivalrous King Vasirius, who ruled some two centuries ago.
Its capital Rima is also the headquarters of the **True Temple**
and the **Argolian Order**. Currently ruled by King Carolus III of
the House of Ambelin, a scheming, ambitious monarch known
also as the 'wily' and the 'greedy' for heavy taxes imposed on
his barons.

Pilgrim Kingdoms   Collective name given to northern **Sassanian**
territories carved out by **Urovian** crusaders a century ago,
consisting of the Kingdom of Ushalayim, named after its
principal city, where **Palomedes** the **Redeemer** was born, the
Kingdom of Keraka and the Kingdom of Ranishmend. Also
known collectively as the **Blessed Realm**.

Pilgrim Wars   Series of crusades – holy wars against the heathen
Sassanians sanctioned by the **True Temple** – begun more
than a hundred years ago that recaptured the holy city of
Ushalayim where **Palomedes** the **Redeemer** was born. Many
factions besides the victorious crusading dynasties have profited
from the Pilgrim Wars, most notably the merchant houses of
Mercadia, most southerly of the **Free Kingdoms**. However, the
Pilgrim Wars have not been endorsed by all Palomedians: the
Orthodox Temple has openly voiced its disapproval, whilst
the **Argolian Order** has refused to condemn or condone them.
And few knights from the northerly Free Kingdoms of **Thraxia**
and **Northalde** have taken the **Wheel**, with most crusaders
originating from Mercadia, **Vorstlund**, **Pangonia** and Thalamy.

Platinum Age   A thousand-year epoch during which the **Elder
Wizards** ruled all of the Known World from the Island of **Varya**;
during this time mankind, though in bondage to the Priest-
Kings, reputedly lived in a state of ease, comfort and luxury
unparalleled in mortal history. According to some scholars the
average lifespan exceeded a century and even the lowest of birth
were well educated and literate. This era came to an abrupt end

some five millennia ago when the **Unseen** punished **Ma'amun** for daring to challenge their authority by destroying Varya and much of the Known World, laying waste to the great civilisation it had built.

Princes of Perfidy   Collective name given to the seven most powerful **archdemons** who serve **Abaddon**: Sha'amiel (**avatar** of greed and bigotry); Azathol (vanity and hubris); Zolthoth (wrath); Ta'ussaswazelim (cruelty); Chreosoaneuryon (gluttony); Satyrus (lust and sexual depravity); and Invidia (envy). The Seven Princes are themselves dark emanations of the **Seven Seraphim** and thus have their celestial opposites among the **archangels**, whose virtues they seek to corrupt and subvert.

Purge   Calamitous event a generation ago that saw the **Argolian Order** falsely accused and tried for witchcraft by clerics of the mainstream **True Temple** in Rima. Many Argolians were tortured and made false confessions which they later retracted. The Order eventually succeeded in refuting the charges and even turned the tables on their accusers – a divination led by Hannequin, Grand Master of the Order, revealed many of their accusers including the Supreme Perfect to have been themselves acting under the influence of the **archdemon** Sha'amiel. The guilty perfects were burned alive in the main square at Rima. However, in another twist, since then the Temple has been held to be itself 'purged' of all wrongdoing, its traitors having been brought to justice, whilst much suspicion continues to fall on the Argolians, whose psychic and spiritual abilities are held by many to be akin to sorcery itself.

Purple Garter   Also known as the Crescent Table, this elite Order of thirty knights was founded by King **Vasirius** and is supposed to comprise the flower of **Pangonia**'s chivalry. Nowadays it is more a political tool, used to keep more powerful nobles in check by appointing their younger brothers to key posts of state.

Redeemer   Common epithet by which **Palomedes** is referred to among believers of the **Creed**.

Rent Between Worlds   The name given to the gap between the mortal vale and the **Other Side** that wizards of all kinds use to draw upon the supernatural powers essential to sorcery, using the Language of Magick and the Sorcerer's Script. This gap was greatly widened during the **Platinum Age** when the **Elder Wizards** ruled the Known World, and is said to be responsible for all manifestations in the mortal vale, be it **elementi**, demonkind,

Fays, Gaunts or other supernatural entities. The Rent widens in accordance with how much sorcery is being used; hence if a warlock is particularly active in one area, the Rent there will be widened, increasing the likelihood of possessions, hauntings and other apparitions.

Reus Almighty   God; responsible for the creation of the Universe and everything in it, including the Known World, the **Other Side**, **archangels**, angels, spirits, **elementi**, mortalkind and the animal kingdom. Sages differ on whether His power is truly infinite or simply incalculable according to the reckonings of mortalkind. The Almighty was unknown to pre-Faith mortals, who worshipped the archangels and **archdemons** as gods in their own right during the **Platinum** and **Golden Ages**.

Right Hand Path   More benign white magic originally taught to the **Varyans** by the **Archangels** to help them fashion their civilisation during the **Platinum Age**. Some thinkers, the **Argolians** among them, hold that all magic is a mistake, and that even the Right-Hand Path can be used to do evil in the wrong hands. Others such as the pagan followers of Kaia The Moon Goddess – who retaught aspects of white magic to the folk of the **Island Realms** during the **First Age of Darkness** – disagree on this point.

Ryøskil   Treaty signed by the **Northlanders** several generations ago forcing them to stop officially raiding mainland **Northalde** (though clandestine raids have continued sporadically). The Northlanders were brought to the treaty after being defeated decisively in battle by the **Northlendings** under King Aelfric III.

Sassania   Lands of the hot south lying beyond the Sundering Sea that comprise the Four Sultanates, the **Pilgrim Kingdoms** and various other petty principalities. Principal religion is the Faith, founded by the First Prophet Sha'abat several generations before the coming of **Palomedes**.

Scandia   Central principality of the **Frozen Wastes**, the largest in extent but with limited access to the sea. Ruled by Magnhilda, also known as the Shield Queen, a berserker maiden of fearsome repute.

Second Age of Darkness   Another period of decline marked in Western **Urovia** by the destruction of the Thalamian Empire after Tyrannos was sacked by Wulfric of Gothia more than nine hundred years ago. It is generally agreed to have ended with the consolidation of barbarian petty kingdoms into the six **Free Kingdoms** more than three centuries ago, ushering in the advent of the present **Silver Age**. Note that other cultures differ in their reckoning of the Second Age of Darkness; for instance the **Urovian New Empire** dates its ending with the completion of the Hundred Years Conquest slightly earlier, while the **Sassanians** date its beginning from the demise of the last Rightly Guided Sultan, two generations after Wulfric sacked Tyrannos.

Seven Schools of Magick   The core disciplines of sorcery practised by warlocks and witches of varying bent and aptitude throughout the Known World. These are: Thaumaturgy, Transformation, Enchantment, Scrying, Alchemy, Necromancy and Demonology. The first five are broadly classified under the more benign **Right Hand Path**; the last two belong to the darker **Left Hand Path**.

Seven Seraphim   Foremost among the **Archangels**, those that sit at the right hand of **Reus Almighty**. They are: Logos (**avatar** of prosperity and tolerance); Siona (grace and dignity); Virtus (courage); Stygnos (stoicism and fortitude); Euphrosakritos (merriment); Luviah (love); and Aeriti (aspiration). The Seraphim are opposed by their dark emanations the **Princes of Perfidy**, who represent twisted or corrupted forms of the virtues they embody.

Silver Age   The present age; regarded by most Western **Urovians** as beginning with the consolidation of the **Free Kingdoms** some 350 years ago. Distinct from the previous **Golden Age** in that it is an era in which **Reus Almighty** has made Himself known to mortalkind – yet civilisation in Western Urovia is acknowledged by the learned to lag far behind that of the preceding epoch.

Sixth Sense   Special talent particular to the **Argolian Order**, honed by years of prayer and meditation. Its abilities are somewhat vague and thus difficult to define, but broadly speaking they allow a monk of the order to detect the following, with varying degrees of accuracy: when a person is lying or concealing something; when danger (particularly supernatural danger) is near; past pain or sorrow that continues to plague a victim; the presence of a warlock or witch and the type of magick being used; and a demon's psychic spoor.

Sjórkunan   Foremost deity of the **Northlanders**, revered for his mastery of the waves and said to preside over the Halls of Feasting and Fighting below the Sea of Valhalla, the Northlandic equivalent of the **Heavenly Halls**. Known as Aqualcus, Baha'muhit and the Salt King in other periods and cultures.

Søren   Legendary hero who hailed from the **Frozen Principalities** and came over with the First Reavers who began conquering and

settling what is now **Northalde** seven centuries ago. Reputed
to have been fathered on a mortal maiden by the archangel
Sjórkunan, Lord of Oceans, whom the Northlanders worship as
a god. Is most famed for his adventures thereafter, when seeking
the westerly **Island Realms** in his magic ship Jürmengaard he
stumbled upon the sorceress **Morwena**'s lair in the ruins of
one of the **Watchtowers of the Magi**. She ensorcelled him into
performing his Seven Deeds, the last of which saw the **Headstone
of Ma'amun** recovered from the Forbidden City of **Varya**. Søren
subsequently slew Morwena and broke the Headstone into four
pieces, before taking his ship and sailing out across the Great
Western Ocean, never to be seen again by mortal eyes. Has gone
by various epithets during and after his lifetime, including the
Doomed, Irongrip, Wavetamer and Wyrmslayer.

Sorcerer's Script   Hieratic script taught to the **Varyans** by the
Archangels and used to express the Language of Magick.
It is used to store and communicate spells and incantations
of all kinds. Like the Language of Magick, its darker modes
constitute the Left Hand path taught by **Abaddon** to **Ma'amun**.

Stornelund   One of the richest of the nine baronies that compose
the realm of **Vorstlund**, neighboured by **Dulsinor** to the west
and Ostveld to the south. Ruled over by the House of Lanrak;
the current Herzog is Lord Hengist – a vain, inept and bibulous
man unworthy of the title.

Succubus   Demonic spirit that can take female form. Conjured
specifically to cater to a **Left Hand** warlock's depraved lusts.

True Temple   The church of the **Creed** that holds sway in Western
Urovia, with the Supreme Perfect headquartered in Rima, the
capital of **Pangonia**. Its name differentiates it from the Orthodox
Temple, which administers the Creed in the **Urovian New
Empire** east of the Great White Mountains. The True Temple
was created by a schism, known as the Sundering of the Temple,
six hundred years ago.

Thraxia   One of the **Free Kingdoms** of Western **Urovia**, composing
the lands west of the Hyrkrainian Mountains that divide it
from **Northalde**. Originally settled by clans fleeing the **Island
Realms** after the Wars of Kith and Kin two thousand years ago.
The last of the kingdoms to embrace the **Creed**, Thraxia has
somewhat more tolerance for right hand magic than the other
western kingdoms, although the **Left Hand Path** is punished
severely. Thraxians are famed far and wide for the excellence

of their poetry and music, and their greatest bard **Maegellin** is celebrated throughout the Free Kingdoms and beyond. Their skill at hunting and their fine mead are also noteworthy.

Tintagael Name given to a haunted forest in the westernmost fiefs of the **King's Dominions** and the ancient **Watchtower of the Magi** on its outskirts. Long the earthly sojourn of the Fay Folk, who exploited the **Rent Between Worlds** caused by the sorcery emanating from the Watchtower to cross over from the **Other Side**. Nowadays few wayfarers dare venture inside it, and of those who do fewer still emerge.

Tyrnor War god worshipped by the **Northlanders**. Reviled in Palomedian culture as Azazel, the archdemon embodying war.

Two Prophets Collective name given to the **avatars**, Sha'abat and **Palomedes**, whose teachings inspired the Faith and **Creed** respectively and brought the knowledge of **Reus Almighty** to mortalkind. Due to religious conflict, particularly the **Pilgrim Wars**, adherents of both religions respectively call the prophets 'true' and 'false' – though some loremasters acknowledge both. Note that the term 'false prophet' is also used to describe those possessed or impersonated by **archdemons** in order to lead mortalkind astray.

Un-angels Collective name given to 'neutral' entities that are considered neither angels nor demons. Foremost among them are **Azrael**, judge of souls; Kaia, worshipped as a nature goddess throughout pagan communities in the **Island Realms**; and Nurë, the archangel of fire, prayed to by smiths of all kinds. The **Fay Folk** are also considered by many loremasters to be lesser un-angels, being far from good but not truly evil.

Unseen Collective noun given to all inhabitants of the **Other Side** after the **Breaking of the World**, when angels and other supernatural entities ceased to walk openly among mortalkind. Throughout the **Golden Age** they are said to have reappeared occasionally, though with diminishing frequency, and by the advent of the **Silver Age** such manifestations had become virtually unknown. Note that demonkind will manifest in the form of possessions and in response to summonings by a demonologist meddling with the Other Side using the **Left Hand Path**.

Upper Thulia Lands adjacent to **Dulsinor** ruled by the House of Ürl, long hostile to the House of Markward. Its ruling Eorl was crippled by Sir Balthor, foremost knight of Dulsinor, during the last war between the Ürls and Markwards, and has nursed a bitter grudge against them ever since.

Upper Vallia   Ancient name given to the northern and central margravates of **Pangonia**, including Rima where the royal seat is. Besides the capital its foremost provinces are Gorlivere, Vichy, Morvaine and Valacia, long rich in arable lands, vinyards and iron ore. Their smiths are renowned for their smelting skills, and the fineness of their wines is surpassed only by that of Armandy province in **Occitania** and Aquitania in **Lower Vallia**.

Urovia   Name given to all the lands lying north of the Sundering Sea and the Great Inland Sea, as far the Steppes of Koth that lie beyond the Mercenary Kingdoms to the east of the **Urovian New Empire**. Nowadays Urovian culture is usually associated with the **Creed**; but note that the Three Emirates lying directly south of the Mercenary Kingdoms and Koth are considered **Sassanian** by virtue of their religion and culture.

Urovian New Empire   The most powerful and technologically advanced country of the **Silver Age**, a land empire comprising seven former kingdoms that were consolidated four centuries ago by the House of Usharok during the Hundred Years' Conquest. Protected by a string of fortresses in the Great White Mountains to the west and the Great Wall to the east, the Empire guards its secrets jealously and trades selectively with its neighbours. It is said to have preserved or relearned much of the lore of **Ancient Thalamy**, and former outlying provinces of that fallen empire are now part of the New Empire. Its capital, Illyrium, is said to be the greatest **Urovian** city since Ancient Tyrannos, and is the seat of the Imperator, the Ruling Senate, and the Orthodox Temple.

Varya   Name given to the civilisation and the island city that spawned it more than six thousand years ago in the midst of the Great Inland Sea. Inspired by the **Archangels**, who regularly visited them and taught them the Language of Magick among many other arts and crafts, the Varyans founded an empire that covered the Known World, from the **Island Realms** in the West to the Steppes of Koth in the East. They were ruled over by the Synod of **Elder Wizards**, said to number some five dozen warlocks of power unsurpassed before or since. This empire lasted about a thousand years until it was destroyed by the **Unseen** at the **Breaking of the World**, by which time it had fallen into demonolatry, decadence and corruption thanks to **Ma'amun**, foremost among the Elder Wizards, who was seduced by **Abaddon** during his astral wanderings through the **Other Side**.

Varya is also frequently referred to in texts as Seneca, the name given to it in Decorlangue, the language of **Ancient Thalamy**.

Vasirius Also known as the Chivalrous King, lauded by poets and loremasters alike for his uncommonly just rule, he was the Scion of the House of Rius who ruled **Pangonia** more than a hundred years ago and instituted the Code of Chivalry, designed to reform knighthood and rein in its worst excesses. Since Vasirius' death at the hands of the Traitor Prince Ancelet at the **Battle of Avalongne**, the code has waned in influence, though it still attracts adherents among idealistic young knights across the **Free Kingdoms**.

Vorstlund Formerly a kingdom until the Partition Crisis some two centuries ago, Vorstlund is now a loose federation of nine baronies, although it is still classed as being one of the **Free Kingdoms**. Vorstlendings are known for their gluttony and generosity, but can also be quick to anger and are doughty fighters.

Wadwo The result of disastrous experiments by the **Elder Wizards** to create a race of superhuman soldiers, Wadwos are generally solitary, near-mindless creatures of humanoid but grossly distorted aspect who dwell in remote forests and mountain lairs. Also known as ogres, woses and beastmen, they are possessed of huge strength but are clumsy and ill-disciplined.

Warlock's Crown Colloquial name given to the ruins of a structure built by the **Elder Wizards** in the southern ranges of the Hyrkrainian mountains between **Thraxia**, **Northalde** and **Vorstlund**. Not thought to be a **Watchtower**, most likely it was a palace or prison colony used to keep **Gygants** enslaved by the priest-kings of **Varya**. It takes its name from the five surviving shards of the edifice, each one bigger than a castle.

Watchtowers of the Magi A series of huge towers built by the **Elder Wizards** to watch over their vast domains across the Known World. Many were destroyed during the **Breaking of the World**, but some survived partially intact, including the Watchtowers of **Tintagael** in **Northalde**, the Valley of the Barrow Kings in the **Island Realms**, and Mount Brazen in the Great White Mountains dividing the **Free Kingdoms** from the **Urovian New Empire**.

Westenlund Richest of the nine major baronies of **Vorstlund**. Ruled over by the House of Drüler, which insisted on retaining the title of principality after the kingdom was broken up two centuries ago, on account of its scion Aelle being the last king of a united **Vorstlund**.

Wheel   Chief symbol of the **Creed**, derived from the execution of its prophet **Palomedes** on a torture wheel in Tyrannos a thousand years ago. The sign of the Wheel is made by first touching the forehead and then splaying the fingers of the hand across one's chest, in representation of the spokes the **Redeemer**'s limbs were broken on.

White Valravyn   Chivalrous order founded by the Hero King Thorsvald of **Northalde** a hundred years ago, in memory of the warrior saint Ulred; charged with upholding Royal Law throughout the **King's Dominions** and bringing justice to all during peacetime, defending the realm in times of war, and the King's personal security. Revived during the reign of Freidheim II after falling out of favour during the rule of King Aelfric III. The Order's prestige means it draws the greatest and most ambitious knights of the realm to its ranks. Its present High Commander is Prince Freidhoff, younger brother to the King. It is headquartered at Staerkvit, one of Northalde's greatest castles, which lies on lands in the Dominions that the Order rules directly on royal grant.

Wyrm   Also known as dragons and wyverns; the ancient offspring of the **Great World Serpent** and Hydrae the Many-Headed. Now an extinct species, after the last of the great venom-spitting reptiles was slain by the Pangonian knight Sir Azelin of Valacia some years ago.

Acknowledgements

A huge thanks to Moonika for believing and her astonishingly quick and efficient beta reading, Snip for funding the start-up costs and general moral support, Niall for his invaluable advice on how to market, Cris for his stalwart critiquing, and last but not least, my mother for putting me up while I got this project off the ground.

I'm not sure if I could have done this without your help, and even if I did it would certainly have been a hell of a lot harder.

I'd also like to say a quick word of thanks to all of you who have read, reviewed, and generally bought into this book series – I hope you'll be around for many more years to come!

Finally, to fans both new and old – thanks for letting the *Broken Stone Chronicle* capture your imagination! Keep spreading the word – in person, on Goodreads, Facebook and Amazon – and let's see if we can't get a few more converts!

damien@damienblackwords.com
www.damienblackwords.com
@TheDevilsFriar
www.facebook.com/damienblackwords/

Lightning Source UK Ltd.
Milton Keynes UK
UKHW040605080719
345781UK00001B/37/P